About the author

Born in Newcastle in 1942, Arthur Clifford was educated at
Rugby School and Newcastle University. He went on to train
as a teacher and subsequently taught in schools in Uganda,
Scotland and England. In the late 1990s he retrained as a
TEFL teacher and taught English in Siberia, Budapest and
Romania. He is a keen mountain climber, having climbed in
the Andes and Siberia, and scaled some of the world's most
famous peaks, including Mount Ararat and Kilimanjaro. As
a teacher, he led expeditions to Peru, Turkey, India and East
Africa. He lives in Durham and this is his first novel.

FAR, FAR THE MOUNTAIN PEAK

Arthur Clifford

Book Guild Publishing

First published in Great Britain in 2016 by
The Book Guild Ltd
9 Priory Business Park
Wistow Road
Kibworth
Leics LE8 0RX
Tel 0800 999 2982
Email info@bookguild.co.uk

Typesetting in Sabon by
Keyboard Services, Luton, Bedfordshire

Printed and bound in Great Britain by
CPI Group (UK) Ltd, Croydon, CR0 4YY

A catalogue record for this book is available from
The British Library

ISBN 978 1 91050 820 6

Prologue

Two Newspapers

TEACHER RESCUES SCHOOL PARTY FROM UGANDAN GUERRILLA BAND

...It had been a triumph for teacher John Denby and the pupils of Mereton College, Norfolk. Despite difficult terrain and dreadful weather, they had finally conquered Mount Margherita, the highest peak of the remote and mysterious Ruwenzori Mountains... They were looking forward to a well-earned rest in Kampala when, quite unexpectedly, the bus in which they were travelling was ambushed near the town of Mubende by armed guerrillas belonging to the so-called 'Army of the Archangel Gabriel'...

'Bliss turned to nightmare,' said Mr Denby. 'It was all so utterly unexpected, a bolt out of the blue ... I really thought they were going to kill us all...'

But by steely nerves and split-second timing he managed to engineer a dramatic escape...

'It was a brilliant operation of which any professional soldier would be proud,' said Major Bill Horton, commander of the Cadet Force with which Mereton College is closely associated. 'It required planning, skill, quick thinking and sheer old-fashioned guts. Denby is a hero twice over – first for getting a very unpromising group of youngsters up a difficult mountain, an achievement which showed real leadership, and, second for masterminding this incredible escape...'

...Tragically, however, on the afternoon of the breakout one of the expedition leaders, twenty-five-year-old Debora Helmsley of Great Yarmouth, went missing. Despite intensive enquiries she has not been seen since and there are fears that she might be dead...'

1

That was the *Daily Mail*.

MADCAP YOUTH ADVENTURE IN UGANDA ENDS IN TRAGEDY

...It has now emerged that the leader of this ill-fated venture was not properly qualified ... Neither the organisation nor the safety procedures were remotely adequate for so hazardous an undertaking... The young people concerned were in no way prepared for the dangers that faced them ... failures, dropouts, inadequates ... the detritus of a pampered and over-ambitious middle class...

'I intend to see justice done,' declared a distraught David Helmsley, the girl's father...

Dr Giles Denby, the Minister for Sport and Leisure, is forthright in his condemnation. 'It is high time that something was done about these crazy ventures which wantonly put the lives of children at risk,' he said yesterday. 'Indeed, the appropriate legislation is already in the pipeline...'

That was the *Guardian*.

What *Did* Happen?

Thirty-six-year-old John Denby scanned the two newspaper reports. Altruistic hero in one; incompetent, egotistical fraud in the other. Fame or ignominy? It all depended on which newspaper you read. It was all a question of facts – which facts you chose to include and which facts you chose to exclude. As to what had *actually* happened in that torrid Ugandan swamp on that crazy afternoon, well, he was damned if he really knew.

Putting the newspapers into his briefcase, he set off down Wild Bull Street towards the solicitor's office. 'The authentic and unchanged heart of medieval Eastwich' was how the tourist pamphlets described the twisting alley of Wild Bull Street with its overhanging half-timbered Sixteenth Century houses. But just how 'authentic' was it? Those brightly painted and immaculately maintained buildings positively oozed modern technological opulence. Behind the glossy facades were offices containing the very latest in computer technology – about as far from the tumbledown squalor of a medieval town as you could possibly get.

It was all a sham. A con trick. All appearance. But, then, what people believed was true was more important than what was true. Just like the court case which was hanging over him.

Relevant Facts

'Well, Mr Denby,' said Croft, 'we might as well start with the bad news. Here's the writ. Here's what Old Man Helmsley has to say about you.'

Denby read quickly through the three pages of closely typed foolscap. He caught phrases like 'ill-planned and totally irresponsible adventure', 'fraudulent claims of expertise', 'total ignorance of the conditions that were to be encountered', 'wilful and culpable negligence', 'the terrible and wholly unnecessary loss of my beloved daughter, Debora', 'selfish and callous disregard for the safety of others', 'inconsolable sorrow...', 'subsisting on anti-depressant drugs'...

In short, a tidal wave of iniquity only to be assuaged by a jail sentence and half a million pounds' worth of damages.

Denby seethed. He wasn't a fraud. He was an experienced mountain explorer who'd braved mosquito-infested jungles and scaled 27,350-foot Makalu, the fifth highest mountain in the world. There was precious little he didn't know about shambolic Third World countries and their problems. 'Ill-planned'? The Royal Geographical Society – no less – had given the expedition its blessing! 'Callous disregard'? He was a distraught as anybody over the disappearance of Debora Helmsley. She'd been his special protégée, the shining example of his altruism. If he hadn't paid for her out of his own pocket, she would never have realised her lifelong dream of visiting Africa and climbing the Ruwenzori. Indeed, her father had even called him a 'saint'.

'There's a pack of lies here,' he eventually said. 'How do people think they can get away with it?'

Croft leaned back in his chair. In late middle age with a shock of white hair and a Roman nose protruding from a wrinkled old face, he was almost the parody of a bishop or a distinguished world statesman.

'You get used to this sort of thing in my line of business,' he said. 'Don't worry too much about the histrionics. They're just the icing on the cake. It's money Helmsley's after. Between you and me and the doorpost, the man's facing bankruptcy. Half a million could be

3

the saving of him. He sees you as a soft touch. Teachers, you know, "Men among children: children among men".'

'But, could I *really* be bankrupted or land in jail?'

'A remote possibility, very remote, but one we shall have to avoid.'

He motioned to his secretary and leaned over the desk. 'Now let's have the facts – all the *relevant* facts.'

Denby sighed. Facts were all right. It was *relevant* facts that were the problem. That was why he'd nearly come to grief in his second-year exams at university. He'd been able to get 'the facts' into a sequence coherent enough to answer an exam question, but new facts kept popping into his brain shattering the intellectual framework he'd so laboriously constructed – rather like those flashes of light that kept appearing out of nothing on your computer screen. Columbus had sailed over the Atlantic: relevant fact. But he would never have reached the West Indies if America hadn't been in an accessible position. That accessible position was the result of plate tectonics. So plate tectonics were an important fact, but were they a *relevant* fact to be included in a thousand-word essay?

'Come on!' said Croft encouragingly. 'Start at the beginning. I mean why did you have to take a bunch of kids to Uganda in the first place? I mean they were hardly the sort of kids I'd want to take anywhere – failures, dropouts – one of them, apparently, mentally unstable. You're quite a celebrity, aren't you? Mountaineer, traveller, adventurer... I've read your book. Surely, with your contacts you could have picked a better bunch? So what was it all about?'

What indeed? Where did it all start? Where did anything start? Where did the Russian Revolution start? In February 1917? In 1905? Or with the Czar's fateful marriage to the disastrous Alexandra? The question had caused him big problems in one of his midterm assignments. He'd started with the bread riots in Petrograd and ended up with the death of the last woolly mammoth at the close of the Ice Age. His tutor hadn't been amused.

What to include and what not to include? There were some things that had happened on that fateful afternoon which few sane people could comprehend, let alone believe...

Origins?

But behind everything there was that compelling urge to do something big and dramatic. Perhaps that could be traced back to a dismal October afternoon twenty-five years ago. A scrawny little eleven-year-old with a mop of white hair and tears pouring out of his big, goggly eyes, was hammering away at a locked door and screaming: 'I HATE you! I'm FAR better than you are! One day I'll be famous and then I'll fucking show you!'

But what was that particular eleven-year-old doing behind that particular door and just what was he screaming about?

Like everything else in the universe – like the trees, the rivers, the mountains, the clouds, the planets, the stars and, yes, even the galaxies – it was the result of past events.

Certainly of an event which had taken place in a village church in the summer of 1969.

1

Growth and Development of a Sort

Genesis

Dr Giles Denby and Mary Ponsonby were stark naked and making passionate love in front of the high altar of All Saints church in the Lincolnshire village of Lower Melthorpe.

They were marching to a nearby American airbase as part of an anti-war protest organised in conjunction with the Campaign for Nuclear Disarmament. All through that long and hot day Giles had become increasingly obsessed with Mary. She was quite preposterously beautiful – that delicate, exquisitely proportioned body, that smooth velvety skin, that rush of glossy white hair falling carelessly over her shoulders and that face with its big, watery eyes and its radiant, glittering smile.

In the bright summer sunshine he had gazed at her perfectly shaped buttocks as they rippled beneath her blue jeans and at the rise and fall of the ample breasts under her loose white blouse. If only she would drop everything and reveal her naked splendours!

He was a twenty-seven-year-old university lecturer – big, burly and ruggedly handsome. She was one of his students. From the very moment of her arrival at the university he'd noticed her. Not just that wonderful body and glorious smile, but the way that she absorbed everything that he had to say – his lectures, his radical ideas, his rethink of conventional bourgeois morality... She never missed a lecture; she always attended the student meetings he arranged – 'Hands off Cuba', 'Legalise Pot', 'Brits out of Ulster', 'The Revolution within the Revolution'...

They were soul mates, made especially for each other. It needed only the final physical act to complete the symbiosis.

But how to do it? It might have been the Sixties – Liberty,

uncontaminated Youth blowing away the fusty old repressions of the clapped-out older generation, the therapeutic necessity of free sex, the dawn of a New Enlightened Age and all the rest of it ... But for a newly appointed university lecturer to start screwing his students?

Well, it wasn't really on. It could even be dangerous and put all he had achieved at risk.

But that night it had happened. The radical young vicar of All Saints had let the marchers sleep in the church hall.

'Great to see you all!' he'd chortled as they'd piled into the rather dilapidated late nineteenth-century building, 'Great to see so many spiritually aware people in this materialistic age. Don't call me "Reverend" by the way, just call me Kev – "Kev the Rev" if you like! Incidentally, the church is open for all who want to use it. So feel free!'

As they rolled out their sleeping bags on the dusty wooden floor, Giles had whispered into Mary's ear, 'I love you. You are so ... well, so right in every respect!' He hadn't meant to say it. It had just slipped out and he immediately regretted it. How would she respond? With anger? With insulted indignation?

But she'd smiled back at him with that intoxicatingly radiant smile of hers:

'Well, you know what to do about it, don't you?'

An electric current had seemed to surge through him: 'Yes, but where?'

'Why not in the church? The vicar said "Feel Free", didn't he?'

'But surely not for *that*!'

'Oh come on! We'll make a radical statement. Sex in front of the high altar. Show the world what we think of the whole fraud of religion. After all, it was *you* who told us that religion was a bit of medieval mumbo-jumbo that had outlived its time! Well, let's get on and hasten its departure!'

That was what he liked about her. The way that she took his radical ideas to heart and wasn't ashamed to implement them. Yet he still hesitated...

'But what about the vicar? I mean we don't want to alienate him.'

'Oh for fuck's sake, he's just a petty bourgeois birdbrain! "Useful idiots"? Wasn't that how you described his sort? If he sees us, we'll just tell him that it's our new radical way of worshipping God. He'll be stupid enough to swallow it.'

So there it had happened, there in front of the high altar in the dark and empty late Victorian church of All Saints, Lower Melthorpe.

Nobody came in, neither the vicar, nor any of their fellow marchers, nor, even, God it seemed. Their conscious blasphemy went undisturbed. The candles in their cheap brass candlesticks did not spontaneously ignite. The sugary-sweet Christ in the cut-price imitation Burne Jones window did not call down a curse. No flash of lightning descended from On High.

'You see, nothing's happened!' cried an exultant Mary. 'It just proves that God doesn't exist!'

'We knew that already,' declared Giles, sensing an unwelcome hint of superstition in his protégée. 'You don't have to do this sort of thing to prove it.'

But she wouldn't stop. 'You know,' she gushed on, 'back in the Middle Ages they used to say that a child conceived in a church was especially blessed by God...'

Giles winced. For all her virtues Mary had an undisciplined mind and was apt to make wild, unsubstantiated statements.

'I'm not too sure about that, Mary...'

'Well,' she continued, 'when our child, conceived in an authentic radical statement emerges, let's bring it up properly!'

'Hang on!' interrupted Giles. 'We don't know if there *is* going to be a child!'

He felt a slight frisson of alarm. A child could cause problems, big problems! In the sheer ecstasy of the moment he hadn't thought that far ahead. It had all just happened in one wild rush.

'Oh don't be so bourgeois!' giggled Mary. 'There's bound to be a sprog. So let's show the world how a sprog ought to be brought up! None of those stupidities and repressions that have made such a mess of our lives. It'll grow up free from religion, free from morality, free to develop as a proper human being.'

'Yes, yes, I get you!' replied Giles, beginning to feel the warmth of her radicalism. 'Together we'll show the world how a child ought to be brought up!'

In a sudden flash the idea intoxicated him. How he loved Mary at that moment! Adored her! His true disciple, leading him on and ever forwards! Passionately he embraced her naked body, running his fingers over those marvellous breasts. He felt a deep, quiet thrill, not the 'Peace of God which passeth all understanding,' but the Peace of Consummated Sex – the ultimate peace, the very meaning of existence. 'Christ,' he sighed, 'I *never* thought it would be as good as this!'

'*Never?*' echoed Mary in a teasing voice. 'You were always telling us that you'd been doing it since the age of thirteen!'

'Not *that*!' he added hastily. 'Doing it in a church and showing religion up for the rubbish it is.'

Actually in an unguarded moment Giles had spoken the truth. This *was* his first sexual experience. All that talk of casual sexual conquests was just image building. Necessary, of course. If he wanted to change society, he had to get the students on his side and they weren't likely to have much use for an unblooded virgin. He had to create the correct persona – bold, liberated and sexually strong.

When Mary had made her suggestion one half of him had been ecstatic, but the other half had been alarmed. He'd never done it before. Suppose it all went wrong? The exposure! The shame!

But he'd been a big success.

Born to Success

Not that there was anything unusual in that, however. Whatever he did, he was always a success. He was one of those people who seemed preordained for success.

The only son of a wealthy London doctor, his life so far had been a continual upward spiral. The head boy of a well-known prep school, he'd won a scholarship to Rugby. Good at Mathematics, good at Latin, good at games, a fine athlete ... good at everything in fact, his career there had been a triumphant progress. Winning all the academic prizes, the star of all the teams, he had become Captain of Rugger and Head of School.

He'd wielded great power. The day-to-day running of School House, the largest and most important of the houses in which the boarding pupils lived, was in his hands. Getting people up in the morning, keeping the place tidy, getting people to bed at the right time; ensuring that everybody obeyed the elaborate dress code – accreted from the time of the revered Dr Arnold – which laid down precisely who could wear which cap, which tie, what jacket and what blazer – and, more important, who could *not* – guarding with an eagle eye those ancient and hallowed rules which stipulated exactly who could put two hands in their trouser pockets, who could put one hand in and who was forbidden to put either hand in... All this and much more: in short, curbing the natural adolescent tendency to anarchy and creating an orderly community. Above all, creating school spirit.

Those who turned up late to cheer the First XV on the touchline had to clean the house prefects' shoes – *all* of them – for a whole week and take a cold shower every morning. Those who failed to turn up at all had to do all of this *and* got a beating in the school library at seven o'clock that evening.

On Wednesday afternoons the school cadet force paraded in Horton Crescent. Those who turned up in dirty boots got a cold shower for the first offence and a beating in his study for the second offence.

He rather liked beating youngsters. Not for any sexual reasons, of course: he despised the sordid perverts who had to bugger little boys. Rather, it was the sense of power, of justice and of the essential rightness of things. That initial cheeky bravado – 'You can't hurt *me*!' The silence after the first stroke, the watery eyes after the second. Then, usually after the third stroke, but occasionally as late as the fifth, the trickle of tears, and, finally, in a good sixty per cent of cases, the crumpling up into a sobbing heap which signified victory and the vindication of right.

It was all for their own good, of course. The lower orders couldn't be expected to manage on their own. They had to be protected against themselves. There was a hierarchy in life with natural leaders like himself at the top. Lesser beings had to know their place.

Then it had been up to Cambridge (scholarship, of course!) and a First in History (naturally!).

But this was the Sixties. A new world was being born. Liberated youth was bursting into the fusty old bourgeoisie, exposing its pretentious frauds, its bigotries, its nauseating cant which posed as morality. Everything was being challenged. Nothing was sacred. Do your thing. Blow your mind. Make love not war.

A rational world was emerging, shorn of the idiocies of the past. Like capitalism, for instance. Why have a dozen makes of cars when one would do? And what did all those middle-class upstarts need cars for anyway? They should be made to use public transport like everybody else.

And why did they have to live in semi-Ds with gardens? That just wasted valuable space. All those leafy suburbs should be replaced with properly designed 'living machines' as Le Corbusier advocated.

The workers were being cheated, corrupted, led astray by vulgar commercialism. What was needed was a properly ordered society

11

with the *right* people running it, people with good university degrees – in short, people like himself. Those middle classes just didn't know their place. That was the problem. It was perfectly clear – clear to any right-thinking person, that was! – that all this parliamentary democracy thing was a sham. It just let the bourgeoisie air its fatuous and uninformed prejudices. Why should the Tory Party – or, for that matter, the so-called Labour Party – be allowed to exist? A scientist didn't tolerate astrology, so why should unscientific political opinions be tolerated?

The Soviet Union did things better. There, at least, properly qualified people were running the show. Not like here!

Elementary Common Sense

It all made good sense. Change a few names around. Get rid of a lot of outdated lumber like religion – all that rubbish about dead bodies getting up and walking round gardens on Sunday mornings! – and the correct solution was Rugby School all over again. The natural leaders, the properly qualified seniors, looking after the irresponsible juniors for their own good.

The working classes? They were the decent chaps who didn't have to be told go and cheer for the First XV on the touchline. They just did it. It was the middle classes, especially the *lower* middle classes who needed stamping on. They were the cheeky little ticks who didn't clean their boots properly on Wednesdays and who gave you lip when you gave them a beating. They were epitomised by a dreadful oik called Dorking. Not on any of the teams, not in the VIth Form, in the bottom sets for French, Latin and Science... as thick as pig shit in fact! When confronted with his filthy boots, he'd actually dared to start on about pacifism, Christianity and human rights! Well, he'd got his human rights all right – six across the rear end and with his trousers down for good measure. (And how the uppity young slob had hated that embellishment!) And some tough guy he'd turned out to be. For all his talk about 'making a firm moral stand', he'd crumpled up on the *third* stroke – which was an all-time record. Ignorant, pompous, weak – downright *pathetic*! A petty bourgeois who didn't know his place.

Yes, it all made good sense.

12

Towards the New World: At the Cutting Edge of History

The next few years had been an intoxicating time. There was the intellectual challenge of his Ph.D. thesis on Working Class Movements on Tyneside in the 1890s. Rigorous, demanding and tough, it had all the exhilaration of a hard-fought game of rugger. Then there was revolutionary politics – that sense of being at the cutting edge of history... Sit-ins, demos, CND marches, being arrested for punching a policeman... He was with the students in Paris in 1968. He was in Berlin to support Red Rudi. He was arrested during the great anti-US demo in Grosvenor Square. He went to Berkley to show solidarity with SDS. He was with Tom Driberg when he went to support the Civil Rights marchers in Ulster. He met the Kray Twins and made a radical speech in the Essex University Union about the 'Revolutionary Necessity of Social Bandits'.

A new go-ahead university

He'd got a lectureship at Boldonbridge University, a new go-ahead university in a modern purpose-built campus on the outskirts of a northern industrial city. Already he was making a big impression among both students and staff.

And now this. This ecstatic union with his best student, a fitting climax to a young life of unalloyed success.

Doubts?

The next morning they reached the US airbase at East Sutton. They duly draped their anti-war banners over the barbed wire of the perimeter fence and then lay down on the tarmac and blocked the main entrance. When the police arrived and began to bodily remove them they set up a chorus of 'Ho! Ho! Ho! Ho CHI MIHN!' As arranged, a BBC outside broadcast team turned up, filmed everything and interviewed Giles who made a passionate anti-American speech... In all, it was another big success.

But as he returned to Boldonbridge on the train that evening Giles experienced little ripples of anxiety. Not second thoughts exactly, but a faint nagging uneasiness. What if he *had* made Mary pregnant? Was he *really* prepared to raise a child? And, more to the point, what would the university authorities have to say about a lecturer who screwed his students? Boldonbridge might be 'a new academic departure, a signpost for the future...' and all the rest of it, but, even there, remnants of 'bourgeois so-called morality' still persisted, especially in the person of his boss, that Christian Socialist, Professor Charles Aubrey.

2

An Awkward Fact

A month later the bombshell landed.

Mary rang him up. 'Giles, I'm pregnant.'

'Oh hell!' he exclaimed. 'I am terribly sorry to hear it! Well, you'd better get it terminated...'

'Bloody hell NO!' she exploded. 'I'm having that child and you're helping me out with it!'

'Oh?'

'Remember what you said about it in the church that night? All that stuff about showing the world how a child ought to be brought up?'

'Yes ... but...'

'NO BUTS! It's time for you to stand up and be counted. Are you authentic or are you just a bourgeois playboy? What's your answer?'

There was only one answer he could give.

'OK. Have the child and I'll help you out with it.'

He put the receiver down and continued with his preparation of a series of lectures on the Chartists.

A Tactical Retreat?

He was about to climb into bed that night when those misgivings he'd had on the way back from East Sutton re-emerged. It might be the dawn of a new age – the liberated Sixties, the tide of history moving inevitably onwards and upwards, etc., etc. – but, even here in go-ahead Boldonbridge, screwing your students and leaving them to cope with the results was going a bit far. He was only at the start of his career and Professor Aubrey – stupid old reactionary that he was – was still head of the History Department. He might be a socialist – or, at any rate, what he *thought* was a socialist! –

15

but he was also a practising member of the Roman Catholic Church with all that that meant where sex was concerned.

He telephoned Mary: '...I really think it would be better if we got married...'

'FUCKING HELL!' she screeched (as part of her 'Born Again Proletarianism' she was assiduously rehearsing all the eff words that she hadn't learned at Roedean), 'I thought you said marriage was a thing of the past? If you think I'm going to be your bit on the side, you can piss off!'

'Mary, please listen! I'm only a junior lecturer. I'm not yet a professor... I'm utterly dependent on old Charlie Aubrey – and you know what he's like...'

'Don't I fuck! Full of Christian Socialist crap!'

'Exactly. Now if I get on the wrong side of him it could make things very difficult for me – and for you, too. It could affect my whole career.'

'Your *career*! Don't be so bloody bourgeois!'

'But I'm far more use to the cause inside a university than out on the dole. We've got to compromise. It's reality.'

'Cowardice, you mean.'

'No, a tactical manoeuvre. You really ought to read a bit more Lenin. Then you'd understand. Now if you play along with me, I could get you started on a Ph.D. thesis at the university. That would be a lot better that sitting around in your bedsit smoking joints and doing nothing. Come round to my flat tomorrow evening and we'll discuss it.'

A Modern *Socialist* Marriage

Discuss it they did. From eight o'clock at night until well past two in the morning at Giles' flat in the opulent suburb of Moorside.

It was on the top floor of a big 1920s mansion that stood in a well-tended garden of lawns and rhododendrons in a tree-lined avenue of similar mansions – a monument to the success of upwardly mobile professionals who had known how to adapt to changing commercial and industrial circumstances. With its plush red curtains, mahogany sideboards and fitted carpets, it was a reassuring setting which seemed to say that whatever upheavals might be in store for the underdogs of this earth, at any rate, those clever enough to live here wouldn't be inconvenienced by them.

The marriage was to be a new kind of marriage. A role model for Giles' students. 'A Radical Matrimonial Statement' as Mary would have it. It was to be an 'open marriage', free of all bourgeois lumber. Both partners could have sex with anybody they liked. Sex, after all, was good for you, both physically and mentally. 'It's just like going to a restaurant,' declared Giles, 'only it's free and healthy. It doesn't make you fat, and it doesn't give you a hangover.'

Also, it was to be a marriage without gender stereotyping. 'None of this working-man-coming-home-to-the-housewife rubbish.' Both partners were to be entirely equal. Both could have paid jobs and both would do the housework.

'My parents really fucked me up,' said Mary. 'No love. Just dumped me on a nanny and then bundled me off to a bloody boarding school. They wanted to turn me into a socialite – you know, finishing school in Switzerland, debutante, London parties, marriage to some gruesome upper-class twit. It took three fucking years at university to straighten me out.'

'It was much the same for me,' added Giles. 'Sent off to an upper-crust boarding school and stuffed with all sorts of religious rubbish.'

'But *we're* not going to make the same mistakes with our child, are we, Giles?' interrupted Mary with vehemence.

'Certainly *not*!' came the reply, 'Our child will have a rational and liberated upbringing, free from all the bourgeois crap that our parents filled us with...'

So that was how it was to be. No bourgeois so-called morality, no religious mumbo-jumbo, free sex, free expression ... in fact, a model upbringing that would be a role model for the students.

'Another authentic radical statement,' announced Mary.

'Absolutely,' said Giles. 'Mary, you really ought to write a book about it. *The Bourgeoisie Destroyed in the Cradle*. A title like that.'

Mary nodded vigorously. She relished the idea.

Two days later they slipped down to the local registry office and got married.

Useful Idiots

Both sets of parents were dumbfounded.

For the Ponsonbys it was a devastating blow. Ever since she'd left Roedean, things had gone wrong with Mary. She'd refused to go to

17

that finishing school in Switzerland, refused to be a debutante and insisted on going to university – but not, alas, to a decent one like Oxford or Cambridge, but to a ghastly new plate-glass affair in the north of England where she had gone from bad to worse. Her home visits had become increasingly rare and, when they did occur, they were marred by a series of dreadful rows.

And now this! For years – decades even – they had been planning their daughter's wedding: the church in Chelsea, the distinguished guests, the union with one of the most illustrious families of England, the glittering reception at the Dorchester, the media coverage, the glossy photographs in the *Tatler* ... all gone!

Giles' parents heard about it indirectly. Old Dr Denby was chatting one day to an ex-patient who had a son who was a laboratory technician at Boldonbridge University. 'He's getting married in October.'

'You *must* be pleased! I do wish Giles would get married. It might settle him down and get rid of some of this leftie nonsense that has got into him.'

'But he *is* married. Will tells me that he was married a month ago to one of his students. How come you didn't know?'

It was a shock. He just couldn't understand it. He was deeply proud of his son and had rejoiced in his success. He'd given him everything – money, a good education, all he could ever want or need. So why this truculent rejection? It was so utterly incomprehensible.

'Poor Mary!' sighed a tearful Mrs Ponsonby. 'Seduced by a hippie! But we can't abandon her, can we, Charles? We must increase her allowance to twenty thousand a year. She'll need it...'

Old Mrs Denby wept: 'Giles was such a promising boy! Why has he done this to us? But we must try to win him back...'

There was to be no question of Giles' annual allowance of twelve thousand pounds being cut. Rather it was increased to fifteen thousand. 'They're still doling out the cheques!' exclaimed Mary. 'You'd have thought they'd have at least cut me off. I suppose they think they can buy me back. So fucking bourgeois!'

'Useful idiots,' commented Giles.

3

Onwards and Upwards

Things began to move. As he had promised, Giles enrolled Mary as a Ph.D. student in the History Department.

There was a bit of sniffing about this: '... But she only scraped a lower second. Ph.D.s should have firsts...'

'Throughout her final year,' declared Giles, 'she has been deeply involved in political activity, thinking of the broad picture rather than immersing herself in her own narrow and selfish personal interests... With her experience and her political maturity, she has much to offer.'

That was that. Few dared to contradict this brilliant young Cambridge man whose recently published monograph on the Tyneside working class was already raising the status of a new and, as yet, insecure foundation.

A Radical Architectural Statement at the Socio-political Interface

Then there was the question of their house. Normally a rising academic would have been expected to take up residence among the successful surgeons, bank managers and company directors in the spacious suburbs of Moorside or Northdene. Giles and Mary could easily have afforded a bow-windowed mansion in one of those sylvan avenues.

'We're not bloody bourgeois, are we?' announced Mary.

'Of course not,' replied Giles, 'We must affirm our commitment to the working class.'

So their house and its location were to be yet another 'authentic radical statement' that would point the university and, indeed, all higher education, in the direction that history was taking it. No gracious tree-lined boulevards for them! Instead it would be an 'affirmation of true working-class grit'.

After much searching they chose Gloucester Road. As Broadfell Road struck westwards out of Boldonbridge over the hills and towards the swelling mass of the Pennines, a series of streets branched steeply down into the Boldon Valley. Gloucester Road was one of these, a street of dilapidated red-brick terrace houses built in the late nineteenth century. As cut price, no frills, by-law housing, it was uncompromisingly bleak. No gardens, no avenues of big leafy trees: just raw, grimy red brick flanking the rain-lashed pavement. 'Pure Coronation Street!' cried Mary who was watching every episode as part of her 'proletarian re-education programme'.

But it was more proletarian than even that. It looked down upon the dreary sprawl of Greenwood. Seventy years ago this had been a pulsating working-class dormitory suburb serving the industrial powerhouse of the Boldon Valley. Now it was a decayed and crumbling wasteland left behind by the advance of technology. It was a world of relentless ugliness: slimy pools, piles of rubble, heaps of windblown rubbish and harsh red-brick walls; here and there were rusting steel

14 Gloucester Road

frames – the weather-worn bones of long-dead factories – and the odd smoke stack waiting to be demolished. Over the grey and polluted river, dim in the foggy haze, rose the grimy pile of once-industrial Southside.

No specious 'beauty' here. Only frankness and blunt honesty. The *real* world. The world of the class struggle.

They bought a house in the middle of the street, a decrepit thing with a blocked outdoor toilet and a backyard full of rubbish. Not that they had the slightest intention of living in a slum, however. Quite the opposite. Their aim was to show the world what a house *should* be like.

No expense was spared on its renovation. Mike Boardman, a brilliant young graduate from the Department of Architecture, gutted the entire interior and replaced it with a design of the most advanced sort. On opening the front door you stepped straight into an 'open-plan living machine', one big multi-purpose room whose very openness symbolised the honesty of the authentic working class. Along the left-hand wall was the kitchen area – an accumulation of sinks, ovens, fridges and pine-wood working spaces, placed deliberately on the left, of course, to represent the toiling masses who did all the serious work in society.

Along the wall that faced you was the study area with its minimalist – and to uneducated eyes – crude and unfinished desk of plain unvarnished wood which represented clear and uncluttered thought. To your right was the relaxing area, a broad space filled with three black leather settees, specially designed to evoke the rugged boulders of the northern hills and symbolise the no-nonsense grittiness of the North Country miners. The trestle table, made of rough-hewn planks, further stressed the blunt candour of the working class.

In the middle of the room a simple wooden staircase, unvarnished and unadorned – a ladder, really with its ostentatious absence of risers and banisters – led up to the first floor. (Its position somewhat to the left of centre was deliberate and emphasised the fact that *all* upward progress moved in a *leftward* direction.) Up there was a single bedroom and a bathroom-cum-toilet. This latter was the very last word in the technology of hygiene. For the Denby couple were not Luddites, but enthusiastically embraced scientific progress.

A further ladder led up – and leftwards as always! – into the attic directly under the roof. Total integrity prevailed here. Warm and waterproof, yes: but the rafters and the roofing planks were left for

21

all to see and the cistern and its pipes were left exposed as a 'meaningful architectural statement'.

The backyard was converted into a garage, but the outdoor toilet was lovingly preserved and retained the authenticity of a Northern 'netty'.

Al Dawson, the rising star of the Art Department, winner of all the prizes and (of course!) a forward-thinking young radical was commissioned to do the decor. The entire wall space was painted black and filled with abstract murals – bold, striking and, above all, 'meaningful'. A revolutionary theme developed as you proceeded upwards and – inevitably! – leftwards. It culminated in the attic where the opposing walls represented the male and female principles and the rafters the 'socialist resolution of the dialectic'.

Meanwhile Giles and Mary were busy covering the rough plank floors with ethnic rugs, each one of which made a 'radical statement'. An Xhosa rug showed their solidarity with the liberation struggle in South Africa. An Afghan carpet stressed their empathy with anti-colonialist peoples with 'alternative world narratives'. A Bolivian mat proclaimed their support for the exploited miners of the Andes.

Soft lighting and artfully placed spotlights completed the 'meaningful and philosophically integrated whole.'

In short, it was a masterpiece of design and was comprehensively reported in all the leading architectural journals. The *Sunday Times* did a feature on it. So did the *Observer*. The *Guardian* was ecstatic. 'It is not just Modernism,' wrote a well-known correspondent, 'but a new dimension which can only be described as "Cerebralism" ... Wherever you look, on the walls, the ceilings, the floor, at the very space itself, you meet a radical statement which challenges every lingering particle of smugness that you might retain...'

It greatly enhanced Giles' and Mary's prestige in the university.

There was, of course, talk of Gloucester Road being demolished to make way for office blocks and high-rise housing, part of an urban-renewal scheme embracing the whole of Greenwood. But, faced with those doughty defenders of the authentic working class, the newly married Denbys, the capitalist developers were forced to withdraw – as far as Gloucester Road was concerned anyway.

4

A New Radical Child Development Plan

As the days passed, Mary thought more and more about the coming child. Bourgeois childrearing, she knew, was oppressive and deeply damaging, producing all sorts of unhealthy repressions – just look at what she'd had to go through!

One day she went to the university library. As part of her research into 'women's movements on Tyneside in the 1890s', she took out a book about the Acholi tribe of North Uganda. There she learned that Acholi mothers did not bother with nappies and let their children run around naked until puberty. It was then that she had a sudden flash of insight – the spark of genius, perhaps?

No nappies? No wonder the Africans were so free and uninhibited! No wonder they were such splendid sexual performers! It was because their mothers didn't brand their nether regions and natural functions as disgusting. She'd often wondered why otherwise sane and intelligent adults were so stupid as to go to church and vote Tory. Now she knew. It was nappies and the anal fixations that they produced. Abolish nappies and you would abolish both religion and the Tory Party. Quite a thought!

There would be no nappies for her child. It would run around naked and perform its natural functions in the open air – and would grow up with a clean and hygienic mind, liberated from all mental sewage.

Naturally it would never be repressed. It would be reasoned with and encouraged to expand its critical faculties. It would become a sentient and critical human being.

To emphasise the point she went down to London and bought a Basuto rug from an expensive and 'ethnically aware' boutique.

A Gender Problem?

The child duly came. Unfortunately it was a boy. They had been hoping for a girl which would have made their planned statements about 'gender stereotyping' much easier.

But what to call it? 'My parents really fucked me about with the names they gave me,' said Mary. 'Mary Samantha-Jane De Lisle, for Christ's sake!'

'Well, you can rest assured that we're having no hidden agendas in the names,' replied Giles. 'We'll be simple and unpretentious – anti-bourgeois. What's wrong with plain John?'

So John it was. Plain John Denby.

Radical Child Development at the Socio-political Interface

'The new radical child development plan' swung into action. Freedom, liberation, reason, awareness – and, of course, no anally fixating nappies...

The trouble was that the child just didn't seem to appreciate any of this. It had no sense of 'socialist community values'. Not only was it totally and irredeemably selfish, but it was horribly demanding as well. Put it down for half a minute and try to get on with something more important and it started to bawl. If it didn't get its food just when it wanted it, it started to scream – just like an arrogant bourgeois in a posh restaurant. And when you did get round to feeding it, it sicked up half of its carefully prepared meal down your 'Support Frelimo' T-shirt. And, as if that wasn't enough, it wouldn't even let you sleep at night. It would start bawling for attention at four in the morning for Christ's sake!

Naked and free from anally fixating nappies, uninhibited by any bourgeois so-called morality? Maybe. But why did it have to go and pee all over their expensive Celtic rug, that symbol of their solidarity with the caring and peace-loving Gaelic culture so brutally crushed by the Anglo-Saxon imperialists? In the end they had to cover the floor with sheets – which rather detracted from the ethical and artistic impact of that 'radical architectural statement' to say the least.

'He's done it again!' cried Mary. 'Your turn this time, Giles!'

'Bloody hell!' groaned Giles, looking up from his half-finished lecture on the General Strike of 1926. 'Does this baby *never* stop shitting?'

Theoretically, whenever Mary looked at the baby she should have been filled with love, tenderness, caring, proletarian motherhood and such like noble emotions. But, instead – like it or not! – she was filled with revulsion. What she saw was a little pink sausage with an autocratic mouth at one end and a complete lack of social responsibility at the other. And the *smell*! That gut-wrenching reek of urine, vomit and shit!

A Necessary Radical Child Development Statement

Still, she needed the little bundle as an essential part of her 'radical child development statement'. She carried it everywhere, tied on to her back with a Zulu tablecloth that her uncle had sent her from South Africa. When Giles gave his lectures, she sat alongside him, ostentatiously breastfeeding it, her more than ample breasts exposed for all to see.

Her reputation among the students spread.

'You want to see Denby's posh totty... She's well worth looking at.'

'You should see those knockers! What a pair!'

Radical Agitation at the Socio-political Interface

Her big chance came when Giles asked her to give a talk to his student Social and Political Awareness Group. Every Tuesday evening at seven-thirty there would be a lecture-cum-seminar: 'Mind Expanding Drugs', 'The Liberation Struggle in Mozambique', 'The Coming Socialist Revolution in the Andes', 'The Repressive Nature of the Bourgeois Family' ... This time it was to be 'Liberated Child Development'.

Though she refused to admit it, Mary was acutely nervous. Public speaking was not her forte. When she had gone to debates in the University Union she'd never actually made any speeches. She'd merely shouted, 'Fascist crap!' at those who did venture to speak. Actually standing up in front of a potentially hostile crowd and trying to deliver a complicated discourse without being put off by interruptions

25

and without forgetting what you were going to say: this was a very different proposition and one which alarmed her. Supposing her mind simply went blank and she was unable to speak a word? Horrendous thought!

Still, it was a golden opportunity to burnish her academic credentials before the mutterers who considered her unfit to do a Ph.D. She had to succeed.

She went at it with a will, preparing her notes with unaccustomed care. The naked child was an essential visual aid. It would create an appropriate image of tenderness and caring and would emphasise all the points she was going to make, especially, when, at the culminating point of the discourse, she breastfed it.

Petty-Bourgeois Obstructionism?

The coming event was well advertised. The politically and socially mature students were eager to hear the radical message. Unfortunately, less desirable elements were, also, interested. Word got round that 'Denby's posh totty' was going to be on show.

'Isn't she the one who shows off her knockers in lectures?'

'That's the girl all right! Jesus, what a pair!'

That night a bunch of Engineering and Agricultural students (hardly the most enlightened of people), descended on the Union bar, got themselves well 'oiled' and, then, spilled noisily into the back of the lecture theatre.

At seven-thirty precisely Mary made her ceremonial entrance with her child on her back, wrapped in the customary Zulu tablecloth. As the lights dimmed, the spotlights focused on her as she mounted the rostrum and sat down on the chair.

Immediately a host of unforeseen problems hit her. With her heart thumping, she took the wriggling child off her back and tried to balance it on her knees. It was a matter of holding it firmly in place with her left hand while she tried to extract the twenty-odd sheets of her notes from her ethnic shoulder bag with her right hand.

The operation might just have worked if the child had been content to lie still. But it wasn't. It set up an almighty wriggle and at a crucial moment gave a colossal kick which sent the notes flying over the floor. In a near panic she put the child down and began scrabbling round trying to pick them up – only to discover that the sheets were out of order and that she hadn't numbered them. Immediately the baby set up a piercing wail.

After three quite dreadful minutes of sheer terror, she managed to get them into a sort of order. While the baby, by now bright red and arching its back, screamed in unassuaged fury on the floor, she launched into her discourse, reading directly from her retrieved notes.

'The bourgeois concept of child rearing is now in the dustbin of history. Modern liberated thinkers are increasingly looking towards the so-called primitive cultures of Africa. Among the Acholi people of North Uganda...'

'Speak up, lassie!' a loud male voice bawled out. 'We canna hear ye!'

'Hinny, yer bairn's bubblin' like!' yelled another, ostentatiously slipping into a deep Geordie, just to highlight the upper-crust cadences of her Home Counties voice, it seemed.

'Howay!' hollered somebody else. 'Yer bairn wants his supper! Get them tits oot sharp like!'

At which a drunken male chorus began to chant, 'Tits oot! Tits oot! Tits oot!'

Roars of laughter erupted and were followed by a stentorian bellow from Giles (back in the familiar role of Head of House calling the junior dormitory to order): 'QUIET! We'll have no loutish behaviour here, thank you!'

The noise subsided. 'Right, Mary,' he said softly, 'you can start again.'

She picked the child up and, with her left arm under its bare bottom, nestled it closely to her chest. Immediately the wails subsided into a gurgling chunter. Then, frantically trying to keep hold of the notes with her right hand, she began reading again, this time in a loud, almost shouting, monotone:

'The bourgeois concept of child rearing is now in the dustbin of history. Modem liberated thinkers are increasingly...

She'd hardly finished the second sentence when there was another explosion of chattering and laughter.

A Geordie voice bawled out: 'Yer wanna look at yer short. Missus, it's all shite!'

She looked down and saw to her dumbfounded horror that her T-shirt – her precious 'Make Love Not War' T-shirt was, indeed, 'all shite'. The baby had chosen that precise moment to have a colossal dump, so copious that it might have been saving it up specially for a whole week. The muck was all down her front and all over her jeans.

'That's what *he* thinks of yer lecture, Missus,' an enormous male voice called out, 'a load of shite!'

An even bigger explosion of laughter and clapping erupted. As a furious Giles berated the audience for its 'lower-class loutishness', Mary fled to the nearest toilet weeping tears of rage and humiliation. Her attempt to prove herself academically had been an excruciating public failure.

As she wiped herself down, she glanced at the baby, which was chuntering merrily to itself on the floor.

'Christ!' she exclaimed. 'You look just like my horrible mother!'

The baby didn't seem to be in the least put out by the revelation. It just flashed a broad, beaming smile.

'You little sod,' she said in a calm and deliberate voice. 'You little sod. You did that deliberately, didn't you? Just to fuck me up.'

From then on, try as she might, she couldn't stop herself hating the child.

A Crisis

A week later Mary and Giles had their first row. 'If you want to understand the feminist scene in the 1890s,' Giles had told her, 'you've got to understand Marx and Freud first.'

So she'd gone to the university library, taking the baby with her as always. Having extracted *Das Kapital*, she went over to a desk, put the baby down and began to read. Immediately the child set up a piercing wail.

'For heaven's sake!' an angry voice called out, 'this is meant to be a quiet place!'

A librarian duly arrived: 'You can't bring babies in here; it's not fair on other people who need to study. You must leave the premises.'

She wasn't used to being told what to do and didn't like it. But, in view of the universal hostility to her noisy child, she had little choice but to obey.

When she arrived back at Gloucester Road she was in a foul mood. Giles was hard at work and so frantically absorbed that he didn't notice her. Sulkily, she put the baby down on a settee and, sitting down at the table, tried once more to make sense of the first page of *Das Kapital*.

An immediate wail went up from the baby.

'Giles,' she said, 'he needs feeding. Can you see to it. It's your turn.'

'Please, dear,' he replied, 'I'm desperately busy. I *must* get these lectures ready for tomorrow. Can you do it this time?'

'But what about the division of labour we agreed on? I've got work to do too, you know.'

'But my work's rather more important than yours.'

The casual assumption of superiority infuriated her. It was a direct breach of their marriage contract. She flared up: 'So YOU'RE more fucking important are you? You arrogant BLOODY PIG!'

A full-scale slanging match exploded with both of them yelling at the top of their voices and the baby shrieking frantically as a background accompaniment. In the end a resentful Giles had to feed it.

A Matter of Place: A Properly Rational Solution

'This can't go on,' said Giles a day later. 'We're both far too busy to look after babies.'

Mary agreed: 'You know, I don't think it's really our place to be doing it. Mopping up spew and wiping bums should be left to trained child minders. Our job is to write the textbooks outlining the general principles of childrearing.'

'Precisely,' replied Giles. 'You've said it. An architect designs a house, but the menials do the actual building. It's all a matter of place.'

Maybe... But just how were they meant to implement this insight? Just what *were* they to do with the autocratic and messy little bundle with which they had so insouciantly saddled themselves? Chuck it in the dustbin along with those gruesomely tasteless wedding presents that their parents had insisted on sending them? Hardly an option in this so-called enlightened age. Auction it off to the highest bidder? Again, not a serious option.

Two days later – almost on cue – the telephone rang. It was Giles' mother asking after their welfare and that of the child which she'd recently heard about.

Giles was relieved. Deep down he'd been having pangs of conscience about the heartless way he had treated his parents and the cruel things he'd said about them. 'Useful idiots' they might be but, when all was said and done they *had* been very good to him – and, just as some people were born colour-blind, so others were born politically blind... It was time to mend broken fences.

He put on his charm: 'I'm so glad you rang. I really appreciate it. Thank you very much for that tea set you so kindly sent us... (on Mary's vehement instructions he'd consigned it to the bin). Yes, Mary adores it and has specially asked me to thank you... The child? I'm glad you mentioned him. A lovely boy, yes... But actually we've a few problems at the minute... Mary and I are frantically busy – up to our eyes in work... If you could take him for a while?'

Take the baby? There was nothing old Dr Denby and his wife would have liked better. He'd recently retired and, for a compulsive workaholic, he'd found that time hung heavily on him. So too did his wife. But a child to look after! Something to warm the increasing emptiness of their declining years! The very next day they drove up from London to collect their trophy.

Days turned to weeks, weeks turned to months, months turned to years. Giles and Mary forgot about the child. Old Dr Denby and his wife became the parents. It was a rational arrangement.

'It just states the case for the abolition of the family,' declared Giles.

'Absolutely,' agreed Mary. 'Children should not be a burden on their breeders. They should be properly reared in appropriate social units.'

5

Towards the Revolution

Immediately things improved. Freed from the unnatural treadmill of motherhood, Mary blossomed. She gave another lecture to the Social and Political Awareness Group. This time it was a success and went some way towards repairing her dented reputation.

Encouraged by this success and egged on by Giles, she embarked on her long-pondered book *Liberated Child Development: The Bourgeoisie Destroyed in the Cradle*. Her repressed sense of grievance burst out in a torrent of words and radical statements and in less than six months the manuscript had been sent to the New World Radical Alternative Press for publication. It was an immediate success and became required reading for all Humanities students at Boldonbridge.

Her academic reputation duly bolstered, she got stuck into her Ph.D. research and began to amass an enormous heap of facts.

Giles' horizons expanded. Despite initial reservations, he joined the ('so called') Labour Party. 'We must reform it from within,' he told Mary when she protested about his 'betrayal of authentic socialism'.

Education began to interest him. This, he realised, was the key to constructing a rational society. Striking up a friendship with Ed Stimpson, a passionate young radical and the rising star of the Education Department, he started a series of seminars in which the very notion of education was dismantled, piece by piece, each part subjected to rigorous examination before being reassembled into a new radical alternative. Abolish private education, get rid of the grammar schools and set up local area comprehensive schools freed from all forms of selection ... that was only the start. It was vital, Ed Stimpson declared, that the authentic working-class culture of Northern England should not be destroyed by the petty-bourgeois pretentions of the lower-middle-class teaching profession. But how to achieve this?

31

Giles had the answer. 'Rugby School!' he said.

An immediate gasp of horror swept though the assembly: 'But that's a *public* school – the very evil that we are in business to abolish!'

'Of course,' he replied, 'but we can use some of its ideas, too!'

'Dr Thomas Arnold', he continued, 'may have been a hopeless old reactionary by today's standards, but by the standards of his time he was a progressive radical. Were he alive today he would almost certainly be an advanced socialist...'

'So bloody what?' snorted a bearded weirdo with dreadlocks.

'So what, indeed?' retorted Giles, rising to the bait. Borne aloft by his sudden insight, he waxed lyrical. By handing the day-to-day running of the school and its discipline to the senior boys, Arnold had made a great educational advance. Having himself run a house full of adolescents and having nurtured them and directed their anarchic instincts into appropriate channels, he had developed real powers of leadership and social awareness. So why not apply the same principles to the new comprehensive schools that were coming into being? The teachers would only teach. Everything beyond the narrow confines of the classroom would be in the hands of the youngsters – the discipline, the sports, the whole ethos of the school. That would rescue working-class culture from the insidious clutches of the lower-middle-class teaching profession!

All heartily agreed. So when the local council set up a new comprehensive in Greenwood as part of its reconstruction scheme, Giles and Ed led a deputation to County Hall. Few of the Labour councillors could resist the great weight of intellectual rigour and socialist passion that fell on them and Giles was duly made Chairperson of the Board of Governors of the new Greenhill School. Immediately, he set to work to ensure that it would be a flagship school of a new educational era, the Rugby School of Dr Arnold, updated and shorn of all its outdated religious and class attitudes, run by its working-class pupils and with any petty-bourgeois teachers put firmly into their place – *down* into their place – as mere instructors. Thus would authentic working-class culture, the culture of the future, thrive and blossom.

More Petty-Bourgeois Obstructionism?

Neighbouring schools supplied the bulk of the initial intake.

'It's a golden opportunity to get shot of that 3C lot,' said the headmaster of St Ostwald's School, 'You know, our friend Danny Millfield and his merry men!'

'That's a bit cynical,' replied his deputy. 'Hardly the right spirit to unload all your troublemakers on to Greenhill. Can you imagine what it's going to be like?'

'Can't I just? But we've got to be realistic. The well-being of our better pupils comes first.'

So the new 'flagship school' began its career with what was described as 'a big educational challenge'.

Exactly as I would have wished,' declared Giles. 'The true authentic working class without a shred of bourgeois pretention!'

The Queer Worm doon the Well

One Saturday evening some years later Mary went into a local pub for a drink. She didn't, of course, like beer, but she felt she ought to drink the odd pint or two just to affirm her socialist identity.

Inside a local musician was singing an old ballad called the

The Queer Worm doon the Well

'Lampton Worm', which apparently was a hallowed part of an authentic North Country culture. Pulling out her notebook, she scribbled down the words as accurately as she could, though the heavy Geordie accent of the singer made them difficult to understand.

Back home she examined her scribblings:

One Sunday morning young Lampton went a-fishing in the Wear
And he caught upon his hook a worm that looked mighty queer.
Now what kind of worm it was young Lampton couldna tell.
He couldn't tyak it hyem so he hoyed it doon the well.
And away he went to Palestine where many queer things him befell
And forgot all aboot the queer worm doon the well...'

Suddenly that set her thinking. What, she wondered, was happening to *her* queer worm, not exactly 'doon the well', but somewhere down in London?

6

Meanwhile, down in London...

The answer was that quite a lot was happening to the 'queer worm' down in the neighbourhood of London.

The child had given the Denby grandparents a new sense of purpose. 'We thought we'd done everything right for Giles,' said old Dr Denby, 'but we must have gone wrong somewhere. We must not make the same mistake again.'

'John isn't ours,' added his wife, 'so we must make a special effort to make him feel that he is.'

'Every valley shall be exalted and every mountain and hill made low...' So everything possible was done to ease his path through life. Twenty-seven Oaktree Gardens, Houghton-upon-Thames, provided a suitable setting. It was a spacious red-brick villa, built in the 1930s, set in a garden of trimmed lawns and luxuriant rhododendron bushes, one of many such villas in a broad tree-lined avenue. In it were books and toys and an affectionate part-time nanny called Mrs Bowles who also acted as a housekeeper when things got a bit hectic for the old couple. It was an ordered world of feeding times, potty times and bedtimes, interspersed with lots of cuddles and affection. There were birthday and Christmas presents galore – almost too many.

'I do hope we're not spoiling him,' sighed old Mrs Denby when somebody had presented him with yet another oversize teddy bear.

But he didn't seem to be the sort of child that you could spoil. As he grew up they began to notice that he was very different from Giles. Giles had been a strong willed and tempestuous child, always wanting his own way and, not infrequently, only to be controlled by physical force. But John rarely did anything wrong. He always did as he was told. A quiet no and a soft voice would always get you what you wanted. Be nice to him and you had him.

He seemed anxious to please. When other children came to his birthday parties he didn't seem to mind if they played with his radio-controlled car and broke it. He'd simply get another toy out of the cupboard and give them that.

'John's so *easy*!' said old Mrs Denby. 'With Giles it was always such a battle – oh those temper tantrums he used to have!'

'I sometimes wonder if John isn't a bit *too* easy,' mused her husband. 'Maybe a bit soft – even rather *girlie*!'

Indeed, with his mop of white hair, his big appealing eyes and his neat little body, he *could* have been a little girl.

The old couple would go to Italy for their holidays, driving down through France in their big car. Young John would be very quiet during the long and boring journey and especially patient when they looked round boring old churches and art galleries. As a reward he was always given lots of ice cream and taken to the fairground for lots of exciting rides. 'We must never forget John,' they said. 'He's always so good.'

Dynastic Continuity

Old Dr Denby had a great sense of dynastic continuity. So young John was to follow in Giles' footsteps, to Rickerby Hall, the local prep school – first to the infants' department and then to the main school – and then on to Rugby School and, hopefully, up to Cambridge.

Rickerby Hall was a Georgian mansion set in an ample spread of playing fields and grand old trees. Once it had been the local manor house, but most of the estate had been engulfed in the suburban sprawl of an expanding London. Now it was a little island of greenery in an ocean of red-brick villas of which Oaktree Gardens was a nearby example.

It was a gentle and comforting ambience, especially on warm summer afternoons – the mellow, ivy-covered pile of the main school with its warren of cosy little classrooms, the spacious grounds with the rustling of leaves and the smell of newly cut grass, the dark mysteries of the gnarled old trees that surrounded the playing fields... Dressed in his purple cap, his grey shirt, his striped school tie, his grey shorts and his purple socks, John quickly became a part of it – the daily walk to and from school, past the beech trees and the well-trimmed hedges, and on through Rickerby Park with its ornamental lake, rowing boats and scattering of ducks; the school library with its piles of old *National Geographic* magazines which transported you into exotic worlds of immense deserts, strange temples in steamy jungles and vast ranges of untrodden snowy mountains... He made friends easily with the other boys and, with his radiant smile and his natural good manners, he was soon popular with the teaching staff.

Paradise of a Sort

Later on he would view this period of his life as a paradise. But at the time he didn't see it that way. Bliss is only bliss when it has misery to set alongside it. White needs black to highlight it. Rather, it was normality – a shade of cream with odd specks of grey and bright white scattered around it.

The grey specks, the bad bits, were a detention for not doing his Latin homework, a lost fight with a bigger boy called Bill Goodhard and being dressed down by Mr Cotton, the headmaster, for losing his temper with a smaller boy called Michael and punching him in the face. Greyest of all was the big row which had followed the celebrated Battle of Rickerby Park Lake. It had been one of those glorious balmy evenings towards the end of the summer term – a cornucopia of green bushy trees, warm grass and the shimmering expanse of the lake. They'd hired rowing boats and, before long, a mighty sea battle had erupted. It was Ben Hur, the Great Armada and Trafalgar all rolled into one – a frantic ecstasy of ramming, boarding enemy ships and life-and-death grapples which ended only when both parties plunged to their doom in the twelve inches of lake water. Of course, the park keeper had blown a fit, ordered them out and reported the whole business to Mr Cotton, who had blown an even bigger fit.

But everything had been sorted out – as it always was. Bill Goodhard had been given a bollocking by Mr Cotton and told that it was wrong to fight boys who were smaller than himself. He'd apologised to John. And John had been told – very sternly! – that he was not to lose his temper and hit little boys. After all, Jesus never hit little boys and he hadn't got to do so either. He had to say sorry to little Michael – and when he bought him a packet of wine gums general approval was registered and he was duly absolved of his wrongdoing. After the Rickerby Lake affair they all had to go and apologise to the park-keeper and spend a whole Saturday afternoon helping him pick up litter.

An Orderly Place

Rickerby Hall was an orderly place – homework, weekly tests, form orders, end-of-term exams, games on Wednesday and Friday afternoons. Unlike Giles, John didn't shine at any of these things. 'He's a very average boy,' Mr Cotton told the grandparents. 'He won't get into Rugby. I think Milton Abbey would be a better place for him.' He was no good at Maths – and hated it! Neither was he much good at Latin or French. History was all right, but a bit boring. Scripture, however, he loved – all those wonderful old stories of long ago.

Which was just as well because God was very much a part of his life. Every day at Rickerby Hall there was morning assembly where you said thank you to God and asked him to help you through the day. Every Sunday his grandparents took him, first to Sunday School where he listened to all those glorious old tales – he particularly liked the one about young David sorting out that big bully Goliath. Then there was the proper church afterwards with its music and candles and where you joined the grown-ups and went up to the altar where the vicar gave you wafers and let you have a sip of wine. God was a nice old man – an upgraded Mr Cotton, who, instead of living in a house, lived somewhere up in the clouds above you.

One morning, however, he learned that there was rather more to God than that. He was walking up the school drive when he saw a tiny little bird, a little chick, lying alone on the gravel. He picked it up and, seeing that it was almost dead, rushed into the school. The first teacher he met was Mrs Selby, the Scripture teacher.

'This poor little bird is dying!' he spluttered. 'Can you save its life?'

'I'm afraid it's already dead, John,' she replied.

Tears welled up in his eyes: 'Oh no! The poor thing! Why was it lying all alone on the ground? Why didn't any of the other birds help it?'

'Probably it was pushed out of its nest by the other chicks. Stronger chicks often kill the weaker ones so that they can get more food.'

The tears began to trickle: 'But that's *horrible*! The poor little thing! All it ever knew was birds bullying it and stealing its food!'

John had suddenly become aware of something dark and nasty in the world. It was a revelation that stayed with him for the rest of his life.

'Don't worry, John,' said Mrs Selby, putting a mothering arm round him. 'It's gone to God now and God will look after it.'

He felt an enormous sense of relief. So the world was not ruled by blind cruelty after all. God saw to that!

A month later he put his pet guinea pig, Fred, on the dining room table to show him off to his friends. Unfortunately, Fred was not over-blessed with brains and walked over the edge. He died instantly. John was devastated. Poor innocent Fred, killed through his owner's thoughtless negligence! He took the earthly remains to the vicar who blessed them and assured him that, yes, Fred had indeed gone to heaven. John buried him with due reverence at the bottom of the garden and put a wooden cross on the grave.

But everything was all right because God was in charge. Everybody had to thank him and try to behave themselves, just as the boys at Rickerby Hall had to behave themselves.

Which, of course, was what John tried to do. He might not be very good at Maths, Latin or games, but he always tried hard. Jesus himself had said that the widow's mites were worth all the gold of the Pharisees – and he *knew*! 'It's not a matter of how clever you are, John,' declared Mrs Selby, 'but of how hard you try.'

And it did seem to work. One day a wonderful moment came – a bright white splash in the cream. At morning assembly he was called up to the rostrum and given the school prize for effort by Mr Cotton himself. It was a twenty-pound book token. With it he bought a big and sumptuously illustrated *Children's Bible*, which he proudly showed to Mrs Selby.

'Yes,' she said, 'Jesus really will be pleased with you!'

And Jesus did, indeed, seem to be pleased with him. Shortly afterwards, on a dull and bleak day in November, he was asked to play in a Second XV match against a neighbouring prep school because one of the wing forwards happened to be ill. Rickerby Hall duly won the match, but he was completely outclassed by the bigger and stronger boys around him and only just managed to keep up with the game. Yet the following morning in assembly, after the plaudits had been given out and the colours distributed, Mr Cotton called him up to the rostrum and gave him a special badge for trying hard. 'John, here', he told the school, 'is a very brave boy. Even though he was smaller and weaker than his teammates, he still did his best and that's what really counts.'

Yes, Jesus really was on his side. That *Children's Bible* had worked wonders for him. It was twenty pounds well spent.

'Who's Giles?'

All the while Giles and Mary were never mentioned. Only on two occasions did the subject ever arise.

One Sunday afternoon, while rummaging in the depths of his bedroom cupboard, he found a dusty old box full of books. Out of curiosity he pulled one out and began to read it. Soon he was transfixed. It was about a pilot called James Bigglesworth who flew fighters in the war and who did wonderfully exciting things. For the rest of that afternoon he luxuriated in high adventure – heroic battles in Spitfires against the massed power of Hitler's Luftwaffe. Finishing the book towards evening, he was thrilled to find that the box contained at least ten more such books – a whole new world of adventure was stacked up there, adventure in wildly exotic places, from the frozen, snow-bound forests of Finland, to the grey, storm-lashed islands of the Antarctic Ocean and the steamy jungles of Northern Australia.

He felt as if he had unearthed buried treasure on one of those Caribbean islands that you read about in pirate stories.

'Mum,' he said to his grandmother, 'I've just found a box of wicked books at the bottom of my wardrobe. Where did they come from? I mean whose are they?'

'Oh they were Giles'. He loved Biggles books when he was a boy. He collected the whole series.'

'Giles? Who's Giles?'

'Oh he's our son,' was the guarded reply. 'But he left us long ago. Now they're yours.'

'Cor, thanks, Mum!'

That ended that.

About a month after this a boy asked him why his gran and granddad were so much older than other boys' parents. 'They can't be your *real* parents. They're far too old.'

Back at home he confronted his grandfather. Why was this so? Were they his *real* mum and dad?

'Yes and no,' replied the old man. 'The mum and dad who actually produced you live in the north of England. They have to work very hard and have no time to look after kids. So Mum and I are looking after you for them. We're your *real* mum and dad.'

That seemed sensible. As far as John was concerned Giles and Mary did not exist. After all he never saw them. They never visited the house. They were never even talked about.

Rational World

Such, then, was John Denby's world. It was a world of clear-cut certainties. Children were silly, rowdy and dirty-minded. They even thought toilets were funny. Grown-ups were sensible. They always behaved themselves. They were always there when you needed them. When you were sick in your bed Mrs Bowles always cleaned it up and gave you new sheets and pyjamas. Grown-ups didn't think toilets were funny.

Above all, his gran and granddad were totally perfect.

Everybody lived in nice red-brick villas. All children went to prep schools and, then, went on to public schools like Eton, Winchester and Rugby. John Denby wasn't very bright, but he was a good boy, brave and tough, too – and certainly not a little weed.

Holding everything together was God who expected everybody to be good and rewarded them when they were.

It was a rational world.

7

A Slide into Badness?

But one day this world stopped being rational.

It was in September when he was just eleven years old. It was a curious day which really began the night before. His grandparents were away visiting friends and Mrs Bowles was in charge of the house. Returning from school that evening, he'd bought two videos, *Tora! Tora! Tora!* and *A Bridge Too Far*. If his grandparents had been there they would have sat him down at the dining-room table and made him do his homework. But Mrs Bowles was less strict and after tea he'd slipped upstairs to watch television in his bedroom, emerging only for a brief supper before settling down to enjoy his two newly acquired treasures. He'd become so engrossed that he'd forgotten all about the vocabulary he had to learn for his Latin homework. After Mrs Bowles had put his light out at nine o'clock, he'd waited till she'd gone back downstairs before carrying on with the Battle of Arnhem, and, when that was finally over, he'd started on *Tora! Tora! Tora!*, wallowing in the explosive pandemonium of Pearl Harbor. It must have been well past 1 a.m. before he finally dropped off to sleep.

The First Obstacle...

He slept in that morning. He was sleepy and grumpy when Mrs Bowles dug him out of bed and, after a makeshift breakfast, bundled him off to school. He dawdled all the way there and was nearly late for assembly.

The first lesson was Latin with Mr Grant. Mr Grant was something of a joke. Was the phenomenon a he or a she? That was the question. It looked like an old woman with its beaky nose and long white hair and sounded like one with its high-pitched, squeaky voice which rose to a scream when it was excited or annoyed. But it had white hair coming out of its ears and huge masses of black hair covering

42

its hands. It also dressed in men's clothes, in particular in a dreadful old sports jacket – all leather patches and loose bits of thread – which it wore term in and term out and never seemed to change. ('It was a present from Julius Caesar when he left Britain in 54 BC. That's why it's so fond of it.') The boys called him 'Hairy Mary'.

But Hairy Mary was no pushover. Acutely aware of his vulnerability to schoolboy attack, he was the master of the pre-emptive strike. Tests, form orders, litter picks, detentions, minus marks, reports to the headmaster, letters to parents... he deployed them all with the deadly efficiency of the US Air Force. He was not to be crossed.

Wilful Negligence

When he handed round the sheets of paper John suddenly remembered the Latin homework that he'd forgotten to do. He waited glumly as the time-honoured ritual went through its course: Name on the top of the paper. Today's date. (Get that wrong and you'd miss morning break!) Title. ('Latin Vocabulary Test' – again, of vital importance.)

It was like being the tenth man in the Roman Army when the centurion went down the line 'decimating' your cohort because it had failed in battle.

'Ready? Wait for it! Number one: Latin for sailor.'

He hadn't a clue. In desperation he wrote 'Sailorus'.

'Number Two. Latin for flower.'

Another ghastly blank. He wrote down 'Pansia'.

'Number Three. Latin for ship.'

Unable to think of anything at all, he simply wrote down, 'I don't know.'

He was shocked at himself. This was suicide – the Charge of the Light Brigade at Balaclava. Hairy Mary would blow at least four gaskets when he saw that. It would mean two minus marks, Saturday morning detention and a major bollocking from Mr Cotton.

A sense of doom descended.

Worse and Worse

He was sleepy and headachy for the rest of the morning. His sin of omission weighed heavily upon him. How to expiate it? He

43

could wriggle out of it by saying that he hadn't done his homework because he'd had to go and see a sick uncle who was very ill with cancer. But that was a lie – and, even if Hairy Mary did manage to swallow it (highly unlikely!), up in heaven, where it really mattered, Jesus certainly wouldn't. He would give him a big black mark in the conduct book he was keeping... It was better to spill the beans. But that meant approaching Hairy Mary in break time – not something you undertook lightly. He could, of course, go straight to Mr Cotton... But, again, that could be a hazardous enterprise.

Pondering these options in the lunch queue, he was not concentrating on the problem in hand – keeping up and not letting other boys get in front of you.

'Wake up, John!' snapped the prefect on duty. 'You're holding things up!'

Suddenly, a scruffy little fellow called Jimmy Stokes darted in front of him. This woke him up. Jimmy Stokes was the school thug. The school was divided into two classes: those strong enough to stand up to him and those who were not. Honour and status were at stake. In a blaze of temper, John grabbed his blazer and threw him on to the floor. Jimmy was notorious for his aggression, a knobbly little boy, all bones and sharp edges. Immediately, he got up and rushed at him, fists flailing.

'Fight! Fight! Fight!' chorused the queue, gleefully gathering round the scrapping bundle of waving arms and flapping blazers

'STOP IT! BREAK IT UP AT ONCE!' bellowed Mr Sedgewick, the master on duty.

The crowd fell silent as the two combatants disentangled themselves and stood red-faced and panting heavily. John descended a step further into gloom. The very least he could expect was to be sent to the back of the queue and having to stand in the corner for the rest of lunch-break. He would probably get two minus marks as well. Four minus marks in a week! That would mean having his name read out in assembly and being put on punishment – litter picks, tidying up the library and even (if the teacher on duty was in a bad mood) having to swill out the bogs. Down and still further down! This day had a jinx on it!

But, then, something very odd happened. Mr Sedgewick didn't consign him to the corner. Nor did he even send him to the back of the queue. Instead, speaking in a very quiet and gentle voice, he said, 'All right, John. Just calm down. Take your place in the queue and, Jimmy, don't try to push in front of him.'

It was weird. Unheard of in the annals of Rickerby Hall where orderly behaviour in the dining room was as much a part of the syllabus as Maths or Latin. What *was* going on?

Weirder and Weirder...

The weirdness continued. It was Wednesday afternoon, games afternoon. The changing room was Mr Bryson, the games' master's domain. Mr Bryson was a part-time soldier in the Territorial Army and, through the changing room, he acted out his frustrated military aspirations. It had to be kept up to the mark, on parade and dressed by the right, the yardstick of his military efficiency.

John was not in the mood for games. He dawdled and dithered, put his rugby shirt on and then remembered that he'd forgotten to remove his vest so he had to take it off again. He was about to go out when he remembered that he hadn't had his precautionary pee and had to dive into the bogs. By the time he reached the rugby field the game had already started. Then he remembered that he'd put the wrong rugby shirt on and that he hadn't hung his clothes up on the requisite hook – two of the most heinous sins in the 'Bryson Book of Iniquity'. Two minus marks at least! Six in one day! This day was plummeting down into catastrophe.

All through the game he stumbled lethargically about, trying to try. He hung limply round the edge of the scrum, dropped every ball that was passed to him and even failed to tackle a little wimp called Jeffrey who jogged round him and scored a try. Normally 'Foghorn Bryson' would have blown a fit and made him run all the way round the touchline. But, instead, he smiled at him and continually praised him for the most pathetic things. 'Well done, John! Well tried!' he said when he dropped yet another pass. It was quite unlike old Foghorn!

'Oh John, you DORK!' a teammate yelled at him when the ball bounced past him and landed in touch.

'Quiet, please,' said Bryson in a soft voice that was quite out of character.

What *was* going on? Just why was old Foghorn being so nice to him when he was being so obviously pathetic?

A Vision of the Future?

In his hazy, sleepy state his mind began to wander. Maybe there *was* a reason. He remembered that conversation with his grandfather – 'The mum and dad who actually produced you live in the north of England. They... have no time to look after kids. So Mum and I are looking after you for them...' That could be it. His *real* father could be somebody very important – perhaps, even, the Duke of Edinburgh? Maybe he was the *real* heir to the throne and Prince Charles was a fake? Now the plot had been discovered and that very afternoon he would be on his way to Buckingham Palace. Crazy? Yes! But, then, there had to be some explanation for this crazy day.

Back in the changing room, however, the tide of disaster flowed on. He failed to shower properly and arrived at inspection with his knees still muddy. Normally, Foghorn would have sent him back again – not much fun when all the hot water had been used up. Inexplicably, he didn't seem to mind and let him go and dress. Neither did he seem to be bothered about his games kit being left all over the floor. Instead, he picked it up for him and chatted amiably about what a good boy he was and how hard he'd tried.

But he *hadn't* been a good boy and he *hadn't* tried! Something funny was going on. So was he *really* the undiscovered heir to the throne? The idea thrilled him.

An Explanation... Grown-ups Are Such Dorks...

He put on his cap and his coat and, picking up his bag, set off down the corridor making for home. It was Maths homework tonight – Yuk! Yuk! – but, after he'd had a good stab at it, he'd go to bed and make up for all the sleep he'd missed the night before. Then in the morning, properly refreshed, he'd straighten things out. He'd make his peace with Hairy Mary, learn his Latin vocabulary and get back to normality. And he'd forget all about that dreamy nonsense about being the heir to the throne – if Jimmy Stokes should hear of that! He'd never live it down!

Mr Cotton was standing in the main entrance, blocking his way, a massive figure in his dark suit and brightly polished shoes. He was the very last person he wanted to see at that particular moment. He'd deal with him after he'd sorted out Hairy Mary and not before.

That was part of tomorrow's task to be performed when he'd had a good sleep and could think clearly. He looked directly down on to the polished wooden floor and tried to scuttle past him.

'John! John Denby!' a calm, but authoritative, voice called out.

Caught! Help! Obviously his accumulation of iniquity had been reported to Mr Cotton and he was in for 'the chop' – whatever that might be.

'Please, please,' he mumbled. 'I'm terribly sorry about the Latin test this morning. I'm going to learn the vocabulary properly tonight, I promise... I'm sorry about the fight in the dining room. I'll buy Jimmy Stokes a packet of wine gums, I promise...'

'Yes, of course you will. But don't worry about that. It's not important, John.'

'Can I go home now? I'm rather tired and I've got a lot of homework to do.' 'No, John, this is rather more important than your Maths homework. Come into my study because there's something we've got to talk about.'

A frisson of fear rippled through him. The headmaster's study! The holy of Rickerby Hall holies! You only went there when you had done something really bad. Unknown to him he must have done something quite dreadful, not just bad, but *wicked*!

'Please, please, not your study! I know I've been bad today, but I'll be good tomorrow, I promise...'

An oddly patient voice interrupted the flow: 'No, John, of course you haven't been bad. You're a very good boy, we all know that.'

Bemused he followed the headmaster into the big, Georgian front room that was the operational heart of Rickerby Hall. He gazed in wonderment. Compared with the rather battered classrooms and halls that he knew, it was quite unexpectedly sumptuous – a beautiful room with its big windows, its white plaster garlands and urns decorating the light-blue walls and its big oil paintings in their gold frames. It was just like those palaces you saw illustrated in history books. Seated in comfortable armchairs round the beautifully carved marble fireplace were the school matron and the local vicar.

Something was up.

The vicar stood up, a big man with white hair and a smooth, shiny face. 'Sit down, John,' he said deferentially, 'now would you like a coke or an orange juice?'

John sat down on the vacated chair: 'A coke, please. This is very kind of you. Thank you very much.'

47

This was going to be something nice. Perhaps he really *was* the heir to the throne after all? He sipped the coke expectantly.

'Now, John,' continued the Vicar, 'you are a very brave boy and I want you to be very brave now.'

John felt a surge of excitement. This was thrilling. Perhaps he had been chosen for some secret mission – like Biggles, maybe?

'It's about your grandparents...'

There was silence. Everybody was looking at him. This was it. Yes, he really *was* the heir to the throne and Charles was a fake after all.

'I'm afraid they've gone to Jesus.'

The vicar always mumbled and he didn't catch the last word.

'Gone to Jersey?' he asked. 'Will I be going there, too?'

This could be the start of a big adventure. His excitement mounted.

'No, John,' said Mr Cotton in a gentle voice, 'They've gone to *Jesus*. I'm afraid you can't go with them.'

'Oh?' This was mysterious. He didn't quite understand.

There was a long and embarrassed silence.

Eventually Mrs Maxwell, the pointy-nosed Matron who always wore a nurse's blue uniform, spoke up: 'They're both dead, John. They were killed in a motor accident this morning.'

He stared open-mouthed. His first reaction was disappointment. No adventures. No going to Buckingham Palace. Just this. What a let-down!

Then came bewilderment. Dead? In his world people just didn't die. People in history, yes – like King Harold in the Battle of Hastings. But that was history. It was different.

Another embarrassed silence followed as he sat there wondering what he was supposed to do. Cry, perhaps? But it was wrong to cry. It was wet and soppy. Only girls and weedy boys cried. Proper boys certainly didn't. So he just sat there and gaped.

Then, to his embarrassed fury, Mr Maxwell put her arm round him and the vicar knelt down and mumbled a prayer. It was all so pathetic – and in front of the headmaster, too! Grown-ups were such dorks!

Caught in an Avalanche

Mr Cotton drove him home in his car and handed him over to a solemn Mrs Bowles who, to his red-faced indignation, gathered him up in her arms and kissed him. In public and in front of the headmaster of all people! The shame of it! Thank God none of his classmates was there. Grown-ups were such idiots. They always thought you were still a baby! They were always showing you up in public!

Sulkily, he wriggled himself free. Without a word he went into the dining room and settled down to his Maths homework. He had to return to normality after this lunatic day. The exercise consisted of equations and 'factorizing', something he couldn't really understand. As he stared at the incomprehensible jumble of figures, something wholly unexpected happened. A tidal wave of emotion overwhelmed him.

In later years, when he was an experienced mountain traveller, he compared it to being swept away by an avalanche. It was like that wild, insane business of tumbling downwards, struggling for breath as the icy boulders crashed into you in a maelstrom of utter madness. The deep, inexpressible love for his grandparents, always felt, but never articulated, his protectors, his everything, the awful, unimaginable and quite irreplaceable loss, the sense of abandonment and loneliness, the sheer horror of what had happened. One after another, sometimes all at once, the boulders crashed into him amid a suffocating swirl of stinging snow, hurling him downwards into a black pit of nothingness. He sobbed convulsively.

Being brave had nothing to do with it. It was like being sick, something which just happened and over which you had no control.

'Mum! Mum!' he sobbed as he dashed into the kitchen and flung himself into Mrs Bowles' ample bosom.

He cried and cried until, inexplicably, the wave seemed to have passed away.

'Don't worry,' said Mrs Bowles. 'They're both in heaven now.'

So there they were, safe and sound, along with the poor dead chick he'd picked up in the school drive and with Fred, his martyred guinea pig. In due course he'd see them all again.

With that comforting thought he went to bed and slept soundly.

Back to Normal?

He awoke refreshed the next morning. The silly irrational day was over. It was back to normality. Mrs Bowles got him up, he washed, dressed and went downstairs for breakfast.

But just as he was about to attack his boiled egg another avalanche engulfed him. Loss, anguish and emptiness swept him away in a torrent of awfulness. Anger, too – wild rage at God's betrayal of him. Why had God done this to him? He'd tried so hard to be good. He'd gone to church, bought Michael a packet of wine gums, spent his twenty-pound book token on a *Children's Bible* ... God was supposed to reward good boys, not kill their treasured grandparents.

When he eventually emerged from the mayhem and the tears had dwindled into a trickle, Mrs Bowles said, 'God didn't kill your grandparents. It was a drunk driver who crashed into their car. He'll be sent to prison for it...'

That made sense.

A New Mum?

He was too upset to go to school that day, so Mrs Bowles took him into London where they bought a Great Western pannier tank engine for his train set, had fish and chips for lunch, and went to the cinema in the afternoon where they saw the latest James Bond film.

At bedtime that night, when Mrs Bowles came to put out his light, he said, 'You can be my mum now and I'll go to school tomorrow.'

Life would continue as before.

Unseen Problems...

But things weren't that simple.

For a start, all boys didn't go to prep schools. Only those with parents rich enough to pay the fees did. And, unless parents paid the fees, prep schools couldn't exist. There was deep sympathy for John at Rickerby Hall – and goodwill in abundance – but survival had to come first. He could only stay there if somebody was prepared to pay the fees.

Neither could Mrs Bowles be his mum. She had a sick husband who could only be left alone for short periods. One daughter was happily married and was living in Australia. But the other had divorced her husband and was living on social security in Lambeth where her two little sons were suffering from the effects of her increasing alcohol problem. Sooner rather than later Mrs Bowles was going to have to move into that council flat and take charge of those two vulnerable grandchildren.

In any case, John was not her problem. Old Dr Denby had never been much good at understanding the legal niceties. A casual arrangement made over the phone – 'Yes, we'll take the baby for a few weeks...' – had become a de facto adoption. De facto, but not de jure. The legal guardians remained Giles and Mary. They were responsible for young John, not her.

8

Success and More Success

And what of Giles and Mary?

Over the past ten years Giles had flourished. Well established at Boldonbridge University, he had published three groundbreaking monographs – one on nineteenth-century Irish immigration in Newcastle on Tyne, another on Chartism in Sunderland and a third on the Suffragettes in Manchester. All had been well reviewed in the learned journals. Now he was deep into another one, this time on the Liverpool working class in World War II. His reputation as a tough academic working at the cutting edge of his subject was burgeoning.

He was by now heavily involved in Labour Party politics – in constant touch with Arthur Scargill and producing a stream of papers on the injustice and deprivation that was rampant in North Country mining villages, all tightly argued and bursting with well-aimed and relevant facts. Nor was that all. Little, it seemed, escaped his rigorous analytical mind – the parlous state of the Tyneside shipbuilding industry, the substandard council housing in Boldonbridge, the outrageous middle-class exploitation of the Welfare State... you name it! And, of course, the sheer nonsense of Thatcherism. Its callousness and its intellectual vapidity were ruthlessly exposed in articles in *New Society*, the *New Statesman* and the *Guardian*.

He was aiming high – beyond the constrictions of mere academia, to Parliament and ministerial office where he could actually change society rather than merely talking about it. The first step was to get himself nominated as the Labour Party candidate for Boldonbridge West when Sam Clarke, the current member, retired before the next election. His public-school background would, of course, be a disadvantage, but this would be more than offset by his concern for the working class.

Greenhill School had been a big success. He had ensured that it embraced all his progressive ideas and that it affirmed working-class culture by allowing the proletarian youngsters to take charge of its discipline and essential ethos. Having seen it successfully launched as the 'Flagship School of Northern England' [*sic*], he had duly relinquished his post as chairperson of the governing body.

There were, of course, dissenting voices – sadly predictable in an unreformed bourgeois society! – that complained of indiscipline, low to non-existent academic standards, vandalism and the intimidation of teachers. Indeed, some of these middle-class bird brains actually went so far as to talk of the school being taken over by criminal gangs...

'Good!' Giles told the Social and Political Awareness Group one Tuesday evening, 'Good! This so-called 'indiscipline' simply means that the authentic working class is finally rejecting the tyranny of the petty-bourgeois teaching profession that has been stifling its aspirations for far too long! So Greenhill has been taken over by "criminal gangs", has it? That's just another way of saying that the local proletariat is asserting itself. So the average length of a teacher's stay at Greenhill is only six weeks? What do you realistically expect from lower-middle-class flea brains with delusions of grandeur? Of course, the proletariat sees through their pretentions and treats them with the contempt they deserve! It's high time these people knew their place. They complain of vandalism, do they? Broken windows, trashed classrooms, so-called obscene graffiti? What's so wrong with that? It's simply the healthy working-class reaction to our unreformed bourgeois society. What do their lordships think the Winter Palace looked like after the October Revolution, for Christ's sake? That is assuming that they have actually heard of the October Revolution – which I doubt!'

All of which Ed Stimpson, now head of the Education Department and a regular speaker at the Social and Political Awareness meetings, heartily endorsed.

With all this Giles had little time to think about his parents. Though he had rebelled against their cloying possessiveness, he didn't really hate them. Much of the time he'd simply used them as a necessary part of a political statement – their reactionary black to highlight his progressive white. At the same time he continued to regret the cruel and ungrateful things he'd said about them. A little thought showed that they *had* been good to him. Despite everything, they'd behaved with unstinting generosity and by taking charge of the baby they'd relieved him of an impossible burden. As the years passed his nagging sense of guilt festered like a persistent stomach ulcer. In his mind he planned a full reconciliation – a visit, a long stay and a heart-to-heart talk. But immediate pressures had always deferred the date. He always *meant* to arrange it, but never got round to doing it.

So, apart from a few brief telephone calls, he'd had no contact with his parents for ten years.

A Little Less Success

Mary had been less successful. Over the years the euphoria of her groundbreaking book had faded. Martha Merrins, the head of the Sociology Department, had 'seriously questioned many of its unsubstantiated assertions'. *Liberated Child Development: The Bourgeoisie Destroyed in the Cradle* was now 'recommended reading' for the Humanities students of Boldonbridge University, but no longer 'required reading' – which was, of course, a step down.

Meanwhile, her Ph.D. thesis remained unborn. She had accumulated masses of facts – heaps and heaps of them – but, somehow, she just couldn't reduce them to any kind of order. It was like trying to build a skyscraper out of a pile of rubble. Where, for Christ's sake, did you even *begin* to start? One day she *would* get it all sorted out. One day in the future, but not just yet...

Meanwhile she led a full life – lecturing to Giles' students on childrearing, lecturing to women's groups on feminine issues, organising a Feminist Support Group for the Striking Miners, setting up a Support Group for the Sendero Luminoso Freedom Fighters of Peru...

Apart from the cheques that continued to arrive every month, she'd lost all contact with her parents. They were now living in Bermuda and were out of reach. The estrangement was complete.

The Apex of the Social Pyramid

The house in Gloucester Road was now the radical centre of Boldonbridge University – liberated, free and pulsating with progressive thought, the very spear point of social and political awareness. On Sunday nights there would be parties. Not, of course, for the plebs, but for the politically and academically mature – selected honours students from the History Department, sociology students doing their Ph.D.s, overseas students from the exploited neo-colonialist states of the so-called Commonwealth ... the vanguard of the revolution, Lenin's 'elite cadre' in fact.

It was an intoxicating mixture of alcohol, sex, revolutionary politics and drugs – though latterly they'd had to go easy on the drugs bit, in public at any rate! To be invited to attend a 'soirée' at Gloucester Road was a sure sign of 'arrival'.

An Awkward Intrusion

Then the bombshell landed.

First a visit from a policeman, then a telephone call from Mrs Bowles, then, a little later, a letter from a solicitor.

Giles broke the news to Mary on Monday evening.

'Both my parents are dead. I thought I'd better tell you.'

'Oh,' she muttered over her bowl of Costa Rican gallo pinto. (This latter, a gesture of solidarity with the exploited peons of Central America.)

Silence followed.

'It means that I'll have to go to the funeral,' continued Giles eventually. 'Also, I'll have to spend some time down there sorting things out.'

'Isn't that rather bourgeois? Funerals and money-grubbing over the will? Can't you just forget about it?'

'No, darling, I'm afraid I can't.'

'Why not?' She fixed him with her 'analytical stare'. (This was a theatrical device she'd been perfecting over the years, a penetrating look which meant, 'I'm right and, despite your pretentious pomposity, you know it.' It worked very well with the insecure first-year students.)

Giles ignored it. He was beginning to find her 'uncontaminated radicalism' just a little irritating. He had a faint suspicion – as yet a single toxic virus in the bloodstream – that, while he had become an adult, she was still a naughty schoolgirl who could afford to break the rules because she never had to face up to the consequences of her naughtiness. Besides, he was genuinely shocked by the sudden and wholly unexpected death of his parents. There could be no reconciliation now. He would carry that nagging feeling of guilt to the grave.

More silence. Mary continued to munch her gallo pinto.

'It'll mean having that kid back again,' Giles finally said.

'Oh *him*! I'd forgotten all about him. Can't he be bundled off to another relative?'

'No, because there aren't any relatives.'

'Well, can't you put him in a home or something?'

'Darling, that would never do. Can you imagine what people would say?'

'Oh for fuck's sake!' (After years of diligent practice, Mary was now fluent in the eff words.)

'I'm afraid I *have* to think of these things. In the eyes of the law we are responsible for him.'

'But what about your views on children being reared in appropriate social units rather than being a burden on their breeders? What about your avowed aim of abolishing the family? Have you forgotten all that?'

'Of course, I haven't. But that's something that's going to happen in the future. We've got to deal with the situation as it is, here and now. It's reality.'

'*Reality* you say? Let's get real, shall we? Where the fuck are we going to put him? This isn't a bloody nursery, you know!'

'He can have the attic.'

'But you *know* what we use that for when we have our parties.'

'Of course I do. It'll be a good biology lesson for him. I bet they haven't taught him anything about sex at that prep school he's been at.'

There was a moment's silence while Mary studied the solicitor's letter.

'You're not going to let him stay at that prep school and go on to some fucking public school, are you? You can't. Not after all you've been saying about private education.'

'Good lord no! The Labour Party would have a fit if I did that. It would be the end of both of us. No, he can go to Greenhill School like any normal working-class kid.' With that he paused. Then an idea struck him and he became animated. 'You know,' he exclaimed, 'this could be the start of something big. Greenhill School could be the making of him. It could get rid of all that bourgeois garbage he'll have imbibed at that prep school and turn him into the real human being we'd hoped he would be. More than that! He'd provide the experimental proof of Ed Stimpson's ideas. He'd show that Ed's "revolution in the classroom" really does work and is not just the leftie nonsense that the reactionaries say it is. I'll get on to Ed tomorrow!'

Mary seemed unconvinced. 'Maybe it will work out,' she sighed, 'but, you know, Giles, you were right. I should have had that abortion.'

'Yes,' he agreed, 'on one level it would have solved a lot of problems. But we've got him now. I'm afraid it's no use crying over spilt milk.'

'Anyway,' continued his wife, 'I *do* hope we're not going to have him crapping all over the floor. I really couldn't go through all that again.' Unpleasant memories were returning to her conscious mind.

'Oh for Christ's sake, Mary!' snapped Giles, 'He's eleven now. He *must* be house trained, surely to God!'

'Well, I bloody well hope so,' she replied with a weary resignation. 'Yes, I suppose we'll *have* to have him. I just wonder what he's like now.'

A Necessary Concession to Outdated Petty Bourgeois Ways

Despite Mary's vehement protests, Giles went to the funeral. However, John was not there. That morning he'd had one of his weeping fits and Mrs Bowles had decided that he was too upset to sit through the service. A few short prayers had to suffice instead.

After a lengthy session with the solicitor, Giles had had to hurry back to Boldonbridge for a vitally important meeting with the Greenwood Labour Party. So father and son had missed one another.

9

A Radiant Future

When John eventually went back to school, Mr Cotton broke the news to him: 'John you're leaving Rickerby Hall at the end of the week. You're going to live with your father in Boldonbridge. He's a very important man who teaches at a university. He is very clever and has written lots of books. He's famous... He'll be collecting you on Saturday morning.'

John listened agape. Apart from fantasising about his father being the Duke of Edinburgh – that bit of silliness on that day when everything had gone mad – he'd hardly thought about him. He hadn't really existed. Now it seemed that he'd been living in ignorance and that a glorious future awaited him. 'A very important man... He's famous'. *He*, John Denby, the undiscovered son of a famous father! It was like one of those stories you read about in books – like that one in his book of Greek legends, the one about Paris, the shepherd lad who'd learned that he was the son of the King of Troy.

His imagination began to run riot. He thought of the big car arriving at Oaktree Gardens – sweeping up the drive with an escort of motor cyclists like that of the President of the United States – the grand mansion up in Boldonbridge with its servants and its ultra-large TV sets, the new and wonderful toys he would have... God *had* been kind to him. But he mustn't get big-headed. He must be kind to the housemaids and remember not to show off in front of other kids who weren't as lucky as he was. With the £200-a-week pocket money he'd be getting he'd start a home for all the poor stray cats in Boldonbridge. (After he'd bought himself a good supply of wine gums and liquorice allsorts, that was!) Jesus would certainly buy that one.

Farewell the Old World

'You won't forget all we've taught you at Rickerby Hall, will you, John?' said Mr Cotton as he said goodbye to him on Friday afternoon. 'You will remember to be polite to everybody and to try hard, won't you? God has been kind to you and so you must repay him by being kind to other people who aren't as lucky as you are...'

Yes, he would. Yes, he *would*. He'd do all these things and more. He'd start by showing his father what a good boy he was. He'd show him the badge he'd been given for being brave in that 2nd XV rugby match. He'd show him the *Children's Bible* he'd bought with the book token he'd won for trying hard at work.

As he walked back home that sunny autumn afternoon, he rehearsed the speech he was going to make when he met his famous father. He was determined to impress him.

10

An Unwelcome Errand

Meanwhile up in Boldonbridge they got ready to retrieve their unwelcome burden.

When he went to the funeral Giles had thought it appropriate to wear a dark suit and black tie. But now, as he set off to collect his son, he had Mary with him and, at her insistent behest, he had to be properly dressed.

Clothes, as Mary was constantly reminding him, were an 'important statement at the socio-political interface'. They were going to venture into the darkest recesses of bourgeois suburbia and it was essential that the correct signals were sent out. So they had both climbed into their academic uniform – big, muddy boots, grubby jeans and building workers' donkey jackets.

Their battered old delivery van completed the statement. It confirmed their rejection of the vulgar, consumerist society which regarded flashy motor cars as a sign of superior status.

But it also had a more mundane function. The Greenwood proletariat did not, as yet, fully understand the concept of socialist community values. At least, the younger element didn't and was inclined to throw bricks at posh cars and yell 'Muvvafukkas!' at the occupants – all quite understandable, of course, after generations of capitalist exploitation, but nevertheless posing a problem for their socially and politically aware would-be champions. A grubby old rattletrap was a necessary camouflage.

Likewise, they'd had to put steel shutters on the downstairs windows of their house and reinforce the front door with an extra steel door. On Saturday nights the 'natural revolutionary anger' of the local youths was apt to vent its pent-up alienation by pelting Number 14 with empty beer bottles.

'It's the Tories stirring up the National Front again!' declared Mary as a half-full bottle of Newcastle Brown Ale exploded against the front door.

'Quite so,' added Giles. 'Here we are as much in the front line against fascism as the Red Front Fighters' League was in Weimar Berlin.'

'Thatcher's got a lot to answer for,' continued Mary. 'I think we should send *her* the bill for all those broken windows and steel shutters we've had to install.'

'Well said, darling!' replied Giles. 'We'll make the list out now.'

Into 'Enemy Territory'

It was a sunny Saturday morning in early October when they set off down the A1.

Midday found them meandering along the opulent avenues of Houghton-upon-Thames. Here Giles felt an unwelcome pang of nostalgia. It was one of those beguilingly mellow autumn days. A misty blue light filtered through the grand old trees which were an intricate tracery of black branches and golden leaves. On the neatly trimmed lawns and hedges countless thousands of dewy droplets shimmered in the soft sunshine. Highlighted by the low sun, the expensive red-brick mansions rose up bold and confident against a brilliant blue sky. It was a reassuring and comforting world, a siren song which constantly whispered seditious thoughts into his ear: 'Don't be silly. Come back. This is where you really belong.'

But he took a firm grip of himself. He was a realist who swam *with* the tide of history and not against it. All this was bogus, dishonest, fraudulent and downright illegitimate and should be – indeed, *would* be – replaced by proper proletarian housing units as Le Corbusier so sensibly advocated. Serious people had to be *hard*.

'I went to a prep school just down that street,' he told Mary with an air of confessional confidentiality. 'Brings back memories.'

'I bet it does!' she retorted with venom. 'What a nauseating bourgeois prison!'

Just to stifle any lingering sympathies that might be lurking in her husband's mind she began a recital. Recently, she had begun to detect a possible weakening of his radical ardour and this needed addressing. 'Just look at those hedges! Who keeps them trimmed? I'd like to know that. And who pays for all that new paint on those doors? And I shouldn't think that sun lounge cost much under twenty grand! ... God, the taste! Doesn't it make you want to bloody puke? Well, here it all is! Bourgeois exploitation, bourgeois bad taste, bourgeois fucking everything! Everything we're against!'

Giles let the torrent of words wash over him. He'd heard it all so many times before. Every time they drove through the posher residential areas of Boldonbridge it came out – word for word, the same old rant. Mary would keep saying the same things over and over again. She seemed incapable of new thoughts, stuck in a radical student rut, unaware of complexities or subtleties. That single virus of doubt in his bloodstream was starting to multiply – very slowly as yet, only having split into two, but multiplying all the same.

Sensing his faint disapproval, she rattled on, hoping for a positive response: 'That kid, brought up in this shit pit... He'll have been spoiled rotten! Nursemaids, servants... I wonder if he's even learned to wipe his bum yet. And that prep school will have given him all sorts of ideas well above his station. He's going to need a lot of straightening out, mark my words! Don't you agree, Giles?'

Giles frowned: 'Yes, you're probably right.'

Mary had touched a raw nerve here. All the way down the A1 he'd been worrying about the extra burden he'd suddenly had to take on. At every roundabout, at every bridge, a new problem seemed to emerge. Clothes, shoes, pens, pencils, felt tips, washing kit... It was all going to be so time-consuming. And what about food? Mary was into ethnic cooking in a big way – East African matoke, Ukrainian borsch, Moroccan couscous, Iranian shish kebab... What if the kid refused to eat it and demanded Kentucky Fried Chicken instead?

Discipline was going to be the big problem. Deep down he feared children. They were wayward, banal and utterly unreasonable. They could so easily reduce everything to a mindless anarchy. Give them half an inch and they'd take five bloody miles. Show the slightest hint of weakness and they were on to it. Firmness. Firmness right from the start. Obedience and respect reinforced by a healthy dose of fear. Get on top of the kid. Break him. That was the only way.

He comforted himself with the thought that he'd coped before. At Rugby School he'd kept the potential anarchists of School House at bay and had even managed to crush Dorking. The problem was going to be time. He had far too much on his plate to waste precious time on childish trivia. He hoped that Mary would rise to the occasion and bear the brunt of it – after all, it was she who'd insisted on having the kid in the first place. But deep down in his guts he knew she wouldn't.

What Lies Behind That Door?

They drove along Oaktree Gardens and swept up the drive of Number 27, the well-raked gravel crunching under the wheels of the battered old van. Outside the white Doric-pillared portico (a kind of downmarket Disneyland Parthenon) with its shiny brass letter box, they screeched to a halt. Now for the bit that Giles had been secretly dreading. Just what *would* he find?

Behind the Door

Behind the bright-white door, deep in the comfortable recesses of that opulent mansion, John had spent the morning alternating between exhilaration and anguish. He'd had one weeping fit when he'd remembered that he was leaving the place for good. But Mrs Bowles had cuddled him out of it: 'You're going to a wonderful new home. You've got a famous father. Now you don't want him to think you're a cry baby do you? Anyway, you know that you can always come down and see me.'

The tears had dissolved into the vision of the big limousine, the escort of motorcyclists, the mansion, the servants, indeed of the pauper who was about to become a prince.

'Yes,' he replied, drying his eyes, 'I'll come down with the servants and get them to cook you and Mr Bowles a scrumptious dinner.'

'Yes, I know you will. Now you will try to be good when your father comes, won't you? You must make a good impression.'

Of course, he would try. He'd been rehearsing his introductory speech all morning.

He would show him the badge he'd got for being brave on the rugby field and, of course, his *Children's Bible* – and he'd say how he'd bought it with a book token he'd won as a prize for effort. That was sure to impress him.

Problems with an Apparition

Giles rang the doorbell. As they waited for an answer, Mary glanced disapprovingly through the big bay windows to their left.

'Just look at that!' she said, pointing to a large china vase with

'A gift frae Bonnie Scotland' emblazoned on it in golden letters, 'the *taste*! Worse even than my old man's – and that's saying something, I can tell you!'

Suddenly the door opened and an apparition appeared – a scrawny little boy in a purple blazer, a grey shirt and striped tie and with two spindly legs (a bit like oversized drinking straws) emerging from a pair of over-large grey shorts and disappearing into long purple stockings and a pair of shiny black shoes. He stared at them for a moment, his big goggly eyes peering through a mop of white hair.

'Oh, you're the new gardener, are you?' he eventually said in a high-pitched, tinkle-bell voice. 'Well, you should come round to the back door and Mrs Bowles will give you the rake and the wheelbarrow. Gardeners don't use this door.'

With that, he shut the door.

'Jesus Christ!' hissed Mary. 'What the bloody hell was that?'

'I think it was *him*,' sighed Giles, shaking his head.

'Gawd all fucking mighty!' she replied. 'What *are* we to do with *that*?'

'Well, I'm not going round to the servants' entrance, if that's what he thinks!' snorted Giles. His dignity – always a touchy point with him – was upset and he rang the bell again, long and hard. Somebody needed to be taught their place.

This time a dumpy, middle-aged woman answered the door. Her gaudy flowered dress was a shade too tight for her rather ample figure and her podgy face was rather too heavily made up with powder, lipstick and eye shadow.

'Can I help you?' she said with just a hint of being patronizing.

'Yes you can,' declared Giles in his 'commanding voice'. 'I happen to be Dr Denby and I've come for my son, John.'

The woman giggled nervously: 'Oh, so *you're* Dr Denby. Well, I'm Mrs Bowles, the housekeeper. I'm terribly sorry about the muddle. You see we're expecting a man to come and tidy up the garden – all these leaves, you know – and John thought you were him.'

She smiled expectantly: 'Well, do come in.'

Giles sized her up at once. He knew the type. (He knew all the types.) This one was the semi-literate lower-middle housewife with ideas above her station. 'Mere workers' shouldn't be allowed to use the front door? Who the bloody hell did she think she was? She needed to be put into her place – *down* into her place!

They walked through the hall, their big boots leaving muddy

imprints on the soft blue carpet. It was a cloying, cosy world of dark oak-panelled walls and mock-antique furniture. All over the place, on the tops of tables and on shelves, were gaudy bits of china, mostly souvenirs from Wales and Scotland – a tartan plate with 'The Bonnie Banks and Braes of Loch Lomond' on it, an electric blue jug with 'Love from Llandudno' on it, that sort of thing.

Mrs Bowles ushered them into the lounge. Mary grimaced when she saw it – the mock-Tudor fireplace with its accompanying horse brasses, the mantelpiece with more ghastly souvenirs on it – a china horseshoe with 'Good Luck from Brighton' on it, a grotesquely awful Santa Claus emblazoned with 'Merry Christmas from Eastbourne' ... Then the flowered wallpaper and the reproduction 'Old Masters' in gilt frames – Constable's *Haywain* was there, so was the *Mona Lisa* – quintessential suburban awfulness!

'Even worse than I thought it would be!' she hissed.

Giles kept silent. He knew – as Mary clearly didn't – that good taste hadn't figured in his father's decorative schemes. He'd liked to receive presents, and if somebody gave you something, however hideous, you always displayed it. It was really a display of tribute – the rent paid to the Lord of the Manor by the forelock-tugging peasantry, in his case by the grateful working-class patients he'd treated in the course of his medical duties. What he did not know was that some of the most gruesome things – that especially awful Leaning Tower of Pisa on the coffee table and unbelievably dreadful Big Ben on top of the television had been bought as Christmas and birthday presents by John who loved buying people things and who was even more pleased when the results of his generosity were put on show for all to see.

'Take a seat, please,' said a rather flustered Mrs Bowles, pointing to a large flowery sofa. 'Are you sure that you wouldn't like a cup of tea? You must be very tired after your long drive down from Boldonbridge.'

'No! No! No!' replied Giles dismissively. 'We haven't time to wait around. I've got a load of *university* work waiting for me back in Boldonbridge. We must be quick.' (He stressed the word 'university' just to show old Bowles that, unlike her, he moved in high intellectual circles and didn't need petty-bourgeois pretentions to compensate for a lack of intelligence.)

'Well, I'll get John,' said Mrs Bowles, 'and do please be gentle with him. He was ever so fond of your mum and dad and was terribly upset when they were killed. He's been so looking forward to meeting you...'

She stood for a moment, not quite knowing what to do. When she got no response from either of them she turned and left the room.

Giles' silence was deliberate. He'd heard the 'be-gentle-with-him' thing so many times before. It was the regular litany from parents depositing the new boys at Rugby School. 'Do please be gentle with him. He's a bit nervous, you know. It's the first time he's been away from home.' That was a euphemism for 'spoilt brat who needs to be squashed.' After the front door incident and now this coded message, his anxieties mounted.

The lounge door opened and a rather flustered Mrs Bowles re-entered.

'Come on, John, don't be shy. Come and meet your father.'

The little elf crept timorously in and then stood gaping inanely.

'Oh, it's *you*! I thought ... er I thought.'

'You thought I was the gardener,' said Giles reprovingly. (Go on the attack first, get the high ground, seize the initiative.)

'And a gardener was too lowly a being to be *your* father, I suppose?' added Mary.

The little creature continued to gape.

'Christ, he's half-witted!' hissed Mary into Giles' ear.

'I'm terribly sorry, really I'm sorry,' the boy eventually managed to mumble.

Then, straightening himself up, he launched into his prepared speech: 'I am very pleased to see you. I'm a good lad... I played rugby for the second XV and got a badge. I'm a member of the Scripture Union and I read my bible every night... This is my *Children's Bible* that I bought with the book token which...'

'Yes, yes, yes,' interrupted Giles impatiently. 'That's as may be. Now, if you don't mind we'd better be on our way. I've a lot of work to do.'

'But don't you want to see my *Children's Bible*?'

John was both bewildered and rather hurt. He hadn't expected this kind of curt dismissal. His grandparents had always made a big point of listening to everything he had to say.

'Come on!' snapped Mary. 'Into the von!'

'Please, what's a *von*?' (Inadvertently, John had walked into a linguistic problem here. 'Van' posed serious pronunciation problems for Mary. Pronounced in her normal voice it came out as 'vain' – which was an embarrassing revelation of her upper-crust origins. After numerous attempts to get her tongue round Geordie vowels, she'd ended up with 'von', a sort of halfway house that would have to do.)

'Your mother means the van!' snapped Giles. 'Now hurry up and let's get going!' (This little tick was proving to be a dab hand at the dumb insolence game.)

'But we'd better get his luggage,' said Mrs Bowles. 'There's quite a lot of it. It's all in the kitchen...'

'Yes,' added John, desperately trying to repair the damage he'd apparently done with a show of helpfulness. 'If the chauffeur brings the van round. I'll help your servants load it up.'

'Chauffeur? *Servants*?' exclaimed Giles. 'Young man, you've got some funny ideas!'

'Please,' interjected Mrs Bowles. 'If one of you drives the van round to the kitchen door, we can load it up quickly. I'll give you a hand.'

'Round to the servant's entrance, I see,' said Mary. 'Put into our place, I suppose?'

'Please, darling,' sighed Giles. 'We haven't time for the class struggle.'

'No time? You always told me there was time for that.'

'You go into the kitchen,' he replied briskly. 'I'll bring the van round.' (Mary's posturing was starting to get on his nerves. Gestures were all very well when you had time for them. At this particular moment he didn't. He was horribly conscious of the gap that this whole London trip had blown in his carefully planned schedule and of the looming mountain of work that awaited him back in Boldonbridge.)

He duly parked the van skilfully and neatly outside the kitchen.

'Bloody hell!' he groaned as he opened the door and saw the mountain of boxes and suitcases that were piled up within. 'This poses problems!'

But, helped by Mrs Bowles and a fluttery John, he eventually managed to squeeze it all in. The main difficulty was fitting it round the crate of Newcastle Brown Ale that was a prominent feature in the back of the van.

'Wouldn't it be better to leave that crate here?' said Mrs Bowles. 'I mean you don't really need it, do you?'

'*Of course*, we need it!' announced Mary grandiloquently. (She spoke the truth. Neither she nor Giles could stand Newcastle Brown Ale, but they always kept a crate of it in the van. It was an important statement which showed their commitment to the authentic working-class culture of Northern England. But there was no point in wasting time trying to explain *that* to a petty-bourgeois bird brain, was there?)

'Well, that seems to be that,' declared Giles. 'Now in you get, young man.'

The elfin creature looked puzzled: 'But where's the car?'

'Car?'

'Well, this isn't a proper car. Granddad had a proper car... An Austin Princess with a Rolls-Royce engine...'

'This *is* the car. Isn't it good enough for you?'

'Oh, I'm sorry...'

A sharp pang of disappointment swept through John. No big limousine with a motorcycle escort. Just this grubby old builder's van. What WAS going on? First his 'Famous Father' had turned up like a scruffy old gardener, then for some unknown reason the *Children's Bible* hadn't interested him – and now this! This was fast becoming another of those crazy days...

'Come on, into the back!'

'But I must say goodbye to Mrs Bowles.'

'OK, but be quick about it!' (Giles knew this game from Rugby School. It was spin out the departure in the hope of generating sympathy.)

A long, lingering hug and a big kiss from Mrs Bowles followed as Giles and Mary squirmed with embarrassment.

'Have you seen what's in those boxes?' whispered Mary to her husband. 'Enid Blyton books, *Just William* and bloody *Biggles* for fuck's sake! Along with that *Children's Bible*, that's all we need!'

'Yes,' sighed Giles guiltily, 'I'm afraid he's inherited all my old library.'

'But you're not going to let him read all that fascist crap, are you?'

'Please, dear, not now! Let's get him home first.'

The long farewell was irritating him.

Meanwhile John was crying. He'd had another of his weeping fits as the sheer awfulness of the hour of departure struck him. Down, once more, came the icy boulders and the snowy slurry.

'Come on, John,' said Mrs Bowles. 'You've got to go now. You'll

68

be fine when you get up to Boldonbridge and you know you can always come and see me.'

In truth, she was starting to get a bit impatient. She was fond of the boy – who couldn't be? – but he just wasn't her problem. There was her sick husband – and, then, her elder daughter with her alcohol problem. And, on top of that, there were her two little grandsons – one of whom had been punched in the face by his mother in a drunken rage. There were tales, too, of bed-wetting and truanting. In short, the sooner she got to grips with that situation the better. Poor little John Denby! Yes, he'd had an awful shock and deserved sympathy, but there was money in the Denby family, pots and pots of it. Which was more than could be said for her own family! *She* was the one who deserved a bit of sympathy – she and those two forlorn little grandsons of hers, deserted by their father and living in terror of their mother's alcoholic temper tantrums. She had to get shot of the Denby connection, get another job and start clearing up that mess in Lambeth pretty damned quick!

Giles walked over to the kitchen door: 'Come on, John, you're a bit old for this sort of thing.'

Somewhat shamefacedly the boy pulled himself together. He couldn't let his father think he was a cry baby.

'Yes, I'm coming now, but, please, can I go to the toilet first?' (A relic from old Mrs Denby here: always go to the toilet before you go on a journey.)

'On come on, you don't need it!'

'But I *must*!'

'Oh, for Christ's sake!'

'Let him go,' said Mrs Bowles. 'There'll go and be a disaster if you don't.'

'OK. But hurry up about it!'

Giles was getting exasperated. His worst fears about this kid were fast being realised. He was a smarmy little oiler, his head stuffed full of all sorts of pernicious rubbish, clearly spoiled rotten and an accomplished player at the obstruction game. What with Mary smouldering away in the van and the little toerag winning one little victory after another, he was in danger of losing face. It was time to be firm.

So, when the boy eventually emerged from the toilet amid the slooshings of chains, he grabbed him firmly by the shoulder and marched him over to the van.

'But I haven't washed my hands yet!' (Another relic from the Grandma Denby past.)

'You don't need to do that. We've got to get started.'

'But what about my spuke pills? I haven't had them. I get sick in cars.'

'You don't need pills at your age. Now get in!'

11

'They've Taken Him off in a Dustbin with all the Dog Shit'

John clambered into the back of the van, squeezing himself into a narrow canyon between the box containing his train set and a suitcase containing his clothes. The crate of Newcastle Brown Ale formed a kind of pillow. He snuggled down, trying to make himself as inconspicuous as possible. If any of his Rickerby Hall schoolmates should see him in *this*! The shame of it! He could just hear Jimmy Stokes' high-pitched squeal of delight: 'They've taken him off in a dustbin with all the dog shit!'

It was all so strange. So unexpected. Was this scruffy, grizzly bear of a man really the 'very important man' Mr Cotton had told him about? Had Mr Cotton lied to him? Impossible. Mr Cotton was a proper Christian and proper Christians didn't tell lies. So was it all a con trick and was he being kidnapped by a criminal gang? Again, silly. That sort of thing only happened in adventure books.

No, it was perfectly obvious that he'd been fantasising. Worse still, he'd behaved badly and upset his father. Precisely how he'd behaved badly he didn't quite know – but, then, you never did quite know with grown-ups, did you? They could be so odd at times. Be that as it may, however, he must try to be good and try to impress his father.

The Thrill of the Open Road

Off they went. Ensconced behind the wheel, Giles felt a surge of relief. He was a good driver and he loved driving. It was a relaxation for him, almost a necessary therapy. Here he could revel in his natural superiority, weaving artfully in and out of the traffic, dodging round the lumbering incompetent who was hogging the outer lane and should never have been allowed on to the road in the first place, and, then, roaring off into the big, wide, blue beyond. It was speed, skill, daring, aggression. War really.

'He's got a Jag and he's only doing fifty, for Christ's sake! Probably learned to drive on a lawnmower in Surbiton. They shouldn't sell cars like that to those people... There, that scared him!'

It was roar past a big lorry, brake sharply, swing round a dawdling Cortina, surge away down the open road. Bowling past this Saab, that Metro and the other big removal van, he felt like a Battle of Britain pilot leaving a trail of Nazi aircraft plunging earthward behind him. Absorbed in the sheer exhilaration of the chase, he forgot all about the funny little bundle in the back of the van.

A Catastrophe

After a while John was faced with a dire emergency. He was going to be sick at any moment. He was desperately anxious to show the alarming man who was his 'famous father' that he was a proper boy and not a little weed. But – being sick! It was the next worse thing to filling your pants, a quite awful disgrace. The sort of thing that pathetic little wets did.

'Please, God,' he prayed, 'don't let me throw up. I'll give half my pocket money to the poor, starving children of Africa, honest I will.'

But that afternoon God seemed to have more important things on his mind than the stability of John Denby's innards. As Giles flung the van round the roundabout at the Sheffield – Worksop turn-off, cutting in front of a big articulated lorry and zooming off past an accelerating Vauxhall Viva, he could hold it no longer. Out it all came, a repulsive yellow-green mess, all down his blazer, all over his shorts and into the crate of brown ale.

Horrified by the appalling catastrophe, he lay huddled in dumbfounded despair, dreading the awful moment of discovery. It soon came.

Mary turned and sniffed ostentatiously: 'You'd better stop, Giles; he's been sick!'

'Bloody hell!'

Giles pulled into the first convenient lay-by, got out and opened the back door. With a spurt of anger he saw the Vauxhall Viva and the big lorry he'd so skilfully overtaken go roaring away past him – defeat in the competitive battle of the road, loss of face! And a kid being sick all over himself! What the hell was a leading historian supposed to do about that? Mopping up kiddiewink spew wasn't what he was there for.

'Come on,' he growled, 'out you get. Oh, God, you stink! Now clean yourself up and be quick about it.'

John clambered out and just stood there overwhelmed by shame and degradation. What to do? On the rare occasions that he had been car sick his gran had always cleaned him up. Silly kids might run round holding their noses, but adults got on and sorted things out.

'But can't you?'

'NO, we CAN'T! With us you face up to your responsibilities and clean up your messes yourself. We're not your servants, you know.' (Worse and worse! Already – before they'd even got home – this kid was proving a major handful. Not even house-trained, it seemed, and expecting everybody to run round after him. 'Spoilt rotten' was a feeble euphemism. Firm handling needed.)

Sulkily, the boy pulled out a handkerchief and, dipping it into a convenient puddle, managed to get the worst of the gunge off his blazer and trousers.

'Now the mess in the van.'

He climbed into the van and managed to scoop up a reasonable amount the green goo from the brown ale crate. A proper clean-up, however, would entail removing most of the boxes.

'OK. That'll have to do for now. You can wash the van out when we get back home.'

John threw the repulsive handkerchief away and settled down once more into the canyon between the boxes and the suitcase. Giles closed the back doors and climbed back into the driving seat.

'And you assured me that he would be house-trained,' sighed Mary as they inserted themselves into the ongoing flow of the traffic and accelerated up the motorway.

In the back John cringed with shame.

Down the Great Black Tube...

The little van plunged on up the road. A wet, blustery evening closed in. All that John could see through the dirty back windows was an endlessly unfolding film strip of motorway scenery – brutish concrete bridges, forlorn rain-swept lay-bys and metallic crash barriers. That and cars and lorries, always lorries, great big lorries with roaring engines hurtling frantically along amid clouds of grey spray. As the black autumn night engulfed everything, even this limited vision dwindled into a chaos of glaring headlights, burning into you like the sightless eyes of aliens in a science-fiction story. It was all a bit mad. On, on, on, hurtle, hurtle, hurtle, down the great black tube... To where? It was like that Narnia story when two kids had jumped into a magic pool and gone careering down into a strange new land. That had been an evil land ruled by a monstrous witch. Was he plunging into an evil land? Who knew?

Lying uncomfortably on the hard metallic floor of the van with his head resting on the hard edges of the brown ale crate, however, he was acutely aware of a more immediate problem. The gut-wrenching smell of spew. His own spew, continually rubbing his nose in his own degradation.

Your innards were always a problem – to boys at any rate. Grown-ups and girls didn't seem to be threatened by nasty embarrassing liquids coming out of them. Perhaps it was God's way of stopping boys getting too big-headed. He remembered the time that little David Galway had had the squits and hadn't been able to reach the bog in time. How they had all swooped down on him in his distress! 'Galway, don't you know what the bog's for?'

It could, of course, have happened to him – but, well, he was too old for that sort of thing and, anyway, it served little Galway right for being such a pathetic little weed. But now something similar had happened to him – and in front of the man he was so desperate to impress!

Maybe it was God's punishment for teasing David Galway, His main task now was not to be sick again and to stop himself crying.

After a time he slid into a dreamless haze, not really sleep, but a sort of semi-anaesthetised coma.

12

Landing in an Alien World

Suddenly he was aware of metallic doors opening and closing. Opening his eyes, he saw a big, burly man who looked rather like a scruffy version of James Bond.

'Wake up! We've arrived. Out you get and we'll get this stuff into your room. Then we'll have supper and after that you can clean this van out.' All crisp and authoritative.

He blinked for a while. Then it came clear. This was his father, the 'famous father' whom he had to impress.

He clambered out of the van and then reached for a box, the important one containing his train set and his radio-controlled car. He stared around. He was in an alien world – a terrace of raw red-brick houses with stinging rain lashing down on to a rubbish-strewn pavement, no trees, no gardens, just dirty window panes, some of them broken, all illuminated by the harsh monochrome of concrete street lamps.

'Is this it?' he blurted out. 'I mean where's the garden? Where's the drive?' (People in his world just didn't live in this sort of place.)

His father, the big James Bond man, unlocked a battered red door and then set about opening a second door behind it, a massive steel-plated affair.

'Why do you have two doors here instead of one?' He was genuinely bewildered.

Giles ignored the babble: 'Come on inside. Don't hang around getting wet.'

Inside John stared in wonderment at the black walls with their strange, brilliantly colourful patterns and grotesque African tribal masks. It was completely different from the kind of house he knew.

'Cor, this is exciting! It's just like the ghost train at the fairground!'

'Yes, yes,' snapped his father. He wanted to get the kid bedded down for the night as quickly as possible so that he could catch up on the backlog of work that lay piled up on his work table. 'This way,' he said, climbing up a wooden ladder that disappeared into a hole in the ceiling.

'This *is* great!' chortled John, genuinely excited by the quite unexpectedly strange place. 'It's just like a pirate ship... You know the one they have at Brighton ... or is it at Folkestone?'

It was up another ladder and into another weird room – all rafters and painted pipes. 'This is your room and there's your bed,' said his father, pointing to a black lumpy object covered with a brightly patterned rug.

John put the box down. The car sickness had passed off and the cold, damp air of the street had revived him. More than ever he now wanted to impress this strange, stern man who was his father. He must make amends for being sick all over himself like a little wimp by showing him that he was a proper boy – well brought up, polite and grateful and, above all, that he was a *real* boy, strong, lively and full of life and fun.

He began a frenetic babble: 'Cor, this is great! Thank you very much! I shall be really happy here! Why, it's just like being in a spaceship!'

With that he plunged down onto the bed with his arms outstretched: 'Takkannakka! There! Shot down an intergalactic invader!'

But his father did not seem to be impressed. 'Come on!' he growled. 'Let's get your things out of the van.' (So, as well as being manipulative, this kid was noisy and obstreperous. That was all he needed!)

Bemused – and with hurt feelings – the boy followed him back down to the van.

Encounters with Aliens. Mutual Problems

For the next half-hour father and son worked in silent tandem lugging the boxes and suitcases up the ladders – an awkward business, necessitating elaborate teamwork. As he balanced precariously on a rung and passed yet another load through the hole in the ceiling, Giles began to wonder if a few bourgeois fripperies like easily graded staircases with banisters might just be a touch more practical than these dangerously minimalist ladders. What if he slipped and broke a leg? Think of the time *that* would consume! But he soon put that sentimentalism behind him.

When everything was in the attic – the boxes and suitcases strewn randomly over the brilliantly patterned ethnic rugs – they went down to the 'recreation area' for supper and sat down at the plain, unvarnished trestle table.

'Is this the conservatory table?' asked John.

'No, it's the dinner table.'

'But why isn't it a real dinner table?' The grubby, splintery thing was quite unlike any dinner table he'd ever seen.

'It *is* a real dinner table. It just doesn't happen to be a petty-bourgeois pretend table. It's authentic and honest...'

'Please, what's *bourgeois*?'

'Oh for heaven's sake, shut up and eat your supper!'

John fell silent. He was nonplussed and rather wounded. Nothing he did seemed to work with these strange, alien people. Politeness, expressions of gratitude, boyish bounciness... What *was* he supposed to do?

He looked at the pile of grey-brown grains heaped up on the plate that his mother had thrust in front of him. It was like nothing he'd ever seen before. If anything, it resembled the yucky sago muck that they sometimes served up at Rickerby Hall at Friday lunchtime. 'Sago-shit' was what they called it and he'd always returned his plate untouched and filled himself up with crisps and chocolate from the tuck shop. 'What's this?'

'Couscous.'

'What's couscous?'

'Oh just get on and eat it!'

He took a spoonful and shoved it cautiously into his mouth. It was even worse than the Rickerby Hall sago-shit – and that was saying something!

'Please, I don't like it. Please could you ask the cook to get me some egg and chips?' (This was a perfectly sensible suggestion. Everybody had cooks to prepare their meals for them. Back at Oaktree Gardens he'd always got the food he'd liked.)

'And just *who* might the cook be?' said his mother, fixing him with her 'analytical stare'.

He wilted under the intense radiation. She *was* a weird mother, this silent, hard and elegant woman! Mothers were gushy, cuddly and a bit soppy. They loved you and looked after you – even when you didn't want to be looked after. But not her. All she did was stare at you and make nasty remarks. It was odd, not right.

He took another mouthful and then another and then decided that this coocoo – muck or cow shit – or whatever they called it – was quite inedible.

'I'm not hungry. Please may I get down?'

He took the silence for assent and left the table. He wanted to go and explore the exciting rooms up those ladders.

'Hey!' his father called out in a loud voice, 'And just *where* do you think you're going?'

He spun round, frightened. He'd made some awful mistake, but he couldn't imagine what it was.

'Are you just going to leave your dirty plate on the table?'

'Sorry, but I thought the housemaid or the cook dealt with dirty plates.'

His father gave him a withering look and spoke in a stern voice: 'In this house, young man, you wash your *own* plates. Now go and do it!'

'Put the food you've refused to eat back into the bowl first,' added his mother harshly. 'If it isn't good enough for you, it's certainly good enough for your betters.' Trembling slightly, he shovelled the offensive mush into the big, crude earthenware bowl in the middle of the table. (It looked like one of those crude things he'd made with the modelling clay that somebody had given him last Christmas. Why did they have to have bowls like this? Couldn't they afford proper bowls which were glazed and had nice patterns on them? That particular bowl, however, was an 'authentic Berber artefact that Mary had bought in Tangier as one of her 'anti-imperialist statements'.)

'Where do I go?'

'The sink's over there behind the ladder.'

'But what do I do?' (He'd never washed up before and didn't know where to start.) 'Oh just get on and *do* it!' (This situation was spiralling out of control. This was dumb insolence raised to an art form – like the creative stupidity of juniors at Rugby School who would have you believe that they couldn't sweep out the library because they'd never been taught how to use a brush!)

John scuttled over to the sink where he was confronted with a space-age tap which reared up like a streamlined teapot spout and had two round knobs on either side of its base. It was, of course, a deliberately designed phallic symbol, an integral part of the award-winning decorative scheme which stressed the biological equivalence and necessity of water and semen... All of which, however, was lost on John who grabbed the right-hand knob and twisted it hard. A sudden gush of boiling hot water shot out with the force of an erupting geyser, ricocheted off an unfortunately positioned spoon in the sink and landed on an ethnic rug where a steaming puddle began to form.

'Are you trying to be funny?'

'NO! NO! Please, what do I do?'

'Turn the tap off you bloody fool!'

Tiredness, confusion and desperation made his mind go blank. Frantically, he grabbed the left-hand knob and twisted it furiously. Upon which the explosive geyser turned into a veritable Niagara which gushed up into the air and filled the puddle on the floor to overflowing so that it soon became a miniature lake.

Giles rushed over and turned the water off.

'Are you half-witted or plain insolent? Now get the washing-up liquid.'

'What's washing-up liquid?'

'Oh for Christ's sake!'

In the end he found a bar of soap and managed to clean the spoon and the plate with that.

He was now near to tears with bewilderment and frustration. He desperately wanted to go and lie down and sort his thoughts out. He put the plate and the spoon on to what seemed to be a rack and which he assumed was the right place – how was *he* to know it wasn't?

'Not *there*! On to the draining board. You haven't dried them!'

He duly put them on to a grooved surface which he thought was the 'draining board' and then started to climb the ladder.

'Hey!' his father called out after him. 'What about the mess in the back of the van? You haven't cleaned that up yet!'

By now he was beginning to get angry. They had no right to treat him like this. He was a good, decent boy who only wanted to do the right thing. It wasn't his fault that he'd been sick in the van, was it?

His temper flashed out: 'I wasn't sick on purpose. It was because you wouldn't let me have my spuke pills and because of your rotten driving! Clean it up yourself!' Giles groaned. This was one step up from the dumb insolence. It was open defiance. If he was to have any kind of a life afterwards this nonsense had to be squashed. Crushed. Flattened. Exterminated. Right now. Jesus bloody wept!

Was this Dorking all over again? Well, he knew the form. Stage One: sudden shout. And, if that didn't work, go to Stage Two – get physical!

A stentorian bellow which seemed to shake the whole building blasted out: 'GET ON AND DO IT NOW!'

John jumped up in sheer terror and nearly fell off the ladder. This wasn't a Hairy Mary screech, nor even a Foghorn roar. It was a quite different order of things.

'Sorry! Sorry! Yes, I'll do it!'

'WELL, DON'T JUST STAND THERE! DO IT!'

'But what do I do? I'm all confused.' In spite of himself the tears began to trickle. Turning on the taps! Giles knew this one only too well – and it never worked with him. He advanced on his son who cringed in terror as he took a firm hold of his shoulder and marched him back to the kitchen area.

'There's the bucket. There's the soap powder. There's the cloth... Now fill the bucket up... With HOT water, not cold and NOT all over the bloody rugs!'

Then he propelled him out of the front door and into the cold, wet street where the van still stood. Unlocking the back doors, he opened them wide.

'Now get on and clean up the mess. Properly mind. I'll come and inspect it in ten minutes' time.'

Too bewildered to think of tears, John climbed into the darkened interior and attacked the repulsive green sludge with the wet cloth, wringing it out in the bucket at intervals. He was relieved to discover how easily it all came off once you got hot water on to it. He was angry and confused. He'd never been manhandled like this before and wasn't sure how to react. A big tough boy would have lashed out, but faced with the overwhelming strength of this strange, hot-tempered man, that just didn't seem to be an option. Something deep inside him said that survival was the name of this game.

So he worked diligently. Ten minutes later – on the dot – the big, frightening man appeared again.

'OK. That'll do! Come on in. Bring the bucket and the cloth! For heaven's sake, don't just leave them in the street! Empty the water down the drain. We don't want your mess in our house, thank you!...'

John scuttled around, trying desperately to obey the stream of orders – so utterly unlike anything he'd ever been used to.

Eventually, he was allowed back into the warmth of the house. The bucket and the cloth were duly put away. He waited expectantly for the next scene in this crazy and unpredictable film.

'Come here,' said his father. 'Stand there and look at me.'

He promptly obeyed.

'You've got a few lessons to learn, young man. I can see that my parents have spoiled you rotten. That school you've been at has given you all sorts of ideas above your station. You can forget all about cooks and housemaids and egg and chips for supper. In this house we don't exploit the working class. We do all our domestic work ourselves and from now on you'll do the same. It's time you knew your place. Is that clear? Now off to bed.'

John stood and gaped. Glancing at his mother, he saw that she was fixing him with that disapproving stare of hers. Gradually, it dawned on him that he was being given a telling-off. More than that; a rocket. But why? All right, he shouldn't have answered back when he was told to mop up the spew in the van, but there was nothing about his good manners. Nothing, indeed, about his *Children's Bible* or his membership of the Scripture Union. Not a word of praise. Just a lot of stuff about his being 'spoiled rotten' – and nobody had even said that to him before. And what on earth did 'exploiting the working class' mean? He was a *good* boy, not a bad boy. After all, that's what Mr Cotton had said – and he *knew*!

'But, please, I...' he tried to say.

'NO BUTS! DO AS YOU'RE TOLD!'

In terror he scampered up the ladders to the attic. He looked at the boxes and suitcases strewn all over the floor. Should he unpack them? Maybe not. His gran and Mrs Bowles had always unpacked his things after he'd been away. ('Don't *you* do it, John, you'll just get everything muddled up...') If he unpacked his things and got everything into a mess, God alone knew what that odd couple downstairs would do to him. They'd flaming kill him! Best to lie down and wait for his mum – if you could call that weird, bitchy thing a 'Mum'! – to come up and say goodnight to him. After all, every mum did that.

But she never came. Nothing was normal in this strange new world – and it was all quite unlike the palatial mansion he'd been expecting.

Suddenly another weeping fit hit him and he lay down on his bed and just cried. His sobs echoed through the house.

Thatcherism Again...

'Just listen to that!' sighed Mary.

'Ignore it,' said Giles. 'He's just doing it to get attention.'

'Cocky little sod, isn't he?'

'Yes, spoiled rotten, just as you said he would be. Well, we'll have to break him before he breaks us. We can't give in to him.'

'The class struggle?'

'In its way, yes. And I'm afraid I'll need your help. I've got far too much on my plate to be bothered with spoilt brats who won't do as they're told.'

'Trying to shove it all on to me?'

'Well you *are* his mother. You wanted to keep the kid when I suggested an abortion. Be fair, darling!'

The temperature rose: 'So kids are woman's work, are they?!' cried Mary, 'What about that article you wrote in last month's *New Society*? What was it? "Men can no longer leave the essential and vital business of childrearing to their wives while they indulge in the luxury of a career..." or words to that effect!'

'Yes, yes! I know all about that! But we have rather landed in it, haven't we? A noisy, opinionated little brat who's never been properly socialised and is out of control? Have you thought what that's going to do to our way of life? I mean what about tomorrow night's do? What *are* we going to do with him?'

But just them a more immediate problem arose. The Saturday night drunks were spilling out of the pubs on Broadfell Road and erupting down the hill into Gloucester Road.

'NAAEEH! YER ROTTEN FUCKIN' BASTARD!' a female voice shrieked.

'AW FUCK OFF YER FILTHY COW!' a male voice roared back.

Coughings and splashing were heard.

'Christ!' groaned Giles. 'They're being sick on our doorstep again. Why do they always have to be sick *there*?'

'You know as well as I do,' replied Mary. 'It's the National Front again.'

'Thatcher, you mean. She's responsible for all this.'

'YAH! YER MUVVAFUKKAS!' came an even louder male bellow. It was followed by an almighty crash and the sound of broken glass.

'There goes the windscreen of our van,' sighed Giles. 'I should have remembered to put it in the garage.'

'That'll be a hundred quid at least,' added Mary. 'We can put that down on the bill. The one we're sending to Thatcher.'

'Of course. She's responsible. She should pay. Fair's fair!'

Mary took a large notebook down from the bookcase: 'That makes one thousand, five hundred and eighty-five quid to date.'

13

The Strange New Land

When John woke up he didn't know where he was.

He was lying on a lumpy settee-like thing in an attic full of brightly painted rafters and pipes. The walls were black and covered with weird patterns. Above him brilliant sunlight streamed through a large uncurtained skylight. Strewn over the floor was a muddle of suitcases and cardboard boxes. It was all odd and unfamiliar.

For a start he wasn't wearing his pyjamas. He was still in his school uniform – he hadn't even removed his blazer or his shoes. A sickly, tangy reek of spew hung over everything. Where was he? What had happened to him?

Slowly, it came back to him. He'd lain down on this settee-like thing, had a weeping fit and dropped off to sleep. Nobody had come up to check that he'd cleaned his teeth or put his light out. He was still in the clothes he'd spewed over in the van. He'd left Oaktree Gardens and was in a strange new land where everything was topsy-turvy. Walls were painted black instead of white and covered with funny patterns and not pictures. There were ladders instead of stairs. Somewhere down below were those two weird and frightening grown-ups who were supposed to be his mum and dad. But they weren't like a mum and dad. Grown-ups were always neat and tidy – apart from Hairy Mary, of course, but then he was a freak. Yet these two went round in dirty old clothes like a pair of scruffy kids. At Rickerby Hall, if anybody had turned up dressed like that, Mr Cotton would have blown a gasket – probably half a dozen major ones! At Rickerby Hall and at Oaktree Gardens he was a good boy. Here he was bad enough to be manhandled and shouted at. It didn't make sense.

He eyed the unpacked boxes and suitcases. Should he start unpacking them? Or should he wait till the grown-ups came up and did things properly? If that big handsome man who looked like James Bond came up the ladder and found a mess, he would start shouting again

– and that really was scary! All things considered, it was best to lie there and wait till a grown-up came up and told him what to do.

Explorations and Discoveries

He waited for nearly an hour and nobody came.

Meanwhile his insides started to play up. He needed the bog – and pretty quickly, too! Sooner rather than later he was going to have to go down that ladder and 'unload'. The alternative was quite unthinkable.

Screwing up his courage, he clambered down to the lower floor and was confronted with two doors. Which one was the bog? Nobody had told him if there even was a bog in this place? Perhaps these strange people didn't need toilets? Perfectly possible, but how was he to explain to them that he did? Timorously, he tried the right-hand door, silently turning the handle and opening it the barest few inches. Peering in he found – salvation!

There before him was everything he needed – bog, bath, washbasin ... the full works, all black, shiny and streamlined. So these people had the same kind of innards as he did! He could have weighed his sense of relief on a pair of scales. Locking the door, he was relieved to find that the lock was an ordinary bolt and not some hideously complex thing like that ghastly tap in the kitchen area. Then he availed himself of the facilities.

Enthroned in splendour, he stared in wonderment at the sheer sumptuousness around him. The bath was set into the floor like a miniature swimming pool, the washbasin swept out of the wall like an overgrown mushroom as did the bog he was sitting on. The shiny black walls were covered with strange blue and green swirls which enfolded the whole place in graceful curves. It was utterly different from the very ordinary bathroom he'd known at Oaktree Gardens. With the hum of the air conditioning it was like being in a spaceship. (Though he didn't realise it, he was sitting on the cutting edge of toilet design, admiring a bathroom that was a prize-winning example of state-of-the-art architectural Modernism.)

Suddenly the door handle opposite him began to turn, slowly at first and then with an increased urgency that rose to a frenzy. Somebody wanted to get in. It was like being in a science-fiction story when a stricken spaceship was being threatened by evil, alien forces. A violent hammering on the door began.

Caught in an act which he'd hoped would be secret! Frantically, he finished the job – paperwork and all – and pressed a large blue button which he assumed was there instead of a chain. Mercifully it was and everything vanished with a calm and efficient swish. The battering on the door had now risen to the level of a cannonade. God, had he done something awful? Was he about to be manhandled again?

He undid the bolt and yanked the door open – and gaped, open-mouthed, at what he saw.

There was his mother. Apart from a towel draped over her shoulders, she had absolutely nothing on at all. The only naked women he'd ever seen were pictures in those rude magazines which Jimmy Stokes had smuggled into Rickerby Hall and which you'd giggled over in the bogs at break. Now, for the first time ever, he was confronted with the real thing. He gaped in bewildered curiosity at the large breasts and the white hairs – like the fur on Fred, his beloved guinea pig, now waiting for him in Heaven – that emerged from between her legs. It was all frightfully embarrassing and he felt himself blush bright red.

'I'm terribly sorry!' he eventually blurted out. 'Really I am... I didn't know!'

He cringed, expecting a shriek of rage or even a slap for daring to look.

But, instead, she just smiled at him, a sweet and gorgeous smile. 'Take a good look,' she cooed. 'Go on! Don't be shy. You've got to learn sometime, you know.' Once again, things didn't make sense.

'Sorry about being in there,' he mumbled. 'I didn't know you were going to need it.'

'Oh don't worry,' she said sweetly. 'It's such a relief to know that you have finally learned to use a toilet.'

'Of course I can!' he replied, smarting. 'I'm not a little baby, you know!'

She seemed to think he was a little baby, still at the potty stage, and this was about as deep an insult as you could give a proper boy. Nevertheless, he felt he ought to take advantage of the unexpected sweet temper.

'About my things upstairs, should I start unpacking them now, or should I wait for you to do it?'

'Just get on and do it. Haven't you done it already?'

He noticed that she had a funny glazed look in her eyes. Weird! Weird!

But at least that was one decision made. He would unpack and arrange things himself.

What to Do?

He climbed up the ladder feeling reassured. He'd located the bog – a vital piece of intelligence – and now he knew what to do with his luggage.

But where to start? A glance at what he was wearing and a big sniff soon answered that question. He was still in the clothes he'd been sick all over and they smelt yucky. He'd better get something else out of one of those suitcases, though he wasn't sure which one contained his clothes. He remembered that it was Sunday, too, and a glance at his watch showed that it was well after nine o'clock. Time for church! He'd better hurry – if he were late that would mean another bollocking.

He'd have to look decent if he was going to church. Frantically, he opened a case and found – to his great relief – that it was the one containing his spare school uniform. Hastily, he climbed into it. The soiled blazer and shorts he left in a heap on the floor. He wasn't sure what to do with dirty things – presumably the grown-ups would sort that one out: they always did.

He'd been bad yesterday. He hadn't meant to be: it had just sort of happened. He didn't know why. But his father had shouted at him and manhandled him – and he wouldn't have done that if he hadn't been bad. Grown-ups always had reasons for things. So he'd better make amends. He'd go down to the living room – or whatever they called that weird open space on the ground floor – all neat and tidy, his tie done up properly, his hair brushed, his shoe laces tied, his shirt tucked in and with his *Children's Bible* in his hand and he would tell his father that he was ready for church. This would obviously impress him: and the vicar would, too, be impressed, especially when he showed him his *Children's Bible*. That would set things right after yesterday's upsets.

Sorting himself out took a long time – especially when he couldn't find his comb – and he had to forgo cleaning his teeth because he didn't dare venture again into that exotic bathroom. He'd had one lucky escape there and might not be so lucky a second time.

Topsy-turvy Land. Good is bad. Bad is Good...

At last, spick and span – and proud that he'd managed to do it all himself for once – he went down the ladders. The big James Bond man – his father – was sitting at a rough wooden table, surrounded by a mass of papers. Nervously, he crept up to him, feeling a bit like the man who'd crept up to a sleeping dragon in one of those stories he'd read about in his book of *Old Legends of Long Ago*.

'Dad?'

No response. The James Bond man continued to scribble away on a large sheet of paper.

'Please, Dad, excuse me.'

James Bond looked up rather irritably: 'Oh it's *you*, John? Well, what is it?'

'I just want to say sorry about last night. I didn't mean it. I was just a bit tired.'

His father looked blank. (Absorbed in correlating complicated pieces of hearsay about a Liverpool dock strike in 1943, Giles' mind was at full stretch. He'd forgotten all about last night.)

'Oh, don't worry. That's all right.'

Silence. Giles went on writing.

Eventually, emboldened by his absolution, John ventured further: 'Dad, I'm ready when you are.'

Giles looked up irritably: 'Ready for what?'

'Ready for church. Look I've got my bible to show the vicar.'

This produced an alarming and wholly unexpected reaction – as if he'd accidentally set a firework off. The big James Bond man seemed suddenly to come alive, almost to start fizzing and emitting sparks. He stopped writing, pulled himself up, and turning round, glared at him.

'Look, young man,' he barked sternly, 'we don't go to church in this house and you're not going either! So forget it. Understand?'

Setting off a metaphorical firework was, in fact, exactly what John had done. Religion – 'bloody religion!' – was one of Giles' pet hates. Ever since he'd got back from London the problem of his son's religion had been niggling away at him. The Liverpool dock strike of 1943 faded into the background as his temper rose:

'Look,' he continued as his anger gathered momentum, 'your mother and I are atheists. We don't believe in fairies and we don't believe in God. We grew out of that nonsense long ago – and it's about time you grew out of it, too! Look at that book you're carrying! You should be ashamed of yourself reading that sort of stuff at your age. It's high time you threw it out. We're not having bibles in this house. Is that clear?'

John gaped. This was mad. Worse than mad. Bad. Was he hearing right? He felt bound to stand and argue. After all, what would Jesus think of him if he didn't?

'But what about the Archbishop of Canterbury? He's not a little kid and he believes in God...'

This tremulous objection only produced a further incomprehensible explosion: 'The Church is a medieval racket which exists solely to deceive and exploit the working class. No intelligent person takes it seriously nowadays.'

'But...'

'NO BUTS! When you are an honours graduate with a Ph.D. I might just be prepared to listen to you. Not until. It's time you knew your place, young man!' (Nothing exceptional about this dressing-down. It was Giles' standard putdown for first-year students who presumed to question the proven science of atheist socialism.)

Seeing the boy still standing there with his mouth open, the torrent of his rage flowed on: 'Christianity is a thing for the weak and feeble-minded who can't face reality. If you must know, it's been a burden on Western civilisation for far too long. It's encouraged sentimental delusions. All this gentle Jesus crap has simply meant that we've tolerated the weak and the useless who just get in the way of progress. The Russians have denounced Christianity and that's why they are overtaking us...'

'But the Russians are *communists*! They're *bad*!'

'And just where did you learn that? *Where*? Come on, tell me!'

'But ... but...' Under the onslaught John's brain had stopped working.

'You can't tell me, can you?' concluded his father with the triumphal air of a heavyweight boxer who'd just floored his opponent. 'You can't because you don't know anything. You're just a silly little prep-school brat with ideas far above your station and it's time you knew it.'

John was blown away by the blast – stunned, knocked sideways.

What was it all for? Why the venom and the sheer hate? What on earth had he done wrong? You'd have thought he'd committed murder or something.

While his father resumed his writing, he walked away and sat down on one of the black, chunky things that were supposed to be sofas in this nutty place.

The bottom seemed to have fallen out of his world. Good was bad and bad was good. His *Children's Bible* – that outward and visible sign of his goodness and maturity – was a sign of stupidity and childishness. It was mad. Worse than mad. It was awful. The dying chick he'd found on the Rickerby Hall drive, poor silly Fred who'd walked off the table ... all they'd ever known was a life of cruelty. So they weren't in heaven being comforted by God. Neither were his grandparents, his good, kind and wonderful grandparents, up there waiting for him. They had ceased to exist. They were nothing. And the poor, helpless Jews sent into the gas chambers, also, were nothing. Those horrible Nazi guards who'd jeered at them hadn't been punished: they'd got away with it. It was only the weak and the helpless who were ever punished. It was ghastly, vile ... whatever big word you could think of. The world was full of nasty bullies like Hitler who could do as they liked. It didn't make sense. Nothing made sense in this loony world.

Slowly he climbed back up to the attic. Sitting down on his bed, he began to cry.

The Christian in the Catacombs

Then something happened.

Idly fingering through his *Children's Bible*, he happened to open it at the end where there was a picture of Saint Paul in front of Nero. He'd always found that picture exciting. The evil Nero was accusing the Christians of deliberately setting Rome on fire. But Paul, alone and facing the full might of Rome and braving the terrible tortures that were in store for him, had actually dared to defy Nero. 'You lie, Nero!' he'd said. There was a real hero, not a pathetic little wimp who went away and cried on his bed.

That set him thinking. If he had any kind of guts in him at all, he'd have to be like St Paul. Of course, his father wasn't quite Nero and this place wasn't quite Rome, but, still, he'd have to try. Stand up and be a man. He couldn't, of course, defy his father openly – that was far too dangerous! – but he'd keep his bible and say his prayers every night.

He stopped crying and suddenly felt better – bigger, stronger, more of a grown up, even. This was going to be exciting. He would be like one of those Christians hiding in the catacombs. Indeed, it would be like one of those games he'd played in the woods at Rickerby Hall where he'd pretended to be a member of the French Resistance in the war, hiding from the Nazis and sending secret radio messages to London. But this time it wouldn't just be a game. It would be *real*.

Out into the Unknown

Full of a new confidence, he rummaged round in the suitcase he'd opened and fished out his casual clothes – a sweater, jeans and pair of trainers – and changed into them. Leaving his school uniform in a heap on the floor, he climbed down the ladders to see what was happening about breakfast.

Nothing, however, did seem to be happening. His mother was sprawled over one of those black lumpy things that were meant to be sofas. She was now wearing a pink dressing gown, but nothing else and, with the gown wide open, everything of note was on display. Once again he blushed bright red and gaped.

'Oh... er... I'm sorry!'

But she didn't seem to notice him and simply stared vacantly ahead. Again, there was that funny glazed look in her eyes.

There didn't seem to be any food on the table. Over by the sink there was the big earthenware bowl full of that revolting coocoo muck or cow shit, or whatever they called it. No way was he eating that crap. He'd have to go out and buy some crisps at a shop. But he'd better ask permission first. His father was at his table writing away with a furious intensity. Approaching that fiery dragon was out of the question – not unless you wanted to commit suicide. So tremulously he crept up to his mother again.

'Please, Mum, can I go out and explore?'

No reply.

He repeated the question.

Still no reply.

'Yes, go on out!' his father called unexpectedly from his table. 'Ring the doorbell when you want to come in again.'

Sliding back the bolts of the big steel door and then undoing the latch of the wooden door behind it, he crept out into the strange world beyond. It was a bit like emerging from a spaceship on to the surface of an unknown planet. Immediately, he put his foot into a yellow-green sludge on the doorstep. He wasn't the only person to have been sick the previous day – but for some reason this miscreant hadn't been made to clean it up. For a moment he stared at the strange world around him.

The street of harsh red-brick terrace houses which climbed up the steep hill to his left was like a rubbish dump – all over the battered road and pavement were empty beer cans, broken bottles, crisp packets, fag packets and black plastic bin liners overflowing with rusty tins and rotting bits of vegetables. There was even a plastic syringe lying in the gutter. What on earth did people need a thing like that for? He thought only doctors had them. For a while he gazed in disbelief. Oaktree Gardens was neat and tidy, so why wasn't this place?

Down the hill the street plunged into a nothingness of bare earth, piles of rubble and pools of slimy water. It was not unlike that picture in his *History for You* book of Stalingrad after the famous battle.

Where to find a shop which sold crisps and sweets? Not in that seemingly irradiated desolation down the hill – that much was clear. So he strolled up the hill and eventually came to a big road full of cars and buses – Broadfell Road, in fact. This was more like it. There was a semblance of civilisation here. Sure enough, down to the right where the road seemed to be sweeping into a big city, he found a little newsagents full of just about everything he wanted – not only newspapers, but bottles of coke, packets of sweets and packets of crisps ... the lot! An Indian in a turban served him and he used up most of the five-pound note he had on a big packet of smoky bacon crisps – Yum! Yum! – three packets of wine gums and four boxes of liquorice allsorts.

The food problem solved, he strolled back to his new home. Though he was hardly yet aware of it, he'd been born with an acute awareness of beauty. The sheer, unmitigated ugliness of everything he saw around him depressed him deeply – that dreary desolation at the bottom of the hill with its tangled mess of red-brick walls and rusty girders and the grey pile of grime that rose up on the far side of the dirty river in the forlorn valley below. It was a new and dismal land.

A New Freedom

His father answered the door and admitted him without a word. Unwilling to face another confrontation – for what would that unpredictable James Bond dream up to confuse him with this time? – he climbed up the ladders. There in his eyrie under the weirdly painted rafters, he stuffed himself with the crisps and sweets. At least here no grown-ups came along and confiscated them on the dubious grounds that 'sweets and crisps' were 'bad for you' and would 'spoil your dinner'.

Then he started to unpack his clothes. He hadn't the first idea of how to fold them up properly – that was part of the secret feminine lore of his gran and Mrs Bowles – so he simply screwed them up and stuffed them into a convenient cupboard that was next to the water tank with bright red and yellow pipes. In everything went – trousers, jeans, sweaters, T-shirts, blazers and caps, all in one big, incoherent bundle.

After a while he got bored with this and thought he'd better apologise to God for not going to church. He knelt down – as he always did every night – and began to pray in a loud and clear voice so that God would hear: 'Please God, I'm sorry I didn't say my prayers last night, but I was tired and in an epi-sweat and I forgot. Sorry I haven't been to church today, but my dad doesn't go to church. He says it's crap. He says that you're crap, too. Could you please tell him that you're not crap. And could you tell my mum not to walk round the house with no clothes on. It's embarrassing. I mean, what if the neighbours saw her? I'm still a member of the Scripture Union. I promise to read my bible every night. Do send my best wishes to my gran and granddad. I really miss them, you know. And remember me to Fred and to the little chick I picked up at Rickerby Hall. I'll try to be good. Amen.'

Then he remembered his train set. He could spend the whole afternoon playing with it undisturbed by grown-up demands to tidy up, do his homework and get things ready for school. Eagerly, he unpacked it and laid out the track all over the floor in an elaborate

93

series of curves and gradients, making full use of his flyovers, bridges and tunnels. A station here, a house there, a signal box beside the station... The system grew and grew till it covered most of the floor. Eventually, he had to shove the unpacked boxes and the anarchic heap of the clothes that he couldn't squeeze into the cupboard into a pile in a convenient corner. Finding a socket in the wall, he set up the transformer and the controller. All ready! Yes, the electric points worked and so did the signal lights. He felt a spurt of pride. For the first time ever he'd set the whole thing up by himself!

Now for the good bit. Which engine? He chose his best one, the *Flying Scotsman*, hooked it up to its carriages and soon it was hurtling round, roaring through the tunnels, lumbering up the flyovers and stopping at the station to pick up passengers. Next he tried out the new Great Western pannier tank engine that Mrs Bowles had bought him. With a couple of trucks and a guard's van it became a second train. Two trains at once! It took a lot of controlling if you were to avoid a collision...

14

What about Lunch?

After a long time he noticed that it was four o'clock. He felt he'd better go down and see if he was expected at any meals. God, if he'd gone and missed one! And what would he be bollocked about this time? Would they shout at him again? This new world was so odd.

He crept down the ladders to find the ground floor transformed. His father wasn't at his table any more, but was in the kitchen area stirring a pot. His mother – thank God! – was fully clothed. (So maybe his prayer *had* worked and God had had a quick word with her?) She was wearing a strange long skirt thing of brilliant blue and a sort of veil. She looked exactly like one of those pictures of Indian women in his *World Encyclopaedia* (Which, of course, was precisely what she meant to look like: it was her statement of 'Solidarity with the Exploited Peoples of the Indian Subcontinent'.) She was busy putting rough clay bowls on to the trestle table. They were full of weird, yuckie things – the coocoo muck that had so disgusted him last night, a concoction of stringy things and bits of prawn (which, on inspection, turned out to be like that chow mein stuff you got in Chinese restaurants) and an extraordinary cold soup full of bits of salami and cucumber (Russian okrushka, though he didn't know it and a statement of 'Solidarity with the Aims of Scientific Soviet Socialism'). Bottles of wine and vodka were everywhere.

Curiosity got the better of caution and he approached his father: 'Dad, what's all this?'

James Bond looked up: 'I'm not Dad. That's a baby expression!'

Another telling off! What *were* you supposed to call your father? 'Sir'? 'Mister'? 'My Lord'? 'James Bond'? 'Biggles'? It was beyond him. He just stood and gaped.

His father continued to stir the pot. Suddenly he turned round:

95

'Call *me* Giles and your mother Mary,' he snapped. 'Understood? Good!'

'Oh, by the way,' he added after a moment, 'you'll have to be prepared to feed yourself. Mary and I can't always be cooking your meals. You'll need money. Here's twenty pounds to be going on with.'

He pulled out his wallet and handed him two crisp ten-pound notes.

Twenty pounds! John had rarely handled this amount of money before – you only got that sort of sum after months of carefully putting coins into your piggy bank. 'Cor, thanks, Dad – sorry I mean Giles!' he spluttered. 'Thanks a bomb!'

If somebody was nice to you, you had to be nice back to them – that had been part of the moral code of Oaktree Gardens. 'You've got a lot of work to do,' he ventured tremulously, 'so can I give you a hand?'

'Yes you can,' came the unexpectedly warm reply, 'You can stir this pot while I help Mary with the table.'

'But mind you don't spill anything,' he added.

Eagerly John took the wooden spoon and started to stir the seething purple sludge. 'AND I MEAN DON'T BLOODY SPILL ANYTHING!' continued Giles, his voice rising to a shout.

John jumped. 'I'll try not to,' he replied, 'but please don't shout at me. It's scary!' This plaintive appeal just slipped out accidentally. Giles ignored it. As well as being an oily little manipulator, this kid was a wimp. Dorking rides again? It looked depressingly like it.

John enjoyed stirring the pot. He'd never done this sort of thing before. The kitchen at Oaktree Gardens had been strictly out of bounds. Peering into the steaming cauldron, he smelt beetroot. He'd always liked beetroot and he began to feel hungry.

'Please, Dad – sorry, I mean Giles!' he said when next his father entered the kitchen area. 'This smells good. What is it?'

'Borsch.'

'What's that?'

'Beetroot soup.'

'Can I taste a bit?'

'Yes, just a bit.'

This was encouraging. At last he seemed to be doing something right. Eagerly he dipped the spoon into the pot and scooped up a mouthful.

'Cor, this is magic! Can I have some more?'

'Yes, but don't put the bloody spoon back into the soup when it's been in your dirty mouth!'

'What?'

'Wash it first, you idiot!'

Stern, sharp reprimand. Back to normal.

After half an hour's diligent stirring he was finally allowed to help himself to a bowl of the steaming purple brew.

'This is great!' he exclaimed. 'Where does it come from?'

'The Ukraine.'

'That's a communist place, isn't it?'

'Socialist, yes.'

'That's interesting. At Rickerby Hall Mr Harris said all the communists had to eat was stale brown bread. He was wrong, wasn't he?'

At this, Giles actually smiled at him. 'You're learning, boy,' he said encouragingly. 'You're learning!'

Progress of a sort. John felt a flicker of optimism. But it was only a flicker and it was soon dashed.

'Now you listen to me, young man,' said Giles, reverting to his stem 'bollocking' voice, 'Just listen to me...'

John cringed, mentally bracing himself for yet another dressing down – or horror of horrors, perhaps even a slap or two! What was it going to be *this* time? Fortunately it turned out to be a list of instructions.

'Mary and I are having a party tonight. It's not for kids. It's for adults – *intelligent* adults, that is. So we don't want you down here. You're to stay in your room ... Yes, *of course*, you can use the toilet, but don't go and lock yourself in as you did this morning. That caused a lot of problems. Now off you go!'

'Can I have a bath?'

'Yes, of course you can. But, again, don't lock the door and, whatever you do, don't make a mess. Understand? Good!'

Free Again

John climbed up the ladders again. He was completely free now. This *was* a strange place! No meal times. No bedtimes. Kids allowed to choose whether or not they would have a bath. It was all so bewilderingly different from the old days when grown-ups had planned everything for you.

He couldn't be bothered with the rigmarole of having a bath, so he finished off his last box of liquorice allsorts, started on his wine gums and played with his trains.

Then he decided to set up his television and his video player. Normally, grown-ups would have done this for him, but no way was he going to ask Giles to do it! Think of the epi-fit! He'd had quite enough bollockings for one day. Enough to last a whole week, in fact...

He soon found another socket and, to his great satisfaction, he managed to get both the television and the video working. All on his own and without any help at all! He basked in a warm glow of gratified accomplishment. It was rather delicious this business of being able to do what you wanted without adults interfering all the time.

He watched his *Battle of Britain* video for a time.

Then from the hole in the floor noises began to emerge. Human voices. Deep men's voices. Shrill women's voices. Loud laughter. Loud jazzy music suddenly blasted out. A funny, rich smell percolated upwards... Something interesting was going on down below.

He knew he shouldn't go and investigate, but ... well ... curiosity got the better of him. His heart thumping, he crept down the ladder. It was exciting ... like Biggles scouting out that Nazi camp in Norway. And if he was caught he could always say that he was going to the toilet. Ever so cautiously, he peered down into the big lower room.

It was full of all sorts of scruffy people – men and women in jeans and brightly coloured sweaters, some men with long hair, some with beards. Didn't grown-ups know how to dress properly in this place? A blue smoke with that funny rich smell was everywhere. Everybody seemed to be smoking. That was bad. His Granddad had always insisted that smoking was bad for you – and *he knew*!

He went back up the ladder. It was time for his bible and his prayers. He felt another tingle of excitement. He was a Christian in the catacombs of Rome, hiding from the evil Nero. Then he became a French Resistance hero sending secret radio messages to Churchill in London...

Oddly enough – he didn't know why – no weeping fit occurred as he asked God to remember him to his grandparents and to Fred

– and not to forget that little chick he'd found on the Rickerby Hall drive.

Suddenly feeling tired, he changed into his pyjamas and, leaving his clothes in a heap on the floor (so delicious this not having grown-ups telling you to hang your things up properly), he put the light out and climbed into his funny-shaped bed.

Sleep came quickly.

An Encounter with Aliens

Eruption. Loud voices. Bright light. Eyes hurting. Blinking. Deep male voice – not his father's voice.

'Christ, there's a *kid* in here! You never told me you had a sprog!'

'Don't worry about him. He won't mind!' Female voice. His mother's voice.

He rolled over to see... his mother, Mary, again with no clothes on, and a big man in his underpants, his huge flabby belly covered intermittently with repulsive black hairs so that he looked not unlike a gorilla that had had a misadventure with an electric razor. He stared in bewilderment and disgust.

His mother purposely marched over to the lumpy thing that served as his bed, got hold of one end of it and tipped it up so that he slid out on to the floor.

'Move over, John! Give us a bit of space!'

Her speech was slurred and she had that funny look on her face.

'Hey! This is my bed!'

Both ignored the protest. Then, to his utter disgust, the hairy man removed his underpants and the two of them clasped each other, kissed passionately and, in a wild frenzy, rolled over in a tight embrace on to the bed – on to *his* bed! Grunting and groaning the man heaved up and down as if he was trying to pump up a mattress or something. His vast and repulsively hairy backside wobbled furiously.

John stared in horrified disbelief. They seemed to have no shame at all. They were doing something quite disgustingly rude – and in front of a kid, too! Worse still, Mary was kissing a man who was not her husband. What would Giles say when he found out? He wouldn't blow just one gasket: he'd blow at least twenty!

And they'd turfed him out of *his* bed! They'd no right to do that!

He'd been told to stay in his room, but this was a new situation. He'd have to tell his father what his wife was doing. That would put him in his good books – and, maybe, he could put in a word for God? After all, if didn't like his wife kissing other men, then neither did God. God would be on his side in this business. He ought to be told that.

Puffed up with righteous indignation, he scuttled off down the ladders, his bare feet testing the unvarnished wood for splinters.

When he entered the noisy cauldron on the ground floor everything suddenly stopped, even the loud thump of the music. He blinked as he saw a sprawling mass of unkempt men and women turn round and stare at him. His father was sitting cross-legged on the floor in the middle of a circle of raffish exotics from Africa and India. Immediately, he stood up and stared angrily at him.

'John,' he said in a firm and measured tone, 'I told you to stay in your room.' (This sudden apparition was the last thing he wanted. His anger rose, but in front of all these influential people, he had to control himself. He couldn't be seen to browbeat a child. Bad politics.)

'But, Dad – I'm sorry, I mean Giles...'

John's plaintive voice was quickly drowned in an outburst of excited comment.

'What's a *kid* doing here?'

'I never knew you had any seedlings, Giles.'

'Been having a bit on the side, eh?'

Gusts of laughter burst out. Then came a firm female voice: 'QUIET! Do show a little adult responsibility!' It was a big, fat woman who looked like an elderly mermaid with her straggle of yellow hair and her long, tube-like green dress.

Silence. All eyes were on Giles.

'Well, John, what is it?'

'I've been thrown out of my bed.'

'What do you mean?'

'They're in my bed.'

A gust of laughter erupted.

'Who is?'

'A man and a woman. It's embarrassing.'

Even louder laughter.

'You see, the woman's Mary and she's kissing another man. That's very bad, isn't it?'

100

This detonated an explosion of raucous laughter that left John blinking in bewilderment.

'All right!' snapped Giles. 'You wait here.'

With that he scrambled quickly up the ladder. He was livid. He had specifically *told* Mary not to go up into the attic. 'Use our room,' he'd said, '*not* the attic!' But would she bloody listen? No way! It was another of her 'statements' and he was getting pretty effing sick of these 'statements'. All very well when you were a student, but he, at any rate, had moved on. He had his reputation to consider. Either that or she was so stoned up on those bloody amphetamines – or whatever else it was that she was always taking – that she didn't know her arse from her elbow! And that was another developing issue that would have to be faced...

The last thing he'd wanted was that kid romping round the living room. Awkward questions were sure to be asked. Merrins. Martha Merrins. That was the problem. Head of the Sociology Department, well known expert on child abuse, close ally of his, dedicated colleague working alongside him to create a properly socialist society, etc. etc. etc. *But* the old bag desperately wanted to be nominated as the Labour candidate for Boldonbridge West and was quite prepared to use any means, fair or foul – most probably, foul – to get what she wanted. Unpleasant facts. Guilty secrets. Repressed sexual desires finding untoward outlets. That was her line. If she started on that kid ... well, it could be awkward, bloody awkward!

Meanwhile, John suddenly found himself the centre of attention.

'Come here,' said the big, fat mermaid woman. 'Sit down and tell me all about yourself.'

There was nothing he'd have liked better. Sitting on the floor beside her, he snuggled up to her, resting his head on her large and comfortably feminine breast.

'Now then, young man, what's your name?'

'John.'

She took a pencil and a big notepad out of her ethnic shoulder bag and began scribbling away.

'Well, I'm Martha. Now where've you sprung from?'

'Well, I've been living in London and have only just arrived here.'

'Why's that?'

'You see, Giles and Mary, that's my mum and dad, they hadn't time to look after me so they sent me down to my grandparents in London.'

'You mean that Mary and Giles didn't want you?'

Scribble, scribble, scribble.

'But my grandparents were ever so nice. I really loved them...'

'So why are you here now?'

'Well, they're both dead. They were killed in a car crash.'

'Oh dear!'

'It's very sad, I know, but they're both in heaven now and God's looking after them – and Fred.'

'Fred?'

'That's my guinea pig. I put him on to the table to show my friends and he walked over the edge and died. It was all my fault. I should have realised that he didn't understand tables. But I took him to the vicar who gave him a Christian burial. He says he's gone to heaven and I'll see him there.'

Scribble, scribble, scribble on the notepad.

'Go on. This is very interesting.'

'Can you keep a secret?'

The woman's fat, jowly face wrinkled up into a conspiratorial grin: 'Yes, of course. Come closer and whisper it into my ear.'

He snuggled even closer to the soft feminine flesh: 'I read my bible every night. Giles tells me not to do it because he thinks God's crap. But I still do it. It's exciting – like being a Christian in the catacombs. Also, I pretend that I'm in the French Resistance in the war and am sending secret messages to London. You won't tell, will you?'

'No, of course not! But go on. Is there anything else you want to tell me?'

'No, that's all.'

'Are you sure? Are you *really* sure that you don't want to tell me anything else?'

Just then everybody's eyes went elsewhere. Giles had reappeared. He looked at John chattering away to Merrins and scowled. She sure was quick off the mark, that one! What was he saying to her? Or, more likely, what was she *getting* him to say to her? But, control your rising temper...

'Come on, John,' he said gently. 'Off to bed now. It's well past your bedtime.' (Why this sudden concern for bedtimes? It was the first time he'd heard his father use the word.)

'Aw! Do I *have* to? I was having a nice talk to this lady.'

'Yes, come on now.'

Bidding everybody goodnight, he reluctantly climbed up the ladder.

He found his room empty. There was no sign of his mother or of that fat, hairy man. Maybe Giles had duffed the man up? After all, if the sight of a bible threw him into an epi-sweat, what would a bloke kissing his wife do? He'd go flippin' bananas! Perhaps he'd killed them both and thrown the bodies out of that skylight thing? Then the police would come round and take him off to prison. But he'd put in a good word for him and get him released. Then, maybe, they'd start to be friends. He would convert him to Christianity – God would really dig that!

He crawled back into bed. But he couldn't sleep. He was wide awake now. He really wanted to go back down the ladders and continue talking to that nice fat mermaid woman. But, for some reason or other, his father didn't seem to like him doing that.

Then he remembered the bath. That was a good idea. It was so big that it was really a swimming pool – just the place to try out his model ships – much better than the bath at Oaktree Gardens. Getting up, he rummaged round in one of his boxes and pulled out his *Titanic* – which had an electric motor – and his clockwork tugboat. Grabbing a towel, he clambered down the ladder and entered that exciting spaceship-style bathroom.

The taps were easy enough and soon there was a lovely big pool, easily big enough for his ships to sail around in. Remembering to leave the door unlocked, he stripped off and, plunging into the warm water, began a glorious game. The scale of the two ships was a bit out – the tug being bigger than the *Titanic* – but not to worry! The *Titanic* sailed round in a large circle and narrowly missed the tugboat. Then a sponge became the iceberg and hit the *Titanic*. The tugboat dashed to the rescue – but Smersh wanted all the passengers to die and had planted a bomb on the tugboat... But Smersh had reckoned without John Denby – alias James Bond – who was lurking underneath in a submarine! The drama developed.

Suddenly, the door burst open and a small man with an untidy mop of red hair and a straggly beard came charging in.

Caught starkers by a stranger! Desperately John grabbed the iceberg – now back to being a sponge – and held it in front of the bits of him that mattered.

The man didn't seem to notice him. He lurched over to the toilet and, before he had even managed to lift the lid, he had vomited loudly and copiously, mostly over it, but with a sizable dollop landing on the floor.

'Jesus fucking Christ!' he spluttered, and then proceeded to kneel down with his knees just missing the revolting pile on the floor. He groaned and then suddenly coughed and retched and produced an even greater volume of spew, again without managing to lift the toilet lid.

'Bloody hell!' he sighed. 'Oh God!'

With that he got up and staggered out, leaving the door wide open.

John stared with a mixture of bewilderment and disgust. A grown man being sick all over everything? This *was* a weird place! Then came fear. Normally only messy kids did that sort of thing. Giles would think it was *he* who had made the mess, not the man. God, just imagine the bollocking he'd get! Didn't bear thinking about! He'd better get down that ladder pretty quick and put the record straight.

He scrambled out of the bath and, scarcely bothering to dry himself, slipped into his pyjamas and scuttled down the ladder, his wet feet leaving footprints on the plain wood.

A loud cheer greeted him: 'Coming back to the party, lad? Come and join us!

Don't be shy!...'

'Ah, John!' cried the big, fat mermaid woman. 'Come over here and sit down. Let's continue our little chat.'

Out came the notebook again. (Was she a newspaper reporter or something?) 'John,' said his father in a quiet voice, 'I told you to stay upstairs.'

'But I've got something very important to tell you.'

Another cheer went up from the crowd: 'What's it this time? ... Go on tell us! We're all listening!'

A pregnant silence fell. John felt very grand, something he'd rarely felt before and he relished the new sensation. Playing to an audience was fun.

'Please,' he said with an attempt at oratorical solemnity, 'it wasn't me who was sick in the bathroom. It wasn't. Honest, it wasn't. Cross my heart.'

He stood bewildered as roars of laughter erupted.

'So, please,' he continued, 'don't blow a fit on me and make me clean it up...' 'Well said, laddie!' the fat, mermaid woman called out. 'Very well said!'

He turned round and saw her scribbling furiously on that notepad of hers.

'It was me, actually,' said the red-headed man with the straggly beard.

Cheers and roars of laughter.

'Bloody hell!' he added defiantly. 'What do you expect? Special brew, red wine and half a pint of vodka! You need a cast-iron gut to handle that.'

The laughter continued.

'All right, John,' said Giles when it had finally subsided. 'You've had your say. Now back to bed.'

'But can't I stay and talk to that nice lady over there?'

'Yes, *do* let him!' echoed the mermaid woman.

'Please, Martha, *no*,' replied Giles firmly. 'Not now. It's far too late.'

'Aw, Dad, I mean Giles, please!'

'NO, up to bed! NOW if you don't mind!' (He'd noticed Merrins scribbling away. God alone knew what landmine was evolving on that pad of hers.)

Sulkily, John did as he was told.

As he climbed into bed he pondered a while. What a strange, confusing day! He desperately missed the certainties of Oaktree Gardens, yet in its way this odd place was so much more exciting. Weird! Weird!

Eventually he fell asleep.

Unwelcome Problems

At three a.m. the last of the guests staggered out and tumbled into their waiting taxis. Giles and Mary sat down and contemplated the room. The effects of whatever dope Mary had been taking had now worn off and she was hollow-eyed and sullen.

'The place is a mess,' she eventually said. 'I suppose you'll expect me to clear it up for you.'

'I'll do my share as I always do. You know that.'

Silence.

At length Giles spoke up: 'Mary, why did you *have* to go up to the attic? It just caused a lot of shit.'

She ostentatiously ignored him and lit a cigarette.

More silence as she blew smoke at the ceiling.

'I mean,' continued Giles, after another interval, 'that kid came down. And the little sod milked the situation for all it was worth. He certainly knows how to play to an audience. Needless to say, Merrins made a beeline for him. He'll need watching, that one. If we don't get a grip on him, he'll lead us a merry dance!'

15

'You're going to a *real* school today!'

Monday morning.
'You're going to school today.'
'Beg pardon?'
'You heard. School.'
John blinked. In this strange new world surprises were normal. A house which had ladders and not proper stairs and black walls instead of white ones ... a rough trestle table of the sort you had in a greenhouse instead of a normal dining room table, but, at the same time, a positively space-age bog ... a place were women walked round naked and grown men were sick all over the floor...
What next?
Handling his father – or, rather 'Giles' – was a problem he hadn't solved. You never knew what was going to send him up in smoke. He didn't mind the mess in his room – his gran (his wonderful, ever-beloved Gran who was in heaven!) would have blown a mega-fit at the sight of his spew-stained blazer and shorts lying in a heap on the floor. Yet mention something good – like going to church on Sunday – and he went bananas.
Still, if he didn't want another bollocking – or worse! – he'd better sound interested. That was the safest policy.
'Ah good! Now will I be in the A stream, the Latin one, or in the B stream, the non-Latin one? You see I'm down for Milton Abbey and they don't need Latin in Common Entrance...'
He faltered as he noticed his father closing his eyes with an 'Oh-for-Christ's-sake-belt-up!' expression on his face. He seemed to have said the wrong thing. Why? All boys took Common Entrance and some public schools wanted Latin and others didn't. Nothing daft about that.
The silence continued for a moment as the time bomb ticked ominously away.

'But, what about my school uniform?' he said, anxious to defuse the thing before it exploded. 'I can't go to school in my jeans and sweater. The other kids will laugh at me and the teachers will give me detention.'

Suddenly the bomb went off with a force that made him jump: 'SHUT UP! You can forget all about public schools, Common Entrance and school uniforms. Your days of exploiting the working class are over. Finished. Done. Understand? From now on you're going to a REAL school where they don't waste time on rubbish like Latin or school uniforms. Now put your pens and pencils into your bag and Mary will take you there.'

Another bollocking. You'd think he'd deliberately broken a window.

'Is *this* it?'

A silent and sullen Mary descended the ladder. With a sense of profound relief he saw that she was wearing some clothes. A filthy old sweater and grubby jeans, it was true, but at least she wasn't naked. Taken to school by a naked mother! He'd have just died of shame! But, judging from her sulky expression, she was going to need careful handling this morning. What could it possibly be this time? These grown-ups were worse than kids. It would be a relief to get to a sensible place like school where the teachers, at any rate, were sane human beings.

He followed her out into the grey world beyond. They walked down the hill and turned left along a road that cut across a piece of waste ground that looked like a World War II bombsite – all piles of rubble and pools of dirty water. Then it was into an alley between the backyards of two rows of bleak red-brick houses, stepping carefully over piles of rubbish – black plastic bags full of rotting cabbages and rusty old beer cans, polystyrene cartons oozing half-eaten chips covered with tomato sauce and empty cigarette packets.

Eventually, they came to a big, modern building with a flat roof – a shabby, run-down affair with lots of dirty windows and blue and red panels all of which were peeling and scratched. The brick wall surrounding it was covered in graffiti. A bemused John picked out a slogan: 'SANDRA SUCKS COCKS.' From the yard behind the wall came a seething roar of human voices, like a fire blazing out of control.

'Is *this* it?' he blurted out. It was like no school he'd ever seen – that filthy graffiti for starters.

'Not good enough for you?' snapped Mary, the first words she'd said that morning.

'Well, here you are,' she added.

'But what do I do? Where do I go?'

'Just ask a teacher where Form 1E is,' she replied hurriedly.

'And, by the way, here's your dinner money,' she added, handing him two fifty-pence pieces before turning round and scuttling off.

Into the Inferno

Left alone, John paused. Entering that raging inferno beyond the wall was scary. It was a bit like the time he'd gone for a swim at Brighton on a wild and stormy day.

But though the big waves had been cold and alarming at first, they'd been good fun once you got in. And, anyway, what had he got to worry about? They were only kids and he was as strong as most other kids – after all, he'd even taken on Jimmy Stokes! He walked boldly through the entrance.

Immediately, his confidence dissolved. The sheer *size* of the youngsters was daunting. So was their scruffiness and the volume of their voices.

Something seemed to be happening in the middle of the yard where a crowd of boys and girls was milling around, shouting and bellowing. He cringed as he caught phrases like 'Fuck 'im hard!' Somebody was going to cop it when the teachers heard this disgusting language!

Nobody seemed to notice him as he elbowed his way through the heaving mass of arms and legs to see two enormous male lumps bashing away at each other with an animal ferocity. Cheers and clapping erupted with a volcanic violence as one of the youths crumpled onto the ground and the other began kicking him with a seemingly lunatic frenzy. Bang! Bang! Bang! On the head, on the back, all over.

A gut-wrenching shudder rippled through him. He'd seen fights before – they were part of a boy's life. But this was something else. The sheer uncontrolled savagery. These were wild animals. Not humans. And where were the teachers who should have stopped the fight before it got out of control?

Suddenly a whistle blew and about half the crowd surged towards a door where a smallish man in jeans and a sweater stood aside as it swept past him. He did nothing about the howling mob seething round the youth who continued to kick the prostrate lump on the ground.

John was propelled into a battered corridor by an incoherent tumble of elbows and knees. Desperately, he looked for a teacher who might explain things to him, but he couldn't see one anywhere.

'Please,' he asked a black-haired boy next to him, 'where's 1E?'

'Hoo the fuck duzz Ah knaa!'

'What?' He couldn't quite understand. What language was this? It wasn't French or Latin, but neither was it really English either. And why the hostility? He'd just asked a normal question.

He stopped as the knobbly mass of arms and legs jostled past him. 'Please,' he said, addressing two largish boys, 'where's 1E?'

They just barged past him.

The he saw a girl – an untidy red-haired thing in purple jeans – who looked about the same age as himself. Boys might be rough and violent, but girls were supposed to be gentler. He might get somewhere here.

'Please, where's 1E?'

'Eh?' she replied with a screech, 'Divvent yer bluddy knaa?'

'What?'

'Is yer's new like? Well, 1E's wor class ser yers is berra gannin' wi' us like.'

That seemed to mean 'follow me'. Progress.

The 'Posh Git'

They went upstairs and eventually poured into a classroom. Most of one wall was a window, but one of the panes had been broken and had been blocked up with a sheet of plywood. On it was a large penis delineated in black felt tip. A notice board covered much of the opposite wall. There were no notices on it, just a mass of felt-tip graffiti – bums, tits and vaginas, red ones, green ones, blue ones... All the desks were covered in the same graffiti. It was like the moss grew over the stones in Rickerby Park. It wasn't remotely like any classroom he'd ever seen before.

He went to a desk at the front and sat down. Behind him a burst of screeching and bellowing suddenly erupted – a girl and a boy were having a fight while half the class gathered round them cheering with delight. Eventually, a small, well-dressed lady with spectacles bustled in carrying a pile of papers. About a third of the pupils sat down while the rest continued to mill around at the back, shrieking away. Seemingly unconcerned, she handed worksheets out to those who'd condescended to sit down.

John looked round in disbelief. Continuing to scrap about while the teacher was taking the lesson? Something awful was bound to happen. Yet it didn't. The teacher seemed to be scared. A teacher scared of the kids? What kind of nonsense was that? It certainly wasn't like Rickerby Hall.

The worksheet – when he finally got one – turned out to be about geography. It consisted of a blank map of Britain on which you had to mark in the main rivers, cities and surrounding seas. Alongside it was a map with everything you needed clearly shown on it to help you. It was grotesquely easy – the sort of thing he'd done as a seven-year-old at Rickerby Hall. But he had to make a good impression. So out came the felt tips and he did a first-class job, printing all the names carefully – using black for the cities, brown for the mountains, dark blue for the rivers and light blue for the seas.

He walked up to the table at the front and presented the finished product to the teacher. A look of gratified amazement spread over her anxious, worrity face.

'Well done!' she cooed, '*Very* well done! But I haven't seen you before. What's your name?'

'Denby,' he replied, 'John Denby.'

At that precise moment a sudden explosion of noise blasted out from the back of the classroom where two girls had started a fight and were screeching at each other like a pair of embattled cats.

'Sorry, I didn't quite hear you. Say it again.'

'DENBY,' he called out in a loud voice, 'JOHN DENBY.'

As luck would have it, the noise at the back suddenly abated and the whole room heard his high-pitched, tinkle-bell voice.

'Eeeeow! Weely cheps! ... Weely!' A loud male voice began to caricature his Home Counties accent.

'Wee's the posh git then?' yelled another.

John turned round and stared in confusion. This had never happened to him before. His voice was perfectly normal, so what on earth was all this about?

111

The teacher made no attempt to stop it. Instead, she whispered nervously in his ear: 'I think you should go and sit down.'

He returned to his seat to find that his felt tips were missing. He turned to the boy next to him: 'Where's my felt tips?'

'Eeeuuh! Weely cheps!' the lad crowed. 'Eeeuuh I sey!'

At which – on cue – the whole room took up the chorus: 'Eeeeuuh! Weely cheps! Eeeuuh weely!'

While John gaped in confusion, the teacher remained glued to her chair and pretended to study her pile of worksheets as if nothing was happening.

This was ridiculous. He walked boldly up to the table, ignoring the jeers and the catcalls: 'Please, Miss, somebody's nicked my felt tips.'

The woman threw an alarmed glance at him and shooed him away. She didn't *actually* say, 'Don't be a suicidal idiot!' But that's what her rabbity gesture obviously meant.

An even louder deluge of catcalls engulfed him as he sat down.

'Borrow them if you want,' he said to his neighbour in an attempt to repair the damage he'd obviously done. 'Only do let me have them back.'

'Aw fuck off!' the boy snarled.

A buzzer sounded and, without waiting for the teacher, the class surged out into the corridor. In the maelstrom of arms and legs he forgot about his felt tips. He was hardly out of the door before two boys and a girl – big, tousle-haired limps with dirt behind their ears and blackheads on their noses – grabbed his arms.

'Lookah, kiddah!' snarled the girl in a quite ungirlish way. 'There's nae teecha's pets heor! Gerrit!'

With that she punched him in the ribs.

'Oyer!' he gasped. The punch hurt.

'Aye!' added a boy, 'Yer wanna belt up in the lessons else we is doin' yer!'

And he punched him hard on the other side of his chest.

'Oyer!'

'An' there's more where that came from!'

'Posh git!' growled the other boy as he spat in his face.

At Rickerby Hall you had to make the new kids welcome – or the teachers blew a fit on you. Here it seemed to be different. Why? At Rickerby Hall, too, he wouldn't have let those punches go unpunished. He'd have fought back – and how! But here ... it was all so strange and frightening – the sheer animal ferocity of that fight in the yard! At the very thought of it his insides seemed to melt.

Educational Achievement?

Confused and steaming with humiliation, he followed the mob into the next classroom – another desolate, graffiti-strewn desert. There he sat huddled at the front, feeling like a hedgehog surrounded by a pack of hungry dogs. All around him a tumult of shrieks and yells exploded as a young teacher in a sports jacket and baggy grey trousers tried to hand round worksheets which had something to do with history.

But before he could even read the one placed in front of him somebody had screwed it up and thrown it at the boy behind him. He achieved precisely nothing in that lesson.

Pure Heroism

When the buzzer went the class erupted out into the schoolyard. It seemed to be break time – though nobody had told him. With a shudder he recognised the youth who'd won the fight earlier in the morning – a vast, thickset tank of a thing with black hair and an incipient moustache on his upper lip. He was holding a cat by the scruff of its neck. John felt an almost physical shock hit him as he saw the brutal way he was swinging the poor helpless creature round. He loved cats – he'd repeatedly asked his gran to let him have one. Here was the cat he'd always wanted, a beautiful black-and-white creature. It was wide-eyed with terror, seemingly pleading directly to him – 'Help me! Save me!' A wave of pity surged out of him, dissolving any sense of reality. He was ready for anything.

A crowd was rapidly gathering round. Something awful was going to happen. With an incredulity that turned to horror, he saw another youth produce a bottle of yellow liquid and pour it over the wretched creature. The big youth then placed the dripping bundle on the ground, and, pulling a cigarette lighter out of his pocket, proceeded to set fire to it. A colossal roar of delight went up as the animal exploded into a sheet of flame and ran screeching over the tarmac.

113

Now's your appointed hour, John! St Paul before Nero! 'You lie Nero!'

Biggles defying the might of the Swastika! Be a hero! Win the crown of glory!

A wild, exhilarating madness followed. He dashed into the circle of bodies, grabbed the screaming cat, crying out with pain as his hands were caught by the flames.

Rolling it against his sweater, he somehow managed to put out the fire – he never knew how. Then, with the tortured animal yowling and tearing at him with its claws, he rushed frantically for safety, pursued by huge, terrifying bellows – 'FUCK THE LIDDELL BASSTADD! DAMAGE THE LIDDELL CUNT!' All in a few crazy seconds.

Gasping for air, his breath coming in frenzied pants, he found himself in a corridor inside the school. Quite how, he didn't know – it was all in one mad tumult.

There was no noise. Nobody was after him. He was safe.

He paused to look at the squirming bundle he held. The sight appalled him. Half its fur was burnt away and the exposed skin was all black and running with liquid fat. It looked and smelt like one of those pieces of barbecued steak that his Granddad had served out when they had summer parties in the garden. It continued to yowl piteously. Heaven alone knew the sheer hell it must be going through.

He just *had* to get it to a vet. Now. Right *now*! That meant dealing with grown-ups. So he marched along the corridor looking for what he thought might be the staffroom.

Suddenly he found his way blocked by a vast burly man, bald-headed, heavy- jowled and wearing a tracksuit.

'*You!*' he bellowed, pointing at him, '*Out!*'

John jumped with fright and nearly dropped the cat. But ... be a hero, John, stand your ground.

'Sir... This cat ... you see. Where can I find a vet? ... I must...'

'Are you arguing with me, son?' A menacing growl, masking heaven alone knew what awful consequences behind it.

There was no way round that humanoid mass of concrete. The heroism evaporated and he scampered back the way he had come.

Before plunging into the shrieking hullaballoo of the yard, he took another look at the cat. The screeching had subsided into a whimper and its wrigglings had ceased. A horrible thought struck him. 'Please don't die!' he said. 'Please stay alive. Try! I'll take you to a vet. He'll make you better and then I'll take you home and you can be mine. I promise. I swear to God.'

Remembering that he still had his bag draped over his shoulder, he unzipped it and, with infinite care, wrapped his treasure in his handkerchief and laid it gently among his pencils and rubbers. 'Have a rest,' he said, 'Go to sleep ... but *please* don't die!'

Out in the yard another fight was going on so, mercifully, nobody noticed him. Then the small man in the jeans and sweater came out and blew his whistle.

A Proletarian Maths Lesson

He followed the onrush into the school and, by keeping some of the 1E people in sight, seemingly arrived at the right place. There, standing in front of a door was that big, burly man in a tracksuit. With his arms folded, he radiated menace and aggression.

'What's this lesson?' an alarmed John asked one of the girls.

'Maths, yer dick!' she hissed as the class lined up along the wall. 'Double Maths with Boobs.'

'And divvent yer try them poofy tricks o' thine on 'im neither,' she added, digging him in the ribs. 'Cos 'e's Boobs an' 'e's a boxer like. He'll fuckin' do yers!'

Under Boobs' ferocious glare the class filed sullenly into the room and condescended to sit down. It was another bleak classroom, just a window and bare walls, though, oddly enough without the tropical growth of graffiti that seemed to be the natural vegetation in this weird place. It wasn't long before John found out why.

A low murmur of conversation continued among the larger pupils at the back. Immediately Boobs went into action: 'SILENCE!'

John jumped. It was as if a commando had flung a hand grenade at an enemy patrol. But at least some of the enemy seemed to have survived, for one of the boys continued to talk. With the ostentatious swagger of an unbeaten boxing champion, Boobs marched up to him.

'Ready, Simpson?' he said calmly. 'Are you ready? Come on out into the corridor and I'll show you.'

The boy muttered to himself and fell silent.

'Yeah! Scared, aren't you?' sneered Boobs.

115

'Now,' he continued, facing the class. 'Money. Shopping. Get these sheets done proper like and you can have your lunch. If not ... we'll just have a very long wait, won't we, Dixon?' He glared at a fair-haired boy who glared back at him.

With that, he handed each pupil a photocopied worksheet: 'Get started, NOW!' John studied the sheet. It was a series of sums. Number One was: 'If I have two pounds and buy a packet of chips for 50 pence, how much money will I have left?'

So it went on down to number 40 at the bottom of the sheet which was more complex: 'If I buy a motorbike for £645 how much change will I have from £1,000?'

He completed it in ten minutes' flat and then sat in silence. He didn't want to risk another punch for being a teacher's pet. Besides, his mind was entirely taken up with the cat in his bag. It had gone ominously silent. Did that mean it was ... dead?

'Please, God,' he prayed under his breath. 'Don't let it die! Please!'

Suddenly a paper dart flew across the room: a direct challenge to the power and the dignity of Boobs. Entirely predictably, the gauntlet was picked up – and with the inevitable relish.

'That were you, Robson, weren't it?' he growled advancing purposely on a red-haired lump of a boy at the back who looked up defiantly.

'It weren't bloody me!'

'Yes, it were. I saw you!'

WHAM! A colossal blow in the ribs tipped the boy off his chair and sent him sprawling onto the floor. The class stared in respectful silence. John cringed. He'd never seen a teacher do this before. At Rickerby Hall things never got beyond the shouting stage. Besides, weren't teachers supposed to get done if they beat up kids?

A triumphant Boobs swaggered back to the front of the class.

'CUNT!' yelled a voice from behind his back.

Before John's bewildered eyes a sort of slow-motion Japanese wrestling match occurred. Boobs turned round and walked slowly up to a smallish black-haired boy in the back row. (How on earth did he know it was *him*? wondered John.) He picked him up by the front of his shirt and pulled him close to his chest.

'Did ye call us a cunt?'

'It weren't fuckin' me!' the boy protested.

'It was an' all!' And he banged him against the wall. Thump! Thump! Thump!

Then he dropped him back into his chair. 'There's naebeddy as calls us a cunt!' he declared triumphantly as an almost tangible silence fell on the class.

Another boy glanced up and half-opened his mouth.

'Yes, Hallstead. Any comments?' growled Boobs, advancing menacingly towards him.

The boy looked down again. The rebellion was over – finished, crushed. A deathly hush ensued – the hush of a stricken battlefield – and lasted for the remainder of the double lesson.

John sat in benumbed anguish. No sound was coming from his bag. The worst had probably happened, but he didn't dare look. Any unauthorised movement would bring the whole weight of an enraged Boobs down on him. Not an option.

At long last the buzzer went. Nobody stirred. Eventually, with an air of pained condescension, Boobs walked over to the door where he positioned himself like a jailer who had been ordered to release his prisoners much against his will.

'Front row come up and hand in your work.'

The front row duly filed out. As each pupil handed in their worksheet, he examined it carefully and then nodded silently. When John's turn came he looked him squarely in the face: 'You're the gobby new one, aren't you? Well, I don't want any more lip from you. See!'

What about Lunch?

Out in the corridor John frantically unzipped his bag and peered in. The worst *had* happened. The cat was dead. An involuntary tear trickled down his cheek.

But there was little time for sorrow. It was lunch-break and he had the mysteries of the dining hall to unravel. He followed the seething mob that surged along the corridor and poured into a big hall where there was a canteen. But he was unable to get anywhere near it. The way was blocked by a seemingly solid wall of bodies and every time he tried to push his way into what he thought was a queue some big lump – male or female – rudely pushed him aside. There seemed to be no teachers on duty.

He stood there bewildered for a while until one of his classmates – the red-haired girl in purple jeans who'd shown him how to get to the first lesson – called over to him.

'Ey! Marmaduke, yer casnnae get nee dinner till yer've handed in yer dinner money like!'

'But what do I do? Where do I go?'

'Nae frets, son,' she replied in a kindly voice. 'Jus' gee us yer money like an' I'll get yer the ticket yer needs.'

'Cor, thanks!' he exclaimed as he handed over his two fifty-pence pieces. He felt a spurt of relief. At least, they weren't all hostile here. He might even be able to make a few friends.

He stood aside as the crowd jostled past him and waited for the girl to return. But she never did and, after three-quarters of an hour, a buzzer went and everybody poured out of the hall. Bewildered, he walked up to a white-coated lady at the canteen.

'Excuse me, can I have my lunch, please?'

'Too late, sonny,' she replied. 'We're closing now.'

Rage filled him. That girl! She'd cheated him, taken his money and run away! She was a nasty thief! But what could he do about it?

Sullenly he walked out. A more immediate problem now preoccupied him. He needed a pee – desperately and ever more frantically with each passing minute! But, where, oh where was the bog? He couldn't hold out much longer. The unthinkable was about to happen. And pretty soon!

'Where do I go for a pee?' A New Friend

He ambled down the corridor towards the yard – perhaps somewhere out there he could 'unload'. Suddenly, he noticed a small rabbity boy with a mass of mousy hair staring at him with a pair of big, goggly eyes.

''Ere you!' the creature hissed, 'Over 'ere!'

John obeyed. At least he didn't seem hostile. He needed a friend – *any* friend! – who could guide him through this hostile jungle and, most important of all, show him where he could have a pee.

The creature beckoned him and then scuttled off down another corridor, looking furtively round to see if anybody was following him. They reached a quiet spot which seemed to be a cloakroom – there were frames with hooks on them, but nobody seemed to hang anything up there.

'Noo,' said the boy, 'if yer divvent skelp wor like, Ah'll be yer mate!'

John didn't understand. What *was* this language? What did 'skelp' mean? He looked carefully at him. He was more like a gnome out of a fairy story than a boy. He had a tiny, skinny little body with a funny, misshapen head stuck on top of it. His face, with its big eyes and its long, pointed nose, was strangely old-looking, almost the face of an old man. His hair was like an unkempt haystack, all matted and greasy, and there were grey tide marks in the wrinkles of his skin. His grubby jeans and filthy old sweater emitted a stale smell of sweat and a sickly faecal odour.

'What do you mean "skelp"?'

'Ah means if yer divvent hit us like.' And the creature imitated a swipe on his head.

'Of course, I won't hit you,' said John. 'I don't hit people.'

'Reet, then. Wees is mates like.'

That seemed to mean that they were friends.

'Who are you?'

'Well, the lads calls us 'Loppy' like. Burra 'aven't got nee lops like me. Promise.'

'What's lops?'

'Divvent yer knaaa noot, son? Why lops is fleas like. Burra 'aven't got nin, me!'

'Of course you haven't.' (He was quite sure he *had* got fleas, but in this incomprehensible jungle he needed a friend. *Any* friend – fleas or not!)

'But what's your real name?'

'Well me mam like, she calls us "Billy". Me other name is "Lees".'

'All right, I'll call you "Billy" then.'

'Yer berra stick wi' us like. Affer skyerl.'

'Why?'

'Fuck me! Divvent yer knaa? They thinks yer's a posh git like, a smarmy basstad an' that. They'll fuckin' do yers!'

'But I haven't done anything wrong?'

'Not done nuttin'? Fuckin' 'ell, man, yer fucked up Freddy Hazlett's do wi' the cat in break. Yer shuddent o' done it! They'll fuckin' DO yer, yer knaa!'

'Do yer'! A burst of fear surged through John as he recalled this morning's fight with the loser cowering on the ground beneath that manic frenzy of kicks... But there was a more immediate problem.

'I'm bursting for a piss. Where's the bog?'

A look of grave concern spread over Billy's wrinkled old face.

'The bogs! Yer divvent wanna gan theor, man. No yer divvent! That's where Freddy Hazlett hangs oot. 'Im 'an Shorly like. If them two sees yer there... Bye they won't 'arf do yers!'

'But where *do* you pee?'

'Yer gans doon ter the boilers like wot Ah does. There's naebeddy theor. Lest the caretaker like. Yer berra watch oot cos 'e divvent jus' skelp yer. He fuckin' BRAYS yer! Hadaway I'll show yers.'

They scurried along the battered and trampled corridor, sneaking carefully past the huddles of youths that blocked their path like boulders. When they came to a big red door with 'Cleaning and Maintenance Staff Only' on it, Billy motioned him to stop while his big eyes and ears seemed to revolve – almost like those radar scanners they had at RAF bases.

'Howay!' he whispered and opened the door, the tiniest bit. Signalling to John to follow, he slipped through the crack. Finding themselves on a small landing at the top of a flight of stairs, they paused. Footsteps sounded from the cavernous depths below.

'Aw fuck, the caretaker!' hissed Billy. 'Quick in 'ere!'

He opened a door beside them and they squeezed into a darkness full of pails, mops and brushes.

'But we're not meant to be here,' said John anxiously. 'Hadn't we get out before we get done?'

'Where's yer gannin' ter pee, then? Shhhhhh!'

The footsteps grew louder and louder and went right past them. They heard a door open and close and then the sound of a key in a lock.

'Oh lor! We're locked in!' This whole adventure was going crazy.

But it didn't seem to worry Billy: 'Nae frets! We can gerroot the back dooah an' if it's locked like, there's the windee.'

He carefully opened the door, peered out and then whispered, 'Howay!'

They scampered down the staircase into the blackness below and found themselves in a world of concrete floors and vast metal drums, draped with pipes and dials – obviously the 'Boilers', the domain of the dreaded 'Caretaker'. Clambering over some big, cladded pipes, they squeezed into a dark and dusty corner behind a large green tank.

''Ere! 'Ere's where Ah gans!' said Billy, unzipping his flies and spraying the red-brick wall in front of him.

John followed suit – immensely relieved as he unloaded a whole morning's accumulation. Disaster averted! Something achieved! But it was all so mad – this business of having to break the rules because you couldn't use the proper bog. Who was running this place, the teachers or the big louts? And what if they were caught down here?

But any worries on that score were quickly swamped by a wave of anguish about the poor, martyred cat. For one ghastly moment he thought he was going to have another weeping fit – the very last thing he needed in this frantic madhouse. But, mercifully, the wave subsided.

'Reet, we'd berra gerroot!' whispered Billy.

They clambered quickly over the pipes, paused while Billy sniffed the air for danger – again the humanoid radar scanner – and then made for a big double door at the far end. Easing it open just the tiniest bit, Billy peered out and then said, 'Ah reet!'

Slipping out, they found themselves in the open air. They were in the bottom of a small pit where a flight of concrete steps led up to ground level. John heaved a big sigh of relief. They weren't trapped. They were safe. Or so he thought as he climbed up towards the schoolyard above. They were directly under a big, steamy window through which he could make out white-uniformed ladies rinsing plates in a sink and putting them into a large dishwasher. Suddenly, Billy grabbed him and pushed him flat against the wall directly under the window.

'Ey! Yer divvent wanna be seen by them cooks like! Coz yer'll get done!'

Squashed flat against the bricks, they slithered under the window and eased themselves round the corner at the top of the steps, finally reaching safety.

Or was it 'safety'? To John it was more like leaping out of the frying pan and into the fire. They were in the school 'playground' – a deadly jungle where clumps of boys and girls roamed round in predatory packs looking for prey. Like a tourist guide in a safari park, Billy pointed out the more dangerous beasts.

'Yin's Beth. Yer wanna watch oot for hor. She's rock 'ard hor... See them sheds. Them's the bike sheds. That's Shorley's place. Divvent nivver gan theor...'

A whistle sounded.

'See yers affer lessons in the broom cupboard at the top o' them stairs like. If the dooah's locked then gan roond ter the back dooah, but divvent let them cooks see yers...'

With that Billy scampered off leaving John nonplussed. Why, amid all this hostility, had this little gnome chosen to befriend him and to be his protector?

An Outcast

As the mob surged along the corridor he soon had the answer to that question. They passed an open classroom door and there in the middle of a pummelling mob was Billy.

'FUCKIN' LOP!' bellowed a brawny youth in an open-necked shirt as he punched him in the stomach. Billy crumpled up into a heap on the floor, wailing like a baby.

Obviously, he was the outcast at the bottom of the heap who needed a friend – *any* friend, even a posh git would do.

An Unwelcomed Alien

John followed 1E into the next lesson, wriggling through the door into yet another desolate classroom, devoid as usual of any kind of decoration save the customary fungus-like graffiti. Clearly no Boobs ruled this corner of the jungle. Trying to look as inconspicuous as possible, he squeezed himself into a desk at the left-hand end of the front row. The back rows were dangerous and forbidden territory – two big girls had started a fight and were welting away at each other amid a chorus of shrieks and cheers. (Did these people *ever* stop fighting?)

After a while a small teacher, bearded and dressed in grubby jeans and an old jacket, scuttled in. Ignoring the fight, he sat down at a table and opened a register. Glancing round the room, he made a few marks in it and then began to call out some names.

'Morton?'

'Yeah!' yelled a small white-haired boy.

'Barnes? Tracy Barnes?'

'Yeah!' shrieked a fat girl in jeans.

'Denby?'

No response.

'Denby?' he called out a bit louder this time.

'Howay, it's ye man!' hissed the boy beside John, punching him.

122

'Yes!' he called out.

'Eeeuuh weely cheps... Wot oh cheps! Wee's the posh git?' came the predictable chorus.

Discovery. Exposure. Revealed as an unwelcome alien.

John cringed.

But, mercifully, nothing else happened. No punches. No gobbets of spit landing on his face ... and the teacher continued with the roll call. Then, ostentatiously ignoring the riot at the back of the room, he handed out worksheets to those pupils who had actually condescended to sit down.

John studied the sheet. Written in a kindergarten English, it appeared to be a comprehension exercise. It was about a football match between Boldonbridge United and Sunderland. Under the text were a series of statements and you had to put a tick against the ones which were right and a cross against the ones which were wrong: 'The final score was Boldonbridge United 3, Sunderland 2. Boldonbridge United won the match. Sunderland won the match...' and so on for twenty more lines about who scored which goal and who was sent off for fouling.

It was ludicrously easy and John finished it in five minutes flat. Determined to avoid the morning's catalogue of errors, he sat in silence and acute boredom while the fights went on at the back and the paper darts flew round the room.

Eventually the buzzer went. A few, including John, handed the worksheets to the teacher while the majority just tumbled out into the corridor.

Proletarian Art

About half the class burst noisily into the room next door which seemed to be an art room. The rest – the bigger, stronger and more dominant – simply disappeared into the wilderness. Cutting classes? At Rickerby Hall this was a quite unheard-of crime – you might equally well have gone on a shoplifting spree! Still, it was a relief to see them go. Without that lot messing things up, he might even have a proper lesson for a change.

Seating himself at the end of a long bench in the middle of the room, he gazed around him. It was the same old desolate, scuffed and graffiti-infested scene as before, but to the right of him was a door with a glass window in it. Out of curiosity he went up to it and peered in. Beyond was another world, an Aladdin's Cave of wonders – potters' wheels, kilns and stacks of modelling clay, all neat and tidy, devoid of graffiti and just asking to be used! There had been nothing like this at Rickerby Hall. Excitement flared. Perhaps they were going to be allowed in? He couldn't wait to start playing around with that clay. He'd make a whale... No, an undiscovered prehistoric monster with gigantic teeth and a huge tail!

'YOU SIDDOWN!'

A deep male voice barked out from behind him and he felt a hand grip his shoulder and propel him back towards the bench. Looking round he saw a big, hairy man with an untidy black beard straggling over a dark-blue denim suit. A chorus of cheers went up from the class: 'Good on yer, Bertie! 'E's a smarmy git yin! Yer wanna give 'im the belt! Aye, pull 'is trousers doon an' dee it proper like!'

John cringed in terror. A quite unheard-of fate was in the offing. 'Sorry... I ... er,' he mumbled at the implacable face of his captor, 'Sorry! I ... er...'

To his enormous relief, he was allowed to sit down at the bench. Reprieved! Safe for the moment. Beside that, the continued hail of insults from the class meant little.

'QUIET!' roared Bertie. (Not quite as awful as a Boobs' roar, but of that order of things.) 'Now, today's task. Motion. Movement. Here's the pencils. Here's the paper...'

With that, he went round the benches handing out the requisite articles: 'Now get started!'

Surprisingly enough the class settled down – sort of settled, at any rate. Chattering went on, the odd paper dart flew round the room, but no fights occurred. 'Bertie' – or whatever he was called – seemed to be popular for a change. The atmosphere of hostile confrontation that had been the hallmark of Boobs' maths lesson was lacking. If he could get on the right side of him, thought John, maybe things could improve.

So, determined to impress him, he set out to produce a masterpiece. Beavering away, he created a vast, positively baroque steam locomotive, the very embodiment of power and motion, losing himself in a glorious complexity of pipes, domes, sand boxes, pumps, headlamps and a vast cowcatcher.

Suddenly a hand reached across and snatched his creation from him. Turning round, he saw the boy next to him holding it up in the air and then start slowly ripping it up.

Blind fury made him forget the lesson of the morning – don't ever appeal to teachers in this place. He stood up and called out: 'Hey, Sir! He's torn my drawing up!'

On cue, the chorus immediately began: 'Eeeeuuuh weely cheps! Eeeuuh deeah...'

'Bertie' just gave him a withering glare – loathing, contempt and disgust all rolled into one – and angrily motioned him to sit down. He could have been a nasty mess a dog had done on the floor. Why? He was only trying to do what the man wanted him to do. Was he radioactive? Had he got the plague or something?

Bewildered he sat down and tried to look as inconspicuous as possible as the tide of abuse washed over him. This *was* a nutty place. Or was *he* the one who was nutty, but hadn't realised it? Anyway, no hope in the Bertie quarter. Forget about art lessons here.

Escaping from the Jungle with a Native Guide

Finally the buzzer went. Task now: to get out of this jungle unscathed! To evade that spine-chilling threat, 'They're gonna do yer,' and reach safety. Then he could take the cat to a vicar who would say the proper prayers and ensure that it went to heaven. But to achieve all this he had to contact that odd little creature, Billy. He only hoped he would be waiting behind that red 'Cleaning and Maintenance Staff only' door.

Picking up his bag with his poor, dead treasure in it, he waited till the bulk of the class had tumbled noisily out of the room. Then he quietly slipped out and scuttled along the corridor, carefully avoiding eye contact with any potential predators.

He came to the door and, when nobody was around, tried the handle. To his enormous relief it opened and he slid into the darkness beyond. For a few minutes he fumbled about. Just what *was* he doing in this dark hole where he was not supposed to be instead of going home the proper way as any normal human being would? Mad! And what if he were caught? 'Give 'im the belt! Pull his troosers doon an' dee it proper like!' An appalling fate!

'Billy! Billy!'

'Hist!' A whisper came from behind the cupboard door. Relief! Salvation! Billy was there. Billy the Saviour!

'Howay!' he said as he emerged from his hideout. 'We berra gan afore the caretaker comes! He's oot guardin' the teechas' cars like an' them cleanin' ladies like they always forgets lockin' the dooahs an' that. Ser wee's are reet like.'

It was an almost military appreciation of the situation – like Biggles sizing up the approaching German Army.

They slipped quietly down the stairs, past the boilers, through the double doors at the end, up the steps and out into the area behind the kitchens.

'Reet! Behind them bins!'

'Why?'

'Coz if them cooks sees us 'ere like we's gerrin' done! But we canna gerroot o' the skyerl till all them big buggers is oot like else theys is dooin' us. Ser we gorra wait like.'

John didn't get the full meaning of all this. He never did with anything Billy said. His speech was almost as incomprehensible as yukkie old Latin, but he got the general drift of it. If they wanted to be safe, they would have to wait till the big yobs were clear of the school and the best place to hide was behind the bins where the cooks couldn't see them. One part of him was irritated and bewildered by the whole rigmarole – it was all so silly not being able to go out of the proper door. But another part of him was full of excitement. It was a big adventure, not just playing at escaping from Colditz as he'd done at Rickerby Hall, but doing it for real!

After a group of ladies in overcoats had bustled past, they crouched panting for a while. Then Billy raised his weird old head with its big eyes and long nose seemingly vibrating like that radar scanner: 'It's are reet noo!'

They darted across to the corner of the main school building. Motioning John to press himself flat against the wall, Billy peered cautiously round it.

'Howay!'

They scuttled across the yard, now mercifully devoid of danger – the empty crisp and fag packets strewn all over the wet tarmac being the only reminder of the seething mobs that had once thronged it.

'Gorra gerrot afore the caretaker locks them gates like else wees gerrin' proper brayed like.'

Outside the gates Billy scampered off towards a pile of rubble and dived behind it.

'What's all this about?' panted John as he ran after him.

'Gorra see if Beth an' thems ain't 'ere.'

'Why?' John was beginning to wonder if this wasn't an elaborate game to take the mick out of him.

'Well, there's times them lot an' Freddy Hazlett hangs roond heor in them 'oles, smokin' and fuckin' an' that.'

'Fuckin'? What's that?' John knew that 'fuck' meant something really bad – evil, actually – but he wasn't sure what it was.

Billy ignored this. Perhaps he didn't know what it meant either.

'Howay!' he said and off they went again – exactly where to John didn't quite know. It was a matter of darting from hole to hole, crouching behind heaps of rubble, sniffing the air for danger and then dashing on again. It was all wildly exciting – like being one of those heroic paratroopers in *A Bridge Too Far*.

'See yon hoos?' whispered Billy, pointing to a semi-demolished red-brick thing that rose out of the rubble like a skeleton rising up from a graveyard. 'Divvent ye nivver gan tee yon hoos cos that's Freddy Hazlett's place – 'im an' Shorley like!'

'An' divvent ye nivver gaan doon them streets neither,' he added, indicating a row of red-brick terrace houses as yet left standing. Cos if they gets you in one o' them yer canna gerrroot an' yer's fuckin' fucked!'

Danger seemed to lurk everywhere in his blighted battlefield of a place.

Making Friends with an Alien

As they scurried on, John realised that he was lost. His anxiety mounted. Finally, however, they emerged on to a busy road at the top of a hill. With a great sense of relief he recognised it as the big road he'd discovered yesterday. He knew where he was now. It was the place where he'd bought those sweets and crisps.

But, crisps and sweets! That made him remember that he hadn't eaten all day and he suddenly felt desperately hungry. Soon they came to the shop. 'Wait a minute,' he said. 'I'm going to get something to eat. I'm starving. I'll get you some crisps, too.'

Billy's response bewildered him. His wrinkled old face melted into a broad grin: 'Reely? Will yer reely? Cor that's ever so canny! Yer's me proper mate, ye!'

You'd have thought he'd never been given anything in his life. Perhaps he hadn't. Very odd.

John went in, fussed around and eventually bought five Mars bars, three packets of wine gums, two boxes of liquorice allsorts and four large packets of smoky-bacon crisps. Outside he handed the waiting Billy two Mars bars, a packet of wine gums and two of the big crisp packets.

'Cor, thanks ever so!' the little gnome mumbled and a tear ran down his cheek.

For a moment John thought he was going to start crying and wondered how he was supposed to respond to that. (He was so *odd*!)

Then the creature pulled a packet of Benson & Hedges out of his pocket: ''Ere I'll give yer this.'

'No! No! No thanks!' replied a startled John. 'I don't smoke. But where did you get it?'

'Nicked it of course. Look I've got three more!'

'Stole them? When? Where?' (This was getting alarming. He was getting mixed up in *crime*!)

'Nicked 'em whiles you was talking tee the Paki blerk wot owns the place. Didn't see us, neither did ye?'

'But that's stealing! That's wrong. Come on, you've got to put them back!'

The little gnome looked mystified: 'No, it ain't wrong. Ah've nee nikka like wot ye has. Hoo the fuck else does Ah gerrem? Ah needs 'em, yer knaa!'

'But you *don't* need fags!'

'Fuckin' 'ell, Ah does an' all! Look man, Ah gorra get them fags for Freddy Hazlett an' Beth fuckin' Duffy. If they divvent get them fags, they'll dee us ower like!'

'But why don't you tell the teachers and get *them* done?'

'The teechas? Divvent talk shite, man! The teechas is more scared of 'em that wot Ah is! Ah berra be off noo! Yorra great mate ye! Ye stick wi' us like an' yer'll be are reet. Sees yers tomorrah!'

Off he scuttled, clutching his sweets and crisp packets, and vanished into the cityscape like a lizard running for cover.

What a Strange Fellow!

For a long time John stood staring after him. What a strange fellow! He'd never thought that such people existed – or even could be allowed to exist. He was desperately dirty and ragged. Had he never had a bath in his life? Had he never combed that disorderly haystack that passed for his hair? Lops? Fleas? That can only have been the start: there must have been a whole zoo of creepy-crawlies swarming round in the unexplored jungle which covered that oddly misshapen head! And those weird, ungrammatical and barely comprehensible sentences of his? Had nobody ever taught him to speak properly? And the constant use of the word 'fuck'? Didn't he know that it was a filthy word that properly brought up boys never used? And the stealing? He didn't seem to understand that it was wrong to steal.

He must be a bad boy – *very* bad – not to wash and to be always stealing and using dirty language. Yet he had been very kind to him and helped him out when nobody else had. And why had he been so stupidly grateful to be given a few sweets and packets of crisps? You'd think he'd never even had a Christmas stocking! After all every kid had a stocking at Christmas!

No, Billy Lees just didn't hang together like a normal person.

The Christian in the Catacombs

But other matters pressed. The poor, martyred cat in his bag. He had to find a vicar to give it a Christian burial so that God would take it up to heaven. But where to find a vicar in this strange and hideously ugly land? He could ask Giles ... but then he remembered yesterday morning's eruption about going to church. No, that was not an option. He'd have to bury the cat himself and say a prayer. God was sure to understand.

So he walked down to the waste ground at the bottom of Gloucester Road. Scrabbling round in the dirt, he scooped out a little hole and put the poor charred body into it and covered it up. Then he knelt down.

'Please God,' he said in a quiet voice, 'do take this cat into heaven. Please introduce him to Fred – that's my guinea pig, you know. And give him to my gran and granddad. They'll look after him. I'm sorry to pester you like this and I'm sorry not to have a proper vicar to do this. But, you see, I haven't been able to find one. By the way, I'm renewing my subscription to the Scripture Union and I promise to read my bible every night.'

That done, he went back home and rang the doorbell. Mary answered it – thank God she was wearing some clothes! – and climbed up to his room. Taking a piece of paper out of an exercise book, he wrote a letter to the Scripture Union, informing of his change of address and asking for instructions. But where to get an envelope and stamps? Dare he ask Giles? Not really, but then he had no choice.

Screwing up his courage, he descended the ladders and approached the massive figure bent over a pile of papers on his table in the study area. It was a bit like entering a lion's cage at the zoo.

The lion bestirred itself and turned round. Mercifully, it didn't roar. Instead, it merely growled. 'What do you want them for?'

(Momentary panic! He couldn't tell the truth, could he? That would ruin everything.)

'Just to send a letter to a friend.'

'You're not still thinking of that prep school down south, are you? You've got to forget all about it.'

'No, no, it's just to the friend of a lad I met at school today who's moved to Leeds...'

(He was amazed at how quickly the lie slipped out. Lying, he knew, was wrong. Mr Cotton didn't like liars and neither did God. But then it was so much easier not to tell awkward people things they didn't want to hear. Telling them the truth could sometimes make life very difficult. Tell the truth now and he wouldn't get the envelopes and stamps that he needed – and that would mean no Scripture Union. And what would God have to say about *that*?)

'OK. That's all right. Over there at the end of the bookcase.'

He duly collected what he needed and went back to his room. He addressed the envelope, put a stamp on it and slipped a five-pound note into it along with the letter he'd written. Then he went outside and posted it in a letterbox he'd seen on Broadfell Road. Mission accomplished.

Bewilderment

Back in the attic he lay down and tried to make sense of yet another crazy day.

'A proper school'? 'A real school'? No homework to do. No Latin tests hanging over him like a black thundercloud. The evening was entirely his. That was liberation.

Yes ... but ... He'd learned nothing all day. The lessons had been a complete waste of time. Most of the teachers couldn't control the kids. Those who could were brutal and hostile. No nice Mr Cottons or cosy old Mrs Selbys.

And the kids? They weren't kids. They were wild animals – that fight, the burning of the cat, the continuous foul language ... Having to sneak out of the school unseen because they were 'going to do you'. Their blind hostility ... Why? He wasn't a freak. He wasn't a wimp. He didn't piss the bed like some of the junior boarders at Rickerby Hall. He just couldn't work it out.

Fear rose in him, the same kind of nagging fear that had swamped him when he'd messed up Hairy Mary's Latin test – only worse, much worse. For a moment he thought he was going to have another weeping fit.

But no! He musn't start that again. Be brave, John. Be like Saint Paul before Nero. God would see him through. After all, he'd tried to save the cat and he'd renewed his Scripture Union membership. God couldn't ignore that.

And the kids weren't all hostile. There was Billy. As time went on he was sure to make more friends. Things must get better.

16

A Crazy Life

But things didn't get better.

For the rest of the week they stayed much the same. The lessons were as boring and as futile as ever, his classmates just as boorishly hostile. But he did manage to get some lunch at the canteen and, by doing no work in class, he managed to avoid being punched. It was a matter of keeping a low profile – pure survival, nothing else.

And there was Billy. A friend, yes, but was he really human? First impressions deepened. He seemed more like an animal. He couldn't read or write. He was quite grotesquely ignorant. His world consisted of Greenwood and its streets. Beyond it there were vague and distant areas called 'Boldonbrig' and 'Soothside like'. And beyond them? Nothing. Just a blank void. He didn't know where London was. 'Is yin doon Broadfell Road like?' he asked John when he told him where he was from. He didn't know what England was. He'd never heard of Europe.

But he knew all the ins and outs of Greenwood – the streets, the alleys, the building sites, the shops from which you could steal things without getting caught, the hidey-holes, the warm places in the empty houses where you could spend the night undisturbed.

But why did he have to spend nights in these empty houses?

'Well, when me uncles an' that is all pissed up like an' me brothers an' all yer knaa ... Aye an' when me mam an' me sisters is fuckin' an' that... Why, man, they just hoys us oot like...'

John asked about 'fucking' again.

'Well, fuckin' like. Divvent yer knaa noot, man? Why me big brother fucks us when he canna get owt else like...'

John still didn't understand. He shook his head in bewilderment. It was all so odd, so utterly different from anything he knew. Whatever else he was, Billy certainly wasn't a boy. He didn't do any of the things boys did. He had no hobby, he didn't collect things, he had no model railway, no stamp album. He continually smoked cigarettes and, when he hadn't got one handy, he would pick up fag ends from dustbins and the street. He even drank whisky from the bottles he nicked from shops and was surprised when John refused the offer of a swig.

He didn't seem to have been taught the most elementary things about hygiene. One evening, when they were scurrying home, he suddenly pulled his trousers down and did an enormous turd, and then walked on without even bothering to wipe his backside – all in front of an embarrassed and disgusted John who was very fastidious about such things. It was just the sort of thing that a dog would have done.

But that was just what Billy was – a humanoid dog. His craftiness, his cunning, his eye for danger, his complete integration into the natural habitat of the streets – and, also, his obvious affection for and complete loyalty to him. He was like one of those stray dogs that eked out a marginal existence on the strips of waste ground, sniffing round and emptying the dustbins.

It was weird, out of joint. What *would* Mr Cotton have had to say about his mixing with somebody like this? More to the point, what *would* Jimmy Stokes have had to say?

His life had gone crazy.

17

Caught in an Earthquake: Preliminary Tremors

It was on Friday that the chain of disaster got under way.

It quickly gathered momentum. It was like a film he'd seen about an earthquake in South America. At first there had been the ominous little hints of trouble – the unaccountable howling of the dogs and braying of the donkeys. Then the first light tremors which shook the tiles off the roofs... Then the big shocks, one after the other, each one worse than the previous one and plunging a once orderly world into a wild lunacy of collapsing houses and crashing masonry, and finally culminating in a whole mountainside roaring down and engulfing everything.

He arrived home to find Giles and Mary looking like thunder. He had survived another day in the jungle without being punched and was mentally prepared for two blissful days of relaxation, playing with his trains and eating wine gums. Giles' threatening expression alarmed him. Had the shopkeeper on Broadfell Road seen Billy nicking those fags after all and reported the pair of them to the police? Oh cripes! He really was in for it!

'Come here, young man,' said Giles in his head-of-School-House-sorting-out-the-junior-dormitory voice, 'Come here. Stand there and look at me.'

Trembling slightly and with his insides seeming to melt, John meekly obeyed. (What else could he do?)

While Mary fixed him with her 'analytical stare', Giles continued: 'You've got some explaining to do. How do you account for this?'

With an almost professional sense of drama he brandished a large envelope with 'Scripture Union' on it.

John felt an immediate sense of relief – he hadn't heard about Billy and the fags! He was in the clear.

'Well ... er... They must have sent it on. They have me on their mailing list...'

'That's your story, is it? They had you on their mailing list and just sent it on.'

'Yes, that's right.'

And how did they find out about your change of address?'

Quick thinking needed here: 'Well, Mrs Bowles must have told them.'

Quiet nod: 'I see. It was all Mrs Bowles, was it?'

'Yes.'

Forced grin: 'Then what's your answer to this?'

Giles opened the envelope, extracted the letter and began to read it aloud in a slow and deliberate voice: 'Dear John, thank you very much for your letter of last Monday and thank you for your five-pound subscription. We are delighted that you are continuing to read your bible and we enclose ... blah, blah, blah...'

Silence. Analytical stare from Mary.

'Well?' said Giles eventually, putting on his about-to-get-the-cane-out-of-the-cupboard-voice.

More silence.

Suddenly, the reality of the situation hit John in the face. Why the hell should he put up with this? His red-faced anger exploded: 'That was *my* letter and *my* money... You had no right...'

(No right? No bloody right, indeed? Cocky little sod. Knows his rights does he? That struck a raw nerve. Dorking rides again! Maybe it was time to dish out a bit of the Dorking treatment?) Giles cut him short with a sudden shout that made him jump: 'QUIET! You've no "RIGHTS" at all! That wasn't YOUR money. YOU didn't earn it. It belongs rightly to the working class who have done the work that produced it!'

Speaking in a calm and deliberate voice, he continued: 'Now I told you quite clearly that you were to stop all this religious rubbish. It's crap. It's childish and it's high time you grew out of it. Only sick and twisted minds take religion seriously. We're NOT having it in this house. NOT. That's an order and I don't intend to be disobeyed. Is that clear?'

Red-faced and sulky and with an involuntary tear trickling down his cheek, John turned round and walked away.

'COME BACK!' came a sudden bellow that made him jump. 'I haven't finished with you yet. You said you wanted that envelope to post a letter to a friend. You lied to me, didn't you?'

Semi-audible mumble: 'Yes.'

135

'And you lied about Mrs Bowles.'

'Yes.'

'Well, don't you EVER lie to me again. I don't like being lied to. Anyway you're not clever enough to get away with it and you'll always be found out. Anything to say for yourself?'

He knew what he ought to say: 'You're hopelessly wrong. The Bible's God's word and God is far more important than you are!' That's what Saint Paul would have said. But somehow the words just melted away.

Instead, he said in a calm and clear voice: 'I don't like the school I'm at. Can't you send me to a proper school?'

He didn't know why he said it. It just slipped out – by accident, rather like spilling your tea by mistake. Immediately, he realised that he'd stepped on a landmine.

There was an ominous silence while Giles and Mary exchanged knowing looks. Then Mary spoke in a cold, hard voice, the verbal equivalent of her 'analytical stare': 'And just WHY is Greenhill School not good enough for you?'

To his surprise, he was able to reply coolly and clearly: 'The kids all muck about in the lessons. They're always fighting and using filthy language. The teachers can't control them. You don't learn anything.'

'I see. You think you're better than them, don't you?'

'But I *am* better. Most of the class can't even read.'

Suddenly Giles exploded: 'YOU CAN CUT THAT OUT RIGHT NOW! You're NOT better than them! You're worse. FAR WORSE! You're just a spoilt little prep-school brat who needs straightening out. That's what Greenhill is doing for you. It's a proper school and you're staying there. Understand? So don't come snivelling to me every time they knock a bit of sense into you.'

'But ... but...'

He wanted to say, 'But you've no idea what it's like. The violence, the fights, the burnt cat... Billy Lees...' But the words just wouldn't come.

Giles dropped into that quiet, gentle voice that the School House juniors had learned to dread – that beguiling calm pregnant with hidden menace: 'But nothing. If you don't start shaping up pretty soon, I shall have to beat you.'

John felt a spasm of sheer terror flutter through him. 'Beat you.' He'd never been beaten before and had little idea of what it was like. The only information he had came from a picture in a history book which showed an Elizabethan boy lying over a table with his trousers down. He and his classmates at Rickerby Hall had giggled over it, but secretly he'd been appalled – how could that wretched boy have endured the sheer humiliation of having his bottom bared in front of the whole class, let alone the pain of the beating? Now, apparently, this was what was going to happen to him!

But it was all so unfair! He hadn't done anything wrong. Or had he? You just didn't know in this barmy place. He turned round and walked over to the ladder.

'Not so fast, young man!' said Giles as he was about to climb up. 'Not so fast.

We're still not finished. When I gave you that pocket money I didn't expect you to waste it on a lot of religious rubbish. So from now on you'll have your dinner money and nothing else. No pocket money until I know that you won't waste it. Understand? Now you can go.'

Deflated and crushed, John clambered up to the attic.

A Socio-political Statement

'You were right,' sighed Mary. 'I really should have had that abortion.'

Giles looked wistfully out of the window: 'It's a bit late now, I'm afraid.'

Suddenly his accumulated anger burst out: 'The cheeky little sod! Who the hell does he think he is? We take him out of a reactionary con shop – that's all prep schools are! – and put him into an up-to-date school and one which Ed Stimpson says is at the very cutting edge of educational development – and, mark my words, Ed knows what he's talking about! But, oh no, the little pea brain knows better. The little pig wants to roll in his shit again. Why can't he SEE that Greenhill's a better place than that Rickerby Hall place? And all this religious garbage? Can't he see that it's all crap?'

'He probably can't,' said Mary as the flow petered out. 'He's not very intelligent and stupid people can be very obstinate, you know. Just look at my mother. He'll have inherited her brains – or, rather, her lack of them.'

'Yes, you're probably right.'

Then Giles' anger blazed up again: 'Greenhill is OUR school. It represents all that is right in education. It's bad enough having to listen to the Tories bitching on about it, but for fuck's sake, a small KID! Mary, let's get one thing straight. I'm not, repeat NOT, having a bold educational initiative derailed by a spoilt brat with a brain the size of a pea. NO WAY!'

'Is that a socio-political statement?' asked Mary quietly.

'Yes it is,' declared Giles. 'Anyway, just imagine what would happen if we took him out of Greenhill. What would Ed Stimpson have to say? And what would the Labour Party say about it? We'd lose all credibility. No, he stays where he is.'

'When I think of the hopes we once had for that child...' mused Mary ruefully. 'Yes!' interjected Giles forcibly. 'I'm afraid we drew a bad number in the natal lottery. You know, Mary, if scientists could find a way of predicting the potential brain power of a foetus and gently aborting the inadequate ones, it would be a great social advance.'

Respite and Disappointment

That weekend John was left alone to enjoy his trains and his sweets. But he wasn't allowed to join the Sunday night party. 'You stay in the attic. We don't want you interrupting serious academic discussions as you did before.'

That was a big disappointment. He'd been looking forward to talking to that nice fat woman called Martha who had the big notebook.

Ordeal by Combat

But all this was a preliminary tremor. The first big shock came on Monday.

It was lunchtime and he was waiting in the queue. Suddenly he felt a punch in his back. He turned round to see a big, fair-haired girl in a dirty green blouse and tattered jeans glaring at him. He didn't know her name, but he recognised her as one of the screechers from 1E who regularly reduced the lessons to chaos. Behind her was a posse of supporters.

'Wanna a fight, kiddah?' she yelled at him.

138

He knew the right answer: 'Come on, let's have you!' That's what Biggles would have said before he smashed her to the ground with an upper cut on the jaw. But he wasn't Biggles. He was John Denby. And John Denby was in an alien world which he didn't understand and which seemed to suck the guts out of him and reduce him to a heap of jelly. If it had been Jimmy Stokes, he would have squared up to him – and how! But she wasn't Jimmy Stokes. She was a wild animal in a place where they thought burning cats alive was fun – and, moreover, she was twice the size of him.

'No, no,' he spluttered. 'I don't fight. Fighting's wrong.'

An explosion of jeers burst out: 'Fuckin' hom! Fuckin' poof! Smarmy git!'

'Howay, Joyce lass!' a large red-haired youth bawled out, 'lerruz dee 'im anyway!'

Despite his struggles, he was grabbed by the arms and frogmarched out into the yard. There a raucous mob formed around, barring any chance of escape. He was trapped – just like that poor martyred cat.

He knew he shouldn't run away from a fight – only wimps did that and he wasn't a wimp. But this was different. Sheer terror of a sort he'd never known before engulfed him and he tried frantically to break out of the circle, only to be blocked by a wall of arms and legs and flung back again.

'DAMAGE THE LIDDELL CUNT!' an enormous male voice roared out.

The next thing he knew was a violent blow in his face. Brilliant flashes of light danced before his eyes, a shock of pain blasted through his nose and he found himself crashing on to the ground with blood pouring all over his sweater. Quite automatically, he began to wail like a baby. He knew he shouldn't cry in a fight – that was the ultimate admission of wimpery – but he couldn't do anything about it. It just came out of him like the blood pouring out of his nose. Crumpled up on the tarmac, he curled into a defensive ball as the blows rained down on him, kicking him viciously on the back, on the backside, all over him... All around a wild cheering roared away with the ferocity of a forest fire: 'POSH GIT! FUCKIN' HOM! SMARMY GIT! FUCKIN' POOF!'

It was total, abject defeat. The fallen gladiator helpless before the jeering mob. It was a new and quite awful experience, quite different from anything that had ever happened to him before.

The Price of Failure

Dazed, the tears flowing as copiously as the blood that streamed out of his nose, he stumbled back into the school, his hair all awry, his jeans torn and muddy, his sweater soaked in blood – a picture of abject humiliation.

A chorus of jeers erupted as he entered the classroom: 'Fuckin' hom! Smarmy git! Poofter!'

He crept up to an empty desk in the front row. As he sat down, the boy next to him pushed his big red face right up to his. 'Chinned off a lass!' he sneered. 'Yer fuckin' shite ye!'

With that, he spat in his eye. It was an English lesson with the little bearded teacher. Predictably, the frightened little elf remained silent and pretended to ignore the riot.

'Chinned off a lass': Brotherhood of the Despised

'Chinned off a lass.' Later he came to realise that this was the ultimate sin in this cockeyed place – the deadliest of all the seven deadly sins! You could reduce every lesson to chaos, smoke in the schoolyard, drink whisky, go shoplifting, burn cats alive – anything but be 'chinned off a lass'. There could be no forgiveness for such a heinous crime.

It was the tipping point. From then on sullen disdain turned to open aggression. He was doomed.

But not with Billy. For him John's disgrace seemed to be a bond which tied them together – almost like a marriage certificate. He became more dog-like than ever in his affection – doing everything but actually licking him. 'Eeee yer poor fucker! Noo yer knass like! Yer see Ah canna bray 'em back neither. Yin's why Ah has ter keep nickin' fags an' that for ter stop 'em brayin' us like.'

'Aye,' he added, grasping John's hand. 'Wee's proper mates the noo!'

Proper mates. Two rejects at the very bottom of the heap, despised by all except themselves. This was John Denby's new status.

'Keep nickin' fags...'

'Keep nickin' fags an' that.' That was the next big shock.

The following morning he tried, as usual, to slip unnoticed into the schoolyard. To his horror, his way was barred by the massive bulk of Freddy Hazlett and his entourage of sweaty-shirted thugs. Hovering alongside there was a great lump of a girl with a shock of black hair and tight jeans that hardly managed to conceal her vast, wobbly backside – apparently the dreaded 'Shorly'.

Before he could escape he was grabbed and firmly pinioned by rough, brutish hands – more like animal paws than human hands, it seemed to him. Quite involuntarily, he began to tremble violently as his bag was torn from him and emptied and everything removed from his pockets – his handkerchief, his sweets, his dinner money, the remaining five pounds of his pocket money – the lot.

'Reet, son!' said Freddy, pushing his grubby face right up to his and almost suffocating him in a cloud of foetid breath, 'Wee's 'avin' all this nikker an' that.

'Yer's a rich git, ye, ser tomorrah we wants ten quid off yers. Sharp, mind! Gerrit?' John stared at him in blank terror, unable to speak, let alone resist.

'Gerrit, son? Else yer's gerrin' THIS!'

And he punched him hard in the ribs.

'Oyer!' It hurt.

'Yeah! An' there's a lot more where that came from. Yer liddell two-bob fart. So if yer divvent gerrit, yer fuckin' histry ye!'

'Warraboot some fags an' all, Fred?' cut in Shorly.

'Aye!' added Freddy, 'girrus two packets o' fags an' all. Tomorrah. Sharp mind!'

Another World

A fog of helpless despair descended as he scurried off. 'A lot more where that came from'! There was, indeed: that youth lying on the ground being kicked, the poor martyred cat...

Creeping into the classroom was like dropping a lighted match into a box of fireworks and setting off an incoherent chaos of flashes and bangs. Jeers, catcalls, shouts of 'Chinned off a lass!' and 'Fuckin' hom!' The worrity little teacher buried her face in the register and ignored the uproar. Covered with spit, he eased himself into the front row – hardly safety, but less absolutely lethal than the back of the room. The boys next to him held their noses and edged away from him: 'Cor you fuckin' stink! Shat yer pants again, yer dorty basstadd?'

Bereft of pens and pencils, he could do nothing but sit there in bemused bewilderment. Why all this hate? Why this contempt? He didn't stink. He hadn't messed his pants. But, then 'Chinned off a lass!' Perhaps that was the answer.

Meanwhile, anxiety filled him – as if a black oily liquid had been poured through a hole in his head and had seeped into every part of his body. Two packets of fags. Ten quid. Where, oh where on earth was he to get it? But, if he didn't get it 'by tomorrah' and 'sharp mind!' ... And to think that he'd once been in a stew about failing a Hairy Mary Latin test! This was another world.

David and Jonathan

Hunger. That was the next problem. He had no dinner money – so the canteen was out – and no pocket money – so he couldn't buy any sweets or crisps on the way home. Neither was there ever any food waiting for him back at Gloucester Road. All day hunger gnawed at him.

Going home he explained the problem to Billy.

'Nae frets!' said the little gnome. 'Nae frets! Ah'll see yers reet like!'

A wave of gratitude swept out of John. For a moment he wanted to hug and kiss the misshapen little creature, shitty smell, fleas, creepy-crawlies and all.

'Cor, thanks!' he spluttered. 'You're a real friend. I'll ner forget you!'

They went down into the city at the bottom end of Broadfell Road. While John hung nervously on the pavement outside, Billy disappeared into a big newsagent's shop. A little later he emerged triumphantly brandishing three large packets of smoky bacon crisps, two Mars bars and a packet of wine gums, all of which he handed to John: 'There yer is, son!'

'An' 'ere's them fags an' all!' he added, producing two packets of Silk Cut out of his pocket.

Salvation!

'Cor, you're nifty, you! How *do* you do it?'

John was lost in awed respect. Dirty, smelly, a walking zoo cage of exotic insects, unable even to use a toilet properly... yes! But a world-class expert when it came to shoplifting. More than that. His saviour. Billy the Brave. Billy the Good. He put his arm round him and hugged him – something that in his previous incarnation at Rickerby Hall he would never have dreamed of doing. (Just think of what Jimmy Stokes would have made of a thing like that!)

Oddly enough, Billy responded with a warm embrace: 'Yer me emly mate ye! Why, man, Ah've jus' gorra help yes!'

A strange, warm feeling momentarily welled up in John. For the first time in his life he had a glimpse of friendship, something far deeper than the rumbustious matiness that he'd known at Rickerby Hall. The bond between David and Jonathan? Maybe. But. Oh dear, *what* a David and *what* a Jonathan! Two squalid little rejects clinging to each other like survivors from a shipwreck, cast adrift in a tempestuous ocean, thrown together because nobody else wanted them. But real friends for all that.

'Mind,' added Billy as they disentangled themselves, 'Ah cannae dee oot aboot them ten quid like. Yer've gorra dee yin yersell!'

What *Is* Reality?

That ten quid obsessed John as he walked home, stuffing himself with crisps and a Mars bar. He felt limp and drained. All his energy seemed to have dribbled away. It was as if the black oily liquid that had filled his body all day had leaked out of him leaving a void.

He couldn't ask Giles for the ten pounds. That would mean having to explain the mess he was in – or, to be more precise, admitting that he really *was* a disaster area. After all he was having a 'real education' at a 'proper school' – and Giles was a big professor and he *knew*. The trouble was that Giles' reality and his reality didn't match. Which was the true reality? Probably Giles' reality. He really *was* a spoilt prep-school brat. After all, being 'chinned off a lass'! 'If you don't start shaping up pretty soon I shall have to beat you.' He desperately wanted to 'shape up' – but how on earth was he to do it? And, in the meantime, he had to get that ten quid.

'Please, God,' he muttered, 'I want to be good. Please get me that ten pounds.'

Crossing the Line: A Dirty Little Thief...

Maybe God did hear him – at least, that's what he thought. When Giles let him into the house the first thing he saw was three five-pound notes lying on the floor. There they were, crisp and new, lying on the Peruvian ethnic rug that Mary had bought in a pricey New York boutique to affirm her 'solidarity with the Shining Path Freedom Fighters of the Andes'.

As Giles walked silently back to the pile of papers on his table, he snatched them up and stuffed them into his pocket. 'Thank you, God,' he said to himself, 'Thanks a bomb!'

Then he had a momentary panic. Stealing was wrong. Surely God didn't want him to do that! Perhaps God had left the money there just to test him? He was about to replace the notes when he remembered Freddy Hazlett's warning: 'There's a lot more where that came from.' He stuffed them back into his pocket. Survival came first. (More mundanely, however, God was only very indirectly involved with the business – indeed, if at all. It was Mary he had to thank for the windfall. She was ostentatiously careless about money. Leaving large sums lying around the house was one of her most frequent 'statements'. It proclaimed her emancipation from bourgeois consumerism, her rejection of commercialism and her utter contempt for Thatcher and all she stood for.)

Now John knew that he really was bad. Not just a pathetic little wimp, but, also a thief.

God's Punishment for Bad People?

That night he sunk further into badness.

For a long time he couldn't sleep. He tried getting up and watching a video. But he just couldn't concentrate on it – not even on a programme on the Battle of Britain. The empty void inside him seemed to have turned into a gigantic worm which nibbled away at his brain. Always his thoughts returned to Greenhill School. Freddy Hazlett, the burnt cat, 'chinned off a lass', the contempt his classmates had for him... Why? Where had he gone wrong? And that awful doom hanging over him: 'If you don't start shaping up pretty soon I shall have to beat you.' How could he redeem the situation? How could he possibly 'shape up'? He desperately wanted to be good, but *how*?

When he finally drifted off to sleep, he found himself in a strange, disjointed world. He was back at Rickerby Hall – joy of joys! – back to being a real boy again. He was in a rowing boat on Rickerby Park Lake, fighting the Battle of Trafalgar with his mates. But, then, they weren't his mates, they were 1E jeering at him with the same old words: 'Poofter! Chinned off a lass! Shat yer pants!' Suddenly he was in the Pacific Ocean where a terrifying giant squid burst out of the waves. Each tentacle was a form of badness, stealing, lying, 'chinned off a lass' ... One after another they coiled round him, dragging him down into the cold, wet sea, towards a huge, cruel beak that was actually God himself. 'This is what I do to bad people!'

He woke up screaming in terror. To his immense relief he was safe in his bed. But he must have fallen into a lake somewhere because he was soaking wet. It must have been Rickerby Park Lake... But then he remembered that he was in Greenwood and that there were no lakes in Greenwood. Slowly the full horror of what had happened sank in. He'd wet the bed.

It was an appalling catastrophe which had never happened in living memory. Only dirty little wimps pissed the bed. So that was what he really was. He seemed to be getting badder and badder.

For a long time he wept silently with shame and anguish. Eventually fear took over. What *would* happen when Giles found out? He'd die of shame for starters – but, after that? 'If you don't start shaping up pretty soon...'

Quickly removing his dripping and stinking pyjama bottoms, he stuffed them and the sodden duvet into the cupboard. With disgust he saw his old spew-stained school blazer lying in there, growing a green mould. What *would* Giles say when he opened that cupboard? Another doom hanging over him.

'Twenny quid this time'

The next morning he put the two fag packets into one trouser pocket and two of the five-pound notes into the other. The third five-pound note he put under his sock on the sole of his left foot. He would need that to get food on the way home and to reward Billy for getting the fags.

Freddy and Shorley were waiting for him in the schoolyard. Dutifully, he handed over the two packets of fags and the ten pounds.

'That's me lad!' said Freddy. 'That's me lad!'

'Can I go now?'

'Not yet, son! Not yet!'

To his rage and shame, he was firmly pinned down and everything in his pockets and his bag duly removed, including his last set of felt tips and his dinner money.

'Yorra a rich git ye!' growled Freddy. 'So tomorrah mornin' we wants two packets o' fags. Aye an' twenny quid this time! But we'll give yers till Friday ter get the twenny quid!'

'But I haven't got twenty quid! I can't get it!'

'Is ye tekkin' the piss, son? Gerrit else yer's gerrin' done!'

A thump in the ribs made him cry out in pain.

Then it was back into lessons and back to the hooting derision of 1E.

Your Only Friend in Need...

During lunch-break the next big shock came.

As he scurried down the corridor, he found his way blocked by a seething mob. Judging from the cheering and the great peals of yobbish laughter that erupted out of the throng, something was going on – and it was pretty nasty, too. Squeezing through the crush of bodies, he soon saw what it was. There, rolling round on the floor, trying and failing to dodge the kicks and wailing like a baby, was Billy.

For a brief and awful moment their eyes met. Billy seemed to pleading for help. 'If you really *are* my friend, help me now!'

Now's your hour, John! Wipe out the stain of being 'chinned off a lass'! Be brave! Charge into the fray as you did with the poor burning cat! Remember Saint Paul before Nero! But all the fire had gone out of him. Feeling sick with fear, he pushed his way out of the mob and fled down the corridor.

'There's yer bum chum, Loppy!' a voice called out after him, 'Ain't yer gannin' ter help 'm like? Nah! Coz yer shite ye! SHITE!'

That hurt as much as one of Freddy's punches. It *was* true. He was shite. He'd failed the only friend he had.

The Shoplifter

There was no sign of Billy at four o'clock. For nearly an hour he waited in the broom cupboard, but he never appeared. He seemed to have vanished – disappeared into the brickwork like a cockroach on the run.

His fear grew. It was as if his body was now filled with a corrosive acid which was slowly turning him into a heap of jelly. How was he to get through the lethal jungle which surrounded him without Billy to guide him? 'Two packets o' fags! Twenny quid ... else yer's gerrin done!' The cat: and now Billy being kicked around on the floor. Though he hadn't eaten all day, he wasn't hungry. The fear made him feel sick.

But he couldn't remain in the cupboard for ever, so, with a huge effort of will, he slipped out. Luck was with him and he managed to get out of the school and cross the danger zone beyond.

Now the fags. Without Billy, how on earth was he to get them? Well, he'd just have to nick them, wouldn't he? But, what if he got caught? The police, Giles, prison ... doom!

He came to the shop where he usually bought his crisps and sweets. He went in and hung round for a while. To his utter dismay, he saw that the cigarettes were behind the counter and next to the till, a well-guarded position that was almost impossible to reach.

'Yes, son,' said the turbaned Indian who ran the shop. 'What do you want?'

He remembered the five-pound note under his left sock. That gave him leeway.

'Wait till I get my money out!' he mumbled as he proceeded to take off his trainer and his sock.

'So that's where you keep it?' remarked the turbaned Indian with a kindly smile. 'You're wise. It's best to hide your money round here. Now what do you want?'

He bought four packets of cheese and onion crisps and two packets of wine gums. The man was so nice. How could he possibly steal from him? But...

'Is that all?'

'Yes.'

He went out in despair. Just then two big, fat women bustled into the shop. Without really thinking, he followed them back in. Then – was it a stroke of luck, or God answering his prayers? – the women went over to the freezer at the back and rummaged round in it. After a while one of them called out: 'Hey Ali, don't yer 'ave any mince in 'ere?'

The turbaned man left his vantage point by the till and went over to the freezer where he bent down and began to fiddle around.

Everybody's backs turned! All eyes occupied in examining frozen packets of meat. The counter is left unguarded. The coast's clear! Now's your chance!

John dived behind the counter and, keeping his head well down, crawled along the floor and snatched two packets of Benson & Hedges. His heart thumping, he crawled back to the end of the counter and peered cautiously round the edge. But, horror, panic! The turbaned man and the two women were coming back! *Caught!* Frantically, he dashed out of the door.

'Hey, you!' shouted one of the women. 'Look, Ali, he's nickin' yer fags, the liddell basstadd!'

He ran. Ran as he'd never run before. Fast, faster, faster still, down Gloucester Road, his lungs bursting, and out on to the rubble-strewn wasteland at the bottom where he dived behind a heap of bricks.

For an unknowable length of time he lay there panting. Soon the sirens would sound and the police cars would be roaring down the hill with the blue lights flashing. Then it would be a punch in the face, handcuffs, stuffed into the cells, trial... and prison! He scraped at the bricks and the gravel, wishing that he was a rat that could vanish down a hole.

But nothing happened. Gloucester Road remained silent. He'd got away with it!

Or had he? Almost certainly that turbaned man knew who he was and would have telephoned Giles... And then! Oh, God, the bollocking that awaited him! And, worse than that... 'If you don't start shaping up pretty soon...' He certainly *would* be beaten ... and *how*! Doom descended again. His body filled up with that corrosive acid again and began dissolving his bones with renewed intensity.

What to do?

White Lies...

Eventually, he got cold and, trembling, he slunk back home, mentally preparing himself for the worst. Perhaps a full confession and a plea for forgiveness would save him? Small hope, of course, but worth a try...

But, when Giles opened the door, he saw to his bewildered amazement that he was actually *smiling*.

'Had a good day, John?' he beamed. Obviously, he hadn't heard about the fags and for some inexplicable reason seemed to be in a good mood.

Hope flickered – just a tiny little flame, but, still, hope. Now's your chance. He's in a good mood for once. But it won't last, so spill the beans now while you can. He might even listen to you for once. Cut free from the giant squid that's dragging you into the abyss... He might even be nice about it.

But ... admit to that big James Bond man, that famous man who writes books, admit to *him* that you're not a proper boy at all, but a dirty little squirt who gets 'chinned off a lass' – yes, set crying by a *girl*! – and who pisses the bed like a baby who still ought to be in nappies? No way! You want to impress this man, not make him despise you!

'Yes, fine!' The words just slipped out.

'Settling into your new school?'

'Yes.'

'Well done. Good lad. I knew you would.'

Big smile. Praise at last. He was finally getting somewhere.

But was he? If Giles knew the truth! Yet it was so much easier to tell lies. Let people believe what they wanted to believe. It kept them happy and you got what you wanted. In this case, it had got him a breathing space – for the time being at any rate.

The Dirty Little Liar

Meanwhile Mary was mooning round the place in a yellow dressing gown that covered most of her nakedness – at least the more embarrassing bits anyway.

'Giles, I'm sure I had fifteen quid here. Where the fuck's it gone?'

'How the hell should I know?' snapped her husband. 'Anyway it's only fifteen quid, so what does it matter?'

'But I need to get something for supper.'

'Won't your chequebook do?'

'I've run out of cheques.'

149

'Well, here's thirty quid.'

He pulled three ten-pound notes out of his wallet and handed them to her.

'Thanks.'

She put one note into her dressing gown pocket and left the other two on the table. Then, seeing John, she fixed him with the 'analytical stare': '*You* haven't seen three five-pound notes lying around, have you?'

'No! No, I haven't.'

'You're absolutely *sure*?' The 'analytical stare' intensified.

'Yes. Quite sure.' (How easy it was to lie! You just had to invent another reality and believe in it – exactly as you did when you'd played commandos with your mates in Rickerby Park in the glorious old days.)

'Well, I'm not so sure about that!'

With that bombshell Mary swept up the ladder and disappeared from view.

A new fear smouldered in John, another smoking bomb to take its place beside Giles, Freddy Hazlett, the outraged shopkeeper in the turban, the police. She knew he'd nicked the money and before long she'd tell Giles.

Bad, Badder, Baddest...

That night he didn't get to sleep till well past midnight.

He woke up to find that – yet again! – he'd pissed the bed. He was being dragged deeper and deeper into badness. Bad, badder, baddest. Lying, stealing, 'chinned off a lass', failing his one true friend in his hour of need, pissing the bed. He didn't want to be bad. It was just happening to him.

Thursday came and went. Ghastly, of course, but not quite as ghastly as Wednesday.

The two packets of fags placated Freddy Hazlett. 'But mind,' he growled, 'I want them twenny quid tomorrah!'

Needless to say, he relieved him of his dinner money and the change from the five-pound note that he had in his pocket,

When John entered the classroom everybody put their backsides against the wall and yelled: 'Watch yer bums, lads! Here comes the hom!'

150

He was mystified. What on earth was all this about, and just *what* was a 'hom'? But, at least, nobody hit him and that was something.

But that twenty quid. Where to get it? And what if he didn't...? He felt sick and floppy. He wasn't hungry. In any case he had no money – and, besides, he could hardly enter that shop on Broadfell Road even if he had.

There was no sign of Billy. The little creature seemed to have vanished. He was alone – alone and friendless in the dangerous jungle.

Salvation?

That night he hardly slept at all. There were no duvets left. He'd pissed them all. They were in the cupboard, stinking away and waiting to be found by Giles.

Twenty quid. Twenty quid. Twenty quid. Hammer. Hammer. Hammer. Like one of those pile drivers he'd seen on building sites in London. He could, of course, simply not go to school... but that was playing truant and the police would pick you up.

They always did. No, it was twenty quid... or else!

It must have been at least two o'clock when he went down the ladders. Why? No reason. He was sick of just lying on the bed, that was all.

In the living room everything was dark and quiet, almost spooky. Suddenly, he got a shock – not a nasty shock, but a pleasant, comforting one, like getting into a warm bath on a cold day. There on the table were the two ten-pound notes that Giles had given Mary on Wednesday evening, lying just where she had left them. Clearly, she had forgotten all about them. Enormous relief! Salvation! Quickly, he snatched them up and scampered back to his room.

18

Disaster

Morning came with an agonising slowness. It was dark and rainy. The sky was a grey sponge that sucked the colour out of everything – the harsh, red-brick houses, the pools of dirty water, the mounds of grey rubble – it all became a drab monochrome. At the bottom of the hill, flowing sluggishly through its decayed and abandoned wasteland was the river – forlorn and lifeless, a river of the dead, like the River Styx in that book of Greek legends. The cold, stinging rain was the final seal of despair.

With mounting dread John approached the school, shuddering as the battered hulk loomed out of the murk. He remembered a story that Mr Cotton had once read to his class at Rickerby Hall. It was out of a famous book called *A Tale of Two Cities* in which a man called Sidney Carton was approaching the guillotine. That was just what he was doing now – approaching his place of execution. But Sidney Carton had been brave and noble. He, John Denby, was a dirty little thing who cried when girls hit him and pissed the bed at night.

Suddenly, he needed to pee desperately. Frantically, he unzipped and began to spray the nearby wall. At that very moment a middle-aged woman wearing a brown coat and a pink hat happened to be walking past.

'Eeeeee! You dirty little brat!' she squealed. 'The toilet's where you piss, not the street! Wait till I tell your headmaster!'

Hurriedly, he put his thing away and zipped up. In the process a stream of pee ran down his leg, leaving an embarrassing stain all the way down his jeans. Something else for the mob to jeer at. He hurried off, but, then, seeing a convenient puddle, he pulled out his handkerchief, wet it and tried to clean up the mess, or, at least, to disguise it.

As he did so, he failed to notice that the two ten-pound notes had come out of his pocket and dropped on to the ground. He walked on unaware of the disaster.

He entered the schoolyard, the House of Doom. Freddy and Shorley were there, waiting for him. He cringed as they homed in on him and Freddy grabbed his shoulder.

'Gorrit, kiddah?'

'The twenty quid?'

'Yeah, yer dick!'

'Here it is.'

But, as he put his hand into his pocket, a kind of electric shock hit him. The ten-pound notes weren't there – they had vanished. Vanished without a trace! Frantically, with a wildly irrational hope, he rummaged through all his pockets. But for his disgusting, pee-stained handkerchief, they were empty. The money – his only hope of salvation – had gone. Vanished off the face of the earth.

'Howay! Lerruz 'ave it!'

'But... But... I DID have it! Honest I did! It must have got lost!'

'Ye tekkin' the piss, like?'

A vicious punch in the stomach sent him reeling. A bundle of pain, breathlessness and terror, he began to cry.

'Reet, yer gerrin' it!'

Doom. Catastrophe. The sentence of death. *Ibis ad crucem.* 'You will go to the cross.'

'NO! NO! NO! I'll get the money. Swear to God!'

All in vain.

The whistle blew and they surged into the school.

A Human Being in a Cage of Animals

He crept into the classroom. The jeers seemed remote, irrelevant, happening to somebody else. 'Yer gerrin' it!' The youth lying on the ground being kicked... The fate of the cat. His fate. He squeezed himself into a chair next to the wall and cried silently to himself.

'What's up wi' ye?' the girl next to him asked.

He looked up. For once it was a gentle voice. Not harsh or sneering, but full of sympathy. He tried to reply, but the words wouldn't come. He just went on crying.

'Ah knaa!' the girl said. 'It's Freddy an' them lot. Rotten basstadds! Yer norra a snobby git is yers? It's rotten what they does to yers!'

153

A human being in a cage of wild animals! He wanted to reach out and embrace her. Then the boy behind her thumped her hard in the back and she turned away. In class war you didn't fraternise with the enemy.

The Fox Pursued by the Baying Hounds

At the end of the double lesson the class tumbled out into the corridor. No time for crying now. It's survival. The fox pursued by the baying hounds. Go to ground before they see you!

Silently, furtively, all senses like bristling antennae, he slithered off to the boiler room. With a positively concrete sense of relief he found both the door at the top of the stairs and the door of the broom cupboard open. He darted into the welcoming darkness. Safe for the moment! A little flame of hope flickered. Perhaps he could dodge his impending execution.

The buzzer signalled the end of morning break and it was out again into the jungle of the corridors – tremulous, fearful and with all senses on red alert...

Another Bit of Corridor Cred

The next lesson was Maths with Boobs, alarming, but at least you were safe as long as you kept your head down.

'Eeeeeee, Marmaduke!' a boy hissed into his ear as they filed into the classroom under the baleful and menacing glare. 'Yer berra watch oot in lunch break coz Freddy an' them lot is gannin' ter dee yer proper like!'

The terror which had momentarily lifted during his successful concealment in the broom cupboard swept down again. He sat down in front row next to the wall and began to cry again – silently with his hand over his face for fear of setting the Boobs' bomb off.

The lesson dragged interminably on. Try as he might, he couldn't focus on the worksheet in front of him. In any case, his hand was trembling so much that he couldn't hold the pencil that Boobs had given him. What would Boobs do when handed in a blank sheet? Another catastrophe. One stone after another was falling on him in this avalanche of disaster.

Finally, the buzzer went. Doom. The hangman is waiting for you.

But why submit? Why not escape? Yes, but how? Jump out of the window? No way! It's a thirty-foot drop and you'd kill yourself. Then, a brilliant idea – the stock cupboard. It was at the front of the room beside the blackboard with the door slightly ajar – not locked, no problems about entry. The classroom door was at the back. That was where Boobs always took up position to collect the worksheets. Slip into the stock cupboard while he isn't looking … !

Sure enough, as predictable as the seasons, Boobs went over to the classroom door: 'Front row, right-hand side, first.'

Front row, right-hand side, duly filed up and handed over their offerings.

'Front row, left-hand side.'

That was his row. Being next to the wall, he was at the end of the queue. That gave him time.

Luck – or was it God? – was with him. Boobs bent over the sheet submitted by the boy at the head of the line: 'That's better, Simpson, that's better.'

Now or never. Go for it! Quick dash, Billy-style, and he was inside the stock cupboard. Panting, his heart thumping, he embraced its comforting blackness. Once more, all his senses were switched on to red alert as he listened. Enhanced hearing picked up every tiny nuance of sound.

'Second row, right-hand side … Still can't add up, can we, Blackshaw?'

Waves, gusts, typhoons of relief! Boobs hadn't missed him. He'd got away with it!

'Third row, left-hand side … Fourth row right-hand side … Now, back row, left-hand side…'

Joy of joys! He was safe!

The last pupil went out. The door closed. Then heavy footsteps drew nearer, ominously nearer, frighteningly nearer. Oh God why did Boobs have to come to the back of the room? Couldn't he just go off to the staffroom like any normal human being? No, not Boobs.

The door burst open. An explosion of light flooded in. In sheer terror John covered his face with his hand as he almost peed himself with fright. Caught!

'YOU!' roared Boobs. 'OUT NOW!'

He grabbed him by the shoulder and hauled him into the classroom 'And where's your work?'

John could only tremble in silence.

'Well, where is it?'

John was unable to speak.

'It's like that, is it? Well, I'll see you after lunch!'

With that he dragged him triumphantly to the classroom door and flung him into the corridor, proving, yet again, that nobody – not even posh gits – could get around Boobs. Another bit of corridor cred chalked up.

Off to the Scaffold...

The mob outside immediately swooped. Freddy had told them to bring the 'liddell poofter' along to 'the bogs' where he was 'gerrin' done proper like'. And what Freddy said went. You didn't mess with Freddy. But if Freddy did what he said he was going to do, it was going to be good fun, too, a show worth watching. Also, Justice was going to prevail. It were only right, weren't it? Pooftas gorra get done like!'

In an explosion of wild cheering – 'Good on yers, Boobs! Good lad Boobs!' – John was lifted bodily up and carried off. Blind terror engulfed him, Trapped. Helpless in the hands of a mindless mob. His worst nightmare coming true.

'Please, God, help me! Please!'

But God didn't seem to be listening. 'Ask and it shall be given unto you...'

Maybe, sometimes. But not in this case.

Desperate pleas to his tormenters: 'NO! NO! PLEASE! I'll get the money, honest I will!'

Pointless. Useless. Swept along on a torrent of animal passion, the mob poured into the boys' toilets. There, towering and massive, was Freddy Hazlett, flanked by Shorley and a full supporting cast, the elite of Greenhill School gathered for an important ceremony. Like Aztec priests in the Temple of the Sun they seemed to John.

'Reet, yer liddell hom. Yer gerrin it!'

'NO! NO! NO! PLEASE! I'LL GET THE MONEY!' Screams of abject terror.

Proletarian Justice. 'Stands ter reasons, doan it?'

You poor, innocent little thing! Scream away! That's just what they want you to do. It's much more fun tormenting you than tormenting cats. You shout. You squeal. You cry. But don't expect them to listen to any appeals for mercy. You don't deserve it. This is JUSTICE. Your rightful punishment for... well, for being John Denby, that posh git from 'doon sooth' and not one of them.

But that's not all. There's more to it. The money's not that important. It's only an excuse – 'pretext' is what they really mean, but that word's too difficult for them.

Even if you'd paid up, you'd still have got it!

It was something which, at that time, John couldn't understand. The fact was that he was pretty, very pretty, and, from the moment he'd first set eyes upon him Freddy Hazlett had wanted to... well, we all know, don't we? That Denby, he were a gift from heaven! Not that Freddy knew what heaven was.

Nor bluddy wanted to neither! Bertie, the arty teecha wotsa good blerk reely, says God an' that's all crap from them capitalists like... But every time he's seed the liddell basstadd he's wanted ter get them troosers off 'm like...

Of course, Freddy ain't no fuckin' hom, yer knaa, not one o' them peedos wot shafts liddell kids an' that. Not wor Freddy. He thinks them basstadds oughta be fuckin' hanged them! He screws lasses... But he would like a gan at liddell poofter Denby!

But he berra be careful like! He's been 'avin' a few problems of late. He's 'ad Shorley are reet, but it ain't been that easy an' the fat cow bin gobbin' roond, seyin' Bert 'Arris bin deein' it berra! An' Bert's bin giwen' 'im lip, callin' 'im a fuckin' hom 'an that! Well, 'es sorted oot Bert good an' proper like, kicked the shite oota the basstadd a couple o' weeks past. Nee more lip oota that big gob!

So 'e canna stick 'is tackle up the posh git's liddell wotsit, can 'e? What would Shorley say? An' Beth fuckin' Duffy? He'd be the laff o' the lads, him!

But nae frets! He's 'ad a great idea, him. Gerra a bicycle pump an' shaft 'm wi' that! Aye, 'an fill it up wi' treacle – like wot them doctaz does when they wants ter mek yer shit an' that. It'll be a great laff seein' the posh git runnin' roon shittin' issell like!

But mind, he's deserved it 'im. We's all deprived, ain't we? That's wot ole Bertie sez-yer knaa the arty teecha wot knaas all aboot them things like an' wot's a good blerk even if he's a teecha like! It's coz o' Thatcher an' all them posh gits that weez ain't all gannin' ter Spain for wor holidays like! We needs his nikka dern't we? 'An them fags an' all! Class justice yer knaa! Bertie's posh words! Stands ter reason, doan it?

Justice. Deserved class retribution. Watching the Christians being torn to pieces by lions. Good fun, hallowed by righteousness. Sorry, John Denby, it's time you got it.

Public Execution of a Poofter

The pack fell upon him. Big hands tearing at his clothes. Trainers yanked off. Then socks, sweater, shirt vest... The worst was happening! They were undoing his belt. 'NOT my pants! NO! NOT MY PANTS! PLEASE NO!'

A huge explosion of raucous laughter blasted out as his jeans went spiralling through the air. An ever-bigger roar of delight when his drawers followed. Total catastrophe. Naked. Appalling shame. Collapse into tears.

But worse was to come. Brutish fingers started poking round his most intimate and embarrassing parts... Filthy, vile, unspeakable, comments. Volcanic peals of laughter. Not human laughter. Animal laughter. Never imagined that humans could be so disgusting. But these aren't humans. The flood of tears became a torrent.

But even worse was to come. His legs were yanked up. Everything exposed for all to see. Shrieks of animal guffaws. Appalling remarks.

'Howay! Fred, dee it, son, dee it!'

Horrible, prolonged present tense. Freddy has a bicycle pump full of some liquid! He's going to ram it up my bum! 'What are you doing? NO! NO! NO! NOT THAT PLEASE!' In it goes. Horrible pain. Bestial roars. Dreadful bloated feeling as liquid is forced in. Then the unimaginably awful happens, the utterly unspeakable that you never even dreamed of... In front of everybody and everything an explosion occurs as his insides react violently to the intrusion. Blood and a filthy brown mess burst out of him. They all think this is hilariously funny and clap and cheer hysterically.

' ... I'M FAR BETTER THAN YOU ARE!'

The mob dispersed, leaving him lying on the floor in a pool of filth. A filthy, foul creature. Crushed. Degraded. Shamed beyond belief. Destroyed.

Horror and disgust at the foul liquid dribbling out of him. How could he ever face anybody again, let alone speak to them? He must hide. Hide. Hide from the world, hide from his shame. Hide from his own vile and stinking self.

He got up, dived into the nearest cubicle and locked the door. Tears poured out of him. Desperate, despairing tears such as he'd never known before.

He cried and cried. Cried until there were no tears left in him. Nothing, in fact. Just an empty void. Even the ghastly liquid that dribbled out of his bruised and bleeding nether region dried up, leaving only a dull ache.

For an unmeasured length of time he just sat there, wishing that he was somebody else. Anybody. Any *thing*. But not dirty, filthy, pathetic John Denby.

Then suddenly, like a delayed action bomb, something exploded within him. A frenzied rage blazed out, wild and gigantic. Leaping up, he pounded the locked door with a manic fury: 'I HATE YOU! I'M FAR BETTER THAN YOU ARE! ONE DAY I'LL BE FAMOUS AND THEN I'LL SHOW YOU! YOU'RE JUST THICK, USELESS ANIMALS! WORSE THAN ANIMALS!'

He would become a fighter pilot in the US Air Force and swooping down in his F–111 fighter-bomber, he would drop a hydrogen bomb on Greenwood. Then he would roar away, laughing hysterically as Freddy Hazlett's and Shorley's eyeballs melted and ran down their fat, ugly faces. Circling again, he would shriek with glee as they were slowly burned to death and transformed into scorching radioactive dust in the ever-expanding mushroom cloud.

'YOU SEE!' he screamed. 'I'LL FUCKING DO IT!'

'Eee, Florrie, there's a lad in there!' came a female voice. 'Yer berra come oot because we's locking up now.'

Back to reality. Rescue. Safety. He could finally emerge. But, then, a horrible practical problem intruded.

'I can't. I've got no clothes.'

'What?'

'They took them off me.'

'Well, is these yours?'

A hand pushed a shirt and a pair of socks under the door, followed by a sweater.

'Thanks, but PLEASE I MUST have my jeans! PLEASE!' (Desperate, anguished plea.)

'Is this them?'

Enormous relief as his jeans and his underpants appeared under the door. His trainers followed and eventually he could emerge into the daylight.

He found two kindly-looking old ladies standing in front of him, brandishing mops and buckets.

'Eeee, yer poor wee bairn! What *have* they been doing to you, son?'

He didn't answer that question. How could he? Instead, he buried his head in the warm, soft bosom of the nearest lady – so feminine and so comforting – and began to cry. Then, seeing the repulsive brown mess on the floor – his own mess! – he felt a deep stab of shame. *They* knew that the muck was his! They'd seen him in all his degradation. They *knew* that he was a filthy, worthless and utterly pathetic little thing. He had to escape. To flee – where? Anywhere? To the very ends of the earth!

Roughly he tore himself away from the feminine embrace and made for the door.

19

Go Home... But *Where* Is Home?

Now what? Get back home and hide. But after that?

One thing was certain. He could never go back to Greenhill School again. Never. *Never.* No, not ever. He'd have to tell Giles that.

But where was home? It was blustery and cold outside with flurries of stinging rain lashing down. All around him was a forlorn desolation – concrete lampposts, grey, dripping piles of rubble, swathes of bare earth strewn with rubbish... polystyrene packets filled with half-eaten lumps of fish and soggy chips smeared with tomato sauce, rusty beer cans, black polythene bag ... A hostile and threatening place. This wasn't his home. He didn't belong here. It was an evil

An evil land

land where good was bad and bad was good, a creeping disease of a land where good boys like John Denby became bad boys – just as those packets of delicious fish and chips became soggy and horrible when they were thrown away half-eaten.

Home was another place. Far, far away. Oaktree Gardens, Rickerby Hall, lovely old trees, beautiful old houses, kindly people like Mrs Selby, Mrs Bowles and Mr Cotton...

More Important Matters. A Big Opportunity

Meanwhile, back in *his* home Giles was at his table surrounded by a mass of papers.

It was Arthur Scargill and the Yorkshire miners. Who had said what and to whom at the NUM conference of 1971 when Rule 43 was changed? It was absolutely essential to get all the details right. Yes, every little detail. Reality was the sum of details.

He'd been at it for days, flat out. Into the university library, into the university canteen for a rushed lunch, down to the city library, back to Gloucester Road to sort out the accumulated heap of material with a packet of Marks & Spencer's sandwiches for supper.

Things were starting to move his way – and big time, too. On Monday evening he had to give the Murray Lecture. This was no ordinary lecture, not just bamboozling a bunch of third-rate students, but a high point of the year when the university displayed its academic prowess to the world – or, at least, to that part of the world which knew what academic prowess was. The Vice Chancellor would be there and so would leading academics from universities across the world.

It was a big opportunity and he intended to make the most of it – to milk it dry, in fact! He was going to make a bold and radical statement, to break new ground and to strike out into unexplored territory. He wouldn't just be droning on about some irrelevant topic in the dim and distant past: he would be embracing *relevance*. Explore the past, yes, but link it with the present, show how the past has created the present and how past events have led up to the burning issues of the present day – the exploitation of the working class, the short-sightedness of capitalism, the senseless destruction of viable manufacturing industry in the north of England, the sheer crassness of Thatcherism, the positive and intellectually sound challenge to all this represented by Arthur Scargill... And to round it off, he would illuminate the bright and burning hope for the future as evinced in Greenhill School where, at long last and not before time, either, real, authentic working-class culture was triumphing over the petty-bourgeois arrogance of the lower-middle-class teaching profession.

Moreover, a Cambridge friend of his who was working for the BBC had suggested that he might present a series of television programmes on the evolution of the British working class. Indeed, he and some of his team were going to attend the lecture to check him out and to see whether he really did have that popular touch that would make a complex subject accessible to the man in the street.

Yes, it was a great opportunity! If he played it right, it would go down big with the local Labour Party when it came to selecting the new member for Boldonbridge West who was to replace Sam Clarke who was terminally ill with cancer.

But how to square the circle? Popular appeal with academic rigour? Of course, his eulogy of Greenhill School would introduce an appropriately popular touch. But he would go further. He would ram home the fact that his own son, John, was being educated *there* and not at some snobby little private school and, moreover, he was not just doing well, but *flourishing*! That would provide a down-to-earth personal touch. And it would, also, be a pointer to the future classless society which all right-thinking socialists so ardently desired... That really should please the local Labour Party!

But there were one or two flies in the otherwise creamy ointment, Alan Jennings from Berkley, for example. A formidable academic, indeed, with a positively forensic mastery of petty detail. Not that he deigned to produce many books himself, however. That fearsome expertise was largely focused on demolishing other people's work, poring over it with a metaphorical microscope and pouncing on small errors of fact. He was purely negative, an intercontinental ballistic missile crammed full of the very latest technology whose sole purpose was destruction. Leave one chink in your armour, leave one fact unchecked and he'd be on to it. That meant check, check, check, corroborate, corroborate, corroborate, cross-reference this, cross-reference that...

Then there was Martha Merrins. She'd be there. Giving her full and unstinted support for his radical idealism. Of course. Everybody knew that... But everybody – at least everybody that mattered! –

163

also knew that she, too, would like to be the next Labour member for Boldonbridge West. And there was the little matter of Mary's book, *Liberated Child Development*, an invasion of *her* territory by an unqualified interloper who hadn't even got a good degree. That still rankled – and *how*! Yes, she'd be there all right – all electronic detectors switched on, radar scanner revolving, all antennae quivering, ready to pick up and amplify the first little hints of any unsuitability to represent the Boldonbridge West working class in Parliament.

Lack of compassion, male chauvinism, indifference to child abuse... that's what she would be hoping to find...

It all meant hard, concentrated work. The problem was *time*, how to get everything ready for the Monday deadline. Now what was Sammy Taylor's exact role in the NUM conference of 1971?

Just then the doorbell rang with a jarring screech which shattered his chain of thought.

Irritated he went over to the door, opened it and returned to the 1971 NUM conference. He hardly noticed the sodden and dishevelled little creature that came in from the rain.

The Polish Cavalry Charge the German Tanks...

Boldly John strode up to his father. It was now or never. Go into the lion's cage and brave its claws. Couldn't be any worse than Freddy Hazlett's bicycle pump. 'Dad, I mean, Giles, I must talk.'

The lion didn't even look up. It continued writing furiously.

'Giles, please.'

Eventually the lion growled a little: 'Not now, John, I'm very busy.'

'But I *must* talk!' Childish, falsetto squeal, specially designed to set your teeth on edge.

At this the lion finally raised its head: 'I said NOT NOW!'

'BUT I MUST! IT'S THAT SCHOOL! I HATE IT! I'M NOT GOING BACK THERE! NO! NO! NO! NEVER! NOT EVER!' A more insistent falsetto squeal, up several notes on the scale.

That was all Giles needed. He closed his eyes: 'If it's a whinge about your school, I'm not going to listen to it.'

'But...' (Bloody hell, the cheeky little sod! Back to this again, was it?)

A burst of suppressed temper: 'But NOTHING! How many times have I told you that you're at a REAL school at last? Not good enough for you, is it? Who the hell do you think you are? Now go away and let me get on with more important things!'

'NO I WON'T!' (Rage and exasperation were welling up. Didn't this great block of concrete *ever* listen to anything?)

(Jesus bloody wept, it's Dorking rides again, is it?) 'YOU'LL DO AS YOU'RE TOLD THIS INSTANT!'

'NO I FUCKING WON'T!'

Time to get physical. Time to dish out the long-deserved Dorking treatment! Giles made a grab at him. But the boy ducked out of the way and seized a pile of carefully annotated papers on the table.

'I FUCKING HATE YOU!' he screeched. 'YOU'RE A CUNT!'

Then, after hurling most of the papers over the floor, he ripped the three sheets that remained in his hands into shreds. Mad, suicidal gesture. The naked Zulu warriors charging the maxim machine guns, the Polish cavalry charging the German tanks.

Retribution was swift and devastating. Giles punched him in the side and he crumpled up into a heap on the floor, wailing like a baby.

'Don't you ever do that again,' he said. 'Just remember that I'm far stronger than you in every respect.'

Looking contemptuously at the heap of misery below him, he wrinkled up his nose: 'Christ, you stink! You've messed yourself, haven't you? Doing a thing like that at YOUR age. You should be ashamed of yourself. Now get up to your room and STAY there! I'll deal with you later.'

The Garden of Gethsemane?

In his room John snivelled away.

To his horror he discovered that his jeans were stained with blood and repulsive brown muck. The stink was unspeakable. Giles was right – he *had* messed himself. The stolen money, the shoplifting, Freddy Hazlett – and now *this*! He'd fallen into a deep and disgusting pit and couldn't get out.

Desperately he began to pray: 'Please, God, I know I'm bad. I know I shouldn't tell lies. I know I shouldn't steal. I know I shouldn't piss the bed. I know I probably deserved what they've just done to me at Greenhill because I'm a snobby little git. But I want to be good. Please tell Giles not to come up and beat me.'

After that he waited for a long time, but nothing happened. Jesus might have got an angel to help him in the Garden of Gethsemane. Saint Peter might have got one that time he was in prison. But no angel came down to 14 Gloucester Road to sort things out for John Denby. He would just have to wait till Giles came up that ladder – and then what?

Rebellion and Defiance

Suddenly his temper blazed up again. *He* wasn't bad. It was this place that was bad, this crazy, topsy-turvy place! Why just sit there like a zombie and wait for Giles to come and start kicking you in? Why not escape while you still had the chance?

His brain began to race ahead. Yes, go back to Oaktree Gardens! He'd see Mrs Bowles – after all, she'd said that he could always come and see her whenever he wanted to. She'd wash his clothes for him and give him a proper supper of scrumptious egg and chips. Then in the morning he'd walk over to Rickerby Hall, see Mr Cotton and continue where he'd left off. As for Jimmy Stokes, well, he'd tell him a story about his father going on a secret SAS mission to Northern Ireland.

But how to get there? He would need a car and a grown-up to drive it for him. And who was that grown-up going to be? Not Giles for starters!

Looking disconsolately round the chaos of his room, he saw his model railway – bridges, loops, flyovers and all – lying just where he had left it on Sunday. Of course, get the train! He remembered from one of his railway books that Boldonbridge had a big and famous railway station, the Prince Albert Station, built in Victorian times as the headquarters of the North-Eastern Railway, that railway which used to have all those glorious bright-green steam locomotives! Yes. He'd go there! Maybe he'd even see famous engines like the *Mallard* and the *Coronation Scot*! But, even if they only used diesels now, it would still be a great adventure. He'd never been on a real train before, only on the London Underground, and they weren't proper trains. He began to get excited.

But there was a snag. He would have to buy a ticket and, when he got to London, he'd have to pay for a taxi to take him to Oaktree Gardens. And where, oh where, was he to find the money?

He prayed again: 'Please God, please help me. I promise I'll be good. I'll give all my pocket money to the Save the Children Fund. I'll forgive Freddy Hazlett. I'll even say a prayer for Hitler...'

But nothing happened and no twenty-pound notes came floating down from the ceiling. Instead, a much more mundane problem arose. His nether region began to erupt again, threatening another squalid catastrophe. Frantically, he scurried down the ladder. Mercifully, the bog was unoccupied and he reached it just in time to avert a disastrous 'spill'.

Coming out, he noticed Mary's ethnic shoulder bag lying on the floor outside the bedroom door. Beside it, for all to see, was her purse half-open and, sticking out of it, three twenty-pound notes, crisp and new. A weird, almost ghostly feeling of elation flared up inside him. So God *had* heard his prayers! How else could that money have been so providentially left there?

Quickly he snatched up the notes. Taking them wasn't stealing. When the Israelites picked up the manna in the desert that wasn't stealing, was it? It was gratefully accepting a gift from God – indeed, not to accept it would be downright rude!

He hurried back up the ladder. The escape was on! No time to lose! He opened the cupboard and was engulfed in the landslide of filthy pyjama bottoms and stinking duvets that fell out. From the squalid debris he managed to extract a clean shirt, a pair of Rickerby Hall shorts that he hadn't yet worn and a clean pair of underpants. He noticed with shame and disgust that his blazer was still there with the unwashed spew now sprouting a gruesome green fungus. But, luckily, the spare one, though creased and rumpled, was still all right. Changing into his clean clothes and pulling on a Rickerby Hall sweater, he eased himself into it. Then he unearthed his holdall bag. Into it went all the remaining clothes he could find that weren't too repulsive for human consumption, his Rickerby Hall cap and shoes, his toothbrush and his comb and, of course, his most treasured possession, his *Children's Bible* that showed everybody – at least showed all *sane* people – that he really was a good boy in spite of... well, all those other things! Putting the three twenty-pound notes carefully into it – God's gift kept safely in God's book! – he zipped the bag up. As for his trains and his television, he would have to leave them behind – but Mrs Bowles would buy him some more. Grown-ups always did if you asked them nicely – sane grown-ups, that was, not these idiots up north!

20

Out of the Prison Camp

Leaving his revolting jeans and underpants on the floor – a visible symbol of the mad world he was leaving – he clambered down the ladder, trying hard not to drop his hideously heavy holdall.

On the landing below he paused. The first crisis: how to cross the danger zone of the ground floor and which door to use? The back door? No way! It was between the kitchen area and Giles' work table. He was sure to be spotted and, besides, it led into the garage and the garage door was always locked. It would have to be the front door. That meant crossing ten feet of open space. Everything in that downstairs room was open and visible – and deliberately so. It was open-plan living, working-class frankness as opposed to middle-class deceit, for this was the whole point of Mike Boardman's 'radical architectural statement'. Then there was the front door – or, rather the *two* front doors. The outer one was simple enough – just a latch – but the inner steel door sported an intimidating array of bolts and chains. Vital seconds could be lost if all these were in place. But, hopefully, Giles would be too busy with his papers to notice him fumbling around.

His mind went back to the escape stories he'd read – and, especially, to the *Great Escape* film he'd seen. That ground-floor room became the minefield surrounding the camp, Giles the guard with the machine gun in the watchtower, the two front doors the electrified fence surrounding the compound...

Time to take the plunge!

Suddenly, he froze, his heart pounding almost audibly. A familiar voice had pierced the silence: 'Bloody hell, Giles, can't you give me a hand with these dishes?'

Mary was there and in a foul temper, too.

'Please, lovey,' came Giles' voice, 'I'm desperately busy. I *must* get all this done!'

'But you're supposed to be my partner, not my bloody husband!'

'Get John to help you. It's time that little tick did something useful instead of sponging on us.'

'Where is he?'

'He went up to the attic a while ago. Mind, he's in a paddy so you'll have to be firm with him.'

'Right.'

Crisis! Postpone escape! The Nazis have rumbled the plan!

Mary marched over to the ladder and began to climb up. Hide! Where?

Desperately he dived into his parents' bedroom – a holy of holies that he'd never seen before – and squeezed himself behind the half-open door.

It was red alert again – all sensors on full power, radar scanners revolving, night vision on, acoustic enhancers on... Time expanded. Minutes stretched into hours... Nearer and nearer came the footsteps as Mary panted and wheezed her way up the ladder. The seconds began to stretch out into hours. Right outside the door now! The bathroom door opening and closing. She's in the bog! That means two or three minutes of opportunity. The gap between the patrolling guards. Go for it!

Out on to the landing. Oh so carefully down the ladder – that holdall is so *heavy*! Mustn't make any noise. Peer around. Giles is bent low over his papers on the desk, writing furiously. Down to the bottom of the ladder. Now for the most dangerous bit, the dash across those ten feet of open space – the minefield! But the guard in the watchtower – Giles – doesn't notice... At the steel door. Mercifully, it's not barricaded up with chains and bolts: only the latch to be turned. Slowly open it... The door behind it opens quietly and easily... Moment of panic as the holdall snags on the door. But out! Quietly close the door. You're over the electric fence!

Away into the Night...

Away into the cold, black dampness beyond!

Down the hill he ran, ran and ran, lugging that heavy bag with him which always seemed to want to trip him up. Down to the bottom of the hill. There he paused, panting furiously. He'd done it. He'd escaped from the prison camp. Now he had to cross the dangerous territory of Nazi Germany without being caught.

He looked around him and gathered his thoughts. It was a dismal night, bleak and hostile with a cold drizzle dribbling half-heartedly down. The bare brick walls were relentlessly ugly and the harsh monochromatic light of the street lamps reduced everything to a dreary black and orange.

Now what? He had to move fast. By now Mary would be out of the bog and would have discovered that he was missing. She could hardly have failed to notice the missing sixty pounds. He had a five-minute start before the police cars came screaming along with their lights flashing and sirens wailing. He had to reach the Prince Albert Station and fast. But how?

Beyond the waste ground at the bottom of Gloucester Road there was a busy street full of cars and hurtling lorries – a place of dazzling headlights, roaring engines and swishing tyres. There had to be a bus stop somewhere there.

With much puffing and heaving, he hauled his holdall over the rubble and through the muddy puddles, getting his feet wet in the process. To his enormous relief he found a bus stop with two middle-aged women waiting at it.

'Is this where you get the bus for the Prince Albert Station?'

'It is an' all,' replied one of the ladies. 'But why's a bairn like you goin' there at this time o' night?' she added suspiciously.

'Oh I've got to meet my dad there,' he answered. (A lie. But nothing wrong with telling lies when you're an escaping prisoner of war!)

'Eeeee!' sighed the woman. 'Sendin' a bairn oot on a night like this! Some folk!' For a seemingly endless time no bus came. The drizzle turned into freezing rain which seeped through his blazer and ran down his neck in an icy trickle. He realised that he should have remembered to wear his anorak, but it was too late now. As he shivered, he grew frantic. *Come on*, bus! Please come *on*! Before the police cars arrive!

Finally, at long last, a big double-decker came swishing up, lights blazing and windscreen wipers thumping, and stopped in a slosh of muddy water. He let the two women get on first – good manners: 'Ladies first', as Mr Cotton had always said – and then clambered aboard himself.

'Where are you going, son?' the driver asked him.

'The Prince Albert Station.'

'That'll be fifty pence.'

He gaped in bewilderment. He'd never been on a bus before and he'd always thought that you went on buses for nothing. Desperately, he unzipped his holdall and rummaged round for his *Children's Bible*.

'Howay, laddie, I haven't all night!'

More frantic rummagings.

'Look, son, if you can't pay, you'll have to get off.'

A sudden and quite devastating blow! Involuntary tears began to trickle down his cheeks.

'Oh forget it!' said the driver in a kindly voice, 'but don't you go telling your mates that I let you on for nowt else I'll have the boss on to me!'

'Cor, thanks a million!'

Savouring the excitement of his first bus ride, he scrambled upstairs, lugging his holdall behind him, and sat panting on a front seat. The sheer fun made him forget his troubles for the moment.

But, time, time, time... If only this wretched bus would get a move on! It seemed to be taking a fiendish joy in going as slowly as possible. It crawled along, continually stopping at bus stops even though nobody was there. There seemed to be an endless series of traffic lights, every one of which was red.

Suddenly there was the sound of a wailing siren and a police car drew alongside them, its blue light flashing. He nearly peed himself with fright. Oh God, that's them after me already! He slipped off the seat and crouched on the floor behind his holdall bag.

'What's up with you, son?' asked the man in the next seat. 'Are you a burglar on the run or sommat?'

Caught! The Gestapo have got you! Wild panic! Then, mercy of mercies, he heard the police car go bowling away into the distance. Phew! Narrow escape! Safe after all!

Embarrassed he got up: 'No, just playing!'

'Here's the Prince Albert Station!' the driver called from down below as the bus entered a big rain-swept square.

'Thanks a lot, you've been very kind!' he said as he clambered out into the cold and wet world beyond. Now for the crucial bit: crossing the guarded frontier into neutral Switzerland – or, more prosaically, finding a train that would take him from this evil and dangerous land and back to the safety and sanity of London...

Trains, Glorious Trains!

Before him was one of the great monuments of Victorian railway architecture, a mighty arched portico rising black and tremendous into the dreary October night, its deep recesses dimly lit by faint orange lights. The frontier post!

Trains, glorious trains

After a hazardous crossing of the road – a frenetic conveyor belt of red and white lights and roaring engines – he passed under its huge classical arches and through an immense pair of Roman doors, all bronze-plated and ornate. Somewhere in the brightly lit hullaballoo beyond was The Train that would take him back to normality and sanity. But where to find it? How to get onto it? The only trains he'd ever been on were the fairground-type things on the London Underground – and then his gran had dealt with the tickets.

Staring around, he saw a small booth – a window in the wall – with 'Tickets' in big letters above it. Presumably, that was where you went to buy your ticket. But had the Gestapo already alerted the guards and would he be arrested as soon as he approached it? But that police car had gone racing off somewhere else, so probably they hadn't yet twigged where he was going... Screwing up his courage and, trying to sound as normal as possible, he went over to the booth.

'Please, I want to go to London.'

'OK,' said the man on the other side of the window, 'but where's your mum and dad. You're not alone are you?'

(Help! The frontier guards have been alerted! Quick thinking needed – just like Biggles when he was on the run from the Gestapo!)

Luckily lies came easily to him: 'Well, my uncle's picking me up at King's Cross. My dad told me to go on ahead. You see he's very busy.' (Inventing another reality again: it was really rather fun – like playing knights or pirates. But would this man swallow it?)

Anxious wait while his fate hung in the balance.

'Well, you'd better be quick. There's a train in ten minutes. But if you miss it, the next one's not until one in the morning.'

(Phew! He's swallowed it!) 'Yes, I'll go on that one. I don't want to keep my uncle waiting.'

'You'll be going economy class, child's fare. That'll be fifteen pounds thirty. Are you sure you've got it?' (Faint suspicion remaining!)

Quickly he unzipped his bag, rummaged around and eventually produced one of the twenty-pound notes.

'Here you are.'

'Right, here's your ticket. Now put it away carefully – in your pocket and not in your bag and don't lose it. And here's your change, four pounds seventy. It's Platform 4. That's over the bridge. Ask a member of staff and he'll put you on the right train.'

Success! He'd managed to do a grown-up thing and buy a ticket! Glowing with a sense of achievement, he put the precious object carefully into his inside blazer pocket. Staggering over the bridge with his awkward load, he paused a while, entranced by the wildly exciting scene beneath him – real railway tracks and real trains which he'd read about, but never actually seen. A big, long passenger train came rumbling up, a long line of blue-and-white coaches pulled by a large, growling Deltic diesel-electric locomotive. Maybe he could, also, see some of those famous steamers like the *Mallard* and the *Coronation Scot*? He looked hard, but couldn't see any sign of them.

Hardly had he reached Platform 4, however, before he saw something

174

even more exciting. A long, sleek, blue-and-white train, coaches and power units all of a piece, shiny and streamlined, glided up and came to a gentle halt. It was one of the new 125 high-speed trains – faster even than the *Mallard*! Having lived his life on a world of cars, a train journey was a treat. But actually seeing a 125 *and* going for a ride in it… this was something else!

The doors opened. Some people got out and others got in.

'Is this the London train?' he asked a bald-headed man next to him.

'Hope so,' the man replied, 'or else I'm in a fix!'

He clambered aboard and found himself in a wonderfully exotic place – new, shiny, streamlined and with automatic doors that opened as if by magic when you approached them. For a while he wallowed in the sheer thrill of advancing and retiring and seeing them open and close. This was as good as a fun fair.

'For Christ's sake, boy, make up your bloody mind!' snapped an irritable male voice from behind him. 'Either go through or stay here. Some of us want to get a seat.'

Chastened and red-faced, he went ahead and entered an almost empty carriage – a brightly lit tube, all gleaming and ultra-modern, almost the sort of place where you'd meet James Bond. 'Cor, this is *wicked*!' he muttered to himself. 'WICKED! Thank you, God, thank you!'

Then he remembered that he was on the Great Escape and that, by now, the police would be after him. He mustn't draw attention to himself. Selecting a seat on the far side of the carriage, away from the platform, he sat down and, putting his bag on the table in front of him, put his head behind it so that he wouldn't be seen. As he looked out of the window, he saw to his huge excitement, that, gently and silently, the train was moving. He'd got away!

He gazed in wonderment as the station disappeared and the train clanked slowly through a darkened world of gleaming rails, vaguely defined wagons and green lights. Then, as it rumbled over a long metal bridge, a thrilling vista opened out – an awesome depth and faintly gleaming water far below and, fading into the murky distance, a series of huge, dimly lit bridges, one behind the other. He was actually crossing the Prince Consort Bridge, one of the great historic railway bridges of Britain!

Suddenly, he had a spurt of fear. At the far end of the carriage the magic door slid open and a man in uniform entered. The Gestapo!

175

They'd followed him onto the train and were going to arrest him! Frantically, he put his head behind his bag and tried to hide.

It was no good. The man walked up to him. 'Tickets, please,' he said. 'Come on, lad, I haven't all night!'

Wave of relief! It wasn't the Gestapo. It was the ticket inspector. He remembered the ticket he'd been told not to lose and proudly extracted it from his blazer pocket.

The uniformed man clipped it with a pair of clippers and handed it back to him. 'Travelling alone?' he said. 'The train gets into King's Cross at midnight. Not a place for a lad of your age to hang about. Is somebody meeting you?' (Quick thinking once more! Escaping prisoner dodging the Gestapo. Stick to your story.) 'Yes, my uncle will be there.'

'That's good.'

The man walked on. When he was safely out of sight, he got up and started to explore the carriage. He'd just discovered the toilet when his nether region began to play up again. Would it *never* leave him alone? And there was that ominous ache down there in his most embarrassing and secret part. It kept coming and going. He'd thought it had stopped, but now it had started again. He couldn't tell anybody about it – how could he? It was the old, mad world of Greenwood clawing at him and trying to drag him back again. It would surely stop when he reached London and sanity.

Having availed himself of the facilities, however, he felt better. It was time to play with those magic doors which opened and shut when you approached them. He tried to cheat them by running quickly through them and then turning round and running back again. It was great fun. For a time he was back in ancient Greece, being Jason sailing through the Clashing Rocks.

'For heaven's sake, SIT DOWN!' bellowed an angry male voice.

He swung round to see an elderly man in a cloth cap, his face contorted with rage.

'Yes, YOU!' he snarled. 'If you don't sit down, I'll get the guard to sort you out!'

Panic! 'I'm terribly sorry. I'll sit down now.'

'Bloody kids!' the old man growled. 'Shouldn't be allowed on trains! They should bring back the birch!'

He scuttled back to his seat and hid behind his bag. Suddenly, he felt immensely tired. It had been an extraordinary day, quite the strangest he'd ever known. He'd started off as a pathetic little weed to whom his schoolmates had seen fit to do an unbelievably disgusting thing, something he couldn't even mention, and which he'd deserved, too – because he was a wimp who pissed the bed and had been 'chinned off a lass'. But now he was a different person – a young adult, able to manage himself on a train and, like Biggles, well able to elude the pursuing police.

A wave of exhaustion broke over him and he dropped into a deep sleep.

London!

'King's Cross. Train terminates here.'

A thin, metallic voice broke into a blissful world of a sunny Italian beach with his utterly perfect and adored gran. Slowly, the dazzling blue sky was transformed into an uncomfortable place with a window of cold hard glass and a vague blackness beyond. He felt heavy and drowsy. All he wanted was a proper bed to sleep in.

Slowly, reality came back to him. Then he felt a thrill of excitement blaze up within him. He was in London now, back in the *real* world where he was a good, normal boy and where things were rational. He'd escaped from that mad, horrible world up north!

He clambered out of the carriage and found himself in a vast, echoing tunnel of a place. Far above him were metal arches and, above them, dirty panes of glass and a black void. Before him an empty platform swept away into a muddle of windows and illuminated signs. Vague and exciting railway sounds emerged from a subdued distance – growling diesel engines and the rumble of moving coaches. It all seemed drowsy and half-asleep like himself.

It must be the middle of the night. He would have to wait till the morning before he could get a taxi to take him to Oaktree Gardens. Meanwhile, he needed to finish his sleep. Seeing a bench, he lay down on it and curled up with his bag as a pillow. Nobody seemed to mind and oblivion quickly followed.

An Exciting New World...

'Move over!'

A big, fat woman in a brown overcoat was pulling at his feet.

He blinked and looked around in bewilderment. Then it came back to him. He was in King's Cross Station. It was bright and vivid now with lots of people walking around. Far above him bits of blue light seeped through the dirty panes of glass. Brilliant blue sky could be seen through a big, yellow brick arch at the far end of the platform where crowds of people were milling around. Like him, a sleeping place had woken up.

He felt a pulse of pure joy. London at last! Soon he would be back at Oaktree Gardens, back to being the normal boy that he really was.

Getting up, he delved into his bag and found that he still had forty-four pounds and seventy pence left – more than enough to pay for a taxi. First, however, he would have to find a café and have a big breakfast – all the things he liked! – and he would go to the bog, clean his teeth and get the taxi.

Lugging his heavy holdall along the platform, he soon came to a café. Inside was a cave of wonders. You got a tray and a plate and chose what you wanted from a glittering canteen full of delights – fried eggs, hash browns, black pudding, fried sausages, fried mushrooms, crispy bacon, scrambled egg … just what he'd been longing for ever since he'd left Oaktree Gardens. Parking his holdall next to an empty chair, and with a glorious sense of liberation, he took a plate and piled it high with just about everything. It was magic not having grown-ups there telling you not to have all the nice things because they were supposed to be 'bad for you'. Grown-ups – even his wonderful gran and granddad who were in heaven! – could be such a drag!

The bill came to over twelve pounds. Putting the change carefully into his holdall, he sat down at the table and wallowed in his gastronomic paradise.

He'd hardly finished before his insides began to chum – the regular 'morning constitutional' of the Oaktree Gardens days, but unpleasantly augmented by extra pressure from … a recent unmentionable event!

Following the signs, he found the bog, but was unpleasantly surprised when the attendant demanded twenty pence before letting him through the turnstile. A desperate rummage in his holdall finally produced a fifty-pence piece and he only just managed to reach salvation in time to avert a gruesome catastrophe. Why, oh *why*, wouldn't *that* go away? It belonged to the crazy world he'd left and not to the sane one he'd entered.

Unexpected Problems

Washed and refreshed, however, and with his teeth clean, he pushed his way through the thickening crowds and went out of the station. As he entered the bright morning sunshine outside, he felt that glorious sense of liberation that you had when you walked home from school at the end of term. There in front of him was a row of taxis, black and old-fashioned, just as they were on the postcards that he'd stuck into the geography project he'd done at Rickerby Hall.

Boldly he marched up to the leading one and climbed into the back seat. (Just as he'd seen people do in films.)

'Where to, son?'

'Oaktree Gardens, number 27.'

To his amazement, the driver looked blank: 'Where's that?'

'Well, Oaktree Gardens. You know, it's in London.'

'Yes, maybe it is, but London's a very big place. So where in London is it? Chelsea? Earls Court? Kensington?'

'Er, sorry. I don't know. Well, it's in London.'

A sudden alarming thought hit him: he didn't really know where he lived. He'd always been taken on long journeys by grown-ups. He'd simply assumed that all grown-ups knew where Oaktree Gardens was.

'Look, laddie, I haven't got all day. If you don't know where to go, you'd better get out. If you're lost, get a policeman to help you.'

Policeman! No way! They were the people who'd be looking for him and would bundle him back to Greenwood as soon as they caught him – the very people he had to avoid. Bewildered by this wholly unexpected setback, he humped his holdall back into the station.

Now what? Perhaps he could telephone Mrs Bowles – but then he'd never used a telephone before and, besides, you had to dial the correct number and he didn't know what the number was. That option was out.

He stared around a bit and then he saw another café which sold exotic and mouth-watering ice creams. So he went in and bought himself a magnificent concoction of vanilla, strawberry, banana and raspberry with big sticks of chocolate sticking out of it. It cost over five pounds.

He went back to the bench he'd slept on and sat down. But soon he got bored. He'd have to try the taxis again – and surely this time he'd find an intelligent driver who knew where Oaktree Gardens was! For heaven's sake, *everybody* knew that!

But that would take him back into the custody of grown-ups and he wanted to savour a bit more of his newly found freedom. There was a whole glittering world outside the station just waiting to be explored. He didn't like the idea of lugging his heavy holdall around with him, so he zipped it up carefully and left it on the bench, clearly reserving the place for him when he came back.

More Fun But More Problems

There were lots of exciting things. There was a big W.H. Smith newspaper shop with its interesting comics and train magazines. That took nearly an hour. Then it was out into the exotic confusion of the city. He suddenly remembered Hamley's toyshop where his grandparents used to take him when they visited London. There were some wonderful things in it – 00-gauge trains, for instance, big American ones with headlights and cowcatchers and even those black German streamliners which were nearly as fast as the *Mallard*. He'd go there and have a look at them and, maybe order one. Mrs Bowles or Mr Cotton would pay. Normal grown-ups always did when you asked them politely and smiled sweetly enough.

Hamley's was 'in London', so, in theory, he should have been able to find it. Yet, oddly enough, it just didn't seem to be there. The big road in front of the station was so full of buses and cars – almost a solid moving wall, it seemed – that it was impossible to cross. So he went down a nearby side street instead. To his surprise, it wasn't like the London he knew. Instead of being neat and tidy, it was dirty and shabby. More like Greenwood, in fact. He wandered all the way down it and then turned into another equally shabby street. But at the end of it there was no sign of Piccadilly Circus, Regent Street or any of the parts of London that should have been there. There was just another street, even shabbier than the last one – if that were possible! It was all rather strange and disconcerting.

After about two hours – (or was it three hours? he'd no means of telling – Freddy Hazlett had stolen his watch on that dreadful day!) – he began to feel hungry again. Seeing a big, flashy shop, he went in and was confronted by a cornucopia – sweets, sticky buns, fizzy drinks and huge bags of crisps. Just the job! He grabbed two Milky Bars, three boxes of fruit gums, a box of liquorice allsorts, a Mars Bar and two packets of salt and vinegar crisps and marched up to the till.

'That'll be ten pounds, sixty-eight,' said the cashier.

He put his hand into his trouser pocket only to remember that he'd left all his money in his holdall.

'Sorry, I've left my money behind. Can I take these and come back with it later?'

'No, I'm afraid you can't. No money, no purchases.'

'Please! Please! I'll come back. Honest I will.'

'Look there's a lot of people waiting. Go and get your money and then you can take the stuff.'

Sweet smiles didn't seem to work here.

Red-faced and sulky, he left the shop. That man should have trusted him. Couldn't he see that he was a good, honest boy? (Of course, he'd been shoplifting before – but that was the bad John in a previous incarnation. Now he was good again.) He would have to go back to the station and get some money out of his holdall – what a drag!

A Disaster. Now What?

It took him a long time to get back to the station. All the streets looked the same and for a while he was lost. He was about to start crying when he rounded a corner and there it was.

He rushed through the entrance and hurried panting up the platform. A chilling surprise awaited him. There was the bench all right, but there was no holdall on it. Frantically, he searched all the other benches. It was no good. The holdall was not there. It had gone.

Slowly, the awful reality sank in. All his money was in that holdall. So were his spare clothes ... and his precious *Children's Bible* ... in fact, his everything! He was marooned, penniless in a strange land.

For a moment he cried. But then he remembered that things weren't that bad after all. The grown-ups would sort it all out. When you lost things they might nag a bit, but they always replaced them. The sane grown-ups who lived in London, that was.

Obviously, he had to get to Oaktree Gardens straight away. But,

181

first, there was a more pressing problem. His nether region had started to ache again and now it was getting sticky and, worse still, was threatening another catastrophic explosion. (Couldn't that bad world up north *ever* leave him alone?) He scurried off to the gents'. Mercifully, there was no attendant at the turnstile and he was able to slip under it unnoticed and find salvation in the toilet.

Humiliated by this nasty reminder of his previous incarnation, he went up to the taxi rank outside and clambered into the leading cab, confident that this time the driver would be clever enough to have heard of Oaktree Gardens.

'Where to, son?'

'Oaktree Gardens, number twenty-seven.'

'Where's that?'

'It's in London.'

'But *where* in London?'

'I don't know.'

'But if you don't know, how am I supposed to know?'

'Please, if you take me there, Mrs Bowles – she lives in number twenty-seven – she'll pay the fare. You see I haven't got my money with me.'

'Look, I'm not your nanny. If you haven't got any money and don't know where to go, go and see a policeman. He'll sort you out.'

The police again! Panic! The last people he wanted to see! By now they'd know all about the shoplifting and the stolen money. Giles would have alerted them!

He clambered out of the taxi and scuttled back to the station. Now what?

Phone Mrs Bowles?

Again, he thought of telephoning Mrs Bowles. But when, after a positive marathon of looking and questioning awkward grown-ups, he found a phone box, he was confronted with a slot machine that required money – not unlike the slot machines at a fun fair. But he had no money and, in any case, he remembered that he didn't know the telephone number. Once more, that option was out.

For a long time he mooned about looking at the trains. The sheer power and majesty of a big Deltic diesel-electric locomotive pulling a long line of carriages out into the afternoon sun made him forget his troubles. So too, did a glittering 125 express gliding up to the platform and disgorging its passengers.

A Dire Predicament and a Hiding Place

The day slowly died and the gathering darkness deepened.

He began to feel cold. Then the ache in his nether region started up again and threatened another gruesome explosion. (Oh, God, would this *never* stop?) It was back to the gents'. But this time the road to salvation was blocked by an attendant standing by the turnstile. His predicament was now dire. If he should go and 'spill' in public – oh God!

Frantically, he scuttled out of the station. There had to be a café with a toilet in it somewhere... Over a busy road on the right-hand side he saw a big building with lots of brightly lit windows and with 'Great Northern Hotel' emblazoned on it in neon lights. That would do.

Darting over the road – and narrowly missing being hit by an oncoming car – he scampered up the steps and went in through the revolving door. Immediately, he was enfolded in a delicious warmth and a bright, clean and carpeted homeliness. The big reception desk was empty. Then – joy of joys! – he saw a sign pointing to 'Toilets'. A short way along a corridor he found salvation and availed himself of the luxurious facilities.

In the streets outside it was cold and dark. Here he was warm and safe behind a locked door. Nobody would find him. He lay down on the floor and finding it surprisingly comfortable, curled up. Suddenly, he felt desperately tired. As if he had fallen into a bowl of tepid treacle, a deep sleep took hold of him.

'Excuse me, what's your room number?'

He came to, sore and achy.

Bright sunlight streamed in through a small frosted window high up on the cream painted wall above him. Clearly it was morning. As he climbed to his feet, his predicament slowly sunk in. No money. No spare clothes. The police looking for him. He just *had* to get to Oaktree Gardens, but none of those idiot taxi drivers seemed to know where it was.

The sound of loud male voices and the sloshing of water in basins jerked him into action. He couldn't stay here for ever. They'd soon find him – and then what? He waited till the male voices had gone and then slipped out into the plush, carpeted corridor. It was a softly comforting place. His sort of place. The place where he really belonged... A wonderful smell drifted along from a double glass door at the far end, the gorgeous, scrumptious smell of cooked breakfast... It was too much.

He crept along and opened one of the doors to find – paradise! A self-service canteen where you could take a warm plate and help yourself to fried eggs, fried bread, fried mushrooms, crispy bacon and scrambled egg... Right in front of him was a bowl of hot, steaming croissants. Why not? They wouldn't miss one, would they?

He reached out, grabbed the nearest one and stuffed it into his mouth. It literally melted in a cornucopia of sheer sensual pleasure. He couldn't resist another one and ... into his mouth it went...

'Excuse me, what's your room number?'

He spun round to see a uniformed waiter standing behind him.

Caught! Disaster! In desperation he ran for the door and on down the corridor.

'Hey you!' an angry male voice called out from the reception desk. 'What are you doing here? You're not a guest!'

Crashing into the revolving door, he burst out into the cold, sharp air of the street. Fast, faster, over the road... Then a sudden explosion of events all piled on top of each other. A screech of brakes. A moment – or was it a whole hour or, even, a whole day? – of pure terror as he saw the big, silver radiator of a massive car hardly a foot from him. The jaws of a vast, slobbering Tyrannosaurus... A wild lunge forwards. A louder and even more demented screech of brakes and an almighty crash.

Panting on the far pavement, he looked back in horror to see a crazy scene unfolding. A large black Mercedes had crashed into a bollard next to him. Its door was opening and a big, fat man in a dark suit was climbing out and shouting at him: 'YOU SILLY LITTLE BUGGER! LOOK WHAT YOU'VE MADE ME DO!' Another man was, also, shouting: 'DON'T YOU EVER LOOK WHEN YOU CROSS THE ROAD?'

People were gathering round. A policeman was approaching.

Get away! Away! Fast as the wind! Faster even! He ran and ran ... away down a shabby side street, in among a jostling crowd of people, dodging this woman here, that man there. After a while he could run no more. His lungs ached. His breath wouldn't come. Fearfully, he looked behind him. Nobody was following him. He'd got away.

Now what? That same old question! Obviously, he couldn't go back to King's Cross. He must go to another part of London and find a sensible taxi driver who knew where Oaktree Gardens was. Then all would be well.

Alone and abandoned

All that day he wandered through the streets – big streets with shops, grubby streets full of rubbish, grand streets where posh people lived. He found another taxi parked by the pavement, but the driver was just as stupid as all the others – he hadn't a clue where Oaktree Gardens was.

Then he needed the bog again. (When, oh *when*, would this shameful and disgusting business ever stop?) Mercifully, he found a public toilet that didn't need twenty-pence pieces.

More wanderings followed. He tried another taxi driver with the same result: 'Oaktree Gardens? Never 'eard of it!'

Eventually, he began to cry. A golden dream had turned into a nightmare from which there seemed to be no escape. God? Where was God? Obviously, God had deserted him. He was being punished for telling all those lies, for stealing, for being 'chinned off a lass', for pissing the bed and for simply being that pathetic weed, John Denby. 'Depart from me, ye cursed!' God didn't want bad people like John Denby. That nightmare of the giant squid rising from the ocean bed had been a true vision, a warning of what was in store for him!

It got dark and began to rain. It was cold, far colder than he'd ever imagined it was possible to be. It was a new sort of cold, a numbing liquid that seeped through your skin and made every part of you stiff and achy. Tiredness overwhelmed him, a deep, bottomless pit of tiredness. All he wanted to do was to climb into a dark and warm hole and hide. Hide from the enemies that were pursuing him. Hide from his own badness. Hide from his disgusting, stinking body that kept wanting to squirt its repulsive liquids over everything. Hide from God...

Mrs Bowles! Good, kind Mrs Bowles, who'd bought him that lovely Great Western pannier tank engine, Mrs Bowles who was his true mum now! If only he could find her! She would put things straight. She'd tell God that he really was a good boy and not a bad boy!

He found himself in a backstreet, empty of people, but full of rubbish – overflowing dustbins, plastic bottles, beer cans, sheets of cardboard, even an old mattress lying on the pavement half-covered in dirty yellow blankets. Instinctively, he flopped down on to it and tried to pull a blanket over himself.

Suddenly something unspeakably horrible happened. A face was looking at him. A hideous, evil face. An old man's face, hook-nosed, battered, wrinkled and unshaven and with tiny reptilian slit eyes. He screamed in terror as a long, skeletal hand – more like a claw than a hand – seized his arm. A mouth opened, exposing an array of filthy yellow teeth and engulfing him in a foul, foetid breath. This was not a man: it was a dead thing, a half-rotted corpse that had crawled out of a grave, sent by the Devil to drag him down to hell!

'Gottya!' it hissed. 'Come a liddell closer. I needs some heat I does!'

Later on, he realised that he had disturbed a down-and-out alcoholic in the last stages of decay, but at that moment it really was a fiend from hell.

Screaming in a blind and desperate terror, he struggled frantically and then, as another reptilian claw was clamped over his mouth, he bit into it with a strength that he never knew he had.

'AAAAAHH YER LIDDELL SOD!' the thing screamed.

In a mad frenzy, he struggled free and rushed off down the street. 'Please God!' he screamed, 'PLEASE DON'T TAKE ME DOWN TO HELL!'

It was run, run, run... And then bump! 'Please God SAVE ME!'

He found himself looking up at the big, kindly face of a policeman.

21

Sanity at Last. Mission Successful

A warm and comfortable police station. Seated at a large desk beside a plump and cuddly policewoman with big stick-out breasts under her clean white blouse.

Everybody had been very nice to him. They'd given him a mug of hot cocoa with lots of sugar in it. They'd made up a bed for him and let him have a good sleep. When he'd woken up the nice policewoman had bought him a gorgeous packet of fish and chips wrapped up in a newspaper.

He hadn't been arrested and sent back to Boldonbridge in handcuffs. Strangest of all, they'd no idea who he was. Clearly, Giles and Mary hadn't alerted the police: no Gestapo-style agents had been following him. It was all profoundly reassuring.

'Now then, who are you and what were you doing wandering around London alone?'

'I'm John Denby and I'm from 27 Oaktree Gardens.'

'Where's that?'

'It's in London.'

'Yes, but where in London?'

'Well, it's near Rickerby Hall School. That's the school I go to.'

'But why were you wandering round alone?'

'Well, I was on a visit with Mrs Bowles – that's my gran's housekeeper – and I slipped off to look at the trains in King's Cross. That's when I got lost!' (Again, so easy to tell lies. Just invent a new reality and believe in it.)

'All right, we'll find out where your home is and we'll get you back as soon as possible.'

'Cor, thanks a lot! And thank you so much for the cocoa and the fish and chips. It's awfully kind of you! I'm sorry to have been such a nuisance.'

He basked in a warm glow of elation. Soon he would be back

187

in the sane, orderly world in which he rightly belonged. God *was* with him after all.

Betrayal. Down into the Pit...

Then the landmine went off and blew his carefully constructed reality to smithereens and left him tumbling into a void.

The policewoman came back into the room and sat down at the desk with a stern expression on her face. She was no longer nice. It was as if a cloud had blotted out the sun and turned a warm, sunny day into a cold and rainy one.

'We've contacted Rickerby Hall School. They say you're no longer a pupil there. Nobody lives at 27 Oaktree Gardens any more. You live at 14 Gloucester Road, Greenwood, which is up in Boldonbridge...'

Blank stare. A feeling of falling through empty space...

A stern voice and a penetrating look: 'You've told me a lot of lies, haven't you? Now, perhaps, you'd better start telling the truth.'

The truth. What *was* the truth? A confused muddle of bits and pieces that didn't fit together, that crazy world of Greenwood where nothing made sense... But in all that swirling chaos one thing was clear. His dream of salvation had been blown away. Mrs Bowles had said that she would always be there whenever he needed her. But she'd gone. Abandoned him. Betrayed him. And neither did Rickerby Hall want him! He was alone and without friends. He began to cry. He knew it was bad to cry in front of strangers. Proper boys didn't cry. Only wimps cried. But he couldn't help it. It just happened.

The policewoman became nice again and put her arm round him. (Had he but known it, he had her round his little finger. He was so different from the coarse and abusive youngsters that were her staple diet – truanting young louts on shoplifting jaunts: he was so well spoken and so beautifully polite, always remembering to say please and thank you. And he was so cute – that lovely mop of white hair, those big appealing eyes, that glorious smile... She really wanted to take him home and sit him down on the carpet with her pet spaniel, Charlie.)

Out it all came, bit by disjointed bit, a seemingly incoherent pile of rubble.

'...I'm sorry... I'm so ashamed! So ashamed!... You see I don't really know who I am or what I really am. I used to be good. At Rickerby Hall Mr Cotton gave me a book token for being good and I bought a *Children's Bible* with it... Now I'm bad. Very bad. I'm a snobby little git and all the kids hate me. You see I was "chinned off a lass". A girl set me crying. That's very bad, isn't it?... And there's worse things... Now you won't shout at me or hit me if I tell you? Promise. Promise not to hit me...'

'Of course not!' And she gave him a big hug. (Be careful, woman! Kids can be very manipulative. Don't get emotionally involved.)

'I stole money. I went shoplifting. I know it was wrong. Please, I didn't mean to. But I was frightened of Freddy Hazlett and that lot. They said they'd do me in, like they did Billy Lees... I'm in a terrible mess... I don't know what to do...'

After a while the trickle stopped.

'Is that everything?'

'Yes.'

There was a pause. Then an enquiring look: 'Are you sure? I think something very unpleasant has happened to you that you don't want to tell me about.'

'No, no ... nothing!' (Oh God, she wasn't going to start on about *that*, was she? And how the heck did she know about it? He'd had a particularly messy do in the bog that morning. Had they been in afterwards and seen the mess he hadn't been able to flush away completely? Oh God! This was awful!)

'We're going to get a doctor to have a look at you.'

'No! No! Please no! I'm perfectly all right!'

Despite his increasingly shrill protests, he was marched into another room.

'Now can you take all your clothes off.'

'No I won't! It's embarrassing!' (Undress in front of total strangers, especially a woman? He'd never had to do that before: at Rickerby Hall you'd always showered behind curtains. Besides, it reminded him of something dreadful.)

'Come on, don't be silly. The doctor's got to examine you.'

'NO! NO! I WON'T!'

Tears. Entreaties. Temper tantrum. In the end he had to obey.

All was revealed. The blood and the unmentionable mess in his underpants. Now they knew. He'd never felt so small and so dirty in his whole life. Dirty, disgusting and pathetic. An overgrown baby who should still have been in nappies!

A kindly voice: 'Can you tell us what happened to you?'

How *could* he? How could he possibly tell anybody that his schoolmates had thought him so pathetic that they'd stripped him naked and rammed a bicycle pump up his back end? He could hardly even admit it to himself, let alone to another person. It had to be expunged from his mind, eradicated, obliterated, dissolved in acid, scrubbed out with a wire brush.

He shut his eyes, clenched his teeth and cried even harder. In the face of this they backed off.

A Comfortable Limbo

That afternoon they took him to a big Victorian house made of red brick where there were a lot of other kids. It wasn't a hotel. It was some kind of a home for orphan kids or something. Anyway, everybody was very nice to him. He was given a bath, some clean clothes, a lovely meal of fish fingers, baked beans and chips and a bed to sleep in with glorious clean sheets.

God to the Rescue?

Next morning there was a shock.

'Your father's here to collect you.'

'Please! No! PLEASE! He'll kill me! I've been so bad!'

'Don't be silly. He's very fond of you. He's been terribly worried about you.'

Once again, he had no choice. He was led outside. There before him was the 'von' and there was Giles. Oddly enough, he was all beams and smiles.

'John! John!' he said, 'I've been so worried about you!'

Instinctively, John cowered away.

Giles continued: 'I know I was bad tempered when I shouldn't have been. Let's make it up and start again. I've got something for you.'

With that he handed him a big box. Inside was a 00-gauge *Coronation Scot*, complete with a set of coaches all gorgeous blue-and-white stripes.

John was overwhelmed. Kindness. The one thing he could never resist. Something exploded within him.

'Cor, Dad!' he spluttered, 'The *Coronation Scot*! Wow! Cor, Dad! Thanks a million!'

Forgetting the people looking at him, he did something he'd never imagined himself doing. He leapt up, embraced Giles and kissed him.

What a transformation! What a wonderful, inexplicable transformation! A miracle. Obviously God had spoken personally to Giles. There was no other explanation.

A More Mundane Explanation

Maybe God *had* sorted things out for him. Maybe God *had* dropped a line to Giles and put in a word about the *Coronation Scot*. Perhaps. After all, the universe, we're told, is stranger than we can imagine it to be.

But in this case there was a more mundane explanation for everything.

That Friday night Mary had *not* gone up to the attic to look for him. Instead, she'd slipped into the bathroom to smoke a joint. Normally, Giles wouldn't have minded her smoking downstairs, but, being under dire pressure to get the Murray lecture up and running, he didn't want dope fumes clouding his mind. She'd had a difficult day. Her Ph.D. thesis was getting nowhere and nasty things were being said. She just had to blow her mind. The last thing she needed was a stroppy kid.

After the joint she'd popped a few pills and then crashed out in the bedroom and enjoyed a well-earned trip. She hadn't noticed the missing sixty pounds – and wouldn't have given a damn even if she had.

A Good Party

Neither of them thought about John on Saturday. Giles was preoccupied with the Murray Lecture. Mary went to see some friends and then on to a party.

Sunday came. Giles finally finished his preparations for the Murray Lecture and began to get ready for the weekly Sunday evening soirée. He noticed the dishes in the sink, unwashed since Friday evening.

'Mary, I thought you were going to get John to wash these?'

'Couldn't be arsed to look for him!'

'Where is he now?'

'He's probably up in the attic. Shall I get him?'

'Don't bother. Just ignore him. It'll do him good not to be the centre of attention for a change.'

It was a good party. Having completed his lecture notes, Giles was in a relaxed and genial mood. He was even prepared to come to the defence of a student who'd dared to put in a good word for Kautsky. Mary managed to get Bill Baxter to screw her – which was no mean achievement as he was reputed to be gay or actually impotent.

The Little Sod!

On Monday morning Giles went to the university, while Mary lay recovering from the previous night's trips – sexual, alcoholic and chemical.

At midday, just as she was about to set off for a meeting with her Feminist Awareness Group, the telephone rang.

'Are you Mrs Denby?'

She grunted in the affirmative.

'Well this is the Merton Road Police Station...'

'The what?'

'The Merton Road Police Station in London. We've got your son, John, here.

He's all right, but...'

There followed details of what seemed to be a sexual assault.

'Oh Christ almighty!'

Still a bit hazy and with a headache coming on, she put the receiver down. Slowly it all sank in. That kid in LONDON! That was all she bloody needed! The little sod!

Sneaking off like that just to get attention! The inflammable fumes built up...

And when she climbed up to the attic those fumes ignited into a veritable fireball. The repulsive, fouled jeans stinking away on the floor. The filthy clothes strewn everywhere. That heap of duvets reeking of piss... Jesus fucking Christ, this kid wasn't even house-trained! And he was eleven years old! She'd always known that he was a congenital idiot! Well, he could bloody well stay in London.

192

Go to a special school down there where they knew how to deal with loonies. *She* had better things to do than run round washing shitty pants and pissed duvets. To actually expect her to do it was an insult to her liberated womanhood.

At the university she unburdened herself to the Feminist Awareness Group. Fortuitously, the theme for this week happened to be 'Sexism in Private Education'. High on her pills, she unlocked her subconscious and blew her mind. Just look what private education had done to her son! Spoiled him utterly. Turned him into a fatuous little snob with ideas far above his station... Why he couldn't even use a toilet properly and had been taught to expect – yes to *expect*! – women to clear up after him! He couldn't face the reality of a proper working-class school and had sneaked off to London in the hope of getting back to his prep school again ... and he'd managed to get himself buggered – almost certainly by one of those twisted males who infested private education and, very probably of his own volition, too...

Out the torrent poured in a monologue of pent-up fury. Martha Merrins made deeply sympathetic noises and scribbled away on her notepad. Everything was taken down – especially the juicy details about the 'damaged rectum' which would 'heal in time, despite distressing problems in retaining faeces...' (And just how she relished this bit! At last, she was getting what she'd long been wanting!)

When the monologue finally petered out, she assured Mary of her full support and her total understanding of her terrible predicament.

A Bourgeois Vice... Nurtured in Public Schools

At 5 p.m. that afternoon Martha went into a huddle with the senior members of her Sociology Department.

'... We've only half an hour and so I must be brief. We must keep this strictly confidential for the moment... As you know, our department has a social improvemental role beyond its purely normative academic role... Now we have a very serious case of child abuse before us with explosive potential...'

Very explosive! In fact a lovely big bomb which could demolish the one major obstacle that lay between Martha Merrins and the nomination as the Labour Party candidate for Boldonbridge West in the coming by-election ... and, also, propel her into the stratosphere as a national campaigner – *the* national campaigner! – against child abuse. Fearless, assiduous, deeply caring, totally fair, not afraid to expose it even when a respected colleague – a close personal friend, in fact! – was involved. If she had been a believer – which she most emphatically was not! – she would have thought that God had set it all up specially for her.

With a warm glow of elation and a delicious sense of altruism and nobility, she outlined the case... Dr Denby (hushed and awed tone! But, oh how she relished that name!) had a son, an unwanted love child, in fact. The boy had run away and had been found in a distressed state in London. Examination by a police doctor had shown that he had been sexually abused. Apparently, it hadn't happened in London, but had been done a day or two previously. It couldn't have been anybody in Greenwood. Pederasty, as they all knew, was something that went on in perverted private schools – another reason for abolishing them! The working class didn't do that sort of thing. It was a bourgeois vice, created by the anally oriented lifestyle of the bourgeoisie and nurtured in the public schools... That left...

Well, it was obvious, wasn't it? He filled the profile to perfection: male (and that in itself said a lot!), leading public school where he had made a habit of beating junior boys... (And, here, she pulled out a thick file and rummaged a while before producing a letter.) In particular he'd beaten one James Dorking – at a time and date duly specified – with his trousers down and had (and here she read directly from the letter) '... put his hand into my crutch and fondled my testicles...'

Dr Denby had tried to conceal his son, but during a Sunday night party, the child had managed to slip downstairs and join the group. He had begun to talk to her and had mentioned a secret, but had obviously been too ashamed – and probably too frightened! – to be specific. Before he could go into any details, however. Dr Denby had chased him back to his bedroom. He had not been allowed to join the party the following week. Now he had run away. So it all added up, didn't it?

Vindication. Righteousness. Fighting the good fight... Heady stuff!

Filled with elation, Martha Merrins set off for the Murray Lecture at seven-thirty.

Still More Success

The Murray Lecture that evening was a brilliant success.

The audience hung on Giles' every measured word and he was given a standing ovation. During the question-and-answer session afterwards Dr Jennings, that nihilistic guided missile, had tried to trip him up on some abstruse and trivial fact, but he'd routed him. Caught him out on his home territory of detailed facts and tied him up in knots – the anti-missile-missile had worked to perfection. Professor Aubrey had personally congratulated him and so had the Vice Chancellor, the Mayor of Boldonbridge and – most usefully of all! – the chairman of the local Labour Party.

Professor Stimpson of the Education Department had been especially lavish in his praise and had said that he would incorporate much of the lecture into his forthcoming book, *A Revolution in the Classroom*. In particular, he'd expressed a deep interest in the way that the ex-prep schoolboy, John, was adapting so well to a 'true working-class education'.

'I must interview the young man personally,' he declared as he shook Giles' hand, 'and include his comments in my book.'

And, of course, Martha Merrins had been ecstatic: '...A most memorable radical statement from the socio-academic interface...'

To cap it all, the BBC were definitely going to sign him up to do those programmes on the evolution of the British working class.

He was soaring upwards into the deep, devouring, burning blue...

Shot Down in Flames

Mission accomplished. As Giles left the auditorium with the plaudits ringing in his ears, he felt like a World War II bomber pilot returning from a successful raid. Then BANG! In went a lethal cannonade from an unseen German night-fighter and down he went in flames.

In the corridor a lecturer from the Sociology Department approached him: 'Giles, I think there is something you ought to know...'

Sworn to confidentiality, yes, but Maggie Wright had a soft spot for Giles – in fact, was secretly in love with him! – and, moreover, couldn't stand her boss, that fat, sanctimonious, long-winded and self-obsessed slob, Martha Merrins...

A Blazing Row – Or Serious Ideological Debate

Back at Gloucester Road that night Giles and Mary had a blazing row.

'Couldn't you have told me first before shooting your mouth off to Merrins?'

'So what? Merrins is one of us.'

'That's what you think! But she's after the Labour Party nomination and will stop at nothing to get it.'

'But she can't hurt *you*! Nobody will believe that crap about you buggering the little sod! It's just not true!'

'Of course, it's not true! But truth's got nothing to do with it! It's what people believe to be the truth that matters. As a history graduate you should *know* that!'

'But nobody's going to swallow that one! Anyway that little bitch, Wright, probably made it all up.'

'She's not a little bitch! She's a first-class sociologist!'

'A first-class screw, you mean!'

'Oh for God's sake, can't you *see* that we're both in the shit!'

'Balls!'

'Look, Merrins has got it all sewn up. I've been buggering the little toerag and beating him up. That's why he's run away. Christ alive, she's even got hold of that slob, Dorking – who's told her a pack of lies, of course! ... She's assiduous, I'll give her that.

'Well, just tell her to piss off.'

'I can't do that and you know it. I'm going down to London to collect the little sod. Tomorrow morning prompt!'

'*Why* for fuck's sake? Let them sort him out down there. They can put him into a special home where they know how to deal with loonies. Have you seen the state of his room?'

'Don't start on that again!'

'Yes, duck out of it, won't you! It's a woman's job to mop up shit and piss, isn't it? A man's got better things to do...'

'Yes, I know you've got better things to do with your life than clean up after messy kids. You've said it often enough. But, for fuck's sake, Mary, can't you *see* that this kid's got us over a barrel!'

'How? Who's going to listen to an infantile halfwit? You're a well-known academic, for Christ's sake! Your word counts for far more than his!'

'That's not the point! If Merrins gets hold of him, Christ alone knows what she'll get the little toad to say! I mean just look at what she's squeezed out of Dorking...'

'So bloody what?'

'So bloody EVERYTHING! If he says I've been buggering him, we could both land in jail. BOTH of us! Social pariahs! Careers ruined!'

In his exasperation Giles' voice rose to a shout: 'OH FOR FUCK'S SAKE, CAN'T YOU SEE!'

'You're getting hysterical,' replied Mary coolly. 'Smoke a joint. Chill out!'

That did it. Giles finally exploded into blue smoke. He stood up and bellowed, waving his arms around and brandishing his fists. Tall and well built, he towered over her... Awesome. Intimidating.

When the storm eventually blew itself out, he addressed her in a calm and purposeful voice, laced with a scarcely concealed menace: 'Tomorrow morning I am going down to collect him. In the meantime you had bloody well better do something about that room of his. The first thing Merrins will do is send the Social Services round and if they see all those pissed duvets and unwashed clothes...? Well, need I say any more? Got the message?'

She'd never seen him quite as angry as this before. Yet something deep inside her warmed to him. He was big, strong, properly masculine, far removed from the mealy-mouthed flabbiness that she'd so despised in her father. It touched a deeper layer in her than all her aggressive feminism. A raw sensuality. This was what a *real* man ought to be like...

Damage Control, CCF-style

Giles didn't sleep much that night, but by five o'clock in the morning he'd cooled down. His calm, orderly mind took over. It was a matter of damage control and a decisive response to an unexpected crisis.

He remembered that time, long ago, when he had been the Cadet Officer in the Rugby School CCF. It had been the annual field day and he was in charge of the company attack. Halfway through – and just to test him – the visiting general had organised an unexpected attack on his rear. Cool and collected, he'd managed to turn his company round and deal with it. The general had been deeply impressed and had said that he ought to go to Sandhurst and become a regular officer. For a time he had seriously considered it.

This situation was no different. It was simply a matter of tactics. Preparation for battle. The boy he believed – *knew*, in fact! – was soft-centred and would respond to mollycoddling. Well, mollycoddling he'd get – laid on not with a trowel, but with a whole bloody shovel! It would be big smiles, welcome back ... and then would come the blockbuster bomb, the Grand Slam, delivered by a low-level fighter-bomber à la US Air Force. He'd stop off at York and buy him a new train for his model railway. He knew all about trains from his childhood railway books and a visit to the attic had shown him that the kid hadn't got the *Coronation Scot*, one of the truly great streamliners of the 1930s. So that's what he'd get...

At six o'clock he set off. Stopping off at York, he spent over two hundred pounds, getting, not only the engine, but a set of matching coaches and a whole new station as well. Then he rang up the police station and got the directions to the children's home where his son was staying – so much easier to do without Mary screeching away in the background.

By the time he reached London the whole battle plan was firmly in place.

A Complete Pushover

Yet he was nonplussed at just how easily the plan worked.

It was a complete pushover. Of course, he cringed with embarrassment when the boy kissed him in public. But affection displayed in public and in front of possible prosecution witnesses? It couldn't have worked out better if he'd actually planned it!

But, oh that kid was soft! Not just wet, but downright soggy, waterlogged in fact! He had to fight to control his rising contempt.

All the way back to Boldonbridge it was spuke pills, driving slowly so as not to make him car sick (being sick in cars at his age, how pathetic!) ... And, oh the agony of containing your healthy aggression and letting a Ford Anglia overtake you! Then the business of stopping at cafés and buying him chips and Kentucky Fried Chicken (Thank God Mary wasn't there to start on about the superiority of ethnic food!) and letting him spend an age in the toilet without getting impatient. Apparently there were 'problems in the downstairs

198

department' – or so the police had said, and in graphic detail, too! – but he mustn't mention it in case he embarrassed the wretched child!

Then the process of buying sweets and comics...

Worst of all was having to smile benignly while he drivelled on in that high-pitched, squeaky voice of his about the 125 express he'd travelled in, about aeroplanes and how an ME 109 could out turn a Spitfire, how a Spitfire could shoot down a V2 rocket and how he'd read that Biggles had flown over the South Pole or something... A leading historian having to listen to *this*! How far could you fall?

And, of course, there was the predictable 'statement' from Mary when they got back to Gloucester Road and he gave the kid fish and chips for supper: 'Weak! That's what you are, Giles, weak! You're letting him walk all over you...' And so on till well past midnight.

22

Blissful Limbo

For John the next few days passed in a blissful limbo.

Mary had made an attempt to tidy up his room and had taken one of the pissed duvets to the laundry so he had a bed to sleep in. Giles was ostentatiously nice to him, always smiling at him and buying him fish and chips and packets of wine gums. He even gave him thirty pounds and told him to go and spend it.

If somebody was nice to you, you had to be nice to them. So John made a special effort to be nice to Giles. He was genuinely delighted with his new *Coronation Scot* and station and was touched by the thoughtfulness of the gesture. In any case, he always found it almost impossible to resist kindness. Besides, Giles was a reformed character: God had obviously had a word in his ear.

So for three days he lay around playing with his trains, setting up his new station and watching videos. On the fourth day he ventured outside to spend his thirty pounds and replenish his supply of sweets.

This posed problems. It meant going back to the shop run by that Indian in a turban. But after the shoplifting incident would he let him into the shop? And wouldn't he immediately call the police? But, then, God had been kind to him, so hadn't he better pay God back by going up to the man and apologising for what he'd done?

Nervously he crept up the hill and sidled into the shop. The man was busy serving two fat women in overcoats and didn't notice him at first. So he just hung around dithering for a while. Then the man saw him, scowled and said in a firm voice, 'You, out!'

Hopes shattered! Giles may have forgiven him, but clearly other people hadn't. He was still in that deep, black pit.

Desperately he began to plead: 'Please! Please! I'm not going to steal anything. I've come to say sorry! You see I was frightened. The kids at Greenhill School said they'd do me over if I didn't get them fags. It's horrible at Greenhill School and I was frightened. Here's ten pounds to pay for the fags I stole. Please take it! I'll never steal again. Swear to God. Cross my heart.'

The man's face broke into a big smile: 'Oh, Greenhill School! You should keep well away from that place. Very bad people. Don't worry. Keep your ten pounds. It's good to know that some people round here are honest. Now what can I get you?'

He bought five packets of liquorice allsorts and four packets of wine gums, the things he liked best. He left the shop glowing with success. He'd made amends, salved his conscience and made a useful friend as well. It was good to keep on the right side of God. Paid dividends.

'Leave me alone!'

The only unpleasant thing occurred when Giles took him to see a doctor who made him take all his clothes off and insisted on examining him in an excruciatingly embarrassing way. Being poked around in a filthy, unmentionable place while Giles and the nurse looked on... Having somebody sticking his gloved fingers up *there*! He was so ashamed. Couldn't they just leave him alone? But when the doctor started asking questions about ... well, about *that*! It was just too much.

In the face of his tears and rising temper, Giles signalled to the wretched man to back off. On the way home he bought him some chocolate and a packet of chips.

So the days passed. A week slipped by in a pleasant arcadia of sweets, crisps, trains and videos.

23

Guerrilla war

Round One

Then suddenly his arcadia ended.

On Monday morning Giles climbed up into his room: 'Well, John, it's time to go to school again.'

A bolt of lightning. A flash of blind terror. The worst possible fate.

'NO! NO! NO! I'm not going back to Greenhill again! NEVER! NEVER! NOT EVER!'

John rolled himself into a tight little ball – a sort of hedgehog without prickles – and began to cry. (He knew that proper boys didn't cry and at Rickerby Hall he hadn't cried for over a year. But now he seemed to be crying all the time. In this strange land he'd changed into something else.)

'Now, come on! You know you've got to go to school.'

'NO! NO! NO!' The sobs became wails.

Giles looked on in exasperation. Defied by a pathetic little eleven-year-old! *Him*, a rising historian and potential cabinet minister? A thump and a good shaking would soon sort all this rubbish out. But, under the present delicate circumstances, that was not advisable. Besides, he had a lecture at nine that morning and hadn't got time to hang around.

He withdrew. Round One to John.

Round Two

The next day he tried again – with exactly the same result...

The unthinkable was happening. In a straight contest a weedy little kid was getting the better of him, a big strong man. It was like a guerrilla war with him in the role of the occupying colonial power. He remembered how he had rejoiced when the Vietcong freedom fighters had shot down a super-sophisticated American fighter bomber with a crossbow. Now he began to feel a certain sympathy for that unfortunate American pilot.

Council of War

That evening he and Mary had a council of war.

'He refuses to go to school.'

'Well bloody well *make* him go. You're a big, strong man and he's only a little kid.'

'But *how*?'

'Pick him up and skelp his bum for heaven's sake! It's what he's needed all along.'

'I'm afraid that in the present situation that would be most unwise.'

'Why for fuck's sake?'

Giles sighed. Sometimes Mary was as bad as a thick student: 'We've been through all this before. Merrins says I have been buggering him...'

'Which is not true.'

'Of course it's not true. But that hasn't stopped the old bitch getting on to the Social Services. They could be coming to inspect us any day now. We've got to keep the little toerag sweet. If he starts shooting his mouth off... Can't you bloody *see*?' Mary fixed him with her 'analytical stare':

'Yes I can see only too well. You, a leading member of a progressive university at the very cutting edge of the social revolution, you whose books are changing society, *you* are putting yourself into the hands of a pathetic little birdbrained child. It's grotesque, like something out of the Middle Ages when grown men had to obey small kids who happened to be their feudal lords...'

'I suppose that's one way of putting it.'

'Well, I never thought it would come to this.'

'Neither did I,' replied her husband with a resigned sigh. 'But it wouldn't have done if you'd agreed to have that abortion.'

'Don't start on *that* again!' snapped Mary.

Stalemate.

A Piranha Fish in a Bowl of Treacle?

For another day the siege went on. Giles was starting to get desperate. Time was running out. He just had to get that kid back to school again before the Social Services descended and did its worst. He would really liked to have gone up to the attic and thumped the living daylights out of the little toad, given him the Dorking treatment . . . the full, undiluted works.

But, of course, he knew he couldn't.

He founds kids hard enough to understand at the best of times – so irrational, so banal and so utterly boring! – but this one floored him. At Rugby School the juniors would put up a show of resistance and crumple when you got physical. But not this one! He was so utterly wet – dripping, waterlogged, leaking like the proverbial sieve. Gutless. Always trying to be ingratiating, always saying 'please' and 'thank you' in that ghastly tinkle-bell voice of his. Hugging and kissing him in public, for Christ's sake! Quite pathetically thrilled with his bloody *Coronation Scot* – toy trains at his age, bloody hell!

But there were these unexpected obstinacies underneath. All that fuss about the Scripture Union, for instance. He was still writing to them – he'd seen the letters lying round in his room. And now this refusal to go to school. He was a bowl of glutinous treacle all right, but with a piranha fish swimming round in the middle of it.

The Slippery Slope of Revisionism?

On Thursday evening Giles and Mary had another council of war.

'It's no good,' groaned Giles. 'Whenever I mention school he just curls up and starts to cry.'

'You mean you're letting him defy you.'

Well, what do *you* suggest? If we don't get him to school pretty damned soon, we'll have the truancy officer round. I'm sure Merrins will see to that – if she hasn't already done so.'

'Just pick him up and *take* him to school! Perfectly simple.'

'Fine. You go ahead and do it. But he'll just run away again and Merrins will have a field day.'

'So now what?' Mary switched on the 'analytical stare'.

A long silence followed as Giles' orderly mind explored the options.

'We're going to have to send him to another school,' he said at length.

Mary's 'analytical stare' intensified. The X-ray eyes pumped out an extra dose of radiation: 'You know what that means, don't you? If he goes to another comprehensive it will be breaking the rules. Rules which *you* spoke so forcibly in favour of, remember? Area comprehensives. Not allowing the middle classes to remove their children from schools in working-class areas and turn those in the posh areas into free public schools. Anyway think what it will do to the morale of the Greenhill staff if their best pupils are allowed to desert them.'

'Oh come on, Mary, he's hardly one of their best pupils, is he?'

'That's not the point.'

Another silence ensued. The 'analytical stare' continued apace with a withering intensity.

'So just what *are* you going to do?' said Mary eventually, putting on her well-practised interrogator's voice. 'Send him to a third-rate public school?'

'Good lord no!' expostulated Giles, stung by the rebuke. 'How could you even think of such a thing? It would be professional and political suicide. I mean just what *would* the Labour Party make of that? Especially after all I've said about the need to abolish private education!'

'Well, what then?' The X-ray eyes bored into him.

More silence.

Eventually, Giles replied, his voice dropping almost to a whisper – like an Old Testament Jew pronouncing the word Yahweh: 'There is always Beaconsfield.'

Mary ignited. Went up in a sheet of red flame – almost literally. 'WHAT?' she screeched. 'BEACONSFIELD! That's a special school for idiots and it's PRIVATE, for fuck's sake!'

'Not quite,' replied Giles coolly. 'Not quite. The local authority pays for statemented children to go there. You know things like dyslexia, learning difficulties, too feeble to handle a normal school. Our John certainly fulfils the last two requirements.'

The 'analytical stare' became an interrogator's lamp, turned up to full power and directed onto the prisoner's face. Consciously imitating a practised inquisitor, Mary delivered her punchline: 'Have you forgotten that only last week you openly told the Social and Political Awareness Group that Beaconsfield School ought to be closed down because it provided the middle classes a plausible escape route from the working-class revolution that was taking place in the comprehensives? And you went on to call the female who runs it – Watson or something – a pathetic little petty-bourgeois birdbrain who, because she couldn't handle a real school, had decided to vent her spite on the state system by trying to destroy it... And what did you say she was? Like a spoilt child, wasn't it, who, because she was too stupid to understand her reading book, rips it up and throws it out of the window? Or words to that effect anyway. Don't try to deny it. I heard you say it and Samantha Glenn has got it all on tape!'

Giles folded his fingers and stared at the ceiling for a while. Then, speaking in a clear and calm voice, he replied: 'OK, I agree with everything you've said. But, let's run through our options, shall we? Option One: I carry the kid kicking and screaming back to Greenhill. He runs away again. Merrins gets hold of him and gets him to say that I've been buggering him. We both land in jail...'

'But *nobody's* buggered him!' interrupted Mary. 'It's just a figment of his dirty little mind. He's probably invented the whole story just to get attention...'

'No,' said Giles shaking his head, 'I'm afraid he *has* been buggered. It's in the police doctor's report and quite a juicy read it is, too! And I took him along to old Dr Callander last Wednesday and he confirmed it all.'

'I take your point,' replied Mary in her 'icy voice'. 'But did his little Lordship condescend to say who had done the deed?'

'No, when Callander pressed him he got hysterical and then shut up like a clam.'

'It was probably a policeman in that London police station,' growled Mary. 'They're all perverts. That's why they join the Freemasons. Do you know that the Freemasons...?'

'Yes,' replied Giles, anticipating one of his wife's favourite rants, 'you've said it all before and I totally agree with you, but let's get back to the point...

'Option Two: we transfer him to St Ostwald's. Old Riley, that reactionary in charge of it, sets up a howl of delight. He tells the Tories on the Council that Greenhill is a disaster and ought to be closed down. Why? Because Dr Denby, who has so vehemently championed it, has seen fit to withdraw his precious little son from it. All hell breaks loose. Not a feasible option.

'That leaves Option Three. We send him to Beaconsfield. Nobody need know about it, but if they do find out, we can always say that he had special needs which were a burden on Greenhill. In a word, that he simply wasn't good enough for them either socially or academically.'

'Well, at least that bit's true!' snorted Mary.

'You know when I think of all the hopes we had for that kid,' she added, 'Christ, just how he's let us down! If I were a Christian, I'd start thinking that the Devil had taken him over.'

'Maybe, but what's your conclusion, then?'

'Send him to bloody Beaconsfield. Eat shit, if you must!'

'Well, Mary, there are good revolutionary precedents for eating shit. After all, Trotsky was forced to employ Tsarist officers in the Red Army...'

'Yes, I get you,' she said with an air of weary resignation.

'But there's just one more thing,' she continued, feeling not unlike a victorious admiral, putting the final torpedo into an already-sinking enemy battleship, 'what about that interview that Ed Stimpson was going to have with his nibs? What's *he* going to say when he finds out that you have sent the little toad to a private school?'

'What indeed?' Giles sighed and said nothing. That conundrum would have to wait for the time being.

Later that evening he telephoned Dorothy Watson, the headmistress of Beaconsfield School.

A Disreputable Undercover Operation

'Yes,' said Dorothy Watson, 'we can take your son. When do you want him to start?'

'Tomorrow.'

'That's a bit precipitate. He'll need a uniform and games kit. I'll put a list in the post. I think Monday would be better. It would give you time to get him organised. Now, what about fees? Are you paying or is the local authority?

'No problem about that. Tell me how much it is and I'll put a cheque in the post.'

'You'll find the details in the prospectus that I'll send you... Now are there any problems that we ought to know about – learning difficulties or dyslexia?'

'No! No! No! Nothing like that. He's just not very bright. He lacks personality and just couldn't cope with Greenhill, that's all.'

'Would you like me to get him seen by the County Psychologist?'

(Bloody hell NO! What *would* start coming out? And, more to the point, what *would* Merrins make of it when she got hold of the spicy details? – which, knowing her, she undoubtedly would.)

'No, I don't think that will be necessary...'

These probing questions irritated him. He needed to get things settled as quickly as possible, but the wretched female *would* persist. He saw through the game of course – trying to hide her lack of intellect behind a facade of pseudo-professionalism. Typical teacher. Typical private-school con trick.

'Perhaps you and he would like to visit the school tomorrow. I could get Bill Bleeson, our head boy, to show you round...'

'No! No! No! That won't be necessary! Please no!' (The very last thing Giles wanted was to actually *visit* the place. It was bad enough having to make contact over the telephone. But to *go* there! What if his university colleagues found out? What if the local Labour Party got to know of it? This sordid business had to be done under cover and completed as quickly as possible – like a spy handing over his stolen documents to his contact at the dead of night.)

Mercifully, the session soon came to a close.

'So that's all settled them. He'll start on Monday. I'll meet him at eight-thirty in my study and we'll sort him out.'

'Yes, and the cheque will be in the post as soon as possible.'

Thankfully, Giles put the receiver down. He'd never imagined that he'd be reduced to this sort of undercover operation.

Vindication

On the other end of the line Dorothy Watson basked in a warm radiance. Gratification. The sheer joy of being proved right. It was like being vindicated in the High Court.

This *was* a scoop. Dr Denby had been the most articulate and dangerous opponent of her school. He'd very nearly strangled it at birth by almost persuading the local authority not to subsidise any of her pupils. He'd denounced it as a 'pathetic petty-bourgeois rear-guard action against the onward march of history' and had declared that it should be closed down 'in the interests of mental and social hygiene'. His comments about her personally had been deeply wounding.

Now here he was delivering his precious only son into her hands. Talk about the Road to Damascus!

24

Interlude – The Tale of a Missionary

The Dedicated Teacher

But who was this Dorothy Watson? And just what had she done to earn the disapproval of her intellectual betters?

It was a long story.

First of all, she was a dedicated teacher. Teaching for Dorothy Watson was more than just a job. It was her purpose in life and, indeed, her very identity. She actually liked children. She relished their freshness and the way that they could transform a mundane world into a colourful and exciting place – a bit like the countryside when the sun broke through the clouds and the rain-sodden woods and fields sparkled anew in the brilliant light. She even enjoyed their waywardness and frequent silliness. It added a spark of absurdity which enlivened an often drab world. When there were no children around, she felt empty.

The great sadness of her life was that she'd never been able to have children of her own. She'd always meant to, but it just hadn't worked out. Indeed, her whole life hadn't quite worked out.

The Missionary

At heart, she was a missionary. For her it was not a matter of believing in God. She'd always *known* that God was there. Not, of course, that she was a God botherer. 'I may be a Christian,' she would declare apologetically, 'but I am not a Holy Joe!'

She didn't take the whole of the Bible literally – she was far too analytical for that. But, if God wasn't there, then nothing made any sense. The whole extraordinarily balanced structure of the universe and the quite incredible complexities of the natural world that it was her duty as a Biology teacher to expound: to her all this required a creator. Besides, she reasoned, if God wasn't there, then what was the point in being good? Why not just live for the moment and indulge your appetites? To her, this was a recipe for catastrophe. Years of teaching had convinced her that youngsters, especially the aggressive, testosterone-crazed young males, were bundles of explosive and self-destructive impulses. The whole 'do your thing' cult of the Sixties had appalled her. All it seemed to have done was to let a rampaging demon loose which led to violence, rape and drug abuse. Youngsters needed a firm moral framework to save themselves from themselves.

If God didn't exist, you would have to invent him – just as in elementary physics you invented the notion of waves to explain things like different colours. She felt sorry for people who didn't believe in God. They were simply missing out on something good.

The Making of a Missionary

The only daughter of a skilled shipyard worker, she'd grown up in East Snape. East Snape had once been a stretch of swampy ground on the flat northern side of the River Boldon, not far from the broad estuary where the river faded undramatically into the North Sea. As the Industrial Revolution had gathered momentum, shipyards had mushroomed and the open land had been engulfed in the ugly sprawl of North Boldonside.

The Fulwell Estate where she had lived was on the northern edge of this sprawl, a utilitarian, no-frills place, a gridiron of harsh red-brick boxes hurriedly thrown together as a low-cost response to the post-war housing shortage. All around were litter-strewn expanses of bare concrete and odd bits of withered grass pretending to be lawns. On the grey days when a lid of cloud came in from the North Sea it looked dismal enough, but when the sun did manage to come out it looked even worse. Its sheer, relentless ugliness was fully exposed, rather as if an old man had removed his clothes and revealed the withered flab underneath.

From an early age she'd dreamed of being a missionary in Africa. As she had pored over books in the local library, the dank and dreary world around her had been replaced by brilliant sunlight, soaring skies and vast, sweeping plains, awash with colour and studded with palm trees, acacias and huge herds of exotic animals.

211

Her heroine was Mary Slessor, the factory girl from Dundee who had gone out to Nigeria and carved a school out of the jungle. But she planned to go one better. She'd be a teacher, yes, but she'd be a doctor like Albert Schweitzer who would alleviate pain and suffering as well.

She'd managed to pass the Eleven Plus – to her parent's huge pride and delight – and had gone to the local grammar school. But her A level results hadn't been good enough for university, let alone for the exacting demands of the Medical School at Newcastle. So, she'd had to make do with second best and had gone to a teacher-training college where her main subject had been Biology.

There she'd met Lawrence. He was a trainee Chemistry teacher and, like her, a committed Christian. They'd quickly become friends. For studious, repressed and rather fusty Dorothy, he was a whirlwind of warm and bracing air who'd opened doors and revealed new and exciting worlds that she'd only dreamed of. A keen sportsman and outdoor type, he took her hiking in the Lake District and on extended cycling trips round the Scottish Highlands where they'd climbed Ben Nevis and explored the remote and dramatic mountains of Torridon and the far north. Soon a mere friendship had blossomed out into a passionate love affair.

After graduating they had got married. Their union was blissful – tender and understanding, but, at the same time, deeply carnal. For the first time Dorothy had experienced the sheer, sensual ecstasy of sexual relations. They seemed to be specially made for each other and Lawrence had declared that God had brought them together for a planned missionary purpose.

Shortly after their wedding they had gone out to Uganda as a man and wife team to teach Chemistry and Biology at Apollo Kagwa School, a well-known missionary foundation.

Paradise

At first it had seemed like paradise. It was the early Sixties and Uganda was being prepared for independence. Brilliant vistas were opening up of a new and dynamic society blossoming out in the middle of Africa, a society shorn of all the impediments and irrationalities that so stifled things in old, tired, class-conscious Britain. A new birth. A renaissance.

Apollo Kagwa School seemed to epitomise all this. One of the first schools to be founded in Uganda (the very first according to the Walsall Missionary Society, its progenitor), it was the fruit of seventy years of generous donations and devoted missionary effort. It was, moreover, a showcase which demonstrated for all sceptics to see, the very real and tangible benefits of British colonial rule. As such, it got the lion's share of any government or United Nations grants that were going.

Apollo Kagwa School

It was set in a gracious compound of carefully trimmed lawns and massive brilliantly coloured trees. There were elegant modern classroom blocks and student dormitories, better equipped than many in Britain, a fine modern dining hall and a simple, but beautifully designed, chapel with stained-glass windows, crafted by Fine Arts students from Makerere University. For the all-European teaching staff there were spacious bungalows where dutiful and efficient African servants relieved them of tiresome domestic chores.

It was an open and airy place, caressed by gentle breezes and full of the exotic smells of tropical vegetation and a rich, wet earth. Set on the top of a hill, it commanded an intoxicating view of the oceanic immensities of Lake Victoria, source of the mighty Nile and the second biggest freshwater lake in the world. Blue and mysterious in the cool of the dawn, the lake was a riot of dazzling red and gold as the sun set in the evening. It was all so different from the decaying, industrial desert of East Snape.

The African pupils – the boys in their neat white shirts and shorts and red socks, the girls in their white dresses and red neck ties – were delightfully earnest and eager to learn – so unlike the semi-literate and sullenly hostile oafs that you encountered on teaching practice in so many northern secondary moderns. Moreover, they took their Christianity seriously. The chapel was always crammed to capacity – and, not only with Apollo Kagwa pupils, but with the local people as well. The Scripture Union flourished mightily. Here Christianity was real, not just the self-deluding fantasy of a few inadequates.

The exam results were always uniformly excellent – hundred-per-cent pass rates at both O and A level and with whole clutches of top grades to boot. Definitely a new and dynamic society in the making!

And, as if all that wasn't enough, there was the quite unexpectedly rich and varied social life. Lovely houses to live in, servants to look after your every need, cars, dinner parties, dances and barbecues at the Club in town – officially open to all, but in fact almost exclusively European. And there were the safaris in the game parks, the holidays on the palm-fringed beaches of exotic Mombasa... Most wonderful of all was a climb to the very summit of snowy Kilimanjaro with guides, porters and all the colonial trimmings – something Dorothy had never even dreamed of ever happening to somebody like her.

From dowdy student teachers they had suddenly been changed into privileged landed gentry.

Savouring the Gorgeous Fruits

Lawrence had been swept away by it all. The only son of a dour and puritanical Methodist who ran a small grocery shop in the proletarian heart of Southside, he had always been acutely conscious of class. He was not to play with the other children in the street, his mother had told him, because they were 'working class' and 'common'. They, in turn, had despised him as 'posh'. But when, at his parent's behest – for they were both strong Tories – he had joined the Young Conservatives, he'd found himself cold-shouldered by the smooth, well-spoken public schoolboys from the opulent suburbs of Moorside and North Dene. These self-assured sophisticates had dismissed him as a 'lower-middle-class oik', sneered at his northern accent and excluded him from their parties and dances. You just couldn't win!

But, here in Uganda, class didn't matter. He was fully accepted by all his European colleagues. It was liberation. He plunged avidly into the expatriate social whirl – parties, dances, picnics on the Sese Islands in the middle of enchanting Lake Victoria, even receptions with diplomats at the British High Commission in Kampala. He was savouring all the gorgeous fruits that had been denied him in dreary, restrictive, inward-looking and class-ridden Southside.

Not Quite What They Seem to Be?

For a time Dorothy, too, had luxuriated in it all.

But she had a problem: she was gifted with insight. She saw through the appearance of things and perceived the realities that lay beneath the surface – almost like radar in an aeroplane which could see through a placid sea of white clouds and discern the rugged mountains that lay beneath. The trouble was that she could not articulate this insight – at least not into terms that the people who mattered would listen to. (For who could possibly take a mere schoolmistress without a university degree seriously?) She sometimes felt like Cassandra in the old legend of Troy, condemned to be right, but always ignored.

After a year she began to have doubts. This luxurious lifestyle wasn't what Mary Slessor would have thought of as missionary work. It seemed unreal, almost fraudulent. At the bottom of the hill was a Uganda far removed from the orderly elegance at the top – a sprawl of filthy shanties and open sewers where beggars with elephantiasis and naked, undernourished children defecated in muddy alleys. This was the *real* Uganda, not the beautiful illusion on top of the hill.

The European staff, and, especially Lawrence, honestly believed that they had cracked the problems of education. They seemed to think that the school's brilliant exam results were due to their excellent teaching.

To Dorothy this was a self-indulgent fantasy. The pupils with the highest grades in the Primary School Leaving Exams were automatically sent to Apollo Kagwa. With the very ablest pupils in Uganda, of

At the bottom of the hill

course the exam results were going to be good. If they'd been landed with the slow learners and the failures things would have been very different. She'd met teachers from the less opulent up-country schools and they'd told her of pupil strikes because of poor exam results and of students unable to cope with the rigorously academic curriculum and blaming their teachers for their predicament. And what if they'd had to teach those diseased and criminalised children at the bottom of the hill where drunkenness and violence were rampant? Here at Apollo Kagwa School they were living in a fools' paradise.

Then there were the pupils, so intelligent and so apparently committed to education and Christianity. Quite early on she'd begun to suspect that things were not quite what they seemed to be.

One day she'd unexpectedly sprung a test on a class and many of them had done badly. When she'd read out a list of the marks she'd been surrounded by an angry mob.

'You've put my name against a low mark! ... You are trying to destroy my brain and make me stupid... You want to turn me into a child by making me fail!'

'Don't be ridiculous!' she'd expostulated, taken aback by the sudden vehemence. 'This is only a little test to show you what to revise if you want to do well in the end-of-term exams!'

It was no good and the entire class had stormed out of the room.

The look of sheer terror in their eyes was bewildering. They really did seem to think that numbers scribbled on a piece of paper had a magical power over them.

Later Bill Matthews, the headmaster, had told her never to give them bad marks because it 'upset them so'.

A year afterwards there had been that night-time incident. Lawrence was at a party down at the Club and had left her to do his night duty for him. (During their second year at the school this had become an increasingly frequent state of affairs.) Sometime after midnight she had been woken by a delegation from one of the boys' dormitories.

'You must come quickly. Ojara is dead!'

'Dead?'

'Yes, he is dead and the Acholi boys are going to kill the Langi boys who have killed him!'

Horrified, she had rushed over to the dormitory to find it in an uproar. A crowd of bare-chested and sweating youths was milling round the bed on which the boy, Ojara, lay naked and breathing heavily with his eyes wide open and staring in front of him. Enormously relieved to find him actually alive, she had tried to talk to him.

'Ojara, what's the matter? Do you need a doctor?'

'I am dead.'

'But you are *not* dead. You are talking to me.'

'I am dead.'

One of the bystanders had explained the situation. Ojara was an Acholi from the north of Uganda and he'd knocked a boy from the Langi tribe down in a fight. Swearing revenge, the Langi boy had gone to a local witchdoctor and paid him to put a curse on Ojara.

'If the curse is not lifted, Ojara will die and then we Acholi boys will attack and kill the Langi boys...'

The sight of that seething mob of bare-chested youths, brandishing sticks and machetes, sweat glistening on their quivering bodies, had appalled her. It was mad, crazy. These were not the polite and scholarly young students that she'd been teaching that very afternoon. They were something else.

Out of sheer desperation she'd asked one of the boys to take her to the witch doctor. After a long haggle with the old man, she'd paid him fifteen English pounds to lift the curse. Peace had suddenly returned to the dormitory, but not to Dorothy. As she'd watched the wizened old charlatan cavorting round in his grotesque costume – all rattling bones and repulsive dangling things which seemed to be bits of a long-dead monkey – mumbling and grunting away to himself, she'd noticed with a bewildered alarm how the students seemed to take the whole grotesque charade totally seriously. She'd glimpsed something dark and frightening lurking beneath their seemingly sophisticated exterior.

And then there had been that leprosy clinic business. The missionary society ran a leprosy clinic in the slums of Kampala. As part of their training in Christian duty, the senior pupils would help out. One day all the medicines and much of the surgical equipment disappeared. It had eventually transpired that the head boy and the senior prefects had stolen it all and sold it in the marketplace as a cure for sexual inadequacy. With the proceeds they had had a night of whoring in Kampala and had then set up a highly profitable brothel in one of the school dormitories. The whole incident had been hushed up and the perpetrators had gone unpunished.

Bleak Realities

These young people, Dorothy decided, were not the altruistic Christian scholars that her colleagues seemed to think they were. They were uprooted and confused beings, half in ancient Africa and half in modern Europe, suspended in a limbo and prey to all sorts of wild and irrational impulses. Education was not valued for itself. Physics, biology, geography ... it did not matter what you studied. It was a magic pill which got you a comfortable job in Kampala. Even tiddlywinks would do if it helped you get that office job. Then you had to distribute largesse to the extended family who had clubbed together to pay for you to go to school – get them shirts, jeans, televisions, motor cars and even jobs in your office. Christianity was just another form of magic – OK if it got you the goodies that you wanted, but to be discarded if it didn't.

By the end of three years she had come to the conclusion that Apollo Kagwa School was little more than a racket – a cushy number for the expatriate staff and an avenue to loot for the pupils. Moreover, it was sitting on the top of a volcano that was going to erupt – and sooner rather than later.

The successful pupils would fill up the available jobs in the civil service and milk it dry of all potential loot. The cornucopia of goodies would dry up. The tribes excluded from the bonanza would become resentful and rebel... And what about that seething sewer of deprivation and discontent at the bottom of the hill? How long before it erupted? Those frustrated and restless wannabes wouldn't be content just to gaze for ever at the riches around them, would they? Then what? A bloodbath. The frenzied, wild-eyed and hate-filled fury of those Acholi and Langi pupils in the dormitory was a preview of what could happen.

Already there were riots in upcountry towns, unexplained killings in Kampala and rumours of unrest in the army. It was like being in a luxury car hurtling downhill with no brakes.

Christians: Saved and Unsaved...

Eventually she'd confronted Lawrence with her misgivings.

As Christian missionaries, shouldn't they really be working among the slum children who lived in the shanties at the bottom of the hill? Their present luxurious lifestyle was hardly what Mary Slessor would have called missionary work, was it?

But to her dismay she got nowhere. Over the past three years Lawrence had changed. He'd always been inclined to be a bit dogmatic and to have difficulty in admitting that he could ever be wrong about anything. But this had been a minor blemish, barely noticeable in the warm glow of his generosity of spirit and infectious idealism.

Yet, here in Uganda, the lavish expatriate lifestyle had turned his head. What had once been an irritating foible had mushroomed out into a crass and self-deceiving complacency. The former idealism had all but disappeared. He positively wallowed in the Apollo Kagwa scene. He was convinced that he was a brilliant teacher at the very cutting edge of Ugandan growth and development and that everything was as totally right as it could possibly be. The slums at the bottom of the hill, the pupils in the up-country schools who couldn't cope with the academic curriculum? Irrelevant. Let them wallow in their own mess! He had more important things to do than to waste time on inadequates. God had given him this task to do. Didn't she realise that?

Didn't she know that he was *saved*? Why the proof of the pudding was in the eating! The comfortable houses, the servants, the brilliant exam results, the safaris, the car, the parties at the Club: these were a *blessing* bestowed on him by God! If she couldn't see it, it was because, unlike him, she was not saved!

She'd listened to the outburst aghast. She'd always been a bit worried about his rather simplistic religion and his tendency to incorporate God into his own ego, but this was something different. An irritating little nettle had ballooned out into a whole jungle.

'Just an emotional woman...'

Further problems had arisen. She had discovered that, for some complex medical reason, she was unable to have children. It was a devastating blow which had shattered all her future plans and aspirations. What had made it especially unbearable was Lawrence's scarcely concealed assumption that it was God punishing her for her lack of proper Christian faith.

Then she had learned that he was having a steamy love affair with Marion MacFarlane, a pretty and vivacious American Peace Corps volunteer who taught English at the school. She was bewildered and bitterly hurt by this infidelity – so utterly out of character with the Lawrence she'd married four years ago.

She'd confronted him. Fiercely reproachful, she'd poured out her soul in a venomous torrent – her frustrations, her anger at his habit of continually getting her to do his night duty while he enjoyed himself down at the Club, her conscience about the neglected slum at the bottom of the hill, her fears for the future of Uganda, her anguish about her inability to have children...

'And I might at least have been spared Marion MacFarlane!' she'd yelled at him.

He'd remained unmoved. In a calm and smug voice he'd told her that it was all God's doing. God had obviously wanted him to have children and had directed him towards a new wife who could provide them for him.

'You stuck-up, self-righteous prig!' she'd cried.

'Say what you like,' he'd retorted, 'it doesn't bother me. You're just an emotional woman.'

'Just an emotional woman': that hurt.

Wastelands, Golden Bubbles and Frustrations

Returning from Uganda on leave, they'd divorced. He'd returned to Uganda and had gone out of her life.

She was left with a great chasm in her being. All those radiant and intoxicating dreams of four years ago had dissolved, leaving a dreary nothingness. Deep down, under layers of bitterness and hurt, she still loved Lawrence as passionately as ever.

At times she would let herself believe that the divorce had never happened and that he was still faithful. She would even search the morning post for the longed-for letter of reconciliation which in those moods she confidently expected. But it never came – as, in her sane and analytical moments, she knew it wouldn't.

Meanwhile, it was back to East Snape. Domestic duty called. Both her parents were ailing and needed her help. So it was back to mundanity with a vengeance – into an enclosed world of emptying bedpans, changing sheets, washing pyjamas, visits to the doctor, arranging visits from the district nurse ... all in the colourless wastes of a run-down council estate. Inundated by disappointment and drabness, the missionary idealism had withered away.

After a couple of years both her parents had passed away and had been laid to rest, side by side in the ugly little cemetery that surrounded the dreary and ill-attended parish church.

Alone in the world, and desperately short of money, she got a residential job in a classy prep school in Surrey. It was easy work, pleasant even. The surroundings were agreeable, the accommodation good, the children on the whole docile, polite and willing, and the pay good. But it wasn't really her scene. It was a gorgeous upper-class bubble, oblivious of the outside world. Prep school, Common Entrance, scholarships to Rugby and Harrow, Oxford and Cambridge, that was the universe. The state system, secondary modern schools, grammar schools, comprehensive schools, deprived areas ... all that just didn't exist.

Slowly the old missionary idealism had revived. She wanted to go where she was really needed, to improve the lives of her charges, to alter their lives for the better. These rich and favoured children didn't really need her.

So she got a job in a comprehensive in a run-down part of Sunderland – only to be frustrated once more.

Officially the youngsters were 'deprived'. But what were they deprived of? Most of them seemed content with their lot. They had streets to roam in, fags to smoke, beer to drink – and they could always find some kind of a job at the end of it all. They didn't need to be civilised and neither did they want to be. They didn't need teachers like her.

A Bold New Educational Initiative?

Then she'd heard about the new Greenhill comprehensive in the west end of Boldonbridge.

Billed as a bold new 'initiative' that would eradicate destructive class attitudes, correct age-long educational wrong-headedness and employ the very latest pedagogic techniques to promote 'civilised values', it seemed to fulfil all her yearnings. Vigorously backed by the Education Department of Boldonbridge University and the brainchild of no less a person than Dr Giles Denby, a leading social historian, it would also propel her on to the very cutting edge of educational development. She applied for an advertised post and was flattered and gratified at how readily she'd been accepted.

But a few weeks soon cured her of any illusions. In that part of Boldonbridge the old working class had disintegrated and had been replaced by a shifting population of problem families, down-and-outs, alcoholics and criminal gangs. Added to which, she discovered that the other local schools had used Greenhill's foundation as an opportunity to divest themselves of all their nutters and deadbeats. What was supposed to be a 'flagship school' was in reality a dustbin for problems and head cases.

Structure, discipline, order and, yes, good solid Christian values to curb their anarchic impulses were what these young tearaways needed. What they most emphatically did *not* need was child-centred education, free expression, a lack of formal discipline, project-based learning and 'interdisciplinary enquiry' which was what – in *theory*! – they were getting. Nor, especially, did they need that constant drip, drip, drip of synthetic class hate. It only provided them with a cop-out which prevented them from facing up to their real problems.

And, as for the worthy notion of letting the senior pupils manage the school discipline... Even at the best of times, you had to watch adolescents like an eagle. They were unformed and impulsive creatures. All too often a little authority could be an excuse for bullying and exploitation. It might have worked with Thomas Arnold back in the nineteenth century – though she personally doubted it! – but here it was downright calamitous.

Before long it was clear to her that the teachers did not control the place. It had been taken over by teenage gangs, themselves exploited by outside criminals. Youngsters were being used to tout drugs, case joints for future burglaries and steal cars. There were prostitution rackets and even strong hints of a paedophile racket in which girls – and boys! – were rented out to weirdoes who could then be blackmailed.

Her old insight revived. To her, the whole thing – and, indeed, much of the current educational scene – was like the Gerasene Swine rushing blindly over a cliff. Like Cassandra in ancient Troy, she began to see gloomy visions of the future. With increased competition from the burgeoning economies of Germany and Japan the local industries would collapse. The semi-literate and undisciplined products of this school – and of other schools like it – would be unable to cope with the new and harsher world that was coming into being. Unemployed and unemployable, they could only become the sidekicks and fall guys of criminal gangs.

It would be Uganda all over again. But not a spectacular descent into war and massacre, but a slow and squalid slither into decay – a morass of crumbling houses, uncollected rubbish and underage sex.

The crazy thing was that the academics at the university just could not see it. Dr Denby, for all his brilliant analytical mind, actually thought that Greenhill School represented *progress*! How could clever people be such fools? It bewildered and angered her. It was Lawrence all over again.

But in all this mess there were youngsters who desperately needed help. Those who wanted to learn, but were prevented from doing so. Those whose finer feelings were being bashed out of them. Those who were too weak to hit back at the bullies who made their lives a misery.

A Mission at Last...

So the idea had come.

She would rescue these needy youngsters. Here, at last, was her true mission! She would start her own school. It would be a lifeboat which would rescue the floundering, save the bullied, and provide an escape route for anxious parents appalled by the state schools on offer, but unable to afford the horrendous expense of private education.

There would be small classes so that individuals would not be lost in an amorphous crowd. Borderline cases, teetering on the brink of yobbery, would be removed from an environment which reinforced their loutish tendencies and immersed in one that reinforced their better side. There would be formal lessons to inculcate the basics, but plenty of opportunities to develop creativity through project work as well. The curriculum would be tailored to suit the abilities of the pupils – not just academic stuff, but workshops, art rooms and cookery as well. She was a great admirer of Kurt Hahn and the Outward Bound ideal and so there would be lots of extracurricular education, too. To give her charges pride, a feeling of belonging and a sense of identity and discipline, she would revert to the discredited idea of a school uniform. Underpinning the whole structure would be the Christian faith.

It was heady, liberating stuff... So Beaconsfield School had been born.

At long last the missionary had found a mission.

A Morass of Practicalities

But lofty ideals had soon been submerged in a morass of practicalities.

Indeed, had she known just what would be involved in getting things going Dorothy might never have even started the venture. It took all her persuasive skills to get the council to back the project as a remedial school for needy pupils. Some councillors – the Tories, especially – were surprisingly enthusiastic, but she was taken aback by the sheer venomous hostility of others. The virulent rancour of the Boldonbridge University Education Department – and of Dr Denby in particular – bewildered her. 'Exploiting the working class and making money out of their gullibility'? It was *they* who were exploiting the working class and their gullibility, they with their fat salaries and the best-selling paperbacks that they kept on writing. They with their refusal to abandon their self-serving fantasies. Not her. She was trying to *help* the working class. And she wouldn't be earning a quarter of Dr Denby's salary.

Eventually she'd won through – though she'd felt like a squeezed lemon afterwards. The opposition, far from being beaten, however, had simply made a tactical withdrawal and was regrouping for a counter-attack.

Fortunately, she'd managed to get the backing of some local industrialists and businessmen and to even bring some of them on to the board of governors. The Bishop of Boldonbridge, a vast, hirsute and terrifying man, had agreed to be its chairman. Then – a shot out of the blue, manna from heaven, almost! – a distant aunt of whom she'd never even heard, let alone met, died and left her a £20,000 legacy. (A 'blessing' from heaven, as Lawrence would have had it? Possibly, but you had to be very careful about bringing God into things!)

Next, she'd had to find a suitable building. Eventually, she'd located a nineteenth-century terrace house, named 'Beaconsfield House' for some abstruse historical reason. In a 'decayed gentry' part of Moorside, it was cheap but in a dreadful state of disrepair. That led her into the jungle of bank loans, mortgages, leaky roofs, toilet facilities, science labs, workshops and art rooms...

Teachers...

Then there had been staffing problems.

If the school was to have any credibility, she had to get properly qualified teachers, but few of these wanted to risk a small, insecure semi-private school. Fewer still shared her missionary zeal. Too many applicants were after a cushy nine-to-four number with long holidays.

Early on she'd had a crisis. Mr Mattingly had seemed to be a real find, never complaining about hours and duties and always willing to help out with the boring jobs like supervising changing and showering after games. Then one day, in the course of a conversation, a boy had casually mentioned that Mr Mattingly always insisted on washing *his* crotch and not those of other boys. Had he got an infection down there which needed to be seen by a doctor? A check revealed that old Mattingly had a string of convictions for molesting small boys. He'd had to go and the whole affair had been hushed up. Now, at last, she had understood why that leprosy clinic business at Apollo Kagwa School had been hushed up. Truth was a luxury that insecure institutions could not always afford.

Also, she'd had to learn how to go against her inclinations and be ruthless. Old Mr Timms was a lovely man, a delightful old bean, but since he couldn't control a dead sheep, she just couldn't afford to keep him. Survival had to come first.

But gradually she'd managed to get a workable team together, the backbone of which was Roderick Meakin, a gnarled old veteran of the chalk face who seemed to have seen it all and survived it all.

... Pupils

And, of course, there were the pupils...

She'd started off with a handful of refugees from Greenhill, but, as word had got round of her competence, more began to roll in from other schools. Most were pretty normal, others were dyslexics, several had been sent along to keep them away from criminal influences, a few were deadbeats...

It was all boys. She'd originally envisaged a mixed school. But with so many unstable repair cases coming into her school, she'd had second thoughts. Girls could be a terrible distraction for adolescents. She remembered only too well the mayhem of Greenhill – those lustful stares in the classroom, the endless copulation in the toilets and classroom stock cupboards. No, she had decided, get the place up and running, first, and then think about bringing in girls.

So, after a few years, the school was just about floating. She had good staff and some quite promising pupils. Bill Bleeson, her head boy, was a good-hearted lad, but in no way a whizz kid and certainly not an intellectual.

Stormy Weather Ahead

Yet there were ominous clouds looming on the horizon.

'This Christian remedial stuff is all very well,' declared a local industrialist at a meeting of the governing body, 'very praiseworthy and all that, but isn't it time you produced some real *results*? I mean how about some good exam results? Some success on the games field? That sort of thing. After all, that's what the council is paying for.'

'Yes,' added the bishop, pitching in with one of his withering glares, 'people are starting to say that Beaconsfield is the local "dustbin school" – you know, a cosy little nook where all the deadbeats of the city can sleep, undisturbed. They want value for money...'

'Good exam results', 'success on the games field', success all round? Fine! But just how was she supposed to achieve it with the sort of pupils she had? None of these able and dynamic men seemed to understand the realities of teaching. The crude fact was that without a modicum of ability no amount of exhortations and 'insistence on high standards' could ever achieve the sort of 'success' these people had in mind. They seemed to think that she could just wave a wand. But genetic facts were genetic facts. As a biology teacher, she knew this, even if they didn't.

Yes, she needed some tangible success that the outside world would understand. But where to find the sort of pupils who could achieve it?

A Big Educational Challenge

Recently, however, she'd acquired a pupil who might just save the situation.

He was a 'big challenge' in the guise of a dark-haired, little ferret of a boy, named Robert Napier. With an absentee father, a drug-addicted mother and a brother in prison for 'grievous bodily harm', his background was about as bad as it could be.

Always in trouble, continually truanting and with a string of convictions behind him, the Social Services had turned to her. The boy was intelligent and had potential, but all this would go to waste if he were not removed from his present criminal environment and placed in a totally different one – an environment which provided order, discipline and solid ethical values. Could *she* turn him round?

Dorothy had been both flattered and slightly alarmed at the request. If she *could* salvage this lost soul, what a feather it would be in her cap! What vindication! But, then, a hardened young psychopath could equally well destroy her fragile school.

Yet the first signs had been encouraging. Far from being the surly lout that she'd been dreading, the boy was friendly and, with his impish grin and cheerful patter, even charming. He didn't disrupt the lessons, worked hard and actually came top in Maths and Science. He clearly *was* intelligent. Briggs, the PE teacher, spoke highly of him: 'He's a promising rugby player and could go far...'

Clearly, there was something to young Robert. But precisely *what*? That was the question.

Soon teachers began to report a changed atmosphere in Form One. A former spontaneous friendliness had somehow cooled. 'It's that new boy, Robert,' a boy had confided to old Meakin. 'He's so well ... strange!'

Rumours grew up around him. A boy came to Dorothy and said

that he was extorting money from his classmates. She made enquiries, but got nowhere. Later the same boy said that he'd misunderstood the situation and that young Robert hadn't been extorting money, after all. Then there were tales of unseemly 'goings on' in the toilets. 'That Robert, Miss, he's proper dirty him! Mind, all kids is dirty like, but well ... he's *filthy*!' She'd dismissed this as part of a schoolboy feud.

And then there was that business of Mickey Stuart. Mickey was a great, fat lump of lard who'd been bullied unmercifully at St Oswald's – having had at least ten different kinds of stuffing kicked out of him – and had been sent to Beaconsfield by the local authority. For the first week he'd charged round the school bashing up the smaller boys in an orgy of gratuitous thuggery, clearly relishing the thrill of doing to others what had been done to him. All he seemed to understand was violence. Exhortations and appeals to Christian ethics got nowhere. It was only an 'accidental collision' with Meakin that had eventually put a stop to his rampageous career.

Thereafter he had teamed up with young Robert. The two seemed inseparable. One day a worried Bill Bleeson had told her that he was 'Robert's slave' and that whenever Robert said, 'Owly, do your trick!' he would drop his pants and cavort round in an obscene way.

Robert was duly hauled in and confronted with all this. He denied it vigorously: 'That's disgustin', Miss! It's them other kids like! They's pickin' on us jus' cos me brother's inside like an' I ain't got no proper dad, yer knaa!'

Tears trickled: 'Don't be sendin' us away, Miss! I mean you's me proper mum, like...'

That struck a deep chord within Dorothy. So she *was* succeeding, her mission *was* bearing fruit... More than that, here, perhaps, was the child she'd always wanted. Her very own child who needed her and loved her... Forgetting her 'stern headmistress' role, she'd hugged and kissed him.

A Big Success – or Not?

Robert Napier was regularly discussed at staff meetings.

'He's our big success,' declared Briggs. 'He'll go far, that one ... and, can I just say that he's our real purpose, which is sorting out deprived working-class kids. That's what we're here for, isn't it, Mrs Watson?'

But old Meakin wasn't quite so sure: '...I wouldn't count your chickens before they're hatched. Be careful of that young man. There could be a lot more in him than we can see...'

So the jury was out. Dorothy desperately wanted to believe that young Robert was a good-hearted lad who would come round and earn her plaudits – perhaps, even become her own adopted son, that child for which she secretly longed. Yet, deep down, she wasn't too sure. The 'hard-headed professional' was at odds with the 'emotional woman'.

A Real Asset – or Not?

Now she'd got John Denby. A boy from his background could be a real asset – perhaps, even that role model who would inject a bit of vim into her sluggish clientele. (She knew, of course, that she shouldn't chase after clever pupils. That went against her stated principles: 'The whole need not a physician, but they that are sick.' But in this imperfect world you had to survive – and that meant making compromises.)

The next morning the 'hard-headed professional' got a grip on the 'emotional woman'. She'd better not start building castles in the air. Young Denby could easily turn out to be yet another deadbeat: after all, his own father had said that he was dim and lacked personality – and fathers usually spoke well of their offspring. So she did a little research via the telephone.

She eventually managed to get through to Rickerby Hall: 'John Denby? ... Oh, a very average boy! Perfectly normal... Nice little chap... Definitely not brilliant, though...'

Rickerby Hall, she knew, was one of those golden bubble places that sent pupils to Eton and Winchester. 'Average' there meant pretty bright by normal standards, genius by Greenwood standards. There were possibilities here.

But taking a kid from that sheltered little nirvana of a place and dropping him into the maelstrom of Greenhill! Mad! Loony! Whatever you wanted to call it! No wonder he 'couldn't cope'. It was a wonder that he was still sane! Highly intelligent people could be so blindly stupid.

25

'John, we're going to talk about school...'

On Friday morning Giles climbed up to the attic.

'John, we're going to talk about school...'

Immediately, the boy curled up into a tight little ball on his bed. The foetal position. Wasn't there a name for this sort of thing? Arrested developmental regression? Infantile response syndrome? Not that it mattered. Bloody pathetic was what it really was. A good boot up the back end would soon sort it out. But, of course, you couldn't do that... at least not until the Social Services had been and gone... (Meanwhile, a thought struck him: 'The strength of weakness'? Wouldn't that be a good essay to give his third-year honours students?) So it had to be grit your teeth, swallow your vomit and get stuck into the 'caring parent' role.

'There's no need for that, John. You're not going back to Greenhill. I've got you into a new and much easier school.'

Immediately, the little ball unwound itself and the pouty face dissolved into a broad grin.

'Thanks, Dad – I mean, Giles! Cor, thanks a bomb!'

To Giles' intense embarrassment, the boy embraced and kissed him. (Christ! How long was he going to have to put up with this sort of thing?)

'All right! All right!' he half snapped, 'Don't overdo it! Now this afternoon Mary is going to take you down to Miles & Eden in Shaftsbury Street to get your school uniform.'

A Serious Question of Ideology and Revolutionary Commitment

But Mary wouldn't take him. 'FUCKING WELL WOULDN'T' in fact.

It was a serious question of ideology and revolutionary commitment.

230

'Uniform!' she exclaimed, 'UNIFORM? What does a place like Beaconsfield needs a uniform for? You tell me!'

She fixed Giles with the 'analytical stare': 'It's just another way of screwing money out of gullible parents, isn't it?' she added.

'Exactly!' Giles could hardly deny it: it was what he had been saying for the past ten years.

'Typical private education, isn't it? A con trick. Dress 'em up all smart and people'll think they are something better than they are...'

'Exactly.'

'Disguise the fact that the so-called school is a dustbin. Put your garbage into a pretty box so that idiots will think it smells good...'

'Exactly.' (God all bloody mighty, how *many* times had he heard this rant? She was merely repeating, almost verbatim, what he'd said to the Social and Political Awareness Group back in 1979. She had a good memory: he had to give her that.)

'If a proper school like Greenhill doesn't need a uniform, then why does a tin-pot con trick like Beaconsfield have to have one? You tell me.'

'You *know* why,' he sighed wearily.

'Because it *is* a con trick. Greenhill's a *real* school, working in harness with the Zeitgeist. It doesn't need to dress its students up in a petty-bourgeois costume to prove itself. It can stand on its own true socialist principles...'

'You're absolutely right!'

The 'analytical stare' was cranked up into cosmic radiation: 'Then *why* are we sending his nibs to Beaconsfield?'

'Because we've got to...'

'Got to? GOT TO? Got to dress that little twerp up in a silly red blazer and whatnot? Just to make him think that he's better than he is? Bloody hell, he's no better than the other kids round here. Worse. FAR worse! Have you seen the state of his room?'

'Darling, we've been through all this before! Look, we've got the Social Services coming round any day now. Oh, for Christ's sake, can't you bloody well SEE!'

How many times over the past day or two had they chewed this particular rag? Mary could be so bloody obtuse. She insisted on seeing everything in crude black-and-white terms, whereas he, at any rate, was moving on. That little virus which had started to nibble away at the certainties of his younger days was getting bigger. It had made a little hole in the wall at the top of the neat and orderly intellectual staircase that he had been climbing. Through that minute orifice he could dimly discern an alarmingly convoluted landscape of a quite unexpected complexity – worthy, indeed, of a mathematical fractal.

Yes, *he* could see this, even if she couldn't. So, perhaps it was time to get himself another and more intelligent partner?

In the end it was Giles who had to take the kid down to Miles & Eden to get his school uniform.

Eating Shit

'Eating shit' was the best way to describe the business.

Shaftsbury Street was bad enough. It was a monument to a temporary economic system that had been overtaken by history. As such, it represented everything that was bogus and deceitful about nineteenth-century capitalism. The curve of the street with its pseudo-classical buildings was pompous, reactionary and architecturally dishonest, little more than a vulgar stage set. It arrogantly disguised the mid-Victorian exploitation of the working class under a transparent veneer of pseudo-sophisticated paternalism. It was named after a feudal aristocrat who'd helped to stifle a possible revolution by introducing a few minor improvements in working conditions. This had merely let his upper-class allies continue their exploitation of the proletariat under a fig leaf of Christian so-called 'charity'. Giles had repeatedly called for the council to have it demolished and replaced with buildings properly in harmony with the late twentieth-century Zeitgeist.

Miles & Eden was even worse. 'Gentlemen's Outfitters' in the 1980s, for Christ's sake! Inside it was all brown panelled walls and classical mouldings on the ceiling (had they never heard of Mies van der Rohe?), brown carpets and obsequious old flunkies fawning on you. It was like one of those reconstructed 'Georgian' or 'Medieval' rooms they would keep installing in museums in an attempt to bring history down to the level of the less intelligent. It was a con shop, designed to give petty-bourgeois flea brains the illusion that they belonged to the landed gentry. And, as for the whole school uniform racket, any sentient being with a modicum of intelligence *knew* that it was one big swindle designed to massage the egos of middle-class thicks who didn't know their place. In the interests of elementary mental hygiene Miles & Eden would have to be closed down – and the sooner the better!

So as he went in, Giles had to make a big effort to control his nausea. An elderly man, all shiny and greasy with his pinstripe suit and gleaming bald head minced up to John. 'And is this the young gentleman in question?' he cooed in a glutinously plummy accent.

'Yes,' replied John in that gut-wrenching tinkle-bell voice of his, 'I'm going to Beaconsfield School and I'll have to look my best.'

'Of course you will, young Sir. Now come this way.'

Giles observed the ensuing minuet with academic distain. How that kid ponced around, showing off and preening himself in front of the mirror as he tried on, first, this blazer and then that pair of long grey trousers! 'No, this one's a bit tight under the armpits... I think these trouser legs are a bit long...' The way he played up to that old queer's camping!

When it was all finally finished, the parcels wrapped up and the cheque signed and delivered, he nearly died of embarrassment when the kid embraced him: 'Thanks, Dad, I mean Giles, cor thanks! I'm so grateful...'

He'd suspected it all along and now he knew. This boy was a poof – it stuck out a mile! In a previous age he would have been one of the Emperor Tiberius' 'minnows' in that pool on Capri or a catamite in some Ottoman harem. Of course, he didn't object to homosexuality as such. How could he? Free love. The sexual revolution. Liberation from bourgeois repressions ... you couldn't quarrel with that. That was Ego speaking. Deep down, Id, his real self, despised homosexuals. Inadequates. Mutations. Best if they could be phased out, just as the Nazis had advocated. In fact, the Nazis weren't wholly bad. They did have some sound ideas. Pity they had to be fascists.

26

'Depart from me ye cursed...'

Monday morning came.

The Resurrection. John got up and eyed his new uniform. Bit by precious bit, it went on: the white shirt, the red-and-white striped tie, the long grey trousers – so much more grown up than the baby shorts you had to wear at Rickerby Hall! – and, finally, the icing on the cake, the bright-red blazer with its black, white and gold badge. This was the old John again, the good boy who'd been so brave in that Second XV rugby match at Rickerby Hall. The 'snobby liddell git' of Greenhill who'd cried when he was 'chinned off a lass'? That was buried under the nasty jeans and dirty sweater that Mary said she was taking to the laundry.

Resplendent, he climbed down to the ground floor.

'Giles, I'm ready for school now.'

Giles looked up from the pile of papers on his table.

'All right, off you go.'

'But, aren't you going to take me?'

'No, John, I'm too busy. You're not a baby. You can get there yourself.'

'But where do I go? What do I do?'

'Oh for Christ's sake! Just go up to Broadfell Road and get bus number 30. Then get off at Prince Consort Park. It's not far from there.'

'But...?' His newfound confidence was starting to evaporate with this unexpected setback.

'Look, here's a map with the school marked on it...'

Giles handed him the Beaconsfield prospectus which had just arrived that morning and had a map on the back cover to show prospective parents where to go. With that he got up, went out into the garage and drove off in the van.

Bemused and disappointed, John went out into the cold, grey and desolate world outside.

Feeling rather irritated at the way in which the drizzle was wetting his beautiful new blazer, he went up the hill, picking his way over the layers of rubbish that was a substitute for vegetation in this place. Suddenly, somewhere in the middle of his head, a small black dot seemed to appear – like that famous cloud 'no bigger than a man's hand' in the Old Testament story of Elijah and the prophets of Baal. Was he *really* the old John of Rickerby Hall, brought back to life again like Lazarus in the Bible? More likely he was still that 'snobby liddell git' of Greenhill School 'what were chinned off a lass' and who'd thoroughly deserved it when they'd done *that* to him. Just what was waiting for him at Beaconsfield School? Probably discovery. They'd soon learn what his classmates had done to him at Greenhill – if they didn't know already! They, too, would punish him for being weak and pathetic. Eternal punishment. That was his lot. 'Depart from me, ye accursed!'

The black cloud of fear grew. Almost on cue, he noticed a gaggle of youths blocking the pavement. They were big, sweaty, unkempt and muscular – a pack of predatory wolves seemingly ready to tear him to pieces. Instinctively, he turned aside and started to cross the road.

'WEE'S THE FUCKIN' HOM THEN?' a massive Geordie voice boomed out.

'LIDDELL LORD FUKIN' FAUNTERLOY!' yelled another.

A polystyrene packet of half-eaten chips exploded against the back of his head. The Greenhill terror was on him again. The question was answered: he *was* a 'snobby liddell git' and he had to run for his life. Run, run, run, take cover in a desperate attempt to preserve your squalid little self!

He dashed back down the hill and dived frantically into a side alley... God, they were *still* following him! What were they going to do to him when they caught him?

Run, run, run, splutter, gasp! ... Away down the back alley that stretched behind Gloucester Road. Then, oh wondrous relief! Oh wondrous salvation! The garage door of Number 14 had been left open. He dived into the black haven and slammed the door shut, just as a large missile exploded against it. Saved. 'FUCKING POOF!' a colossal voice roared out.

The back door had, also, been left open and so he could slip in, unnoticed by Mary who was sprawled on one of the living-room couches smoking a cigarette with a funny smell. It was up to his room, up to safety and to the bliss of being able to eat wine gums and play with his trains.

Why leave it? Why *ever* leave it? School kids were dangerous animals who were out to get you. You were weak and pathetic – always would be and always would be punished for it. So stay here and live for the moment.

What Do You Do with Inadequates?

In the evening Giles returned from the university, laden as always with work. But no sooner had he pulled the papers out of his briefcase and started on the Liverpool dock strike of 1943 than the telephone rang.

'...This is Mrs Watson of Beaconsfield School. You said your son, John, was joining us today, but we haven't seen him...'

'Haven't seen him? But you *must* have done. He set off for school at eight o'clock!'

'No, we haven't seen him.'

Panic! The carefully constructed house of cards tumbling down! Christ, the little toad's done another runner! The Social Services! In his alarm he could almost see Merrins' fat, porcine face smirking with delight!

In desperation, Giles rushed up to the attic.

Then... Salvation! Immense relief of the kind you get when a painful boil is lanced. There was John sitting on the floor playing with his trains. Relief was quickly followed by boiling rage and he let out a stentorian bellow: 'JOHN, YOU WERE SUPPOSED TO BE AT SCHOOL TODAY!'

The little elf made no reply. Instead, he immediately curled up into the time-honoured foetal position. (Wild exasperation. Bloody hell, not *this* again!) 'JOHN! I AM TALKING TO YOU!'

No response. Now what? Pick the little sod up and belt him over the earhole? The sensible solution. Yes, but that would leave a mark for the Social Services to see. Lay him over your knee and slap him hard across the back end? But, then he'd go and tell Merrins that you'd been fondling his bum... No, hold yourself in check. Think tactically. Remember that he's as soft as shit. Work on that. Soft-soap him. Smother him in sugary lather.

So a big, creaky smile and a soft 'caring' voice: 'Now look, John, I've been very nice to you. I've got you into a new school – and it's taken a lot of doing I can tell you! – and I've spent a heap of money on a lovely new school uniform for you. Couldn't you just show a little gratitude in return? Just a little?'

As expected it worked. After a while the little ball uncoiled itself and began to cry: 'I'm sorry, Giles, I'm so sorry! I'm so ashamed! You see, I'm so frightened... I mean why do I have to go to school? School's horrible. Why can't I just stay here?...' Sniffle! Sniffle!

Giles looked on in exasperation and embarrassment. This was so *pathetic*!

What *were* you supposed to do with inadequates? Hitler knew. So did Stalin. But, unfortunately, you couldn't get away with rational solutions in this irrational petty-bourgeois society. You just had to play along with the charade of being 'caring' and try to talk them round. So, with a great effort of will, he put on what he hoped sounded like a 'calm and compassionate' voice:

'Now, listen to me, young man, you must try to understand reality. In this country everybody between the ages of five and sixteen *must* go to school. If you refuse to go to school, the truancy officer will come along with some policemen and *take* you, not to Beaconsfield, but to Greenhill which is your *real* school, the one in which you have been registered. There's nothing I can do about it. Now do you want that to happen?' (It was all a load of rubbish, of course, made up on the spot. But this little half-wit didn't know the law and would swallow it – which, of course, he duly did.)

'All right. I'll go... But...'

'No *buts*, John!'

The 'calm and compassionate' voice became harsher. It was time to put a needle into the treacle, a long and sharp needle: 'Tomorrow morning I am going to *take* you to Beaconsfield School, myself whether you like it or not. By force, if necessary. The law says that I am allowed to use reasonable force to restrain you if I see you doing something illegal like refusing to go to school. So you either come to Beaconsfield with me or the police will come and take you back to Greenhill. Is that clear?' (More hastily invented garbage for the half-wit to chew over in the night!)

With that, Giles went back down the ladders. As a precaution, he locked all the doors and pocketed the keys. All of which caused a big row later that night when Mary returned from her Women's Feminist Awareness Action Group without her key and in a state which she described as 'enhancedly and perceptively super-aware'.

ARTHUR CLIFFORD

'Can't go to school...'

John didn't sleep much that night.

When he finally dropped off he awoke quickly to find that he'd wet the bed again. Shame, anguish, disgust and despair! He wasn't just bad he was awful! Always letting Giles down. Why, oh why, couldn't he be normal? He began to cry.

Slowly the skylight above his bed turned from black to grey. The Day of Judgement was at hand. Like a zombie he climbed into his school uniform. But why bother to smarten yourself up? When he got to Beaconsfield the kids would just rip everything to bits, punch him, kick him and probably strip him naked. A dreadful, but thoroughly deserved humiliation, like Guy Fawkes being hanged, drawn and quartered at Tyburn before a jeering mob.

He stumbled down to the bathroom and began to clean his teeth. Just then his insides went crazy – everything inside him from his neck down to his waist seemed suddenly to melt into a hot, seething liquid. He only just managed to disrobe before it all exploded out – blood, too: *that* was still there...

For a long time he just sat there. He was full of fear again, that awful, numbing fear which dissolved your muscles, your bones and your very mind and turned you into a heap of squelchy jelly. It was like being ill, something you could do nothing about. Suddenly he understood how those wretched soldiers in World War I must have felt when they were ordered to climb out of their trench and attack the enemy and found that their fear-absorbed bodies just couldn't do it.

There was no way he could go to school that day. His body wouldn't let him.

'Don't try to escape because you can't'

Down on the ground floor Giles was losing patience. He had a lecture at nine o'clock and wanted to get started.

'John!' he called, 'JOHN! COME ON! It's time to go!'

No reply. Dead silence. What the hell was the little creep getting up to now? Passive resistance? Or was it guerrilla war again?

Exasperated, he climbed up to the attic only to find that he wasn't there. There was no way he could have got out of the skylight and be hiding on the roof, so he went down to the landing again where he noticed that the bathroom door was locked. Bloody hell! Had he gone and barricaded himself in the bog? So, now what? Break the door down and drag him out? ... But, burst into the toilet while the kid was using it? Merrins would just *eat* that!

Instead, he banged on the door: 'John, I know you're in there. Now come on out. It's time to go.'

'I can't. I won't.'

Impasse. Exasperation. The same old ludicrous situation of a big, strong man being defied by a weedy little eleven-year-old. Even sillier was the fact that he was actually scared of the little scrap. If it wanted to, it could make a meal of this situation – one over-hasty and ill-considered action and you could land in court accused of child abuse. That little bundle of feebleness behind the locked door was a primed hand grenade which had to be handled with kid gloves.

So, speaking in a deliberately calm and (hopefully!) kindly voice he said: 'John, you can't just sit there. If you don't come out, I'll be forced to get the police who'll break the door down and take you back to Greenhill. Is that what you want to happen?' (Lies again, but he's stupid enough to swallow them!)

Once again, the ploy worked. There was a shuffling sound and the door opened. To his profound relief he noticed that the boy had pulled his trousers up. So Merrins couldn't accuse him of ... well, paedophile ogling!

'Come on, John, what's the problem?'

Tears and snivelling: '... Can't go to school today. I'm ill. Tummy trouble...'

'Got the squits, have you? No problem there. We'll soon sort that out!' (He was going to get that kid to school even if he had to carry him there on a stretcher, fastened down with a ball and chain and his nether regions wrapped up in an oversize nappy.)

Gripping the dishevelled bundle firmly by the shoulder, he marched it over the landing and into his bedroom. Mary was lying sprawled on the bed, stark naked and apparently making one of her 'sexually liberated' statements. Ignoring her outspread legs, he fiddled around on the shelf where she kept her 'Restoration Kit' which she used to recover from her 'enhanced awareness' trips. Choosing a bottle, he poured a thick white liquid into a plastic spoon.

'Open your mouth – wide! – and swallow this! ... And another... And another...'

Then he picked up a small bottle, undid the cap and shook four little green capsules into his palm.

'Swallow these. Go on!'

'What's all this?' spluttered a bemused John as the sickly, peppermint-tasting gunge dribbled down his chin.

'Kaolin and Lomotil. Triple dose. After about half an hour you won't have any more squits problems. Quite the reverse. You'll be bunged up for at least three days. Isn't that right, Mary?'

The naked form on the bed made no response and continued to stare into space. Which was just as well. He hadn't the time for yet another ideological debate about the ethics of using private education, tactically or otherwise.

Crisp and in control – as he liked to be – he marched his son back to the bathroom and wiped his grubby face clean with a wet flannel – just as you did with a baby.

'Now if you need one more go in the bog, go ahead, but I'll be standing here making sure that you don't do anything silly.'

'No! No! No!' The idea was dreadful ... the sheer embarrassment!

'It was all a little ploy, wasn't it? Right, now tidy yourself up. Tuck your shirt in. Do up your tie. Brush your hair...' (It was back to sorting out the juniors at Rugby School, something that came naturally to him.)

'Now follow me.'

It was down the ladder, into the garage and into the van where he pushed him firmly into the passenger's seat.

'Don't try to escape,' he said as he locked the door, 'because you can't.'

Trapped. No hope. Resigned to your fate. Like that picture in one of your history books which showed a prisoner being taken in a cart to be hanged at Tyburn. Would it hurt? Or would it be timeless and quick? All else was blank. Almost as if he were watching somebody else on a video.

Giles in the Naughty House...

Giles wove his usual artful way through the traffic.

Soon they shook off the bleak wastes of Greenwood and entered a gentler and more inviting land of tidy streets and big, well-built late-Victorian houses. Driving down a long tree-lined avenue, they finally drew up outside a tall red-brick terrace house with large bay windows and yellow sandstone mullions. There were no heaps of rubbish lying around, no broken down walls covered in obscene graffiti and no boarded-up windows. It was all a far cry from the bomb-site nakedness of Greenwood – not quite the homely lushness of Oaktree Gardens, but of that order of things. John felt a faint flicker of hope. This was not unlike home – he felt a bit like a frog being returned to its pond after a spell in a goldfish bowl. Why couldn't Giles live in a place like this instead of in a ghastly dump like Gloucester Road?

Giles got out of the van, marched round and unlocked the passenger door.

'Here we are!' he said, gripping him firmly by the shoulder as he pulled him out.

The gallows. The gibbet. Tyburn Tree. John's legs seemed to give way.

'I'm going to be sick.'

'All right. Not in the van, if you don't mind. Outside.'

He grabbed his neck and pushed his head forwards. After a few coughs and retches, a mass of green liquid came up and splashed down onto the pavement where it formed a little pool.

'Please, please, I *can't* go to school! I'm ill!'

'Rubbish! Now wipe your mouth... Right, in we go!'

With that, he frogmarched the quivering red-blazered bundle up a short tarmac path that led through a mini-garden and up two worn sandstone steps. Passing through a big red-painted door with 'Beaconsfield School' emblazoned on it in big, gold letters, he opened a second door, with two panes of frosted glass in it and painted brown. The lower half of the door had no paint on it and bore unmistakeable signs of clumsy adolescent feet kicking it open.

Immediately, they were engulfed in youthful noise – shrill treble squeals and bovine adolescent bellows. It was almost like falling into a river. They found themselves in an entrance hall, standing on a crude mosaic floor which consisted of a central star surrounded by jagged patterns. In front of them was a carpetless wooden staircase with a line of ornate brown banisters which swept up to a first-floor landing and culminated in a bronze angel holding up what was meant to be a flaming torch. Grubby cream-painted walls reached up to a white ceiling decorated with crude classical mouldings – a late-Victorian cut-price attempt at a Regency ceiling.

241

Giles winced. It was quintessential nineteenth-century atrociousness
– vulgar, pretentious and dishonest. Hopefully, in the not too distant
future, it would be pulled down, consigned to the 'dustbin of history'
and, along with Shaftsbury Street and the Miles & Eden con shop,
replaced with housing units properly in tune with the late twentieth-
century Zeitgeist.

In the meantime, however, he had to get out of this place as
quickly as possible. Better to be caught in a naughty house than in
a place like this! What would his colleagues at the university say if
they found out? But where the hell was that bloody Watson female?

In a largish classroom that opened off to the left gaggles of
youngsters were scrapping about, scruffier versions of John in their
unbuttoned red blazers and with their shirt tails hanging out and
their ties flapping about. One bunch seemed to be having a fight –
playful or otherwise. A sudden explosion of high-pitched laughter
burst out as a bag went flying through the air. John cringed in terror.
Here were the prowling wolves ready to pounce – naked, unrestrained
animal barbarism waiting to sniff out weakness and tear it apart.
He made a feeble attempt to wriggle free and bolt out into the
street, but Giles' vice-like grip was too strong for him. He could
only drift along to his doom – like that man who went over the
Niagara Falls in a barrel.

Brandishing him like a rabbit he'd just shot, Giles entered the fray.

'Right, you lot!' he called out in his Rugby School 'restore order'
voice. 'Can one of you find the headmistress for me?'

Immediately, the room fell silent. The various gaggles untangled
themselves and stiffened up. Ties were straightened, shirt tails stuffed
into trousers and blazers buttoned up. A gangling, black-haired youth
with a dark pencil line of down on his upper lip approached them
deferentially.

'Can I help you, Sir?'

Giles eyed him with distain. This petty-bourgeois grovelling! The
sheer ease with which these boys had been called to order! Pathetic!
And they considered themselves superior to the Greenhill kids! Thank
God Mary wasn't here. She'd have started another of her rants.

'Yes,' he finally condescended to say, 'you can find your headmistress
for me.'

'Yes, Sir, I'll take you to her right now.'

Just then an older and more assured youth entered the room. He
was clean-shaven, spick and span with neatly brushed red hair and

polished black shoes. A large badge with 'Head Boy' on it was pinned onto the lapel of his red blazer.

'You must be Dr Denby,' he said. 'I'm very pleased to meet you, Sir. If you'd come this way, please...'

Giles retched. What the bloody hell *was* this apparition? He certainly didn't feel obliged to return the politeness. This stuck-up prig needed squashing. To be put *down* into his place with the word 'down' heavily stressed.

'No,' he replied curtly, 'I can't spare the time so I'll leave his lordship with you. I've important work to do up at the *university*.' (He deliberately stressed the word 'university' to let this smarmy upstart know that he moved in circles far beyond the reach of his feeble mind.)

'By the way,' he added, handing him a large bag, 'here's his games kit and his pens and pencils. Don't give them to him. He'll just lose it all.'

With that he went out into the street where he heaved a sigh of relief. Mission successful. Goods unloaded. Now he had to get away quick, back into the real world and away from this flea-brain pretentiousness. Yet, as he climbed into the van, he felt the tiniest inkling of doubt. That little virus kept whispering unsettling words into his ear: 'Don't be silly! This is where you really belong...' Those Beaconsfield kids were his people, not the Greenhill desperadoes who, though he hardly dared to admit it, scared him rigid. But he quickly squashed this subversive nonsense. Real people had to be *hard*.

27

'Ah, John, we're so glad you got here!'

Meanwhile the head boy ushered John into a big room on the right-hand side of the entrance hall.

As he went in, he felt a flicker of reassurance. It was the sort of room he was used to. Glass-fronted bookcases climbed up the walls to an ornately plastered ceiling from which there hung a big, flashy chandelier. A thick brown carpet covered the floor and, together with the dark-red curtains which flanked the white-painted window frames, it created a slightly religious hush. The ornate marble fireplace with its swirls and its flanking brass lions was a proper fireplace – like the fireplace in the sitting room at Oaktree Gardens.

Seated behind a large mahogany desk was a dumpy, dark-haired little lady, neatly dressed in a white blouse and brown skirt, yet somehow faintly shaggy, not unlike a big, unkempt sheepdog. She exuded a calm reassurance – the experienced mother who'd seen it all and coped with it all, like that nice policewoman in London. Immediately, she got up and came beaming over to him.

'Ah, John, we're so glad you got here!'

'Thank you, Bill,' she added as the head boy handed her the bag containing the precious games kit and pens and pencils and then left the room.

John was left alone facing her.

'Well, do sit down and relax,' she said, motioning him to a large and rather battered armchair.

He sat down nervously on the edge of its engulfing leather hospitality. It was like being in a warm, soothing bath. If only he could stay here all day and not have to brave the predators who prowled around the threatening jungle outside.

'I'm Mrs Watson, the head teacher here,' the shaggy lady said as she sat down at her desk again. 'You'll be seeing a lot of me... We were expecting you yesterday. What happened?'

A mumbled and scarcely audible reply: 'I don't know.' (The standard response of inadequates who funk things, thought Dorothy. You shouldn't ask these sort of questions: they never get you anywhere.)

'Now John,' she said with a big, comforting smile, 'we're going to make a fresh start, aren't we? I know you had a bad time at Greenhill...'

A sudden shaft of fear! The knife going in! How much did she know? Did she know about *that*? Did all the boys know about *that*? He turned away and stared at the floor. Involuntarily and hideously embarrassingly, tears began to trickle.

'Oh, come on, John, you're not the only one who's had problems at Greenhill. Now all that's behind you.' A warm reassuring voice. He looked up again.

'I've heard a lot about you,' she continued, 'and it seems that you're quite a clever young man. We expect great things from you – and we're going to get them, aren't we?'

'Clever young man'. 'Expect great things from you.' That made him perk up. Nobody had ever called him clever before. He was the dull boy who had to be given consolation prizes for trying hard, not for actually succeeding.

'Now you'll find things a bit confusing at first. But if you have any bother come and see me or one of the teachers. Don't bottle it all up. But, mind, don't come telling me any silly stories!...'

Flash of lightning behind the fluffy white cloud. She might look like a mothering old sheepdog, but there was a wolf lurking underneath. She'd need careful handling.

'Anyway,' she went on, 'I've got a boy from your class, Michael Connolly, to look after you until you have settled in. Oh, don't look like *that* about it! He won't eat you! In fact, if I know anything about young Michael, you'll be the one who'll have to do the looking after. Just be nice to him when he comes. But where's he got to? He's probably forgotten or got the time wrong. Wait a minute while I go and find him.' With that she got up and went out of the room.

Out into the Jungle

Left alone! If only she wouldn't come back and he could stay all day in this lovely, comfortable armchair.

But, alas, his hopes were dashed: she did return.

'Come on, Michael, John's waiting for you,' she said as she opened the door and pushed a dumpy little boy into the room.

John eyed his potential tormentor carefully. He was a plump little ragdoll of a fellow with a round, rather vacant face, topped with an anarchic mop of red hair. His bits of clothes seemed about to fall off him.

'Oh Michael!' sighed Mrs Watson. 'Just look at you! What *have* you been doing? Come on, do up your shoelaces! Now tuck your shirt in ... and, for heaven's sake, do your zip up! ... And what happened to your comb this morning?'

'Sorry, Miss,' the little creature replied, 'but me mam, she slept in like and forgot to wake us... And she hadn't got me breakfast ready nor washed up the supper things neither... So I had to do it all meesell like...'

As she fussed round the little bundle, John watched the scene through slit eyes. The boy spoke with a northern accent, yes, but it was the English language and not Billy's scarcely comprehensible patois. He was allowing a teacher to mother him, yes, even to touch him and do up his tie for him. Not something that ever would have happened in the Greenhill jungle... Besides, if it came to a fight, he wouldn't have too much trouble with this little scarecrow. He felt a glimmer of reassurance, just a glimmer, though!

'Now then, John, this is Michael Connolly. Michael, this is John Denby, our new boy... Oh, come on, Michael, at least say hello. He won't bite, you know.'

With that, she shoved them out into the hall. For a while they stood looking at each other. Eventually, John ventured to speak – more to end the embarrassing hiatus than anything else.

'Well, where do we go?'

Tensed up, he waited for his alien voice to provoke the inevitable jeer, but, to his relief, none came. Another small step in the right direction.

'Er, well... It's Tuesday, isn't it? I think it'll be jog with the Mekon.'

'The Mekon?'

'Well, that's Mr Meakin. He's not bad really, but it's best not to muck about with him. Oh cripes! I've left me homework behind! I'll get done!'

'Done?'

'Yeah, I'll be in the punishment platoon ... you, know detention, sweeping out the classroom an' that.'

246

More reassurance. The teachers seemed to run this place. John felt emboldened to slip in a question that had been troubling him all morning: 'Where's the bog?'

'Cor, are you desperate like?' (A kindly, sympathetic voice, not a jeer.)

'No! No! I want to know, just in case.'

'Well, there's one on the first-floor landing, but that's for the teachers. You can only use it if you're desperate like. Like Sam Hawthorne yesterday. Sick all over everything he were. Old Polly Parrot got right narked when he went in for a sitter. Old Mekon made Sam clean it all up, but then Dolly – that's her wot you've just seen – she says he's bein' too 'ard on him. Can't help it an' that. But Mekon, he says he ain't a babby no more and must learn hissell to be normal like other kids. But when Owly starts teasin' him in biology Dolly blows a fit and he gets done. Anyway yer don't want ter gan to that bog. The proper bogs is in the changing rooms. Oh and there's one in the backyard, but it's cold and the light don't work. Some o' the big lads goes smokin' there an' reads their dirty magazines, but you gotta watch it 'cos Briggsy checks it...'

So the little ragdoll babbled on. More reassurance. The little droplets were starting to become a trickle. The bog wasn't a forbidden place of torture, the teachers seemed to be in control of the kids, you got done if you picked on other kids ... and he hadn't said 'fuck' once.

'Anyway,' he eventually said, 'we'd better go to the lesson or Mekon'll blow a fuse!'

They went upstairs and Michael knocked on a big white-painted door at the end of the landing. Suddenly John's fear blazed up again and the little trickle of reassurance evaporated. What was behind that door? The wild animals who would tear him to pieces! Exposure as a wimp, the moment of truth...

But before he could run away the door burst open to reveal a big, burly man, bald headed and with a bristly black moustache. Jovial and welcoming, he beamed at them. 'Ah, *you're* the new recruit, the famous John Denby!'

John cringed. God, the exposure! The full floodlight turned on him! He'd hoped to slip unnoticed into the back of the room. Now his cover was blown. Grown-ups were such dorks! No social sense!

'Well done, Michael!' the man boomed. 'You've actually managed to get him to the right place. We're making progress. Making progress.'

As he crept self-consciously in, John noticed that the whole class was standing up. Twelve red-blazered boys of all shapes and sizes – long and short, thin and fat – were staring at him. There was even a black boy among them. He could have been stark naked as he slunk up to an empty desk in a far corner of the room and huddled up against the wall.

'All right, sit down!' continued the man as loudly as before. 'There's no need to stare at him, Robert. He hasn't dropped in from Mars. He's human, you know!'

The lesson continued. Michael sat down at a desk and John was handed a large ordinance survey map.

'Right, back to map reading. Sam, what's at 316072?'

A long, thin boy, all flattened out, almost as if he'd been squashed by a garden roller, looked vacant.

Immediately a mass of hands shot up: 'Sir! Sir! Sir!...'

John eyed them warily. He knew the answer, but thought it best to keep quiet. Stay under cover. Spy out the land before you make a move.

'Martin?'

'A bus station.'

'No, not really.'

'Danny?'

'A railway station.'

'Yes, but what sort of a railway station?'

'Sir! Sir! Sir!'

'Fred?'

'A disused railway station. Sir.'

'Exactly. Well done!'

From his hideout at the back John noted a discovery or two. There was no shame about pleasing the teacher here. Neither was there an enforced language code. Some voices were Geordie, others less so. Fred, the black boy, had a refined tinkle-bell voice like his own and nobody had sneered at it. So he *might* be able to talk without being attacked. Might, not *would*. So best to keep quiet for the time being.

The lesson continued and after a while the maps were collected up.

'Homework. I receive.'

The teacher went round the room gathering up exercise books.

'Michael, where's yours?'

'Don't know, Sir.'

248

'Don't tell me that the dog ate it up again... Well, you'll just have to take your usual place in the punishment platoon. See me at four o'clock.'

'Can't, Sir! I've got to take John to the bus stop on the Great North Road. Miss says...'

'Well, we'll just have to postpone your little treat till tomorrow evening, won't we? Unless, of course, you actually manage to produce your homework in the morning.'

Not so good. You got homework here and, if you didn't do it, you got done, just as you did at Rickerby Hall.

Don't Drop Your Guard!

A loud electric bell sounded.

That meant a big crisis: morning break. Would somebody challenge him to a fight? Would they all start kicking him in? Again, low profile, *very* low profile. The spy behind enemy lines who mustn't be found out.

A red-blazered mob spilled raucously down the stairs, through a backyard and out onto a large, muddy playing field, surrounded by a high, red-brick wall. It was a grey and wet place. At the far end the sodden black branches of sad-looking trees dripped cold water into a spreading brown puddle.

While noisy clusters of youngsters coagulated into groups, John hung back. Would one of those babbling mobs make a rush at him? Would they surround him and force him to fight one of the bigger boys? Alone in the jungle. So keep well hidden. He watched warily as a bunch of younger boys chatted conspiratorially among themselves.

Suddenly one of them yelled, 'Tom! You're it!' Shrieking mayhem burst out as 'Tom' dashed madly into their midst, scattering them in all directions. Seeing John standing still, he grabbed his arm: 'Gottya!'

Holding him firmly by the hand, he bundled him firmly over towards the fleeing crowd... Chain tig – part of the break-time lore of Rickerby Hall!

John forgot his forebodings and quickly became absorbed in the game, seizing a running fugitive by the collar... Soon a long, wriggling chain was writhing its way over the sodden grass and pinning the few remaining survivors against a red-brick wall.

A whistle blew and everybody streamed back into the warmth of the building. One crisis over. He'd been accepted – for the moment, at any rate, so don't drop your guard!

'A dab hand at arithmetic...'

A Maths lesson followed with a man they called 'Polly Parrot'.

John soon saw why. He was a fluttery little man, untidily dressed in an oversize sports jacket which flapped around him like a wigwam. He had a long, beaky nose and a big quiff of white hair on top of his head which, apparently, defied all his efforts with a brush and comb and insisted on standing up vertically. So, he did look just like a parrot.

One wall of the classroom was plastered with lists – a list of names, in red felt tip with a red star on top of it; a shorter list in black felt tip with a black diamond on top of it; a silver-starred list and a gold-starred list... A quick glance showed that 'Polly Parrot' lacked the Mekon's easy-going, swaggering authority with its hint of brute force behind it. Marks, tests, red stars, silver stars, gold stars, black marks ... this was his way of staving off juvenile anarchy. This was the Hairy Mary order of battle.

Did it work? Did the potential anarchists accept it? John slipped into a desk at the back and observed the developing scene – the soldier on a recce patrol, spying out the enemy position.

Polly bustled round the room handing out exercise books.

"Ere, why's he got a red star and I ain't? I got more marks than 'im!' That was Danny, the skinny black-haired fellow.

'Because Sam finds it harder than you do and he's tried harder.'

'But I flippin' tried!'

'No you didn't! You didn't number the questions and you made six silly mistakes...'

'It's not fair!'

So, getting red stars and the like did seem to matter here. Obviously. If it didn't how had Polly Parrot managed to survive?

Textbooks were handed round and the lesson proceeded. To his surprise, he found the work easy – not as stupidly easy as at Greenhill, but, unlike Rickerby Hall, comprehensible. They had to do an exercise in percentages and when Polly fluttered up to his desk, he found that he'd got everything right.

'What's your name?'

Awful exposure. All eyes on him. 'Denby,' he whispered, 'John Denby.'

'WHAAT??' (The famous Polly 'squawk' which he later learned was imitated all round the school, ad infinitum!) 'Repeat it! Don't mumble, boy!'

'John!' he called out loudly, 'John Denby!'

Doom. Discovery. The spy unmasked. He waited for the Greenhill-style chorus of jeers. But – amazingly? – it didn't come.

'Well, Mr Denby, you're quite a dab hand at arithmetic, aren't you? I'll give you a red star.'

'But that's not fair! He's a flippin' brainbox, him!'

'Danny, be quiet!'

The skinny black-haired boy subsided into mutters.

An easy Maths lesson! A 'dab hand at arithmetic'? That was something new.

Then – Yuk! Yuk! – homework was set. 'Exercise 6, page 22.' Bang went his cosy evening of TV and wine gums!

Others Even Weedier Than You Are?

So the long journey through the jungle continued.

Lunch came. This was far easier than at Greenhill. There was no long queue to give the thugs a chance of getting at you. You sat at preordained tables to which the food was delivered on a tray by the boy on duty. The teacher at the table saw that you got your fair share.

A quarter of the way through there was an uproar at the far end of the room – boys standing up and yelling and then a stentorian bellow from the Mekon: 'SIT DOWN AND SHUT UP!'

This was followed by quieter order from the Mekon: 'Right, Bill, now go and get the bucket and the mop...'

'What's all this about?' asked John, his curiosity overcoming his caution.

'Oh, it's just Bill Watkins being sick,' replied the boy next to him. 'It happens every time he doesn't like the food. Mekon makes him clean it up, but Dolly gets the cleaners to do it. Wait till he does it when Polly's on duty. That's a show worth seeing...'

More reassurance. He wasn't the only one with 'problems'. Maybe others were even weedier than he was.

ARTHUR CLIFFORD

The Main Crisis of the Day

Afterwards came the main crisis of the day. The crux. The high jump... Whatever you like to call it. The games period.

That meant the changing room, the showers and physical contact with other boys – a host of potential snares. Would they notice the state of his underwear? (*that* was still with him and creating an embarrassing stickiness.) Would they steal his clothes? And when they did, it would mean exposure, ignominy and disgrace. And, out on the field at the back, would the others gang up on him and beat him in? He felt the old fear welling up again.

Yet, to his immense and bewildered relief, things went ridiculously easily. The games teacher was an aggressive little weasel of a man, called Briggs, who was an even bigger fusspot than old Foghorn Bryson of Rickerby Hall. You filed into the changing room in silence. You changed under his eagle eye and hung all your clothes on the requisite hooks – and in the right order, too: pants, vest, shirt, tie, trousers, blazer... And you didn't leave your socks lying around on the floor, either! There was no opportunity here for the predators to attack you.

Out onto the cold, muddy field at the back. Seven-a-side rugby. A slight spurt of confidence here. He knew the form from Rickerby Hall. Neither were any of the boys very much bigger than him: some were even smaller and weedier.

Immediately, they were chased around the forlorn wasteland by Briggs' whiplash of a voice: 'On! On! On! GET INTO HIM, DANNY!'

Seeing one of the larger boys coming towards him with the ball, he did what he'd been taught to do at Rickerby Hall – crashed into the charging mass, arms around the pounding tree-trunk-like legs and down he came.

'WELL DONE, THAT BOY!' cried Briggs. 'THAT'S what I want to see! THAT'S how it should be done!' Compliment indeed!

Shortly afterwards he even managed to pick the ball up and, for the very first time in his entire life, to actually score a try.

'Great stuff!' exclaimed Briggs. 'Great stuff!'

'What's your name?' he added. 'I haven't seen you before.'

'Denby, John Denby,'

'Well, you're obviously quite a rugby player. I can use you on one of the teams.'

John felt himself glow with gratification. This was something wholly unexpected.

But then came the moment he had been dreading. The shower. Unlike Rickerby Hall, there were no curtains and you had to go in naked for all to see. He tried to avoid it by hanging back and starting to change back into his uniform. But it was no good.

'You, yes *you*, in you go with the rest!'

Doom! All the good work on the rugby field undone! Certain discovery of *that*...

But nothing happened. True, he was starkers, but then so were all the others, and being covered in mud, *that* wasn't noticeable. Anyway, with Briggs eying you like a hawk, you were safe from attack. Profound sense of deliverance when it was all over. He'd won through and actually survived.

A Friend...

Fresh, shiny and aglow from the exercise, he found Michael Connolly waiting for him in the hall: 'I'm to show you to the bus stop. Miss says...'

They went out of the school and strolled along the avenue under the dripping black trees and with the red-brick late-Victorian houses towering canyon-like above them. The dank and sodden October afternoon faded into a dark, grey oblivion as if it were trying to forget the dreariness of its existence. The dull orange wash of the street lamps and the subdued roar of traffic emphasised the presence of the sprawling, amorphous metropolis nearby. Crossing a quiet road, they passed through a large Victorian park with its mournful trees, spreading wet lawns and ornamental lake of leaf-covered brown water, and eventually emerged onto a roaring main road – all orange street lamps, dazzling headlights and bowling traffic.

All the time Michael prattled on: 'Now you gets the number 30 bus an' Miss says I've gotta see yous on to it, but I canna 'cos I've gotta get back to feed Herbie and Horace...'

'Herbie and Horace?'

'Yeah. Herbie's me hamster an' Horace is me cat. Herbie's ever so nice, but he ain't got no brains... And Horace, well he's nice really, but 'e's right naughty like. He kills birds an' brings 'em into the parlour an' eats 'em and me mam goes mental...'

'You like animals then?'

'Course I does. Don't you?'

'Yes, I do, but I haven't got any...'

'Well, you can come and see mine at the weekend. Mind, me mam's a bit weird, so I'd berra warn yous. If she 'as one of her turns, you won't start pissing us up, promise?'

'Of course not. I don't tease people. It's wrong. Anyway, I bet she's not as nutty as my mum.'

'What's she like, then?' (Be careful. Don't get carried away! Don't expose too much of yourself.)

'Brainy, but a bit freaky...'

All very comforting. Michael liked animals – he was normal and he also had a freaky family. He, too, was frightened of being teased.

Two Different John Denbys?

A big double-deck bus came and, bidding his new friend goodbye, he climbed aboard and rushing upstairs, secured a front seat.

As the bus spluttered through the traffic, grinding its staccato way through the kaleidoscopic chaos of red, yellow and orange lights that pierced the all-enveloping gloom, he experienced a strange feeling. He remembered a story – a soppy fairy story he'd read long ago! – about a girl who'd swallowed a magic potion which had changed her into somebody else. Well, that was what seemed to have happened to him. He had begun the day as a pathetic little weed who'd pissed the bed, cried because he had to go to school and been sick all over the pavement. Now he had become a different person. The old John of Rickerby Hall again? Perhaps, but maybe something better – 'a dab hand at arithmetic' and 'quite a rugby player'.

He got off the bus at the top of Gloucester Road and walked down the hill. Suddenly a loud voice boomed out from behind him: 'COR LOOK AT LIDDELL LORD FUCKIN' FAUNTERLOY!' Terror! Panic! Back to being the 'snobby liddell git' again.

He pelted off down the street – the fox pursued by the baying hounds. Awful realisation. In his Beaconsfield uniform he might just as well have had a large notice pinned on him saying, 'Snobby git. Kick me in!' He was as vulnerably conspicuous as a bright-white chicken amid a pack of wolves.

Gasping for breath, he reached Number 14. But, oh Christ, it was locked! Frantically, he rang the doorbell. When nobody answered it, he turned round to confront his assailants with a desperate despair.

But – oh wondrous relief! – he hadn't been followed! Still, it was a lesson learned. When he went to school tomorrow he'd have to go in his dirty jeans and yukkie old sweater and change into his school uniform on the way – maybe in the gents' toilet in that park they'd passed through. Tiresome, but elementary survival technique.

'Thank you, God...'

Eventually, after what seemed like a century, the door opened to reveal a big, smiling Giles.

'Well, John, how was it?'

(He's in a good mood. Take advantage of it. Keep him sweet. But there's no need to tell lies this time. For once the truth will do!)

'Great! I got a red star for maths and I scored a try at rugby.'

Effusive smile from On High: 'I am very glad to hear it. Just as I thought it would be. All that fuss this morning was a lot of nonsense, wasn't it?'

'Sorry, I know I was silly. But I won't be silly again! Promise!'

With that, he scampered up to his room. His euphoria faded somewhat when he saw the mess up there, especially the pissed duvet. What would happen when Giles discovered *that* – as sooner or later he was bound to? But cross that bridge when you came to it. In the meantime he'd better make a good impression by working hard at school. At Beaconsfield, the kids didn't kick you in if you did good work, so he had no excuse for not doing his homework. Resisting the temptation to put the television on – and it was *Blue Peter* time! – he sat down and got stuck into it. The exercise was all about triangles – isosceles ones and equilateral ones – and to his surprise he quickly became absorbed in it. He could do it, but not too easily, so he actually found it interesting. To please Polly, he did it all beautifully neatly.

Then he said his prayers: 'Thank you for stopping the kids from kicking me in. Sorry I was sick on the pavement. Please stop me pissing the bed tonight...'

That night he slept soundly and didn't piss the bed. God had been listening.

28

Successful Survival Plan

The next morning the survival plan went into action.

He climbed into his grubby jeans and scruffy old sweater and stuffed his school uniform into his bag. It worked and nobody yelled at him as he sidled up the street and waited for the bus. In the park he found the gents' toilet conveniently open and he was able to change in one of the cubicles. He went in as a Geordie yoblet and emerged as a respectable middle class schoolboy, resplendent in his red blazer and grey trousers.

And it worked equally well in reverse when he went home. One problem solved.

On the Up and Up

Wednesday... Thursday... Friday. The week passed with a string of good things. A silver star for Maths. (Wow!) Another try at Rugby. A magic history lesson with the Mekon – an exciting story about the Wars of the Roses and embellished with a by-the-minute account of Queen Margaret being chased through the forests by a gang of cut-throats: he never knew that history could be so interesting! Top in the Scripture test and a silver star from Dolly. Then a fabulous art lesson with a female they called 'Dracula' – a real freak, this, with her dirty denim suit, her dead white face and her purple hair.

('She's actually a corpse, you know,' one of the older boys told him. 'She's only able to get out of her coffin after she's drunk warm human blood...' 'Laced, of course, with gin,' another boy added...) But she let you do clay sculpture – something which had never happened at Rickerby Hall – and he'd made a prehistoric monster which had been much admired, and, what was more, nobody had screwed it up. In general, then, all on the up and up.

The Ultimate Tribunal?

But the most important thing, the ultimate tribunal, the other kids? What about them?

He wasn't so sure here. They were certainly a very mixed bunch. There were some real cases in Form One. Sam, for instance, the long thin lad who looked as if he had been squashed by the garden roller. He was the oldest in the class, but he could hardly read or write and seemed to have problems with everything he did from dressing himself to tying up his shoe laces. That, at least, was comforting. There was somebody here who was an even bigger drip than he was and who would be the first to catch any bullying that was going.

Then there was 'Army Barmy' Martin. A big, flabby fellow with a puffy white face, he was like a vaguely animated snowman and you felt he would melt if he spent too long in the sun. Physically, he was pathetic. During rugby, he hung back and not even Briggs' most fearsome blasting operations could make him do more than skulk around at the edge of the field. He seemed to be reserving himself for bigger things. He had an encyclopaedic knowledge of military affairs – regiments, cap badges, rank insignia, tanks and guns – and an immense collection of uniforms, belts, berets, sergeants' stripes, even deactivated Bren guns and rifles. He was always brandishing the latest edition of *Combat Survival*. He could talk of little else but 'the Army'. He had every known war video: *Nam*, *Secrets of the Spetsnaz*, *Into Action with the SAS*, *The Israeli Air Force*, *The Selous Scouts*, *Tank Battles on the Russian Front*, *Fighter-Bombers of the US Air Force* ... A freak. No threat here.

And, of course, there was Michael Connolly. He was as effusively friendly as ever, always trying to be helpful, but he soon realised what Dolly had meant when she'd talked about him being the one who'd have to 'do the looking after'. Little Michael was quite desperately disorganised. On Wednesday night he had found himself having to pack his bag for him – 'It's English homework tonight, so where's your comprehension book and what about your exercise book and your pencils?' A friendship was burgeoning, but he was the dominant partner – it was a new experience to find yourself actually needed by somebody else.

The other boys seemed to be more normal and two of them made a point of latching on to him: Danny Fleetwood, the skinny, black-haired little fellow who was always bouncing round with his hand in the air, and Fred Macdonald, the black boy. Danny was heavily into model railways and model aeroplane kits and, when he discovered that John had a train set, too, he became effusive and competitive: no, he hadn't got the *Coronation Scot*, but he had got the *Flying Scotsman* and an American diesel-electric streamliner called the *California Zephyr*...

Fred, who had a similar posh voice to his own, seemed to regard him as welcome ally.

'By the way,' he asked him, 'why are you here? I mean, you're not a head case like some of them, are you?'

(Awkward question! Don't mention Greenhill. Don't spill the beans!) So evasive answer: 'Well, my dad didn't like the schools in Greenwood.'

'I'm not surprised! Neither does my dad, He's a lecturer at the Polytechnic and he thinks the local schools are rubbish. You don't learn anything. Also, he's a Baptist and he wants me to have a proper Christian education. He's a bit worried about some of the nutters they have here, though.'

All manageable. No threats here... At least, not yet!

An Odd Atmosphere in the Class...

However, there was a slightly odd atmosphere in the class.

It emanated, rather like a body odour, from two boys they called 'Owly' and 'Ratty'. 'Owly', whose real name was Mickey Stuart, was a great clod of a youth with a mop of black hair and a round white face, in the middle of which were two large eyes and a small beaky nose – hence the nickname. 'Ratty', whose real name was Robert Napier, was his diametric opposite, a scrawny black-haired little thing, with a long pointed nose, buck teeth and a receding chin, a sort of humanoid rodent – hence, once more, the nickname. For some incomprehensible reason they were inseparable – always performing their double act.

When they were around the class became somehow different – standoffish and distant. While the others would talk normally to him, those two didn't. On Wednesday he'd breezed up to them and tried to break the ice, but they'd simply turned their backs on him and giggled. On Thursday, during lunch-break, he noticed them pointing to him and giggling. He also saw Sam surreptitiously handing each a five-pound note.

Something was going on and it wasn't very nice. The old fear began to revive. It was like that old Saxon legend about a man who'd gone into a cave and found a dragon sleeping on a pile of gold. That dragon was the fear inside him. It had been asleep, but now it was starting to wake up again. Those past few days had been a blissful interlude, the lull in the storm. Grown-ups and teachers might say nice things about you, but they didn't really know anything. It was the kids who knew. Their judgement was harsher and more correct. There probably *was* something about him which made other kids hate him. He always would be rejected – like that chick which had been thrown out of its nest at Rickerby Hall. That scrawny little scrap of wizened flesh was him. For a few days he'd allowed himself to think that the world was a rational place with God in charge of it. Now he began to suspect that it really was a crazy place ruled by blind chance – a place where the strong always bashed the weak.

Back to Greenhill Again?

Friday afternoon ended with English with Clarkson.

Clarkson was so nondescript that he hadn't even got a nickname. Kids bored him and he didn't like teaching, but he needed the money – especially to pay the alimony to his divorced wife. Teaching in this place was as good a way of getting it as any other. The kids were at least squashable – which was more than you could say for the local comprehensives. The only problem was that Watson woman who would keep banging on about out-of-school activities. (The latest one was about a weekend camping trip to the Lake District. Well, he knew where she could stuff that notion!) Screw 'em down to work. Keep 'em busy. Crush any embers of incipient rebellion... And get away on the dot at four o'clock. Musn't be late for that rendezvous with Meggan – her husband was beginning to suspect that something was going on and that could cause big problems.

While Sam and Michael struggled with an elementary grammar exercise ('The cats... (is/are) ... hungry': Underline the correct word.), John sat at the back with Danny and Fred doing a comprehension exercise. It was about how astronauts coped with zero gravity on their way to the moon and he found it interesting. The weekend stretched before him: freedom. Sweets, crisps and videos.

At five to four Clarkson ended the lesson. 'Stop working now. Stand up everybody. MICHAEL PUT YOUR CHAIR UNDER YOUR DESK! As you go out put your books on my desk. By the way, John Denby to go to Mrs Watson's study immediately.'

An electric current seemed to flicker through the class. Everybody turned round and stared at him. Ratty pointed at him and then drew his finger across his throat, after which he poked Owly and the two of them went into a whispering and giggling huddle.

'Yes!' said Clarkson aggressively. 'Can I join the conversation?'

Giggle.

'Well, come on, what's it all about?'

'Nothing.'

'Laughing at nothing? I suppose I'll have to ring up the Royal Infirmary and get the men in white coats with the hypodermic needles, will I?'

Silence.

'Right, out you go. MICHAEL YOUR CHAIR!'

In the corridor everybody crowded round John.

'Gotta see Dolly, have yers?' grinned Ratty. 'She's the 'ed yer know! Cor, you're really for it!'

'Yeah!' added Owly with a smirk. 'You're getting' the cane!'

'The cane?' That dragon called Fear was stirring inside him and breathing puffs of fire.

'Yeah,' continued Ratty with a knowing air, 'off ole Mekon. He's an 'omo an' all.'

'An 'omo? What's that?'

'You'll soon find out. He pulls yer pants down and gives it yer on yer bare bum while Dolly has a good look.'

'I bet he doesn't! That's *filthy*!' Another sheet of fear flared up.

'Oh yes he does! He gives yer twelve and then 'e bums yer...'

'Bums you? What's that?'

'It's wot 'omos does. If yer wanna know jus' ask Bill, the 'ed boy. 'E's Mekon's bum chum an' 'e bums all them liddell kids an' all. Anyway you'll be gerrin' it!'

'But I haven't done anything wrong!' protested John with a mounting sense of desperation.

'Oh yes you has,' said Ratty, 'You was smokin' fags in break.'

'But I WASN'T!'

'Yes, you was. We sawed yer, didn't we, Army Barmy?'

'Yes we did,' replied Martin, nodding his head vigorously.

This was mad. Crazy. The fear flared higher.

'An' yer've broken the new kids' rule,' continued Ratty.

'What *rule*?'

'We sawed yer standin' on that star on the floor in the downstairs hall. An' that ain't allowed.'

'But I saw you standing on it and all the other kids, too!'

'We's allowed. New kids ain't,' said Owly. 'That's right, ain't it, Rats?'

'Not 'arf it ain't! You gets the cane for that.'

'But nobody told me about it!'

'Shoudda asked,' replied Ratty with an evil grin.

'An' wot's more,' he continued, 'the big lads is doin' yer over on Monday at break 'coz you's been gerrin' too many marks an' that.'

'Not 'arf!' added Owly. 'Yous is too big for yer boots. You want takin' down a bit, so theys is doin' yer over proper like.'

That did it. John's mounting fear became a raging conflagration. Despite himself the tears began to trickle.

Sensing victory. Ratty moved in for the kill. 'Yer shite ye!' he snarled, sticking his finger sharply into John's bottom.

'Oyer! That's *filthy*!'

Then he seemed to change his tack. He put on an ingratiating smile and spoke with a kindly voice: 'But we can help yers. Jus' show us a liddell respect an' we'll call them big lads off yers. Jus' give me an' Owly five quid – *each*, mind you. Like wot Sam 'ere does. We stops them big lads pickin' on 'm an' he pays us forrit. That's right, ain't it, Sam?'

Sam nodded bleakly.

'On Monday mornin', sharp, mind. An' ter show proper respect yer berra learn a trick. Owly, do yer trick!'

With that Owly dropped his pants and his drawers and, while Ratty giggled convulsively, cavorted round in an obscene way. John turned away in disgust.

The class dispersed. Alone on the landing, John began to sob silently. The whole rational world that he'd been slowly erecting during the past few days had come crashing down. It was Greenhill again. There was no escape. The whole world was Greenhill. Irrational. Mad. A place where the strong bashed the weak, where chicks were thrown out of their nests and left to die, where schools had stupid, inane rules and punished you savagely, where thugs extorted money from you... Darkness. No God. Just brute force.

261

And, more immediately, how could he possibly face the dreadful pain and humiliation of the Mekon caning that awaited him in Dolly's study?

Impending Crisis

Meanwhile Dorothy Watson was sitting in her study looking out of the window.

The soggy November day was giving up in despair. A forlorn attempt at brightness in the early afternoon had failed to make a serious impression on the blank grey cloud that covered the city like a lid and reduced everything to an endogenous depression monochrome. 'What's the use?' it seemed to say. 'Just crawl into a hole and hibernate.'

As the raucous din of departing youngsters faded into the gloom, it seemed sound advice. But it was a mood that she had to resist. The weekend stretched out before her. Normally, it was a brief respite from being responsible for the blindly irresponsible. But not this time. It was crunch time. On Saturday there was that rugby match against Ascomb House, the first inter-school match in Beaconsfield's history. Though it was only against the third XV of a local prep school it had taken a vast amount of cajoling and arm-twisting to set it up. At stake was the credibility of her school – and more precisely, *her* credibility as a headmistress. 'These lads may not be the brightest lights on the tree,' I'll grant you that,' the chairman of the governing body had said at the last meeting, 'but, surely to goodness, you can get a decent rugby team out of them!'

'Get a decent rugby team out of them?' Easier said than done. Despite all Briggs' efforts, the team was pathetic. The third-years, who should have been its mainstay, were so hopeless that he'd been forced to pad it out with underage first-years. The one boy who might have been some use, Robert Napier, had dropped out – 'I gotta help me mam on her market stall on Saturday. I mean she's bin that good ter us like. An' she works that 'ard forrus an' all. It's only right. Christian, yer knaa...' The residue, that lumpen mass of unwilling conscripts, probably wouldn't even survive into the second half.

All week she'd gone round with her 'think positive' smile on her face. 'We're going to put up a good show, aren't we, lads?' But deep down she knew the match was going to be an embarrassing flop. And then what? An excruciating session with that ghastly man, the bishop, at the next governors' meeting.

But there was one glimmer of hope in the murk – the new boy, John Denby. True, he'd been a disappointment when she'd first seen him on Tuesday morning. Not that bright-eyed and bushy-tailed little bundle that she'd been hoping for, but a snivelling thing that had been sick over the pavement. Quite possibly he was yet another professional failure and ducker-out of things. But, then she'd started to get gratifyingly glowing reports from her staff – 'enthusiastic', 'lively', 'creative' and, according to Briggs, a 'plucky and aggressive player on the rugby field'. In the short term, he might just save tomorrow's match – and in the long term, even save the school. But where was the little creature? He should have been here half an hour ago.

The 'Hot Cocoa Treatment': Back to Sanity

Then there was the faintest tap on the door.

At last! She flung it open to find – disappointment again! Instead of the hoped-for bundle of youthful energy, she saw a wretched little creature crying like a baby. She'd had one like this before – always crying for no reason and eventually diagnosed as an endogenous depressive for whom she could do nothing and who had to be sent to a psychiatrist...

Frustrated anger burst out: 'John Denby, what *is* all this?'

The sobs became a torrent: 'Please, Miss, I didn't mean it! I didn't know it was wrong. And I haven't been smoking. Cross my heart and swear to God. Please don't get Mr Meakin to give me the cane! Please, no! No!'

'Give you the *cane*? What *are* you talking about?' (Oh, my God, is this boy schizophrenic or something?)

Snivel. Snivel.

'For heaven's sake boy, *nobody*'s going to give you the cane! I was going to tell you how *well* you'd done this week!'

Blank stare. The tears stopped. (Thank God! That shows he's not certifiably insane. He does respond to reason!)

'Come on in, sit down and make yourself comfortable. I'll give you a cup of hot cocoa – sugar and milk? – and when you've calmed down you can tell me what your problem is.' (The hot cocoa treatment. A fairly regular occurrence with the Michael Connollys of this earth, for instance, when they had lost their money and couldn't remember the number of the bus they had to take to get back home.)

Fussing around with the cups and jars and the electric kettle that littered the table beside the fireplace, she eyed him as he sat down on the edge of the leather settee.

He *did* look so cute – that mop of white hair, those big, watery eyes, that neat little body in its red blazer, white shirt and grey trousers. Possibly he was neglected and in need of a proper mother. Indeed, deep down, she hoped that he *was* neglected – then he could become *her* child, that child she'd always wanted...

But pull yourself together, Dorothy Watson! You're a proper professional, not an 'emotional woman'! Young mammals – puppies, kittens and, yes, children! – *do* look cute. It's part of their defence mechanism. As a trained biologist, you should *know* that! And, as a trained teacher, you should know that children can be very manipulative, laying on the charm by the bucketful, wheedling, wrapping the unwary round their little fingers... Just beware!

She handed him the steaming mug and sat down on the settee beside him.

'Now what is all this nonsense about getting the cane from Mr Meakin?'

'Well Ratty and Owly – I mean Robert and Stuart...'

Here he paused and looked round the room.

'Go on,' said Dorothy, 'I must know the truth.'

'But you won't say that I've been telling tales, will you? I mean they might do me over...'

'Of course not. There's only me here, so nobody else is going to hear.'

'Well, they said that because I stood on that star in the entrance hall, Mekon – sorry, I mean Mr Meakin – was going to give me the cane. They also said I'd been smoking, but, swear to God, I haven't been...'

'Yes, continue.'

'They said that Mr Meakin was an 'omo who'd pull my pants down and bum me. Please, Miss, what's an 'omo?'

Inwardly, Dorothy sighed. Robert Napier again! Her prize pupil, that white hope of her redemptive skills whose success could make her name! He seemed so positive, so clever, so willing, so charming, Briggs spoke so highly of him... Yet there were these continual stories about him! Was he taking her for a colossal ride? It did look like it. Failure stared her in the face. In accepting him she'd possibly made a disastrous blunder. No way could she redeem the likes of him. He was much too hard a case for her. Dolly, old girl, you're just not good enough! It was not what she wanted to believe.

Meanwhile, there was this muck about Roderick Meakin, the mainstay of her school! Malicious rubbish of course, but it was just the sort of thing that her enemies on the council and up at the university would love to hear. It could destroy her school at a stroke. If this boy was telling the truth, then young Robert was lethal – positively radioactive!

'John,' she replied in a firm voice, 'that is all absolute nonsense and I'm surprised that an intelligent boy like you has been stupid enough to believe it. Pull your pants down! Do you really think that Mr Meakin would do that? If he did, the police would soon be after him. Not allowed to stand on the star in the entrance hall? John, we're grown up here. We don't make silly rules about not standing on bits of the floor. Anything else they told you?'

'Well, they said that the big kids were going to do me over because I was getting too many marks...'

'Of course they're not! Oh John!'

'But, please, Miss, what's an 'omo and what does "bum you" mean?'

Another inward sigh! More corroboration of those tales of filthy goings-on! Boys were smutty creatures – she knew that! – but, again, if any of this were true, Robert Napier's smut was of an altogether different order.

'Something very unpleasant. We'll talk about that later. But in the meantime, John, you really ought to be ashamed of yourself. Fancy letting some one like Robert Napier make a fool of you!'

'Sorry, Miss.' A sense of deep shame engulfed him. What a prat he was! What an utter dork! He stared at the floor and, to his embarrassment, a tear began to trickle.

'Come on, John, there's no need to turn on the taps! Just pull yourself together...' She was beginning to suspect professional wimpery: tactical fits of weeping in pursuit of nefarious ends. She'd seen it many times before and it grated on her.

But then the little scrap *did* look so crestfallen ... and she knew what they'd done to him at Greenhill... Poor, lost soul...

Suddenly her restraint broke down and she did a crazy thing. She hugged him. Immediately, she was aghast at her stupidity. This sort of soppiness could backfire horribly. Boys could be so prickly proud. He could see this sort of thing as an insult to his manhood and shut himself down. Oh, Dolly, you ass!

But, instead, the grubby tear-stained face broke into a glorious smile and the boy embraced her. The child who needed her! The child she'd always wanted...

'Can we talk, Miss?'

'Of course, John. Go ahead.' (How she was just loving this! But, Dolly, control yourself! This one's a charmer. He'll wrap you round his little finger if you're not careful.)

Her restraint broke down again and she gave him another hug and was rewarded with another glorious smile.

'Now, Giles, that's my dad. He's nice really... He gave me the *Coronation Scot* after I'd called him a "cunt" and run away... but, well, he never talks to me and there's so many things I want to talk about...'

'Yes, go on.'

'You say the world's sensible and that I should know that this school's a sensible place. But things aren't sensible.'

'And why not?'

'Well, at Rickerby Hall I did my very best to please God. I bought a Bible and I joined the Scripture Union. I gave fifty pence to the Save the Children Fund and I bought Michael Dickenson a packet of wine gums after I'd punched him in the face, but God still killed my nan and my granddad...'

'No, John, it wasn't God who killed them. It was a drunk driver and he's now in prison and feeling very sorry about it.'

'But why didn't God stop him getting drunk, or grab the steering wheel when he careered over the central reservation? He's meant to be in charge, isn't he?'

'It's not quite like that. God gives us free will – the ability to choose between good and bad. He puts us here to test us. It's like a biology exam. I want to see how good you are at biology. It's no good if I correct you every time you make a mistake.

'We've got to be good because we choose to be, not because we're forced to be. We've got to manage ourselves and at the end of the day God will see how well we've done. You don't pass an exam if the teacher does it for you.'

'But the world isn't sensible, is it? When I went to Greenhill I tried my very best to be nice to the other kids, but they were horrible to me for no reason...'

'Yes, I know they were, John. I know what they did to you there.'

Fear, quickly blazing up into panic, flashed through him – *that*, discovery, exposure, ridicule... 'What do you know? How do you know?'

'I hear a lot about what goes on at Greenhill, John.'

'Oh no! Oh God! But you won't tell anybody about ... well, *that*, will you? Please! Promise you won't! You see I'm so ashamed! So *ashamed*! If the kids here find out...'

Tears began to trickle again.

Another hug, long and warm. He buried himself in her soft feminine breasts. (Oh, Dorothy *was* enjoying this! He needed her. He wanted her. Her own child at last.)

'John, you should not be ashamed of what happened. They are the ones who should be ashamed. One day, perhaps, they will be.'

'But they wouldn't have done it to a good kid, would they? They did it because I was a little wimp, didn't they? You grown-ups say nice things to us kids, but it's the kids who tell the truth...'

'Not really. They did horrible things to Jesus. The Bible doesn't tell us the half of what they did. And it wasn't because he was bad or weak. It was because he was good and strong and so much better than they were. That made them hate him.'

'By the way, Giles says that God and all that's a load of rubbish. You don't think so, too, do you? You're not just having me on, are you?'

'Of course not.'

'But he's very clever. How do you know he's not right?'

'But you're clever and you still believed the nonsense that Robert Napier told you. Clever people can be very silly, you know. Anyway, if he doesn't believe in God, you should feel sorry for him. Think of what he's missing!'

But enough self-indulgence, Dorothy Watson. You're a professional with a job to do. She sat up and changed from a soppy mother to a purposeful headmistress.

'Now, John, I wanted to tell you that you've made a very good start and that all the teachers are very pleased with you. Here's a report on your first week. There's one copy for your parents and there's another for the Social Services who are going to visit you tomorrow morning.'

She handed him two large white envelopes. 'Now you won't be like Michael Connolly and go and lose them, will you?' She studied him with a serious expression. 'Now, John, we're making a fresh start. All that Greenhill business is water under the bridge. Gone. Finished. You've had a good cry today, but I don't want to see you crying again – *ever*. Understand?

'There're boys in this school far worse off than you are. Face up to your difficulties. Don't let the sillies make a fool of you. Now, there're all sorts of things going to happen. Mr Meakin's starting an adventure club – camping, hiking, mountain climbing and canoeing. I want you to take part in that. Mr Rymer – who teaches you Maths – is going to make a model railway. He'll need your help. And Mr Briggs tells me that you're a promising rugby player. There's an important match tomorrow against Ascomb House. You *will* turn up and play for us, won't you?'

'Oh, do I have to?' A cosy weekend of sweets, crisps and videos was under threat.

'Yes, you do.'

'But the Social Services are coming.'

'At nine thirty, John, and they will be gone by twelve o'clock. I'll expect you at two o'clock with your kit.'

'But if I don't turn up, what then?'

'You really will have to go and see Mr Meakin this time.'

A New Gran? A Modern Sir Lancelot

John went back home. Out into the late-autumn gloom, a cold, dripping world of monochrome. Dark-grey sky, orange street lamps, black sodden trees, wet pavements – and then into the gents' toilet in the park, a bleak cave-like place, where he changed from a respectable middle-class schoolboy into a Geordie street arab.

He was elated. His new world was rational after all. He'd found a new gran, Mrs Watson. She'd listened to him, talked to him and – yes! – given him the physical contact, those hugs and cuddles that he knew he shouldn't want, but, nevertheless, desperately did want!

The old John of Rickerby Hall was back in business again. More than that: a new and previously unknown John had been uncovered – clever, good at rugby and from whom 'great things' were expected...

But at the same time he'd been a pathetic little wimp. He'd let

Ratty and Owly make a right dick of him. He'd cried like a baby – and in front of Mrs Watson, too! What a disgrace! It was almost as if he'd messed his pants! What she must have thought of him! Well, that John, wimp John, the John of *that*, must be buried for ever. Yes, buried with a stake through its heart like a vampire from Transylvania so that it would never rise again. Never would he cry again. Never, never, not ever, never in the whole long life that stretched out into the infinity ahead of him.

'You really will have to go and see Mr Meakin this time.' Old Watson might look like a cuddly old sheepdog, but she was no pushover. She could bite. He would have to make her *like* him. That meant proving to her that, in spite of everything, he was *not* the weedy little cry baby that he seemed to be. He'd turn up to that rugby match all right. Yes, and win the game for her. Then she really would like him. It would be like Sir Lancelot and Queen Guinevere in those King Arthur stories.

29

A Bewilderingly Pleasant Surprise

A bewilderingly pleasant surprise greeted him when he got home.

A smiling Giles opened the door. Even Mary was smiling at him – that *was* something!

'And how's your first week at school been?' beamed Giles. (They're being nice to you. Be nice back. Say the right things.) 'Magic! I got a silver star for Maths, I came top in the Scripture test and I'm playing for the first Fifteen tomorrow. Mrs Watson says I've made a very good start. Here's the report she's given me.'

Giles took the envelope and ostentatiously opened it: 'Very well done, John. I'm really pleased. I always knew you could do it.'

It was like warming yourself on the hot pipes on a cold day. Acceptance at last. 'Thanks, Giles, thanks!'

He clambered up the ladders to find his room transformed – all neat and tidy, the rugs on the floor hoovered, his clothes folded up, new clean duvets and, there on the bed, a box containing a new and exotic engine for his railway: a Southern Railway *Bulleid Pacific*. Merchant Navy class! Wow! Danny Fleetwood hadn't got that one!

A little note in the box said, 'From Giles and Mary for trying hard and doing well at school.'

He was overwhelmed, swamped, flattened... It was so thoughtful, so kind. Giles and Mary were so nice really and all he'd done was hate them and run away to London and cause them trouble. He'd even called Giles a cunt. He must thank them right now! And prove himself worthy of them.

He scampered down the ladders: 'Cor, Giles, cor, thanks... Cor thanks, Mary! I'm so sorry I've been bad! I'll never be bad again! Promise!'

Back in his bedroom he knelt down and gave a long thank you to God for sorting things out so well.

'We will never surrender...' A New Biggles

As night closed in he became obsessed by the coming rugby match. It would be an unpleasant ordeal of freezing rain, cold sodden rugby shirts, numb fingers, bumps, kicks and painful scrapes from hard and sharp football boots, icy and gritty mud and sheer exhaustion. But go through it all he must – be brave, dauntless, fearless, selfless, like those pilots who'd won the Battle of Britain, like the soldiers who'd stormed the Normandy beaches in 1944 ... Out came his history book and he soaked up Churchill's great speech of 1940: '...We will never surrender...' In went the video of the Battle of Britain – all those heroic fighter pilots defying the might of the Luftwaffe. By ten o'clock he was doing battle over the fields of England in a Spitfire alongside none other than Squadron Leader James Bigglesworth himself.

Crunch Day of Saturday...

Saturday morning.

Crunch time at 14 Gloucester Road. The visit from the Social Services. Tension in the air. Crackling static. The soldiers on night patrol, cap badges removed, camouflage in place, nothing rattling in the pockets, weapons oiled and tested, loaded and at the ready, all senses on full alert...

Since Tuesday Giles and Mary had been sweating away. All the correct signs had to be in place – and, if there was one thing they knew about, it was signs. Caring, concern, domestic competence, tolerance of personality differences, awareness of childhood realities... The house was immaculate, but John's trains were strewn all over the attic floor – just enough disorder to show tolerance of boy-hood waywardness, and a sympathetic understanding of the need to be creative, but just enough order to show a firm and humane discipline.

Mary, in particular, had had a ghastly few days. At first she'd ridiculed the notion of a threat from Merrins. (Hysterical garbage! How could any properly aware person possibly believe that she and Giles were child abusers? For Christ's sake, they weren't bloody vicars running a prep school, were they?)

But an incident in the university canteen had changed all that.

271

Waiting in the queue, she'd overheard a conversation between two females from the Sociology Department:

'...When the Social Services make their report, he'll be for it ... and so will she... Aiding and abetting... So much for her childrearing expertise...'

Of course, when the good ladies had turned round and realised who was standing behind them, all had been sweetness and light, big smiles and congratulations to be sent to Giles for his magnificent radical statement at the Murray Lecture.

That had set the alarm bells ringing. She'd gone straight back home and plunged head first into the mephitic morass of her son's bedroom. Out of the cupboard came the pissed duvets, the repulsive underpants, the spew-stained blazer. Off to the laundry went the salvageable cases; into the bin went the hopeless cases. Then it was hoovering the place out, picking up the rubbish and down into Boldonbridge to buy new duvets, new underpants, new shirts, new trousers, a replacement Beaconsfield uniform... God how she hated the whole business! Bloody housemaids' work this!

Not the sort of thing she should be doing! She ought to have a housemaid to do this for her... But, then, housemaids were 'in the dustbin of history' ... She'd said it herself and that meant having to do all this effing stuff yourself! Couldn't bloody win, could you?

'I really appreciate this, Mary,' said a grateful Giles. 'I really do'.

For the past weeks they had been going their separate sexual ways – she with Bill (gay?) Baxter and he with Maggie Wright. But, now, in the shared companionship of adversity, they'd been thrown together again and their old love had flared into life once more.

The keystone of their carefully constructed edifice was ... well. *Him!* The whole structure depended on what *he* said, especially about ... *that*!

'We've just got to keep him sweet, lovey. We can't afford any tantrums – at least not until Saturday's over. If he goes and shoots his mouth off to one of Merrins' vampires.'

'Don't I bloody know it!'

So Survival Plan One had gone into action. Sweet smiles, encouraging remarks, no bad language, nothing said when a letter arrived with 'Scripture Union' on the envelope and, the ultimate piece of precision bombing, a lovely new engine for his railway, a *Bulleid Pacific*, strategically delivered on Friday night.

Petty-Bourgeois Factualism versus Objective Reality

Yet again Giles had been nonplussed by the response. He'd expected a positive reaction, of course, but the tidal wave of effusive gratitude had bewildered him. God that kid was so thick! Didn't he realise that he had them both over a barrel? 'Ask and it shall be given unto you.' And, unlike mingy old God, it *would* have been given – a scale model of a Union Pacific 4–8–8–4 *Big Boy* mallet flown over from the USA on a specially chartered Concorde, if that was what he'd wanted! Or a ton of liquorice allsorts delivered by helicopter...

On Thursday a setback had occurred. 'Oh shit!' groaned Mary as she'd put the telephone down. 'They're sending Old Granny Higton along on Saturday! You know, that dreadful old reactionary that you asked them to get rid of. They'll be doing this just to fuck us up!'

Giles agreed. Annie Higton was not what a properly aware social worker should have been. Aged fifty-six – i.e. approaching senility! – she was a bustling, profane little lady who was married to an estate agent (for Christ's sake!), went to church on Sundays (bloody hell!) and helped with the Girl Guides (Christ almighty!). And, as if that wasn't enough, she even helped out with the Salvation Army... She had no idea of historical necessity, the concept of the Zeitgeist eluded her, and, worse still, she was unaware of the sociological need for an up-to-date ideology. 'I just take each case at it comes,' she was wont to declare. Giles had tried hard to get her removed from the Social Services – or, at any rate, side-lined into some irrelevant sinecure.

Yet secretly – and though he couldn't tell Mary this – he was relieved. 'I just take each case as it comes.' She wasn't one of Merrins' dervishes with 'Child Abuse' emblazoned on her battle flag. Without an ideology to stuff the facts into she might even be reasonable.

But no ideology? That created complex historico-philosophical problems. Petty-bourgeois factualism as opposed to objective reality? Tactical retreats to achieve long-term objectives? Lenin's New Economic Policy? Making positive use of reactionary elements? Much food for thought here. He jotted his ideas down for discussion in a forthcoming seminar with his honours students.

'He certainly knows how to play to an audience'

As it turned out things went extraordinarily well.

John played the part of the happy little boy to perfection. A cynical observer might have thought that he'd been specially coached. He beamed and smiled and said all the right things. He clearly charmed old Ma Higton. 'Christ, it's Miles & Eden all over again!' sighed Giles to himself as the boy minced around. 'He certainly knows how to play to an audience. You've got to give him that!'

When he and she went up to the attic for 'a little chat', Giles and Mary clasped each other's hands. This was it! Giles wished he could have bugged the room – just to hear what the little sod was saying to the old bag. (Nothing immoral in that. After all, Stalin had bugged Roosevelt's rooms in Teheran in 1943 – and quite rightly: he had to know what the imperialists were getting up to!)

Yet he would have been surprised if he *had* heard what was being said in that attic. What John was really interested in was buttering old Higgie up so that he wouldn't be sent back to Greenhill again. So he made a big point of showing her all his trains and his books...

'This is my *Coronation Scot* – the one my father gave me... And look at this one, the 'Battle of Britain', a Merchant Navy-class *Bulleid Pacific*. Even Danny Fleetwood hasn't got one of these! It's wicked, isn't it! By the way, would you like a wine gum, or would you prefer some liquorice allsorts? ... I'm saving up my pocket money to buy a new bible, a real one this time, not just a children's bible... I'm in the Scripture Union, you know...'

Old Higgie sat cross-legged on the floor as he prattled on. She couldn't help liking him. He was so friendly, so polite ... that lovely smile! Such a change from the sullen adolescent lumps that were her staple diet. She had to find certain things out, of course, but she was far too hard-bitten to ask direct questions. All you would get was a confused jumble or a pack of downright lies. And it was so easy to get kids to say what you wanted them to say – which then produced an inconsistent muddle which hostile lawyers ripped apart in court. So care, caution, the indirect approach...

'So you're getting on well with your parents now?'

'Oh, yes, they've been very nice to me. Look my dad gave me this... It was very nice of him, wasn't it? Especially after I'd been bad and run away.'

'What happened then?'

'Well, he was angry with me. You see. I'd called him a cunt. What's a cunt?'

'A very nasty word. Don't call people that.'

'But that's what they called me at Greenhill.'

'You didn't like Greenhill, did you?'

'It was *horrible*! Please don't tell my dad to send me back there! Please! Promise you won't!' (Sunny smiles replaced by a look of wild desperation.)

'No, of course I won't. But they were horrible to you there, weren't they? I mean the other children?'

'Yes, but do we have to talk about it? It's embarrassing. Look, this is my collection of Biggles books. I've got them all, you know. People say it's old fashioned, but I think it's great...' (There's one thing you've got to find out, Higgie, old lass, but don't push it. All you'll get is a temper tantrum. So careful circumlocutions around Biggles, maths tests and today's rugby match...)

When the ground was suitably prepared she slipped in the crucial question: 'Now I want you to tell me the truth about this. The absolute truth. God's listening to you. (This'll work with him!) Have any grown-ups ever undressed you and fiddled with your bottom or private parts? I mean apart from doctors or nurses who have to do these things?'

Shocked silence. Blushing bright red. Then eventually: 'No! Grown-ups don't do that sort of thing. Only dirty kids do it. Anyway, do we *have* to talk about this? It's so embarrassing. It's what dirty kids talk about. Now, this is my book about planets...'

Higgie had got the answer she'd been looking for. It was what she'd suspected all along.

'Now, I'll have to have a little talk with your parents.'

With that, she bustled off down the ladders, an untidy bundle of middle-aged bonhomie.

In the living room Giles and Mary were holding hands, nervously awaiting the verdict.

'Well, I don't think you've got much to worry about...'

'Yes,' said Giles anxiously, 'But what about ... well, you know? Has he said anything about who did it?'

'Not in so many words, no, but it's pretty obvious...'

('Obvious'? The warning lights began to flash. Was the old bag playing a cat-and-mouse game?) 'What do you mean "obvious"?'

'Oh, come on! It's not *you*! Grant me a bit of sense.'

'Well, what then?'

'It was one of those kids at Greenhill... Who else?'

'Did he tell you this?'

'No. But if it had been an adult he would have said so. Because it's the other kids he's too ashamed to mention it directly. When kids get bullied they often think they deserve it.'

'Oh, come on!' said Giles. 'It can't possibly have been anybody at Greenhill! You must *know* that pederasty isn't a working-class problem. It's an integral part of a twisted petty-bourgeois lifestyle. Freud said...'

Giles was profoundly relieved to have been let off one particularly deadly hook, but this casual denigration of Greenhill was, in its own way, almost as lethal. It struck at the roots of his self-esteem – his professionalism, his historical insight, his scholarship ... all this and more was at stake. To admit that Greenhill was a place where pupils were allowed to bugger one other and get away with it blew a pretty big hole in most of what he'd spent the past decade proclaiming. And not only him – the very foundations of Ed Stimpson's groundbreaking book on working-class education were being gratuitously attacked. Anyway, probing questions about the validity of established educational truths were the prerogative of qualified research workers with Ph.D.s and the right basic ideas – definitely *not* of a semi-literate do-gooder without a proper degree who messed around with petty-bourgeois rubbish like the Girl Guides. He felt his hackles rising.

Old Higgie didn't argue. What was the point? She'd just get buried under an avalanche of statistics and academic studies. In any case, her remit was to stay strictly neutral. Don't interfere with clients' beliefs, religious or political.

'Yes,' added Mary, cleared of one charge and anxious to refurbish her radical credentials, 'I'd say it was a policeman in London. They're all perverts. That's why they join the Freemasons. Did you know that the Freemasons...?'

'But there are some pretty odd characters at Greenhill, you know,' said Higgie defensively.

Giles signalled for Mary to stop. They'd been cleared of what mattered. He wanted to get the old bag safely out of the house before Mary went and put her foot in it. Let the old thing think what she liked about Greenhill. What did it matter? She wasn't part of the university – she hadn't even got a degree!

But Mary wouldn't stop. The scent of battle was in her nostrils: 'We're both very worried about John's mental hygiene. He's picked up a lot of religious rubbish at the prep school he was at and he's constantly receiving stuff from the Scripture Union. Giles and I are both atheists and find it most unhealthy.'

'Oh, please, that's pretty harmless...'

'Harmless? You call it *harmless*!'

As Mary launched forth into her time-honoured anti-religious rant, Higgie sighed to herself. That woman really ought to see some of the clients she had to deal with. Billy Less, for example, aged twelve, permanently truanting and keeping body and soul together by shoplifting and selling himself as a rent boy. The Scripture Union a problem? There was one born every minute, but you weren't supposed to say that sort of thing...

Meanwhile Giles winced: 'All right, dear, we can discuss this later...'

But Mary wouldn't stop. She was Saint Joan riding her white horse into battle: 'We were very disappointed at his negative and snobbish rejection of Greenhill. He's full of crap. Thoroughly anal...'

'Please!' expostulated Higgie in a gently reproving way. 'He's not really snobbish. He's only eleven. A little upper-class prep school was all he knew. You couldn't really expect him to handle a place like Greenhill...'

'He didn't even try. He rejected it right from the start.'

'They rejected him, more likely.'

'Because he was a stuck-up little snob...'

'No, because he was different... Anyway, Beaconsfield is a much better place for him.'

'You really think so? You *really* think so?' Mary switched on the 'analytical stare'.

'Yes, the only problem you'll have is that he's a lot more intelligent than most of his schoolmates and he could get delusions of grandeur.'

'He's got them already.'

'Please, darling,' said Giles firmly, 'we can talk about all that later on.'

He turned to old Higgie: 'Well, you must have a lot of work to do. Thank you very much indeed for all you've done. You've set our minds at rest. We really appreciate it.'

With beams and a firm handshake, he ushered her to the door.

'God, you bloody creep!' exclaimed Mary, angry that her socially aware statement had been so abruptly terminated. 'You bloody creep! You're not really a revolutionary, are you?'

'Well, I'm not an overgrown student if that's what you think.'

The brief truce was over.

30

The Dustbin

Crunch Day for James Briggs, Cert. Ed.

The rugby team traipsed out onto the scruffy swathe of mud that passed for Beaconsfield School's playing field. The grey lid of cloud that had hung over the city for the past week seemed to have settled down for the duration – as if it were an old tramp who'd found himself a cosy pad, drunk himself silly on his meths and crashed out for good on the floor, snoring away, insensible and immoveable. Everything seemed to be in the last stages of futility – the wet earth; the bare, black bones of the sodden trees; the cold, muddy puddles. Beyond the enclosing red-brick wall, shabbily ornate Edwardian buildings faded into the grey murk. It was a give-up sort of day.

Which was just what James Briggs, Cert. Ed., felt like doing as he eyed his 'team'. What a collection of walking disasters! On one level, a total write-off. But on another level the product of a year's struggling and straining. And on yet another, his apotheosis or, more likely, his nemesis.

For this was crunch day for James Briggs, the PE man of Beaconsfield School.

His future would be decided on a dreary November afternoon, on a scrawny apology for a rugby field in the shabby-genteel Edwardian suburb of a northern industrial city. Daft really, but that was the way the dice had rolled. Had he been of a philosophical bent he might have seen the irony of it all.

He'd done very well at his teacher-training college in Wiltshire and, when his family had moved up to Boldonside, he'd started his job as a PE teacher in a Southside comprehensive full of the highest ideals and expectations. But somehow everything had crumbled. For some inexplicable reason the kids just wouldn't obey him and his lessons had slithered down into a humiliating chaos, turning him into a staffroom synonym for incompetence. A devastating inspector's report had terminated a disastrous career. He'd left before he could be pushed.

For a time he'd thought of leaving teaching altogether, but he couldn't think of what else to do – and his success at college seemed to indicate that, despite this setback, he might just be able to make a go of things. He'd taken this job at Beaconsfield as a last fling. For his future, for his financial security and for his very self-esteem, he *had* to succeed this time.

So it had been correct all the mistakes he'd made before, no matey-matiness with the kids, keep a tight lid on the discipline, pay close attention to detail, clamp down on any nonsense in the changing room and the showers – the number-one danger area! – be prepared for all eventualities, but, above all, *achieve*. That's what Ma Watson wanted, that was the way to success. But achieve with *what*?

He'd jumped out of the frying pan and landed in the fire. The Southside kids may have been uncontrollable tearaways, but this lot, in their own way, were even worse.

A void. An empty void. A nothing. Lumps of putty. Wimpery raised to the level of a creative art. Yet he had to get *something* out of them. Ma Watson had told him that he was 'on probation' – a try-out – and if he got *nothing* out of them?

Muttering and (not-so-vague!) hints of possible dismissal... And the old cow was there on the touchline, in her anorak and green wellies, ready to suss him out – and, doubtless, to revel in his humiliation.

He looked at the opposing team, Ascomb House, standing disconsolately in the drizzle in their yellow shirts and white shorts – bigger, stronger boys, most of whom wore an expression of supercilious boredom.

They were the paltry and unwilling fruit of an exhausting round of politicking, telephonings, pleadings, postponings, cancellations and awkward sessions with Ma Watson who kept on insisting on 'results'... The bleak fact was that none of the local schools wanted to be contaminated by contact with Beaconsfield School, the 'dustbin school'. The state schools feared it for ideological reasons; the private schools for commercial reasons. Ascomb House was the local prep school and was in fierce competition with other prep schools in the area. Old Charlie Morrison, the headmaster, was a rugby fanatic who wanted to establish his school as the leading rugby-playing school in the area. Worthwhile opponents were what he wanted, not the detritus of the garbage heap – for what would influential parents think of *that*?

However, the games teacher, Don Ford, was a kindly soul with Christian tendencies and Briggs had worked on this. 'Give my lot a chance. You know the saying, "Inasmuch as ye did it unto one of these least..." That sort of thing...' And eventually Ford had agreed to field a team, not, of course the First Fifteen, nor even the Third Fifteen, but a scraping of the barrel – all his 'also rans' and deadbeats. 'Yes, give *them* a chance... I take your point...'

Not, of course, that the 'also-rans' and deadbeats had been exactly thrilled at the prospect: 'The dustbin school? You're not *serious*, are you?'

'We'll all have to sit in wheelchairs, won't we? I mean they're all flippin' cripples, aren't they?'

'Wait till my old man hears about this! He'll blow at least two gaskets!'

Neither was Charlie Morrison exactly over the moon with enthusiasm: 'This Christian charity stuff is all very well, Ford, but there are limits, you know...'

No Ascomb teachers accompanied the 'team' on its charitable mission to Beaconsfield – which, at least, spared Briggs the humiliation of being 'shown up' in front of his professional peers. That, at any rate, was a mercy.

The Contents of the Dustbin

Time to start...

Briggs cast a bleak eye over his team. There was big Joe Willis, a fat whale of a thing who could hardly run a hundred yards without keeling over. He was merely 'infill', the ballast with which you filled up empty space. There was old Fatty Coburn, a huge beach ball of a lad who would provide the dead weight in the second row of the scrum – if he could manage to keep up with the game, a very big 'if' in his case. Philip Lawson, a gangling tousle-haired boy, was the scrum-half. He could be reasonably good if only he could overcome his 'duck-out' syndrome. He always had some excuse. Today he'd managed to turn up in his brother's St Ostwald's kit – casting a visual aspersion on Briggs' much vaunted discipline – which the old cow on the touchline was hardly likely to let go unnoticed! He was already moaning about the cold and had his hands clasped firmly under the blue soccer shirt: 'Christ, I'm bloody frostbitten!' There was going to be trouble in that quarter.

How the bloody hell was he supposed to win a match with this load of rubbish? To cap it all, the one boy who might have saved the situation, Robert Napier, had cried off. Which, of course, had gone down like a concrete balloon with old Watson – 'But why couldn't you have persuaded him? You're supposed to create enthusiasm, aren't you? Isn't that what you're there for? Etc., etc., etc...'

He eyed the substitute, the new boy, Denby. Not much hope there. He might have been quite good in the PE lessons, but could he survive a real rugby match against serious opposition? His spindly little frame was bad enough, but his posh accent clearly marked him out as 'soft as shit'.

Then he saw his pet hate, Sam Hawthorne. 'Give him a chance,' the old bitch had said. 'If he does well, it could be the making of him...'

'Does well!' ... Dream on! What a walking catastrophe! And, more to the point, what a brazen defiance of his specific instructions! His skinny frame was draped in a gigantic T-shirt with 'Love from Blackpool' on it – and God alone knew where he had got that from! – which covered him like a child's wigwam. One of his hands was lost somewhere up a long sleeve while the other was holding on to an extra-large pair of Bermuda shorts – again of unknown origin – which were sliding down his white beanstalk legs. As he loped onto the field, a derisory cheer went up from the Ascomb House team, followed by a groan from the Beaconsfield boys.

'Shat yourself again, Sam?' Philip Lawson bawled out, referring to a disaster which had occurred on Sam's first day at Beaconsfield and had been his theme tune ever since.

A crowd of red-shirted Beaconsfield boys began to swarm round him like Red Indians harrying a wounded buffalo.

'Know why Sam wears four pairs of underpants?' somebody asked John, who was shivering on the edge of the mob.

'Why?'

'Because he's got a tiny little willie and his mum tells him that if he keeps it warm, it'll grow bigger.'

'Yes,' added another, 'she pulls it every night to make it longer...'

'And did you know that he puts fertiliser on it, too,' said a third. 'You see, he thinks it's a flower...'

Poor old Sam, thought John, what a life he must lead! He felt he ought to do something to help him. But what? It was easier said than done.

Seeing his team becoming a rabble, Briggs came storming over: 'All right, that's quite enough! Come on, get into line, forwards on the right, three-quarters on the left!'

The crowd responded silently and unwillingly, leaving Sam fluttering in the breeze like an overgrown geranium.

'For God's sake, Sam, sort yourself out!' exclaimed an exasperated Briggs, 'Where's your rugby shirt?'

'Couldn't find it.'

'And what HAS happened to your rugby shorts?'

'He's shat himself again!' cried Billy Nolan, a stringy, white-haired boy in Form Three.

'You shut up!' snapped Briggs, cuffing him over the ear.

Billy subsided into a tearful sulk: 'Right, I'm not playin'! I'm telling me father of you!'

'Oh, don't start that again!' (It was the usual Billy Nolan scenario – all he needed on this ghastly afternoon!)

Briggs turned on Sam: 'No wonder they kick you about! You can't even tie your waist cord! God almighty, do I have to pull your trousers up for you? And what HAVE you got under that T-shirt? Your school uniform shirt and your school tie!' He looked at him in angry exasperation: 'Thirteen years old and you can't even dress yourself!'

'But I'm dyslexic. I can't help it!'

'Yes, and I'm the Sugar Plum Fairy! Don't give me that garbage!'

'His mum has to wipe his bum for him, Sir!' interjected Paul Morris, a non-descript fourth-year with black hair.

'And I'll have none of that from you, Morris!' snarled an increasingly furious Briggs, punching him in the ribs.

'Oyer! Keep yer hair on! I was only joking!' Tears began to trickle – as they usually did with Paul Morris.

Meanwhile Mrs Watson, standing on the touchline in her green wellies and brown anorak, look at her watch and called over: 'Mr Briggs, the match should have started ten minutes ago. Aren't you ready YET?'

Briggs grimaced. Dealing with this lot was like dealing with globules of mercury on a sheet of glass. As soon as you'd got one lot together, another lot scattered into a random muddle. Already Billy Nolan was walking off to the rear, muttering to himself.

He blew the whistle: 'Time to start!'

'We can't. Sir. David Robson's not here and he's meant to be the captain.'

'Where the hell is he?'

'He's in the bog. Sir.'

'Oh hell!'

'Don't bother waiting for him. Mr Briggs!' cried Mrs Watson. 'For heaven's sake, get started before everybody freezes to death!'

Seething with humiliation, Briggs handed the ball to Philip Lawson: 'All right, Lawson, you take the kick off.'

'Oh God, do I HAVE to? It's starting to rain and my hands are cold.'

'Get on before I kick YOU off!'

A glance at the snivelling Paul Morris showed that this was no idle threat, so the boy reluctantly complied. He managed to pump the ball five yards in a vaguely forward direction.

Predictable Flop

The Big Match had begun.

A large, sandy-haired Ascomb House boy caught the ball and ambled his way through the disorderly red-shirted gaggle that was supposed to be the Beaconsfield defence. Reaching the try line, he walked slowly up to the goal posts, held the ball ostentatiously above his head and then placed it firmly on the ground.

Three nil to Ascomb House.

Five minutes later he managed to convert the try – just! – and made the score five nil to Ascomb House.

'It's starting to rain,' called out the Ascomb captain, a big, burly, dark-haired fellow. 'Can't we just pack it in and say we've won?'

'No we can't!' retorted Briggs. His worst fears were being realised. Collapse. Disintegration. A withering interview with the old bag on the touchline... Then, tail between his legs, off into the outside world looking for a new career... Librarianship? Clerking in the Civil Service? Stacking boxes in a warehouse? How was he going to explain this disaster to his wife, Rosemary?

Biggles Defies the Swastika

But, unknown to him, salvation was standing beside him. Salvation. Recovery. Rebuilt career. Wing-forward John Denby's blood was up. This was disgusting! All that these big lumps could do was bully poor witless Sam, yet a bit of rain and a boy running at them with a ball scared them shitless! The mighty Luftwaffe was winning the Battle of Britain. More than winning. It was a pathetic pushover. You could just hear Hitler's evil cackle and Fatty Goering chortling with glee...

From that moment on everything shrank into a frenetic present tense.

'Beaconsfield kick off. Stop sulking, Nolan – it's your turn!'

'Why me? I'm hopeless!'

'You'll be even more hopeless if you don't!'

'You've no right! Wait till me favver comes up!'

'Get ON with it!'

A quarter-hearted pump goes a few feet into the air, lands in the mud and rolls a yard or so forwards. The big sandy-haired Ascomb boy casually picks it up and starts to run. Another disaster in the offing...

But Biggin Hill has been alerted. 646 Squadron may have been shot to smithereens, but one lone, battered spitfire remains, flown by Pilot Officer John Denby. Ma Watson is looking at you, John. You are the only one who can save her. The big, pink legs are pumping away like pile drivers. The cold, hard boots and sharp-edged studs are cleaving the air like knuckledusters. Death and glory! Go for the knees, clasp your arms round them. Sharp pain from the studs scraping your left hand. Freezing mud. Thump! Crash! Down comes the giant. Stars before your eyes. Headache as you crash into the ground...

'Fucking hell, you little git!'

Whistle blows.

'We'll have none of that language!'

'But he knocked me down!'

'That's what he's there for, you idiot! Free kick to Beaconsfield.'

Pick up the ball. Realisation growing. Outclassed at Rickerby Hall. But here better than most of them. Opportunity beckons. Never much good at kicking, but at least the ball goes diagonally forwards and not backwards.

A large, frighteningly large, Ascomb boy catches it and starts to run... The Luftwaffe are coming again, a swarm of Heinkels and Me 109s. Pilot Officer Denby alone against the massed might of Nazi Germany. Get the big bomber. Flailing legs, shot of pain as a sharp-studded boot hits your chin. The rear gunner is pumping a stream of lead into your cockpit. Grab the ankles... And over he goes... The big Heinkel spiralling down in a billow of flame.

'Bloody hell, you little sod!'

'Language!' from Briggs.

No whistle blown, so game goes on. Struggle to free yourself from the entangling legs. The pilot escaping from his burning aircraft. Ball on the ground. Mass of yellow-shirted boys converging on it. The Me 109s are swarming in for the kill. Ball wet and slippery. Freezing cold, but manage to pick it up. Run! Run! Run! The lone Spitfire battling its way through the overwhelming might of the Luftwaffe.

Duck! Dive! Turn this way! That way! A big bloke coming towards you, all guns blazing! He's getting you. Hold on to that ball. Shirt sleeve ripping! But you're free. No whistle blown. On! On! The try line is in front of you! Death and Glory! Over it. Dive melodramatically on to the ground. Whistle blows. You have scored a try!

Back to the centre covered in mud, cheek bleeding, the wounded soldier returning from the battle, the battered Spitfire landing at Biggin Hill having single-handedly beaten off the numberless legions of Nazi Germany. Surrounded by Beaconsfield players. Thumped on the back. 'Well done!' 'You're great!'

'Well done, Denby!' from a bewilderingly gratified Briggs. 'Now let's see the rest of you get stuck in!' Briggs is sensing a faint frisson rippling through the disjointed heap of wayward dropouts that's supposed to be a rugby team. Something unexpectedly good about to happen? Don't count on it. Not yet!

John takes the conversion. The ball goes sideways and barely manages to reach a height of two feet. Timely reminder that you're not ready for the England Squad. At least not yet.

Ascomb kick-off. A big lad thumps the ball halfway down the pitch, well into Beaconsfield territory. It heads for Sam Hawthorne who's having serious problems with the oversize Bermuda shorts which keep sliding off his narrow hips. He's only just able to dodge the muddy bomb plummeting down from the grey sky.

'Yah, Sam you're pathetic!'

The ball bounces up to Philip Lawson who gives it a colossal kick, which, by a benevolent stroke of fortune, sends it spiralling away back into Ascomb territory and over the left-hand touchline. It's the first really successful kick in Philip's life and he glows with pride. He's now got a stake in the game and he'll start to try.

Line out. Ascomb ball. Ball goes straight to a big, fat Ascomb forward who flings it out to the scrum-half. But ace fighter pilot John Denby gets him and sends the Me 109 hurtling earthwards in a plume of fire. Over he goes in a muddle of arms and legs. Whistle blows. Scrum down. Ascomb ball.

'Where's David Robson? He's meant to be in the second row with Fatty Cobum!'

'Here he is.'

'Come on, Robson, get your scrum in order. You're meant to be the captain, aren't you?'

'Get your bloody head down, Fatty!'

'I can't. I've got earache!'

'Get down or I'll fucking do you!'

Whistle blows: 'Any more of that language, Robson and I'LL be the one who does the doing!'

After much scuffling about the Beaconsfield scrum is about as organised as it ever will be. Scrum down. Ball in. The much more efficient Ascomb machine rolls over its disorderly opposition, reducing it to an incoherent muddle of arms and legs.

'Get your fat arse off my face!'

'Ow! You're squashing my arm!'

Ball goes to Ascomb scrum-half. Out to fly-half. Out to the big sandy-haired lad in the centre who starts to run. Crisis! The Luftwaffe is back in strength. But Pilot Officer John Denby – alias Beaconsfield wing-forward – the Lone Ranger of the Skies in his war-battered Spitfire, is on to him. Crash! Over he goes!

'Christ, not YOU again!'

Ball on the ground. Enemy converging on it. Quick! On to it! Pick it up. Go! Go! Go! Denby the Dauntless, sole defender of the Home Islands, battling against the swarming hordes of Nazi fighters while Winston Churchill himself – alias Mrs Watson on the touchline – watches from the white cliffs of Dover as he accelerates at full throttle... Faster, faster, steeper dive, ever steeper dive ... through the sound barrier ... over the line between the two posts. Crash sideways as a big Stuka – alias a large Ascomb boy – rams into him. But touch the ball down. Whistle blows. Yes! Another try!

The turning point. Crux of the battle. Score five-six. Beaconsfield is in the lead. Briggs and Mrs Watson elated.

John takes the conversion. An even bigger disaster than before. Ball not even airborne. No, John, you definitely won't make the England squad this year! Next year? Well, maybe...

Half-time whistle goes. Timely relief. Beaconsfield team gathers round John. 'Great stuff! Wicked! Magic!...'

Hero of the hour. New intoxicating experience.

Briggs shakes his hand in a flush of hardly concealed gratitude: 'Well done, Denby! Keep it up!'

Then he turns to the others: 'Now, if this little bloke can do it, what's to stop the rest of you? By the way, Lawson, well done! That was a great kick.'

Philip glows with gratification.

The warm breeze, that faint frisson, is picking up strength. Perhaps a warm spring is driving the cold and muddy winter away.

Mrs Watson bustles over. Big smiles and congratulations all round: 'Keep it up, lads! Well done, John! Now let's see somebody else score a try!'

Half-time over. Ascomb kick-off. There's a sea change in Ascomb, too. The game's for real now. Beaten by the dustbin school? Charlie Morrison's going to blow at least ten gaskets, probably even fill his pants with fury! We'll all get done... So get your act together, lads!

The big, sandy-haired boy boots the ball hard and sends it plunging deep into Beaconsfield territory. Concerted charge after it. Mass attack.

The ball lands near Sam Hawthorne. He actually manages to pick it up. But the half-time changeover has disoriented him and he's not sure which way he's meant to go. Then CRASH! Over he goes, demolished by a large Ascomb lump. The Wright Brothers 1903 flying machine obliterated by the latest German Me 262 jet fighter. Unequal contest...

Now Ascomb's got the ball! The try-line's only fifteen yards away. Do your stuff, John! Into that Spitfire of yours. England expects. More than that England *needs*! Big, dark-haired lad, dodges, swerves. Nearer and nearer, gasping for breath...

Hand off! Really a punch in the face. Flashes of light. Pain. Tears welling up.

Blood pouring out of your nose. Salty taste in your mouth. BUT DON'T CRY, JOHN! NEVER CRY AGAIN! NOT EVER! After him. Go for the legs. Got him! Over he goes. But he's across the line and touches the ball down. Try. Score six-eight. Ascomb is back in the lead. Fatty Goering has blown up the Houses of Parliament!

The Ascomb attempt at a conversion is almost as pathetic as the Beaconsfield efforts. Jeer from Beaconsfield.

'Don't you start any of that!' snarls Briggs. 'There's nobody here good enough to jeer at anybody else.'

Blood up. And not just Pilot Officer Denby this time. David Robson takes the Beaconsfield kick-off. Got to justify his position as team captain. Supreme effort is rewarded with partial success as the ball goes, not quite forwards, but at least diagonally and in the right general direction. It bounces over the right-hand touchline, decently far enough into Ascomb territory. Face saved!

Line out. Ascomb ball. Big Ascomb forward gets it. Out to the Ascomb scrum half... But fighter ace John Denby is airborne in his Spitfire and down goes the Me 109 in an incandescent sheet of fire...

Ball on the ground. Big sandy-haired Ascomb centre three-quarter picks it up and starts to run. Pilot Officer Denby's out of breath – got a hole in his fuel tank, engine is spluttering. Can't catch him... But Philip Lawson is there. Wild neck-scrag of an attempted tackle results in hand-off. A punch in the face makes Philip cry...

Then Billy Nolan comes to life and actually manages to execute his first ever rugby tackle.

Ball on the ground. Rolls over to Sam Hawthorne. John can't quite reach it. Supercharged, super-everything Rolls-Royce Merlin engine cutting out. Screams at Sam: 'PICK IT UP!'

Sam picks it up and – Wow! – he actually manages to hold on to it!

John screams again: 'RUN, SAM! THAT WAY! THAT WAY!'

The tryline is only fifteen yards away. Glory beckons. Random chance has opened a clear path ahead of Sam. He lopes his way along in slow motion like a giant stick insect. He crosses the line! Then he just stands there, not sure of what to do. The enemy are bearing down on him fast.

'PUT THE BALL DOWN, SAM! DOWN!' screams John. He wants to see Sam get his glory, but the old goof is so bloody clueless!

'PUT THE BALL DOWN AND TOUCH IT!'

Message gets through the interference and the static. In the nick of time Sam puts the ball down and touches it.

The improbable has happened. Sam Hawthorne has actually scored a try. A grin of sheer, unalloyed pleasure breaks over his flattened and squashed face. Life for Sam has been one long lurch from failure to failure. Now at last he has tasted a little success. The unaccustomed taste is sweet indeed.

'Well done, Sam!' Clapping and cheering...

Then his Bermuda shorts fall down. But not to worry: everything that matters is hidden beneath a pair of bathing trunks, a pair of underpants and that oversize T-shirt. Sorting out the subsequent sartorial muddle, however, demands his full and undivided attention and he is out of action for the next fifteen minutes. Eventually Mrs Watson has to come to the rescue and tie up his waist cord for him.

David Robson insists on taking the conversion kick. 'I'm the bloody captain, ain't I?' It's Beaconsfield's best effort yet. The ball actually gets airborne and goes forwards. But it doesn't cross the bar. Score: nine-eight.

Now Ascomb's blood really is on the boil. If this mess isn't sorted out pretty bloody soon, old Charlie Morrison won't be the only one filling his pants. Don Ford will be too and so will you lot when you get bloody done!

Kick-off. Wiry, red-haired Ascomb fly-half follows up and gets the ball. Thunders down the centre of the field at the head of a yellow-shirted horde. Eagle Day. The massed assault of all Hitler's airborne legions to prepare the way for the invasion of Britain. One lone Spitfire rises up to meet them – Denby the Dauntless, John the Brave... Yes, but he's muddy, cold and tired, dropping with exhaustion. More tired than he's ever been in his whole life... and he's got a bleeding nose and a bruised arm... But keep going, screw up that courage of yours, pull out those last feeble scraps of energy, rev up that supercharged, super-everything Rolls-Royce Merlin engine of yours to beyond its limit ... and in you go!

Down comes the twin-engined Ju 88 fighter-bomber in an explosion of fire and black smoke. But he passes the ball to that big sandy-haired Ascomb lad. Try line only a few yards away.

Now it's Joe Willis' chance. Having done little throughout the game but kick fatty Coburn's more than ample rear end, he has had a 'Damascene Conversion' of sorts. Or, to put it in less exalted terms, if that little git from Form One can bring down these big Ascomb tanks, then why the hell can't he? It's a matter of dignity.

So in he goes ... and crunch, down comes that big Ascomb bastard! But he's over the line... Try!

Score: nine-eleven. Looks like old Charlie Morrison won't be needing that new pair of boxer shorts, after all – and, neither, thank God, will anybody else!

The attempted conversion is the usual flop.

Go for it now, Beaconsfield! It's up to you, Pilot Officer Denby! You're near the edge now – dropping with tiredness, aching all over, cold and wet and with a bleeding nose. But squeeze out those last few drops of energy.

Billy Nolan takes the kick-off. No improvement. If anything, even worse than before. The ball goes backwards. But Briggs doesn't blow his whistle and the game continues. Confused, scrappy play.

Scrum down. Ascomb steamroller demolishes the squabbling Beaconsfield tangle of arms and legs. Ball out to Ascomb scrum-half. Roars away down the field... But the lone, marauding spitfire of Pilot Officer John Denby takes the Bf 110 head on ... and over he goes, twisting and turning in a trail of black smoke before exploding in a red flash among the green hedgerows of England...

Confusion. John picks up the ball. But the lone knight of the air is beset by the swarming Me 109s... Run this way. Run that way... But the big dark-haired Ascomb captain gets him and he disappears into the mud under a mountain of thirteen-year-old beef. The heroic little Spitfire, belching flame and smoke, plunges down to its glorious death...

But Paul Morris has managed to get the ball. Sees his chance. Ascomb are all piling on to little Denby... In for the kill. Making sure that the little squirt really is dead and won't rise again. So run, Paul! Run! Run! Run as you've never run before in your whole life of ducking out of difficulties... Over the line!

And Paul Morris has scored a try! His first ever! Score: 12–11. Beaconsfield back in the lead!

Billy Nolan makes the usual mess of the conversion.

Last minutes now. Dusk closing in. The few shreds of daylight in dismal retreat. John gelatinous with exhaustion. Ironed out. Longing for the salvation of the final whistle. In a daze, almost as if he's watching another John Denby going through the motions of trying to survive those last few moments.

Ascomb kick-off. Last frantic attempt to win the unexpectedly hard-fought day. Big dark-haired captain gets the ball and plunges towards the corner flag. Beaconsfield defence scatters...

It's up to you, now, Pilot Officer Denby in your battered, shot-to-bits, barely functioning Spitfire... Over in Berlin Hitler has blown at least fifty gaskets and has given Fatty Goering a mega-bollocking. So now Fatty himself – no less! – is leading the mass attack in his specially designed Me 262 fighter-bomber! The fate of the world depends on you. Pilot Officer Denby! ... Dazed, hands numb with cold, mouth full of salty blood, in a trance, you crash, kamikaze-style into him – and over he goes five yards from the tryline!

Fatty Goering goes cartwheeling down through the blue and explodes in a sheet of flame... You've saved civilisation!

Final whistle goes! Salvation. Release. Beaconsfield has won its first ever match.

Bewildering Victory

Dazed, battered, sodden, miserably cold, covered in mud and with a bleeding nose, John found himself hailed as a hero.

'Well done, Denby!' exclaimed an effusive Briggs, doing something that normally he would never have dreamed of doing, and clasping him firmly by both his shoulders.

'And well done the rest of you!' he added, again letting his carefully preserved guard drop momentarily and thumping Paul Morris and Billy Nolan on the back. 'I never knew you had it in you!'

In his euphoria Briggs felt a great weight slide off his shoulders. He'd been saved! No dismissals now! No signing on for courses in librarianship, male nursing or whatever. But the way that it had all happened was so strange and unexpected. Uncanny even. As if some alien force had entered into that bunch of deadbeats. And it all seemed to be connected with that weedy little new boy, Denby. With his girlie looks and, above all, with that ghastly, toe-curling upper-class voice of his, by all normal criteria he should have been a complete poof. Probably was. It just didn't fit.

Then Mrs Watson rushed over. Full of emotion, she wanted to pick up and hug her new protégé, John Denby. He'd saved the match for her, saved her credibility with the Board of Governors, done her a service that he couldn't possibly be aware of... But she was the 'disciplined professional' and not an 'emotional woman'. So she contented herself with beams and smiles and handshakes all round: 'Well done, all of you! I'm really proud of you!'

Finally she shook John's hand: 'Well done, John! That's the sort of thing I want to see!'

John felt a blissful radiance rippling through his aching and battered body. Sir Lancelot had been worthy of Queen Guinevere.

As they all stumbled off the pitch, Briggs received an unexpected boost. The Ascomb captain came up to him: 'Thanks for a great match. We thought it was going to be pathetic, but it was wicked. Can you fix up a return game?'

'Of course...'

There was nothing Briggs would have liked better.

Then the captain approached John: 'You've got guts! Sorry if I thumped you up a bit...' (Under a rather uncouth exterior Graeme Holdsworth was a kind-hearted lad who'd felt ashamed of Ascomb's sneering at Beaconsfield: 'It's not their fault. How would you like to be them?')

'Remember you are only a man'

There followed the warm paradise of a hot shower – or what *should* have been a warm paradise! As he slipped off his rugby shorts, John noticed to his horrified disgust that *that* was still there. Worse, even. With the violent exercise a little trickle had become a minor stream ... a stinking, repulsive slurry.

His euphoria dissolved. Part of him was still a pathetic little wimp. It was as if he had been one of those triumphant Roman generals and the slave had whispered those famous words in his ear: 'Remember you are only a man.'

But mercifully his shorts and his legs were so soaked and caked in mud that the mess wasn't noticeable.

Bliss

Then came the team tea – coke, sausage, beans and chips and ice cream – and the feeling of feasting with the victorious Knights of the Round Table. A new experience for him. A momentary promotion. A transformation. A metamorphosis, not, of course, that he knew what that word meant.

So back to Gloucester Road and a welcoming bed.

And, after that, a blissful Sunday. Homework – Yuk! Yuk! But then sweets, crisps and playing with your trains. Not allowed to go to the party in the living room, but an evening spent watching *Tora! Tora! Tora!*, which was much more interesting.

31

A Day of Glory

The first bit of Monday was a day of glory such as John had never known before and would only fleetingly know again.

It started, almost spookily, with a change in the weather. He woke up to see an unfamiliar red glow streaming in through the skylight above his bed. Looking out, he saw that the deadening pall of grey cloud that had hung over the city for so long had lifted. In its place was a rising sun, brilliantly red and beaming down from a clear and radiant sky, revealing a new and fresh world. In the damp air everything gleamed and sparkled. The grey slate roofs, the piles of rubble, the brash new tower blocks stranded amid swathes of litter-strewn wasteland ... all seemed revitalised as if it had recovered from a lingering disease.

Down in the valley the glum old River Boldon was no longer a dismal grey smudge, but smiled out to the world in a multitude of shimmering ripples of light. On the far side, clear and precise, the massive blocks of flats marched slab-like up the hill. Far beyond, bright-blue hills surged away, rising layer after layer, to the distant ridges of the Pennines. 'Away! Away! Come away!' they seemed to cry, 'Here in our hidden folds you will find freedom and adventure!'

He got up with a feeling of exhilaration – born again like the vibrant world outside. It was time to collect the trophies won in Saturday's triumph.

Reality came first, however. He had to cross that dangerous belt of enemy territory. That meant the usual disguise: dirty jeans and scruffy sweater and face fixed in an aggressive scowl: 'What the fuck are ye lookin' at, son?' Get off the bus at Prince Consort Park and into the gents'. In as a Geordie yoblet: out as a polite middle-class schoolboy in your red blazer, striped tie and grey trousers.

Unfinished Business...

As soon as he entered the school hall for morning assembly he sensed a wave of excitement rippling through the lines of red-blazered youngsters.

'You were great on Saturday!'

'Wicked, John! Wicked!'

Bill Bleeson, resplendent in his neat uniform and his head boy badge, shook him warmly by the hand: 'Well played on Saturday, John, very well played!'

Joining the Form One line, he was greeted with smiles and thumps on the back. Only Ratty stood aloof, his rodent face twisted into an ugly leer as he pointed at him and made an obscene gesture with his fingers. Unfinished business from Friday night...

Glory

There was silence as the teachers filed in. Mrs Watson announced the hymn. Prayers were said. Then came the announcements. 'First the bad news...!' So and so had got four minus marks for bad behaviour: 'See Mr Meakin in break and collect your punishment...' Somebody else had been reported by a member of the public for bad behaviour on the Dunfell bus: '...See Mr Meakin at break...'

'Now the good news...' Bronze stars for Maths and Geography for Mark Smith and Andrew Hughes... Round of applause as they came up and collected their certificates... Then: 'Our new boy, John Denby – a silver star for Maths, a silver star for Scripture and a gold star for Art...' There was a louder round of applause as he marched out to collect his certificates and receive a big smile and a warm handshake from Mrs Watson. A wonderful and exhilarating experience – and so new. He rejoined Form One glowing.

More was to follow.

'Now,' declared Mrs Watson, 'Mr Briggs wants to say something about Saturday's rugby match against Ascomb House...'

A beaming Briggs mounted the rostrum. This was the first bit of success he'd had since he'd left St Martin's College in Wiltshire and he intended to make the most of it – to savour the cup of nectar, delicious drop by delicious drop.

He launched into his rehearsed oration: on Saturday an 'historic event' had taken place... The school had played its first-ever rugby match against another school ... and it was no ordinary school either. Ascomb House was a school with a strong rugby tradition... Its First Fifteen had been the champions of the Junior schools' Rugby League in 1972, 1974 and...

'For heaven's sake get *on* with it, Jamie lad!' hissed Meakin from behind him. 'Some of us have work to do today!'

But James Briggs Cert. Ed. was not going to be denied his moment in the limelight and the peroration continued: '... In 1978 they won the Hilliard Cup which is etc., etc., etc...'

At long last he came to the point. He hadn't expected the team to win against such a formidable opponent, but they'd pulled together and played far better than he'd dared to hope. A new spirit had entered into them and this had been provided by the new boy, Denby, who'd inspired his teammates to achieve great things... During the match he'd ... etc. etc. etc...

Eventually the said Denby had to come forward and receive his 'Man of the Match' Award and his Rugby Colours, the 'first ever to be given in the history of Beaconsfield School...'

Tumultuous applause erupted into wild cheering as John marched up to receive two gleaming badges to pin on to his blazer. A vigorous handshake from Briggs was followed by a wonderful smile from Mrs Watson and thumpings on the back as he returned to his place.

He was a new John now. The drab little grub had turned into a gorgeous butterfly, talented, clever, brave and a great sportsman. Giddy with his success, he walked on air.

The Waterloo of Form One

But even more glory was to come.

The first lesson was Maths with Polly Parrot. Polly's lessons always started at least five – and, sometimes, ten – minutes late because he had to get all his props together.

He could barely survive forty minutes of potentially rebellious anarchy without massive logistic support in the shape of lists of marks, charts of bronze, silver and gold stars awarded, multi-coloured graphs showing topics covered and pupil performance in each one of them, a complex chart showing the interaction of ability, effort and achievement, exercise books arranged in appropriate order of the best down to the worst ... and so on.

So, while he fluttered round amid reams of semi-organised paper, there was time to sort out Friday's unfinished business as Form One waited on the landing. The stakes were high. This morning's coronation of 'smarmy liddell turd Denby' had come as an unpleasant shock to Ratty and Owly. They'd confidently imagined that they'd sorted him out on Friday. And so they had! The little git had burst into tears without even being hit. Now he was being hailed as a 'fuckin' hard'! The praise heaped on him by the big lads in Form Four and Five was especially unsettling. Unless he were 'done over pretty fuckin' sharp like', their little empire – indeed their whole tribute system and the fags they enjoyed on the proceeds – could collapse. Time to act!

The crucial battle began – the Naseby of Form One, the Waterloo, if you like.

Owly pushed in front of John. Ratty took up station behind. The rest of the class hung back in fear – ready to join the winning side when the outcome was clear. And, if past experience was anything to go by, they were pretty damned sure what that outcome would be... Poor little John, he really was for it! The teachers didn't rule Form One: Ratty and Owly did.

'Ey you!' hissed Ratty, poking a finger obscenely into John's bottom. 'Warraboot me five quid?'

'And mine an' all?' added Owly, turning round.

This was it. Decision time. Surrender now and you're still a pathetic little wimp and always will be. Not an option. Screwing up all his new-found courage, John pronounced the portentous words.

'Piss off!'

The reaction was immediate and alarming.

'Did ye tell us ter piss off?' snarled Ratty, outraged by the unexpected defiance. 'Reet, yer's gerrin it!'

'Hey, lads!' he called out to the class in ready anticipation of their usual support. 'Yer shoudda seen liddel fart Denby 'ere cryin' on Friday night! He got the cane like what I said. Twelve off Mekon on 'is bare bum while ole Dolly 'ad a fuckin' good look. An' ole Mekon bummed 'im an' all, good and proper like!'

'Crap! I never got the cane and Mekon wasn't even there!'

'Liar! We was lookin' in the windee an' we sawed it all, didn't we, Owly?'

'We did an' all!' chortled Owly.

'Crap!'

'Howay, dee yer trick like what yer were told! Drop yer pants an' show us the red marks on yer bum!'

'No I won't!'

'Reet lads! You 'old 'm whiles Owly an' me pulls 'is pants off!'

This was war. War to the death. High noon. Gunfight at the O.K. Corral. Oddly enough, he wasn't scared. It wasn't like Greenhill where his whole body had turned into rice pudding at the sight of the baying mob. The Greenhill lot were wild animals. This lot were human. They could bleed. He'd seen that on Saturday afternoon.

Quick military decision. Blitzkrieg. Go for the enemy headquarters. Knock out the brain and then mop up the decapitated body afterwards.

So a savage pre-emptive strike on the unsuspecting Ratty. Smash his ugly face to pulp! Ferocious punch on his beaky nose. Blood streaming. Punch his ear so hard that it hurts your knuckles. Violent punch in the eye.

Offensive succeeds with gratifying ease.

'Oyer! Ow! Fuckin' hell! Give ower will yers!' Sob! Sob! Sob!

Ratty's crying. Enemy headquarters a smoking ruin. Now go for the disoriented mass of Owly.

Kamikaze punch right into the middle of his big, fat face. Tiger claws on his blazer, pulling it off and ripping the sleeve...

'Gerroff us, will yers!'

A feeble and uncoordinated attempt at retaliation quickly crumbles under a hail of blows. Total victory with minimal casualties in sight...

EH?AHER?ERWHAT'SGOINGONHERESTOPITATONCEISAYST OPITATONCEISAYSTOPIT!'

All in one multi-syllable compound word. The celebrated squawk elongated and red-shifted out into a prolonged high-pitched falsetto screech. The best yet with the added delights of arms flapping and hair standing on end. A real bravura performance which was imitated round the school for weeks afterwards. ('Should have seen Polly Parrot on Monday! He nearly lost all his feathers!')

End of war. Arrival of UN Peacekeeping Forces.

They filed into the Maths Room with Polly squealing away about 'Ten minus marks' and 'seeing Mr Meakin in break'.

'And, yes, I MEAN seeing Mr Meakin! Seeing Mr Meakin in break! Yes, I REALLY MEAN it!' (Old hands, however, knew that whenever Polly said he *really meant* something it was a sign that nothing was going to happen. That was part of the accumulated 'Science of Polly-Watching'.)

While John lost himself in the areas of rectangles. Ratty snivelled away at the back and Owly did his feeble best not to cry.

The destiny of Form One had been decided. 'The King and the Kingdom were lost at Naseby.' Likewise Ratty and Owly's kingdom had been lost on the landing outside the Maths Room of Beaconsfield School. Henceforth there was a New Dispensation in the junior end of Beaconsfield School.

When they went out on to the playing field for morning break Form One crowded round John.

'Nifty! ... Wicked! ... Magic! ... You're great!'

Fred, the serious West Indian boy, shook his hand: 'Great stuff! It was about time somebody sorted those two out. They've been making poor old Sam's life a misery. They were getting money out of him – five pounds a week – and forcing him to steal fags for them.'

'But why did you let them do it? I mean Ratty's as soft as shit!'

'Dunno! There was something about him that made everybody scared.'

'Wow!' chortled Michael Connolly. 'You don't look it, but yous is rock 'ard you ... Where were yer last school?' he added. 'I mean why is you here? We're all here for a reason, you know.'

'Er, Greenhill.' It just slipped out and John immediately regretted it. Intoxicated by the adulation, he'd dropped his guard – and now the ghastly truth could leak out and destroy everything.

'Cor! That's an 'ard school! Was yer bashed up like?' (Answer: YES! Underlined in red! But nobody must know that. NOBODY!)

'No, I was expelled because I hit a teacher...' (He lied easily and fluently. Again, it was so much easier to invent a more agreeable reality, yes, so much nicer to pretend that you were the person you wanted to be rather than the person you really were. Anyway, who would check up on the facts?)

'Crikey!' whistled an awe-struck Michael. 'Hear that, lads! John were expelled from Greenhill for hittin' a teacher! You really is rock 'ard you!'

'But you doesn't go round hittin' other kids, does yer?' he added nervously. Victory and success had John feel big, wise and noble – grown up. 'No, I don't,' he replied in a solemn and pompous voice, trying to sound like Mr Cotton of Rickerby Hall. 'I only hit people when they hit me for nothing. God says you're not to hit people for nothing, so I don't.'

Danny Fleetwood sidled up to him: 'I'm glad you kicked Ratty in. He and Owly are real dirty. They're always talking about bums an' that. They was tryin' to make me do filthy things in the bog with them. They're a couple of homs. They do *it*, you know...'

John didn't know what a 'hom' was, but it was obviously something far dirtier than anything he'd ever encountered before. To preserve his new 'rock 'ard' image, however, he couldn't admit that he didn't know. So he pretended that he did. 'Cor, you mean they do *it*!' (Not that he had the first idea what 'it' was!)

'Yeah, they do!'

'But what do the grown-ups have to say about it?'

'Grown-ups don't know half the things we know about kids,' added Danny sagely, tapping into his accumulated experience of adult innocence in the face of juvenile criminality.

John could only nod in agreement.

Surrender on Lüneburg Heath

Out on the playing field during lunch-break the final surrender occurred. Appomattox, Lüneburg Heath ... call it what you will.

Ratty and Owly came up to John, all ingratiating smiles: 'Let's be friends. I mean we was only 'aving a birra fun, weren't we, Owly?'

This was the glorious moment of triumph. Victor. Conqueror in war. Something that he'd never imagined ever happening to him. But in his euphoria he remembered Mr Cotton's words when he'd left Rickerby Hall: 'God has been kind to you and so you must repay him by being kind to other people who aren't as lucky as you...' Remember to forgive your enemies. God got pretty shirty if you didn't do that. Other images flashed through his mind – the dying chick on the gravel of the drive at Rickerby Hall, the poor burnt cat at Greenhill ... and poor, helpless old Sam Hawthorne! Here was his chance to keep on the right side of God! Paid dividends.

'All right, but you've got to stop kicking Sam Hawthorne in and taking his money...'

'Yes, but...'

'Well, if you don't me and the lads really will do you over this time, won't we, Danny?'

'Not 'arf we will! And there's ten of us and only two of you!'

Ratty glanced round and saw to his dismay that the whole of Form One was surrounding him, fists clenched and ready to pounce. Trapped! An alarming new situation.

But he'd been in this sort of corner before and his quick intelligence recognised military reality when he saw it. Change of tack needed.

'OK. It's a deal.' The treaty was signed and sealed.

Later on an almost tearful Sam came up to him: 'Thanks, John, thanks... You're the first friend I've ever had...'

As John looked at Sam's strange, flattened face twisted into an expression of supreme gratitude, he had a vivid flashback. Similar things had been said to him before by an even more wretched creature that had clung to him for protection – Billy Lees. It was almost as if he actually saw the little gnome standing like a ghost before him. He'd failed Billy utterly. Now, at least, through Sam, he'd made a kind of recompense. But that vision was from a forbidden past and was quickly expunged. No place for it in the New Dispensation.

A Perfect End to the Day

Only one thing remained to complete the glorious day – a hug and a kiss from Mrs Watson.

He knew he shouldn't want this – it was what soppy little wets wanted, not what proper boys wanted. And, supposing his classmates found out? He'd never live it down! But, well... Well, he just couldn't help himself! It was what he'd been secretly missing ever since his utterly perfect gran and granddad had been taken from him.

At four o'clock he waited till all the kids seemed to have left the school and then, looking carefully around him to make sure that he really was alone, he crept timorously up to her study door. Nervously, he knocked. But as soon as he'd done it he had a moment of panic. What was he to say to her? What if she was angry at being disturbed?

But before he could run away the door opened and there she was – the Mother Goddess, the Queen of England, call her what you will – beaming radiantly at him.

He fumbled for words: 'Sorry to disturb you, Miss, but well... Can I just say thank you for everything...'

Unknown to him this was exactly what Dorothy had been waiting for all day. She could hardly have ordered him to come and see her, could she? That would have looked like favouritism – and she was a proper professional, *not* an 'emotional woman'. Also, it would have been a dangerous admission of weakness – and kids could home in on weakness with all the deadly efficiency of a guided missile. Best not to go chasing after kids, but to let them come to you. But *would* this one come to her? Did he *really* need her? Oh, how she'd been hoping he did!

But there he was, her *own* special child, smiling his glorious smile!

Quite forgetting herself, she closed the door and hugged and kissed him: Well done, John! Very well done!' (Oh, Dolly! You silly woman! Don't let yourself go like this! You'll only regret it! But, something tells you that this one won't exploit you. He needs you as much as you need him! Woman's instinct, perhaps?)

To her relief he responded fulsomely, seemingly luxuriating in the warm feminine embrace. Did she but know it, at that moment she was his beloved gran come down to earth again...

Somewhat shamefaced, he disentangled himself and, bidding her a polite good night, slipped out of the room. As he went out of the front door, he met Danny Fleetwood standing on the pavement outside. He had a moment of panic – had he been spotted being soppy little mummy's boy with Dolly?

'Cor, John!' cooed Danny. 'You're a real hero, aren't you? You know like Robin Hood...'

John heaved a big sigh of relief. His newly acquired 'rock-hard' image was still intact.

Cinderella Returns from the Ball...

The hero went home in a state of exaltation.

'One day I'll be famous and then I'll fucking show you!' That day could be coming. Budding scholar, artist and rugby star! Victor in the Form One Civil War, deliverer of Sam Hawthorne! He just had to tell Giles and Mary all about it.

When Giles answered the door, he exploded into the house: 'Giles! Giles! I've got silver stars for Maths and Scripture and a Gold star for Art! I've got my rugby colours, too!' All in a prolonged, high-pitched falsetto squeal.

Without a word Giles returned to his table and continued writing, seemingly immersed in his mountains of paper.

'Giles! Giles!'

303

The humanoid typewriter motioned him to go away.

'But Giles, I've got...'

'Not now, John.' Low menacing growl.

'But...'

'GO AWAY!'

The sudden explosion made John jump with fright. For a moment tears welled up in his eyes. But, don't be a cry baby, John! You're a 'hard' and hards don't cry! Still, it was all so unexpected and deflating.

Crestfallen and feeling physically reduced in size, he clambered up the ladder.

Mary was on the landing, smoking a cigarette, but fully clothed, thank God!

'Mary, Mary, I've got a gold star for Art and...'

But instead of being impressed, Mary screwed her face up into a scowl. 'I don't care if you've been given the Nobel-bloody-Prize for Physics!' she said, 'Have you seen the state of your room?'

'But ... but...'

'But NOTHING! And those bloody games' clothes! What the fuck have you been doing in them? Rolling in the mud? Am I supposed to wash them for you?'

'Sorry ... but...'

'And those stinking shorts! Messing yourself at your age! Has nobody ever taught you to use a toilet or bog paper! Jesus Christ!'

He blushed bright red and felt himself shrivel up. God, did she *have* to mention this in public? He didn't *want* to do it! It wasn't his fault. It just happened – well, because of *that*!

'Now you'll go and get them and wash them yourself. THIS INSTANT!'

'But... But...'

'Are you trying to defy me, young man?' A cold, threatening look that made him cringe.

He scuttled up to the attic and gathered up the offending articles. Mary was right. The shorts *were* disgusting – downright repulsive. Oh God, when *would* this business ever end? And what if the kids at Beaconsfield found out about it? Didn't bear thinking about. Not so much a hard now – more a dirty little shit-pants.

He climbed down on to the landing, went into the bathroom and turned on the tap in the wash basin.

A screech in his ear made him jump: 'NOT THERE! I don't want to wash myself in your muck. DOWN BELOW!'

'Sorry ... er...'

Fighting back tears, he scrambled down the ladder and made for the only other washbasin in the house, the one in the kitchen area. Giles, writing frantically at his table, didn't notice him. The dragon in the cave was asleep, a gentle coil of smoke coming out of its nostrils.

So be careful! But he faced an immediate problem. The sink was full of the remnants of last night's supper – wine glasses, spoons and forks, ethnic plates with funny patterns on them and big, crude earthenware bowls. Moving this conglomeration would be a noisy, clattering process which would almost certainly wake the smoking monster at the table up.

So what to do? Washing clothes was one of those feminine mysteries accessible only to Mrs Bowles and his beloved, adored and perfect gran up in heaven. It was wholly unexplored territory – and, anyway, girls did that sort of thing, not boys.

After a moment's dither, he turned on the tap – and, thank God, no water spurted over the floor this time! – squeezed in some washing-up liquid and set to work. The most embarrassing and disgusting thing went in first – the rugby shorts. A revolting sludge soon filled the basin.

Suddenly a violent banshee screech exploded into his ear: 'YOU DIRTY LITTLE PIG! ARE YOU DELIBERATELY TRYING TO POISON US!? WE'VE GOT TO EAT OFF THOSE PLATES, YOU KNOW!'

He swung round to see Mary, her face contorted with fury. A stinging slap landed on his left cheek and then another on his right cheek. It hurt – and this time the tears came thick and fast. There was nothing he could do about it.

Then a deep male voice boomed out over the cacophony: 'Oh, for Christ's sake! Can't I have a bit of peace!'

The sleeping dragon had woken up. Total catastrophe. He cringed in terror as the monster approached him.

'All right! All right!' said Giles in a calm reassuring voice. 'There's no need for that! I'm not going to hit you! But you don't wash your dirty clothes among the supper things, do you? Take them up to the bathroom and wash them there.'

Crazy confusion. 'But Mary told me *not* to do that... Please I'm all confused...' John dissolved into baby sobs. The 'hard man' image was shot to hell.

305

'Oh, come on, boy, there's no need to turn on the taps. Just get up to the bathroom and get on with it. There's a good lad!'

'Take his bloody side, won't you?' exclaimed Mary. 'Make a fool of me in front of him! What about my authority?'

'Darling, PLEASE!'

He Must Make Amends

Eventually John settled down for the night with his wet clothes draped over the 'meaningful statement' of the cistern and pipes.

He was about to turn off the light when Giles clambered up the ladder and sat down on the bed. Instinctively, he cringed. What had he done wrong this time?

But, oddly enough, Giles seemed to be in a good mood: 'Well done, John! That's the place to hang your wet things... By the way, I'm sorry I was a bit bad-tempered when you came in this evening. You see, I've got a lot of work to do. Anyway, I'm very pleased that you've done well at school...'

Peace treaty.

Gratified, John embraced and kissed him. But Giles brusquely pushed him off.

'There's no need for that! You're not a little baby any more.'

An awkward silence followed and, without a further word, Giles went back down the ladder.

For a while John lay and mused. It had been another of those strange days. Glory that he'd never known before alongside tears and infantile degradation. He seemed to be two separate people. He remembered the story of Cinderella. It was, of course, a soppy fairy story for little kids – something he'd grown out of long ago. But the image had stayed with him: glorious princess at the ball and then grubby little kitchen maid after midnight. That was the way he was: glorious hero at Beaconsfield, dirty little cry baby at Gloucester Road. Which was the *real* John Denby?

And why this sudden change in his parents' attitude? They'd been so kind to him – forgiven him for running away, tidied up his room for him, bought him presents...

But now, when he had done *good* things, they'd shouted at him, blamed him for something he couldn't help and slapped him on the face. Obviously, they didn't like him – but why?

He rolled over and caught sight of the Merchant Navy *Bulleid Pacific* that they'd given him only three days ago. That *had* been kind! But what had he given them in return? Nothing! Nothing but a heap of filthy rugby kit left stinking on the floor! No wonder they didn't like him. Grown-ups were sensible people who always had reasons for things. So he must do his bit to make Giles and Mary like him. Yes, he would save up his money and buy them the best Christmas present they'd ever had. That would put everything right – and, what was more, God would approve of that!

32

Different Conceptual Universes

But things weren't that simple.

It was a matter of conceptual universes. Forty or more years before this some tribesmen in the remote mountains of New Guinea had seen aeroplanes dropping parachutes laden with goodies into the jungle. They didn't know what they were, but their logic told them that they were big birds. So if they built similar birds on the ground, then those birds would drop their goodies on to them. Thus the Cargo Cult had been born.

Wildly mistaken? Certainly, it was in no way connected with the reality of military supply drops in World War II, but was it illogical? Not really. Those tribesmen just lived in a different conceptual universe.

It wasn't so different from the situation at 14 Gloucester Road. John and his parents lived in different conceptual universes.

The *Real* World – Problems with Dinosaurs and Uppity Inferiors

Giles' attitude to John had nothing to do with expectations of gratitude.

The kid was simply in the way. Over the past two weeks a great hole had been blown in his work schedule. But with old Mother Higton's satisfactory report to the Social Services – 'absolution' you could call it – that particular chapter had been closed. It was time to catch up on developments in the *real* world.

And a lot had been happening – not all of it very positive either. Securing the Labour Party nomination for Boldonbridge West was proving a lot harder than he had imagined. The younger party members were no problem. They all talked the same radical language.

It was the old Labour dinosaurs who were being awkward. Typical of them was George Dawes of ASLEF whose natural habitat was the cab of a 1930s steam locomotive and who kept banging on about 'public school professors an' that' not being 'proper workers' – whatever that was supposed to mean! And then there was that dreadful old fool, Robertson, who ran the local Salvation Army hostel and was always grinding on about 'caring' and 'Christian values'…

He was going to have to hold his nose and pay a visit or two to the Working Men's Club on Greenwood Road and – yes! – drop in at the Sally Army HQ if he was going to square those two Neanderthals. (And what was Mary going to say about 'bloody religion' when he spent next Sunday with the Sally Army?)

More immediately, of course, there was that monograph on the Liverpool Working Class in World War II. It was behindhand and the publisher was demanding to see some specimen chapters… And, on top of that, the BBC was wanting an outline of the proposed programmes on the evolution of the British working class. This was an opportunity not to be missed. Time, that was the problem, *time*!

But just as he was beginning to get a grip on some of this problem, another of those wholly unexpected night-fighter fusillades had slammed into him. It could almost have been a nuclear attack by some rogue American-backed Third World dictatorship…

It was inferiors again. Inferiors like John who didn't know their place. This time it was students. It was bad enough having to wade through the dreary, second-rate rubbish that his specialist honours group churned out in their weekly essays. (A few of them, it was true – a *very* few! – did have something between their ears and they were the ones who were admitted to the Sunday evening soirées at Gloucester Road. As for the majority, however? Forget them!) But when it came to setting essays for his 'Broad Humanities' students… Well, he knew where they could stuff that notion! They were only doing history as part of a 'Broad Humanities' course, officially described as 'a new academic development of the interdisciplinary dimension of knowledge'. But, as anybody with an atom of sense knew, the 'Broad Humanities' lark was a dustbin for students who were too thick to cope with a proper honours course. All that those future primary-school teachers and clerical-grade civil servants needed to do was to remember enough of the notes he'd given them to be able to regurgitate some of it in their finals. Period.

Yet a group of them had gone snivelling to the Vice Chancellor and complained about the lack of seminars and set work. And – would you believe it? – old Jacobson had actually *listened* to them! A frosty little interview with the old fool had followed and he'd been forced to set his 'Broad Humanities' students some essays. When it came to marking them, of course, he'd simply written 'Delta Minus' on each script and handed them back – no point in actually *reading them*: he knew in advance what a load of rubbish they would be. 'Broad Humanities' students were as thick as pig shit – which, of course, was why they were doing 'Broad Humanities' in the first place.

But these boneheads just didn't know their place. Among them was a ghastly public schoolboy called Mark Leverage. Not only did he have a gruesome toffee-nosed accent (Giles, of course, had a similar accent, but that was different!), but he had no idea of the Zeitgeist and not the faintest idea of how to dress properly. While the student dress code stipulated grubby jeans and building-site workers' donkey jackets, he insisted on poncing round in a 'Hooray Henry' sports jacket and grey flannel trousers. He'd collected those essays and given them to Brian Beezley, a newly-arrived lecturer in the History Department. And the silly young ass had gone and given two of them alphas and most of the rest beta plusses... Thank God he was soon going off to Australia to take up an academic post in Brisbane. Hopefully, they'd send him there shackled and chained up in the sodden hold of a convict ship! But, of course, that was too much to expect in this sentimental age.

And then – surprise, surprise – that stuck-up little toad, Leverage, had gone and dumped the essays on Jacobson's desk... Semi-literate articles had appeared in the student newspaper 'exposing' 'academic snobbery and corruption'. All of which had resulted in yet another gruesome interview with 'His Nibs' and a humiliating climb-down and grovelling excuses about being 'overloaded with important work'. (Actually true in this case!)

And, to cap it all, that very morning Ed Stimpson had been on to him about that interview with John. 'I really must get it done quickly... The publisher has set me a deadline... Could I come round to your place this evening?' Fending off that invasion had taken a lot of prevarication. How could he possibly admit that he'd allowed the little creep to buck the system and escape into a private school? One day that was going to take a lot of explaining away...

310

Eating Shit...

So, here he had been on that Monday evening, wasting valuable time wading through a pile of 'essays' written by his 'Broad Humanities' students. Talk about eating shit!

Then just what should come bouncing up to him but John, the arch-fiend itself, or rather the arch soggy dishcloth. He couldn't have chosen a worse moment to start squealing on about rugby colours and silver stars for Maths...

Frustrated Feminist Liberation

Neither could John understand Mary's conceptual universe.

In his universe adults were sensible people. Mums always loved their children, just because they were mums and that was what mums did. And children always loved their mums because that was what children always did.

But Mary didn't love her mum – or her dad for that matter. They were the oppressors who had tried to stifle her aspirations and force her to be a brainless upper-class dolly. It had taken a vast amount of emotional energy to break out of the cage they had designed for her. They were the enemy.

And she certainly didn't love that child of hers. At Boldonbridge University she'd tasted honey. Demos, sit-ins, the sheer thrill of the forbidden fruits of drugs and promiscuous sex, the feeling that you were highly intelligent and were at the very cutting edge of the social revolution, that, above all, you had the freedom to be yourself and to achieve undreamed of things... Motherhood threatened to put an end all this and to trap her in a banal world of baby talk and dirty nappies. One small dose of it had been quite enough.

But now she'd been landed with it again and in a shape of an obstinate little squirt of a thing that somehow always managed to cause the maximum amount of trouble. Running off to London and getting himself rogered by some perverted old policeman down there; smearing her and Giles with allegations of child abuse; causing them both an immense amount of embarrassment by refusing to go to a proper state school and having to be sent to a private school instead; and, as if that wasn't enough, messing his bed and his trousers and actually expecting her to clean up after him – and

311

succeeding, too! – in short, an insult to her liberated womanhood.

She desperately wanted to prove her academic credentials to her colleagues and to herself by getting her Ph.D. But somehow she just couldn't focus her mind on it. How to build a coherent structure out of the heaps of factual rubble she'd created? Where to even start? The last thing she needed were the continual distractions of a tiresome, time-wasting child.

John was not a beloved son. He was a burden that threatened to crush her. More than that, a political principle that embodied the whole bourgeois world against which she had rebelled. He could buy her all the expensive Christmas presents he liked. It wouldn't make the slightest bit of difference. As well to make a wooden aeroplane in the middle of Gloucester Road and expect goodies to come floating down from the sky.

Normality

In the following weeks the roller-coaster of John's life subsided into a semblance of normality.

His school career flourished. He continued to get bronze and silver stars for work, but no more gold stars. Word had got round that he was 'very clever' and that things 'should not be made too easy for him'.

He continued to be the star of the rugby team. The return match against Ascomb House duly occurred. This time Ascomb won, but only after a hard-fought game which did both sides credit. Word spread that Beaconsfield wasn't quite such as dustbin after all and fixtures against other private schools began to trickle in.

And Mrs Watson was always there to provide the cuddles that he needed – when nobody was looking, of course!

Above all, he was now accepted by his classmates and began to make friends – especially with Danny and Fred.

Still Two Separate People

He duly went round to Michael Connolly's place to see Herbie and Horace.

'Mind, me mam's a bit weird!' hissed a nervous Michael. And

'weird' she certainly was – a great fat lump of a thing, looking like a half-drowned mermaid as she flopped around in a dressing gown with her long, straggly hair and a damp cigarette hanging out of her mouth. The little council house was quite extraordinarily untidy – piles of unwashed dinner plates overflowed from the kitchen sink and were strewn around the living-room floor where they joined heaps of old newspapers, empty fag packets and un-emptied ashtrays.

As Herbie, the hamster, ran up his sleeve and as he chased Horace, the cat, round the piles of empty beer bottles, he remembered his Old World. There, it was only kids who were untidy: grown-ups were always tidy. That was one of the differences between them and kids. He'd never imagined that a house like this could exist. But then his own house was almost as weird and at least Michael's mum wore clothes – not like Mary!

For a moment he thought of inviting Michael round to play with his trains on Sunday – that would make the afternoon a lot less boring. But then he thought not. What if Mary started on about his messy underpants or punched him in the face and made him cry? His carefully constructed 'hard' image would be gone for ever.

For, despite his recent success, he was still two separate people: the clever, dashing schoolboy who won fights and the pathetic little flea-brain who, even at the age of eleven, had embarrassing 'problems downstairs' and cried when he was hit. Best to keep the two of them well apart.

Something's Going On...

So things were going well. However, all was not plain sailing.

There remained the question of Ratty and Owly. They were friendly enough and Sam was no longer being bullied. The threat to 'do them over' seemed to have worked wonders. Whatever Mr Cotton had said to the contrary, brute force did seem to work with some people.

Ratty even started to turn up for the Saturday rugby matches and, to Briggs' huge delight, performed enthusiastically and well.

So far, so good.

But John had the feeling that his victory had been only temporary and that they were planning a comeback. There were little hints. Ratty struck up a friendship with some of the third-year boys, especially with Billy Nolan. Billy was seen exchanging ten-pound notes for fags and small bottles of whisky. He, Ratty and Owly were seen going into the outside toilet together. 'There's sommat right dirty going on in there,' said Danny Fleetwood. The three of them would walk home together after school and sometimes they were joined by other senior boys. In break, they would go into a tight little huddle on the edge of the playing field, occasionally pointing at John and giggling among themselves.

Something was going on. But exactly what?

What's Got into Briggsy?

Then, for some strange reason, Briggs turned hostile.

It all happened suddenly. After that first climacteric rugby match he'd seen Briggs as a new-found and valuable friend. He felt he had to work on this, impress him and get him to really like him. So he'd thrown himself into the PE lessons, giving them all he'd got. The evening before, he would dig up his encyclopaedias and ferret out sporting facts. At the end of each lesson he would sidle up to him and talk sport, ostentatiously trying to impress him with his interest in it and his knowledge of it.

'Now, can you tell me what happened to Jesse Owens after the 1936 Olympic Games?'

'Can you tell me who won the Tour de France in 1972?'

For a while it had worked well and Briggs had been all smiles and ready with his answers and encouraging remarks. Then suddenly he went cold and hostile.

At the same time he started to openly favour Ratty. Ratty was good at rugby and he and John soon became the backbone of the team. But, while Ratty was showered with praise, John got none. In one especially hard-fought match, John had scored two tries and Ratty none. Yet in morning assembly Ratty was praised to the skies – 'Man of the Match... Single-handed, he won the match for the school...' John wasn't even mentioned.

After each PE lesson Ratty would grease up to Briggs and the pair of them would go into an enthusiastic huddle. But when John tried to join in, he was brushed off.

'Yes, Denby, I know you've got lots of encyclopaedias and can actually read them, but I happen to be talking to Robert.

'Robert', please note, for Ratty: 'Denby' for John.

It all hurt.

So even more effort in the PE lessons, more sporting facts from his encyclopaedias and his newly bought *Guinness Book of Records*. But it just didn't work. Why?

Real Kids versus Spoilt Upper-class Brats...

The fact was that Briggs moved in a different reality from John.

He occupied a mini-universe which John with his belief in sensible adults just couldn't comprehend. It was that New Guinea Cargo Cult again. John's conceptual universe said that, by making his metaphorical wood-and-grass aeroplane of effort and enthusiasm, he could get the goodies that came floating down from the aeroplane – Briggs – that flew over the mountains.

But he couldn't.

After that first rugby match against Ascomb House Briggs had settled down. Freed from the threat of dismissal, his mind began to expand beyond issues of mere survival. When he reviewed his situation he felt ashamed of himself.

'The inner city. The deprived kids. The challenging pupils. There's your *real* task. Private education? Forget it. That's just an escape route for the failures who can't handle real kids...' That was what they'd dinned into him at St Martin's College.

But what was he? A failure who'd had to hide in a private school. He was always receiving newsletters from St Martin's filled with fulsome reports of former students who were doing great things at their comprehensives. Along with this were invitations to attend student reunions. It was salt rubbed into an open wound. How could he possibly go to a student reunion and confess that he, too, was one of those failures only able to survive in private education? He'd die of shame.

At first he'd taken to young Denby – so enthusiastic, so responsive, so full of life... There was something there. If he could get results out of him, he could possibly salvage a few rags of kudos from his truncated career. But when he'd made enquiries about his background an ugly truth had emerged. Posh prep school from down south. Couldn't cope with a Boldonbridge comprehensive so he'd had to hide in this dump! Spoilt upper-class brat who needed squashing. Exactly what he should *not* be teaching!

Robert Napier, however, was something better. Pure working class and from an impeccably deprived background, to boot. Make something of him and you might just be able to face your student friends at a St Martin's reunion!

That Denby creature merely advertised his failure to the world. He could have been a messy boil on the end of his nose. The very sight of him and, worse still, the *sound* of him, set his teeth on edge. When he prattled on in that ghastly upper-crust voice of his about this or that sportsman, the underlying message was: 'You're such a pathetic failure that *I'm* the only person you're able to teach. You'll just have to put up with me!'

As far as young Denby was concerned, it was: 'Fetch the sick bucket!'

Affirming Working-class Culture...

Meanwhile, in Giles' universe, life also went on.

He finally screwed up his courage, swallowed his vomit and, gritting his teeth, made his long-promised visit to the local Working Men's Club. It was a dreary and wholly uncompromising November night as he and Mary made their way along the desolation of Greenwood Road. The glow of the street lamps reduced everything to a monochrome black or orange. The moribund red-brick terrace houses and the harshly utilitarian tower blocks that were replacing them were all bleakly negative.

By the time they reached the Working Men's Club it was raining hard and they were both soaked.

'Working MEN's Club!' sighed Mary. 'What about working WOMEN?'

'Quite,' added Giles as he eyed the pseudo-baroque Edwardian edifice erected in 1903. 'It is a touch passé.'

As they mounted the steps towards the ornate pseudo-classical entrance, the altercation which he had been dreading began.

'Do we *have* to do this?'

'Yes, I'm afraid we do.'

'But you're obviously the best candidate! Why can't they just accept you?'

'Because I've got to prove myself first.'

'But you *have* proved yourself! How many of the other candidates have written groundbreaking monographs?'

'That's not the point. If I'm going to represent them, I've got to affirm their working-class culture.'

'But you *have* affirmed it!'

'Not in their eyes. They don't read scholarly monographs, you know...'

'Which means that they're all as thick as boards. Can't you just ignore them?'

'Darling, I can't. They've got the votes. In any case. I've promised to pay them a visit. I can't get out of it.'

Boldly, Giles pushed through the red-painted double doors. The whole scene inside was upsetting. Downmarket, cut-price Edwardian pretentiousness. Ornate glazed tiles – sickly green and spuke brown. Dark polished wood. Elaborate plaster casting on the ceiling. The gullible working class trying to ape their exploiters by trying to appear gentrified...

Beyond the lobby they entered a large, dimly lit room, full of billiard tables, big leather armchairs and dart boards with a brightly lit bar at the far end. A thick miasma of cigarette smoke hung over everything.

An elderly man greeted Giles: 'Welcome to the Working Men's Club.'

'Working *Men's* club?' said Mary, switching on the 'analytical stare'. 'What about working *women*?'

'Please, darling,' cautioned Giles, 'Not here...'

'And I don't see many women here,' continued Mary, cranking herself up into 'righteous feminine warrior' mode. 'Where are they all?'

'Most o' them will be at home lookin' after the bairns an' that.'

'I see. Woman stays at home while man goes down to the pub and drinks himself silly...'

'Please, darling!'

Her righteous indignation gathering momentum, Mary rounded on Giles: 'Well, if you're going to stand for this petty-bourgeois sexism. I'm fucking not!'

With that she sailed majestically out of the room, swelling with pride at having made yet another 'radical statement'.

'She wants proper skelpin' that one,' said somebody.

'Bloody women!' sighed Giles, forgetting his ideology in his frustrated anger.

Now he faced the difficult bit. 'Affirm working-class culture'?

317

Fine. Proper socialist idealism and all the rest of it… But just what was he supposed to do? Talk about football, which bored him to insanity? Talk about stotty cake? Sing the 'Blaydon Races'? Talk about pigeon racing or the 'lotties' (whatever they were supposed to be)? It was as bad as trying to talk to that retarded little son of his.

'Have a pint on me,' he eventually said to the elderly man next to him.

Marching up to the bar, he stood a round of drinks for all and sundry and ordered a pint of Newcastle Brown Ale for himself.

'Just what I've been waiting for all day,' he said as he braved the obnoxious liquid.

For the next two hours he diligently enquired about the footballing fortunes of Middlesbrough, Newcastle United and, of course, Boldonbridge United and listened dutifully – or as dutifully as he could! – to the interminable details of somebody's holiday in Benidorm.

Before he left he downed a double whisky to fortify himself for what he knew would be waiting for him at home.

'You're Weak…!'

And he needed that fortification.

Mary was in full rant: 'What the fuck's come over you? Standing there and taking all that sexist crap! You've changed, you know. Changed for the worse. First letting the kid go to bloody Beaconsfield and now this! You're weak, that's what it is… WEAK! So what's it going to be next? Bloody religion, I suppose!'

Bloody Religion…

And it *was* 'bloody religion' next. That Sunday he'd agreed to drop in at the Salvation Army Hostel – just to square Old Man Robertson. ('… Yes, *of course*, I value Christian caring! It's what socialism is all about…') He fobbed Mary off with a story about having to do some extra marking up at the university. It was so much easier not to tell some people the truth.

33

Christmas

The Culmination of the Year

So the days slipped by.

As November passed into December one thing began to dominate John's mind: Christmas. In the Old World it had been the culmination of the year – a wonderful, magical time. It had begun slowly after the excitement of Bonfire Night had passed. Coloured lights and Christmas trees began to appear in the streets. In the shop windows lovely, shiny Santa Clauses, and colourful streamers appeared along with red-breasted robins perched on snowy logs.

Then the delicious question was asked: 'John, what do you want for Christmas?' The Christmas calendar would be put up in the hall with the numbered days leading up to Christmas – each day you opened up a little door and another Christmas scene would be revealed: snow-covered forests, a Christmas tree, the Three Wise Men ... right down to the big one you opened on December 25th, which showed the birth of Jesus at Bethlehem. Slowly, the house filled up with gorgeous Christmas cards, the best ones with lots of lovely tinsel and glitter on them. On December 21st Grandpa put up the Christmas tree in the lounge and, after helping him decorate it, you wrapped up the presents you were going to give people in beautiful Christmas paper and placed them carefully round the bottom of it.

The exquisite magic of Christmas Eve followed with its hot mince pies for tea and the evening ritual of carol singing where you joined a group of grown-ups and kids from the local church and, wrapped up well, processed through the dark and rainy streets, knocking on neighbours' doors and singing one of the beautiful old carols that you so loved.

Then came the night when, almost exploding with suppressed excitement, you made an attempt at sleep. And then the radiant joy of Christmas morning: the stocking with its store of little treasures, the delicious excitement of opening your big presents under the Christmas tree, the lovely service at the church ... and, of course, the Christmas dinner with turkey, cranberry sauce, roast chestnuts, Christmas pudding and Christmas cake... And then, on December 28th the visit to the pantomime in London.

Why couldn't you have Christmas once a week instead of once a year?

Paradise Lost?

It all hit him one Saturday morning when he was in Boldonbridge with Danny Fleetwood.

Danny had got some money for his birthday and he was coming along with him to help choose a new engine for his model railway. As they went down Gladstone Street, they passed Millward's, the big department store. The whole of its long shop window was taken up with a Christmas tableau of Snow White and the Seven Dwarfs. As he gazed in wonder at the purple light, the gleaming heaps of artificial snow, the robins on the logs and the glittering tinsel, the memory of his lost paradise suddenly hit him. For one dreadful moment he thought he was going to have a weeping fit – the very last thing that should ever be allowed to happen in front of the likes of Danny Fleetwood. Only by covering his face with his handkerchief and pretending to sneeze was a catastrophe averted.

But the question remained: was he going to get any presents this Christmas?

Indeed, was Giles even going to celebrate Christmas?

A Criminal Waste of Money

The answer to that question was: not if Giles could help it!

Christmas encapsulated everything Giles despised about bourgeois society. Pathetic fairy stories about stars which moved across the sky and animals that worshipped a baby born without insemination: and, worse still, children being encouraged to believe such infantile rubbish. The glutinous sentimentality and the sheer dishonesty of all that 'peace and goodwill' stuff. The blatant and quite appalling commercial exploitation. The excruciatingly awful taste – those dreadful polystyrene

Santa Clauses, those gruesome Dickensian Christmas cards with their twee stage coaches and snow-covered villages ... the tinsel, the glitter... And the utter hypocrisy of the whole business. It was positively pornographic. And, above all, a criminal waste of money.

He'd had a gutful of it all with his parents. Old Dr Denby had always made an awful fuss about Christmas. As a little boy, of course, he'd lapped it up – the Christmas tree, the stockings, the presents, the stately ritual of Christmas dinner with its retinue of aged and infirm patients specially bussed in for the occasion to emphasise the 'spirit of Christmas' by remembering the 'sick, the lonely and the needy'.

But when he'd grown older and more aware, it had all begun to cloy. The 'spirit of Christmas'? Bloody hell! All those obsequious old derelicts, seated round the dinner table, were only there because Old Man Denby had a psychotic need to play the lord of the manor dispensing trinkets to his forelock-tugging serfs. Instead of being allowed to pass peacefully away in their hospitals, they were stuffed with pills, medicine and heaven alone knew what else and wheeled along to be stage props in the 'Devoted and Caring Family Doctor Show.'

'Devoted and caring'? Crap! He was an old egotist who had to be the boss at all times. That was why he had so resented Giles growing up. Every year it was the same ritual, the same place at the bottom of the table, the same old business of being a childish appendage to the 'great and good' Dr Denby. At sixteen he was still being given a stocking and at seventeen he was still being dragged off to the pantomime. The shame of it! He, the head of School House and the captain of rugger, having to sit among all the little squealing kids as if he were one of them! He'd even been seen there by one of the School House fags who'd had a field day spreading stories about his being a pederast who'd fondled little boys' bottoms in the back row of the dress circle. (And the little sod had paid dearly for that one with a full-scale beating in the Temple Library!)

The following Christmas there had been a monumental row and he'd gone off to a party with some friends and got wildly drunk.

Long ago Giles had given Christmas the sack.

'A Nauseating Bourgeois Swamp'

To Mary, Christmas was a 'nauseating bourgeois swamp'.

As a teenager she'd come to hate it. It was a dreadful round of obligatory parties and social events. You were forced to wear clothes you disliked and were always having to be polite to people you didn't want to know and who bored you to insanity. You had to endure the awful tedium of 'dancing classes' and, as you got older, the dreary nonsense of dances and debutante coming-out balls.

As she'd matured, she'd started to read widely and discovered a whole new world – a world of grinding poverty in places like Africa and South America, of class oppression in Britain and of the unjust inferior status of women... In her A level History course at Roedean she'd learned of artists like Courbet, Van Gogh, Kokoschka, Matisse and Picasso and whole new dimensions of social and aesthetic awareness had opened up before her. It all contrasted so blatantly with the smug philistinism around her. Secretly, she'd begun to read 'forbidden books' about sexual liberation and free love.

These were the things she'd wanted to talk about with her peers, but instead she was supposed to tittle-tattle about hunt balls, who was getting engaged to whom and who was 'coming out this season'. The real world with all its problems and injustices was deemed 'boring' and 'bad form'.

She began to feel immensely superior to the whole set-up – her parents, the jejune adolescent smoothies, the budding debutantes ... the lot. And, as for all those 'invitations' that her parents would plaster round the house! Their sole purpose was to show those gullible enough to swallow it that chez Ponsonby was part of an 'in group' from which lesser beings were excluded. She felt she was highly intelligent and destined for great things – if only she could break out of the prison she was in and be her proper self!

She'd stuck it till she was eighteen and then she'd made her first, most dramatic and most meaningful statement. Barging stark naked into the family Christmas dinner, she'd waggled her bum and her tits at the 'distinguished guests' and shouted 'fuck' at the top of her voice.

Her father had called in a psychiatrist who'd said it was 'just teenage rebellion augmented by the pressure of A levels...' 'Just teenage rebellion'? It was a lot more than that. It was a rejection of a whole set of false values – snobbery, hypocrisy, commercialism, exploitation, gruesome kitsch posing as art... How many kids in the Third World were starving because their parents hadn't got enough money to feed them? And just so that rich gits like her parents and their 'distinguished guests' could get indigestion and pyloric spasms by stuffing themselves with food to which they had no right in the first place!

The whole notion of Christmas made you want to puke.

So when John made tentative enquiries he was given short shrift.

'Christmas?' snorted Giles. 'That's just for little kids. You should have grown out of that long ago!'

A Lonely Old Frump Gets a Big Idea

And Christmas for Dorothy Watson?

Certainly not a 'nauseating bourgeois swamp'. And not a 'magical occasion' either. The Biology teacher in her saw it as a necessary social event which gave a bit of structure to an increasingly fragmented society. The believer in her saw it as marking a supremely important occurrence.

More prosaically, however, it was a time of sadness and frustration which exposed the emptiness and essential failure of her life. It was a matter of going to a dreary church service, listening to some badly sung carols and an execrable sermon and then going home to sit alone in her living room. The few friends she had were all busy with their families. She had no relatives and no family. There she sat in her armchair – a fast-decaying middle-aged frump, pushed into a siding and marginalised, a loser in life's obstacle race.

Above all, she had no children to share it with. That was what was so frustrating. She had everything that was needed to make Christmas a wonderful experience for children – all those years of experience in dealing with them – but no children on which to work her magic. A conductor without an orchestra to conduct.

So she mused on a dismal Sunday afternoon, sitting in the armchair in the living room of her downstairs flat, fitfully glancing through the *Sunday Times*. Outside, the steady rain dribbled down the window panes blurring the view of the once opulent, but now slightly seedy, Edwardian terrace houses that made up Fern Avenue. The trees, which in summer gave it an air of leafy luxuriance, were bare and black – the last-surviving and diseased remnants of a defeated army it seemed. 'Give up! Hibernate! It's all futile in the end!' That was the day's message.

Then suddenly the idea came. Children? She *had* children! Those 'lost souls' of Beaconsfield School. Some of them were well catered for over Christmas – too well catered for in a number of cases! But others most emphatically were not.

John Denby, for instance, her great catch – the clever, enthusiastic little fellow with that lovely smile and those delightful manners. With those parents of his he would probably be having a pretty dismal time over Christmas. In fact, she hoped he *would* be having a dismal time because he would *need* her... And she'd get the child she'd always wanted. So bring him over. Give him a real Christmas with all the works – crackers, Christmas trees, polystyrene Santa Clauses, the lot. Forget about the bad taste. Children weren't bothered about sophisticated aesthetics. A positively electric thrill surged through her. Why hadn't she thought of this before?

But, hold on Dorothy, old girl! Don't be an 'emotional woman'! You mustn't start having favourites. That's a recipe for disaster! They will exploit you and get away with murder. The others will resent it and will start to hate you. Discipline will collapse and the vultures will swoop. If you're going to keep the lid on that adolescent volcano you've created, you've got to be fair. Kids respect fairness.

As a trained teacher, Dorothy, you should know that.

So she would have to get some other lads along, too. Sam Hawthorne? ... Oh heavens! But it wasn't his fault that he was physically repulsive. And with that drunken oaf of a father and that promiscuous tart of a mother, he would almost certainly be having a ghastly Christmas... She'd have to have him – but could she stand the mouldy, faecal aroma he carried round with him? The first thing she'd have to do with him was put him into the bath and scrub him down.

Michael Connolly? His mother probably wouldn't even know it was Christmas and whatever money there was in that dysfunctional household would certainly be earmarked for her two main priorities – fags and alcohol. Forget about the father. He had never paid a penny of the alimony and was somewhere in Canada, untraced and untraceable.

And then there was Robert Napier. Be careful here! Remember what John Denby said about him... Yes, but Briggs had been giving him glowing reports... And there had been no more stories of extorting money and dirty goings on in toilets. He *did* seem to be coming round. She *was* succeeding. So reinforce this good behaviour. Welcome him warmly into the fold. Yes, she would have to invite Robert Napier.

A Plan

Bit by bit the scheme took shape. A party for the deadbeats on Christmas Eve.

Start at five o'clock with a Christmas tea – the full works: mince pies, Christmas cake, the lot. Then get them to play games – wink murder, murder in the dark... Monopoly, perhaps. For youngsters who spent most of their spare time stuck in front of the television this could be a new experience.

At eleven o'clock they'd go to a midnight Christmas service in the local church. She'd circumvent old Vicar Wood and rope in young Steadman, his curate. He was very high church and would dress his charges up in white cassocks and march them round the darkened church with candles and lots of genuflections before Christmas cribs. Mumbo-jumbo? Possibly, but kids loved mumbo-jumbo...

Then they'd go back and have a midnight Christmas dinner – turkey, crackers, Christmas pudding and all the rest of it. Early on Christmas morning they'd go home.

There were pitfalls galore and it would take a lot of organising. She'd need help. Bill Bleeson, her head boy, was fully occupied over Christmas, but he was a very decent and willing lad and his parents were thoroughly good people who'd certainly lend a hand – on Christmas Eve, if not on Christmas Day. (Involve the parents. Cornerstone to running a good school!)

She'd need male reinforcements to provide a 'physical deterrent' if things started to get out of hand. Hyper-excited kids from unstable backgrounds having a new and exotic experience? They could explode like the pent-up fizz in a bottle of coke. Bluff old Roderick Meakin would fill that slot – if only to get away from his nagging millstone of a wife.

34

End of Term

John's term ended with a flourish.

In the last week a Christmas tree appeared in the dining room and they decorated the classrooms with streamers and balloons. On the last day reports were handed out in sealed envelopes addressed to parents and there was a Christmas lunch with turkey, Christmas pudding and crackers – ruthlessly policed by Meakin and Briggs to avert a threatened outbreak of anarchy.

Then came a final assembly in the hall. Mrs Watson made a short speech and prizes were given out. John collected four: the form prize for coming top of the class, a History prize, a Scripture prize and an Art prize – a blaze of glory that could never have happened at Rickerby Hall. 'Good King Wenceslas' was sung, a short prayer was said and the liberated, hyped-up mob surged away.

After promising to come and see Danny Fleetwood's celebrated *California Zephyr* and to pay another visit to Michael Connolly's equally celebrated Herbie and Horace, John slipped quietly into the bog and stayed there till the noise of the departing mob had died down. Then he crept out and scuttled along the corridor. Making sure that nobody was around, he knocked on Mrs Watson's study door.

Immediately, it opened to reveal a beaming Mrs Watson.

'Yes, John?'

He launched into his rehearsed speech: 'Excuse me. I'm sorry to disturb you, but I just wanted to say thank you very much for...'

'Oh John!' she cooed, 'There's no need for that! Come in and we'll have our little chat...'

She pointed to the settee and sat down beside him. She was elated. This was what she had been waiting for all day.

'Now, John, tell me what you are doing over Christmas.'

There was an embarrassed silence followed by a mutter: 'Well, er,

I don't think ... anything, er nothing. You see, Giles, that's my dad, he thinks it's all rubbish...'

'So you won't be doing anything?'

'Well, no.'

'I see. Well, in that case, would you like to come round to my house on Christmas Eve and join me in a little party I'll be having?'

'Yes, Miss, *rather*!'

The little bundle positively glowed. He flashed his glorious smile. (Dorothy glowed, too. It was just the response she'd been hoping for all week. Her child. Her very *own* child! He *needed* her! The old frump mattered after all!)

'Right. 27 Fern Avenue. Here's a map to show you where it is. Five o'clock. Not before. Don't come too early because I've got to get things ready...'

'Cor thanks, Miss! You're wicked!'

A wonderful, warm hug. (Dorothy, *be careful*!)

Into a Dismal Cave

John felt an immediate chill when he got home. It was like leaving a warm and sunny meadow and entering a dank and dripping cave.

Mary – when she eventually condescended to answer the door and let him in – was mooning around, draped in a dressing gown which only very partially covered her naked body and smoking one of her funny-smelling cigarettes. She had a vacant and glazed expression on her face.

'Mary,' he said, summoning up the few surviving remnants of his previous elation, 'I've won four prizes and here's my report.'

Without answering, she shooed him away. Leaving the report on Giles' table, he went up to his room.

A Bleak Emptiness

A bleak emptiness followed. No fairy lights. No Christmas cards. No Christmas tree. Nobody to talk to.

The emptiness went on all the next day. Slowly, he realised just how much he needed his classmates. Their noise, their jokes, their ragging around and their acceptance of him as a mate. And, yes, even the teachers, too. Their barminess – Polly with his squawks, Dracula with her polychromatic hair-dos ... those chats with the Mekon and – and, oh how he hated admitting it! – those cuddles from Dolly.

It was all topsy-turvy. He was a *boy*. Boys should hate school and love the holidays. William Brown, in the *Just William* books he loved, was the sort of boy he felt he ought to be – tough, bold and, above all, fiercely anti-school. 'The term has ended and the holidays have begun' ran a passage in the Narnia books he devoured. The holidays *should* have been a time of liberation. But they weren't. He actually liked school and hated the holidays. It wasn't right.

'I Suppose You Want a Christmas Present...'

December 21st came, that magic day of the Old Dispensation when Granddad put up the Christmas tree. There was no sign of anything here – not even a single Christmas card. Was there going to be no Christmas at all? No Christmas dinner? And – dreadful thought! – not even a single Christmas present?

In desperation, he went down the ladders. Giles was at his table typing furiously surrounded as usual by piles of paper. Timorously, he crept up to him.

'Giles, is anything happening about Christmas?'

Giles looked up and scowled: 'I've told you before that we don't bother about Christmas in this house. It's high time you grew out of all that childish rubbish!'

His worst fears confirmed, John let out a long groan: 'Awwwwww! Can't we even have a Christmas tree?'

Giles eyed the disconsolate little bundle in front of him. Christ, was it going to start crying? So bloody what if it did! But then he remembered... Merrins and her dervishes! The satisfactory report from the Social Services hadn't ended the war: it had only bought a fragile truce. He still had to keep the little squirt sweet – sound insurance policy...

'All right!' he sighed. 'I suppose you want a Christmas present.'

Fumbling with his wallet, he pulled out a bundle of crisp new ten-pound notes.

'Here you are. Go and buy yourself something.'

'Cor, thanks... I mean I wasn't ... well er...'

Before he could formulate his sentence the telephone rang. Immediately, Giles picked it up and began a long conversation, shooing him away in the process.

A Noble Gesture

As John turned round to go back to his room, he noticed the envelope containing his school report lying on the table unopened and exactly where he had left it two days ago.

Sitting on his bed, he counted the notes. Sixty pounds! Wow! Immediately, he ranged over the things he could get – more engines for his railway, new videos, a radio-controlled tank, a set of encyclopaedias... But then a sobering thought struck him. He remembered his resolution of a month or so back. Giles and Mary didn't like him. Obviously, they had their reasons. Grown-ups always had sound reasons for things. Only kids didn't have reasons for things. Clearly, Giles and Mary considered him greedy and selfish, thinking only of himself.

A fine, noble feeling seemed to flow through him. He wouldn't spend the money on himself. Instead, he'd buy Giles and Mary the very best Christmas presents he could ... yes, and he'd get Mrs Watson a magnificent present, too. God would really like that. And he'd reward him well. His renunciation was a noble gesture, all right, but it was a sound investment, too. Keep God sweet and he'll see you through!

He knelt down and said a short prayer: 'Sorry to pester you, God, but thank you for telling me what to do with the money...'

'Oh you *are* a good lad...'

He set off for Boldonbridge in an exalted frame of mind.

Outside Millward's he paused. The Christmas tableau was really rather soppy – all those dwarfs and fairies: ugh! But he did like the red-breasted robins and the snow-covered logs which glittered in the purple light. Apparently, it was all an advertisement for the pantomime at the Empire Theatre. But this was going to be his first Christmas ever without a visit to the pantomime. How he had come down in the world! However, he steeled himself: today's good deed was a sound investment. God was sure to reward him with more than a visit to the pantomime.

Inside, he duly found a department full of expensive china. Slipping into 'best behaviour mode', he went up to a shop assistant at the counter.

'Excuse me, can you help me, please. I want to buy three china plates. They're presents for my mum and dad and for my teacher so they must be the best you have...' He flashed his 'ingratiating smile'.

The lady was duly charmed.

'Yes, dear,' she cooed. 'But are you sure you can afford it? They're very expensive, you know.'

'Yes I can. I've got sixty pounds which I've been saving up specially.' He brandished the bundle of crisp ten-pound notes.

'Oh, you ARE a good lad! Well we'll do what we can.'

After a lengthy process, he bought two glossy wall plates with Regency ladies and roses on them for Giles and Mary. The one for Giles had 'Dad' on it in gold letters and the one for Mary had 'Mum' on it, also in gold letters. For Mrs Watson he chose a wall plate with a hunting scene on it.

'And, please, can you wrap them up in Christmas paper so that they look really nice...'

'Of course, dear. Your mum and your dad really will like this.'

Yes, he thought, they couldn't fail to. And they'd start to like him, too.

As he left, clutching his treasures, the lady sighed and turned to her colleague: 'Eeeee, Joyce, warra luverly bairn! Some mums is right lucky! Warra luverly bairn!'

The bill had come to fifty-four pounds. He went downstairs and spent three pounds fifty on a gorgeous Christmas card for Mrs Watson. It had all the trimmings – snow-covered logs with robins on them, a Dickensian stagecoach, holly and bells and lots of silver paper and glitter. He deliberately denied himself a visit to the toy fair on the top floor but, as he left the store, he spent the remaining two pounds fifty on wine gums and liquorice allsorts. After such an heroic gesture of Christian charity, God couldn't begrudge him a little self indulgence. God *was* human after all.

35

Impatience...

Time hung heavily. Empty. Boring. Drab. The 21st was followed by the 22nd and the 23rd. A slow funereal procession. Giles working furiously at his table. Mary drifting round in a haze, as often as not stark naked. Always the same grey sky. The one bright spot in the gloom was Mrs Watson's Christmas Eve party. 'Come round at five o'clock...'

When Christmas Eve finally came he could stand it no longer. Climbing down the ladders, he saw that there was nobody in the house. Carefully, he placed the two plates on Giles' table along with a covering note written in his very best handwriting: 'To my wonderful Mother and Father from their loving and grateful son, John.' As he did so, he noticed the envelope containing his school report lying just where he had left it five days ago and still unopened.

Huddling in his anorak, he went out into the bleak world outside and braved the cold, stinging rain. It was only nine o'clock and Mrs Watson had most emphatically said *not* before five... But when she saw the present and the Christmas card he was going to give her she'd soon forget about that.

Fern Avenue was easy to find. It was a quiet street of red-brick Edwardian terrace houses not far from the school, fronted by trees and small gardens. In most of the windows there were lighted Christmas trees.

Seeing a large number 27 on a neat, well-painted gate, he passed through a small garden – little more than a soggy lawn with a black and empty flower bed at one end and a rusty wrought-iron bench at the other, but with no broken bottles or empty fag packets lying around. (Why couldn't Giles live in a place like this instead of in a World War II-style bombsite?)

As he stood before the shiny maroon-painted front door, he had a moment of panic. It was only ten o'clock and Mrs Watson had insisted on his *not* coming before five ... and Mrs Watson *had* to be obeyed! But, when she saw the present, well ... that would be different!

So he screwed up his courage and pressed the bell labelled 'Watson'.

Behind the Door: The Thorns of Memory

At that precise moment Dorothy was hard at it in the kitchen.

Her day had not begun well. She had spent the first hour or so brooding in her living room. The world outside the bay windows was bleak and hostile. The usual wintry desolation – bare, sodden tree trunks, freezing black puddles on the garden path, droplets of icy water on the scrawny apology for a hedge, the gloom of the rain-washed red-brick street ... a feeble sun failing to break through the ceiling of grey clouds. A metaphor for her own situation?

Inside, it was warm and reassuring, of course. A comfortable room with its electric fire and good 1950s furniture – two armchairs, a settee, a sideboard and a mock-mahogany dining table. An anaesthetised oblivion perhaps?

On the cream-painted walls – seemingly mocking her present status – were relics of her African adventure. Two Makonde masks, a big leather Acholi shield, a couple of spears from Buganda. Then a scatter of framed photographs: herself in a Buganda village, elephants and lions in the Serengeti National Park, a leopard in a tree, the icy summit of Kilimanjaro... Largest of all, and given pride of place in the centre of the display, was an enlarged colour photograph of the snow-covered crags of the 16,873-foot Margherita Peak, the highest point in the Ruwenzori.

Remote and beautiful Ruwenzori! Fabled 'Mountains of the Moon' whose snowy crests rose out of a sodden jungle and were swathed in an almost perpetual pall of cloud. Here was the ultimate source of the mighty Nile, the most evocative and romantic river on earth! It had all meant so much to her.

Fulfilling a dream, she'd staggered up to the 16,042-foot summit of Mount Speke, the easiest peak in the range. As she'd stood panting amid the improbably bulbous mounds of snow, the clouds had parted and there, for a fleeting moment, was Margherita Peak, an immense icy wedding cake, seemingly floating freely on a sea of turbulent clouds and dazzlingly white against a brilliant blue sky. There had just been time to take the photograph of a lifetime before the mists had swept down again.

It had been the high point of an arduous, but magnificent ten-day round trip – a saga of swamps, rain, extraordinary almost science-fiction vegetation and sudden visions as grey mists had parted revealing shimmering snowy splendours lurking in stormy skies. Perhaps the high point of her life.

Yet it was a bitter-sweet memory, for immediately afterwards she and Lawrence had had their first serious row. But there it was, the great 'might have been' of her life taunting her present banal status.

Would any of the dreary deadbeats she now taught even notice that picture, let alone understand its message? Almost certainly not.

White-water Rafting down the Unknown River

In the meantime she had gone and landed herself with this Christmas party – out of the dying embers of her misguided missionary impulse.

There were hazards galore. It was like pushing out into a turbulent river in a rubber dinghy. You would be hurled uncontrollably along by unpredictable currents, thrown against hidden rocks, swept down towards unseen cataracts and over plunging waterfalls ... and at the end of the chaotic voyage? What? Probable disaster or, at best, a very moderate glory. Who knew?

Children could be such little savages – selfish, cruel and stupidly short-sighted, all too often seeing kindness as weakness to be exploited. Suppose the whole thing got out of hand? Authority, reputation and perhaps even survival itself could be on the line. 'Keep your distance... Don't get too close to them... Don't get emotionally involved with them...' That's what they'd dinned into her at St Aiden's College. And here she was, breaking these elementary rules. Inviting a group of potential predators into your inner sanctum? Talk about putting your head into the lion's mouth. Dolly, you idiot!

So it had to be damage control. No hostages left to fortune. No letters lying around. No dirty linen for smutty little eyes to see. No money left in unlocked drawers. The bedroom with its store of personal secrets firmly locked...

Then everything organised, table set, mince pies and turkey cooked, crackers and sweets in place, the game of Monopoly readied for use (make sure that you still have two dice and all the various cards!)...

No hiatuses left to give anarchists the chance to disrupt the smooth flow of things... She'd been at it for the past three days and now she had to tie all those loose ends up. The multitudinous tasks to be done stretched away before her like a foaming river full of rocks.

But – and this was the worst scenario of all! – suppose nobody turned up? Where would that leave her? A marginalised old frump that nobody needed. The 'emotional woman' in her desperately wanted little John Denby to come. But the 'proper professional' sounded a warning note. Her relationship with the little shrimp hadn't gone unobserved. Word had reached her of staffroom mutterings... 'The old girl seems to have taken a real shine to that little creep. You'd think he was her boyfriend...'

At the end-of-term staff meeting Briggs had all but openly alluded to it:

'You want to watch that one. He's brighter than the rest and he knows it! ... Oily little thing ... thinks the rules don't apply to him... Just because he's come from a classy prep school, he thinks he's special... Needs squashing!' After which he'd launched into his now-familiar eulogy of Robert Napier: '... A promising lad... There's a lot there... That's our real challenge ... winning over lads like Robert... We're not here to pamper spoilt prep-school brats...'

Brooding alone in her living room, she'd begun to have doubts. The 'proper professional' gained the upper hand. Yes, John Denby might have charm, but he probably *was* a spoilt little prep-school brat in need of squashing. But, even if he wasn't, he was still middle class and a pedagogic pushover. There was no kudos there. Robert Napier, on the other hand, a feral rat boy of whom the Social Services had despaired? That *would* be a professional scoop! What a brick to throw at Professor Stimpson! And, she *did* seem to be succeeding, too. There had been no more ugly rumours about him. He *was* coming round.

Rat boy Robert would make her professional name, not pampered prep schoolboy John.

A Spoilt Prep-School Brat?

So here she was in the kitchen, frantically trying to get her act together before the five o'clock deadline.

Just as she was manoeuvring the massive turkey out of the fridge, the doorbell rang. Her irritation rose to the level of anger when she opened the door and found a dishevelled John Denby standing on the doorstep. 'Spoilt prep school brat ... thinks the rules don't apply to him ... needs squashing...' Here he was exploiting her weakness by deliberately disobeying her instructions, exactly what Briggs had warned her about! Message delivered: 'Be strict! Slap him down *now* if you don't want the whole thing to end in disaster.'

So stern teacher-cutting-unruly-child-down-to-size voice: 'John Denby, you're rather early! I said not before five o'clock! Now go away and come back at the right time!'

As she started to shut the door, the bedraggled little elf pleaded with her: 'Please, Miss. I'm sorry, Miss, I forgot... I thought you might need some help. Here's your Christmas present...'

Dorothy paused. He looked so forlorn standing there in the rain, so helpless, so downcast ... and so cute! (And, oh Lord, was he going to start crying?) It was a rapier thrust into her soft centre.

'All right, come on in, John!'

But decidedly mixed feelings. On the one side immediate regret: letting herself be exploited by an oily little charmer. The first breach in the orderly schedule: the little pebble tumbling down to start a whole landslide? On the other side enormous relief: the very worst scenario – nobody turning up at all – being averted and by the boy she really wanted!

John flashed his glorious smile: 'Thank you ever so much, Miss, you see I thought you might need some help. So that's why I came early.' ('Rubbish!' thought Dorothy to herself. 'You were bored stiff at home. Your parents were ignoring you and you wanted a bit of attention. But, at the same time, I'd better make you welcome.')

'Thank you very much for the present. No, I won't open it now. I'll put it under the Christmas tree and open it tomorrow morning.'

She ushered him into the living room.

'What a lovely cat. Miss! Can I stroke it?' (Just the right thing to say! This boy *was* a charmer! But an angel or a devil?) 'Yes, but be quick about it! We've got a lot of work to do. Now while I deal with the turkey, you can decorate the Christmas tree for me. Everything's in the box next to it. Be careful and for heaven's sake don't bust the lights!'

John picked up the gently purring cat, luxuriated for a moment in its silky black and white fur, and then put it down and set to work. Decorating the Christmas tree and seeing that the lights worked was something that his granddad had never let him do. This was promotion and he swelled with importance.

For a blissful two hours he worked away, unloading all the exquisite treasures on to the spiky, pine-smelling branches: all those green, blue and gold balls, those lovely Santa Clauses, those long streams of glittering tinsel...

At intervals he would run into the kitchen – ostensibly to ask Miss where she thought this or that purple bell should go, but actually to reassure himself of her continued favour. That initially hostile reception on the doorstep had jolted him.

Then he saw the African masks on the wall. His grandparents were wonderful and perfect, but just a little ordinary. This, however, was something exotic.

'Cor, Miss, have you been to Africa?'

'Yes, I lived in Uganda for four years.'

'Wow! Did you see lions and leopards and that?'

'Yes, look at these pictures. I took them in Serengeti National Park.' (And just how Dorothy warmed to this!)

Then he noticed the picture of Margherita Peak. He gazed in awe.

'Wow! Look at that! Is that the Himalayas?'

'No, it's Margherita Peak in the Ruwenzori.'

That name rang a bell. Here was his chance to impress Miss and show her that he was something special.

'Ruwenzori. On the border of Uganda and Zaire. Biggest glaciers in Africa. Wettest place in the world...' Out came the data from his much-thumbed geography encyclopaedia.

'Well done, John, well done. You obviously know your geography.'

'Did you *really* go there? I thought only explorers went there.'

'Yes I did. I took that photograph from the top of Mount Speke, the mountain next to Margherita.'

'Wow! You're a mountaineer then? Are you friends with Chris Bonnington and Edmund Hillary?'

'No, John, I'm not quite in their class.'

'I'd love to go to the Ruwenzori. You haven't any more pictures, have you?'

'Yes, lots. But they're all slides. I'd have to get the projector out...'

'Could I see them? Please, Miss. Please!'

Dorothy glowed, positively radiated! How she liked this boy! The Ruwenzori had been her great achievement. But nobody in Britain had been remotely interested in it. The kids in Sunderland had found Africa 'dead boring' – as, indeed, they found everything more than ten miles from Sunderland. At Greenhill, the staff had sneered: '*Boys' Own* imperialism... Why not go and tell Baden Powell about it? It's his scene not ours... It's all irrelevant...' But here, at long last, was somebody who actually was interested in her travels and climbs – and it was the child she wanted for her very own! It was almost too good to be true!

'Yes, John, when the party's over we'll have a look at them.' (Dorothy, be careful! Don't let this one beguile you into favouritism. Keep the tempter at arm's length if you want to preserve your professionalism!)

Reining in her emotion, she put on her orderly headmistress voice: 'When you've done the tree, you can start setting the table.'

John duly beavered away. He was in paradise. Things were going his way.

Plunging over a Waterfall

Half an hour later the doorbell rang.

'Answer the door for me, will you John?' called Dolly from the kitchen.

Eagerly he did so. But as soon as he opened the door paradise dissolved in a puff of smoke.

There, standing in the rain was a scrawny, beaky-nosed girl of about fourteen dressed in jeans and a grubby sweater with a cigarette hanging out of her mouth. Leaning on her was a dishevelled Sam Hawthorne with odd bits of clothing draped round his skinny frame. All his buttons were undone and his famous trousers were halfway down his thighs. Muddy and sodden with his hair all awry, he looked like a waterlogged guy on Bonfire Night.

'Oh God, what do *you* want?' groaned a bitterly disappointed John. He'd thought the party was only for him. Now it seemed that others had been invited, too. He wasn't so special after all. For the past two hours he'd had Dolly all to himself and had been getting all the attention he'd so sorely missed during the last dismal week. Now this would go – and all because of a pathetic, overgrown stick insect that couldn't even dress itself!

'Where's Miss?' the girl screeched. 'She's jus' gorra sort Sam oot!'

337

'Go away!' growled John, as he began to shut the door. 'She's not in!'

'OH YES I AM IN, JOHN!' came a whiplash voice from behind him.

Dolly had emerged from the kitchen, greasy spoon in her hand – and not shaggy sheepdog Dolly, either, but stern headmistress Mrs Watson.

'Oh Sam!' she exclaimed. 'What *have* you been doing?'

On cue the girl let fly a tirade: 'Divvent ye start fuckin' pickin' on 'im, Miss! It weren't none o' 'is bloody fault! It were that dad o' his! Reet cunt 'im! Thrown 'im oota the house 'e 'as! Oyed 'im oot into pissin' fuckin' rain. Spent the neet in the bins 'e 'as ... Yer gorra 'elp 'im!'

'All right!' sighed Mrs Watson. 'Come on in and tell me what's happened. John, will you keep an eye on the turkey for me?'

'Gawd! Do we *have* to have him in?' groaned a glowering John. 'He'll ruin everything, the half-eaten baboon!'

'John, we'll have none of that!' The stern-teacher voice of Mrs Watson, headmistress. The alarm bells were starting, not quite to ring, but to tinkle ominously. This display of infantile selfishness by her treasured protégé was disturbing. She wanted a paragon, but what she'd probably got was an oily little toad who was exploiting her weakness.

As she ushered the sodden Sam into the lovingly nurtured cleanliness of her living room, she wrinkled up her nose. The wretched scarecrow wasn't just dirty. He was filthy. Mephitic. His back end wasn't only covered in black mud, but evinced alarming hints of his alleged inability to use a toilet properly. Hastily, she grabbed a newspaper and slipped it on to the armchair before the pristine purity of her cushions was permanently soiled. The sooner Sam was in the bath the better.

'John, can you run the bath for Sam?'

'No I won't!' came a shrill squeak from the kitchen. 'Shat your pants again, have you, Stick Insect?'

(Open defiance! The start of that long-dreaded loss of control and slide into anarchy? Don't let things get out of hand!)

So fierce-teacher-in-control voice: 'John Denby, you'll do as you're told! If you can't behave, you'll go home THIS INSTANT!'

John jumped with fright. Not the cosy old shaggy sheepdog, but a savage wolf. Message received: if he wanted to have any kind of

Christmas, he'd have to stay in Dolly's good books … and that meant being nice to that shitty old stick insect called Sam. He scuttled into the bathroom and turned on the taps.

'Now, Sam,' said Mrs Watson, sitting him carefully down on the newspaper, 'tell me all about it.'

Meanwhile the girl had draped herself over the settee and rested her muddy pumps on the coffee table. Ostentatiously, she threw her fag on to the carpet and proceeded to light up again, making a great show of blowing the smoke through her nostrils and flicking the ash onto one of the cushions.

Before Sam could open his mouth she plunged in: 'It were that cunt o' a dad of his. He works on them oil rigs in the sea like … Well 'e comes home all pissed up wi' the whiskey an' that like wot 'e always does when he gans ower hyem like. Well, Sam's mam, yer knaa, she's gannin' oot wi' me uncle Bob an' that. So 'e starts skelpin' 'er, yer knaa, geein' 'er a birra fist an' callin' 'er a fuckin' slag. Well, she gans roond ter wor place where me uncle Bob is an' 'e fuckin' follows 'er an' the pair o' 'em start fightin' like. Well, me uncle Bob – he's a boxer like an' 'e brays the pissed 'ard cunt proper. So 'e gans back ower hyem. Then 'e sees Sam an' starts on 'im. Says 'es nowt burra a poofter and 'e brays 'im reet proper like. Well, Sam's cryin' like. 'E's only a bairn, yer knaa, an' 'e couldn't gee owt fist – could yer, pet? So the 'ard cunt hoys 'im oota the hoos. He's that scared that he spends the neet in the bins. Yer jus' gorra help 'im, Miss!'

Dorothy sighed. Through the semi-coherent jumble several messages were emerging. She *was* needed. No doubt about that! A son battered by his drunken and aggressive father was a matter for the Social Services, if not the police – deep waters here! But the sooner that girl could be eased out of the house the better. The flagrant insolence with which she simply took the place over, the fag ends on the carpet, the muddy feet on the coffee table, the continual smoking and not to mention the foul language … What kind of a message would that send out to the potential anarchists who were about to invade her inner sanctum?

Keeping as calm and magisterial as possible, she interrupted the flow: 'Of course I will. Now, Sam, the first thing you're going to do is have a good bath.'

Turning to the girl, she said: 'Thank you very much for your help. Now you'd better get back to your family: they'll be wondering what's happened to you.'

'Not fuckin' likely I will! I'm stayin' 'ere to 'elp Sam wash 'issell I am!'

With that, she uncoiled herself and, picking up her trophy by the scruff of the neck, marched him forcibly out of the room.

'Please, Sam is perfectly capable of washing himself. Now will you go home and leave this to me.'

'But I gorra wash 'im, Miss! He's that upset that he canna dee owt hissell!'

'I gorra wash 'im': Dorothy wasn't born yesterday. She knew what that was all about: sex. Get the old goof naked and then 'work him up'. Girls weren't always the sugar-sweet innocents that some people imagined they were. They matured earlier than boys and could be sex-mad maniacs... Which was why she hadn't had any girls at Beaconsfield.

She followed them out into the hall: 'Please will you go home and leave Sam to me.'

'Fuck off!' snarled the girl as she elbowed her way into the bathroom.

Grabbing a bewildered John by the arm, she flung him out into the hall where he landed in a heap on the floor.

'Will you leave my house at once.'

'Piss off, you old cow!'

Dorothy quailed. Worst-case scenario. House taken over by a female thug... Now what? Stern expressions? Headmistressy admonitions? They just bounced off this creature. As well to try and shoot a rhinoceros with a peashooter. Brute force was the only answer. But a middle-aged lady tangling with a tough, wiry street girl with years of violence behind her? Hardly a feasible option. Besides, like those Greenhill tearaways, she'd know her rights and she could end up being charged with assault.

The only answer was to call in reinforcements.

'Look, if you don't go now, I'll call the police.'

'Call in the pigs if yer fuckin' wanna! Divvent scare us!'

The dinghy plunging headlong over a waterfall. About to capsize. Occupants hanging on for dear life! Trying to look as calm as possible, Dorothy marched over to the telephone. After a moment's reflection she decided that it might be better not to involve the police at this stage – it could land you in all sorts of complications. Instead, she rang Meakin. And, thank God, he was in!

'Yes, I understand. I'll be over right away.'

340

Meanwhile in the corridor John was trembling on the floor. That girl had unnerved him. It was like a science-fiction story in which the fabric of the universe had been torn apart. Through the hole in 'space-time' he'd seen... Greenhill! It had been a glimpse of his utter helplessness before brute, animal force. Supposing Dolly got sick of him and he was sent back there again? Oh God! More than ever he needed her protection.

With a mixture of horror and disgust, he peered through the open bathroom door. The girl was busy pulling Sam's drawers down and was starting to manipulate his thing – and the silly old stick insect was just letting her do it! God almighty, had he *no* sense of shame?! He also noticed in passing that the legend was true. Sam's thing *was* minute.

Stepping over John, Mrs Watson marched into the bathroom – brave and bold Mrs Watson, his one defence against evil.

'I've rung up the police and they're coming over now. If you don't leave the house you'll be charged with illegal entry.'

Quite untrue, of course. Pure bluff. But to her immense relief it worked.

'Fucking cow! Mother-fucking bitch!...'

In a cloud of raucous obscenities the girl stormed out of the house, slamming the front door so hard that a china plate fell off the wall and broke.

A collective sigh of relief on all sides.

'Right, John,' said Mrs Watson in full headmistress-in-charge persona. 'Can you look after the kitchen while I deal with Sam. It's an important job, so don't let me down.'

'Yes, Miss.' That glimpse of Greenhill had shown him just how much he needed her protection. He just had to keep in her good books – pure survival.

A little later, amid clouds of steam, a pink and shiny Sam emerged from the bathroom swathed in towels. As he was ushered into the living room, John fussed over him: 'Great to see you, Sam! Can I get you a mince pie from the kitchen?'

If the price of Mr Watson's protection was greasing up the shitty old stick insect, then so be it. Pile on the grease, squirt the syrup over him with a hosepipe...

Sam sat on the settee in a state of bewildered bliss. For once, nobody was shouting at him or being nasty to him – a new experience.

Meanwhile Dorothy was phoning the Bleesons: '... It's Sam

341

Hawthorne... Can you possibly buy him some underwear, a shirt and some jeans? ... You can give me the bill.'

Reinforcements. The Dinghy Righted. Smooth Water Again

As expected, the Bleesons promptly agreed – and, moreover, insisted on paying the bill. It was a timely reminder that there *were* some decent people in the world after all.

Then Meakin arrived, all bustle and bonhomie, his legendary pipe emitting its customary clouds of smoke: 'All's well. Mrs Watson. The US Cavalry's here...'

And, shortly afterwards, in came Mrs Bleeson and her son laden with a Christmas cake, a chocolate mousse, more mince pies and, more important perhaps, a bundle of new clothes for Sam. Despite further protestations from Dorothy, Mrs Bleeson still insisted on paying the bill. After which she left, leaving her son to help out, as arranged.

With much fuss and feminine bustle, Sam was duly levered into his new and glossy outfit. Meakin eyed the finished product, resplendent in its red T-shirt and bright-blue jeans.

'I say, Mrs Watson,' he said, 'I think you'd better ring up the police and let them know that His Nibs is here... You know what old man Hawthorne is like when he's had one too many.'

Dorothy promptly did so and it proved a wise move.

Meanwhile, under Bill Bleeson's guidance, John and Sam set about readying the living-room table for the coming feast. So all was in order once more. After the trauma of the waterfall, the dinghy had been righted and was drifting gently down the calm waters beyond.

The Planned Schedule in Shreds. An Unwelcome Guest...

A little later the doorbell rang. Dorothy answered it and found a scruffy Michael Connolly standing on the doorstep in his school uniform.

'Michael, it's only two o'clock.'

'Oh dear, I thought it was six o'clock.'

'Well come on in and help us get things ready.'

The carefully planned schedule was now in shreds.

'What's that in your blazer pocket?'

'Oh, it's just Herbie.'

'Herbie?'

'It's me pet hamster. I couldn't leave him all by hissell like whiles I were havin' a party, could I? Ain't right. I mean what would he think o' us?'

'Well, do try to look after him properly...' (Another potential crisis in the offing. What would happen when the cat saw the hamster?)

But before she could do anything an excited Michael had bumbled his way into the living room. Having laid out the knives and forks, John was sitting next to Sam on the settee stroking the cat. Seeing Michael he felt another stab of disappointment – somebody else to get a share of the attention he wanted all for himself. More people invited to the party he'd thought was only for him... Still, if he wanted to stay in Dolly's good books, he'd better continue to play the kind and unselfish boy who welcomed others – even though it stuck in his throat.

He stood up: 'Come on in, Michael, great to see you!'

At that moment there was a sudden explosion of anarchy. As Michael's blazer brushed against the table, the long-imprisoned Herbie made a bold dash for freedom, leaping out of the pocket and scampering off among the newly laid-out mince pies, Christmas cake and meringues. Here was a heaven-sent opportunity for the cat: the chase, warm living flesh instead of boring old tinned stuff ... its very being as a real cat, a hunter, strong, deadly and brimming with testosterone! With a single bound it leapt on to the table.

A glass landed on the floor, followed by the plate of meringues... Herbie, displaying a quite unexpected athletic prowess, dived through the void, landed on the armchair and scuttled under it. The cat, after desperate attempts to reach him with its claws, settled down for a prolonged siege. John picked up the angry creature, its tail swishing furiously, while a frantic Michael tried to coax a traumatised Herbie out of his refuge.

Eventually, a distracted Mrs Watson came into the room and surveyed the wreckage – the overturned glasses, the scatter of meringues on the floor and, also, the unmistakable evidence of Herbie's trauma in the shape of a trail of 'biological elimination' across her spotlessly clean tablecloth.

'Give me the cat, John.'

The cat, protesting furiously, was deposited behind the locked door of her bedroom.

'Now, Michael, let's have that hamster. We really can't have it running wild.'

'But can't Herbie come to the party? He's been so lookin' forward to it.' (How to explain to a not-over-intellectual eleven-year-old that hamsters didn't have the same social awareness as human beings? And why did he have to bring the blasted thing along in the first place? ... Kids! ... But control your irritation, Dorothy Watson! It's when kids want to kill animals that you should get worried, not when they sentimentalise them.)

'No, Michael, I think Herbie would be much happier in a little box of his own. This place must be very frightening for him. I mean, how would *you* like to be dumped in a giant's castle full of strange monsters? That's what Herbie must feel like.'

Luckily, there happened to be a suitable wooden box in the kitchen with piles of newspaper in it. Deposited in that, with a mince pie to nibble and placed in a corner under the Christmas tree, Herbie seemed content. Getting out a new tablecloth and picking up the meringues off the floor, Dorothy rearranged the table. That crisis was over. But what was next on the long afternoon of anarchy?

Tensions Aboard the Dinghy...

A quiet period ensued. The dinghy was drifting lazily down a peaceful stretch of the river. Luxuriating in his new-found sartorial splendour, Sam sat on the settee enjoying the unaccustomed sensation of being clean and tidy for once. While Dorothy and Bill Bleeson beavered away in the kitchen, Meakin produced a game of Snakes and Ladders to keep the three boys occupied.

'We don't want any riots, do we?' he said as he spread the game out over the coffee table. 'So let's get stuck into this. Two mince pies for the winner, one for the runner-up. You start, Michael...'

John found it hard to concentrate on the game. As a stream of excited chatter flowed out the kitchen, his frustration grew and turned into resentment. Bleeson was having Dolly all to himself. He, John, the bearer of an expensive gift, had been elbowed aside, first by shitty old Stick Insect and then by brainless little scatterbrain Michael ... and now by arch suction pump Bleeson. The pressure was building up. 'The Sweet Little Boy' act was becoming increasingly hard to sustain.

Disaster. Over the Waterfall and into the River.

At about four o'clock the doorbell rang.

'Somebody see to it!' called Dorothy from the kitchen.

'You go, John,' said Meakin.

Rather grumpily, John did so. When he opened the front door he got an almost physical shock. He felt the last vestiges of any sweet temper evaporate. There, leering aggressively at him, was... Ratty!

'Oh God, what are *you* doing here?'

'I comes to the party. I were invited an' all! An' I gorra pressie for Miss an' all!'

He brandished a large, beautifully wrapped parcel. John sank deeper into dismay – that 'pressie' was probably far more expensive than the one he'd bought for her. Outdone in the bribery stakes by his deadly rival! The dream of a party specially for him had finally dissolved.

'What is it, John?' came Mrs Watson's headmistressy voice from the kitchen.

'It's Robert Napier.'

As he mumbled the words, John prayed desperately to himself: 'Please, Miss, tell him to go away! PLEASE!'

But all in vain. A radiant Mrs Watson burst out of the kitchen, hot-foot from the oven, complete with greasy spoon and stained apron. Seeing Ratty, she seemed to glow, to positively radiate: 'Ah ROBERT! How WONDERFUL! DO come in!'

It was as if an electric light had been switched on inside her: 'Robert, this is WONDERFUL!' she gushed. 'So you could come to the party after all! We're all SO pleased to see you, aren't we, John?'

John merely stared disconsolately at the floor.

Ratty put on his 'ingratiating smile'. (And as the proud possessor of a similar weapon, John knew the stratagem only too well.) 'Well, as you was that kind in askin' us along like I jus' had ter come, didna? An' as yer's bin that good ter us I've brought yers this Christmas box special like.'

With ostentatious ceremony he brandished the superbly wrapped parcel that he was carrying.

A smile of sheer radiant joy flowed over Dolly's face. How kind of the little street arab! How thoughtful! And, more to the point, what vindication! Despite old Meakin's mutterings, she *had* managed to break through the crust of Robert's gutter culture. A new and better Robert Napier *had* emerged. Her professionalism had worked after all. Now she really did have that brick to throw at Professor Stimpson.

But there were disturbing thoughts, too. Young Briggs had been proved right about Robert Napier, but what about that other protégé of hers, little John Denby? Briggs hadn't minced his words where that particular baggage was concerned – 'Thinks he's special... If you don't get a grip on him, you'll regret it.' By openly favouring him was she making an ass of herself? Agonising reappraisals...

'Thank you so much, Robert!' she purred. 'Do come and join the party. Give the present to Mr Meakin – he'll put it under the Christmas tree.'

As she swept back to work and Ratty slipped into the living room, John lingered in the corridor. He listened disconsolately to the excited babble of conversation that erupted from the kitchen.

'Bill, you'll never guess! Robert Napier's actually managed to come... And he's even brought a present as well... We really *have* succeeded with him...'

Solemnly and portentously – for he was a solemn and portentous youth – Bill pronounced: 'I do believe he's seen the light at last. Born again, you know, like Nicodemus in the Bible.'

'I'm sure you're right. It's what I've been praying for every night... We must make the most of this... Be especially nice to young Robert...'

John writhed. Ratty 'born again'?! What a load of crap! Why, only the other week Michael had told him that he was part of a burgling gang... Michael might be a scatter-brained little thickoid, but in certain areas he was wired up all right. Grown-ups were such dorks. They let some kids run rings round them. And here was suction pump Bleeson telling the old fool what she wanted to hear!

'Come on, John – back to the party,' the 'Mekon Voice of Authority' boomed out of the living room.

As the game of Snakes and Ladders resumed, John noticed that an icy chill seemed to have fallen on things – like what happened in horror films when Dracula arrived. Sam and Michael seemed to have shrivelled up.

'Can somebody come and collect the sweets and sausage rolls?' came Mrs Watson's voice from the kitchen.

'All right. I'll come,' said Meakin.

'Right, you lot,' he added, putting the game back in its box, 'time to work.'

As he left the room. Ratty sidled round the coffee table and poked his finger obscenely up John's bottom – the timeless Ratty signature tune for all who really knew him.

'Yer not gannin' ter be teecha'z pet no more,' he hissed, 'coz I's gannin' ter tell on yers!'

Sam and Michael looked away and seemed to freeze. Ratty was making his long-awaited comeback. And without the rest of Form One to help him, John could well lose the impending battle. Their brief respite could be over.

Suddenly, Ratty darted over to the fireplace where his hand shot out like a chameleon's tongue and grabbed a silver cigarette case and an embossed ashtray on the mantelpiece and stuffed them into his trouser pocket. Then, with equal split-second timing, he snatched a heap of mince pies and sweets and added them to his loot. A brilliant professional job in the same league as Billy Lees' shoplifting.

A delighted John saw his chance. As soon as Meakin returned with the next tray-load, he piped up: 'Please, Mr Meakin, Sir, Robert's been nicking things off the mantelpiece...'

But Meakin shook his head dismissively: 'What the eye doesn't see, the heart doesn't grieve over. No tales, please.' (Years of experience had taught him to stay out of children's internecine wars. Anyway kids were such accomplished liars.)

John sank further into frustrated anger.

When Meakin went out again Ratty retaliated. 'Little sneak!' he hissed as he grabbed another handful of sweets.

Then, turning to Michael, he said in a loud and clear voice, 'Jonny boy weren't expelled from Greenhill for hittin' a teecha, yer knaa...'

A deep wound was being reopened and John reacted fiercely: 'Yes I was!'

'Liar! The big lads pulled yer pants off an' bummed yer with a bicycle pump coz you was a poof! I knass all aboot it coz Freddy Hazlett told us. So THERE!'

'Crap!'

'Yer shooda seen him, Mickey lad, runnin' roond starkers, cryin' like a babby an' shittin' hissell an' all!'

347

Horror. Exposure. John's whole world was about to collapse.

He was about to fling a punch at the little demon when Meakin returned with a tray-load of crackers and bottles of coke. The blitzkrieg was postponed.

'Yer soft as shite, ye!' Ratty hissed in his ear.

As soon as Meakin went out again, the war began. The stakes were high. Survival for John. The recovery of a lost empire for Ratty.

John struck first – the devastating Stuka attack – flinging a punch straight on to Ratty's beaky nose. Blood flowed.

'Reet, yer gerrin' it!'

Ratty hadn't been taken by surprise this time and fought back ferociously with all the fury of long-suppressed hatred. He landed a stinging punch on John's left eye. Literally seeing stars, John grabbed his assailant's flailing arms and together they rolled on to the floor, dragging the tablecloth with them and bringing down an avalanche of plates, mince pies, sweets and spilt Coca Cola. Thrashing round amid the debris and fighting desperately for his life, John managed to wrestle his enemy to the ground and bang his head savagely on the carpet. As he did so, his right foot tangled with the Christmas tree and brought the whole precarious structure crashing down. The tinkle and crunch of broken glass followed as they battled furiously amid the ruins of the morning's labour of love.

Retribution was immediate. A stentorian bellow from Meakin which made Sam and Michael cringe: 'WHAT THE HELL'S GOING ON HERE?!'

And with it a nerve-shattering screech from Dolly in full Mrs Watson-headmistress mode: 'STOP IT AT ONCE, THE PAIR OF YOU!'

John felt hands grabbing him as Bill Bleeson pulled him to his feet. Trembling, red-faced and panting, he glared at his antagonist.

'What IS all this?' demanded a thunderous Mrs Watson. 'We leave you for five minutes and you start fighting like babies!'

'I ain't done nuttin', Miss,' piped up Ratty. 'But he went an' hit me.'

'Is this true, John?'

'Yes, but he was stealing things. I saw him take a cigarette case and an ashtray off your mantelpiece. And he was nicking mince pies and sweets...'

'No I weren't' interrupted Ratty. 'It were *you* what were nickin' things!'

'Rubbish!'

348

'I sawed 'im, Miss, and when I took 'em off 'im he blew a fit on us. Here they are, Miss, I saved them for yous.'

With great ceremony he handed her the ashtray and the cigarette case.

'These are among my most treasured possessions,' gasped Mrs Watson. 'They were given to my poor old father when he retired from the shipyards! Oh, John, how *could* you?'

'But it wasn't me, it was *him*!'

Dorothy was aghast. Her worst fears were being realised. She'd gone and let a thief into her house. But *who* was the thief? That was the pregnant question. Trying to keep as calm and magisterial as possible, she fixed a disconsolate Sam with her headmistressy stare: 'Sam, you were here. Who was the person stealing my things? Now don't be frightened to tell the truth.'

Which, of course, was exactly what Sam *was* frightened of doing. He flashed a nervous sidelong glance at Ratty and then, in a barely audible whisper, said, 'John'. John felt himself almost literally sinking into the floor. A frantic rage blazed up.

'Crap!' he snarled and flung a vicious punch on to Sam's ear.

Sam crumpled up and started to cry.

'John Denby, behave yourself! HOW DARE YOU!' cried Mrs Watson, flaring up in turn. 'You've betrayed my trust in you by stealing my things and, what's more, you've tried to get another boy into trouble by telling lies! You can go home now!'

Wild, outraged fury: 'PISS OFF!'

In a fit of blind exasperation, Dorothy slapped him on the face.

It was too much. The bomb exploded: 'FUCK OFF, YOU OLD COW! I HATE YOU! I'LL NEVER COME BACK TO YOUR ROTTEN SCHOOL AGAIN! YOU'RE A CUNT!'

Riding the whirlwind of his wild and crazy fury, John stormed out of the house and into the cold rain beyond.

Of course Briggs Had Been Right. On the Side of the Under-privileged...

The dinghy had plunged over a waterfall and capsized. One member of the crew had been swept away in the raging torrent, while the others were clinging on for dear life. Talk about inept rivermanship!

Dorothy surveyed the wreckage of her missionary enterprise – the all-too-literal wreckage strewn over the carpet, the grinning Robert Napier and the snivelling heap on the floor that was Sam Hawthorne. It was a moment of truth. What an ass she'd been! Of course, Briggs had been right. Little John Denby *was* a 'spoilt prep-school brat'. He'd cynically buttered her up and exploited her kindness for his own nefarious ends. He'd stolen some of her most treasured family mementos and lashed out viciously at another boy who'd dared to confront him. 'If you don't get a grip on him ... you'll only regret it...' Regret it, she did – and how! Poor, wronged, deprived Robert Napier... That was where her efforts would lie from now on... On the side of the under-privileged of the inner city, no more wasting time on pampered upper-class dropouts. She'd seen the light.

'I think I'd better go after him,' said Meakin.

'Don't bother,' replied Dorothy. 'We're well rid of him.'

Meakin ignored her and went out into the rain.

Ratty Triumphant

Game, set and match to Ratty. He'd been on the point of losing the battle, but he'd won the war. He exulted in his triumph. Little shite Denby were gonna cop it. Callin' Dolly a cunt! Well, ole Mekon were after him. Gonna give him a birra fist like. Bray 'im over proper. Then Dolly'd give 'im the cane. And he'd tell her to do it proper like: pull his pants down and give 'im twelve. That'd get 'im cryin'! He was looking forward to that.

But he'd had a lucky escape. Freddy Hazlett had told him to be sure and nick a few things. He was privileged to be in Freddy's gang – not something had happened to many little kids! – but Freddy had to be obeyed ... or *else*! Little turd Denby had seen him nick that ashtray and that fag case and had grassed on him, but he'd managed to drop him in the shit. Luckily, Dolly was as soft as shit and would swallow anything... However, while nobody was looking, he'd been able to nick a gold pocket watch thing he'd seen lying on that mantelpiece. That should fetch a birra nicker like! And keep Freddy happy which was what mattered...

Meanwhile, without Denby there, he could start on Sam. As the old stick insect got up off the floor, he nudged him: 'Well, that's the enda him. Now then, yous is owin' me a canny birra nicker, ain't yer? An' Owly an' all!'

'What's that, Robert?'

'Oh, nuttin'. Miss! Just sayin' thank you to Sam for tellin' the truth like.'

'Good for you, Robert.'

Swept Away by the Raging Torrent. Fished out. Abject Surrender...

Outside, John stormed away down the street. Going? Nowhere.

Consumed with blind fury, the cold rain didn't matter. Nothing mattered. Not the future. Not Christmas. Nothing. Only justice. And revenge. Revenge on everything that had shattered his world. Ratty. Grown-ups... Yes, even God. They were all such idiots. Couldn't Dolly *see* what Ratty was? *Why* did she have to believe his lies? Didn't the old bag know how he and Owly had forced the pathetic old stick insect to give them money and go shoplifting for them? And what the hell was God doing letting it all happen? If he'd had any sense at all, he'd have rewarded him for spending his Christmas money on presents for other people. He was as much of a brain-dead buffoon as the rest of them!

Crazy, mad, lunatic. He was too angry even to cry.

Glancing round, he saw Mekon coming after him. Danger! Retribution! Well, he wasn't going to let the old fool catch him. He started to run.

But the old bastard was surprisingly quick on his feet. He caught up with him and grabbed his arm. He wriggled frantically.

'FUCK OFF! LEMME GO!'

'No I won't. And when you've cooled down, young man, you and I are going to have a little talk.' Calm, assured voice of authority.

'FUCK OFF! I'LL CALL THE POLICE!'

With all his strength he punched his captor in the side with his free hand.

Whereupon Meakin retaliated with a massive blow in the ribs. He was bigger than him and far stronger and he crumpled up into a soggy heap. Burying his head in the prickly tweed jacket that smelt of tobacco, he burst into tears. Not anger. Not fury. Just anguish and utter helplessness. Big boys didn't cry, but he wasn't a big boy any more. He was nothing.

'John Denby,' came a calm voice, 'don't you *ever* try to hit me again.'

351

'Sorry! Sorry! I didn't mean it. But I'm so angry. It's all so *unfair*.'

Meakin glanced nervously around. Thank God the street was deserted. Punching kids in public wasn't a good idea. It just needed some sanctimonious old trout with frustrated missionary tendencies to see you and all hell could break loose.

He looked at the utter heap of misery sobbing away into his bosom and shuddered. It reminded him of something he'd rather forget. Something that should have been dead and buried, but, like a corpse in a ghost story, kept climbing out of its grave.

He didn't like hitting kids – and he hated it when they cried on him. But they pushed you into it. Sometimes they gave you no alternative. A short, sharp physical shock could be the only thing that brought them to their senses and saved them from themselves. And what was the alternative here? Let the kid run amok on a wet and freezing winter afternoon, lose himself in the city and end up suffering from hypothermia, or even worse? Kids were so short-sighted and self-destructive.

The tears flowed. Out it all came through the gasps, bit by incoherent bit: 'Why does Miss call me a thief? I *didn't* steal those things off the mantelpiece. It was Ratty. I *saw* him. Why don't you believe me? Can't you *see* what Ratty's like?

You people are so thick! He and Owly were getting money out of Sam and forcing him to go shoplifting for them – until I did them over, that is. Why does Miss pick on me? I try to be good. I even bought her a present...'

So it trickled on like the rivulets of freezing rain dribbling down his neck: the presents he'd bought with the money Giles had given him, the lack of a Christmas tree at home, the way that nobody had bothered to read his report... 'And I was *so* looking forward to this party...'

'Yes, I quite understand you,' said Meakin, reverting to the avuncular mode that he preferred. 'Now we'll go back to the party and sort it all out.'

'But what will Miss say? She told me to go home. I won't get the cane, will I?' The awful truth was dawning. He'd never called a teacher a cunt before. What would have happened if he'd said that to Mr Cotton? Didn't bear thinking about. And Dolly was just as strict. He was for it now. He could even be sent back to Greenhill!

'No, no, no, of course not,' said Meakin in a comforting voice. 'Just say you're sorry and we'll sort it all out.'

John wasn't reassured and, as he was frogmarched back to the house, he began to tremble.

Creeping timorously into the living room behind the bulky shield of Meakin, he noticed that it had been tidied up. Another fresh tablecloth was on the table. The Christmas tree was erect again with the lights working, though it was shorn of some of its former splendour.

To his alarmed dismay, he saw that Dolly was in 'Mrs Watson-stern-headmistress' mode. He shrivelled as she fixed him with her X-ray eyes.

'So you have decided to come back, have you, John Denby? I thought I told you to go home.'

'I know you did,' said Meakin, 'but I think there may have been some misunderstandings here.'

'What *misunderstandings*? My instructions were perfectly plain and I don't like being disobeyed.'

Meakin sighed. It was Dorothy's much-vaunted 'credibility' again. Beneath her cultivated air of headmistressly gravitas, insecurity lurked – lose her 'credibility' and she'd lose control of her school: that was her nagging fear. She'd need careful handling...

A pregnant silence followed while Dorothy mused. The crude reality was that in this precarious situation she needed old Meakin. So, after a theatrical interval, she pronounced: 'All right, John Denby, you can come back. I'll deal with you later. In the meantime, however, what have you to say for yourself?'

'Sorry, Miss, I just lost my temper.' Scarcely audible whisper.

'I should hope you *are* sorry!' came the whiplash voice. The 'affronted headmistress' was not in a forgiving mood.

'And what have you to say to Robert whom you attacked and wrongly accused of stealing?'

'Sorry, Robert.' Even less audible whisper. Total, abject defeat. Despite himself, the tears began to trickle.

'Aw howay, Miss!' piped up Ratty with a triumphant leer. 'Ain't yer gannin' ter give him a birra fist or sommat? I mean 'e called yer a cunt an' that's deesgustin'! Yer too soft, you! That's what me mam says. Yer wanna give him the cane. Pull his pants down and dee it proper like! That's what he's been wantin' him! Howay, me and Sam'll help yer.'

John slipped behind the bulk of Meakin and cringed. It was going to happen! The HUMILIATION!

'Robert, be quiet!' came Mrs Watson's commanding voice. 'You'll do no such thing!' (Kids! They were such little sadists. Thank God they'd abolished public hanging. Just think of all those kids milling round Tyburn Tree ogling at the dangling corpses. And one kid was as bad as another. This party was sliding out of control...

Underlying message: Dolly, old girl, you're out of your depth here.)

However, no option now but to soldier on and try to redeem what was left of the situation. Bail the dinghy out and try to keep it afloat. While Dorothy returned to the kitchen, Meakin and Bill Bleeson organised a game of Monopoly round the coffee table.

You've Made a Mess of This, Dolly Old Girl...

The frigid little game had hardly started before Bill Bleeson went into 'head boy' mode: 'Robert, what's that in your pocket?'

'Nuttin!'

'No, it's not. There's a mince pie there.'

'No there ain't!'

'Yes there is.' And he leaned over and stuck his hand into Ratty's trouser pocket.

Ratty reacted like a coiled viper: 'GERROFF, YER BENDER! Hey, Miss, he's fiddlin' with me dick!'

He wriggled frantically, but couldn't prevent Bill from extracting a crumpled mince pie and a handful of sweets.

'I think there's something else in there, too,' added Bill.

But before he could do anything, Dolly came flying out of the kitchen: 'What's all this?'

'Robert's been stealing sweets and mince pies.'

'So John wasn't the only one, then? Robert, I'm surprised at you.' (And 'surprised' she was. More than that. Worried: the 'redeemed Robert' vision was under threat.)

'Howay, Miss. It were jus' a liddell bit o' fun...'

'That's your word for it, is it?'

The cold, icy voice was unsettling. Seeing the gains of the past hour being lost, Ratty went on to the offensive: 'Yer wanna watch that bugger Bleeson, Miss. He's a filthy hom, him. Pulls the pants off the liddell kids, fiddles with their dicks an' then bums 'em... Don't he, Sam? Yer should knaa like!'

John saw a fleeting chance to redeem himself in Mrs Watson's eyes. 'Liar!' he squealed in high-pitched falsetto. 'That's a dirty lie!'

'Wanna fight then?' hissed Ratty.

For a moment it looked as if the carefully restored room would be reduced to bombsite chaos again as the two antagonists squared up to resume their war.

'SHUT UP!' A stentorian bellow from Meakin made everybody jump. Order returned.

'Right,' continued Meakin, 'sit down the pair of you. Robert, you can put your loot back on the table. And you can keep your smut to yourself. We don't want to hear it. Now let's get on with the game. Sam, it's your turn.'

Dorothy went back into the kitchen. Her worst fears were being realised. Self-absorbed little egotists wanting to monopolise her attention and exclude others, sex-mad teenage girls, lies, stealing, fights ... and now this torrent of filth about the one honest boy in her whole wretched school... What next? It was Africa all over again. Nothing solid. Everything sinking into a morass of lies and deceit... She felt she'd fallen into a sewer...

'Keep your distance ... Don't get too close to them ... You'll only make a cross for yourself.' How right those lecturers at college had been! You've made a right mess of this, Dolly, old girl! But you've made your bed, now lie on it. Bail out the dinghy, brave the white water and try to reach the finishing line without capsizing and drowning everybody.

A quiet period followed. Despite his anxieties, John began to enjoy the game. It was much more fun than watching videos.

Over Another Waterfall. 'You teechas oughta listen to us kids'

But the peace didn't last long.

Ten minutes later the doorbell suddenly erupted in an orgasm of noise followed by a frantic banging on the door.

'Go and see what it is, Bill,' said Meakin.

Bill did so and a cacophony of shouting and screeching ensued.

'Is this ole Watson's place? I jus' gorra see that ole bag!'

Ratty tightened up, his little eyes darting round in their sockets, his long nose quivering.

A flustered Bill returned: 'There's a lady here. I don't know who she is or what she wants.'

A youngish woman dolled up, tart-style, in skin-tight jeans, a leather jacket and lurid-red lipstick burst into the room behind him and pushed him aside, her peroxided mound of hair bobbing up and down like an iceberg in a stormy ocean. She was obviously a bit drunk.

'Yes, Mrs Napier?' said Mrs Watson emerging from the kitchen – the 'ole bag' tag uttered in the hearing of her charges was a challenge to her 'credibility' that could not be ignored.

'Would you like a mince pie, Mrs Napier?' said Bill doing his 'polite head boy' act.

'I'd rather have wor bairn... So there yer is, yer liddell sod!' she exclaimed, pointing aggressively at Ratty. 'Runnin' off like that an' leavin' yer mam all alerm with yon pissed bastard an' his fuckin' tarts!'

'Please, Mr Napier,' said Mrs Watson, 'There are *children* here.'

'Bluddy 'ell, 'e nivver were no fuckin' child him! Like his rotten fuckin' father, him!'

'Mrs Napier, can you *please* mind your language.'

Ignoring Mrs Watson's appeals, she marched over to the Christmas tree and picked up Ratty's present.

'That's what I were lookin' for!'

'If you don't mind, Mrs Napier, that's Robert's gift to me.'

'ROBERT'S gift! Fuck me! Not if it's what I think it is!'

Before anybody could stop her, she had ripped the parcel open. A glittering silver teapot was revealed – possibly a genuine Georgian antique worth more than a thousand pounds.

'Robert Napier!' gasped Mrs Watson, 'where *did* you get that?' (She could feel her head starting to spin. What *was* she getting into?)

A Christmas present

'Nae frets, Miss!' answered Ratty, putting on his 'ingratiating smile'. 'Ah gorrit in the market doon on the quayside with the tweeny quid I saved up special from me paper round. Don't yer like it?'

'Yer liddell lying sod!' screeched Mrs Napier. 'It's me fambly hairloom what were given us by me ole granddad what's passed away!'

'No it ain't an' yer fuckin' knaas it an' all, yer ole cow!' snarled Ratty.

Then, with his lightning-quick chameleon reflexes, he snatched the teapot from her. As he did so, it dropped onto the table and the lid fell off, spilling a red plastic package into the sweets and mince pies. A white powder dribbled out of a tear in its side.

'EEEEE! That's where it were! God, yer liddell fucker. I've been lookin' forrit all bloody morning!'

With the deft movement of a professional, Ratty scooped it all up – teapot, lid, package, the lot – and dashed out of the house pursued by his screeching mother.

The dust settled.

'Thank God we're rid of him!' exclaimed Michael.

'MICHAEL!' Dorothy's beatific vision of a 'reformed Robert' had taken a battering – along with that brick she was longing to throw at Professor Stimpson – and she felt sore.

'Shall I go and get him back?' said Bill, trying as always to act the 'responsible head boy'.

'Don't bother,' cut in Meakin authoritatively, 'Mrs Watson, I think it's best to let that lot sort themselves out. Young Master Robert has caused enough problems for one day.'

'Yes, you're probably right,' she replied. 'But I wonder where that teapot came from?'

'Best not to ask. Curiosity killed the cat, you know.'

'It'll have been nicked,' said Michael in a knowing way.

'Michael, you don't know that!' snapped Mrs Watson.

But Michael wouldn't be browbeaten: 'But, Miss, Brian, that's me mam's new partner, he says that Robert's a burglar. He's in with Freddy Hazlett, that Greenhill kid what John knows, an' he nicks things forrim...'

'Michael, that's quite enough!'

But still the babble continued: '... That were dope in that packet, dope like what me mam uses. Gets it off Kev what's Mrs Napier's new partner ... and it weren't John what were nickin' your ornaments neither. He were tryin' to stop Robert what was nickin' them, but

357

Robert false accused him like and you believed 'im. It were John what stopped 'em being nicked. Yer shouldn't of bollocked John, yer knaa. You shouldn't pick on him like what Mr Briggs does jus' cos he talks posh like. Ain't his fault any more than it's my fault that I talks Geordie... I mean I know he's a bit big-headed an' that...'

'Yes, Michael, you've had your say...'

Mrs Watson turned to Sam: 'Sam, who *was* stealing my ornaments? Now let's have the truth.'

Sam replied in a surprisingly firm voice: 'It were Robert.'

Mrs Watson groaned audibly: 'Oh, for heaven's sake! Why didn't you tell me this when I asked you before? You let a perfectly innocent boy get into trouble!'

'But, Miss,' interrupted Michael, 'he couldn't of said it. Not with Robert there.'

'And just WHY not?'

Undaunted by the X-ray eyes, Michael babbled on: 'Yer see, Robert's rock 'ard him and we's all afeared of him. Specially Sam like 'cos he does him over sommat awful. It's John what stopped it by doin' 'im an' Owly over on the landin' outside the Maths room...'

'But why didn't you tell me this before?'

'But yer wouldn't of believed us like. You teechas oughta listen to us kids. Us kids knows more what's gannin' on than what you grown-ups does...'

'All right, all right. I take your point, Michael. I owe you an apology, John. I was told lies about you. But it's all water under the bridge. So let's forget it and get on with the party.'

With that Dorothy returned to the kitchen. She felt deeply humiliated. She'd let a young criminal run rings round her. An antique teapot of dubious origin with drugs in it had been planted on her... She'd let some of her most treasured possessions be stolen from under her very nose and had allowed herself to be conned into blaming the boy who'd retrieved them for her. No wonder the wretched kid had thrown a temper tantrum! ... And, here she was, being told a few obvious truths by an immature and not-over-bright little eleven-year-old who thought that hamsters had the same social awareness as human beings! Not very good for the 'professional headmistress' image! Still less for the much vaunted 'credibility'. A big defeat.

Back in the living room, John couldn't contain his glee. He was exonerated. Freed from the ghastly possibility of 'getting the cane' and being sent back to Greenhill. He clasped Michael's hands: 'Thanks, Mike! You're a great mate!'

'All right,' said Meakin, taking charge, 'all's well that ends well. Now let's get on with the game. John, it's your turn. Are you sure you can afford to buy Mayfair?'

Peaceful Waters Again. But Something Missing?

Peace at last. The overloaded dinghy seemed finally to have reached the tranquil lower waters of the river.

In the street outside the grey, apathetic day finally fizzled out and a soggy, black dishcloth of a night closed in. Yet again the orange street lamps reduced everything to a monochromatic emptiness: black or orange. Nothing else.

Inside the Christmas tea got under way with its hot mince pies and great chunks of sticky, glutinous Christmas cake – a paradise of fruity mush, marzipan and icing sugar. It was everything that John thought Christmas ought to be: the dimly lit room; the tree aglow with its magical blue, green and red lights, the gorgeous golden balls shimmering mysteriously amid the sparkling points of colour; the smell of roast turkey wafting out of the kitchen... Only one thing, one massive thing, was missing ... the presents waiting to be opened to disgorge their hidden treasures! But, then, he'd deliberately made a big sacrifice and spent Giles' money on presents for other people. If he had any kind of decency at all, God would surely take note of that.

A Vision of Another World?

At eleven o'clock they forsook their comforting cocoon and ventured out into the bleak and wet blackness beyond.

At the little red-brick church Steadman did them proud. Here at last was a chance to display his considerable, and as yet unrecognised, artistic and theatrical skills – and he made the most of it. He was a dab hand at model-making and had got his Sunday-school kids – all four of them! – to do a first-rate job on the Christmas cribs. A master of all things electronic, he had turned the stark and dismal nave into an Aladdin's Cave of flickering candles, twinkling lights and cunningly illuminated Christmas tableaux.

To compensate for the lack of a choir he had rigged up a tape recorder to play a series of carols at carefully timed intervals.

John was swept away by it all. It was all so different from anything he had known before. The thrill of being up late. The cavernous gloom of the church pierced by the sparkling brilliance of the candles and coloured fairy lights. Those wonderful Christmas cribs... The exotic ritual as he and the boys were dressed up in white robes and processed through the darkness holding their candles... That, and the sheer beauty of the carols. 'O come all ye faithful... Yea, Lord, we greet thee, born this happy morning...'

Suddenly, John experienced something that amounted almost to a vision.

Everything came clear. More than clear. Brilliantly lucid. It was all right. Everything was all right. Jesus had come. His gran and his granddad were up in heaven, there with Fred, his poor martyred guinea pig and that wretched chick which had been so cruelly thrown out of its nest at Rickerby Hall.

More even than that. There was a 'Beyond World', a place where everything was clearer, more beautiful and of a deeper, richer and more meaningful hue. A fleeting glimpse of something grand and majestic that shimmered through the boiling clouds, focused for the minutest instant and then was gone. A far-off, distant mountain peak.

He prayed silently; 'Thanks, God, for the reassurance. But do please give me a Christmas present. It's not Christmas without presents.'

The Dinghy Home and Dry?

At twelve-thirty they traipsed back through the darkened streets.

The rain had stopped and the clouds had begun to dissolve, revealing a black, velvety sky studded with brilliant stars. A pale moon emerged and in its soft, restrained light the damp pavements and the wet slate roofs of the Edwardian houses exuded a reassuring calm. In the dim bay windows the odd brilliantly coloured Christmas tree glimmered through the tangled branches of the black and leafless trees.

Back at Fern Avenue the midnight feast began with all its exotic trappings. The dark room mysteriously illuminated by the flickering pinpoints of the Christmas-tree lights, the steaming turkey, the brandy burning on the Christmas pudding, the creamy sauce, the chocolate mousse, the meringues... To John, it was Paradise Regained – except, of course, for the lack of presents. To Sam and Michael, it was heaven on earth, an entirely new experience.

To Dorothy, it was vindication. Her plan was finally working properly. The dinghy was triumphantly sailing down the last calm reaches of the Wild River.

'What are we going to do about Sam?' whispered Meakin as he and she were sorting out the ice cream in the kitchen. 'I mean we can hardly send him back to Dad, can we?'

Dorothy sighed: 'Yes, I hadn't thought of that one... I suppose we'll just have to cross that bridge when we come to it.'

The dinghy wasn't home and dry yet.

Class War. 'I'm Gerrin the Law on to You!'

They'd just dished out the roast chestnuts when there was an almighty crash as the unlocked front door was flung open. A vast, sweaty man erupted into the living room.

'So there yer are, yer liddell bastard!' he shouted, pointing at Sam. 'Yer comin' home NOW!'

Huge and gangling, he was smartly dressed in a bright-blue suit and a jazzy tie. Damp with rain, he had obviously been tramping the streets for some time. Equally obviously, he had been drinking heavily. Radiating aggression, he towered over the assembly. A look of pure terror spread over Sam's wrinkled face and he slithered under the table.

'Come 'ere yer liddell sod!'

'Excuse me, but this is my private house.' The sheer arrogant loutishness had infuriated Dorothy.

'Excuse me nuttin!' snarled the man. 'You got my lad in 'ere! You no bloody right! If yer've done owt to him I'll fuckin' do yers ... an' Ah divvent care if yer's a bloody 'eadmistress or what!'

Taken aback by the massive male aggression, Dorothy looked round for support.

'Please, Mr Hawthorne,' said Meakin, putting on his avuncular front, 'no harm was come to Sam. We're just having a little Christmas party. With you being so busy we thought...'

Reason versus alcohol-fuelled resentment. Unequal contest.

'His own home ain't good enough! Ain't good enough, eh? Ain't good enough forrim? Workin' class ain't good enough! Middle class gorra take over! I'll have ye know, son, Sam's WOR bairn and NOT thine! An' I loves me bairn me! I'm not havin' neebeddy tekkin wor bairn off us, SEE! Why I gorrim the best Christmas box ever. Trainers. Two hundred quid an' all. Top o' the range. Worked me bloody balls off forrit an' all. An' proper work an' all! Oot on them rigs in the North-bloody-Sea, gerrin' the petrol what you lot takes for fuckin' granted. Not jus' poofin' roond what you lot does... But when Ah gans hyem like, worra find? Liddell bastard's gannin' roond ter see you lot. Own fuckin' dad not good enough? Workin' class not good enough...'

The alcoholic maunder dribbled away to nothing and he sat down heavily on the settee.

Stunned silence.

'Please, Mr Hawthorne,' a threadbare Dorothy finally ventured, 'I did send a note about this party in Sam's report and I thought...'

The mere sound of a female voice was enough to detonate a further explosion: 'Sent ME a note? Sent ME a note! Crap! Yer sent it to bloody Beth, yer did. Just ter shame us like!'

'But she IS your wife and with you being away...'

'My bloody wife?! She's nae bloody wife HOR! Why man she's jus' the fuckin' bike! The hale bloody toon rides hor! Ah comes back hyem like an' worra find eh? She's roond at Raby-bloody-Terrace shaggin' roond wi' Bobby fuckin' Hebborn... Ay an' where's me bloody bairn an' all? Well, nae more, lads! Nae more! He's commin' hyem wi' us. Aye, an' 'e's not stayin' nae longer at yon bloody skyerl o' thine neither! Yer've not learned him nowt! Why man he canna fuckin' read!'

He lurched unsteadily to his feet: 'Howay, we's gannin' hyem!'

Then he glared threateningly at the empty chair where Sam had been sitting: 'Where the fuck 'ave yer hidden 'im?'

'I think he's under the table,' said a tremulous Dorothy. 'Sam, dear, come on out. Your father wants you...'

No response from under the table.

'Aw Jesus Christ!'

With that Mr Hawthorne lifted up the tablecloth and hauled his trembling son out of his refuge, upsetting a bottle of coke in the process. Boldly brandishing his trophy as if were a rabbit he'd just shot, he marched towards the door.

Throughout the encounter a frightened John and Michael had huddled closely to Mrs Watson – chicks seeking refuge in the reassuring feathers of Mother Hen. But John felt ashamed of his fear. It was weak and soppy. Not what a real boy should be like. It was just like the time when he'd watched them doing Billy Lees over at Greenhill. But not any more! Now was the time for redemption. Save yourself, too, from the distant, but awful, prospect of getting the cane for calling Mrs Watson a cunt. Show yourself to be brave and good by rescuing Sam from this monster and get back into her good books. Saint Paul before Nero...

So kamikaze charge with fists flailing: 'Leave Sam alone, you big bully!'

'John, PLEASE!'

Commotion... The naked African warrior charging the maxim machine guns of the colonial invaders... Massive retaliation by overwhelming force.

'AW SHUDDUP, YER LIDDELL SNOB!'

A punch in the face sent him sprawling on the floor, his nose pouring blood.

One final grenade was flung into the enemy trench by the infuriated Mr Hawthorne: 'Reet, you lot, I'M GERRIN' THE LAW ON TO YOU!'

The front door slammed and the whole house shook.

The Wounded Hero

John's ploy worked. To his huge delight, Mrs Watson lifted him up and, oblivious to the blood soiling her cardigan, cuddled him and laid him out on the settee. The heroic soldier, wounded in battle and rescued by his faithful comrades. He even managed not to cry. He was a big boy now.

Meanwhile in the general uproar Herbie's box had been upset and the precious hamster was running wild. While John wallowed in the attention he craved, Michael set up a wail.

'HERBIE! Where's Herbie? He'll get stood on!'

Bill eventually found him on the table nibbling the Christmas pudding.

After a while a sort of normality began to return.

'Come on, John,' said Meakin, 'you've done your wounded soldier act, now get up and help us tidy up.'

'I wonder what's next on the list?' he mused, lighting his pipe. 'This is almost as good as the war. You never know what's going to happen. Just when you think you're over the worst, that's when

Jerry starts playing silly buggers... Oh, sorry about the language, Mrs Watson!'

Dorothy didn't reply. She was finding it difficult to take it all in. Tarty foul-mouthed girls, priceless Georgian teapots with drugs in them, the attempted theft of her precious family heirlooms, lies, fights, temper tantrums, violent drunken fathers, 'gerrin' the law on to you' ... What else? Did the Good Samaritan have all this hassle when he'd rescued that man who 'fell among thieves' on the road to Jericho? Things were so much more complicated these days.

The Mouth of the River. The Dinghy Safely Ashore at Last?

Half an hour later Mr Bleeson arrived to take the boys home.

'What about you, John?'

'Well, there was nobody in the house this morning and I don't have a key.'

Mrs Watson duly telephoned Gloucester Road. There was no reply.

She eyed the tousle-headed little scrap in front of her. She'd probably lost one potential child, Robert Napier, and it still hurt. She'd nearly lost the other one by wrongly accusing him of stealing her things, hitting him and causing him to storm off in a temper tantrum. She'd been lucky to get him back. Time to make amends.

'Well, John, you'd better sleep here. We can't have you wandering around the streets at this time of night. I'll make up a bed for you on the settee.'

Michael and Bill left amid effusive thanks and with Herbie safely ensconced in Michael's blazer pocket. When the bed was made up, John settled down on the settee. Sleep followed at once.

Dorothy heaved a long sigh of relief. The dinghy had finally reached the placid waters of the river mouth and the surviving crew were safely ashore.

Or were they?

Alone and Unsafe on an Alien Shore?

John opened his eyes. He seemed to be floating on a cloud of sheer bliss. The Old World. The Sensible World. Christmas with his perfect gran and granddad.

Then a limbo... A creeping disappointment. It was just a dream. Then a panic. Where was he? It was Christmas, yes. The lights were winking on the Christmas tree. A grey light was poking through the slit between the thick, red curtains. But what was that sinister, grinning mask doing on the cream-painted wall?

Slowly, it all came back to him. This was the New Dispensation. Mixed feelings, big splashes of black and white. A feeling of triumph. He'd won yesterday's battle with Ratty and vindicated himself before Mrs Watson... But, at the same time, he'd been such a pathetic little cry baby! Crying like that when Mekon had hit him! Proper boys didn't cry. What would Jimmy Stokes have said if he'd seen him? More important, what did old Mekon think of him? He wanted to impress him and tough old men weren't impressed by little cry babies.

And Mrs Watson? He'd thought he'd got a new gran here, but he hadn't, had he? Her coldness when he'd arrived early and then the way she'd believed Ratty and accused him of stealing things... 'You can go home now.' It was horrible. HORRIBLE. And it could happen again. He suddenly felt terribly alone, frighteningly alone and unsafe.

And Christmas morning, that magic time when Granddad said you could start opening the presents under the Christmas tree? Not any more. The first Christmas without presents. A dreadful comedown. He was about to start crying when he remembered that big boys didn't cry.

But when Mrs Watson saw the lovely plate he'd given her, then, hopefully, she would start to like him. So, too, would Giles and Mary when they found their plates. Besides, if God had any sense in his silly great head, he would reward him for being so kind and unselfish. All was not lost.

Dolly, You're a Failure! Time to Recover Lost Ground...

He got up and, finding that he was in his underpants, hurriedly dressed.

Entering the kitchen, he found Mrs Watson bent over the sink, sloshing round amid piles of dirty dishes.

'Merry Christmas, Miss.'

There was no reply. He tried again.

'Merry Christmas, Miss.'

'Yes, John, I heard you the first time.'

Cold and hard. 'Stern headmistress' mode. His heart sank down through his trainers and on to the floor. What NOW?

It was conflicting universes. That New Guinea Cargo Cult again. Something beyond his understanding.

Dorothy had survived the Christmas party – but only just and it hadn't done her 'credibility' much good either. 'Keep your distance... Don't get too close to them...' By flagrantly ignoring this sound advice, she'd made a right idiot of herself. How weak she'd looked when old man Hawthorne had barged into the house! (If Meakin hadn't been there, what *would* have happened?) Robert Napier had run rings round her and shown her up... 'Weighed in the balance and found wanting.' Not the 'proper professional' of her aspirations, more like the 'emotional woman' that Lawrence had so sneeringly called her. It was time to recover lost ground.

And, to add to her discomfort, early in the morning, while John was still asleep on the settee, she'd crept into the living room and found that the gold pocket watch, given to her poor, sick father by his workmates on his retirement, was missing. Then she'd opened John's parcel and had discovered a hugely expensive plate inside it – far beyond the pocket of a normal schoolboy. That Georgian teapot again? Kids were not always what they seemed to be. They could be so deceitful, so wheedling and so devious. In the cold, grey light of the morning her doubts about John Denby had re-emerged. Oily, self-centred little charmer? Very probably. Robert Napier was a thief, all right, but this one was almost certainly in the racket as well. How else did he get enough money to pay for that plate? Almost certainly they'd met a day or two ago and cooked a little plan between them. That fight? A fight between thieves, nothing else...

Surreptitiously, she'd searched his clothes. She'd found nothing, but he would have handed it over to Robert, wouldn't he? Down had come another airy castle. Dolly, you're way out of your depth here! You're letting these little scamps rung rings round you. Face facts, old girl. You're simply not up to the job. You're a failure.

She turned round, her gloved hands covered in soap suds: 'Now, John I want you to tell me the truth about this. Where did you get the money to pay for that plate you've given me? It can't have been from your pocket money, can it?'

As the death rays bored into him, a heavy, leaden feeling came over John. He felt himself sinking and darkness closing over him: 'Please, Miss, I didn't steal it! ... Cross my heart! ... Swear to God!'

Out in bits and pieces came the story of the sixty pounds. It sounded very improbable to Dorothy.

'And I'm supposed to believe that, am I?'

Desperate pleading. Drowning man clutching at a floating twig: 'But it's TRUE, Miss! I was trying to be CHRISTIAN! I thought you'd like it!'

Despite himself, despite Herculean efforts, the tears began to trickle.

Dorothy was unmoved. 'Turning on the taps.' Another weapon in the childhood armoury. Don't be fooled by it.

'And you don't know what happened to a gold watch that was lying on the mantelpiece, do you? It was there yesterday morning, but it seems to have gone missing. How do you explain it?'

'*What* gold watch? ... Please, Miss, it must have been Robert...'

'Robert? That's very convenient, isn't it?'

Despite all John's efforts, the dam broke. The tears poured out. It was like being sick, something you could do nothing about.

'Please, Miss, I'm not a thief! Why don't you *ever* believe me...?'

He went back into the living room and sat down on the settee. Hopeless, utter despair. The darkness closing in on him...

Clarification

A little later the telephone rang. It was a panicky Giles: 'Is that Mrs Watson? You haven't by any chance seen my son, John, have you? Christ, I hope he hasn't run away again... That's all I bloody need...'

'Oh, no! Whatever gave you that idea? He's here with me. I told you he was coming over to spend Christmas Eve with me. I put a note about it in with his report.'

'Thank God for that!' (If the little toad had done another runner...!? Merrins! Didn't bear thinking about.)

On the other end of the line Dorothy could almost feel the warm blast of relief engulfing her.

'Yes,' he continued, 'I must have seen it... But I've been very busy, lately...' (Of course he hadn't seen it. He hadn't even looked at the report. He'd simply dumped the envelope unopened into its appropriate place, the bin.)

'Now, Dr Denby, there's one thing I must clear up...'

'...Oh, yes, I gave him sixty pounds... Shouldn't have done, though... He went and wasted it all on two gruesome plates... You never saw the like of them... God, if Al Dawson were to see them, what would he say? ... It'll be his way of trying to buy respect instead of earning it by behaving properly ... needs more discipline ... hope you'll provide it...'

'Thank you, that makes things a lot clearer...'

'Now I wonder if you could do me a favour? You see Mary and I are off to a friend's place for the next few days. It's not the place for a kid...'

(Most emphatically *not*! Releasing tensions through free sexual interchange... Serious discussion of revolutionary theory... The progressive elements of the Psychology Department beginning a series of groundbreaking experiments on chemically enhanced awareness... The very last place for a stuck-up little prig, especially when Merrins would be on a fighting patrol in enemy territory...)

'...Oh you *can* keep him for the next few days! That's awfully good of you. Mary and I really appreciate this...'

Right after All!

Dorothy entered the living room and sat down on the settee next to the snivelling heap of misery.

'That was your father on the telephone, John.'

'Oh God!'

'Don't look like that about it. He was very pleased with your presents and he wants you to stay here for the next few days. Now, John, it appears that you *were* telling the truth about the sixty pounds. That was very good of you. Very adult and very Christian. I shall treasure that wonderful plate and put it up on the wall. I'm sorry I didn't believe you at first, but you know when people start stealing things it does make life very difficult for innocent people. Of course, you're not a thief!'

At that the little bundle seemed to light up, to glow with warmth as if he were an electric fire that had been switched on. He flashed his glorious smile.

Suddenly, Dorothy lost control of herself. Poor, pathetic little scrap! Tossed about, discarded, wronged. Of course, he wanted attention. He needed it! Of course, he told lies – that silly story about being expelled from Greenhill for hitting a teacher! Admit to his classmates that he'd been stripped naked and raped by a gang of thugs? Impossible! After a thing like that he had to invent a story to restore some semblance of self-respect. Trying in his own clumsy way to love his silly and misguided parents. How could she tell him what his father had really said about the plates? Truth wasn't a simple issue. She'd been so blind, so wilfully incompetent.

'Robert Napier... That's where your efforts should be directed, not wasted on middle-class dropouts.' What a load of academic codswallop! She should have seen through it long ago. Hardened, streetwise Robert Napier was beyond her redemption. Probably beyond anybody's. This one wasn't. She could do something with him.

She hugged him effusively. To her huge delight, he responded. Her *own* child! ('Dolly, don't be an emotional woman!' 'Get lost!' replied her deeper self.) God had given her a child at last? That's what Lawrence would have said. Well, maybe the sanctimonious old prig was right for once.

'Now, John, tell me the truth. Are you getting any Christmas presents?'

'No.'

'Well, when the shops are open I'll get you a present because you've been so good and kind. But you mustn't go round telling everybody about it. You must keep it a secret. Understand?'

'Cor thanks, Miss!'

A blaze of euphoria followed, but then came caution. He was back in favour – but only for the moment. It could all go wrong again. So he'd better consolidate his position by erasing the selfish little weedy thing.

'But what about Michael? He won't be getting any presents, will he? We should get him something, too.'

'Yes, of course we will.'

Dorothy was loving this.

Bliss. A New Gran. Another Vision from Beyond...

The rest of the day was bliss.

At last John had Mrs Watson all to himself and he could get the undivided attention that he so desperately wanted. He lay around in luxury, gorging himself on the plentiful remains of the Christmas feast, stroking the cat and playing Monopoly.

Outside, the bleak, wet day made a half-hearted attempt at brightness. A few patches of blue sky made a fitful appearance before surrendering themselves to the omnipotent greyness. In the late afternoon, as the all-enveloping blackness closed in and shut everything down, he popped the question that had been on his mind all day.

'Please, Miss, could you show me your photographs of Africa?'

An electric thrill surged through Dorothy. This was just what she'd been hoping for ... those slides in their dusty old boxes, consigned to the depths of that fusty cupboard, abandoned, half-forgotten, the great might-have-been of her life ... deemed 'irrelevant' by all the clever people. But, here at last, was somebody who might appreciate them.

So out from under the blankets and old clothes in the hall cupboard came the screen and the projector.

John had never seen a slideshow before. He gazed in wonder as, out of the blackness of the curtained living room, one after another, a succession of glowing panoramas flashed up in front of him. African villages, brilliantly clothed Buganda women in markets, the mysterious oceanic emptiness of Lake Victoria under a blazing red sunset, the vastness of the African savannah sweeping away to infinity under a tremendous sky... Exotic animals – elephants, lions, giraffes, hippos ... a stunning shot of a black-and-yellow leopard in a gnarled old tree... Then the snowy dome of mighty Kilimanjaro rising over the dusty plains ... the otherworldly walls of ice in its lonely crater, aglow with the ethereal orange of the dawn...

'Cor, Miss, have you actually climbed Kilimanjaro, the highest mountain in Africa?'

It was something his perfect gran and granddad had never done. Good, kind, yes, wonderful, but they'd never had adventures like this.

'You're not bored, are you, John?'

'No! No! This is wicked! I'm loving it!'

This time he spoke the unvarnished truth. He was slowly becoming aware of something rather odd about himself, something that made him different from other kids. He was acutely sensitive to his surroundings. The fresh and brilliant green of the trees in May, the subtle vividness of those occasional snowy days in winter ... it all mattered greatly to him. And here, in this darkened room, was a window through which he glimpsed a world of extraordinary colour and beauty.

'Now this is the Ruwenzori which you were asking me about...'

So, picture by picture, Dorothy relived the great adventure of her life. Indeed, the Paradise before that Fall which had sent her back into mundanity, childless, husbandless and irrelevant.

John watched entranced as the screen lit up with an exotic world of sodden jungles, dense and dripping and filled with weird, oversize flowers – the sort of things that space travellers found on other planets. Menacing elephants were glimpsed through tangled foliage. Dark and sinister lakes brooded sullenly in forested ravines. Dazzling snowy spires reared up into vividly blue skies. Then, larger, grander and altogether more splendidly real, was the photograph he'd seen on the wall: Margherita Peak, a soaring vision of shimmering icy draperies and plunging black crags, rearing up into a crown of pure snow, brilliantly-majestically! – white against a tumult of grey and purple clouds.

Suddenly something happened to him. It was that unearthly, exalted feeling he'd experienced in the church the night before when he'd heard that carol 'O Come all Ye Faithful'. It was as if the fabric of the universe had been torn apart and a door had opened revealing a Beyond World. A world of deeper meaning where Jesus was with his beloved grandparents.

The show ended. Mrs Watson switched the lights on.

'Cor, thanks Miss!' he exploded. 'When I grow up I'm going to be an explorer. I bet there's mountains in the Ruwenzori that nobody's discovered. I'm going to be the first to climb them!'

'Oh, John!'

Dorothy hugged him warmly. (Dolly, get a grip on yourself! You'll only regret this. He's manipulating you for his own nefarious ends... Rubbish! This boy is the first person who has actually appreciated my richest treasures. He's my soulmate. Part of me. *My* child!)

A Happy Ending – Almost...

On the twenty-seventh, together with a wildly excited Michael Connolly, they went into Boldonbridge and bought a new and very elaborate cage for Herbie the hamster and a 125 diesel express with all its accessories for John. Two days later Mrs Watson took them both to the pantomime. So those glossy china plates had done their stuff. God had responded – and so he bloody well should have done: those plates had cost a fortune.

John was bewildered – and deeply hurt – when he went home and found his precious gifts in the dustbin along with his unopened school report.

36

Life Moves On

The New Year came in amid rain, sleet, blustery showers and occasional patches of blue sky.

Giles appeared on television alongside well-known politicians and trades union leaders. He performed brilliantly and work began in earnest on his BBC programmes about the evolution of the British working class.

Martha Merrins finally finished her 'scholarly amendment' of Mary's blockbuster, *Liberated Child Development*. To Mary, at a meeting of the Feminist Child Abuse Awareness Action Group, she described it as a 'developmental enhancement of your brilliant radical insights'. In fact, it was a scurrilous hatchet job. Unfortunately, it was couched in such convoluted and impenetrable jargon – one sentence being a whole page long – that not even the New World Radical Alternative Press could consider it for publication. Martha had to think of other ways of sorting her rival out. Resentment smouldered. Knives were sharpened.

Meanwhile Mary's Ph.D. thesis continued to get nowhere.

Aftershocks. Disappointments and Vindications...

For a while the aftershocks of Dorothy's 'Christmas good works' continued.

A few days before term began a beautifully wrapped parcel suddenly appeared in her living room. A lavishly elaborate label declared that it was 'a present from your very grateful pupil, Robert Napier'. How it got there was a mystery. She'd thought that all the doors and windows were locked.

After a momentary blaze of euphoria – a resurrection of the 'redeemed Robert' vision – she thought it best to take the exotic thing down to the police station unopened. It was just as well. Yes, it did contain that celebrated silver teapot; yes, it was a genuine antique worth at least a thousand pounds... No, it certainly was not a Napier 'fambly hairloom'. It had been nicked from a nearby stately home called Coldbeck Hall. Yes, the plastic packet inside it did contain cocaine. Michael Connolly had been right after all.

Robert Napier didn't appear at Beaconsfield that term. Instead, Dorothy got a probation officer's report. It made juicy reading – part of a gang of juvenile burglars working for an underworld syndicate, working as a rent boy for a paedophile and blackmailing ring ... a vicious knife attack on a thirteen-year-old boy... Depths far beyond the scope of Dorothy's remit. Meakin felt vindicated.

Deprived of his lifeline to respectability, Briggs sank into gloom. It was made all the worse by the fact that he'd written a letter describing his success with a 'deprived working-class child' which had been duly published with great fanfare in the *St Martin's College Newsletter*. ('St Martin's Graduate's Success in the Inner City' had been the banner headline.) Now he was left stranded and looking silly. Bang went that reunion he'd been telling his wife about! Subconsciously, he began to blame the debacle on that 'posh prep school brat', Denby, who'd smarmed his oily way round old Watson and sabotaged his rival...

Micky Stuart – 'Owly' to the boys – disappeared. He just seemed to fade away – appearing less and less frequently at school and finally not turning up at all. Without his master, 'Ratty', he seemed diminished – as if an arm or a leg had been cut off. Rumours went round of his moving to another town or, even, his involvement in a road accident.

True to his word, Mr Hawthorne 'got the law' on to Dorothy. Solicitor's letters and affidavits flew round, wasting a vast amount of time. But facts were facts. Hawthorne's drunkenness, his philandering, his notorious propensity for violence, Sam's bruised body and his nights spent out on the streets... Not even a hardened old legal shark like Rodney Jamieson could alter that. The case never got to court and ended up with Hawthorne having to pay costs. Sam was taken into care, but continued to be a pupil at Beaconsfield School.

'What did Jamieson think he was doing putting old Hawthorne up to it?' sighed Dorothy, 'He must have *know* what would happen.'

'Of course he did,' replied Meakin, 'but it hasn't done him any harm. He's laughing all the way to the bank. He just leads fools like Hawthorne on. It isn't only the yobs who are muggers, you know. The middle classes are into mugging, too, only they are a bit more subtle about it.'

Still Two People

For John, things settled down into a sort of normality. With the departure of Ratty he felt a great sense of liberation. Briggs continued to be inexplicably cold and distant, but this was compensated for by the increased warmth of old Mekon. Handle him right and he became an uncle – or even a possible replacement for his utterly perfect granddad. Dracula, too, for all her freakiness, could be very nice if you kept on the right side of her. He continued to get plaudits for doing well.

Mrs Watson was ostentatiously formal and distant in school time, but she was always there for cosy chats afterwards and – yes! – even for little cuddles when nobody was looking. In later life he compared it to having an illicit love affair.

But he continued to be two people: a 'clever and promising young man' at school and a 'retarded little birdbrain' at home. Which was the real John? He still didn't know. One thing was certain, however: he still couldn't ask any of his pals down to Gloucester Road. That part of him had to remain secret.

Trains, Glorious Trains

The Model Railway Club eventually materialised in a disused attic far up among the school rafters. It got off to a shaky start with Polly squawking round in an anarchy of saws, paint, glue and heaps of soggy paper mash.

Indeed, it was very nearly stillborn. Seeing Polly perched on the table, trying to nail down a length of track, Danny Fleetwood couldn't resist surreptitiously painting an RAF-style roundel on his upended backside. The predictable explosion occurred with the metaphorical feathers flying round. This time Danny really *did* have to 'see Mr Meakin'. He duly 'got the cane' – 'Ole Mekon only gave us two, but cor, it flippin' well hurt! He's got a hard hand that old man!'

But eventually out of all the chaos a miniature world of mountains,

375

trees and cities began to take shape. It absorbed a large part of John's Friday evenings.

A Dream Lesson

But perhaps the most significant event of the term occurred on a Friday afternoon in February.

It was the last lesson of the week – traditionally the worst lesson of all when bolshie, demob-happy kids battle it out with exhausted teachers. It should have been English, but Clarkson had suddenly vanished. The official reason was 'an unexpectedly severe attack of migraine'. In fact, he'd had to rush off to do a frantic repair job on his relationship with Megan who was threatening to tell her notoriously violence-prone husband about their illicit affair...

So at the last moment a grumpy Meakin had been told to stand in. He had nothing prepared and in desperation had scooped up a pile of maps.

'Right, you lot, we'll finish the day with a bit of map reading.'

Sullen groan: 'Not AGAIN! Do we HAVE to?'

''Fraid so!'

Danny Fleetwood's acute antennae sensed weariness and vulnerability: 'Why? I mean, what's the point?'

'Well, you'll be pretty lost in life if you can't read a map.'

'But I never read a map when I go into town,' replied Danny, pushing his luck.

'Maybe, but what if you didn't know your way?'

'But I'd just ask somebody, wouldn't I?'

'But supposing you were in a foreign country and didn't speak a word of the language?'

'Well, I'd buy a guide book. That's what me dad does when we is in France.'

'But sometimes you can't get a guide book.'

'Of course you can. You just get 'em in the shops.'

The boy's mixture of cockiness and pig ignorance was starting to annoy Meakin. 'Young man,' he snapped, 'when I was in Italy on the run from the Germans I could have done with an accurate map, I can tell you!'

'Cor, was you in the war then?'

'Yes he was,' put in 'Army Barmy' Martin with a knowing air.

'He's got the Military Medal, you know. I saw him wearing it on the Remembrance Sunday parade last November.'

Meakin sighed. Things were sliding out of control. The last thing he wanted to do was to trade on his war record. He'd made that mistake at the Stirling Academy back in the Sixties. It had backfired horribly and he'd found himself caricatured with all the malicious mockery of which adolescents were capable. Colonel Blimp always banging on about the good old days when men were men... He'd been mimicked all round the school – even within his hearing in the corridors. No way was he going to fall into that pit again.

He tried to retrieve the situation: 'All right, Fred, what's at 345809?'

But the class was in sticky-cement mode: 'Come on, Sir, do tell us what you did in the war. We won't muck about, honest!'

'Well, I was a prisoner of war and I escaped, if you must know.'

Martin looked wise: 'He was one of those blokes who got away during the Great Escape in Germany. I've read about it in *War Monthly*.'

'No, Martin, I wasn't in Germany. I was in Italy... Now come on, let's get down to a bit of work...'

'AWWWWW! Sir, this is much more interesting...'

Clearly, the map-reading lesson was dead. Meakin had three options. Drive yourself crazy by flogging the dead horse – but to what end? Squash the rebellion by a monumental fit of rage – but he hadn't the emotional energy for that. Or take the easy way out and swim with the tide. He chose the latter course.

'Yes, I was taken prisoner.'

'But why didn't you just mow them all down? Brrrrrr! Rat-a-tat! Tat! Splat! I mean the Germans were just a lot of dumb Daleks, weren't they?'

'No, Martin, they weren't. They were the most professionally skilled army of modern times, if you must know. If was we who were the dumb Daleks.'

'But that's rubbish! The British were far better than the Germans. Everybody knows that.'

'That was just wartime propaganda, my boy. It wasn't like that. That day we just walked into it.'

'What happened?'

There was a deathly hush. All eyes were staring intently at him. It was a teacher's dream lesson.

The intense experiences of forty years ago were crystal clear to old Meakin, clearer indeed than those of yesterday. They were like a brilliant colour film, vivid in every detail, but a film locked away in the bottom of a drawer that nobody ever opened. On the rare occasions that he did try to view it people found it 'boring', so he quickly put it away again. Ever since the Sixties debacle at the Stirling Academy the film had remained unseen – but not forgotten.

Now, faced with an appreciative audience, it came out. Like the accumulated fizz in a shaken coke can, the lurid, long-hidden images burst forth.

'Well, I was eighteen. A private soldier in the infantry... No, Martin, I wasn't a general and I wasn't James Bond either. It was in 1942 in North Africa, just after El Alamein...'

'But the Germans was in France... You know, in the trenches an' that.'

'Wrong war, Martin, old man.'

'You mean you've been in Africa in the jungle like Mrs Watson?'

'No, Michael, it's desert in North Africa, not jungle...'

'Was you ridin' camels like the three Kings of Orient?'

'No, Michael, we weren't. It was like this.'

Here he took a piece of chalk and drew a simple sketch map on the blackboard.

'The British Army was here in Egypt. The Germans under Rommel were here. There'd just been a big battle at El Alamein – here! – and Rommel had been beaten. He was on the run, retreating all the way along the coast right up towards Tunis, which is here. He was retreating so fast that we couldn't catch him. He always slipped away. But he'd leave tough little rear guards behind him, which would play hell with us, hold everything up and then just vanish into the desert – poof!

One morning we were fired on by a group who'd occupied a hill by the side of the road...'

Here he drew a simple diagram on the blackboard.

'They were somewhere up here. They only fired a few shots, but that was enough to set the cat among the pigeons. The transport refused to move until they'd been dealt with. Captain Burford – he was our company commander – decided it was a section job. Just the job for us, in fact. You see we were new arrivals and we hadn't seen a shot fired in anger. We'd missed the big show at Alamein and we were desperate to prove ourselves.

Boy, were we excited! This was the real thing. So off we went.

Number Three section under Sergeant Ellis with Joe Barnes on the Bren. There's something unique about going into battle. All your caveman hunter's instincts take over. The adrenalin pumps away. You actually feel yourself becoming a proper man. Daft when you think about it. Perhaps it's Mother Nature's way of hyping you up to attack the mammoths that you need for food, you know rather like a dog getting excited when you take it for a walk ... It's a delicious feeling while it lasts.

Anyway, we put in a classic section attack, just as we'd been taught ...'

Again he paused and drew a diagram.

'V formation, five-yard intervals. Ellis here, Bren group here, myself here ... We picked our way carefully round the boulders, our eyes peeled, our ears ready to pick up the slightest little sound ...'

Here he mimicked the action, crouching down and creeping along in front of the blackboard.

'Then it was takka-nakka-nakker! We were fired on. So it was dash, down, crawl, observe, sights fire ... Just as we'd done over and over again on manoeuvres in Britain ...'

More mimicking of the actions occurred as he spoke.

'You mean you just ran away?' interrupted Danny. 'Why didn't you stand up and fire back at them? Show 'em that you weren't scared!'

'Because, dear boy, that's exactly what the enemy wants you to do. Stand up, make a lovely target and get yourself killed ... Anyway, nobody was hit and Ellis soon located the enemy. They were in the obvious place on top of a spur with the road winding round the bottom of it. It was like this ...'

He paused and drew another diagram on the blackboard.

'... Here on the left-hand side was a little gully leading up the side of the spur. It was what we called 'dead ground'. The enemy couldn't see you until you were within a few feet of him. Jerry must have overlooked it. For once he'd made a mistake. That gully could have been specially designed just for us. Well, we crawled up it with Joe Barnes and the Bren group giving covering fire to keep Jerry's head down. At the top of the gully Ellis motioned us to be quiet, crouch down and wait ...'

Once more he mimicked the action.

'We checked our weapons, saw that the magazines were loaded, saw that there was a bullet up the spout, saw that the safety catch was off ... and waited. Yes we were frightened. You had a prickly

379

feeling in your stomach, almost as if you'd swallowed a bunch of holly... You could hear your heart thumping. It was our first contact with the enemy. Just what *was* up there beyond that skyline? In your mind you peopled it with all sorts of monsters and grotesque machines. When the Bren group stopped firing, Ellis flung a grenade...'

More mimicking of the action.

'We waited. Then bang went the grenade and we leapt up, screaming like devils and jumped into a little trench. But it was empty. Jerry had scarpered.'

'So the Germans were cowards like what I said.'

'No, Martin, they were just properly trained soldiers. They waited till we were all there and the Bren group had joined us. You see, we had committed Infantry Sin Number One. When you take an enemy position, never occupy it. Move out...'

'But why? Isn't that what you want to have?'

'Because, my dear John, the enemy will have zeroed his mortars, and perhaps even his artillery, on to it. At least that's what Jerry would have done. And that's exactly what he *had* done! While we were busy congratulating ourselves on our little victory, suddenly – and quite out of the blue! – it was bang! crash! bang! An almighty din like a load of dinner plates being smashed. Mortar. Dreadful stuff mortar. All too often you don't see it coming and don't even hear it. The first thing you know about it is when it hits you.

'What a mess! Ellis was in bits, literally. Jonny Rawlings and the radio were strewn all over the place. Jonny Leach was pouring blood from his chest and his stomach. More mortar came over. Bang! Crash! Bang!

'There was no point in firing back. There was nothing to fire at. You just rolled up into a ball at the bottom of the trench. You said your prayers. You had a long chat with the Guy Upstairs. You get pretty religious in a bombardment, I can tell you.

'Then the bombardment stopped. There was dead silence, but for Jonny Leach moaning. He died soon afterwards. We just lay and waited at the bottom of that trench, waited for darkness to come so that we could get away. You think the desert's hot, don't you? Well, it is – in summer, but not in winter. As we lay there, it began to rain... So there we were, soaked and shivering, not daring to move in case Jerry dumped another load of mortar on to us. That delicious feeling of going into battle? It had gone. An illusion, like a lovely dream fading away in the morning.

'At long last night came. Release from our prison. Phil Williams

– he was the corporal – tapped us on the shoulders and whispered: "Time to go lads, follow me!"

'So we did – the six of us who were left alive, that is. One by one we rolled over the parapet and into the gully. My God, it was nerve-wracking. One just prayed that for once in his fanatical, militaristic career, Jerry might have missed a trick or two. You had the feeling of being stark naked under a floodlight. It was a matter of creeping down that gully, squirming through the dirt like a snake...'

More mimicking of the action...

'Darkness does things to you. Everything seems bigger. That gully could have been fifty miles long. Wriggle. Stop. Listen. Wriggle. I remember the brilliant, starry sky and getting the idea that Ellis, Leach and Rawlings were up there, watching us and checking us, seeing that we were doing things properly...

'But, by the time we'd reached the bottom of the gully, the moon had risen. Everything was grey and very spooky. Full of black shapes. Your eyes start doing things. Making things move. Stop. Listen. Listen for ages. Silence. Enormous relief. Somewhere in the darkness ahead of us was the transport column and safety... We'd made it!

'Then suddenly – it was rather like a horror film – the boulders around us seemed to come alive. They stood up. There were blokes all around us. Our mates who'd been waiting for us. Phil called out the password: "Kangaroo!"

'But – oh God, and I'll never forget it! – a stream of German answered it! It was Jerry. He was all around us. How the hell he'd managed it, God alone knew! He'd just filtered his way round. It was terrifying. Your legs go soggy. You want to throw up. Christ, are they going to shoot us? Drop rifles. Hands in the air. Desperate prayers to the Guy Upstairs...'

'You mean you just gave in?' exclaimed Danny. 'Why didn't you shoot them all? Bang! Brrrrrrrr! Splat!'

'Commit suicide, Danny? You want to stay alive. So you try to be friends with them. Grease them up. Offer them fags and chocolate...'

'You mean you sucked up to the Germans?'

'Fraternization with the enemy is strictly forbidden under military law,' said Martin, looking wise.

'No, Martin, it's not that simple. You're dependent on them and you want to stay alive. Anyway, this lot were quite a decent set of lads. Showed us photos of their families and that and then handed us over to the Italians...'

381

'But you were fighting the Germans and not the Italians!'

'Yes, Martin, but the Italians were their allies, their friends.'

'But the Germans had no friends.'

'Yes they did. They had allies just like us.'

'But the Allies were the Yanks an' that...'

'Of course, they were...'

'But what were the Italians doing with them? I thought you said they were friends of the Germans?'

'Anyway, they sent us to Italy. Now when Italy surrendered in 1943 we had to make our way south to where the Allies had landed...'

'But the Allies landed in Normandy in 1944. Not in Italy...'

'Oh, for heaven's sake, Martin!'

'Sir! Sir! Sir!' chorused the class, 'This is great! ... Tell us how you got your military medal... Tell us how you...'

Just then the bell went.

'Awwwww!' from the class. 'Please, Sir, go on!'

'No time now, lads. Another time!'

Bonding

As the class spilled out of the room, John sidled up to Meakin: 'Cor, thanks, Sir! That was magic! You're a real war hero!'

Meakin was touched. Touched by these words. He was surprised, too. Surprised at himself. Like water long dammed, those memories had just poured out. And he'd found the words to express them. At last he'd managed to run through that Technicolor film. And it had gone without a hitch.

He was surprised, too, at the way that the class had listened to it all. They hadn't groaned. They hadn't sneered. It had been quite unlike the pampered sophisticates of the Stirling Academy. He felt he'd broken through a barrier. A bond was forming between him and Form One, deeper and more lasting than any bonds he might have formed before. These kids were *his* kids.

A New Granddad

The bond was strongest with John. His granddad was utterly perfect, but he'd never been a war hero. This was the first time he'd actually

382

met a real live war hero. He was awed by old Mekon, even scared of him – that hefty punch on Christmas Eve! But now his task was clear. He must get the old man to *like* him – even to become another granddad. He must stop being a little wimp and win his admiration by being a proper boy – good, strong and brave.

The Glory Days Again

That April, Argentina invaded the Falkland Islands. In Boldonbridge it was a replay of the New Guinea Cargo Cult. More disconnected universes.

John's universe was one of excitement, exhilaration and heroism, the glory days of World War II come again. He devoured the news, bought magazines, stuck a map of the Falkland Islands on the attic wall and carefully marked each British advance on it and the name and position of each ship that was sunk. He cut pictures of battle scenes out newspapers and added them to his ever-enlarging mural display. He bought Airfix models of Harrier jump jets and Super Étendards, painstakingly assembled them and suspended them from the cistern pipes in attitudes of deadly combat.

The Battle of Goose Green enthralled him. Colonel Jones became his hero, his role model, his aspiration ... his all! He stuck a large colour photograph of him in the middle of the display, wrote the words 'A Great British Hero' under it and surrounded it with a montage of pictures of the Paras in action.

At school he compared Airfix models with Danny and Fred. Together with 'Army Barmy' Martin, who knew all the military terminology, the three of them worked out a plan for the recapture of Port Stanley and sent it to the Ministry of Defence. They were wildly excited when a letter arrived thanking them for 'their contribution to the war effort', praising their 'idealistic patriotism' and assuring them that their plan was 'being considered'. (John had to translate these difficult words into simpler English for Martin's benefit.)

When Port Stanley fell Martin made a solemn declaration: 'It's our plan they've used.'

'But why haven't we been on telly?' asked Danny.

Martin looked wise: 'They'll be keeping our names secret. If the Commies knew it were us what made the plan, they'd get us. We're marked men.'

Heady stuff.

But among the more intelligent and properly aware people up at the university it was very different.

Their universe was one of outrage. Anger and sheer disbelief that in the late twentieth century such blatantly jingoistic imperialism could still exist. The sheer brass neck of Thatcher was breathtaking... It wasn't long before their superior minds saw the whole squalid charade for what it was: a pathetic attempt by her and her clique to divert attention from the destruction of British industry and the disenfranchisement of the working class. Dazzle the workers with banal and shoddy nationalism and ship them out to die in some useless and anachronistic outpost of empire which should have been handed back to its rightful owners, the freedom-loving Argentinians, long ago. In this way, there would be fewer workers to rally behind Arthur Scargill and the miners. So simple. So obvious. And so wicked. The outrageous plot had to be exposed, challenged, shown up for what it was...

In a surge of idealistic altruism old rivalries, vendettas and failing love affairs were put on hold. Meetings were held, resolutions were passed, sit-ins, protest marches ... joint letters bearing weighty academic signatures were published in the *Guardian* and the *New Statesman*. Giles and Mary reaffirmed their position as the leading radical partnership of the university. For a few intoxicating weeks the glory days of the Sixties were back again.

Every evening Mary shouted 'Fuck!' outside the TA headquarters in Mafeking Road.

Heady stuff.

37

Summer finally came.

With it came long, warm days and clear blue skies. The stark nudity of Greenwood was exposed as never before – the mouldy armpit of Calderside with its piles of rubbish and windblown dereliction. But over in Moorside where Beaconsfield School was, the bleakness of winter was replaced with a lush greenery as the bare, sodden trees suddenly erupted into shimmering masses of leaves. The revival of hope. Resurrection, even.

Up at the university exam time came. Giles was inundated with marking – great mounds of scripts delivered on a seemingly endless conveyor belt. Mary felt isolated, more than ever an irrelevant hanger-on.

Heroic Epic?

John's double life continued, if anything more accentuated than before. Bright Young Thing at Beaconsfield School. Pathetic disaster area at 14 Gloucester Road.

For him the culminating point of that summer term was the adventure weekend in the Lake District.

In his later life that weekend became a kind of heroic epic, a legendary time when colours were brighter and everything glittered with freshness – the early morning when the dew on the young leaves shimmers in the long rays of the rising sun. It was a time of discovery – of dark frightening woods at night, of rushing streams, of tumbled, craggy mountains lost in swirling blue mists. And also of excitement, achievement and close comradeship. The battle with the gods of the plains of windy Troy, the Quest for the Holy Grail. A time when everything was simple, pure and vividly colourful. The world seen through the innocent eye of youth.

Well, perhaps? We tend to invest childhood adventures with a sticky treacle of nostalgia, inventing a golden age which was only very partially there, if indeed it ever was. Children are not a separate species: they are us. But crude, undeveloped versions of us. Curiosity, freshness, sensitivity, wonder: they can be there, but they are fragile growths, all too easily blighted by a coarse animal egotism which flounders round in a blinkered world of aggression, fights and bodily functions in all their manifestations.

Yet, through the accumulated detritus of carnality, he had another glimpse – more than a glimpse, another vision – of that Beyond World which he'd found so unexpectedly in that Moorside church on Christmas Eve. It was as if he'd been travelling in a train, enclosed in a world of sweets, fights and toilets and then, glancing out of the window, had seen a different land, a higher, better and more colourful land.

Not Too Tough for John Denby...

It happened late in June, not long before the end of term.

One morning at Assembly Mrs Watson announced that after the exams Mr Meakin and Mr Briggs were going to organise an 'adventure weekend' in the Lake District. The idea was to climb Scafell Pike, the highest mountain in England, but for the tougher and more adventurous souls there would also be an 'escape and evasion exercise' which would involve sleeping under the stars like escaping prisoners of war. The weekend was aimed at the older boys and not at the younger ones who would find it too tough for them.

Something flared inside John. Mountains, adventure, escape ... a chance to show Mrs Watson that he was embarking on his mountaineering and exploration career ... and a chance to show his hero, Mekon, that he was a *real* boy and not just a silly little wimp who cried when he was hit. 'Too tough'? Not for John Denby.

Sitting through the morning lessons was an agony. Try as he might, he just couldn't concentrate on Polly's fractions or Clarkson's comprehensions. At the end of the PE lesson – a rather desultory game of cricket – he approached Briggs:

'Please, Sir, can I go on the adventure weekend?'

Briggs was more than usually cold and dismissive: 'Forget it, Denby! It's not for you. It's for senior boys.'

Not 'John', still formal and distant 'Denby'. Other kids got Christian names.

386

Not him. Why? What had he done? He always gave maximum effort, even when others were skiving. He was always cheerful, always ready to chat about rugby – even enquiring about how to be selected for the England squad. Would nothing ever satisfy the wretched little 'Action Man'?

'But, Sir?'

'No buts, Denby. Just because you've come from Rickerby Hall doesn't mean you can jump the queue. You're not the only boy in the school and certainly not the best.'

He sounded almost like Giles. What had Rickerby Hall got to do with it? He never even mentioned it to him. Grown-ups could be worse than kids.

Sulky and resentful, he began to scheme. He could ask Mrs Watson... But, well, that would be a bit too obvious. And you had to be careful with old Dolly. She could be a right cow when she was in the wrong mood. He hadn't forgotten that slap on the face on Christmas Eve. And, above all, he desperately needed to keep her sweet.

A Plan

In Mekon's Geography lesson the idea came. Of course, go and ask Mekon. You got on well with him and, what was more, he was the Deputy Head and senior to Briggs. But ... hold on a moment! ... Do a proper job. Get some of the other kids involved. Show that you thought of others as well as yourself. Sam – be nice to him, that always went down well with Dolly – and how about Michael as well? Work on these two and then come to Mekon with a petition – not just for yourself, but on behalf of the bullied and despised kids as well. Dolly would certainly eat that one when she heard of it. Sound politics.

So before he went home, he buttonholed Sam and Michael.

'You know this adventure weekend ... you ought to go on that...'

'But it's only for the big kids. It's not for us...'

'That's just to show everybody how tough it's going to be... Miss wants you two to go on it, just to show the school that you're not the little wimps that everybody says you are. And Mekon says that if you go on the escape thing you'll be excused Geography homework all next term...' (Lies, the lot of it. But they were daft enough to

387

swallow it. Anyway, it was lying in a good cause and God couldn't get too shirty about that.)

Hanging around behind them was 'Army Barmy' Martin. Hearing the words 'escape thing', he became interested. 'Great Escapes' from POW camps? That was his territory. He decided to come along as well.

Mission Successful...

The following day at lunch-break the deputation knocked on the staffroom door. Dracula opened it.

'John spoke up: 'Sorry to disturb you, Miss, but could we speak to Mr Meakin?'

Meakin bustled out amid the usual clouds of pipe smoke: 'Disturbing my well-earned rest? I hope it's something important. For your sakes and not for mine.'

Slipping into 'best behaviour' mode and flashing his 'ingratiating smile', John recited his carefully rehearsed speech: 'We're sorry to disturb you, Sir, but it's about your adventure weekend. I know we're only juniors, but, please, could we be allowed to come?'

'Are you sure you know what's involved?' replied Meakin. 'It's going to be very tough, you know. It's not a jolly. Are you really prepared to get wet, cold and exhausted?'

'Please, Sir, we know it will be hard. That's why we want to come. Your stories about the war were magic. They've made us want to be strong and brave, like you...'

Meakin's gnarled old face creased up into a broad grin: 'Good on you, lads! Yes, of course I'll take you. Hold on while I get you the parental consent forms and the kit lists...'

He disappeared into the staffroom for a while and then returned and handed each of them two sheets of paper.

'Show this to your parents and get them to sign it and then return it to me. See me if you can't get hold of any kit and I'll sort you out. Come along to the meeting after school on Tuesday. Geography Room...'

'Cor, thanks a bomb, Sir! You're wicked! A real doss! We won't let you down, will we, lads?'

Mission successful. It had been a pushover. John went away bright-eyed and bushy-tailed.

Fallout...

Inside the staffroom the atmosphere was less euphoric.

'Was that young Master Denby's voice I heard?' asked Briggs suspiciously. 'What was His Nibs trying to wheedle out of you this time?'

'Oh, he and his mates were asking about the adventure weekend.'

'And you sent them packing, I hope.'

'No, I've just given them the parental consent forms and the kit lists.'

'Oh, for Christ's sake! Do you realise that only yesterday I told Little Lord Denby – or whatever he calls himself – that he was most emphatically *not* wanted on this thing? So what does the little toad do? He comes snivelling to you and you let him get away with it! What do you think that does for my authority? What does it do for anybody's authority?'

Briggs appealed to his colleagues who were sitting in their armchairs, hiding behind their newspapers and not wanting to get involved.

Meakin sighed his 'don't-be-an-idiot' sigh: 'Oh come off it, Jamie lad!'

Cat among the Pigeons

Though he didn't know it, John had set the cat among the pigeons. There was rather more to that adventure weekend than was apparent to childish eyes. Status, authority, territorial imperative, personality clashes, smouldering resentments ... it was all there. A miniature minefield.

It had originally been Meakin's idea. He'd always loved mountains and, at the age of fifty-eight, he was still an enthusiastic hiker. Whenever he could he would slip off to the Lake District or Scotland. Every summer he spent a fortnight in Austria. A little bit of the great outdoors was just what these Beaconsfield deadbeats needed. Besides, trapped in a loveless and childless marriage, it would add a bit of purpose to his increasingly empty life. After much dithering he'd taken the plunge.

Dorothy had enthusiastically backed the project. But he would need a helper – and, as the PE man, Briggs was the obvious choice.

The Professional PE Teacher

Briggs was not enthusiastic.

Physical Education meant football, rugby, cricket, gymnastics and swimming. Of course, he'd done a bit of the 'Outdoor Education' stuff at St Martin's. You had to. It was 'on the syllabus' and you couldn't get out of it. But he couldn't really be bothered with it. It lacked the thrill and the dash – the sheer adrenalin – of a game of rugby. Still, it *was* Physical Education and that was *his* department. He remembered the valedictory address to the PE students at St Martin's: '...You'll find that everybody thinks they can take PE lessons. Don't let them. Take a firm grip. Never forget that you're the professional and that they're just untrained amateurs...'

And, if ever there was an 'untrained amateur', it was old man Meakin. So he hiked a bit and had made the odd alpine ascent in Austria? That didn't make him a professional. It didn't mean that he knew anything about the all-important business of safety! Without a Mountain Leadership Certificate, he just wasn't qualified, was he? Suppose something went wrong? He, the properly qualified PE man, would have let himself be overruled by an unqualified amateur. The coroner would have his balls for breakfast. It would be the end of him.

But that wasn't all. More than ever the business of having to work in a private school rankled. More than ever he blamed the departure of Robert Napier – his one lifeline to respectability – on the machinations of Meakin and his nauseating little protégé, Denby. That little toad had far too much influence. Old Watson had got a crush on him and let him get away with murder... And here he was oiling his way on to an activity specifically aimed at the senior boys only. It was time to make a stand.

A Sense of Purpose

For his part, Meakin despised little Briggs.

What did *he* know of the real world? What did he know of anything? School, college, school ... that was all. He'd never been in the army. He'd never been into battle. He'd never seen starving Italian peasants. He'd never climbed a proper mountain in his life. Apart from a fig leaf called 'qualifications', he was as naked as a new-born babe. For the past week he'd been banging on about 'safety'. There hadn't been much 'safety' in the war, had there? Not when Jerry had been playing silly buggers in Italy

Besides, something was happening to old Meakin. Arid, desiccated old buffer, fast fading into a late-middle-aged futility. Alone with a store of vivid memories, the accumulated treasures of his life, but now mouldering away into dust. He was an irrelevant old bore whose only future seemed to be a rocking chair in the nearest geriatric home...

But those Form One kids had reignited him, breathed air on to the sputtering embers. They'd listened to his war stories. They hadn't sneered. They'd been interested, quite pathetically interested. And then there'd been Dolly's Christmas party. How little Briggs had grated on about 'professionalism' and 'losing authority' if you 'got too close to your pupils'. ('They'll see all your weaknesses and will just exploit them. Once you've lost discipline, you won't be able to get it back again...') But it hadn't been like that. Of course, there'd been problems – only to be expected with kids like those – but 'authority' hadn't been lost. Instead, something deeper had been created. A relationship. A bond. You could feel it whenever you took that class – a frisson, a warmth. And now there were those bright-eyed and eager faces pleading to be allowed to come on the adventure weekend, *his* adventure weekend!

Turn them away? Not bloody likely! He was starting to become a daddy to those little creatures and he liked the role. It gave him a sense of purpose.

Internecine War...

The lines were drawn up for a battle and it duly occurred.

'No, Meakin, I WON'T come off it! You're letting that boy, Denby, run rings round you. And not only you. He's always in and out of Dolly's study. I've noticed it and so have the senior boys and they don't like it, I can tell you!'

'But he's just a pathetic little thing. He wants a proper mum, that's all! Just say boo to him and he curls up.'

'I'm glad you think so. But do you seriously imagine that he won't be a liability when he gets to the Lake District? He's that big-headed that he'll run wild and wreck the whole thing.'

'Rubbish! He'll be all right. I'll see to that!'

'Take him if you must, but, mark my words, he'll let you down! And I, at any rate, don't want to be involved in any accidents. There are serious safety concerns on a venture like this. As a trained professional...'

'Oh, for heaven's sake! Not safety again!...'

The Parental Consent Form

Blissfully unaware of the situation he had created, John went home that evening.

He walked on air. Climbing the 'highest mountain in England'! Great! Not quite the Ruwenzori, perhaps, but still 'the highest mountain!' – and you had to start somewhere. Promotion. Running with the big boys. No longer a little kid... And, what was more, he'd recruited Sam, Michael and Martin... He'd been unselfish ... responsible ... aware of the needs of others... Mrs Watson would just eat that!

But there were problems. That 'parental consent form' had to be signed – and the kit list was alarming: rucksack, boots, sleeping bag, waterproofs...? Where was he going to get hold of all this? He was going to have to grease up Giles and Mary big time, pour on the treacle by the bucketful.

Mary answered the door – clothed, thank goodness, but clearly in a foul mood.

'Please, Mary, could you sign this?'

She glanced at the 'parental consent form'. It was Meakin's concession to Briggs who'd taken full advantage of the chance to proclaim his superior status as a professionally qualified Physical Education teacher. He'd done a thorough job, spending a whole weekend trawling through his college textbooks in search of appropriately professional phrases with which to decorate his dissertation. 'A developmental initiative exploring personality improvemental potential.' 'An experimental initiative at the socio-academic interface.' 'Preparation for the socio- environmental-awareness learning situation of the Duke of Edinburgh's Award Scheme.'

Evil memories of gruesome 'character-building' weekends at Roedean came flooding back – rain-soaked moors, wet tents, 'guts and character', 'showing the chaps at Oundle a thing or two' ... The fraudulent banality of the bourgeois world that she'd long rejected.

Mary returned the form without a word.

No change out of her. Better try Giles ... and if that failed, there was always Mrs Watson as a last resort.

As usual, Giles was at his table surrounded by piles of paper and writing furiously. (Did he *ever* do anything else?) John put on his 'ingratiating smile' and went into 'best behaviour' mode: 'Erm, I'm very sorry to disturb you, Giles, but you see I've been specially selected to go on a mountain expedition with the school... I've been chosen to represent my form... It's a great honour...'

Not, of course, that the 'good little boy' act worked with Giles. Quite the opposite. He looked up and scowled. It was that Miles & Eden business all over again: the nauseating little poof poncing round like a catamite that had escaped from a Turkish harem in Constantinople... Neither did he bother to read the parental consent form that was thrust in front of him. What was the point? It was just a load of pretentious teacher training college garbage... His first instinct was to tell the little squirt to get lost.

But then ... things were getting complicated. He still wasn't the Labour Party candidate for Boldonbridge West. Old man Robertson was still banging on about 'Christian family values' – whatever that was supposed to mean in this post-Christian world! And there was that old dinosaur of ASLEF, George Dawes – a sentimental ass of the Frank Cousins vintage who should have been put out to grass long ago. He was going to have to square him: invite him round to supper and grease him up – and he'd need the little sod in front of him as a vital prop in his 'caring family man' act...

And, of course, there was always Merrins skulking resentfully in the background like a terrorist waiting to plant a bomb.

Giles signed the form.

'But, please, I need some mountain kit... Boots, waterproofs, a rucksack...'

'How much do you need?'

'I don't know.'

Giles fumbled in his wallet. He hadn't much ready cash, so he pulled out his chequebook and wrote a blank cheque.

'Go down to the Mountain Adventure Emporium in Hackworth Street and get what you need. Here's my driving licence and my visiting card for identification. Right, off you go!'

ARTHUR CLIFFORD

The Full Works

On Saturday morning John set off on his purchasing expedition.

He had little idea of what he needed. He'd never set foot on a mountain before, let alone actually climbed one. But on those car journeys to Italy with his perfect gran and granddad they'd passed through the Alps and he'd noticed that, as well as rock, there was lots of snow around. The Ruwenzori, also, had lots of snow and rocks. Scafell Pike was much lower, but, if it were a proper mountain, it presumably had some snow on it as well as lots of rocks. Obviously, he'd need the full works. In any case, if he were going to be a proper mountaineer, he'd better start collecting the kit he'd be needing.

In 'best behaviour mode' and wearing his 'ingratiating smile', he entered the Mountain Adventure Emporium.

'Please, Sir, I'm going to climb a big mountain with snow on it and I'll need the proper kit... My dad has signed this cheque... He's a professor at the university and he's very important...'

The young shop assistant could scarcely credit his good luck. It was his first job and he was still on probation. He had yet to prove himself. '... We're a highly professional company,' he'd been told at his interview, 'we're not cowboys. We make sure that our sales staff know what they're talking about. Safety first: that's our motto. We strive to ensure that our customers are appropriately equipped with due regard to safety...' At the company's behest he'd duly done his Mountain Leader training and had acquired the requisite certificates: he was well versed in the arcane labyrinth of 'safety'.

Equally relevant was the fact that Wilderness Paths, the deadly rival company, had just set up shop in a neighbouring street. He had to work his passage as a salesman – or else! This kid was manna from heaven.

'...A cheap cagoule won't do, not for where you're going. You'll need something breathable – only Gore-Tex will do... Snow and ice? You'll need a proper ice axe and crampons... And you'll have to have a proper harness... You'll not be sleeping in your back garden so you'll need a decent sleeping bag able to withstand sub-zero temperatures... Emergency rations? These must be properly nutritious if you don't want to collapse from hypothermia... Rucksack? You'll need a large one, top of the range...'

The bill was appropriately astronomical – hundreds of pounds. John wasn't sure exactly how much.

The Highest Mountain in the World?

Weighed down with his exotic loot, he staggered home. When she opened the door, Mary was not impressed.

'What the fuck's all this? Do you think we can SHIT money? Christ, you're not climbing bloody Everest!'

He winced. He'd done the right thing. Kitted himself out properly. Indeed, the bloke in the shop had complimented him on his 'adult awareness of safety'. Would nothing ever satisfy the old cow? But he couldn't face a row, so he just went very red and scampered up to his room.

That night he dressed up in his boots, gaiters, waterproofs and woolly hat. Squeezing into his sleeping bag, he picked up his junior edition of *The Ascent of Everest* by Colonel Hunt and began to read. So Hillary and Tenzing thought they'd climbed the highest mountain in the world? Poor things, he, John Denby, was going to climb a higher one which he would discover in the unexplored recesses of the Ruwenzori.

Unwanted Interlopers?

The Tuesday afternoon meeting was awkward.

The Geography Room was full of senior boys. Occupying the front desks, they formed a solid wall of beefy, red-blazered backs. As John led his little band of disciples in, they were engulfed in a chorus of jeers.

'Get out you lot! ... Get lost, Denby, this isn't for babies!'

Immediately a scowling Briggs rose from the teacher's chair before the blackboard: 'Denby, I thought I told you that this weekend was not for you.'

Red-faced and pouty, John stood his ground: 'But Mr Meakin said...'

'Did he indeed? That's news to me.'

But mercifully, directly on cue, Meakin burst through the door.

'Yes, Mr Briggs, for my sins I did!' he boomed.

'Well,' declared Briggs, putting on his professionally-qualified-Physical-Education-teacher voice, 'be it on your own head, Mr Meakin. You are responsible for this lot, not me.'

With that, he turned to John: 'And I hope that Mr Meakin is good at changing nappies, because I'm not.'

Led by Billy Nolan and David Robson, the wall of red blazers exploded into raucous guffaws.

John winced and blushed an even brighter shade of red. How much did Briggs know about *that*? It had started again this week in a most embarrassing way. Indeed, he'd had to stuff a handkerchief into his nether region to absorb the disgusting trickle in case it became too obvious. God, had Briggs examined his underwear in the changing room? Appalling thought!

Still, none of those teenage lumps had got the kit he'd got. What did they know about ice axes, crampons and Gore-Tex breathable cagoules? When it came to checking out kit he'd show them all right!

The four juniors duly sat at the back of the classroom and listened intently as Mekon outlined the forthcoming adventure. They were to come to school on Friday in their school uniforms. At four o'clock they were to change into their hiking kit which they had brought with them. The minibus would be loaded up and they would drive to the Lake District where they would camp at a campsite which had already been booked. On Saturday they would climb Scafell Pike. While the majority would camp at Sty Head Tarn, the escape group would bivouac somewhere on the mountainside and would be picked up the following morning...

'Command Tasks': Into the Adult World?

On Wednesday evening they practised putting up the school tents on the playing field.

While Martin stood aside giving a stream of military-style orders – 'You'll have cam the tent up properly. It's your FRP and the enemy mustn't see it...' – John and Michael managed to get their tent up before any of the seniors.

'Well done, lads!' said Meakin.

'You've done a lot better than that lot over there,' he added, pointing to the far corner of the field, where, amid an anarchy of flapping canvas, Paul Morris and Billy Nolan were almost coming to blows.

John's morale revived. Yes, he *would* show them!

Then came the exotic excitement of the 'Cooking Command Task'. Trangia stoves, a bottle of methylated spirits, matches, boiling water. Heady stuff for John's little group, especially when they were the first to cook their baked beans and Irish stew and when, over at the far corner, Philip Lawson nearly succeeded in setting a tent on fire.

Mekon responded with predictable roars and bellows and then with a stern admonition: 'Things are a bit topsy-turvy, aren't they? It's the little kids like John and Michael who are the big kids and the big kids like Philip and Billy who are the little kids, if you get my meaning!'

More heady stuff for John.

A Clever Young Man

Even so, the week crawled by with an agonised slowness.

In the classroom it was filled with the end-of-year exams. John found them far easier than the Rickerby Hall exams. Which was hardly surprising because the new John of Beaconsfield School was a 'clever young man' of whom 'great things' were expected. The old plodder of Rickerby Hall who tried hard and never got anywhere belonged to another universe.

Denby the Dauntless...

But it was the adventure weekend that dominated his thoughts.

On the Thursday night he lay on his bed absorbed by a book he'd got out of the library. It was about K2, the second highest mountain in the world, a fantastic, cloud-wreathed spire of rock and ice and, according to the book, only ever climbed once before. But it would soon be climbed again – by John Denby, Denby the Dauntless, no less!

Spreading out his treasures once more, he dressed up in his woolly hat, waterproofs and gaiters and snuggled down into his sleeping bag. Soon he was at 27,000 feet, desperately trying to ward off the numbing cold as the gale rose to a shrieking crescendo and threatened to hurl his flimsy tent into oblivion.

...But, battling through the crazy inferno and gasping for breath in the thin air, he managed to scale those impossible icy cliffs and make the first British ascent of K2.

Fame and fortune followed. Amid the cheering crowds, he saw Freddy Hazlett and Shorley on their knees begging for mercy. With great magnanimity he solemnly forgave them. Up in heaven God

The first British ascent of K2

duly took note of it and told the Archangel Gabriel to put a big tick against his name.

'Off to Climb Mount Everest, Are We?'

He awoke early in the morning to see bright sunlight streaming into his room.

Looking out of the skylight, he saw a vivid and vibrant world. The sad dereliction of the valley below was still shrouded in shadow, a mysterious smudge of blue with chunky black shapes looming out of the murk. But beyond the river was a land of light and colour. The long rays of the rising sun lit the massed ranks of the terraced houses and the slab-like tower blocks with shafts of brilliant light which transformed them into a glittering abstraction of squares and rectangles. Up they went, tier after tier, up the hill until, far above the valley, the rolling green fields took over and swept away into the luminous uplands of the distant Pennines. 'Come away! Come

398

away, John!' they seemed to sing, 'Come away to the great blue beyond. This is your real home!'

Eagerly he dressed up in his new treasures – boots and harness as well as the gaiters and waterproofs. Stuffing his crampons and his self-heating survival rations (... 'as used by the British Antarctic Survey') into his rucksack, he pulled his balaclava helmet over his woolly hat and squeezed his hands into his mitts.

Brandishing his ice axe, he set off for school. Yes, he was going to show David Robson a thing or two about proper kit! Of course, Mekon *had* said something about turning up in your school uniform ... but, when he saw all this mountain bonanza on display, he'd change his tune...

'Off to climb Mount Everest, are we?' said the driver as he climbed aboard the bus.

'Where's your school uniform?'

As he had hoped, he duly caused a stir when he entered the hall for assembly.

Immediately, he was surrounded by an admiring crowd of his classmates.

'Cor, look at that! Is it for cutting steps in the rock?'

'No, it's for cutting steps up steep walls of ice. Martin, take a look these self-heating compo rations! It's what the British Army had in the Falkland Islands...'

Just as Danny Fleetwood was binding the crampons on to his stockinged feet, the jamboree ended.

'John Denby, where's your school uniform?'

John swung round to see Mrs Watson staring at him in full headmistress mode with her X-ray eyes boring into him.

'Go and change at once.'

'But ... er ... well. My school uniform's at home.'

'In that case you can join the punishment squad in break and do a litter pick. Two minus marks.'

He blushed bright red as a jeering snigger rippled through the ranks of the senior boys. The unexpected onslaught left him deflated and crestfallen. He'd confidently assumed that he was in Dolly's good books.

But his humiliation was somewhat diluted when shortly afterwards another altercation occurred.

'Billy Nolan and David Robson, why are you not in your school uniform?' Further dose of radiation from the X-ray eyes.

'But Mr Meakin said we were to come to school with our kit for the adventure weekend.'

'Quite so. But he said you were to come to school in your school uniform and change into your hiking things at four o'clock. He did not tell you to break the school rules. You can join your friend, John Denby, on the litter pick in break. Two minus marks each. That means six in one week for you, Billy Nolan. I can see that you're going to be pretty busy next week.'

Getting Out of Hand Already?

In the staffroom at break Briggs voiced his concern: 'I really think we ought to call this adventure weekend off. Already they're using it as an excuse to break the school rules. Pretty soon things will get right out of hand and we'll have an accident on our hands...'

'No, no,' replied Meakin, 'it's just a few silly kids getting overexcited. If things do start to go haywire, a few atrocities will soon sort them out. You know, severed heads on London Bridge exposed *in terrorem populi*, as they used to say...'

'I'm glad you think so, but, frankly I don't share your confidence. As a matter of elementary safety...'

'Showing off again, are we?'

Lunchtime came. Time to check kit. For John, vindication time when his treasures would be fully revealed before the admiring crowd of boys and teachers. 'No, Sam you don't need to take your football boots or your school blazer...' 'No, Michael, you can't take Herbie, your hamster. Put him back in his cage and give him to Mrs Watson for safekeeping...'

'John, what *is* all this? Whoever told you to bring an ice axe and crampons?'

'But in Geography you said that the Lake District was glaciated...'

'That was twenty thousand years ago. Get your dates right, young man...'

'Showing off again are we, Denby?' added Briggs. 'Always have to be the centre of attention, don't we?'

John blushed bright red as Philip Lawson and Paul Morris dissolved into a fit of derisive giggles. To his embarrassed chagrin, he had to leave the bulk of his treasures behind – his crampons, his ice axe, his harness, all those exotic self-heating survival rations '...as used by the British Antarctic Survey'.

A Shaky Start

Four o'clock finally came.

Followed by a disorderly crowd of red-blazered onlookers, a hyped-up bunch of boys in scruff order spilled out on to the pavement in front of the school.

As soon as a sour-faced Briggs drove up in the hired minibus it was stormed by an anarchic mob.

'Bags the back end! ... Dave and Billy ... you two next to me! Fuck off, Denby! We're not having you in here! Nor you, shitty old stick insect!...'

John's little group stood forlornly on the pavement as the five senior boys – great bulky lumps – took over the bus, sprawling over the seats and draping their belongings haphazardly round the floor. Briggs got out of the driving seat and walked nonchalantly into the school. With any luck the riot would get completely out of control and Dolly would come storming out and cancel the trip. Then he could go home and watch the test match on TV.

Suddenly a stentorian bellow blasted forth with volcanic violence: 'EVERYBODY OUT OF THE BUS THIS INSTANT!'

Meakin had arrived.

'Right, line up on the pavement... Yes, you too, Philip! We're going to have a little law and order, if you don't mind.'

He turned to Bill Bleeson who was standing beside him, dressed in full hiking kit and wearing his head boy badge on his anorak: 'Bill, can you see that the bus is loaded up properly? Then I'll decide who sits where.'

Bill Bleeson assumed his sergeant-in-the-Army-Cadet-Force persona: 'Billy, take these tents... John, you take that box... Come on, Philip, look sharp!...'

Order prevailed.

'Now,' said Meakin when all the baggage had been stowed neatly under the seats and on the floor, 'Spewk pills. You younger lads take two each... We don't want you being sick all over everything, do we? Any older lads need a pill? No. Right, we'll have you, Billy and Philip, sitting near the front where I can see you... Sam, you by the window in case you're sick... Paul, you sit next to him...'

'I'm not sittin' next to *him*!'

'Well, stay at school then.'

Sulkily and with a very bad grace, Paul Morris obeyed. 'Fucking flid!' he hissed at Sam. 'Cor you stink!'

'We'll have none of that, thank you!' snapped Meakin, clipping him smartly over the ear.

Tears trickled as they always did with Paul Morris.

'John, you sit by the window... Darran, you next to him.'

Briggs duly appeared in his tracksuit.

'Right, Mr Briggs, we're all ready. You can take the first stint at the wheel.'

'But I haven't done the minibus driver's course.'

'For Christ's sake, man, you can drive the blasted thing... I mean you've just fetched it from Quick Hire.'

'Yes, but I'm not qualified to drive it when it's full of kids. If there was an accident...'

'Oh Christ! I suppose I'd better do the driving then. Somebody has to...'

The overloaded minibus finally lumbered off.

They crawled slowly along the sunlit streets of benign Edwardian terraces and opulent greenery, waited by the traffic lights, joined the main road and then launched out onto the bypass.

At a prearranged signal from Billy Nolan, the older boys burst into a raucous song:

> 'OOOOOOOOO! We don't give a FUCK
> For old Von Kluck
> And his mightee
> German armeeeee!'

Meakin slewed over on to the hard shoulder and slammed on the brakes. A tangle of bodies landed on the floor.

'We can do without the choir, thank you very much.'

A grumpy silence followed.

402

'I told you this trip would get out of hand,' said Briggs sitting in the front passenger seat.

When Meakin failed to reply, he resigned himself to two days of concentrated tedium and ghastliness.

A Top-notch Job...

The minibus spluttered on. They had just passed through the old market town of Hexham and were heading out into the open country beyond when there was an explosion of noise in the back.

'Ugh! Gads! Sam's been sick!'

'No I ain't!' came Sam's thin, high-pitched voice.

'Sir, it's Billy. He's been sick all over everything!'

John could hardly contain his glee. He'd secretly been dreading a public spill. He remembered that awful journey up from London with Giles and Mary when he'd thrown up all over the back of the 'von'. But – hooray! hooray! – it was big loudmouth Billy Nolan who'd messed himself like a little baby and not him.

The minibus came to a juddering halt in the first convenient layby. Meakin got out and opened the back door.

'Oh, my God, Billy, you have! A real top-notch job, too! All down your sweater and all over the floor...'

His eye lighted on a half-empty bottle of vodka.

'Is this what you've been drinking?'

No reply. Just a white ashen face with tears trickling down it.

'He's probably nicked it from his dad's cocktail cabinet,' said Bill Bleeson.

'I'll never do it again, Sir,' mumbled Billy with a woebegone expression. 'I didn't know it did this to you... It was Philip what dared me.'

'That's as may be,' said Meakin. 'Now out you get and, when you've wiped yourself down, you can clean up the mess you've made. I don't see why anybody else should have to do it for you. In the meantime, I'll take your little treasure. I'm sure Dad would like it back again... Now let this be a lesson to you... No, I'm not going to wallop you... In future, just remember what alcohol can do to you...'

Throughout the little drama, Briggs sank further into an almost biblical gloom. Christ, if any of his St Martin's mates could see him now!

ARTHUR CLIFFORD

Bloody Kids...

By six o'clock they were heading over the Pennines.

The minibus climbed slowly out of the grassy fold in which the little stone town of Alston lay crouched and onto the broad moors above. John gazed at the sprawling emptiness around him which swept away to far-off rolling hills, bare, brown and boundless, seemingly devoid of human habitation. He'd never seen anything quite like this before. Glowing in the bright evening sun, this was a new and undiscovered land.

Suddenly there was an uproar: 'Sir, Martin's desperate for the bog!'

'Well, he'll just have to be desperate. We can't stop now. We're late.'

'But there'll go and be another disaster if you don't!'

'Oh for Christ's sake!'

Meakin stopped the minibus by the side of the road: 'Right, out you get, Martin, and be quick about it.'

'But I need the proper bog with paper and that!'

'Oh for heaven's sake! Well, don't just stand there, boy! Get over the blasted wall! Paper? What do you think the good Lord made grass for?'

'Bloody kids!' he confided to Briggs.

'Well, you *would* insist on this weekend.'

Into Narnia... The Wells of Anarchy...

Seven o'clock found them grinding slowly along the shores of a big lake.

John stared out of the window. Gnarled old forests, rushing streams, mossy crags rearing up improbably out of masses of dense foliage, the mysterious expanse of the lake, the tumbled blue mountains in the far distance ... it was all so new and exciting. When he'd gone to Italy with his perfect gran and granddad he'd slept most of the way. The landscape had mostly been a blur outside the car windows. But now he found himself right in the middle of a land he'd encountered in those *Narnia* books and in those Ruwenzori slides.

'For those of you who might be interested,' announced Meakin, pointing to a pile of mountains, stacked up on the horizon like a heap of blue cushions, 'that's our objective, Scafell Pike, the highest mountain in England.'

Soon they turned off and ground slowly up a steep side-road which wound a tortuous way through dark, dripping woods and over noisy, boulder-filled streams. Finally, they emerged into the brilliant light of the evening sun and juddered to a halt in a broad field, hemmed in by scraggy trees and steep, rocky hills. Here was the campsite which Meakin had booked some weeks ago.

Immediately, a torrent of boys exploded out of the minibus.

'Let's chase those sheep!'

'I'm bursting for a pee! Where's the bog?'

'Let's see where that stream goes!'

'Let's climb that tree!'

Around the field other campers – mostly sedate middle-aged couples – looked askance at the sudden barbarian invasion. A small group set off towards an old stone farmhouse at the end of a muddy track. A week of careful planning was dissolving into anarchy.

'COME BACK, THE LOT OF YOU, THIS INSTANT!'

Meakin had got out of the minibus.

'Right! Into your groups – and that includes YOU, Billy Nolan! First we pitch the tents... Over THERE, that far corner!'

He pointed to a distant extremity of the field where the tufty grass lapped up against a steep, wooded hillside.

'That's Yobbistan where you won't be annoying the other campers...'

'...Sleeping bags, litter bins, rucksacks... Now we're going to cook supper. Water? Bill, can you see to that...'

Bill Bleeson, sergeant in the Army Cadet Force went avidly into action: 'Juniors! That's you, John and Co. Take these containers up to the farm and fill them up...' Acutely aware of their need to placate higher authority in the interests of survival, John's group set off for the farm armed with an array of plastic water containers. They entered the muddy quadrangle of the farmyard with its garages, barns and smell of manure. Seeing an outhouse marked 'Toilets and Washrooms', they duly found the appropriate taps. Just as they were about to start filling the containers, a big, burly man in green wellies and a cloth cap bustled up to them.

'Are you them bloody kids what's just arrived? Well, if there's any crap out of you lot, you can just fuck off! Off the fuckin' site, see! Gerrit? Aye an' I doan want none o' yers pissin' and crappin' all over the field like what the last lot did neither! Gerrit?'

With that he stomped off.

'Well, he wasn't very friendly,' said Michael.

'You know he SWORE!' added John in a shocked tone. 'But if we did that, we'd really get done by old Mekon. It's not fair!'

'And I didn't like that bit about crapping all over the field either,' he continued. 'I mean we're not little kids who just crap anywhere, are we?'

'Martin is,' sniggered Michael.

'You belt up!' snapped a wounded Martin, 'Just you wait till you need the bog in the middle of nowhere!'

Grown-ups!

The 'Command Task' of cooking supper began. Under Meakin's and Bill's eagle eyes Trangia stoves and bottles of methylated spirits were issued along with packets of soup powder and tins of stew and baked beans.

'Be careful with the stoves – especially, you, Philip. Try not to set everything on fire this time...'

Again the hot steam of anarchy threatened to blow everything apart.

'You boil the water first and THEN you add the soup powder.'

'No you don't, you twit!'

'Sir, Mr Meakin Sir! There's a fly landed in our stew! What should we do?'

'Just pull it out – or, if you can't, just eat it! Good protein. It's what kept prisoners alive on the Burma Railway.'

'But my mum will go apeshit if she knows I've been eating flies.'

Eventually, a patchy sort of progress was made by these groups of dogmatic superintendents and culinary experts.

While Meakin and Bill cooked their meal on a shared Trangia, Briggs remained aloof in the minibus, munching the ham sandwiches that his wife had given him.

'He looks a bit sad,' Michael whispered to John, 'all on his own like. Mebbe we oughta give him a cup o' tea?'

'Good idea,' agreed John. 'It might put him in a better mood. He's got a down on us for some reason.'

Here was a chance to try to mend those inexplicably broken fences of the past six months. Timorously, John crept over to the minibus with a steaming mug of tea. 'Please Sir, would you like some hot tea?'

Sullenly, Briggs waved him away: '*Do* stop trying to suck up, Denby. You know it doesn't work with me.'

'Still sulking like a babby?' asked Michael when a forlorn John returned.

'Grown-ups!' sighed John. 'First the farmer and now him!'

'Quite right,' agreed Michael. 'You should see me mam when she's havin' one o' her turns! Talk about little babbies! You know, it's not always the kids what's babbies, it's the grown-ups!'

Twilight...

A cool, velvety twilight closed in, punctuated here and there by the sputtering blue of a Trangia flame.

'Right, you lot, Command Task Number Three: washing up! David, who told you to sneak off into the woods? Philip, where's the rest of your group? They're supposed to be helping you with the washing up!'

Eventually, the washing up was done.

'Can I go to the bog, Sir, I'm desperate!'

'OK. But there's no need to tell the whole campsite about it! They don't want to hear the thrilling news!'

'Sir, here's the farmer coming down to complain about the noise.'

'Oh hell!'

Sure enough, right on cue, having duly worked himself up into a paedophobic frenzy, the farmer stormed up to them: 'Can you lot shut your fuckin' rattle, else I'm throwin' the whole lot of you off the site, see!'

'No problem,' replied Meakin. 'I'm busy settling them down. It's their first time in tents and they're a bit excited, you know.'

Darkness Deepens...

The darkness deepened as the last dying embers of the day finally faded into a sombre midnight blue.

'Right, into your tents the lot of you! SILENCE! Billy, if you don't shut up this instant, you're getting my boot on your tent – and I don't care if the innocent suffer as well as the guilty!'

Gradually, a fragile silence was established and a weary Meakin crawled into his tent.

In the minibus, aloof and in a 'properly qualified state of being', like Zeus enthroned on his professional Olympus, Briggs looked disdainfully down on these amateur goings-on. Finally, he inflated his rubber mattress and draping himself over the back seats, settled down for the night.

Out into a Subdued and Shadowy Land... A Night Patrol...

Across the darkened field peace at last seem to reign.

But in John's tent war had broken out. The tent was really too small for the four juniors and any sleeping arrangement always resulted in a tangle of knobbly elbows and sharp pointed knees. It was a matter of territorial acquisition and disputed hegemony, a low-key war fought out with kicks and punches and soft whispers for fear of dire retribution from a hovering Mekon.

'Move over!'

'You're on my leg!'

'Oyer! That hurt!'

It simmered down with the victors, John and Martin, semi-comfortable in the middle and the losers, Michael and Sam, squeezed up in acute discomfort on the sides.

John couldn't sleep. It was all too new and exciting. Outside was a world waiting to be explored – darkness, mystery, adventure...

After half an hour he could wait no longer.

'Move over, Martin,' he hissed. 'I'm going outside. Stick Insect is gassing me out!'

'Yeah, I'm coming, too!'

'Better see if the coast is clear. We don't want Mekon in an epi-sweat!'

John stuck his head out. A subdued and shadowy land was revealed – a cloudy moon and a silvery field surrounded by dark, looming shapes, bigger and more meaningful than in daytime. It was almost as if the trees and the rocks had come alive and were murmuring softly to each other. There was no sign of Mekon.

'OK. It's all clear!'

'Let's go on a night patrol,' whispered an excited Martin. 'You know, check the perimeter like what they does in 'Nam!'

'Yeah! Great! Coming, Michael? Sam?'

'But what if Mekon sees us?'

'No sweat, Michael; he's asleep!'

'Come on, Sam!'

'No... I'm scared of the dark!'

'Poof! Shit-pants!' A punch in the ribs.

Martin took charge: 'We'll go at five-yard intervals, no torches, no talking ... eyes peeled for any sign of the enemy.'

'Bags me be Colonel Jones!' whispered John.

'Shhhhhhh! The Argies'll hear you!'

Hearts thumping, all senses sharpened, led by Colonel H. Jones and General Douglas Macarthur, the SAS/Green Berets patrol crept quietly over the silent, moonlit field towards the Argie/Vietcong position. John was in a state of exaltation. Nothing as great as this had ever happened before.

At the edge of the field the woods loomed up before them – a silent black wall, sinister, secretive, almost alive.

'Cor, I wonder what's in there?'

'Better not hang round here,' muttered Michael. 'Goodness only knows what's in there looking at us!'

'Scaredy! It's only trees!'

'But there is things what comes alive at night.'

'You don't believe in fairies, do you?'

'No, but there's nasty old men – tramps and that – what sleeps in the day an' wakes up at night an' kills kids!'

'Crap!'

'No, it's real! Me mam, she read about it in the papers...'

Just then a twig snapped in the depths of the wood.

'Oh God!' gasped Michael. 'It's a tramp!'

He turned round and scampered back to the tent.

John and Marin froze with fear. John remembered that horrible old tramp down in London. He longed to follow Michael, but he wanted to be like Colonel Jones and Colonel Jones wouldn't have been scared of a dirty old man who lurked in the woods.

'There's something in there,' whispered an equally frightened Martin.

'It probably *is* an old tramp,' replied John. 'He'll be waiting to come out and kill us, just like Michael said.'

They lay trembling on the damp grass for a while. Eventually, Martin spoke. His reputation as a military expert was on the line: 'We'd better make a recce first and then tell Mekon and he'll set a guard on the camp.'

'Yeah!' added John, hyping himself up with visions of military glory. 'We can tell Robson and that lot that we've saved their lives!'

A blaze of heroic ardour began to swamp his fear.

'A real lad! One of us!'

So they crept into the threatening black wall of the wood in front of them. Martin ostentatiously performed a 'Special SAS Night Patrol Crawl' which he'd discovered in *Combat Survival*. John tried to imitate him, but found it impossible. The wood was a pitch-black lunacy, an impossible tangle of prickly things and sharp, knobbly stones covered with slimy wet moss. It reminded him of a television documentary about coral reefs.

'There's something over there,' whispered Martin. 'Look!'

John peered into the solid blackness. A tiny dot of red light appeared, then another and another, brilliant pinpoints in the cavernous dark. Through the faint rustling of the leaves and the soft gurgle of a nearby stream came a barely audible murmur of voices. Panic flared up. There was a whole crowd of tramps there!

'God! We'd better scarper!'

'Yeah! Tell Mekon to get the police and call in a helicopter!'

Turning round was an appalling problem. Somehow John found himself slithering down a mossy crevasse between two huge and smooth rocks. Frantically, he grabbed a small branch above his head. With a loud crack it broke and he tumbled forwards and fell sprawling onto a flat, leafy platform.

A voice called out of the darkness: 'Fags out, lads! There's somebody there!'

John closed his eyes and prayed in sheer terror. When hands grabbed him, he tried to scream, but his mouth was blocked by a huge, fleshy paw.

He opened his eyes to see David Robson glaring angrily at him. A great gust of relief! Not a monster! Not a murderous old tramp! Just a boy. Next to him Philip Lawson was sitting astride Martin.

'Spying on us for old Mekon, are you?' growled David. 'Dolly's little pet going to grass up the bad lads and get a cuddle, eh?'

'No! No! No!' pleaded John. 'Please no! We're not going to grass on you. We were just having a midnight patrol...'

'Little kids playing bang-bangs!' sneered Philip, poking a prostrate Martin in the ribs.

410

Billy Nolan emerged from the gloom, a fag dangling from his mouth. John cringed. The baddest boy in the school. Always getting minus marks, always 'on punishment', rumoured to have 'got the cane twice' ... the 'Lord of Misrule' himself.

Like Ratty, he seemed to have an uncanny hold over senior boys like David Robson and Philip Lawson.

'So it's Dolly's little suction pumps!' he growled threateningly. 'Well, we're going to sort them out, aren't we, lads?!'

John cowered. Trapped! Greenhill! Freddy Hazlett!...

'Howay, lad!' added Billy in a paternal sort of way. 'We ain't gonna do you over. We've more sense. You'd just go cryin' to Mekon and get us all done! No we're gonna make yers as bad as us. That'll really piss Dolly off!'

He pulled out a packet of cigarettes, extracted two filter tips and brandished them in front of John's face.

'Stick this in your gob, Denby darling – and you, too, Army Barmy, and smoke it. Here's a light.'

He ostentatiously produced a cigarette lighter.

Aghast at the revelation of his true status among the senior boys – oily little suction pump with its shades of Greenhill – John promptly obeyed. It was *vile* ... the daft things that grown-ups did! But he had no choice – not if he didn't want to be a pathetic little wimp. Somehow he managed to finish the fag without throwing up.

'And now there's this,' continued Billy, producing a small bottle of whisky, 'Take a swig... Go on! ... And another!'

A quite appalling stream of fiery liquid – almost a stream of lava, it seemed – burned its way down John's throat. Immediately, he retched and spat it out.

'God almighty! I never knew it was like that!'

'You're learnin' lad, you're learnin'! Now you, too, Army Barmy, you're not getting' away without it neither!'

'Right,' concluded Billy, screwing up the top of the whisky bottle. 'Now you're as bad as what we is! Don't go grassing up to Mekon because we'll just tell the truth – tell the ole bastard that you've been smoking and drinking an' all. That'll really piss him up. You'll get the cane, Denby. Pants down so everybody can see your little pink bum!'

'Can we go now?' asked a deflated Martin.

'No, because you're gonna help us do a liddell job!'

They sat down among the leaves, the damp ground soaking through

John's climbing breeches and wetting his backside. (He'd thought they were waterproof and was annoyed to discover that they weren't.)

Billy assumed a conspiratorial air, like a guerrilla chieftain addressing his band of partisans. 'That farmer', he whispered, 'is a mingy old bastard. Me and Dave went up to the bogs and he told us to bugger off...'

'Yeah,' added an aggrieved David, 'I mean what was we supposed to do? Crap in the fuckin' fields like the cows?'

'I'll shit on his bloody doorstep for him,' growled Philip.

'Don't be daft!' snapped Billy. 'All the kids would laugh at you! Say you were like Stick Insect and can't stop shitting yourself! I've got a better idea. We'll sneak up to the farm and let his tractor tyres down. That'd really piss him off!'

'God!' gasped John. 'But we'll all get done! The police and that!'

'Only if we're caught,' said Billy sagely. 'But he'll never know it's us. He'll just think he's got a load of punctures.'

'Well, count me out,' declared John. These were deep and dangerous waters. A flashback – Billy Lees and his shoplifting.

'No, Denby, darling, you're comin' wi' us – an' you an' all, Army Barmy!' 'But...'

'Wanna dose of this?'

Billy brandished a fist, but then added in a kindly voice, 'But we're giving you a chance, Denby, to be a proper lad, not just a liddell pet like. One o' the lads, a *bad* lad, just like what we is. Gonna take it?'

Excitement flared up in John. Accepted into the elite. One of the lads! Redemption. Squashing for ever the little wimp thing, that 'Dolly's little pet' business. Big, bold, *bad*! Only one possible answer.

'Yes, you bet!'

They set off in single file with Billy leading the way, creeping through the woods towards the farmhouse which loomed up, black and threatening against the ragged, moonlit sky. John was consumed with excitement. Going on a real-life patrol in enemy territory – and with the big, bad lads, too! He really was Colonel Jones.

They reached the entrance to the courtyard. Billy motioned them to stop.

'Wait in the shadows while I make a deco!'

As he crept forward, a dog growled ominously. He scurried back.

'It's no good. There's a bloody dog there. We'll be sussed. Let's try the other side.'

They slunk round, keeping carefully in the shadows, to where the wood lapped up to the back of the house. There in front of them, clear in the bright moonlight, was a stone-walled shed with a flat corrugated-iron roof abutting on to the main building. About four feet above it was an open window. The shed was about eight feet high, but, providing a convenient way on to its roof, was the large, mossy branch of a nearby tree which leaned towards it like a gangway.

A whispered conference began.

'There's a way into his house. Look, look... Get up that branch and on to that roof! Then get in that window...'

'Dead easy,' said David. 'We get in there and trash the place!'

'Crap!' hissed Billy. 'That's vandalism! That's what the yobs do! I say we go in there and empty a few drawers and turn a few chairs over. That'd really piss him off big time!'

'But that's housebreaking!' said John. 'The police would do us! We'd be sent to Borstal or something!' Fear was swamping his excitement. These big lads were so *thick*! They couldn't put two and two together.

Martin remained silent. John saw that he was trembling. He had a sudden thought: was all that army talk just a pose hiding a fat wimp?

'We'll only get done if we're caught,' said Billy, steadying his troops. 'And we're not going to get caught, are we?'

'Well, up you go then, Billy,' said David.

'Hold on a minute,' he replied, looking worried for the first time. 'I'm pretty big. So are you, Dave – and you, Phil. That roof looks pretty weak. We could fall through it... Then what? We need a small, light bloke to do the job...'

There was a silence for a while and then, simultaneously they all looked at John. 'There's only one small and light bloke here,' declared Billy, 'You, Denby. *You'll* have to do it!'

John had a fit of blind panic: 'No! Please no! I mean I'll get done!'

Billy grabbed his shoulder and addressed him with an unexpected warmth and friendliness which deeply touched him. 'Go on, be brave, be a *lad*! Be one of us! Be our best mate!'

It was too much – acceptance, promotion to an exalted rank! John eagerly agreed: 'OK. But how do I get on to the roof?'

'We'll give you a lift up.'

Climbing on to David's shoulders, he grasped the wet, soggy bough above him and then, with the hands of the others pushing onto his backside, heaved himself on to it. Sitting astride it, the cold clamminess of the moss soaking into his groin, he shuffled his way along it and lowered himself carefully on to the flat corrugated-iron roof. Mercifully, it bore his weight as he crawled up to the open window, his heart pounding furiously. God, this was great!

For a moment he crouched beneath the windowsill, and, then screwing up his courage to breaking point, he heaved himself up and peered in. The clouds had parted and the uninterrupted moonbeams flooded into the room. The clear, silvery light revealed a bedroom full of furniture. There in a big double bed were the farmer and his wife, snoring away gently. No way was he going in there. He crept back to the edge of the roof.

'Well?' whispered Billy.

'It's his bedroom. He's in there with his wife.'

'So you can't get in then?'

'No.'

'Why not stick your head in and tell him to fuck off?'

'God, no! He'll *kill* me!'

'Go on! Dare you! Give him a scare. Get him to shit himself in front of his wife. Disguise your voice. He won't know it's you.'

A silence followed as John weighed up the risks of the venture.

'Go on,' said Billy. 'You'll be our mate for ever. We won't call you Dolly's little pet any more, honest!'

'OK. But what do I say?'

'Fuck off, you filthy fucking mother-fucking cunt!'

'But that's *filthy*!'

'Proper lads *is* filthy. Only little kids is pure.'

'I'll get killed.'

'Go on! Be a real lad! We'll give you a fiver!'

That did it. Filled with a wild courage – Colonel Jones storming Goose Green at the head of the Paras – John crawled back to the window and peered into the room. He counted three and then in a shrill voice screamed, 'FUCK OFF, YOU FILTHY FUCKING MOTHER-FUCKING CUNT!'

A few grunts emerged from within the darkened room and then there was silence. No reaction. Still asleep...

He tried again: 'FUCK OFF, YOU FILTHY FUCKING MOTHER-FUCKING CUNT!'

Immediately in wild fear and exaltation, he rolled back along the roof and was received into Philip's and David's waiting arms.

A great explosion blasted out from the window: 'I KNOW IT'S YOU FUCKING KIDS! JUST WAIT, I'M BLOODY DOING THE LOT OF YOU!'

As fast as they could they dashed into the black and crazy tangle of the woods. There they crouched down among the prickly branches and mossy slime.

'God, this is great!' gasped John.

'Shhhhhhhh!' hissed David, 'Here he comes!'

Sure enough, a door opened emitting a flood of yellow light and a massive gorilla-like silhouette emerged.

'COME 'ERE, YER LIDDELL BASTARDS! COME ON OUT AND I'LL FUCKING HAVE YOU!'

The boys hugged the ground. John felt he was with the British Army on Mount Tumbledown, braving the Argie bombardment.

After a while the abuse petered out and the farmer stumped back into the house, slamming the door. Silently, the victorious patrol crept back to the campsite. In the shelter of the dark woods Billy addressed his partisans.

'That was just WICKED! Denby, you're a lad! A real lad! One of us!'

John swelled with pride.

'Now,' added Billy, 'back to the tents and don't be seen. Final word. When the balloon goes up tomorrow, remember it wasn't us! Gerrit?'

Positively radiating satisfaction, John went back to his tent with Martin. Sam and Michael were fast asleep. But while Martin snuggled down and dozed off, John stayed awake. He was too stirred up. John the guerrilla fighter! John the lad! John the brave! John the equal of Colonel Jones!

It was almost too good to be true.

A Far-off Mountain Peak...

Restless, John eventually crawled out of the tent.

In the cool, damp air he paced around. The moon had set and the sky was a mass of glittering stars. But the land was black, a blackness so seemingly solid that you could have carved your name on it with a penknife.

Then something wonderful began to happen. Slowly, very slowly, the darkness began to dissolve. In the immensity of the sky above the stars began to disappear and a dark-blue dome appeared, pure and unsullied. In the dim, blurred distance, mountains began to appear, vague at first, but seemingly growing like living plants. Around him the random black shapes changed into leafy trees. Down below the murky gloom became a valley where a sheet of water glinted, mysteriously at first, as fleetingly fragile as a soap bubble. It was like being present at the Creation – as if that story in his *Children's Bible* was true, after all, and he was watching God create the world out of nothing.

Silently, the revelation developed. A rich blue light suffused a rolling land of rocky hills and huge trees, extravagantly opulent in their feckless leafiness, merging into lush green forests which tumbled down into a vast, glittering lake. Here were islands, hidden coves and rocky coves, and, in the distance, huge, shadowy mountains.

All was still and expectant, promising something wonderful – like the lounge at Oaktree Gardens at Christmas when his presents were waiting unopened under the Christmas tree. At the memory of his lost paradise an involuntary tear trickled down his cheek, rich, warm and infinitely sad.

Then came comfort and reassurance. A brilliant sun rose and began to probe the twilight with golden fingers and setting the nearby crags ablaze with colour. Here was rebirth, resurrection, excitement, the very spirit of life itself. 'Yea, Lord, we greet Thee, born this happy morning... Don't worry, John, your grandparents are safe and well. So is Fred, your guinea pig, the cat they burned alive at Greenhill and that dead chick you picked up on the drive at Rickerby Hall. Jesus has come. All is well.'

O beautiful, beautiful, beautiful – beautiful beyond the power of human thought to encompass! The Beyond World. God was calling him. Calling him to some far-off mountain peak. But where was it? What kind of a mountain peak?

Down to Earth... 'It is a far better thing that I do than I have ever done'

Suddenly an angry bellow shattered the morning calm.

'EVERYBODY UP NOW! GATHER ROUND ME! MOVE YOURSELVES! NOW! THIS INSTANT!'

Meakin was in full flight.

A tangle of scruffy youngsters tumbled out of their tents and gathered on the wet grass – hair awry, some with their shirt tails hanging out of their jeans, a few clad only in their underpants, most barefoot. Sam was in his school blazer and, oblivious of the potential ridicule, was clutching his teddy bear. They huddled together like terrified villagers surprised by an enemy invasion.

'God, Mekon's in an epi-sweat!'

'Something's pissed him off big time...'

'Someone's gonna cop it!'

'Weren't me!'

In front of them stood a grim trio. A red-faced and fuming Meakin like a volcano on the verge of a cataclysmic explosion – Mount St Helens plus: you could almost *see* the smoke pouring out of the vents. Beside him, like the public executioner on the scaffold at Tower Green, stood the farmer, scowling ferociously and clearly in the throes of a major paedophobic paroxysm. A few feet away, neat and composed in his blue tracksuit, was Briggs, standing with his arms folded and wearing a smile which, though not exactly triumphant, was definitely of the 'I've-been-proved-right' sort.

A terrible sense of doom – almost of Greenhill proportions – fell on John. Retribution was coming. The bill for last night's adventure had to be paid – and it was going to be far costlier than he had ever imagined.

As he joined the nervous throng, Michael whispered in his ear: 'It's *you*, John, ain't it? What *was* you up to last night? You shouldn't of... Really you shouldn't of.'

John began to tremble.

'Right, sit down all of you,' said Meakin.

Specialists in 'Mekonology' noticed that there was none of the usual avuncular bonhomie: just a white-faced fury that they'd never seen before. Alarming.

'Last night some of you broke into the farmhouse and shouted obscenities at the farmer and his wife. That's breaking and entering. I need hardly tell you that's a matter for the police...'

John went white. His stomach seemed to oscillate inside his torso. He felt sick.

'...We're going to sort this out, NOW, THIS INSTANT! If nobody owns up we're going straight back to school and you can forget about any more adventure weekends. Now and in the future. I'm not going to be made a fool of by a bunch of silly kids. Is that clear?'

A groan rippled through the huddle of boys followed by a stunned silence.

'Come on, you know who it was.'

Silence. John's trembles became visible.

Right, we're going back to school now...'

A big groan.

John had a flashback. He remembered that story which Mr Cotton had read to his class at Rickerby Hall. It was out of a boring old book called *A Tale of Two Cities* written by some ghastly old fossil called Charles Dickens (Yuk! Yuk!). But there had been one good bit in it. During the French Revolution a bad man called Sydney Carton had gone to the guillotine to save the life of a much better man. 'It is a far better thing that I do than I have ever done,' he'd said as he faced his terrible death.

At the time John had almost cried at the sheer heroism of the act. Now was the time to be a hero like Sydney Carton.

He stood up and said in a loud and clear voice: 'It was me. I shouted the swear words through the window.'

'Denby! I might have known it!' declared Briggs, grinning broadly. 'What did I tell you, Mr Meakin?'

'Come here, Denby,' growled Meakin – (Not 'John' any more. Just formal 'Denby'. Oh Lord, what a mess he was in!) – 'Stand there. At least somebody has had the guts to own up. Now who else was involved? Don't try to tell me it was only little goggle-eyes here.'

A frantic burst of whispering broke out among the senior boys. Darran Simms and Paul Morris gesticulated furiously at Billy Nolan who glared at the ground, red-faced and sulky.

'There seems to be an interesting discussion going on over there,' said Meakin. 'Can I join in?'

Darran stood up: 'It was Billy Nolan. He was the ringleader.'

'Come here, Nolan. You've managed to make a pretty good idiot of yourself, haven't you? First drinking and being sick all over yourself and now this. Not a very good start, is it?'

Glowering villainously and muttering to himself, Billy shuffled up to the front. John noticed that tears were running down his cheeks.

'Come on, who else was involved?'

With his face twisted up into a vengeful scowl, Billy pointed to Martin: 'Him, he was.'

Martin seemed to deflate – like a lilo when the stopper is pulled out: 'Weren't me! Please, weren't me!'

He began to snivel and tears trickled. A picture of terrified misery, he slunk out to the front.

'Right, that'll do,' said Meakin. 'The trip's on again.'

A low cheer emerged from the boys.

'But, because of this nonsense,' he continued, 'we've been chucked off the campsite. So I want all the tents taken down and the minibus loaded up. Bill, can you see to it while I deal with these beauties.'

'What about breakfast?'

'We'll think about that when we're off the campsite. Now MOVE!'

'Right you lot,' he said, addressing the three malefactors, 'you're going to get a good walloping from me and then you're going up to the farmhouse to say sorry and that'll be the end of it!'

To show that he meant business, he brandished an old-fashioned leather tawse. 'Warrabout me rights?' protested a tearful Billy.

'OK, if you want your rights I'll hand you over to the farmer here and he'll take you down to the police station and you'll be charged with attempted burglary...' (All bluff, of course, but very effective with cosseted adolescent poseurs like Billy Nolan.)

'But I ain't done nowt!'

'Don't give me that rubbish! Now what's it going to be, me or the police?'

A barely audible mutter: 'You.'

'Right, over here behind this wall.'

An expectant crowd assembled.

'Cor, Denby,' whispered David, 'you're really going to cop it. Mekon's rock hard, you know. It'll be six of the best, pants down like what Billy said.'

John shuddered. This was the first time he'd ever been beaten. That picture in the history book flashed into his mind: the Elizabethan boy lying bare-bottomed over the bench while the teacher wielded the birch and the whole class looked on. The shame, the sheer degradation, the awful pain! He'd wondered how the wretched kid could have possibly endured it. Now it was going to happen to him...

The voyeurs began to swarm.

'GO AWAY!' roared Meakin.

Everybody jumped. They'd never seen old Mekon quite like this before.

419

'Bloody little sadists,' he muttered.

The malefactors duly filed their way to their place of execution behind a big stone wall. Martin was sobbing like a baby, Billy mumbling ferociously through his tears, John white-faced and trembling.

The farmer followed them, glowering angrily.

'I wanna see you do this properly,' he told Meakin. 'Hit 'em hard! Set 'em cryin'! No namby-pamby crap!'

'Please, Sir,' said John, desperately clutching at a straw. 'Do I have to get it? I mean I DID own up.'

'Of course, you get it, Denby. You're not oiling out of this one.'

No mercy in that grim countenance. No reprieve. He could only prepare himself for the worst. He remembered a story he'd read in a book he'd got out of the library. During the American Civil War a soldier had been a coward and had run away, but later he'd redeemed himself by getting wounded and winning the 'Red Badge of Courage'.

They lined up.

'Right, who's first for the firing squad?'

Silence.

Then John put up his hand: 'I'll go first.'

'That's my lad. Now bend down and touch your toes.'

John felt a partial relief. At least he was spared the humiliation of dropping his pants – which was something! But could he bear the pain without crying? He bent down and shut his eyes. 'Please, God,' he muttered to himself, 'don't let me cry. It is a far better thing that I do ...'

'That's the one what did it,' said the farmer. 'You should have heard the language coming out of him! Never heard such muck in all me life and in front of the Missus an' all! Hit 'im real hard! Set 'im crying!'

WHAM! A sheet of fire flamed across John's rear, far more painful than he'd ever thought possible. He gritted his teeth to stop himself crying out.

WHAM! WHAM! WHAM! (Please, God, no more! PLEASE! Please don't let me cry!)

'Right, that's you.' (Relief. Profound relief.)

'Is that all?' snorted the farmer. 'He's not even bloody crying! You've just tickled him! Go on, give him a bit more!'

'All right, Denby,' said Meakin, pushing John's head down. 'Here's one more for honour's sake.'

WHAM! Not quite as hard as the others, but enough to make him emit an agonised 'OOOOOOOO!'

420

'Go on, give 'im six! Smarmy little so and so! Wants taking down a peg or two him!'

'As you please. Last one, Denby.'

A great swipe ending in a light tap. Then merciful release. Through the ordeal. He'd won the Red Badge of Courage.

'Bloody pathetic! Call that a hiding? He's still not crying!'

'Right, Mr Nolan, your turn now.'

'But it weren't me! I didn't do nowt me!'

'Yes, and I'm the Man in the Moon. Don't try to tell me that you weren't the ringleader!'

With tears running down his cheeks, Billy half bent down: 'You've no bloody right...'

WHAM!

'Oyer! That bloody hurt!' The tears flowed faster.

WHAM!

Billy jerked up. 'No more! PLEASE! I can't take it!' he sobbed.

'All right. That'll do! That's you!'

Sob, sniffle, waffle: 'I'll bring me father up!'

'You do that and I'll wallop him and all!'

Meakin pointed to Martin: 'Right you are, Davidson.'

'Please no! Please no!'

'Oh come on!'

Sobbing nosily, Martin made a gesture towards bending down.

WHAM!

He immediately collapsed on to the ground, wailing away in a sodden heap of infantile misery.

With his backside throbbing painfully and fighting back his own potential tears, John looked on in bewilderment. Army Barmy, the hard man, the great military expert, the possessor of the hidden secrets of 'Nam and Goose Green, rolling round on the ground like a little baby? Whatever next?

Moments of Truth...

Meakin, also, had a moment of truth. That pulsating heap of childish misery lying on the grass was the spitting image of something else. Something which should never have happened. That something which just wouldn't go away.

And, God, how he hated this business of hitting kids! It was all

421

so squalid. But kids were such silly creatures. Short-sighted. Wilfully self-destructive. They pushed you into a corner which gave you no alternative. He was furious. Seething. Christ, he'd sweated blood enough getting this adventure weekend off the ground... 'They're not worth it! They'll just let you down! Call it off before they land you in it...' That had been Briggs' litany. And what had the little sods gone and done? Just that! Briggs couldn't have asked for more. He was having a bloody field day.

And little Denby! He'd allowed himself to be hoodwinked by his greasy charm. Stuck his neck out for him. Given him what he'd wanted in the teeth of Briggs' 'professionalism'. Stood up for him in the staffroom: '...Oh he's all right... Good lad...' And his reward? Dropped right in the shit! Briggs had been right after all. He didn't just want to wallop little Denby. He had to restrain his impulse to put a fist into his smarmy little face...

Still, one thing was certain. He was going to see this weekend through. Simple pride. Couldn't let Briggs win the battle...

The Red Badge of Courage...

'Bloody pathetic!' growled the farmer as he strolled off. 'Whole country's down the toilet! No bloody wonder neither when you've got a *woman* as prime minister! It's all Thatcher's fault! Bloody woman!...'

He turned round briefly: 'I want the whole lot of you off. NOW! And don't bloody come back neither else I'm fetching the polliss...'

The three malefactors filed back to the minibus. The tents were down and Bill Bleeson was busy getting it loaded. An excited crowd gathered.

'Cor, Billy's crying! Mekon must of hit 'im real hard!'

'Denby? How come you're not crying? Did yer manage to grease yer way out of it?'

'Course he did!'

'Mekon couldn't hit Dolly's little pet, could he?'

'No, he *did* hit me!' retorted John, stung by the assertion. 'He gave me six! Billy only got two!'

'Liar!'

'No, I'm not!'

'Go on prove it then! Show us your bum!'

This was awful. (Suppose *that* started. He'd never live it down!)

But there was nothing for it. Hideously embarrassed, he dropped his breeches, pulled down his underpants and lifted up his shirt.

An excited murmur swept through the onlookers.

'Cor, look at that! Yer bum's all red stripes!'

'Wow! One, two, three, four... Mekon must have really laid it on!'

'And you didn't cry, neither!'

'Hey, lads, come and look at Denby's bum!'

Standing there, face as red as a beetroot, with a crowd gawping at your most intimate and embarrassing part? Could you fall much lower? He'd won the Red Badge of Courage all right! But how he wished it could have been in a less embarrassing place!

'Cor, John, you really is rock hard,' sighed Michael, as thankfully John at last pulled up his breeches. 'And you didn't cry neither.'

'But', he continued with a sad reproach, 'you really shouldn't of done that, you know. I mean ole Mekon went to all that trouble to take us out and he took us little kids special like in spite of what Briggsy said... An' you start pissin' round with Nolan an' them lot. It ain't right, yer know. I mean what's Dolly gonna say to ole Mekon when we gets back?'

That hurt. More even than Mekon's tawse. More than ever John had to stop himself crying. His hero. His defender. The man he desperately wanted to impress. How he had betrayed him! How could he say sorry? Would he ever be forgiven?

'Right! Now before we leave, you three criminals are going up to the farm to apologise...'

They set off up the track, Martin still crying, John red-faced and nervous, Billy muttering angrily to himself.

'Why did you have go and grass us up, Denby?'

'I didn't grass on you. It was your mates. They didn't want to go back to school.'

'Fuckin' weekend! I never wanted to come! It were me old man who said it would do us good!'

They entered the farmyard and rang the farmhouse bell. After a while the farmer's wife answered it. They stood awkwardly for a few moments and then John spoke up.

'We've come to say sorry about last night... We're really very sorry...'

'Nothing to do with me,' said the woman, shutting the door. 'Go and see Arthur. He's over there in the garage.'

They crept timorously into a wet and cavernous garage where a large, green-trousered backside was bent over a Land Rover's engine. Again it was John who ventured to speak.

'Er, we've come to say sorry about last night...'

A ferocious red face looked up: 'You kids again! You just FUCK OFF BEFORE I FUCKING DO YOU!'

They scuttled away.

'You know,' sighed John as they reached safety, 'I think he just hates kids. He really deserved to be called a cunt.'

Soon after, the minibus lumbered off down the road.

'Surely you're not *still* going on with this?' said Briggs.

'Of course I am,' replied Meakin. 'We can't let the idiots win, can we?'

So Far, So Bad...

They parked in a convenient lay-by beside a cove on the wooded shores of Derwentwater.

'Breakfast now,' said Meakin. 'Bill, can you deal with it?'

With that he retired to a nearby boulder and pulled out his pipe. After the morning's melodrama he needed a little nicotine to calm his still seething rage.

So far, so bad. A boy swilling vodka and being sick all over himself. An infantile inability to cooperate with each other over cooking. Pathetic little squabbles. Crazy, semi-criminal goings on at night. Ignominiously chucked off the campsite.

And all this before they had started the serious business of climbing Scafell Pike!

And at the end of it all? A smug little Briggs giving Dolly a Bill of Pains and Penalties and a Monday-morning visitation from Billy Nolan's ghastly father.

'What's you been a doin' with my lad then?' With a father like that no wonder that kid was a screwed-up inadequate!

Still, look on the bright side of things: he'd been spared his usual gruesome weekend with Molly. The excruciating boredom of sitting trapped in their overheated semi-D and having to placate her by stuffing yourself with the endless stream of buns and cakes that she would keep on cooking with an obsessive, almost manic, frenzy – all to the detriment of his figure and his bodily health. The constant fusillade of grievances! How she cherished her grievances, polishing them up lovingly, storing them away carefully and then firing them at you with all the skill of a veteran sniper! This time it had been: 'Aren't all those mountain holidays *enough* for you? Do you really *have* to waste your time with a lot of silly children?' And, of course, the usual chorus line:

'When I married you I thought I was marrying an army officer, not a child-minder...'

And, yes, he *had* let her down. He'd been unable to provide her with any children. He hadn't given her the social status that she'd wanted. Differences in aspirations which had, at first, seemed so trivial had, over the years, grown into unbridgeable chasms. Life at home was a state of undeclared war.

'Don't you agree, Roderick?'

'Yes, dear.'

'But why do you always say "yes, dear" when obviously you don't agree?'

He felt deeply sorry for her: poor, lonely, limited and frustrated thing... But she did so little to help herself! She complained about loneliness, but she refused to join the YWCA, scorned the Inner Wheel, wouldn't get involved with the local church, wouldn't have visitors in the house... She'd become positively agoraphobic. What *could* you do with her?

Still angry, he glanced towards the minibus, fully expecting to see yet another dose of idiocy requiring yet more blasting operations. Instead, he got an unexpected surprise. There was no squabbling, no litter was being chucked around, they were managing to share out the beans and the sausages without the older boys stealing them from the younger ones, they were coping with the Trangia stoves safely and sensibly...

It was all so different from last night. A new atmosphere. You could feel it, like a change in the weather, as if a night of storm and rain had blown itself out and had been succeeded by a cool and calm morning. Perhaps they *had* sobered up – peeped into the abyss into which their silliness was leading them and recoiled in alarm?

Soothed by the nicotine, his rage subsided. He began to feel benevolent. Poor things, it wasn't *their* fault that they were thick and inadequate! And now they *were* trying to make amends. Pathetically eager to please, in fact...

The Troublemaker?

He saw little Denby running round with a bin liner, assiduously picking up rubbish. Oiler, plummy-accented greaser, the troublemaker who had betrayed his trust and got them thrown so ignominiously off the campsite... His rage welled up again.

But ... but ... but, then, he *had* owned up, he *had* taken his punishment without grizzling and yowling like the other two. What was more, in his fury he'd gone and hit him very hard, far harder than he'd hit the other two. Too hard perhaps? He could well have damaged him – and not just physically, either. He'd been so keen, so positive, so eager to involve his classmates... All that stupid and expensive kit... And, poor silly thing, it had all ended in disaster! Better start mending that fence before it was too late and he rebounded into yobbery. But, wait a minute, let *him* come to you, not vice versa. Don't look weak. Kids homed in on weakness like Exocet missiles.

Anguish

His backside still throbbing painfully, John drifted round with his bin liner. He was a split personality. He listened to David Robson's loud voice booming away to Bill Bleeson: '...Well, I tried to warn Billy... Christ, I tried, but he just wouldn't listen! ... And Denby? Oh, he's hard all right. You don't get chucked out of a place like Greenhill for nothing ... hit a teacher... Mind, he's a nutter, a bit of a head case...' One part of John swelled with pride. Denby the hard! Denby the bad! Denby the dauntless! No longer 'Dolly's little pet'!

But the other half of him could have wept with anguish. What *had* he done? Mekon would go to Mrs Watson and tell her that he was bad. She would expel him and he'd be sent back to... Greenhill! He desperately wanted grown-ups who would be kind to him and support him. He'd had them, but now he had gone and messed it all up. John, you fool!

'Call me John instead'

When breakfast was over, Briggs came to life. Seeing an opportunity to assert his authority as a 'professional PE teacher', he took the boys for a swim in the lake.

His brilliantly emblazoned 'life saver' bathing trunks duly proclaimed his yet unrecognised talent as a swimmer.

While the more timid souls – Martin, Billy and Sam – stood nervously on the edge, the more enterprising braved the frigid waters. John, meanwhile, crept timorously up to the ominously smoking Mekon volcano.

'Yes, Denby?' Withering glance. Clouds of blue smoke.

'I'm very sorry about last night, Sir... Honestly I am.'

'So am I, Denby.'

'I mean, Sir, you went to all that trouble to arrange this trip for us and you specially took us younger kids on it in spite of what Mr Briggs said ... and, well. I've messed it up for you, haven't I?'

Involuntarily, the tears began to trickle.

'Come on, boy, no need for that...'

Then a stern look: 'Now I want you to tell me the truth, young man, and I mean THE TRUTH! Did you, or did you not go into the farmhouse as the farmer said?'

'No! No! Honestly. Cross my heart! I just shouted swear words through the window...'

'You'd better not have gone into that house, because if you had, the police would have got involved and then you really would have landed in it, I can tell you!'

Silence.

Meakin continued: 'Young man, you just don't realise the problems that you cause when you do these things. I'll have a lot of explaining to do back at school. I only hope Mrs Watson's going to be in a good mood. For your sake and not for my sake.'

The tears started in earnest: 'I won't be expelled, will I?'

'Don't be silly! Of course not! You've just been a bit daft. The big lads were calling you Mrs Watson's little pet and you didn't like it. So when young Nolan dared you to go up to that window you did it... Just to get a little street cred.'

'How do you know that?'

'I wasn't born yesterday. You're young and daft. I was once young and daft, too.'

'What did you do?'

'I was dafter than you can imagine. One day I'll tell you about it, but not now...'

Silence.

John began to scheme. How to get back into favour? How to redeem himself?

One way: show enthusiasm by going on the Great Escape...

Tentatively, as if he were creeping out onto a pond covered in thin ice, he popped the question: 'Can I go on the Great Escape? I promise I'll be good.'

'Of course you can!' replied Mekon with unexpected gusto, 'That's the way to say sorry!'

He felt himself warming to the little bundle with its dirty, tear-stained face. 'Oh, do stop snivelling!' he said. 'Look, it's all over now. You owned up. You took your punishment like a man. I respected that. And I hit you a lot harder than I hit the other two. Did I hurt you?'

'Not half, you did!'

Momentary panic by Meakin: Christ, have I gone and battered a child?!

'You're not seriously hurt, are you? Sure?'

'No! No! No! I'm all right, honest!' (I'm not showing *you* my bum! No way!) 'Good lad ... Well, now we're back to normal, then.' (Enormous relief: but press home your advantage. Grease up Mrs Watson in advance to soften the bollocking you're sure to get back at school! Show a 'caring and unselfish attitude' – that usually works with her!)

'Please, can Sam come on the Great Escape, too? You see everybody calls him a flid and a stick insect...'

'Just as you do.'

'Yes, but if he can do the Great Escape, the big lads will see that he's not a poofter after all.'

'All right, you can bring him along. But mind, he's *your* responsibility. Don't let me down, not a second time. Once is quite enough!' (Sam on the Great Escape! That would be one in the eye for Briggs!)

'OK. Now off you go!'

John walked off. But then he turned round, blushing bright red. 'Please, Sir,' he said. 'Can you stop calling me Denby and call me John instead?'

'Is it that important?'

'Yes it is. If you call me John, it means you're not just a teacher. You're like the dad I want you to be.'

That just slipped out by mistake and, scampering off, he blushed

428

even redder. Denby the dauntless didn't want a *teacher* as his dad, but John Denby did.

Preparations

Preparations began for the 'Great Ascent'.

'You're *still* going ahead with it, are you?' sighed Briggs.

He shook his head as Meakin nodded and began to marshal his troops.

'Gather round!... Rucksacks... Sleeping bags... Bivvi bags... Trangias... Darran, you've got Michael in your group. Look after him properly. He's your responsibility... Bill, your Escape Group... No Trangias ... no tents ... bivvi bags ... hard tack ... chocolate... Everybody got waterproofs?...'

Restored to favour, John bounced round in an orgy of obsequiousness.

'Sam, I won't piss you up... I won't call you Stick Insect, promise! Look, I'll carry your sleeping bag... Robson, I can take your sleeping bag, too... Simms, I've got a big rucksack... I can take those cans of beans...'

Martin was desperately trying to salvage the few remaining rags of his shredded 'hard man' image: 'Morris, I can take your sleeping bag...'

Sensing weakness, the senior boys homed in on the two juniors. Never one to pass up an opportunity, Billy Nolan donated his entire load – what were little kids for, anyway? A huge heap of junk piled up beside John's and Martin's rucksacks.

'Oh, come on, John!' exclaimed Meakin. 'There's no need to go over the top!

You can't possibly carry all that! ... Come on, Paul ... and David, *you* can carry your *own* sleeping bags... And you, too, Billy!'

Somewhat to his gratified surprise, the boys obeyed promptly, even cheerfully, except for Billy who glowered and muttered: 'Mekon 'ad no bloody right ter hit me! Wait till me favver comes up on Monday!'

But he made little impression on the atmosphere of eager cooperation. Instead, he found himself in the new and uncomfortable position of being the odd man out.

'Yes,' observed Briggs reluctantly – as if he was having a tooth pulled out – 'There does seem to be an improved attitude. What's come over them?'

'Nothing really,' replied Meakin with a condescending air. 'It's normal. First time they've ever done anything like this. They get hyped up, go over the top, probe the extremities ... and then get a fright. Seen it all before.'

One up to Meakin in the ego stakes.

'All packed up, now, lads?' he continued. 'Right, briefing. Sit down and get your maps out. Where are we, David?'

'Er... Er... Beside Lake Windermere.'

'Wrong end of the map, old man. Anybody else?'

John stuck up his hand: 'Sir! Sir! Sir!'

Meakin let him wriggle for a while as he waited for somebody else to answer.

'All right, John, you tell them.'

'Beside Lake Derwentwater, Sir, at 269204.'

'Showing off again, Denby?' hissed Briggs.

'OK,' continued Meakin, ignoring the interruption, 'we're driving to Seathwaite, here at 235122, walking up to Styhead Tam at 222099 where we'll pitch the tents and cook lunch. Then we're setting off for Scafell Pike... OK, maps away and all aboard the minibus. Same places as before...'

'Martin needs the bog.'

'Not again! Why didn't you go after we'd had breakfast?'

'I tried, but they kept following me and laughing at me.'

'Well, off you go now and be quick about it... And, for heaven's sake, bury your offerings! Paul, if you think it's so frightfully funny, I'll personally rub your face in it!'

Off into the Wilds. Matters of Safety?

The minibus spluttered off along the twisty road which wound its way through leafy woods and past noisy streams and lumpy grey cliffs.

Shortly it turned off down a narrow side-road. Hemmed in by high stone walls covered in wet moss, it followed the floor of a deep, green valley. By now the clear skies of the dawn had filled with dark, brooding clouds. Misty hillsides loomed up on either side. Far above the shifting grey occasionally parted to reveal tumbled black cliffs.

They parked on the grass verge near an old stone farm called

The great ascent

Seathwaite. It was a subdued mob that tumbled out on to the wet grass beside the road. What the others thought, John didn't know, but the setting certainly awed him – the enclosing valley, the plunging mountainsides, the waterfalls, the gorges, the grim, threatening crags which brooded in their misty fastness... It was all so big and so ominous, a new and desolate land, seemingly alive and warning him of impending cold, fear and exhaustion.

Meakin was in 'avuncular mode' – which was how he liked to be, if only the kids would let him. 'Right, lads, Phase One, the hike up to Styhead Tarn... Remember all I've said about mountain safety... We've got to stay together... Nobody is to go racing off ahead... Mr Briggs will be the back marker and will look after any tail-end charlies... We're going to walk at alpine pace... The hard men will think it's pathetically slow, but it's how Austrian alpine guides do it and nobody will get exhausted... Exhaustion is a highly dangerous state...'

They set off in a straggly line following a broad track which wriggled its way along the banks of a big, foaming river. Coming to an old stone bridge, they stopped for a short rest.

'Are we at the top yet?'

Groans from the boys.

431

'No, Sam, we've got a long way to go yet.'

'Look at the weather,' said Briggs. 'It's getting worse. I think we should go back.'

'No problem,' declared Meakin. 'Put your waterproofs on, lads, in case it starts to rain.' (As if he didn't have enough on his plate already with getting this bunch of under-achievers and duck-out artists up the mountain! He could do without this constant non-stop drip, drip, drip, undermining what little morale they had. It was almost as bad as Molly...)

'Oh, Sir, I've left my cagoule in the minibus!'

'Here, take mine,' said John. 'I don't mind getting wet.' (Unselfish. Thinking of others... Mrs Watson would eat that... It would help to offset the impending stink about the farmer affair.)

'Don't be daft, John!' said Meakin. 'We don't want you dying of hypothermia. Luckily, I always carry a spare cagoule with me... Take this... Now the hard work begins. Put your rucksacks on and, when you've sorted yourselves out, we'll start... Into line. Nobody overtakes me.'

They crossed the bridge and, passing through the stone wall beyond, mounted a steep and rocky path which twisted its tortuous way up a boulder-strewn hillside. As they plodded slowly and steadily upwards, a chilly mist closed in, shutting them into a restricted world of greyness, wet grass and big, black rocks.

'Cor, I never knew it would be this knackering!'

'Keep going, Martin, you're not dead yet.'

They stopped for a short rest.

'Concern for the Lives of Children' and 'Safety Awareness'

Briggs, resplendent in his badge-covered tracksuit, bounced up to Meakin: 'Look, we'll never get anywhere at this rate! We're far too slow! I'm going on to Styhead Tarn... You, David, Darran and Paul, follow me!'

Without waiting for a reply, they jogged off up the path and disappeared into the grey murk.

'Shouldn't we follow them?'

'No you should *not*! You lot stay with me.'

Meakin fumed inwardly. This was just the kind of open challenge that he'd wanted to avoid. The simmering conflict between 'qualifications' and actual experience, which had rumbled on in the staffroom for the past two weeks, had finally burst into the open. The gauntlet had been publicly thrown down in front of him. He sighed: kids were less trouble than adults.

'We'll see how far they get,' he said. 'Bill, can you be the back marker?'

They marched slowly on, up the steep path which eventually levelled off and followed a white and angry river which roared boisterously through a wide and stony valley. At intervals the mists parted, revealing grim and inhospitable mountainsides sweeping up on either side of them.

After a while a small wooden bridge loomed out of the fog. Crossing the seething river, they found a woebegone Paul and David sitting on a rock.

'We're knackered. Sir, Mr Briggs says we ought to go down.'

'Where's Darran?'

'Dunno! He went on with Mr Briggs.'

'Well, you're not going down,' declared Meakin forcibly. 'You're staying with me. I hope you've learned your lesson. If you charge off like kangaroos with hyperactivity problems, you just exhaust yourselves. Stay with me and you'll get there.' (Inwardly, he glowed with a smug radiance. Proved right in front of the kids! It couldn't have turned out better!)

A little later they came across an equally woebegone Darran Simms. There was no sign of Briggs.

Soon they came to a small lake. Its green and inviting shores were hemmed in by grey crags; its still waters were sombre and sinister. It reminded John of one of those enchanted lakes you read about in ancient legends.

'Right, David, where do you think we are?'

'Er... Er... Er...'

'You tell him, John.'

'Styhead Tam, Sir.'

'Sir! Sir! Sir! There's Mr Briggs in the lake! Yes, he's *in* it!'

'Flipping maniac!' somebody muttered. 'Like you, Denby, he's always showing off!'

Relieved to have all his party together again, Meakin took charge. 'Here we are. This'll be our base camp. We'll put the tents up and then we'll cook lunch.'

A dripping and shiny Briggs emerged from the lake.

'Cor, Sir, you're rock hard, you!'

Briggs grinned. The object of the exercise had been attained.

The cooperative mood continued. The tents were erected, lunch was cooked and eaten and all the mess tins washed up with a bewildering smoothness.

'Amazing!' sighed Briggs with more than a hint of resentment. 'They're actually doing it without fighting with each other!'

He looked at the sky. The weather was showing signs of clearing. The clouds above them were white and scattered patches of blue were starting to appear. But the big mountains around them still remained buried under towering masses of cloud; grim, black and forbidding. He approached Meakin with his face screwed up into a 'seriously professional' expression, denoting, for the cognoscenti at any rate, 'concern for the lives of children' and 'professional safety awareness'.

'We'll have to pack it in. The weather's getting worse. Anyway, the kids can't handle it. I mean, just look at David, Darran and Paul. They're deadbeat. If *they* can't cope, how do you expect the little kids to?'

Meakin was ready for the attack: 'If we take it gently, they'll manage. You went far too fast for them, young man. No Austrian guide would let you go at that pace.'

'That's as may be, but the MLTB doesn't recognise Austrian qualifications... Anyway, if you insist on going ahead with the climb, you can count me out. I'm staying here.'

'As you wish. You can guard the camp while we're on the hill.'

'You *do* realise that it's illegal for teachers without a Mountain Leadership Certificate to take children above a thousand feet?'

'I *had* heard of that. But it only applies to state schools and we're not a state school.'

'But the local authority pays for most of our pupils and that means...'

'Oh for Christ's sake! Look, if they all get killed, I'll carry the can. Is that good enough for you?'

'Can I have that in writing?'

'As you wish.'

With a resigned sigh, Meakin pulled out his notebook, extracted it from its polythene container and wrote out a legal disclaimer: '...I go up this mountain, Scafell Pike, with these children entirely of my own volition... I hereby absolve James Briggs, Cert. Ed. from any responsibility... Signed R. Meakin...'

He carefully tore out the page and handed it to Briggs.

Then he addressed the boys: 'Gather round. Briefing. Everybody will take rucksacks and waterproofs. Those not going on the Escape will leave their sleeping bags, stoves and tins here ... but take chocolate and biscuits to eat on the mountain... Escape Group – that's you, Bill – make sure you've got sleeping bags, bivvi bags, waterproofs and plenty of chocolate and biscuits... No, John, you're not taking Trangias... When we've reached the top, you go down towards Wasdale. Find a good hidey-hole for the night and don't get seen. You're in enemy territory. The Argies, the commies or whatever after you... Meet us at eleven hundred hours at 181076 ...

Mr Briggs, if my lot aren't back here by eleven o'clock tonight, you can call out the Mountain Rescue... Oh yes, I *have* told the National Park office about our proposed antics...'

The Great Ascent

They formed up in a line with Meakin at the front and Bill Bleeson at the back. They were about to set off when Billy Nolan stuck up his hand.

'Do I *have* to go? My foot's hurting and I'm knackered.'

'I'm afraid you do, Billy Boy.' (A potential crisis here. Let one wimp out and others would jump on the bandwagon. An escalating avalanche would follow. Failure would reinforce the duck-out culture which it was his aim to destroy. Success could be the start of a new and more positive era. And, whatever happened, it was vital to get them clean away from Briggs and his subtle undermining of morale. He had imagined that professional PE teachers were meant to *encourage* physical activity not to keep finding excuses for stifling it. Most undoubtedly did, but not this one – which probably was why he was at Beaconsfield...

Billy looked furtively round for the expected support. But none was forthcoming. Inexplicably, his magic had ceased to work. He relapsed into a muttering sulk:

'Mekon can't fuckin' MAKE me! Wait till me favver getsa hold o' him!'

Finally, the procession got going, plodding with a slow, measured tread along a broad, stony track. The mists had rolled back and

435

more mountain grandeur was revealed. Reaching the crest of the pass, they branched off to the left and followed a smaller, rockier path which led them through some grassy swamps and then cut slantwise across jumbled spiky rocks and up on to a vast, precipitous sweep of mountainside.

As the grey mists swept down again they entered a grim and threatening world.

The path picked its tortuous way through a tumbled incoherence of deep, rocky ravines, steep slabby slopes and huge brutish boulders. It was up, up, up, always up. John stared around him with a mixture of dread and wonder. He'd never seen a place like this before. It was so empty – no people, no houses, no cars. Just a hostile land of coarse wet grass, enormous dripping rocks and savage chasms. He was in a new place, bigger, grander, crueller and altogether different from anything he'd previously known.

At the same time he became acutely aware of his body and its weakness. It seemed to swell up and take over. He was exhausted. His rucksack was pulling him down as if it had invisible arms which grasped at the passing rocks. He panted furiously as he clambered up yet another muddy slither of stones. The frequent rests became a longed-for paradise and Mekon a kindly father who always seemed to know when to stop. Then there would be the fateful words, 'OK. Let's get moving again,' heralding yet another return to the business of squeezing a bit more activity out of your unwilling body.

He looked around him. Thankfully, the others seemed to be making even heavier weather of things than he was. Paul and David were struggling. Billy was clearly having problems. It was taking all Bill Bleeson's coaxing to keep Martin moving at all. On the other hand, Sam and Michael seemed to be doing all right, at least no worse than him – which was a relief. (One in the eye, too, for the big lads who'd said they were too weak to cope!)

The mist began to lighten. The heavy grey became white.

'Are we at the top yet?'

'No, still some way to go. Keep going and you'll get there.'

Eventually, they turned off the main path and struck up a steep valley where a brown stone shoot loomed out of the murk, seemingly flowing down from the misty crags like a monstrous waterfall. Nearby, lurking under a huge, overhanging slab of wrinkled rock, was a mass of cold, wet snow. To John, it seemed like a lurking monster, watching them and murmuring, 'Be careful! This is *my* country, not yours!' Through his tiredness he could hardly contain his excitement.

'Look – *snow*! Look at those cliffs! We must be really high! Cor, this is great! A *real* mountain!'

It wasn't just the need to impress old Mekon: he was genuinely thrilled.

They had another golden rest.

'Now, lads,' said Meakin in full avuncular mode, 'this is the hard bit, a taste of real mountaineering. Those are screes ahead... We must be very careful of falling stones... So keep close together and watch where you put your feet.'

They got up and a long, panting scramble up the great swathe of loose rubble began.

'WATCH OUT! STONE!'

'Christ you idiot, you nearly killed me!'

'DAVID! LOOK OUT!'

Halfway up Martin collapsed in a heap: 'I'm staying here. I can't go on.'

Sensing carrion, the vultures swooped.

'Look at him!' sneered Billy Nolan. 'The great Vietnam hard man, the SAS hero!'

'Sussed to a crust!' jeered David Robson. 'Christ, even old Stick Insect is better than you!'

A chorus of jeers erupted from the senior boys.

'Bury him under that rock,' said Billy Nolan. 'Or mebbe he needs the bog again! Or do you just want a little tommy tank, Army Barmy? Are you sure your little thing really works?'

'SHUT UP!' roared Meakin. Inwardly, he groaned. No, some of these kids hadn't really changed. Under a seemingly serious exterior the same old inadequate beast still lurked. They just *had* to have something to bully. Sam Hawthorne – surprise, surprise – was doing quite well and he hadn't messed himself – at least, not yet! So the knives had gone into Martin instead. Poor, silly kid! Always acting the hard man, but always ducking out of everything. Whenever he faced any difficulties fantasy always came to the rescue. Now he'd been hoisted on his own pathetic petard.

'They don't make you do this sort of thing in the SAS,' he groaned. 'They have helicopters like in 'Nam!'

'Well, you can't have a helicopter here.'

Martin began to cry.

At this, John saw his opportunity. The Monday bollocking from

Mrs Watson still loomed ahead. The more he was seen to be a caring and responsible boy, the better it would be. Good politics.

'Come on, Martin,' he said, 'it's not far now. The top's just up there. If you lie here, the others will just kick you in. If Sam and Michael can do it, so can you. Just get up to that big boulder there and have another rest.'

Slowly, his face contorted with simulated agony, Martin heaved himself up and, attacking the sliding heap of rubble in front of him, staggered up to the boulder indicated.

'Get your breath back now,' said John, 'and when you're ready we'll get up to that big rock there...' (He was hugely enjoying his sense of superiority. In his mind's eye he envisaged the handshake from Mrs Watson, yes, and even God up on his cloud short-listing him for a halo and wings.)

Up they crawled, up the tumbled stones and muddy gravel, engulfed in the cold, clammy mist and the smell of wet earth. Eventually, they emerged on to a little pass between two grey and forlorn heaps of rock. By now the mist was brilliantly white.

'Nearly there!' declared Meakin encouragingly. 'It's just up these rocks to the right.'

'Oh hell, not MORE!' groaned Martin, rounding angrily on John. 'You told me this was the top! Inadequate briefing. That's a military offence, you know!'

Hoots of derision erupted from the senior boys.

'Don't you bloody laugh!' he protested. 'Wait till you hyperventalizz...' (Here Martin's medical vocabulary fizzled out into a petulant splutter.)

'Yeah! Just as you always do whenever it's games, you fat flid!' By now Billy Nolan was well into his new-found role as leader of the vultures swarming round the carcass of Army Barmy.

'Oh, pack it in!' growled Meakin. 'Well done, Sam, by the way, and you, too, Michael! Now one last heave and we'll be there.'

So they clambered up the knobbly rocks and struggled up the last steep slopes. Then something wonderful happened – at least to John, if not to the others. The white mist became blue and then shredded into long wispy streamers and suddenly they burst out into brilliant sunshine. Gone was the dismal world beneath them and they found themselves on warm rock, basking under a friendly sun.

This is what it must be like when you go to heaven, thought John.

A short distance away was a circular stone structure like an oversized drum. A small crowd of hikers of all shapes and sizes was milling around it – men, women and even some quite small children.

'The top!' announced Meakin.

John felt a stab of disappointment – all those people, even kids! 'So lots of kids come here? I thought we were going to be the first kids to do it!'

'I'm afraid not, old man,' replied Meakin in a fatherly way. 'If you want to make first ascents, you'll have to go the Himalayas or Antarctica.'

'There, sussed, Denby darling!' hissed Billy Nolan.

John winced.

'But that big stone thing,' he said, anxious to regain a bit of mountain cred, 'I bet that's very old. It'll probably date from Celtic times. You know it could have been made by King Arthur.'

'No, John,' said Meakin, 'you're wrong there, too. It's a memorial to the men killed in the First World War.'

'Sussed again, Denby!' sneered Billy Nolan. 'You don't know everything, do you?'

'Well, it could have been! And I bet you've never even heard of the Celts, you thickoid!'

By now John had sussed Billy Nolan out as a loud-mouthed wimp who thrived on bullying those weaker than himself. He wasn't going to take any crap out of him. Clenching his fists, he squared up to him.

'No need for that!' snapped Meakin, nipping an impending fracas in the bud.

'We're here now,' he added, 'so let's savour our little triumph. Well done, everybody! Very well done, Sam! Makes a change to achieve something, doesn't it? And, you, too, Michael, well done!'

Sam and Michael glowed with pride as Meakin shook everybody by the hand.

'Right, now the summit photograph.'

Hearing the word 'photograph', Martin suddenly brightened up – almost like a corpse rising from the dead. He smoothed down his camouflage combat jacket, carefully adjusted his red paratrooper's red beret and twisted his face into a purposeful frown.

'You'd really think he *was* a Para,' Michael whispered into John's ear.

Billy Nolan, also, struck a hard-man pose, pulling his black woolly hat down to his eyes and screwing his face into an aggressive scowl.

Then they all sat down and ate the crisps and Mars bars that

439

Meakin and Bill Bleeson dispensed. John was awed by the place. They seemed to be perched on a small rocky island in the middle of a vast ocean of white cloud. Here and there other lumpy mountain-tops poked through the white plain. For a moment he felt he had discovered a warm and friendly group of islands in the middle of the Antarctic ice cap. Nearby was a dramatic, castle-like mountain whose enormous wrinkled cliffs rose sheer out of the mists in a riot of gullies and slabs.

'Cor, Sir, what's that mountain?'

'That's Scafell... Those are the biggest cliffs in England.'

'Wow! I bet nobody's ever climbed them!'

'I'm afraid they have, Jonny boy! A bloke called Slingsby did it back in 1888!'

John began to fret. There must be *some* unclimbed mountains around, surely!

'Time for the big show' ... The last we've seen of them'?

Meakin stood up: 'Time for the big show. Bill, are you ready? Who's going? David? Good. Philip? Good. Paul?'

'I don't think I can hack it, Sir.'

'All right, you come down with me.'

Michael put up his hand: 'Please, Sir, Mr Meakin Sir, Could I go? I'll take Morris's place. I'll take his sleeping bag... He can have my place in Darran's tent.'

'Is that all right with you, Bill?'

Bill nodded: 'Yes, he'll do! He's done well.' (Secretly, Bill was glad to be rid of one of the seniors. His big dread was of losing control of his party and making a fool of himself. With the likes of little Michael Connolly he had the physical edge. If it came to the worst, he could always belt him over the earhole. It wasn't that easy with the older and bigger boys.)

'John? Sam? You're still going? Good!'

Martin put up his hand.

'*No!*' said Meakin firmly, 'We're not having *you* swanning over the mountains at night. We don't want to have get the mountain rescue helicopter out!'

'Helicopter! Wicked! We can go in a helicopter? I told you the SAS always went round in helicopters!'

440

'No, Martin, you're *not* getting a ride in a helicopter. You only get a ride in a helicopter when you have an accident and have to be rescued – and that's the mountaineering equivalent of filling your pants.'

That word 'helicopter' had touched a raw nerve. Under the breezy confidence Meakin *was* worried. On the surface it was all so silly – this business of getting steamed up about a bunch of kids walking down an easy path on one of the most frequently climbed hills in England! Not remotely like going into battle against ultra-tough German paratroopers at Monte Cassino, was it? Yet, in its own way, it was almost as dangerous. Not-over-bright kids alone on a mountain? Would they perform? Or would they just go silly? Bill Bleeson was a thoroughly reliable lad, but he was not over-endowed on the upper deck. Did he *really* know where he was going? Would he be able to control his party? If all went well, he, Roderick Meakin, could chalk up a major victory. If not, Briggs would have a field day for starters ... followed by heaven alone knew what! At Monte Cassino you were responsible for yourself. Here your reputation – indeed, your whole future! – was in the hands of a bunch of kids. Talk about putting your head in a lion's mouth!

'Right, all of you listen to me...'

The boys obediently fell silent and listened attentively.

'Bill, your scenario...' He repeated the whole thing for the third time – communist takeover etc., etc., but with the added tag of 'three brilliant scientists who have vital intelligence – that's you, John, Sam and Michael. Yes, Sam, you're a brilliant scientist now! You've just been liberated from a prison camp and it's vitally important that you reach the Resistance headquarters alive...'

Then came the heartfelt plea: 'Bill, I'm depending on you. Whatever you do, don't get lost or have an accident. Seriously – and I'm in deadly earnest here! – this is your first taste of real responsibility. Your first task is to get your group down the mountain *safely*. Look after your group – especially the juniors. See that no harm comes to them...'

He turned to the Escape Group: 'Now you lads have got to do what Bill says. Support him and for Christ's sake don't start mucking about as soon as I am out of sight. Scafell Pike isn't a kiddies' playground. It's a dangerous mountain, not a muck-about place. Bill, if there's any rubbish out of any of them, you've my permission to thump them. I know it's probably illegal, but safety's more important

441

than legal niceties. Discipline, chaps. Discipline. Be adults and not little kids...'

He fixed John with a hard stare: 'John, listen to me. After last night's little effort some people will think I'm a great big softie for trusting you to go on this thing. You're on trust now. If you start showing off and going daft ... well, I won't answer of the consequences. You know me!'

He brandished a clenched fist. John bowed his head and blushed scarlet.

'That's all, lads. You're on your own now.'

As Meakin led his group back down the track, Darran spoke up: 'Well, that's probably the last we've seen of them!'

The boys giggled, but Meakin winced.

'We're in the army now...'

As Meakin's group disappeared over the rocky brow of the mountain, Bill stood up and began the speech he'd been rehearsing for the past two weeks.

He was acutely nervous, frightened of the responsibility placed on him. He had a horrible premonition of his little army going silly

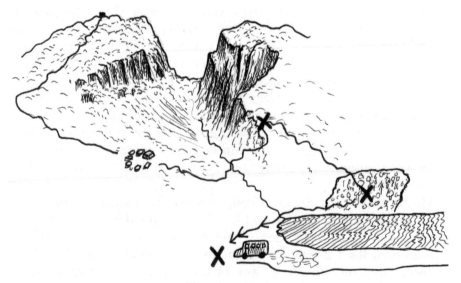

The great escape

and refusing to obey him. Indeed, he'd dreamed about precisely that the previous night.

'Right. You heard what Mr Meakin said about discipline. Right. Denby. Denby you're lucky to be here after all that crap last night. Right. Any more shit out of you and you're getting this!'

He thumped him hard in the ribs.

'OYER! That hurt!'

'It was meant to. Right. Remember that there's a lot more where that came from.' John was silent and blinked back potential tears. Message understood.

'Right, men. Sitrep.'

'What the fuck's a sitrep?' asked David.

'Situation report. Right. We must use proper army language. We're in the army now. Right. Briefing. You're going into battle for the first time. You're probably scared. Right. No shame in that. Control your fear like proper soldiers. We're in enemy territory. Right. The communists are all around us...'

'Oh for fuck's sake, Bill!' exclaimed David. 'You sound like Army Barmy playing bang-bangs!'

Shut up! This is a serious military exercise.'

'Jesus Christ, we're only a bunch of lads on holiday!'

'That's what *you* think! But any day now it could be for real!'

'Crap!'

'No it's not crap! Major Allen says the Russians are planning to take over Britain. They've already infiltrated undercover communist agents into all the important trades unions...'

'Shit!' exclaimed Philip. 'My old man's a member of the Transport and General Workers. All he's interested in is Newcastle United and beer...'

'That'll be what he wants you to think...'

'Bloody hell, Bill, he's never even heard of Russia! He thinks Moscow's in Argentina...'

'Right! Major Allen's an army officer and he knows. Right. Look at the Falkland Islands. The Russians are planning to do the same thing here. Right. We must be prepared...'

As his limited vocabulary dried up, Bill brandished a clenched fist. He was big and strong enough to make any assault a potentially hazardous operation so the opposition momentarily subsided.

'Right. Briefing. Orders. Intention. We intend to reach 181076 at eleven hundred hours... Method. We will march on a bearing of 360 degrees to 210207...'

'Oh for fuck's sake!' groaned David. 'Get a shift on! We want to get there by tomorrow morning, not in the middle of next week...'

'Shut up! We're doing this properly... From there we march in single file to our FRP...'

'What's an FRP?'

FRP in Enemy Territory

They eventually set off, following a bemused group of hikers down a broad and well-marked path. Bill led the way with his map and compass ostentatiously held out in front of him. David brought up the rear. The others walked in the middle of the line. After a few minutes they passed a family man and his wife and two small boys dressed in shorts, T-shirts and trainers.

'Where are you going?' asked the bigger boy.

'We're on an army exercise,' replied Philip genially. 'We're going to sleep out on the mountainside...'

'That sounds wicked!' cooed the boy. 'Dad, could we join them?'

'Yes, come on!' said David subversively. 'The more the merrier!'

'Certainly not!' cried Bill angrily. 'Fraternisation with the enemy is strictly forbidden. We must guard against enemy infiltration...'

David grinned wickedly at the boy and, as they marched off, pointed at Bill's back and whispered, 'He's a bit of a nutter, you know.'

The path led them off the summit dome and over a flatfish expanse of boulders before plunging down into the surrounding mists. Once more they entered a grey uniformity of wet rock and soggy grass. Before long the steep, stony slopes levelled out on to what was obviously a broad pass and they joined a big track which led off to the left. Here they stopped while Bill fiddled around with his map and compass.

'Sitrep. We seem to be at 210077 ... er...'

'Oh come on, we know where we are! Wastwater's obviously down there...'

'Shut up, David. We're doing this properly. We don't want to get lost!'

John kept strictly silent. He knew where they were from studying Mekon's map, but he didn't want to be accused of showing off. He had to get through this this weekend without any more disasters.

When at long last Bill had managed to work out where they were they marched off to the left, following the trail down into a rocky valley. Gradually, the greyness thinned, became whiter and then began to dissolve into shreds. Blue sky appeared, fitfully at first and then with more determination until a brilliant sun burst through and revealed a vividly green land dotted with huge boulders. They were in a kind of hole in the sky, surrounded on all sides by a white wall of cloud.

Bill stopped: 'The weather's clearing. Right. We've lost cover. The sky belongs to the enemy. We must go to ground.'

Which presumably meant that it was time to bed down for the night. While the older boys winced, John wallowed in the military fantasy.

A little further down they found themselves among a scatter of gigantic, house-sized rocks. Here they found a place so ideal that it might have been put there on purpose. It was a sort of natural fortress consisting of a tennis-court-sized enclosure surrounded by a rectangle of massive square-shaped boulders. One especially big one leaned out over a large cleft which was protected by a little rampart of rocks. On the opposite side of the rectangle a tumble of huge rocks formed an arch over a dark hole which led down into a deep, sandy cave.

John was beside himself with excitement: 'Cor! This is wicked! It's just like *The Hobbit*! I bet it's an old castle from the days of King Arthur!'

'Shut up, Denby! No talking on patrol!'

He immediately fell silent.

Bill studied the cave.

'No,' he declared, looking wise, 'we can't use that. Poor field of fire and if the enemy rolled a grenade down it we'd all be taken out. No quick escape route either... We'll basher there.' He pointed to the cleft.

Three years of concentrated ACF training went into action. Two army ponchos emerged from his rucksack and were duly spread out over the gap between the overhanging rock and the ground and secured by stones. Moss and grass camouflaged it. ('The enemy'll be up there in their gunships searching for us.') Heather and grass were plucked up and spread over the gravelly ground inside the shelter. The entrance was concealed by stones heaped up by John, Sam and Michael. When all was completed they crawled inside and spread out their bivvi bags and sleeping bags.

A magic den

John could hardly contain his excitement. He'd made the odd den before in the grounds of Rickerby Hall, but this was something else! And part of a grown-ups' military exercise as well!

'Cor, Bleeson!' he exclaimed with unfeigned exuberance. 'Thanks a bomb! This is magic!'

Warmed by this unstinting endorsement of his efforts, Bill began to unwind. 'Good on you, Denby!' he said. 'You're doing fine. Keep it up! And you, too, Hawthorne and Connolly, you're doing fine, as well!'

John luxuriated in his senior's approval. Things were back on track.

As they squeezed into the shelter, the inevitable squabbles began over space: 'Shift yourself, Hawthorne! ... Shift your butt! ... Move over, you're squashing my arm!...'

In the end David and Philip got the prime estate in the middle while the juniors were banished to the less comfortable outer extremities. Bill took up station crouching at the entrance.

A falsetto squeal from John: 'COR, THIS IS WICKED!'

'Shut up! The enemy will hear you!'

446

Bill looked outside: 'OK. No commies in the area. We can have our scoff now.'

'Scoff?'

'Yes, emergency rations.'

He burrowed in his rucksack and produced some Mars bars, dry biscuits, bars of chocolate and handfuls of raisins, which he duly distributed.

'Scoff this lot, but be quiet about it and hand the wrappers back to me.'

A long silence followed. A strong sun beat down on the little shelter and bright blue showed in the gap between the two ponchos.

'This is dead boring,' declared David eventually. 'How long do we have to stay here?'

'We'll move out at four hundred hours tomorrow morning.'

'Fucking hell. Bill, it's not yet five o'clock! That's nearly ten bloody hours!'

'So what? The SAS often spend days in their OPs. On Pebble Island they spent a whole week just sitting there observing the Argies.'

'More fool them!'

'No it's good military discipline... Shhhhhhh!'

They heard the sound of human voices getting louder and coming nearer. As they huddled together with thumping hearts, John's adrenalin flowed fast and furious. This was as good as last night's raid on the farm. The voices grew louder and then faded away. Everybody relaxed.

'That was a near thing!'

Another long silence followed.

The Inconvenience of Nature... 'Against the rules of the National Park to foul the mountains'...

Then for John the worst happened.

A looming catastrophe swelled up and threatened to ruin everything and reduce all his achievements to a squalid ridicule. He needed the bog, Martin-style, and ever more desperately as each agonising minute passed. With all the upheavals and dramas of the day, he'd forgotten about his 'morning constitutional', that daily event of whose cardinal importance his wonderful and perfect gran had so forcibly insisted. Now, with the large morning breakfast, the vigorous exercise and the recent voluminous intake of Bill's 'scoff', the internal traffic was on the move in a big way. He tried to ignore it, but it was no good. With each passing second more traffic piled up...

He screwed himself up for the confession: 'Please, Bleeson, I need the bog!'

'Well, you'll just have to wait. You can't move with the enemy all around us.'

'But I'm *bursting*!'

Giggles from Philip and David.

'All right,' said Bill fishing in his rucksack, 'You can pee into this empty coke bottle. It's what the SAS do.'

'But I need the *real* bog, you know with paper...'

'Well, you'll just have to hold your fire.'

'Oh God, I *can't* ... I'm desperate!'

Faced with a quite unimaginable catastrophe, John began to whimper: 'Oh God! Oh God!'

'Oh for Christ's sake, let him go!' hissed David. 'If he goes and shits himself, Mekon'll blow another fit on us. You heard what he said about looking after the little kids.'

Bill relented: 'All right, Denby, permission to crap granted. Out you go, but don't let the enemy see you.'

Immensely relieved, John scrambled out into the brilliant sunshine. Where to go? He'd never done this sort of thing before. It had never occurred to him that it might ever be necessary. After all, what had Henry V done at Agincourt? The history books didn't tell you about that sort of thing, and, if you asked the teachers, they blew a fit on you. But he had to make a quick decision. Stumbling out of the rocky fortress, he found himself on a great sweep of open hillside with no obvious hiding places. But there was no time for niceties. Then and there, he heaved down his breeches and his underpants.

To his immense relief, everything slid out of him without any embarrassing noises. Catastrophe averted! Conscious now of the unaccustomed cold on his nether region, he became aware of another problem.

He called over to the basher: 'Has anybody got any bog paper?'

Loud giggles erupted.

'Use your finger and lick it!'

'Get Dolly to wipe your bum for you!' sneered David. 'That's what she usually does for her little pet, doesn't she!'

That stung: 'Shut up, Robson! I got the walloping off Mekon that you should have had! And I didn't cry like that wimp Nolan, either!'

'Quiet!' shouted Bill. 'Denby use the grass, that's what the Paras do. Major Allen says...'

There was no suitable grass in the immediate vicinity, so he waddled over to a nearby tussock with his shirt held up and his breeches round his knees, a sort of shuffling motion that reminded him of a three-legged race at Rickerby Hall – God, if anybody was to see him like this! There he took a clump of grass and used it, eying the mess with utter revulsion. Why did God have to invent crap? Surely there was a better and less nasty-smelling way of doing things. He'd mention it the next time he said his prayers.

Suddenly, a cultivated South Country voice brayed out from behind him: 'Young man, what *do* you think you're doing?'

Appalled, he swung round, dropping his breeches round his ankles. A large man was staring angrily at him. Impeccably dressed in a Gore-Tex cagoule, grey climbing breeches, black gaiters and shiny brown boots, he looked exactly like the tailor's dummy in the Mountain Adventure Emporium. His thick, horn-rimmed glasses and neatly trimmed beard gave him an alarming air of 'official authority'. Beside him was a mousy-haired little woman, equally well dressed and draped with whistles, compasses and shiny plastic map cases. Her pointy face was screwed up into an expression of intense 'official disapproval'.

John was speechless with horror – God, he's seen my bum and my crap! The awful shame of it! An abortive attempt to pull up his breeches merely resulted in getting them tangled up with his boots.

'Well, come on,' said the man. 'You've just done a thoroughly dirty and irresponsible act. Don't you know it's against the rules of the National Park to foul the mountains?'

John continued to gape and blush bright scarlet.

'Well, explain yourself.'

More red-faced silence.

At length, Bill emerged from the basher: 'Excuse me, Sir, he's with me. It's all right.'

'That's exactly what it isn't. Are you a school party? Where's your teacher?'

'Our teacher isn't here. He's at Styhead Tarn.'

'And he left you *children* all on your own?' exclaimed the woman.

'Yes, because we're on an army exercise.'

'That's no excuse!' she replied with venom. 'Children should not be abandoned by teachers on dangerous mountains! Don't you know that it's illegal for children to go on to mountains without an adult leader who holds a Mountain Leadership Certificate?'

'Malcolm,' she continued, turning to the man, 'this is a matter for the police. I think I'd better record the incident for possible use as evidence...'

With that, she whipped out a small camera and, as a frantic John desperately tried to conceal the bits of him that mattered, she took a photograph.

'You children wait here,' the man said to Bill. 'We're going down to Wasdale to inform the police. The Mountain Rescue will come up and escort you down to safety.'

'And *you*, young man,' he added, pointing to John, 'are going to have some explaining to do!'

'But... But... I couldn't help it!'

Ignoring the pleas, the couple strode briskly down the track.

'We'll have to report this incident to the Education Authorities,' said Malcolm, 'It's lucky we happened to be around. Those children could have died of hypothermia...'

'Precisely!' said his wife. 'And allowing a child to pollute the mountain like that! The very idea! I can't say that I liked the look of him either. By the way he spoke he was probably from some moneyed private school. Obviously, he thinks he can do as he likes!'

'Well,' replied Malcolm, 'when all this comes out, he'll be singing a different tune!'

They both worked for local government in a London borough, he in educational administration, and she as an 'Inter-Ethnic-Cross-Cultural Coordinator for Child Abuse Awareness'. Their remit was 'a pro-active improvemental role', an important part of which was 'limiting the abuse of children by teachers'. This was just the kind of scoop they needed. Accolades, recognition, promotion ... and a juicy increase in salary... It all beckoned.

The Brotherhood of the Hunted

A crestfallen John was finally able to pull up his breeches.

'I'm terribly sorry, Bleeson!' he gasped, 'I couldn't help it!'

The encounter had touched Bill on a very tender spot. 'Illegal for *children* to go onto mountains...?' Bloody hell, he was a *lad*! He wasn't a *child*! *And* he'd done three years in the Army Cadet Force.

He'd got all the badges... This was his big day. Wait till the Mountain Rescue came? Hell *no*! His whole being as Sergeant Bill Bleeson of the ACF and head boy of Beaconsfield School was at stake. His blood was up.

'Don't worry, Denby,' he said. 'It wasn't your fault. I authorized the crap and as an officer I am responsible for my men. You're a great lad!'

John glowed with pride.

Bill marched over to the basher: 'Men, we've been spotted by the Reds. They'll be alerting Moscow and calling in a Spetsnaz unit with helicopter gunships...'

'Jesus Christ!' exclaimed David. 'What *are* you on about, Bleeson? Stop playing soldiers like a little kid and talk sense!'

'No, Robson, this is serious. A couple of mongs spotted Denby while he was having his crap. They said we weren't allowed to be here and they're going to get the Mountain Rescue to take us in and hand us over to the police. And, by the way, the Mountain Rescue *do* have helicopters. I've read about it in my *Mountain Leadership* book.'

'The fuzz after us?' cooed David. 'That's more like it! Now it's a *real* escape! Come on, let's get moving!'

'Yeah!' echoed Philip. 'This is great!'

An idea germinated in Bill's mind. 'That bloke', he declared, 'was probably a right bender. I mean looking at Denby while he was having a crap! I bet he followed him deliberately, just to have a good look...'

'Yeah!' added David, grinning wickedly, 'just to have a good look at his bum!'

'And that woman actually took a photograph of Denby's dick!' continued Bill.

'That proves it then!' chortled David, hugely enjoying the escalating scenario, 'They were deliberately following him to get photos for a porno mag.'

'Whooooah!' cried Philip with a lascivious leer, 'you're going to be a star now, Denby boy! Front cover of *Gay News*!'

Hovering on the edge of the conversation, John was bewildered: 'What's a bender? What's *Gay News*? I don't get it...'

'Shall I tell him, Bleeson?'

'Certainly not!' declared Bill sententiously. 'We don't corrupt little kids in the ACF. Major Allen hates benders!'

'I see,' giggled David. 'Keep 'em pure! It's easier that way!'

'Shut up! This is not funny. It's deadly serious, in case you didn't know it!'

The scenario was rapidly enlarging in Bill's mind. 'It won't be the Mountain Rescue they'll be getting,' he said solemnly, 'they'll be alerting their homosexual friends and bringing them up...'

'I get you!' said Philip, grinning broadly. 'If they catch us, we'll all get shafted!'

'Exactly! Major Allen says that homosexuals form secret bands that follow youth groups and prey on them. It's all part of a plot by the KGB to undermine Britain...'

Saving his charges from the evil clutches of Marxist-inspired homosexuals – that dark conspiracy that his hero, Major Allen, was always banging on about! How Bill just wallowed in the idea! He now had a serious purpose. 'This escape's for *real*!' he declared. 'We've got to move out quickly and leave no traces behind us. If they find out who were really are, we could be in the shit!'

Michael and John were nonplussed by the whole business. But not Sam. Disastrously dyslexic and dysfunctional, a real basket case and generalised disaster area ... yes! But in some areas he was wise beyond his years.

A bond of shared adversity and adventure now united the disparate little group – the Brotherhood of the Hunted. John could almost touch its warm inclusiveness as, quickly and efficiently, they dismantled their shelter and packed everything away.

Weighed down by their rucksacks, the little band of fugitives stumbled off into the brilliant sunshine. Immediately, John was struck by the mountain grandeur. By now the last of the mists had dissolved and there before him, bold and dramatic, was a great amphitheatre of towering crags, such as he had never seen before. Surging upwards in an anarchy of twisted rock, every minute wrinkle was sharply illuminated in the clear light of the late afternoon.

'Cor, look at THAT!' he exclaimed in an awed voice.

'Shut up, Denby!' snapped Bill. 'Silence on patrol!'

They followed the path down into a deep valley. The long summer day was slowly dying and there were no hikers left. They were alone in the silent mountain magnificence. Bill stopped for a while.

'If we stay in this valley,' he whispered, 'they're sure to find us.'

He studied the slopes on the far side of the stream in front of them. The massive crags of Scafell plunged down into a chaos of screes and boulders, but further down the valley they relented and merged into a steep rocky hillside covered with carpets of green ferns.

'We'll skirt the bottom of that cliff,' he finally said, 'and then strike up that slope there. When we reach the top we'll find somewhere to lie low until it gets dark. Then we'll head for Wastwater. Come on, we've got to hurry.'

They left the path, splashed over the stream and attacked the great sweep of mountainside in front of them. After the path the going was anything but easy. It was a muddle of big, mossy rocks, partially hidden beneath a jungle of overhanging ferns. You were always tripping up and getting your foot jammed in some rocky crevice. Puffing and gasping they struggled upwards.

'Hang on! I'm knackered!'

'Give me time to get my breath back!'

'I can't keep up with you!'

'Come ON! They'll be here soon!'

Gasping for breath, they finally reached the crest of the slope and found themselves confronted with a broad sweep of tussocky grass which swept down to the wooded shores of Wastwater. Utterly different from the craggy grandeur of the valley they'd left, it was open and empty with not a hiding place anywhere.

'Just like Goose Green,' observed Bill, screwing his face up into an intense professional frown. 'No cover. Even if they don't have helicopters, they'd soon spot us if we tried to cross that. We'll have to wait till it gets dark.'

'There's plenty of hiding places back there,' said Philip helpfully. 'Look among those ferns and rocks. We'd never be seen there.'

'Good on you, Phil!' said Bill. 'Right, lads, over there.' The warm bonds of the shared adventure encouraged intimacy and Christian names. Things were changing.

They moved over into a small hollow full of mossy boulders and tussocky grass and covered by waist-high ferns. Removing their rucksacks, they lay down on the warm, dry ground beneath the green canopy.

'This is ideal,' said Bill, 'we'll just check the perimeter...'

They crawled up to the rim of the hollow and, peering through the lattice of ferns, scanned the broad rocky valley that they'd just left. It was empty and peaceful.

'Wait till the Dark Riders come!' whispered John. It was all too good to be true – a real live adventure with the possibility of the odd hobbit or wizard to add the final touches.

They crawled back to the hollow. Bill rummaged in his rucksack and produced a large bottle of water and a small cardboard box.

'What's this?'

'Hexamine stove like they had in the Falklands. It burns with a smokeless flame so you don't give your position away to the enemy.'

He opened the box and extracted a small metal frame and some white, waxy blocks which he crumbled and laid on the frame. Then he produced a plastic mug and a much larger cardboard box.

'What's this?'

'Army compo rations. Twenty-four-hour ration pack... We're having a brew.' Pulling out a mess tin, he poured water from his water bottle into it and lit the little heap of crumbled white blocks on the frame with some matches he extracted from a polythene bag in his pocket. Soon the water was bubbling merrily. Then, opening the big cardboard box, he produced a pile of goodies – packets of cocoa, packets of sugar, packets of biscuits, tins of jam, tins of baked beans and tins of fruitcake...

There, under the vast empty dome of the evening sky, they gorged themselves. John was in paradise: 'Thanks a bomb, Bill! This is magic!'

'But where did you get all this army stuff?' he added.

'From the ACF.'

'What's that?'

'The Army Cadet Force. They train kids in army things.'

'Can I join?'

'How old are you?'

'Eleven, but I'll be twelve at the end of the month.'

'You're a bit young, but, you know, you're a good lad. A bit daft, but you've got guts. I'll have a word with Major Allen.'

John glowed and felt six inches taller.

Bill assiduously fed Sam and Michael while Philip and David became increasingly protective of them. The group was bonding ever more closely together. The Brotherhood of the Hunted. A richly warm sensation.

The day finally died in a flourish of visual splendour. For a final few moments the wrinkled complexities of the ancient, eroded mountains burst into life as the slanting rays of the sun caught them for the last time. Then came a fiery red and a deep, rich blue. One by one the stars appeared as the muffled silence of the gloaming covered the darkening land. Again, John experienced that surge of emotion which he could hardly understand, let alone articulate. He only had an awareness of a vague something that was altogether grander than himself – that hint of a Beyond World.

A blue darkness enveloped them. David wriggled up to Bill: 'Hey, take a look at what's going on down in the valley!'

Hearts thumping, they crept up to the rim of the hollow and peered through the ferns. Just discernible on the path below was a line of dark figures with the odd yellow torch stabbing the gloom.

'The Dark Riders!' whispered John.

'Shhhhhh! They'll hear you!'

Bill pulled a small pair of binoculars out of his cagoule pocket: 'It's those benders who jumped us! Christ, there's a whole crowd of them! ... They've even got stretchers...'

'So we'll *all* get shafted!' sniggered David. 'Watch your bums, lads!'

'Shhhh!'

'We'd better scarper!'

'No! Lie absolutely still until they've gone!'

'Cor, this *is* nifty!' whispered John as they all huddled together.

From the gloom below them came the sound of voices calling and whistles blowing. Finally, the noises died away.

'Right,' whispered Bill, 'they've gone to search the basher and the surrounding area. Now let's move away quietly... No noise.'

They crawled slowly over the crest of the ridge.

'Keep down!' hissed Bill. 'Don't skyline! They'll see you!'

Safely on the far side, they stood up and set off over the vast grey emptiness of the moor before them, carefully testing each step and pausing at intervals to listen for any sounds of their pursuers. It was wonderfully exciting – the darkness, the cool night air, the sense of escaping from a lurking danger.

Eventually, the black wall of the woods loomed up ahead of them, silent and sinister, as if it were alive and waiting for them.

'Suppose we went in there and don't never come out again,' whispered Michael nervously. 'You know, became rocks or summat?'

'Shhhh!' Bill cautioned him.

'Now, listen to me,' he added. 'There's a wall here. We're getting over it and finding a place to kip. No noise!'

'But what if there's an old tramp in there what kills kids?' said Michael.

'I'd like to see him try. There's six of us. We'd soon sort him out, no sweat! Come on, David, I'll give you a lift up!'

The wall wasn't high and they had little trouble hauling themselves over it. As they entered the pitch-black chaos of the wood the three juniors huddled together.

'God, this is scary!' whispered Michael. 'I bet there's something there looking at us... You know waiting for us, like!'

'Piss off, Michael!' hissed John. 'You're making me scared too!'

After a short time their way was barred by an unseen prickly trellis of a thing. 'OK, lads,' whispered Bill, 'we'll kip down here ... and if you little kids are scared of the dark, you kip in the middle and we big men will kip on the outside...' (His successful essay in leadership was making him protective and paternal – the juniors were *his* troops now.)

The ground was mossy and dry. Soon they were bedded down in their sleeping bags with their plastic bivvi bags adding extra insulation.

'We must use our own body heat to keep warm and protect against hypothermia,' said Bill knowingly as they huddled closely together.

The close proximity of friendly bodies was more than just a matter of warmth, however, for the three juniors. It was reassurance. Protection from the unseen and unspoken things that they knew lurked in dark places at night.

Blissful Morning

John couldn't sleep. Once more he was too hyped up. What a day! The longest day in his life. It had begun in shame and degradation, but that had been expunged by honesty and courage. ('Cor, John, you really is rock hard...') He had re-established himself with his hero, Mekon; he had proved himself on the mountain, shown himself to be 'a proper lad' ... and now this glorious adventure and sense of oneness with the seniors. The pathetic little Greenhill creature was gone for ever.

Eventually the morning came. He watched its silent, unfolding majesty with a religious awe.

Slowly, very slowly, the black void around him dissolved. First a deep-purple sky began to appear above a framework of branches and leaves, then out of the darkness twisted old trees emerged, then boulders and clumps of grass. Again, he had that sensation of being present at a biblical creation in which things emerged inexplicably out of nothingness. And that sense of resurrection and rebirth as the warm rays of the rising sun poked their golden fingers into the mossy depths of the wood – the very breath of God which created life.

Soon Bill was in his element, filling his mess tin with water from a nearby stream, dropping in the requisite purification tablets, playing around with his Hexamine stove and producing yet another twenty-four-hour ration pack from the depths of his rucksack... Mugs of sugary cocoa followed along with biscuits, butter, strawberry jam and tins of baked beans. A glorious feast in the warm, enclosing depths of the wood... Comradeship, the Brotherhood of the Hunted.

'Now then,' said Bill when everything had been packed tidily away, 'before we start, you should answer your call of nature – you especially, John.'

Sniggers rippled through the group.

'It's not funny! Major Allen says that soldiers on active service must never forget to let nature take its course. You can't beat nature. We don't want a repetition of yesterday, John. In the army you'd have been put on a charge.'

John duly availed himself of the opportunity – it was back to normal in that area. Again, as he carefully buried the disgusting mess, he wondered why God hadn't thought of a better way of organising things.

'A credit to your school'

In the sharp light of the early morning they stumbled through the woods, scrambled over a wall and walked briskly along a road which led them to the rendezvous point where a bridge crossed a fast flowing river.

All around them everything was calm and friendly. The clear blue sky, the green wrinkled mountains with their grey crags, the vast, empty sweep of the lake: at this early hour they had it all to themselves and it seemed to be confiding in them, whispering words of encouragement: 'Well done! Welcome to the brotherhood. You're part of us now.'

When they reached the bridge Bill became emotional and shook each one of them warmly by the hand: 'Well done, men! Good show!' (It was a conscious imitation of Major Allen after a successful night operation during last summer's camp.) Once more, John glowed with pride and satisfaction.

A long boring wait began. Eventually, the three juniors began to play in the river, constructing a mini dam out of stones.

Suddenly, a police car drove up and stopped. Philip and David stood gaping at the side of the road while the juniors dived behind a nearby bush. Downcast and nervous, Bill approached the big, burly policeman who climbed out and shut the door. His triumph seemed to have been shattered – leaving behind an incomprehensible debris of accusation and blame. Why? He'd tried to do everything right – and he *had* succeeded, hadn't he? In Meakin's and Major Allen's eyes, *yes*! But in the eyes of those two mongs last night he was a bloody delinquent! What *was* a bloke supposed to do?

Yet, oddly enough, the policeman was smiling and friendly. 'Are you the school party that was bivouacking on Scafell Pike last night?' he asked.

'Yes we are,' mumbled Bill. (Confess! No escape now, you're caught!)

'All right, no need to panic. You haven't done anything wrong – at least not as far as I know. Your teacher, Mr Meakin, asked me to check that you were all safe, that's all. And it seems that you are... By the way, can I have a quick look at your kit?' There was nothing that Bill would have liked better. 'Come on out, lads!' he called. 'Bloke here wants to do a kit inspection!'

Out it all came – the bivvi bags, the sleeping bags, the maps, the compasses, the Hexamine stove, the emergency rations, the first-aid kit ... each item lovingly decorated with its correct military name ... and finally the pièce de résistance: 'Here's the bin liner containing all our rubbish. Nobody will ever know that we've been there. That's the way the SAS do things, isn't it?'

The policeman was suitably impressed: 'Yes, I can see that you're properly equipped and thoroughly sensible. Well done, you're a credit to your school. If only everybody was as sensible as you...'

He drove off leaving Bill radiant with pride: 'It's all right, lads! Nothing to worry about. He's just been sent by Mekon to see that we're all right. And he thinks we're bloody marvellous, too!'

John, also, swelled with pride.

Triumph, But Is 'Nothing ever simple with these kids?'

Eventually, amid clapping and cheering, the minibus drove up.

'There, Jamie lad!' exclaimed a beaming Meakin, 'they're all alive and kicking! I told you they'd be all right.'

'They've been lucky this time,' replied an unsmiling Briggs. 'I'll grant you that.' As he climbed out of the driving seat and marched over to greet his protégés, Meakin became emotional: 'Well done, lads! Very well done! I knew you could do it!'

To their intense embarrassment, he embraced and hugged each one of them.

'What's got into the old man?' whispered David. 'Has he gone doolally or something?'

'Senile decay I'd say,' replied Philip. 'He's long past his sell-by date. Really should be joining my gran in the old people's home.' (What none of the youngsters could grasp was the sheer intensity of Meakin's relief. After all the staffroom politics and despite the constant drip, drip, drip of Briggs' negativity, he'd won through in the end. His gamble had paid off. His little band hadn't let him down and he felt profoundly – indeed, gushingly – pleased with them.)

They cooked a large breakfast, cleared everything away and then had a wild game of football. ('Just to burn off any excess anarchy that might still be lurking in the woodwork.')

As the minibus finally lumbered off, a police car appeared and ordered them to stop. Meakin's euphoria dissolved in a puff of smoke. (Oh, bloody hell, did I speak too soon? Not *another* bloody stupid incident?)

'Yes,' he sighed as he walked over to the policeman (a different one this time). 'And what have my young beauties been up to now?'

'Don't you worry,' the policeman replied, 'you're in the clear. You did all the right things and your lads behaved excellently. But unfortunately we had a couple of people calling out the Mountain Rescue last night...'

'Christ! I *told* you they'd be sleeping out on the hill...'

'I know you did, but they wouldn't listen and insisted that they were all dying of cold... They went and telephoned the Mountain Rescue... They weren't exactly overjoyed to spend half the night on a wild-goose chase, I can tell you.'

'Some people!'

'I agree, but I thought I'd better tell you in case there's a stink. You know what lawyers are...'

'What was all that about?' asked Briggs as Meakin climbed back into the driving seat.

'Just checking that everything's all right...'

Meakin sighed to himself. More complications to be sorted out. When they got back to school he'd have to have a session with Bill to find out just what *had* happened. Was *nothing* ever simple with these kids?

The Hero Returns to a Mixed Reception

That evening a muddy and triumphant John lugged his rucksack down Gloucester Road.

For a long time nobody answered the door. The muffled throb of pop music thumping out into the warm sunshine indicated that the usual Sunday night 'seminar' was in full swing at Number 14.

After nearly ten minutes of ringing the doorbell, a clothed, but dishevelled, Mary flung open the door: 'YOU? What the fuck are you doing here? I thought you were away for the weekend.'

'But...' Faced with the 'analytical stare' words failed him.

'What's the problem, Mary?' Giles' voice boomed out through the clouds of funny-smelling smoke and over the buzz of conversation and thumping music.

'John's here... You said he was away for the weekend.'

'Oh, sorry, I must have forgotten to tell you that he'd be back on Sunday.'

'Thank you for nothing! What are we going to do about Mervyn and Judith?'

'I'll sort that out.'

Giles levered himself up off the floor and, disentangling himself from the muddle of arms and legs around him, climbed purposefully up the ladder.

Mary turned to John: 'Just look at the state of you! I hope you're not expecting *me* to wash those things for you! And watch where you're putting your muddy feet! Those rugs are valuable, you know!'

Back to normal. As soon as he entered this house he changed, not from a princess into a housemaid in that soppy Cinderella story (ugh!) but from a big, bold lad into a pathetic little retard.

The conversation had died down and he found a crowd of weirdoes looking at him – beards, bangles, ponytails, scruffy denim suits. In the throng he recognised Martha, the big, fat lady who had been so nice to him that weekend when he'd first arrived.

'Ah, John!' she cooed, 'how wonderful to see you again! Come over and tell me all about yourself.'

That was exactly what John wanted to do. He waddled over to her and, dumping his wet rucksack – muddy stains and all – on the 'meaningful Ethiopian shamma', squeezed himself next to her. Surrounded by a circle of curious onlookers, he flashed his ingratiating smile.

'Great to see you again!'

'Yes, I've missed you!' she cooed, giving him a warm hug (and how he loved that!). 'Now do tell me what you have been doing.'

'I've been to the Lake District. It was wicked! We climbed the highest mountain in England and then we had to escape from the communists!'

'Communists?' Puzzled frowns all around.

'Yes, they were benders and we had to do a runner. And then there was a farmer who used dirty language...'

Out came the fat lady's notebook: 'Benders? Now tell me more...'

But before he could say anything Giles came down the ladder, angry and scowling: 'All right, John, your room's free. Up you go now – quickly!'

A groan of disappointment: 'Awwwww! Can't I stay and talk to this nice lady? Please!'

'No, John, you can't. We've got important things to discuss.'

He marched over and, gripping his son firmly by the right arm, hauled him to his feet: 'Now pick up your things and off to bed. And for God's sake wash these mucky clothes before Mary gets annoyed. It's *your* responsibility, not hers.'

As he clambered up the ladder, John seethed with resentment. Sent up to bed like a little kid who'd been naughty. It was so embarrassing! And why *shouldn't* he talk to that nice Martha woman? It wasn't fair!

In his room he found his bed all crumpled up and the duvets strewn across the floor, along with a litter of fag ends and empty fag packets. A half-empty gin bottle was on top of the television. He seethed again. Why was it wrong for kids to smoke and drink when grown-ups did it? Grown-ups weren't just dorks: they were hypocrites, too.

Extracting himself laboriously from his hiking things, he went down to the bog, carrying his muddy climbing breeches and his cagoule. If he didn't want a mega-bollocking, he'd better do as Giles had said and wash his things.

After his precautionary pee (that nightly ritual inherited from the old days at Oaktree Gardens), he filled the basin with hot water and put the offending objects into it. He was staring at the glutinous black mush that ensued, not knowing quite what to do with it, when there was a frantic hammering on the door. Hurriedly he opened it and a long, skinny woman in a funny Indian-type dress pushed past him.

'Can you leave, please?' she said in a commanding voice. 'I need the bathroom.'

Leaving the mephitic mess in the basin, he promptly obeyed and the woman locked the door. He waited for a while for her to come out, but when she didn't he clambered back up to his room. There he changed into his pyjamas and lay down on his bed.

Suddenly, he was overwhelmed by an immense tiredness. The hard exercise and the two sleepless nights caught up with him and he fell into a deep, dreamless sleep.

38

Monday was another of those crazy up-and-down, triumph-and-disaster days.

He woke up to see the brilliant summer sunshine flooding in through the skylight. His legs were achy and his feet were sore, but at the same time he felt rested and refreshed. As the events of the weekend came back to him he felt a rich contentment. He'd won through on all sides, not only by proving himself a lad, but also by impressing Mekon by climbing Scafell Pike and surviving the Great Escape. His gran and granddad would be proud of him as they looked down from heaven. Also, though he could scarcely understand it, he'd had a glimpse of something majestic and wonderful, far beyond himself.

But, looking round the room, he came down to earth with a bump. Scattered among the relics of last night's disgusting grown-up goings-on – the overflowing ashtrays, the fag ends on the floor and that half-empty gin bottle on top of the television – was the detritus of his adventure – muddy boots, sweaty socks, repulsive underpants, a soggy rucksack full of heaven alone knew what mouldering horrors... All of it ominous premonitions of impending humiliations. A simple bollocking was the least of his worries. It was the slaps and punches – if not worse – that might lurk behind that bollocking. Mere survival meant attacking that mess.

He went down to the bog. It was strewn with empty fag packets and plastic bags. There was even a medical syringe lying on the floor. God alone knew what weird things had been going on here! His climbing breeches and his cagoule were still in the basin floating in their lake of liquid mud, but, to his utter disgust, he noticed that somebody had been sick all over them.

Retching, he extracted his garments and dumped the sodden pile into the bath. Several sloshings with hot water removed the worst of the spew, but the mass of glutinous mud remained obstinately intractable.

Temporarily abandoning the struggle, he went back to his room to collect his socks and his underpants. Returning, he found the bog occupied, so he went down to the ground floor. What he saw reminded him of a photograph in his *Battle for the Falkland Islands* magazine which showed Port Stanley after the Argies had been booted out – a wilderness of fag ends, empty glasses, overflowing ashtrays, gin bottles, wine bottles and dirty plates, full of some half-eaten mush that looked like dog sick. There was no sign of either Mary or Giles, so he crept over to the kitchen area.

The sink was crammed full of greasy plates and wine glasses, all swimming round in cold, scummy water. Removing these could cause a major volcanic eruption, so he simply squirted some washing-up liquid on to his socks and underpants and started to rinse them out alongside them. Suddenly, he glanced at his watch. It was past eight o'clock! If he didn't get a move on, he'd be late for school – and, in view of the delicate diplomacy needed to placate Mrs Watson after the 'Farmer Affair', lateness was a luxury he could not afford.

Leaving his socks and underpants to soak among the dirty dishes, he scuttled back to his room, dressed, picked up his bag and dashed down again. There, sprawled stark naked over the settee, he found Mary, gazing at him with an aggressive, misty-eyed stare. It was far too dangerous to try to remove the offending articles from the sink, so he scurried out into the street. With any luck she was so far gone that she wouldn't notice what was there.

A Big Bold Lad

At school the squalid little retard became a big bold lad.

As he went into morning assembly a grinning Danny Fleetwood accosted him: What's this about you breaking into a farmhouse and being shot at by a farmer?'

Billy Nolan had been at work and the 'Farmer Affair' had lost nothing in the telling. They'd also had to fend off a pack of mad dogs, foaming at the mouth with rabies.

'And is it true that you were chased over the mountains by a bunch of sex-mad benders?'

David Robson had been at work and the 'Great Escape' was becoming the stuff of legend.

'I wish I'd come,' sighed Fred. 'You seem to have had a great time.'

After the hymn and prayers came the announcements. Ominously, Mrs Watson was in 'stern headmistress' mode: 'Mr Meakin tells me that the Adventure Weekend has been a great success... Plus marks are given to Bill Bleeson, David Robson, Philip Lawson, Michael Connolly and Sam Hawthorne...' (But not to John Denby. Ominous development. Cold shiver down the spine ...)

'...Unfortunately, the weekend was very nearly ruined by some silly behaviour on Friday night... Can I see Billy Nolan, Martin Davidson and John Denby in my study immediately after assembly...' (Doom! Oh Lord, another execution!)

Necessary Diplomacy

Silently, the three malefactors filed into Mrs Watson's study.

The X-ray eyes bored into them from behind the desk: 'Well, what have you got to say for yourselves?'

Silence. (You never get far with these sort of questions.)

'I've just had the farmer on the phone. Not the sort of message I like to receive first thing on a Monday morning. Do you realise that you very nearly wrecked the whole weekend? Mr Meakin was in two minds about cancelling it.'

Silence.

Then a withering outburst: 'Mr Meakin went to an enormous amount of trouble ... and all you could do was play the fool and let him down! THAT'S SIMPLY NOT GOOD ENOUGH!'

Stony silence from Martin and Billy. An impasse.

John realised – though the others clearly didn't – that a symbolic surrender was needed to restore the situation. And he *was* full of remorse. He knew he'd landed old Mekon in the shit. So when the tears began to trickle he made no attempt to stop them.

Sob, snivel, sob: 'I'm terribly sorry, Miss. I just got a bit over-excited...'

Abject surrender. Grovel in front of victorious enemy. Required gesture made. Mrs Watson switched off the X-ray eyes and became normal:

'But it's all water under the bridge now. You've all had your punishment from Mr Meakin and I gather that you all redeemed yourselves by behaving well afterwards – especially you, John. Bill Bleeson speaks very highly of you...' (Mission successful. Back in favour. 'Turning on the taps' has its uses if employed in moderation and at the right strategic moment...)

'...But before you get your plus marks I want you to write a letter of apology to the farmer. I think you'd better do that, John, since you were the one who shouted the swear words through the window. Join Mr Meakin's detention class at four o'clock and hand me the letter when it's finished...' (Also – hidden message between the lines! – you are the only one who's remotely literate, so it'll have to be you ...)

Glory

The rest of the school day was uninterrupted glory. He'd come top in all the exams – brilliant marks in History, Scripture and Geography... He'd even managed to get 80 per cent in the Maths exam. Polly went clucking round the classroom in a state of statistical ecstasy. ('...80 per cent! This only happens once every three years... A probability factor of...' 'Watch out, lads! He'll be losing all his feathers pretty soon...')

Passing a Maths exam for a change! That was a new development...

After lunch Meakin gathered the Escape Group together.

'No, it's not a roasting! Whatever you did manage to get up to that night hasn't reached me. And what the eye doesn't see, the heart doesn't grieve over... As far as I know you all behaved very well. The police were certainly most impressed... No, a friend of mine from the *Boldonbridge Journal* would like to do a story about you and take a photograph...'

They went into Meakin's classroom where the reporter was waiting.

'Now tell me all about your great adventure...'

Bill, as usual, was tongue-tied and so, garrulous as ever, John did most of the talking. Out it all came: training for guerrilla activity when the communists took over, dodging funny characters at night (but be careful not to use dirty words like 'benders'!) compo rations, brew-ups, the night in the woods...

'And Bill says he's going to speak to Major Allen so that I can join the Army Cadet Force...'

The photo was duly taken outside the school next to the 'Beaconsfield School' sign.

More Diplomacy

At four o'clock John joined the detention class and, under Mekon's eagle eye, wrote the prescribed letter:

> Dear Mr Farmer
> We are all very, very, very sorry that we were so silly and bad on Friday night. We are very, very, very, sorry about the dirty swearing. We know you never swear and we are all very ashamed... If you let us come back and camp on your beautiful farm we all promise to be very good...

Timorously, he presented it to Dolly and was rewarded with a big, warm smile.

'Well done, John... Now that's all behind you... Oh, don't keep on apologising. You don't need to tell me why you were silly... A little word of advice. If you want street cred, don't go down that path... You'll just get a bad reputation and, I'm afraid, you'll find that there will be more than enough people in the world wanting to do you down without you actively helping them... That's life! But, think positive.

You did very well on the mountain and I was really pleased that you helped people like Sam, Martin and Michael... I'm very pleased that you have done so well in the exams... But don't get big-headed. Because you're clever, I will expect you to come top – always!'

A big, warm hug. He had his mum again!

Home?

So back home a hero. A recital of his triumphs would surely offset any bollocking about the messy clothes. Anyway, given the mess the house was in, it was a bit rich if they started to create about a few muddy socks. At least rational grown-ups wouldn't... But the problem was that neither Giles – and certainly not Mary! – could be described as rational – at least not in the way that he understood the word!

However!

He rang the doorbell.

An irritated Giles opened the door.

'Dad. I mean Giles... I've come top in the exams and I'm going

to get my photo in the *Boldonbridge Journal*...' (Get in first, bury
the dirty underpants in the sink under a heap of 'glad tidings'...)

'Not now, John. I'm terribly busy...'

An Old Tape Revamped

What then unfolded was a rerun of that Monday evening after the
rugby match last October. All the old ingredients were there – a
frantically busy Giles beset with difficulties, a frustrated and foul-
tempered Mary, piles of muddy clothes – only enhanced, jazzed up,
sexed up, painted in more lurid colours.

The room was still the same old bombsite mess that John had
seen in the morning – perhaps a little worse because two of the
plates of dog-sick stew had been spilt over the expensive rugs. Giles
was obviously in an 'unexploded bomb' mood and best not handled,
so he went up to his room.

Losing Control? A Morass of Problems...

It was a wise move. Giles was extremely fraught. Indeed, almost for
the first time in his life, he was starting to feel that things were
sliding out of his control. However, his analytical mind came to the
rescue and itemised the problems.

Problem One: a mountain of exam scripts that had to be marked
by the end of the week. And, after last winter's contretemps, he
couldn't just put a line through the 'Broad Humanities' papers and
give them all the delta minus that they deserved. If he wanted to
avoid another of those ridiculous confrontations with old Jacobson,
he was going to have to go through Mark Jenkins' script with a
toothpick and be ready to explain precisely why – quoting chapter
and verse – he hadn't given him the alpha plus that the repulsive
toad seemed to think was his due... Talk about 'eating shit'.

Problem Two: the publisher was making increasingly shrill demands
for the corrected proofs of his monograph about the Liverpool
working class in World War II.

Problem Three: those BBC programmes about the evolution of the
British working class... Couldn't the bloody man see that he could
do nothing before the middle of July?

Problem Four: he still hadn't secured the nomination as Labour Party candidate in the forthcoming by-election. That lumbering old dinosaur George Dawes was continuing to bang on about 'working-class family values' (to give the nebulous concept its meaningless title!). Squaring the old fool meant squashing the 'upper-middle-class hippie' burr and presenting himself as a 'competent and caring family man...' Which, of course, led to...

Problem Five: Mary. This was more of a crisis than a mere problem. What had once been an all-consuming love affair had finally fizzled out. She was no longer the ravishingly lovely creature that had so bewitched him a decade ago. Drinking, smoking and what she called her 'enhanced awareness experimental explorations' had left their mark.

Worse still, she was now a liability that threatened his whole future. Any pretensions she might have had to academic respectability were now in shreds. Her book, *Liberated Child Development: The Bourgeoisie Destroyed in the Cradle* – so successful in the early Seventies – had been rubbished by a Ph.D. student. And not just rubbished either, but ripped apart and torn to shreds, each sloppy, unsubstantiated assertion exposed, every non-sequitor mercilessly analysed for all to see. It was now a standing joke. The Ph.D. thesis had still not materialised – and, by all accounts, never would.

Her lifestyle, her dramatic 'statements', once so groundbreakingly radical, now seemed like adolescent exhibitionism. She just couldn't connect with ordinary Labour voters.

Indeed, the only people she could connect with seemed to be the local Tories who positively adored her as a caricature of the 'Loony Left'. They'd invited her to Tory meetings as part of a 'public debate', which had resulted in frantic telephone calls from the Labour Party... 'With all this Falklands Island stuff, we can do without your wife antagonising our traditional supporters... They don't like upper-class hippies, you know...'

She was simply a case of arrested development, stuck in a time warp, still the adolescent student out to shock the fusty old establishment. Fine in the Sixties, but times had moved on.

Besides, he had now fallen deeply in love with Maggie Wright. Not only was she in the full bloom of unsullied maidenhood – those tits, that glorious bum, that soft, sensuous skin! – but she was an adult companion with whom it was possible to discuss things without rantings and tantrums. Mary was such a drag, always saying the same things over and over again, a cracked Sixties disc with the needle stuck in a groove.

The simple fact was that Mary belonged to the callow, youthful part of his life that he had outgrown. It was time for a change, time to slough off the mistakes of the past... And that led to the biggest mistake of all...

Problem Six: John. If only he'd insisted on Mary having that abortion! How much hassle that would have avoided! But it was no use crying over spilt milk. He was landed with the little creature. He was more than a mistake; he was a landmine that could blow everything apart. Ed Stimpson was continually demanding details about his progress at Greenhill and was grinding on about that interview with him which was to be the final chapter of his forthcoming seminal work, *The Destruction of the British Class System: A Revolution in the Classroom.* How could he possibly tell him that the little toerag had run away after barely two weeks and had been enrolled in a private school?

Then, lurking in the shadows like a serial killer, was Merrins. What did the little bastard have to do last night but make a beeline for her! God alone knew what the old witch had got him to say...

Yet, ludicrous as it was, he actually needed the little creep. He would have to convince bovine voters – blinded by Thatcher's militaristic jingoism in the Falkland Islands- – that he really was a normal, caring family man and not just the clapped-out hippie left over from the Sixties that the Tories would have them believe he was.

In particular, he needed a 'happy little boy' to parade in front of Dawes on Wednesday evening.

He surveyed the devastated room. It was worse than a student pad after a weekend orgy. If Dawes and his frowsy little wife should see it when they came round for supper...

He had hoped that Mary would see to it – bloody Christ, she had precious little else to do! But the merest hint had caused the predictable explosion.

'Little housewife does all the work? You're not into that again?'

'But, lovey. I've just *got* to get this marking done...'

And out had come the same old mantra – word for word – that he'd been hearing, off and on, for the past five years! Could she *never* think of anything new to say? Definitely time for a change...

Resentfully, he went on with marking the semi-literate morass of drivel that the 'Broad Humanities' students called their end-of-year exams.

Landmine!

On the landing outside the bathroom John ran into Mary.

'Mary! Mary! I've come top in the exams and...'

The sheer ferocity of the ensuing blast took him aback: 'HOW MANY TIMES HAVE I TOLD YOU NOT TO WASH YOUR SHITTY KNICKERS IN THE KITCHEN SINK?!'

Unwittingly, he had stepped on a landmine...

A Downward Spiral – Betrayal

Recently, Mary's life had been falling apart. It had been one thing after another in a relentlessly downward spiral.

For a long time she had been aware that Giles had changed. Slowly, by almost imperceptible stages, he had become more and more bourgeois. Always having to placate his 'superiors' at the university. Always having to make excuses for the Neanderthal attitudes of the local working class. 'Men only' bars, anti-Irish racism, the obsession with beer and football? 'Well, it's their culture and we must try to understand it...'

At those debates arranged by the local Tories she'd really blown her mind, rammed the whole 'radical alternative' down their petty-bourgeois gullets – and how the stuck-up little birdbrains had retched! In the old days Giles would have backed her to the hilt. But not now. Instead, he'd wittered on in a sulky way about 'student politics' and the 'pressing need' not to alienate 'potential middle-class voters'.

Neither had he backed her up when Damien Clark had made those vicious attacks on her seminal book, *Liberated Child Development: The Bourgeoisie Destroyed in the Cradle*, her pride and joy, her very self. He'd distanced himself from her with remarks like, 'I think you'd better handle this, not me...' What about that 'radical partnership'? Dead and buried, apparently – to use his favourite phrase, 'consigned to the dustbin of history'.

Nor had he continued to help her with her Ph.D. thesis. She'd amassed an enormous amount of material... All sorts of choice nuggets, not only about women's issues on Tyneside, but also about Acholi childrearing procedures in Uganda, Huron Indian views on sex, Iroquois attitudes to homosexuality, the Spanish anarchists of the 1930s ... all this and much more. But how to organise it all? It remained like a bombsite, an immense heap of rubble ... and her supervisor had been getting ever more shirty by the day. She desperately needed Giles' orderly mind to sort it out for her. But would he help? No way! At first, he'd made excuses about having 'too much work to do'. 'Next week, maybe.' Recently, however, he'd started getting onto his high horse about 'academic integrity' – sounding just like his ghastly old father when he'd started on religion.

All along the signs had multiplied. Now there was that little bitch, Maggie Wright. Originally, of course, their marriage had been a 'radical matrimonial statement' in which both partners were free to have sex with whoever – and whatever! – they wanted. And, indeed, she'd taken full advantage of the ensuing freedom – getting herself screwed, for example, by that gay little virgin Bill Baxter. Neither had she given a damn about Giles' playing around, jokingly comparing him to a tomcat rutting among the dustbins. But this business with Maggie Wright was altogether different – ominous and redolent of a major sea change. She was being supplanted – and that hurt.

It had all come to a head that morning. Having smoked her morning joint, she'd gone upstairs to dress. Coming back down again, she'd found Giles surveying the devastation of the living area.

'Darling, I'd be very grateful if you could sort this mess out. I've got George Dawes and his wife coming round on Wednesday and I must send out the right vibes...'

'Not him! Isn't it time you told that old fool to bugger off, told him, that is, in language that even he can understand? There's a new and better age coming. He's dead! Finished!'

'Maybe, but I still need his support in the constituency party. Look, I'm sure you'll understand...'

'Yes, I bloody understand all right! It's corruption. Compromise. Everything you once said you were against!'

'That was years ago.'

'And why the fuck should I do all the clearing up? What about you?'

'Please, I'm desperately busy...'

'Little housewife does all the work? You're into that again?'

'But, lovey, I've just *got* to get this marking done...'

'Well get your beloved Maggie to do the clearing up.'

'She can't. She's got her thesis to write up.'

'And what about *my* thesis? Doesn't that bloody matter?'

Giles had given her one of his hard, contemptuous looks: 'To be perfectly frank, it doesn't matter. It's getting nowhere. It's become a laughing stock. It's time you packed it in.'

A Bitter Blow

She'd stormed off to the university – only to be told by her supervisor that it really was time to chuck the whole thing in: '... Frankly, you're wasting everybody's time, including your own.'

It was a bitter blow.

Revolutionary Rage

When she'd come back home she'd ostentatiously ignored Giles. Engrossed in his exam scripts, he, too, had ignored her. Having popped a few pills and smoked a couple of joints, she'd gone over to the kitchen area to get a slug of vodka.

There in the sink, floating among the glasses she intended to use, were John's disgusting underpants...

The flames blazed up. The cheeky little berk! It was a deliberate, sneaky, underhand defiance of her specific instructions! That little beast had been nothing but trouble from the word go. He was everything she despised. Thick, snobbish, his mind – if you could even call that mishmash of infantile garbage a 'mind'! – was stuffed with all kinds of petty-bourgeois crap: trains, adventure stories, religion... He was a spoilt brat with ideas far above his station. As soon as he faced any real problems he yowled. Unable to cope with a real school, he'd run away and had to be sent to a private school – and, Christ, how embarrassing that had been!

It was all so unjust! Intelligent, meaningful people shouldn't have to waste time on children – especially squalid little retards like this one. That was what trained child-minders were for. No wonder she hadn't been able to concentrate on her thesis with this millstone round her neck. It was all very well for Dr Shanks to be dismissive about her thesis: that old bag didn't have a whingeing, messy little

473

disaster area to deal with morning noon and night. (She did have a Down syndrome daughter, but, well, that was different – proletarian and not fascist.)

High on the dope, reinforced with three glasses of neat vodka and seething like a superheated pressure cooker, she'd lurched up to John's room, ready for ... anything! What she found proved just how right her 'woman's instinct' had been. What a disaster area! Bed unmade, toy trains and bits of model railway lying all over the place, dirty clothes everywhere – shirts, socks, underpants, trousers... And, oh the fascist crap! *Biggles Defies the Swastika*, *The Ascent of Everest* by Colonel Hunt, 'Especially abridged for younger readers', *The Chronicles of Narnia* ... even a bloody bible!

Then she saw what was on the wall. That particular wall was the culmination of Al Dawson's meaningful decorative scheme, a seminal work of abstract art depicting the resolution of the dialectic through the Feminine Principle – what the *Guardian* had called a 'major radical statement for the late twentieth century'. But all over it the little fascist had plastered imperialist propaganda of the most banal militarist sort. A map of the Falkland Islands, pictures of Goose Green, a large photograph of that mercenary thug Colonel Jones. Suspended from the 'significant political metaphor' of the painted cistern pipes were plastic aeroplanes – a Hawker Harrier jump jet, a helicopter, an anti-imperialist Argentine Super Étandard obviously meant to be crashing in flames...!

Talk about desecration, statements of evil! It was the searing moment of truth.

Time for the countervailing radical statement! On the wings of righteous fury, filled with hyped-up revolutionary ardour, she ripped it all down and crushed the offending plastic aeroplanes to smithereens under her feet. Seeing a big blue toy train, the *Coronation Scot*, the very epitome of 1930s anti-socialist bourgeois exploitation of the working class, she kicked it against the wall and stamped on it till it, too, was in smithereens. The Barcelona anarchists burning down churches. Christ cleansing the Temple – for what was Christ but a socialist revolutionary hijacked by the Catholic Church for its own nefarious purposes?

Descending the ladder, she slipped into the bog ... and what should she see but John's filthy trousers floating in their sea of liquid mud.

Then she ran into the little fiend itself on the landing. That ghastly tinkle-bell voice... It was petrol thrown on to the conflagration.

Rebellion and Retribution

John cringed like a cornered mouse: 'I'm sorry, but I was in a hurry this morning...'

'YOU'RE NOT BLOODY SORRY! YOU DID IT DELIBERATELY! AND HAVE YOU SEEN THE STATE OF YOUR ROOM? HOW DARE YOU PLASTER YOUR INFANTILE CRAP OVER THE WALLS!' Full-blast megaphone shriek.

Doggedly, he tried to divert the current: 'I want to tell you that I've done very well in the exams...'

'Done very WELL?' she echoed with a sneer. 'Done very WELL? Don't give me that crap. That Beaconsfield place is just a dustbin for thicks.'

There was no point in arguing. As well to reason with a rampaging rhinoceros. With a resigned resentment he clambered up to his room.

But when he saw the wreckage that awaited him up there, that resentment blazed up into a blind fury. One after another the blows fell. His Falkland Islands display? Ripped to shreds. The precious Hawker Harrier jump jet that he was going to show Danny tomorrow morning? Smashed up on the floor ... And his pride and joy, his *Coronation Scot*, that blue-and-white engineering marvel of the 1930s? A tangled heap of debris beside the far wall, its casing cracked, its connecting rods twisted beyond recovery, its wonderful matching coaches shattered. Why? Why?

Tears came. Not baby tears of sorrow, but red-hot tears of blind fury – reckless, heedless of any consequences. Steaming, boiling, exploding, he scampered back down the ladder. Bursting into his parents' bedroom, he found Mary lying face down on the bed.

'MY PLANES! MY *CORONATION SCOT*! WHAT HAVE YOU DONE WITH THEM?' (High-pitched falsetto squeal. Once more the naked Zulu warrior charging the massed rifles of the British Army.)

She turned round and glared at him, her face full of contempt: 'Do you REALLY think that I'd allow all that fascist crap in my house? Do you know what was on that wall?'

'All my pictures!...'

'YOUR pictures? Jesus wept! One of the truly great paintings of our time, a real radical statement! And all you can do is plaster your infantile fascist crap all over it! You're so THICK!'

'I'm not thick! Mrs Watson says...'.

'Crap! You can't even use bog paper properly! Have you seen the state of your knickers? Like a baby's nappy!'

475

'That's all you can think of isn't it? Shit.'

Years later he was to describe her as a 'fantasising, sex-obsessed, coprophiliac, sociopathic fraud', but he hadn't learned those words yet. At this stage all he could manage was: 'You're a dirty old cow!'

That was too much for Mary. Would nothing bring this arrogant little birdbrain to heel? Would nothing ever puncture that iron-plated sense of superiority? Rising up, she slapped him across the face.

It hurt.

'OWWW!'

Bits of words and phrases whirled around in his mind like random fragments of a jigsaw puzzle. He flung what he could find at her: 'I HATE you! God hates you!'

'You're just like your horrible old grandfather, aren't you?' she snarled. 'God and all that!'

'He's not horrible! He's far better than you! He's in heaven listening to everything you say!'

'Crap! He's dead and gone! And good riddance!'

This was too much. Blasphemy. The most disgusting thing anybody could say. With all his strength he punched her in the stomach.

'AHHHH! You little shit!'

Retribution was immediate and devastating. She was bigger than him, far stronger, drugged up and filled with righteous fury. It wasn't a scruffy little boy in front of her. It was Fascism, Religion, Philistinism, the Oppression of Women, all those reactionary forces that had wrecked her life, a mighty dragon with which she, the feminist Saint George, was locked in mortal combat. She struck massive blows for the Good, straight into his insolent little face. WHAM! WHAM! WHAM!

Light flashed before him, intense pain and he felt blood streaming from his nose. No question now of 'not crying'. His body had taken over. 'WAHHHHHH! WAHHHH!'

Fists flailing Mary waded into the bawling wreckage: 'Right, I'm going to give you the hiding you have asked for!'

Wild terror now. He struggled free and dashed down the ladder. 'COME HERE!'

'I'M GOING TO THE POLICE! I'M TELLING THE SOCIAL SERVICES OF YOU!' High-pitched scream.

One Problem Solved

From his table Giles let out a cry of sheer exasperation: 'For Christ's sake, SHUT UP! I'm trying to do some work!'

Hearing the words 'police' and 'Social Services', however, the alarm went off. Crisis. Forget about sensible work tonight.

He leapt up and grabbed his son by the arm.

'GERROFF, YOU FUCKER! I'M GOING...'

'No you're not! Now sit down over here.'

As he manhandled the wriggling and sobbing heap over to the settee and sat it down, he noticed a stream of blood pouring out of its nose and mouth and leaving a trail of red over the rugs and the cushions. A battered child? Bloody hell, was he going to have to get a doctor? That was all he needed! Game, set and match to Merrins!

But ... damage control. He hadn't been cadet officer of the Rugby School CCF for nothing. Battlefield first aid: 'Now lie back, pinch your nose, cool down and lie still... No, there's no need to cringe. I'm not going to hit you...'

Mary swept down the ladder – the Avenging Angel of the Lord, or, rather, of the Anti-Fascist Good, of Reason, of the Wave of the Future.

'Giles, this is it. I've had enough of that fucking kid!'

The little ragdoll on the settee wriggled frantically: 'LEMME GO! She's mad. She'll kill me!'

Tightening his grip on his trophy, Giles faced her: 'Mary, what IS all this?'

'Like I said. That kid's got to go.'

The kaleidoscopic jumble of words tumbling around in John's brain flashed momentarily into coherence: 'Why do you hate me? What have I ever done to you? I've tried to be good.'

'Done to me? DONE TO ME? You've ruined my life!'

She moved threateningly towards him.

'Mary, PLEASE!' said Giles, fending her gently off. He'd never seen her quite like this before – heaven alone knew what she was capable of in this state...

She cooled down momentarily: 'You can take him away from Beaconsfield for a start. Send him back to Greenhill where he belongs.'

'I'm not going there again! NO! NO! NEVER! I'll run away again!'

Even Giles' strong and capable hands had a hard time containing the wriggles: 'John, nobody's going to send you back to Greenhill.'

The wriggles partially subsided.

There was a short silence while the message worked its way through the layers of chemically enhanced idealism encasing Mary's consciousness. Then she spoke with an ominously threatening calm:

'I see, so you're still taking his side are you?'

Immediately this was followed by a lucid torrent. The pills, the joints, the vodka, the radical conscience, the voluminous research, the historical conscience, the bitter sense of rejection ... all the raging streams coalesced into a fast-flowing and stately river, clear and icy cold. She really was the Spanish anarchist Nin facing down his Stalinist persecutors in that Spanish Republican jail... Galileo before the Inquisition... The dialectic of history.

'Where's your radicalism? Where's your idealism? Can't you see what's in front of you? A vicious little fascist who needs straightening out. A spoilt bourgeois brat. Have you seen what he's been doing to Al Dawson's paintings? Plastering imperialist, fascist, Thatcherite crap all over it. And you let him get away with it. You give in to him all the time. You're weak, that's what it is, WEAK!'

'Mary, be reasonable!'

But the stately river flowed on to its climax. Right versus wrong. Ying versus yang. The up-to-date version of Genesis where the feminist Eve defied the sexist wiles of those male chauvinists, the serpent, Adam and God...

'Giles. This is the turning point. You must choose between me and him.'

There was another silence. Giles could scarcely credit his good luck. The Gordian Knot which had bedevilled him for the past year was cutting itself cleanly and neatly.

'It'll have to be him.'

In a solemn and portentous voice full of historical awareness, Mary pronounced;

'I knew it. I've known it for the past year. Well, that's it. I'm leaving you.'

With that, she sailed majestically out of the house, slamming the door as she went. Everything shook for a while.

Giles heaved a sigh of relief: 'Well, that's solved one problem.'

The Next Problem – How to Talk to a Gorilla?

Now he faced the next problem: the grubby little heap of weakness and inadequacy whimpering away on the settee. Somehow he had to get it to perform the required role and, above all, not to upset any apple carts by blathering away in inappropriate quarters. But how to communicate with it? A colleague in the Zoology Department had claimed that you could actually teach gorillas simple sign language. Great! But did gorillas ever say anything that was remotely worth listening to? Still, he'd better start talking some gorilla language to this humanoid ape.

'Now, John, what was all this about?'

Sob, snivel, whiffle, a babble of incoherence: '... She smashed up my jump jet, the one I was going to show Danny. I took a whole week making that... She bust my *Coronation Scot* ... She started to do me over for nothing...'

No sense out of him at this stage. He remembered the matron at Rugby School giving cocoa to homesick new boys. How he had despised it at the time! Giving in to the spoilt little wimps when a good root up the arse was what they really needed! But it had worked. It had cooled them down.

'All right, you lie there and I'll get you a cup of cocoa. When you're feeling better we can have a talk.'

First, however, he locked the front door and pocketed the key. The last thing he wanted was the little ape doing another runner and ending up in the hands of the police or the Social Services. God alone knew where that would end!

Then he went over to the kitchen area and plugged in the electric kettle.

'Sugar and milk?' (Christ, he didn't even know what his son liked to drink! The Social would have a field day if they cottoned on to that one!)

'Lots of sugar, please, and not too much milk.' Coherence was returning.

He handed him the steaming mug and returned to his marking. The uproar had cleared his head and in less than an hour he got through four scripts. Then, his mind sharp and lucid, he began his essay in Zoology. He was awkward and stilted. Gorilla talk did not come naturally to him.

He sat down on the settee. First the application of treacle: 'Now then, John, I'm sorry I couldn't talk to you when you came in. You see I was very busy. I've got all this marking to do. I'm very pleased that you're doing so well at school. I really am...'

The pouty, tear-stained face broke into a broad smile. (He was making progress.)

'Do you really think so?'

'Of course I do. And I'm not going to send you back to Greenhill.'

'I'm so pleased! I'm so pleased!'

To Giles' intense embarrassment the little thing embraced and kissed him.

Inwardly, he recoiled in disgust. It wasn't that he disliked physical contact as such. With a woman it sent a tingling thrill through his body. But he actually found small boys physically repulsive – especially this one! The pathetic immaturity. That oversized head. That skinny underdeveloped body. That white, maggot-like skin which showed under his wrenched-up shirt... The creature was like an overgrown foetus, the sort of thing you put into a jar and handed over to a biology lab. And that baby smell he carried round with him – a compound of soggy flesh and ammoniacal liquids. (Jesus Christ, had he gone and messed himself again, like he did last October? Not more pissed duvets!) But, in the interests of more important things, Giles had to control himself – just as he'd had to do during that gruesome Salvation Army service he'd been forced to attend the other Sunday.

'That's all right, John. Don't worry, I'll get you a new aeroplane and a new *Coronation Scot*...'

Another hug. (Ugh! But, so far mission successful. Now for the important bit.)

'Now, John, I wonder if you could help me? I really need you. You see I've got this man and his wife coming to supper on Wednesday night. He's an engine driver and he's very nice.'

'A *real* engine driver? *Wicked!*' (Bait is working. It's going to be a pushover...) 'Now this place is a bit of a mess. I'd be really pleased if you could help me tidy it up. Don't worry about Mary. She's gone and you *are* staying at Beaconsfield...'

'Of course I will! Of course I will!'

John felt a spurt of elation. Perhaps at long last Giles was starting to like him.

'By the way,' he added ruefully, 'I'm terribly sorry about the muddy clothes, but, you see, I don't know what I'm supposed to do with them.'

Now that Mary had gone, Giles could get down to practicalities without sparking off an ideological confrontation. (For some reason Mary vehemently opposed laundries – 'exploitation of Chinese immigrants', that sort of thing...)

'Give them to me and I'll take them to the laundry.'

Confusion

Calm rationality reigned. The sun had come out after the storm. The muddy clothes were collected and handed over.

'Now, John, I really think you should go and have a bath. You don't smell very nice you know.'

(That was an understatement. The accumulated grime behind his ears was bad enough. Heaven alone knew what mephitic horrors lurked in the unseen regions beneath the shirt and jeans!)

As the little elf scampered round, desperate to please, Giles shook his head in bewildered bemusement. What a pushover! Just soft-soap him and you had him. How the hell did Mary manage to make him lose his temper? Yes, he was well rid of her!

That night, working into the small hours, he managed to finish his marking.

Up the ladder, John luxuriated in a warm, soapy bath – the first he'd had for over two weeks. Clambering out, he caught a glimpse of himself in the mirror. He had a massive black eye and a swollen, blood-stained upper lip – the fruits of his kamikaze assault on Mary. How was he going to explain that away when he got to school? He felt so ashamed. Bashed up by a woman. Howling like a little baby. God, if Danny Fleetwood should get to know, if Bill Bleeson...? And what if old Mekon found out? He desperately wanted to be like him, a tough, bold war hero with medals...

What was the real John? The big, bold lad of Beaconsfield School or the soppy little baby of 14 Gloucester Road? Giles was being nice to him again, but how long would it last this time?

Things were so confusing.

'We're famous!'

Things remained confusing the next morning.

481

He arrived at school and changed into a lad – the usual metamorphosis.

'Been in a fight?' asked Danny, observing the by now vividly black eye and massively swollen upper lip.

'Not half!'

'Got done over, did you?'

'Sort of, but you should have seen the other kid. BAM! POW! THUMP! WHAM!' He mimicked the beat-up job with his fists, battering his imaginary opponent into the ground and kicking the fallen hulk as a climax.

'Cor! Who was he?'

'Just one of the Greenwood kids that gave me a bit of lip.'

'Gee!' cooed Michael. 'You really is rock 'ard, you!'

It was all a big lie, of course, but it had the required result. In any case, how could he possibly tell the truth? Beaten up by his mother and wailing like a little baby. He'd never live it down. Once more, it was so much easier to invent a better reality and believe in it. Besides, who could possibly check up on the facts?

That was all before morning assembly. The story grew taller with each telling. By break he'd been attacked by a whole gang and had felled their knife-wielding leader single-handedly.

Then Bill Bleeson breezed up to him with a copy of the *Boldonbridge Journal*: 'John, look, we're famous!'

There, grandly displayed on the 'Features' page, was a photograph of the Escape Group with himself prominent in the foreground.

'Schoolboys Prepare to Resist Communist Invasion' ran the headline.

Eagerly he devoured the article: 'For Beaconsfield School pupils Bill Bleeson, David Robson, Philip Lawson, John Denby, Michael Connolly and Sam Hawthorne merely climbing the highest mountain in England was not enough... They, also, insisted on spending a night on a cold, windswept mountainside, under the stars and without tents... Eleven-year-old John Denby explained why: 'After what has happened in the Falkland Islands we must be ready for anything. What would happen if the Russians invaded and the communists took over? We'd have to fight a guerrilla war in the mountains...'

John walked on air. Famous! That was one in the eye for Mary and, also, for Freddy Hazlett. More important, Giles would be pleased and would continue to like him.

Down to Earth Again

But after lunch everything changed. He met Dolly in the corridor. She was all sweet smiles and maternal friendliness: 'Come and see me at four o' clock and we'll have a little talk...'

That was great. Just what he wanted! But suddenly the alarm bells started up – not ringing, but gently tinkling. Why was she asking him to come? He usually went to her, not vice versa. She was being very nice so it couldn't be a normal bit of trouble – not those mongs belly-aching about that crap on the mountainside, for instance. It must be something much more serious. He remembered that awful day at Rickerby Hall when everybody had started being very nice to him for no apparent reason. Probably Mary had come back and persuaded Giles to return him to Greenhill ... and Dolly was going to break the news to him.

The ebullience dissolved and he felt sick.

Getting through the afternoon lessons was an agony. He just couldn't concentrate. When four o'clock came his guts melted and he had to rush to the bog. He could feel his heart pounding away like a pile driver as he knocked on Dolly's study door.

When it opened he was engulfed in a torrent of maternal warmth: 'Ah, John, do come in and sit down! I'm so pleased about the photograph in the newspaper! You've had an excellent term... You must be so proud of yourself...'

So she gushed on for almost five minutes. (Oh, for God's sake, get on with it, woman! Come to the point! I know I'm back in favour again, but something's gone and happened. You're obviously sugaring some ghastly pill...) The torrent ended with a big hug.

He squirmed free of the embrace: 'Please, Miss, I'm not going to have to leave Beaconsfield, am I?'

'Oh John! Of course not! Whatever gave you that idea?'

Profound inexpressible relief. Even a trickle of tears. (God, why did he have to keep crying like a little kid? It was like that soppy Cinderella story all over again. He wanted to be a lad, but for some reason he kept changing back into a little drip.) Dorothy was just wallowing in this – it proved how much he wanted her.

'Oh John!' she cooed as she embraced him again.

Then she popped the question that had been on her mind since mid-morning: 'You've been in a fight, haven't you? What happened?'

Back to being a lad again: 'Some kids cheeked me on the way

483

home last night. I really sorted them out. BAM! WHAM! POW!'

Again he mimicked a beat-up job.

'John, that's not true.'

Pouty face: 'Yes it is.'

'No, John, it isn't. I happen to know that it occurred at home last night. It was your mother, wasn't it?'

'How do you know?'

'I get to know most things.'

He shrivelled up, contracted back into the messy little retard. As he gazed at the floor, the tears started to trickle again: 'All right, yes. It was my mother. She blew a fit on me and did me over. Please, please... Please don't tell anybody. I'm so ashamed. If the other kids find out, they'll take the mick.'

'Of course I won't tell anybody.'

'Promise. Swear to God?'

'Yes, promise and swear to God. Now you must tell me what's been going on. I can't help you if I don't know, can I?'

Out, bit by semi-coherent bit, came the story.

Behind the Scenes

Indeed, lots of things had been going on behind the scenes. Once again, John was unwittingly in the eye of a not inconsiderable disturbance.

That night Mary had swept like a hurricane into her friend Karen's house. Karen had summoned the 'Woman's Support Group' and Mary had poured out her woes.

Her partner had turned against her and denied her her right to academic fulfilment – all in the cause of a latent male chauvinism. Her precious child – for whose radical education she had cherished such high hopes – had been torn from her. Sent to a reactionary private school by her renegade partner, he had turned into a fascist storm trooper: imperialist, militarist, Thatcherite, racist, indeed the very embodiment of the Hitler Youth... In her state of 'enhanced awareness' she had revelled in the exact details of how she had struck those fierce blows for 'The Good' – literally right into the grinning face of Thatcherite imperialism.

Great sympathy and understanding had been expressed by the group. This, indeed, was an outrage and a wrong that had to be righted...

After caring hands had put Mary to bed to get the rest she so

richly deserved, Karen had telephoned Martha Merrins, telling all
and with special emphasis on the 'fierce blows for The Good' struck
into 'the grinning face of Thatcherite imperialism'. Merrins had hardly
been able to contain her glee. Now at last she really had got Giles
by the short and curlies! The next morning she had telephoned the
Social Services: 'I think there's something you ought to know...'

Sadly for her, however, Maggie Wright had got wind of this and
told Giles.

'That Merrins bitch is accusing you of child abuse again...
Apparently, you beat young John up last night...'

'I expected as much, but not to worry I'm in the clear... It was
me who rescued the kid from Mary and, if it comes to court, the
kid'll support me...' (One more reason for keeping the boy sweet.
Don't forget to buy that new *Coronation Scot* ... Damage control,
you know!)

Meanwhile the Social Services had telephoned Dorothy: What did
she know about the situation at Gloucester Road? Sniffy remarks
had followed about the need to be aware of the signs of child abuse.

Yes, protested Dorothy, she had been aware of certain ominous
signs during the past few weeks: the same shirt worn for three weeks,
a musty smell denoting a lack of personal hygiene...

But mere awareness wasn't enough... Didn't she know that ...
etc., etc., etc.?

Dorothy's credibility as 'a professional' was on the line, emphasised
by the fact that she hadn't come too well out of the Hawthorne
and Napier affairs. 'Battered child. Danger signs ignored by headmistress
of private school!' She could just see the headline in the *Daily Mail*.

Once a Drip ... Always a Drip

Another hug for John: 'Now there's nothing you've got to be ashamed
of...'

'But at Rickerby Hall I was able to take my friends home. I mean
Danny's asking to see my trains. What can I tell him? I went to
Fred's birthday party and he wants to know when I'm having my
party...'

A possessive mothering impulse got the better of Dorothy: 'When
the term's over and I am able to breathe again, you can have your
party at my house.'

'Can I? Wicked!' (Oh, Dolly, what have let yourself in for this time? Wasn't last Christmas's wallow in the sewage enough for you? But, no going back now! Once you've made a promise to a kid you've got to keep it! You should have learned that by now!)

'By the way, Mary says I'm thick and that this school is just a dustbin for thicks. It's not true, is it? I mean, you're not telling lies when you say I'm clever?'

'Of course not! If I told lies, the school inspectors would soon get on to me. And boys like you and Fred are here to show that Beaconsfield isn't just a "dustbin for thicks". That's why I want you to do well. Anyway, I don't like that word "thick". It's cruel and unchristian to sneer at what some people can't help. You wouldn't like it if everybody laughed at you because of what happened to you at Greenhill, would you? So don't you start laughing at people like Sam and Michael...'

Stern headmistressy lecture. John blushed bright red.

'Now then,' continued Dorothy, back to being Mother Hen, 'you must tell me if things are getting difficult at home. You can always stay with me, you know. What are you doing tonight?'

'Well, I promised Dad – I mean Giles – that I'd help him clear up after the disgusting party on Sunday night. He's been very nice. He saved me from Mary when she was doing me in and he's promised to buy me another *Coronation Scot*...'

'Yes, I think you should help him. But if there are any problems, see me.' (Secretly, she was hoping there would be a few problems...)

John slunk home that evening feeling deflated. Once a drip, it seemed, always a drip. Even at Beaconsfield where he thought he was a proper lad.

Meanwhile there was a more immediate problem. What would Giles be like when he got home?

Dealing with Scandalous Revelations

As it happened, Giles was in a 'mending fences' mood. Tactical withdrawal. New Economic Policy. That sort of thing.

He'd had a difficult day at the university. First of all, he'd had to sort out the 'John business' with Social Services – no, he hadn't beaten the child, he'd rescued him and consoled him as indeed the child would say.

Then there'd been that seminar with next year's Cert. Ed. students. It was a long-standing arrangement with Ed Stimpson to ensure that tomorrow's teachers started off with the right socialist ideas.

He'd hardly started before a student had handed him a copy of the *Boldonbridge Journal*: 'That's your sprog, isn't it, Giles? I can't say I like the company he's keeping...'

'What's this about Beaconsfield School?' added another. 'It's private, isn't it? I thought you said private schools should be abolished?'

'Prepare to fight a communist invasion?' echoed a third. 'What's going on?'

Giles scanned the article and seethed. The devious little shit! He'd not breathed a word about being photographed for the *Boldonbridge Journal*. Neither had he said anything about what he'd been getting up to during that 'Adventure Weekend' – or whatever it was called. 'The grinning face of Thatcherite imperialism'? Maybe Mary had been right after all... But, then, he hadn't read that parental consent form, had he? He'd just dropped it into the bin. He'd let himself be taken for quite a ride, hadn't he?

But the immediate task was damage control. His quick and orderly mind went into action: '... Of course I still believe in the abolition of private education. But, it's all a question of timing... Greenhill is the flagship school which is tune with the Zeitgeist and is blazing the trail of the future... Naturally, it is beset on all sides by the bourgeois enemies it is supplanting... They are on the wrong side of history. They are the losers and, what's more, they know it! Of course they traduce and slander Greenhill for their own counter-revolutionary ends... Greenhill is at a crucial stage of its development. It simply cannot carry inadequates who might lower its standards... The unpleasant fact is – and how I hate to have to admit it, even to you – that my son is just not up to it. Of low ability, his already weak personality has been so brainwashed by a snobby upper-class prep school that he simply cannot cope with the rigorous demands of a modern, progressive and working-class school... Out of concern for Greenhill I have reluctantly had to remove him...

Anyway, Beaconsfield isn't really a private school. The local authority is subsidising it as a temporary expedient. It's a sort of cage where the inadequates and thickoids can be kept out of harm's way... When Greenhill's up and running it will be closed down... You can rest assured of that!'

'Ah, I get you!' exclaimed a Jesus freak in shaggy jeans and a sheepskin coat. 'Fill the private schools with all the rubbish and give the best to the state. Then the private schools' exam results will be crap and the state schools' will be brilliant. That'll sink the public schools, all right!'

'Exactly,' replied Giles.

'But what about this communist invasion crap?' put in a girl with straggly mermaid hair and a long 'ethnic' dress. 'You can't possibly approve of that.'

Giles smiled benevolently: 'Perhaps you're making a mountain out of a molehill, Sharon. The kid's ESN – educationally sub-normal... He's just playing. Typical *Boldonbridge Journal*, of course, to sensationalise the whole thing. I'll drop them a pretty stiff letter...'

At the end of the seminar he'd heaved a sigh of relief. He appeared to have survived the scandal.

Ed Stimpson – Professor Stimpson! – who telephoned him that afternoon had been less of a pushover: '... Frankly, Giles, it makes both of us look pretty silly ... I had thought that you were being straight with me... And all this communist invasion stuff... Did you know that that Bleeson boy is in with Major Allen, our local fantasising fascist... I've repeatedly been on to the council about him. All his ACF business, it's almost Hitler Youth. And there's the safety angle. I gather that man, Meakin, isn't properly qualified... Frankly, it doesn't look very good, does it?'

And so on for nearly twenty minutes.

Despite Giles' protestations. Professor Stimpson was anything but 'understanding'. As he put the receiver down, Giles groaned. This was going to take some sorting out. Like it or not, the cat was out of the bag.

'Bloody newspapers!' he growled to himself, 'they shouldn't be allowed to get away with it! In the Soviet Union they certainly wouldn't be.'

Then he had run into Merrins, all greasy smugness as usual: 'I *did* enjoy that little chat with John on Sunday night. But, Giles, what *have* you been doing to him?'

That could mean any number of things... What was the scheming old cow up to now? The rage intensified...

But, leaving the Malthusian anthill of the university and its hot-house internal politics, he felt a sense of liberation – like escaping from an overheated bottle. He became reflective. It was all very well for those academic paladins to get frothed up about ideological purity.

They didn't have to deal with the Neanderthal masses out in the real world. As a prospective Member of Parliament, he did. And that meant tactical withdrawals – the NEP, using Tsarist officers in the officially proletarian Red Army ... that sort of thing! By the time he'd reached the centre of town his ideological integrity was intact.

Meanwhile he had to keep that pathetic little ape at home sweet, so he slipped into the requisite shop and bought four model aeroplane kits, a *Coronation Scot* train set – coaches and all – and a set of coloured light signals... The bill came to over £250.

Ed Stimpson may not have understood the motivation, but Trotsky would have done...

A Lad with an Assignment

So, to John's bewildered surprise, it was an effusively friendly Giles who opened the front door.

'Ah, hello, John! Did you have a good day at school? Wonderful! Well done! Now here's something for you...'

He handed him the tribute. Quite predictably, it had the desired effect.

'Cor, Giles, magic! Thanks a bomb! I'll try to be good! Really I will!...'

Which was duly followed by the usual excruciating hug and kiss...

'Now then, John,' said Giles, disentangling himself. 'We must get this place tidied up before Mr and Mrs Dawes come to supper.'

John set to work with gusto. As always, he could never resist kindness. It had happened before, but this time it seemed that Giles really was starting to like him. So he must make the most of the opportunity. Build on it, make sure that things didn't change back into the old contempt. Make sure that he stayed a lad and didn't metamorphose into that little retard again.

Besides, housework was fun. Here he was being allowed to use the hoover, something that had never happened at Oak Tree Gardens where housework was an arcane ritual whose mysteries were only understood by an exclusive priesthood of women like Mrs Bowles and his wonderful and perfect gran.

By eight o'clock everything was in order – the dog-sick stew mopped up, the fag ends picked up, the ethnic rugs shaken and hovered, the dirty dishes washed and cleaned.

'Now, John, can you go up to your room and set your railway up. I'm sure Mr Dawes would like to see that. He's interested in model railways, you know.'

What better assignment could he have had? A chance to perform in front of an appreciative audience... A chance to impress a real live engine driver. By ten o'clock he'd produced a bravura display – flyovers, tunnels, stations, the full works.

Then he dug out his railway books and spent an hour boning up on the names of the iconic steam locomotives of the 1930s and their named trains.

Things were on the up.

Another Awkward Revelation

There was a slight jolt the next day at school.

At lunch-break Mekon asked to see the Escape Group. Experienced Mekonologists read the signs and pronounced him to be in a bad mood.

'Mekon's gonna do you lot! What did you really get up to that night, eh?'

A flutter of anxiety rippled through John: it was those two benders who'd spotted him having his crap...

Bill Bleeson, however, was defiant: 'It'll be those two mongs. Don't worry, men. I'm standing by you.'

They duly filed into Mekon's classroom where the old man was puffing away at his pipe and in an ominously 'pre-eruption' mood.

'Well, sit down. Now I've just received a communication from the Wasdale Mountain Rescue Team. It seems that you were found in dire straits on Saturday night – wet, cold, starving and all the rest of it. But instead of waiting for the rescue team as you were told, you bunked off. They wasted a whole night on a wild-goose chase. There's talk of the school being taken to court.'

Silence.

'Well, just what did happen?'

Ominous puffs of the pipe.

Eventually, Bill spoke up: 'Well, we'd stopped for a brew and a bit of scoff. These two mongs said we were all starving and that, but we weren't. We didn't know they were going to call the Mountain Rescue out... Yes we saw them coming up the valley in the evening, but we thought they were after another group.'

'I see. Now, John, what's this about you fouling the mountainside?'

Snigger, snigger, snigger from David and Philip. John blushed bright red and wished he could crawl into a hole and hide.

'Well come on, just what *did* you get up to, young man?'

Bill spoke up: 'John was taken short and well ... er ... well he had to go for a crap.' Giggle, giggle, giggle from David and Philip.

'Sorry, Sir!' from a beetroot-red John, 'But well I couldn't help it... I was BURSTING!'

Giggle, giggle, giggle all round.

'And then what?' from Mekon.

More puffs of smoke.

John just gaped. This was *awful*! Why did they have to go on about it?

'Well?'

Scarlet-faced silence.

Eventually, Bill came to the rescue: 'Those two mongs who found John. Well, they were benders... Homosexuals!'

Explosive giggles all round.

'Oh yes, but enlighten me. How did you know?'

While John writhed on the end of his metaphorical hook, Bill explained: 'Well, they kept following John round ... looking at his bum and that... They even took photographs.'

'Yes,' chortled Philip, 'he'll be on the front page of *Gay News*.'

'Shut up, Phil, it's not funny! Well, not very funny.'

With that Bill creased up into giggles. John continued to squirm.

'John, is this true?' (Meakin sighed inwardly. Going into the squalid details of a schoolboy dump on a mountainside! The situations kids landed you in! Molly would just eat this one if she got to hear of it.)

'Yes... I did have my trousers down... It was so embarrassing... They kept looking. Shut up, Robson! What if it had been you?'

'I'd have let them have a good look. The poor things must have been frantic.'

'And you would have enjoyed it, too!'

'Belt up, Phil! I'm not a pervert like you!'

'All right, all right!' growled Meakin. 'We don't need to discuss your proclivities here!' (For Christ's sake, don't let a bunch of adolescents start on sex!)

'Then what happened, Bill?'

Bill became pompous: 'Last week Major Allen told me to be very

491

careful about homosexual paedophiles. He says that the communists are using homosexuals to subvert Britain from within. And, as a serving soldier, he *knows*. Well, Sir, after what you'd said about me being responsible for the little kids, I realised that we had to get away quick! I mean they were benders. Looking at John's bum and that... It was *filthy*! I mean what would you have said if he'd been shafted?'

Giggle! Giggle! Giggle!

'And the rest of us, too!' sniggered David who was hugely enjoying the whole business.

'I see,' declared Meakin amid soothing clouds of tobacco smoke. 'I get the picture. You did the right thing, Bill. You've got nothing to worry about – any of you. You all did very well. The police were full of praise. I'll sort it all out.'

Game Two Can Play

'Well, I think that's dealt with,' Meakin told Dorothy that evening. 'A storm in a teacup. Young Denby was caught short and was spotted having his dump by a couple of idiots who decided that they needed rescuing and called out the Mountain Rescue people. You know the sort, always having to interfere and "do good"! Basically paedophobic, hate kids and when they encounter them they pitch into them. Unfortunately, the Lake District's full of them. They're as much a hazard as the actual mountains. Anyway, young Bleeson thought they were paedophiles and they scarpered...'

'You don't really think they were paedophiles, do you?'

'Of course not. That's just one of Major Allen's obsessions that Bill's picked up, but anyway it gives us the moral high ground. The safety-child abuse thing is a game two can play.'

That night he went on to the attack, writing a long and detailed letter. Strict truth was irrelevant. Impression was what mattered. The boys were well equipped and were led by a responsible and experienced leader. (True.) The local police had been informed of the proposed adventure. (True.) While they had stopped for a rest, a young boy had slipped off to answer a call of nature. (Largely true.) In the midst of this operation he had been seen and even photographed by a pair of seemingly prurient adults in a most embarrassing and intimate posture. (True.) He was an especially sensitive boy who had been deeply distressed by the business. (True.) The two adults had then proceeded to make suggestions of a very pornographic nature. (Not true, but it was his word against theirs which was backed up by the rest of the group who had witnessed the exchange.) The boy in charge of the group had been briefed in paedophile awareness as part of his ACF safety training, and had considered it his duty to protect his charges from possible paedophile abuse by strangers. (True!) So he had hustled them away as quickly as possible. The police had praised their good sense and maturity. (True.) The boys concerned were deeply embarrassed by the whole affair (not true) and did not want it to get into the hands of any solicitors. However, if they persisted ... etc., etc., etc.

The letter was duly dispatched. Up on the Olympian heights of Islington there was a predictable furore. Liberal hackles rose. Outrage was expressed. But, under the delicate circumstances ... well ... it was deemed wise to drop the matter!

39

'It's all a matter of signals, you know'

Back at 14 Gloucester Road that evening an important political meeting took place. When John arrived he found Giles all smiles and, for once, wearing a collar and tie. 'Ah, John!' he beamed, 'I think you should go and have a bath and then get into some clean clothes. I want you to look smart when Mr Dawes arrives.'

'Right, I'll wear my school uniform.'

'No! No! No! I don't think that would be appropriate.' (Very *in*appropriate, in fact! His son seen in the uniform of a *private* school? What kind of a message would that send to a chippy, class-conscious old Labour dinosaur?)

'But that's the only smart clothes I've got.'

'Don't worry, I've got you some new clothes.'

He handed him a pair of new jeans and a Newcastle United football shirt.

'But I never watch Newcastle United...'

'That doesn't matter. Just say that you do. It'll please Mr Dawes... Now do make sure that your railway is in working order and do brush your hair...'

Fuss, fuss, fuss. Like an old hen! Something was up. But he was being given a central role and he always liked that.

In the midst of this a strikingly pretty young lady – all silky hair, big breasts and vivacious smiles – erupted into the house carrying a large box.

'Here's the shepherd's pie and the stottie cake you wanted, Giles,' she cooed.

'That's great, Maggie,' he replied. 'Just shove it into the oven to keep it warm.'

'Do you want me to stay and help out?'

'Thanks for the offer, but I honestly think it would be better if you weren't seen. Dawes is an awful old prude and his wife's even worse. It's all a matter of signals, you know. We don't want him to think that I'm the sort of bloke who plays around...'

He turned to John who was all ears: 'Go on, up and start your bath. This is nothing to do with you.'

John scuttled upstairs. Giles becoming a puritan? Yes, something *was* up. Maybe he'd become a Christian? Who knew?

A Political Evening...

An hour later the doorbell rang.

'Go and answer it, John,' said Giles, 'and do remember your manners!'

Flashing his 'ingratiating smile', John opened the door to find a big, burly and heavily jowled man standing on the pavement outside. He was dressed in a tweed sports jacket, grey flannel trousers and a tie. Beside him was a dumpy little lady, heavily made up and squeezed into a brightly flowered dress.

'Good evening, Mr and Mrs Dawes, do come in.'

Feeling awed, John stood back as they entered. With his closely cropped grey hair, deeply lined face and rather bristly chin, the man looked a bit like that Lake District farmer. He'd need careful handling... And, like him, he seemed aggressive. Immediately he attacked Giles.

'What der yer wanna live 'ere for, eh?' he boomed, speaking in a deep Geordie accent. 'Ah mean it's all gannin' ter be pulled doon like. And not aforetime neither! We've gorra new scheme oot, yer knaa!'

Immediately Giles felt threatened. He knew this game only too well – the ostentatious Geordie accent used to put him in his place, *down* into his place among 'them doon sooth wot's not wor lads like' ... It was going to be a difficult evening.

'Aye,' added the lady, pointing to one of the African tribal masks on the wall. 'What der yer want with them things? I mean yer's not an African, is yer?'

'Well, it is rather striking and it is a statement of the relevance of the colonial exploitation of so-called primitive cultures...'

'Hadaway man!' she scoffed. 'Yer can get berra stuff at C&A's – yer knaa nice wallpaper wi' bords an' flooers on it. Ah mean, wot's wrong wi' the decorations that ordinary folk have, eh?'

Bad start! ... The enemy artillery was lobbing shells into sensitive rear areas... Hastily, Giles changed the subject: 'Well, do sit down. What can I get you to drink?'

'Yer can gee us a proper drink, Giles me bonny lad,' replied Dawes. 'Pint o' broon ale – yer does knaa worra mean, divvent yer?'

'Oh yes, of course, I never miss a day without my pint of brown ale!' (Lie! He loathed the stuff!) 'And you, Mrs Dawes?'

'Yer can gee us a birra wine, Giles. Me doctor says it's berra for us than the broon ale.'

Dawes and his wife sat down heavily on the settee and received their drinks.

'An' worraboot the bairn?' said Mrs Dawes, pointing to John who was hovering nervously in the background. 'He wants lookin' after an' all, yer knaa! Gee him a glass of coke.'

Another enemy shell landing in the sensitive rear areas! Giles hadn't thought of that one. There was no coke in the house – Mary had banned things like Coca Cola and Fanta as 'epitomising capitalist consumerist exploitation'. How to get out of this one?

But, flashing his 'ingratiating smile', John came to the rescue: 'Don't worry, Giles, I'm not thirsty. I drank three bottles of coke on the way back from school...'

Dawes turned round and studied him carefully: 'I've seen ye afore, lad. Ye were in the papers yesterday, weren't yer, son? Cleemin' moontins an' that? Gannin' ter join the cadets, are you? Good lad! Yer dad wants ter be prood o' yer son!'

(While John glowed with pride, Giles squirmed. Was the old fool going to get on his high horse about Beaconsfield? Did he know it was a private school?)

But the attack came from another direction: 'Yer should get some of yer students to join the cadets or the Territorials, Giles, me bonny lad. Gee 'em a birra discipline!'

'Oh I don't think that's necessary!'

Giles sensed the drift of the conversation. It wouldn't be long before the old dinosaur started on his hobby horse: how he hadn't had the chance to go to university and had had to start work at fourteen... Inwardly, he grimaced: he'd heard this particular tape at least five times before.

But it was no use. The floodgates were open: 'We pays for them students yer knaa! An' wet does they dee like? They just muck aboot, protestin' an' that. Aye smashin' windees an' that...'

496

'But they *are* making a serious political point. They're on our side.'

'Hadaway, man, they's just playin' aboot! They wanna bring back the borch.'

'The birch? That's a barbaric old punishment. I mean how would you like it?'

'Why I got the borch mesell when I were a lad?'

'Did you?' piped up John who was interested. 'What did you do? Were you bad?'

Dawes turned round and addressed him: 'Sonny, Ah were young and Ah were daft. We was fifteen-year-old, me an' the lads, and we'd just gorra our pay packets like. Well, we was in Sunnerlan' for ter see Newcassell play like. Well, Newcassel won an' we thart we'd show them Sunnerlan' buggers.'

'George!' exclaimed his wife, 'mind yer language! Yer's talking to a bairn!'

'Sorry, but I were with Freddy Willis. Worra lad Freddy! Compared wi' him Ah were the Archbishop of bloody Canterbury.'

'George, your language! He's only a bairn!'

'Well, he jus' had ter nick a bottle of gin, diddent he, the daft bugger?'

'George, I'll not be tellin' ye again to watch yer language in front of a bairn!'

'Well, we was as drunk as lords. Smashin' windees an' that, an' then the Sunnerlan lads comes alang... Worra battle! Then the polliss comes an' what does Freddy Willis 'ave ter gan an'dee? Why man, he just has ter bray the polliss like? Gorrim reet in the gob an' all! Well, we was hauled in an' given the borch for being hooligans an' that!'

'Cor!' gasped John. 'Did it hurt?'

'Aye, lad, it did an' all! But yer just had ter tek it like a man!'

'I've been walloped too,' said John, warming to the man's friendliness. 'Last Saturday off Mekon – that's my teacher – and he said I took it like a man.'

'That's me lad! And wot was yer deein' son ter get walloped?'

'Well, my mates dared me to shout swear words at a farmer who'd sworn at us.'

'Ye've gorra canny lad there, Giles me lad! Mebbe he's another Freddy Willis. Great lad, Freddy! Were in the Durham Light Infantry him in the war like. Didn't half sart them Gormans oot him! Got the Military Medal, yer knaa. Great union man wor Freddy!'

(Giles groaned inwardly. 'Great union man' was he? Corrupt old fossil was more like it – in cahoots with Sam Watson, drinking mate of Joe Gormley... Vehemently anti-Arthur Scargill. This conversation was running out of control. That kid seemed to be taking it over...)

Seeing Giles screw up his face ever so slightly, Dawes went on to the attack: 'If we lads can get the borch, why can't them students o' yers? Tee posh like? One law for the gaffers an' one for the workers, is that it?'

'Please, Mr Dawes, times have changed and my students are workers, you know...'

'Workers? Them lot? Why no! An' some o' them lecturers an' that 'aven't never done a proper job o' work in their lives neither.'

'But...'

It was no use trying to stem the flood which poured forth: 'Wait till Ah tells yer this. Ah left skyerl at fowerteen year ald me. There were nay cushy universities in them days – not for the likes o' us anyways. We had ter gan ter work us. Not like some Ah could mention! Well, me Dad put us into the railway depot at Gateshead like. Ah were shovellin' ash oota the smerk boxes o' them locos, polishin' 'em up an' that. We was up at fower in the mamin...'

'You drove steam engines, did you?' John's eyes were wide open with awe. 'Did it take a long time to learn?'

'All right, John,' said Giles with a hint of impatience. 'Mr Dawes can tell you about that later. We've important business to discuss. Now what about...?'

To Giles's embarrassed chagrin, Dawes waved him aside and faced the boy. (Giles wasn't used to being snubbed in this way and it touched a raw nerve: Christ did this old idiot think a kid was more important than a well-known academic? He felt himself losing control...)

'Aye, son, it did that. Yer had ter start at the bottom in them days, shovelling the ash outa the smerkbox an' cleanin' the tubes an' that... Then they let yer be a fireman... But it weren't just shovelling coal, mind. Yer had to keep the fire right. Nae fire, nae steam. And if there's nae steam, the loco weren't gan... Yer was always gerrin' herls in the fire an' yer had ter put the coal in the right place else half yer fire went up the chimney like. Why, man, it were an art... Ah once had ter gerra load of freight over Shap. Twenty-mile gradient from sea level up ter nigh on a thoosand feet... It all depended on the fireman, yer knaa. Build up the fire proper like ter get the steam pressure else yer wouldn't gerrup nae gradients...'

'I love trains,' interjected John. 'I've got the *Mallard*. Did you drive the *Mallard*?'

'Not the *Mallard*, son, burra drove the *Sir Nigel Gresley*.'

'Cor!' John stared in open-eyed wonder. Here was a real person to be set alongside his hero, Mekon.

'She were a lovely engine,' continued Dawes. 'Work of art. Ran like the wind. Mind, yer had ter get to know her like. See what mood she were in...'

'Mood?'

'Aye, son, Yer see with them steamers it all depended on the weather, the humidity, the air pressure an' that...' (Here the old man launched into a technical discourse.) '...Drivin' ... hor ... were an art. Hard work mind... Yer were concentratin' all the time... Checkin' the steam pressure, watchin' the cut off ... an' yer had to look oot for them signals all the time... Gerrit wrong an' yer could have a smash... You was proper worn out at the end of a big run, Ah can tell yers.'

'Do you like the diesels better?'

Dawes pondered a while: 'In a way, lad, in a way. It's like drivin' a car. Yer don't get dorty and the controls is not hot like ... but yer knaa it's not the same. When yer'd got that express up the line yer felt yer'd done soomat big – like climbin' Moont Everest... An' you an' yer fireman, yer was a team. Proper mates like...'

'But the days of steam are past,' interrupted Giles, 'and we must get on and talk about the present. Now if...'

Dawes ostentatiously ignored him and went on talking to John: 'Yer knaa, lad, Ah once had that Field Marshal Montgomery in me cab...'

'Monty!' exclaimed John. 'The El Alamein man? You mean you knew *him*? Cor!'

'Nah, son. Ah didn't exactly *know* him like. It were wartime an' Ah were just a fireman in them days... Well, he were givin' a pep talk ter us railway lads. A load of old cobs it were an' all! Then he got hissell inter the cab – *wor* cab, mind – an' he starts tellin' us hoo ter drive the engine like... Well, Ah says to him, I says, "Monty, me bonny lad, yer wanna shut thaa gob!"'

'Why, George, yer never?' expostulated his wife.

'Hinney, Ah did an' all. "Monty, Ah says, yer divvent knaa noot aboot locos. Ah'll handle the locos and ye stick tee the Gormans, son!"'

'Eeee, George!' sighed his wife. 'Yer cheeky thing! It's a wonder yer worn't arrested!'

'Why, man, he just grinned an' says to us, "Good lad! Yer'a proper chap, ye!" An' we all starts laughin'. He were a bit posh, like, burra a good blerk, yer knaa...'

A visibly irritated Giles finally managed to get a word in edgeways: 'It's time for supper now... There's shepherd's pie in the oven and beer in the fridge ... and wine for you, Mrs Dawes. And, you know, we really must get down to some serious discussion...'

They sat down round the table and waited while Giles retrieved the steaming bowl from the oven.

Mrs Dawes eyed the rough and splintery table – that 'frank and honest working class domestic statement': 'Eee, where did yer find this thing, Mr Denby, in the builders' yard, was it? Yer wanna gerra proppa table. Why, man, the bairn'll be gerrin' spelks an' that in his hands an' yer'll have Social Sorvices roond...'

'Actually...' Giles began defensively.

Immediately, Dawes interrupted him: 'Hadaway, Giles, lad, yer may be a professor an' all that, but yer divvent knaa noot aboot furniture! Yer wanna gan doon tee C&As an' get yersell sommit proper like.'

Giles winced.

There was a pause while the food was downed and Giles saw his chance to steer the conversation towards politics. But before he could do so Dawes had started again.

'Eee, lad,' he said, turning to John. 'Where does ye gan ter skyerll? Canna be roond heor like. Yer divvent talk like a Geordie. Is it one o' them posh skyerlls? Yer knaa, one o' them public schools, doon sooth?'

Giles reacted sharply – almost as if he'd been stung by a bee. This was getting a bit too near the bone again!

'No! No!' he spluttered. 'He goes to school on the far side of town. Now about that business of Clause Four...' (For heaven's sake, change the subject before the deadly word 'Beaconsfield' is uttered!)

But it was no good. Before he could continue Mrs Dawes had leapt in with an unexpected venom: 'Quite right, too, Mr Denby, you divvent want ter send him ter that Greenhill place...'

Giles winced again – another attack to be fended off.

'Oh, come on, Greenhill's a fine school. It's got all the right ideas. It's the way things are going...'

500

'Rubbish! It never were...'

'But...'

But before he could say anything the little lady had launched out on to what was clearly one of her hobby horses: 'Mr Denby yer divvent knaa what's gannin' on there... Them kids... Why they cheek the teachers, they smoke an' drink... There's even drugs there... An' they steal from the shops... There's no discipline...'

'And Ah'll tell yer this much, Giles lad,' cut in Dawes fiercely, 'that place were rotten from the start. All the other places, they just shovelled their rubbish there... All them lads and lasses they wanted shot of like. It's nowt burra dustbin yon place!'

His wife continued: '...And that's not all... The lads an' lasses like theys is 'avin' sex an' that in the toilets... Yes, George, I knaa he's a bairn, but he's that young yet an' he divvent knaa aboot them things yet... Ah think it's deesgustin' ...' Grandiloquent in her rage, she confronted Giles, pointing an accusing finger at him: 'Mr Denby, I'm gonna say this to yers. If yous is our member, you've gorra do sommat aboot that place. Florrie Jackson, that's me friend what works as a cleaner there, she tells us that the big kids is allowed to do horrible things to the little kids. No, not just normal fights an' that, but deesgustin' things.'

'What things precisely? I must have facts. Solid facts.' (These wild, uneducated allegations were so typical of these dinosaurs ...)

'Well, Florrie tells us that they got one little lad, took all his clothes off him and stuck a bicycle pump up his back end. Cryin' his eyes out he were, poor little mite. An' them teachers they did nowt, nor the headmaster neither... An' Ah'll tell yer this, Mr Denby, if it had been wor bairn Ah'd 'ave been up ter that school, playin' war. Man, Ah'd 'ave given 'em ALL the borch me, startin' with the headmaster. Wouldn't Ah, George?'

'Yer would an' all, lass, yer would an' all. Yer wanna see wor lass when she's playin' war, Giles lad! By...'

'Ah mean what would you do, Mr Denby, if it had been your bairn?'

Meanwhile, as the dialogue had developed, John had felt his whole substance change. The bright, ebullient young thing that climbed mountains and was going to join the cadets became the dirty little wimp of Greenhill who was 'chinned off a lass', who pissed the bed at night and who was so awful that his classmates had done *that* to him. He went pale and floppy as if his bones had dissolved.

Before Giles could frame an answer to that pregnant question, John left the table and scampered up to his room.

'Now lass,' exclaimed Dawes, 'yous is the one that's upset the bairn with yer kak!'

Inwardly, Giles groaned. That bloody kid! He'd wanted him as a polite and dutiful decoration in the background. But, oh no, the little squirt just had to monopolise the conversation, didn't he? Steer it on to trivialities. And he didn't like the way that Dawes and his wife were using the little toerag to humiliate him... But now what? Had he gone into one of his moods again? He couldn't have timed it better, had he tried? Which he no doubt had – just to get attention! The little sod!

Excusing himself awkwardly, Giles went upstairs after him.

He found the sulky little bundle sitting on its bed in the attic.

'John, what's the matter?'

There was no reply. The little creature curled itself up into the foetal position. (Oh God, not this again! A good belt across the back end was what was needed... But ... well ... under the present circumstances ...)

'John, I am talking to you. What *has* come over you? You were fine before.'

To his immense relief, the little ball uncurled itself: 'Do we *have* to talk about Greenhill? I *hate* it. It's so boring...'

'All right, we won't talk about that. We'll talk about business instead...'

(Again, the absurdity of the situation! Dr Denby, leading historian etc., etc., etc. having to kowtow to a pathetic little eleven-year-old!)

'OK. I'll come down. But promise not to talk about Greenhill...'

'All right, I promise...' (Victory to the kid. That super-sophisticated American jet fighter downed by the Vietcong crossbow.)

They duly returned.

'Nothing to worry about,' said Giles,' Just a quick visit to the loo...'

'Actually, I was just checking up on my model railway,' interrupted John, anxious to erase the 'little-baby-who-had-to-run-to-the-toilet' thing. 'Have you got a model railway, Mr Dawes?'

'Has he got a model railway?' echoed Mrs Dawes. 'Why lad, he's just a bairn like you – a great big bairn! It's all ower the parlour like. He's always playin' with it...'

'Howay lad,' added Dawes, seeming to light up, 'let's gan oopstairs to see yer railway...'

John glowed with gratification. Giles groaned again. Would he ever bring old Dawes down to earth? He was being deliberately evasive...

Dawes and his newly found disciple clambered up to the attic, two connoisseurs for whom differences in class and background were drowned in a common enthusiasm.

Lovingly, John displayed his treasures: '... And this is the *Coronation Scot* which my dad's just given me...'

Dawes eyed the blue-and-white object lovingly: '... Lovely engines, these. Stainier's best... With them locos it were like ridin' a rocket... Yer had to herld tem back.' They was always wantin' ter rush ahead them Big Lizzies... Mind, they had their problems. Smerk, yer knaa. If it were wet and humid like there couldn't see owt for the smirk... An' that could mean yer might miss the signals... That's what happened at Harrer, yer knaa... Worst smash ever that, barrin' Quintinshill, that is...'

'Were you in it?'

'Na, lad, burra hord all aboot it like...'

He eyed John knowingly: 'Do yer wanna come and see some real locos, lad?'

John lit up like a table lamp: 'Cor, yeah!'

'Mind, Ah canna show yers any steamers, 'cos we don't have them now. But yer could 'ave a look at the Deltics and the D4s. Mebbe you could drive one o' them. A short way urnly, mind.'

'Magic! Could I bring my friends?'

'Of course, son! Ah'll fix it up. And yer dad can take yers all there.'

'Yer wanna be learnin' yer dad a thing or two...'

Down below, Giles seethed. Vital business was not being discussed. Instead, he was having to fend off accusing questions about 'that school' and the silliness of 'modern art'.

'Now when you is elected as our member, Mr Denby, will yer promise ter dee sommit about that school? I mean warrif it had been your bairn?'

'Yes, I take your point, but we've discussed this. Now about Thatcher...'

'Ah knaa all aboot that, Mr Denby. But you politicians is that airy-fairy. I'm a woman and we thinks about real things...'

Just then Dawes and John returned.

'If you brings the lad an' his mates doon ter the depot, I'll show 'em some locos. Telephone us an' Ah'll fix it up.'

'Visit the railway depot? Excellent idea! Leave it to me.' (Oh hell! Trapped into that one! How the hell was he going to fit that into his schedule? And taking a bunch of Neanderthal kids to look at trains wasn't exactly his scene – to put it mildly! That bloody kid again! But he couldn't wriggle out of this one – politics, you know!)

'Now then,' he continued, 'at last month's meeting...'

But before he could complete the sentence, Dawes looked at his watch: 'Why man, just look at the time! It's time ter gan hyem!'

As they moved towards the door, he fired a parting shot at Giles: 'Giles, lad, Ah'm all for the miners. Yer knaa that. An' Ah'm all for comprehensive education, burra Ah divvent dee this progressive stuff me. What the lads needs is readin' writin', arithmetic and religious instruction.'

'We've moved on a bit since the days of the three Rs...'

'Hadaway, man, if yer canna read, yer canna dee owt. Yer canna drive locos for a start. Some buggers have to read, yer knaa.'

'George, your language!'

'Oh, Ah were forgettin'!'

Dawes turned to John: 'Yer a canny lad, son. But yer wanna be learnin' yer dad a thing or two.'

Then he addressed Giles, wagging his finger like a teacher: 'Giles lad, I'll support you as our member on condition that yer listens ter yer bairn. He knaas more about the real world than you does, me bonny lad...'

With that the old couple finally left.

Moment of Truth

As he closed the door, Giles pondered. Successful encounter? Yes and no. Old Dawes seemed to have accepted him? Or had he? A clapped-out old peasant, yes, but he was crafty. You had to give him that. If he was to become the member for West Boldonbridge, it would be on his terms. Dawes' terms. How he'd homed in on that kid and used him to humiliate him! To put him firmly down into his place. And how the little beast had played up to him!

'Well,' said John as they cleared away the supper things, 'thanks a bomb for that. He really was a nice man, wasn't he?'

Giles didn't answer for a while.

Then he addressed his son, sternly: 'John, when I told you to be polite, I didn't mean that you were to start showing off and dominate the conversation. Because of you we didn't get down to serious business.'

John felt a cold chill.

'And there's another thing,' continued Giles, 'that boy at Greenhill Mrs Dawes kept talking about, it was *you*, wasn't it?'

Again, the evil magic was on him and the bright bouncy lad changed into the snivelling wimp: 'No, it wasn't. Really it wasn't!'

Giles put on his Rugby School getting-to-the-bottom-of-the-riot-in-the-dormitory voice: 'Don't try to tell me lies. I know it was you.'

John said nothing. Involuntarily, tears trickled down his cheeks.

Giles fixed him with a stare of utter contempt: 'So *that's* what they thought of you! I might have known it.'

It was a moment of cold, bleak truth. Forget about trying to get Giles to like you.

He never will. If you want a dad, you'll have to look elsewhere.

Trains. Glorious Trains... The General versus the Particular

At Beaconsfield School the summer term stumbled towards its ragged end.

The visit to the railway depot was a great success. For Dorothy, it was a heaven-sent opportunity to contain a potentially riotous mob on the last day of term. To the hyped-up anarchists of Forms One, Two and Three it was a new and exotic experience. For old Dawes, it was a chance to play the elderly patriarch and display his expertise. For John, it enhanced his growing reputation as 'quite a lad'.

Giles, of course, had been dreading it. Playing trains with a bunch of biologically retarded inferiors from a private school was not exactly his scene – what if Ed Stimpson got to hear of it? (Better to be caught with your pants down in a naughty house!) Worse still was the probability – nay, certainty! – that Dawes, that crafty old peasant, would use the situation to humiliate him, not only in front of the railwaymen, but especially in front of the kids. But, mercifully, one of the Beaconsfield teachers – that old fascist, Meakin – agreed to take them. That got him off the hook. ('Yes I'd love to come along – good socialist education for the children, you know – but, unfortunately, I'm just far too busy at the moment!'...)

Meakin duly went into action in his time-honoured way: 'Now, before we start, lads, a few words of advice. Enjoy yourselves, but if there is any nonsense, I think you know what will happen...'

They 'knew' all right: news of the Lake District 'firing squad' had got round and lost nothing in the telling.

Dawes hugely enjoyed himself, showing off the various engines and acting the experienced veteran among the younger drivers who held him in awe, not only for his years of accumulated experience, but, also, as a senior union man with connections in high places. The kids loved starting up the shunters and driving them for a few timorous yards along the track.

When the fun was over, under Meakin's whispered orders, they lined up, thanked the drivers and presented Dawes with a bottle of whisky. All of which went down a treat.

'Canny set o' lads them Beaconsfield kids,' Dawes told Giles at the next constituency party meeting. 'Mannerly, yer knaa. I see they gives 'em a proper birra discipline like...'

Giles waited anxiously for what he'd been dreading for the past week: the discovery that Beaconsfield was a private school and the ritual denunciation of Labour Party members who dared to send their offspring to private schools – and with all that this would mean for his selection prospects... But, oddly enough, it never came. He heaved a sigh of bewildered relief. But didn't the old fool realise what that squalid little con shop, Beaconsfield, really was? Apparently not...

What Giles' orderly mind failed to grasp was that Dawes didn't connect the General with the Particular. Socialism, grand, simple and hardline: upper classes, not quite sent to the guillotine, but to be stripped of their ill-gotten gains and set to doing real work in factories and on the streets: that was the General. Kindness and generosity to individuals, sentimentality towards kids – provided they behaved themselves! – a picture of the Royal Family in the parlour: that was the Particular.

40

Summary Holidays?

The Beaconsfield academic year formally ended with Final Assembly.

Danny Fleetwood was ecstatic: 'Holidays! Wicked! My dad's got a villa on the Costa del Sol... Can't wait!'

'I'm off to Barbados next week,' cut in Fred, getting competitive. 'My uncle's a headmaster there... You should see the beaches ... the surfing... What about you, John?'

What indeed? He thought quickly: '...Er... I think it's Italy this year.'

Another lie. He wasn't going anywhere. Giles hadn't mentioned holidays. Presumably, like Christmas, he didn't believe in them. But you couldn't let Danny or Fred know that.

In the Old Days before the Fall it had all been so different. After Christmas the summer holiday had been the high point of the year. Gran and Grandpa had packed the car – a ceremony taking two whole days – given you all sorts of games to play with and comics to read so that you wouldn't 'get bored', stuffed you with spuke pills so that you wouldn't get car sick, ensconced you in the back seat amid exciting things like bathing trunks, beach balls and flippers, and then set off for Italy or the south of France. There had been the voyage on the boat – a wonderfully exciting place where you ate chips, drank coke and played Space Invaders on flashy machines – the exotic cafés on the way and finally the seaside with its old towns and churches, its fun fairs and scrumptious ice creams... You were the centre of attention, the prize exhibit that was fussed over by the adults and given special treats for being good in boring old museums and art galleries.

Now all that was gone. And in its place? A vista of emptiness and boredom. The big, bold lad of Beaconsfield would turn into the little retard of Gloucester Road... There was nothing ecstatic about the school holidays now.

After the assembly a chaotic mass of youngsters erupted out into the warm sunshine and dispersed among the leafy avenues. John hung back. He'd been given prizes and praised to the skies, but he wanted more. 'So *that's* what they thought of you! I might have known it.' After that cold, hard moment of truth, he was desperate to find a real mum or dad. He had to make sure that Dolly still liked him. Perhaps – hope of hopes! – she could arrange a holiday for him?

Nervously, he knocked on the door. There was no answer. He knocked louder. Still no answer. In desperation, he opened it. Dolly was at her desk, bent over a pile of papers.

'Please, Miss...'

She fixed him with her X-ray eyes – not shaggy sheepdog Dolly, but Mrs Watson, Headmistress.

'John, I'm very busy. I can't see you now. And don't come into my study without permission.'

She waved him away.

It could have been Giles. It was a heavy, almost physical blow. Another moment of truth. Dolly *was* sick of him. No mum, no exotic holiday. Dismal reality. He went home despondent.

Adult Realities

Moment of truth? Dismal reality? Not quite. Rather an adult reality which John didn't understand. Dorothy was up to her eyes in the annual reports. These were very much more elaborate than the relatively simple things handed out at the end of the Christmas and Easter terms. They had to sum up a whole year's development. And because Beaconsfield was a private school these reports had to be better than the parents would get from a normal state school. Moreover, duplicate reports had to be sent to the local authority and because the local authority was suspicious of private chools – if not downright hostile – these had to be impeccable... All of which meant writing screeds about each individual pupil, and not just about classroom work either, but about personality and social development as well.

There could be no spelling mistakes or bad grammar. (For how the class warriors at the Town Hall would home in on that one!) Which in turn meant confrontations with a chippy Briggs who continually confused 'their' and 'there' and with Clarkson who actively resented having to write more than one word... It all added up to hours of concentrated tedium. The absolute deadline was ten o'clock the following morning.

To Lose a Battle, But Win a War?

Back at Gloucester Road, John's despondency got worse. As usual, Giles was hunched over his table typing furiously. When he tried to talk he waved him away.

He went up to his room, played with his trains, put on his Battle of Britain video and soon got bored with that.

The next day was the same. Nobody to talk to. Giles went out and nothing moved in the sepulchral house. Eventually he got hungry and ventured out into the ugly and dangerous yob-infested streets to buy some liquorice allsorts and smoky-bacon crisps. Not having a latch key he had to hang around for several hours until Giles eventually returned and let him in.

Sunday was the same.

On Monday morning his report arrived through the letterbox.

'Giles, this is my report.'

Giles laid it aside and went on typing.

'Aren't you going to look at it?'

Giles waved his son away.

He went up to his room. By midday he could stand it no longer and came down to confront his father. He was in a desperate, almost kamikaze mood. Ready to do anything – start smashing up dinner plates, throwing the cushions round the room, even peeing on the ethnic rugs – anything, just to get a response – any response! – from the grim, monolithic bent over the table.

'Giles.'

No response.

'GILES!' High-pitched falsetto squeal.

The thing came alive at last: 'Oh, for Christ's sake, what is it?' it growled.

'Have you read my report yet?'

Obviously, he hadn't because the envelope was still lying unopened on the table.

'No, not yet... Now for heaven's sake, leave me alone.' Angry threatening glare.

A strained silence followed while John screwed up his courage to pop the question that had been tormenting him for the past few days.

'Giles, where are we going for our holidays?'

Menacing growl: 'Holidays?'

Well, Danny's off to the Costa del Sol and Fred's off to Barbados... So where are we off to?'

Aggressive snarl: 'I'm not into the business of petty-bourgeois trophy holidays if that's what you think...'

'Does that mean that we're not going anywhere?'

'Oh for Christ's sake, GO AWAY!'

Declaration of war. John's temper blazed up. He became the kamikaze pilot crashing his blazing aircraft on to the American aircraft carrier.

'AW FUCKING HELL!'

He started flinging the cushions round the room.

As usual retribution was swift and potentially devastating. Giles got up and grabbed his arm. He cringed in terror.

For a moment Giles thought of flinging a fist into his cheeky little face, but, in the nick of time, he managed to control himself... Another black eye would not be a good idea! Especially with Merrins and her dervishes on fighting patrol. With a great effort of restraint, he spoke in a calm and clear voice: 'Don't start that silly game or I won't answer for the consequences. Now go up to your room and cool down!'

Then, as he eyed the servile wreckage before him, another thought struck him: he hadn't yet secured that Labour Party nomination. While old Dawes seemed to have been won over (but with emphasis on the word 'seemed'!), others remained unconvinced. He still needed that kid as part of a carefully constructed 'caring family man' image. He still had to keep him sweet. With a great effort of will he managed a creaky smile: 'Yes, I know you want an exciting holiday. But we can talk about this when I've finished this work. We adults have to work for our living, you know. You'll learn that one day.'

John scampered up the ladders. He'd lost the battle – big time! – but maybe he'd won the war...

More Adult Reality

It was another glimpse of an adult reality that John didn't fully understand. His utterly perfect gran and granddad had been able to devote their entire attention to him because they were retired and he was what had filled the yawning gap in their lives.

With Giles it was very different. He was aiming high, into a stratosphere far above the comprehension of a small boy. Did Trotsky have to waste time on kiddies' trips to fun fairs, for Christ's sake?

The long vac had nothing to do with 'holidays' in Giles' book. It was the time when you were shot of student morons and could get down to serious work. He could put the finishing touches to the overdue monograph on the Liverpudlian working class in World War II, he could start on those TV programmes for the BBC. He could work the constituency... The schedule was brim full.

And there was that conference of Marxist historians in Vienna. He'd promised to read a paper on the historical roots of Thatcherism and the appropriate response to it. He was particularly looking forward to this. At last he would be among equals, rubbing up against like minds, exploring new radical insights, operating for once at his proper intellectual level. But that paper would need a lot of intensive preparation if he wasn't to make a fool of himself in public...

Late in the afternoon he finished the final draft of the concluding chapter of the Liverpudlian monograph. That was one major obstacle out of the way. Now he could relax a little.

But, as he poured himself a slug of vodka, a disturbing thought struck him. He was off to Vienna in just over a week. What to do with John, that little time bomb smouldering away in the attic? He couldn't leave him alone in the house. The Social Services would go bananas – and Merrins would just love that! He would have to take him with him.

A nightmare vision rose up before him. An unending torrent of silly inane chatter, gorilla talk, sulks, temper tantrums, sticky cakes, ice creams, tacky fun fairs, being hugged and kissed in public ... and the possibility (or, rather, the *probability*!) of pissed bedclothes in the hotel! And then there was old Helmut Hasslebach whose hobby horse was 'socialist family planning' and 'safeguarding the gene pool'. What would *he* make of a little mutation like that? Didn't bear thinking about... The very last thing he needed was an eleven-year-old kid hanging round his neck like the celebrated albatross of yore – especially this one!

In fact, he had no alternative but to 'eat shit' again. Screwing up

his courage, metaphorically swallowing his vomit and holding his
nose he telephoned the Watson woman.

'... I would just like to say how delighted I am with John's progress.
His report was a delight to read. (He certainly hoped that it was
'a delight' because he hadn't bothered to read it and never would
... but you had to 'prime the pump'... Historical Necessity and all
that...) Now I've got a bit of a problem... I must be in Vienna
next week for a conference. It's not really the place for an eleven-
year-old... Would it be possible, I wonder...?'

Pause.

'Oh you can take him! That's wonderful! Awfully kind of you...
I really appreciate it!'

Profoundly relieved, Giles climbed up to the attic where the grubby
little bundle sat sulking on its bed.

'It's all settled, John. Mrs Watson's going to take you off on a
holiday...'

John smiled in appreciation, but somehow he couldn't bring himself
to embrace his father. Those days were over. 'So *that's* what they
thought of you! I might have known it.' Any affection had died.
The relationship was purely commercial.

41

A Happy and Fulfilled Woman

Have John for the duration? What more could old Dorothy Watson have wanted? *Of course* it was possible!

Having finally got shot of her reports and tied up the remaining loose ends of the term, she had spent that Sunday sprawled in her living room in a state of near catalepsy. Drained of energy. A flat battery that needed plugging into the mains.

The warm, friendly sunshine that flooded in through the lace curtains, the soft mellow brick of the street outside, the fresh vibrant green of the leafy trees ... it all sent a soothing message of hope and progress. It had been a good year. The school was flourishing. Things were on the up.

Then she had seen that Ruwenzori photograph on the wall, that memento mori, that eternal reproach. What now? Six empty weeks. Maybe another package holiday with the Hikers' Association? 'Don't you realise that you're too old to climb that mountain? You stay with the older group in the hut. Don't you realise that you'll just hold the younger members back...' A marginalised old frump, parked in a convenient lay-by so as not to spoil other people's fun.

Years ago, back at St Aiden's College, she'd produced a dissertation on the creative use of leisure for youngsters in which she'd outlined an ideal summer holiday. It had been a judicious blend of education, life skills, adventurous challenges and sheer fun. It had got an alpha and had respresented the culmination of her academic career. But nothing had come of it. It remained like that Ruwenzori photograph, a nagging reminder of unfulfilled potential. She needed youngsters to work on, but how to get them?

When she'd tried to get involved with the local Girl Guides she'd run into a brick wall in the shape of Margaret Perkins, a Home Economics teacher at one of the more successful comprehensives in the dormitory suburbs of the city, who'd managed to seize the commanding heights of the local organisation. She fiercely resented any interlopers and her sour puritanical face with its Medusa eyes had created an unscalable rampart round her little empire. It was much the same with the other youth groups. They were mostly a series of stoutly defended and mutually antagonistic stockades which did not welcome outsiders. No hope there. She was like a bird without a territory, consigned to outer darkness.

That left only... Beaconsfield! But after last year's Christmas party and the 'Hawthorne Affair' ('I'm gerrin' the law on to you!') she would have to tread carefully. She knew which child she wanted, but, in the interests of 'professionalism' and sheer survival, she hadn't got to make it too obvious.

Then on Monday morning the telephone had started. First it was Martin Davidson's mother in a state of near hysteria.

'...It's me man, Jim! Ah canna take owt more of it me! So I'm off wi' Fred – that's me new partner, like! But Jim sez he's gannin' ter sort us oot like... Mind he canna talk him what with his carryin' on with that Maureen bitch!'

'Yes, Mrs Davidson, but I'm not the person to sort out your marital problems...'

'But yer gorra dee sommat for wor bairn, Martin... Whiles me an' Fred's away an' Jim's carryin' on wi' Maureen, he's gonna be all alone by hissell... And, yer knaa, he's ernly a bairn.'

So she was going to be landed with 'Army Barmy' Martin. And just what was she supposed to do with that sticky lump of semi-congealed porridge? (But, Dolly, control yourself! Be a professional!)

Then it was the Social Services. What to do with Sam Hawthorne? The other kids were picking on him (surprise, surprise!) and he couldn't very well go back to *his* home, could he? Not now at any rate? Had she got any ideas?

So she'd got two youngsters to work on – not admittedly very inspiring ones. Then – joy of secret joys! – Dr Denby had rung and she'd got her favourite pupil, John Denby, *her* child! In the hullabaloo of the end of term she'd rather brushed him aside, perhaps even hurt his feelings. Now he was hers again.

Dorothy Watson was a happy and fulfilled woman.

An Ideal Kids' Holiday...

The professional went into action. The ideal kids' holiday. Teach them essential, but neglected life skills like cooking, washing up and organising their clothes. Open their eyes to the natural world that lay, sprawling and unappreciated, around them. Provide adventurous challenges. Provide lots of fun, too.

Things would have to be cheap. John might have unlimited funds, but Martin and Sam most emphatically did not. That would mean camping, which had the additional advantage of sparing her the agony of trying to get potential savages to be civilised and not upset the paedophobes who were apt to infest hotels and youth hostels.

They would go to Scotland. She knew an excellent place on the west coast near Arisaig. They would explore the seashore, go boating on Loch Morar and, as a climax, sail over to the Isle of Rhum and climb Askival, its highest peak – only 2,630 feet high, not exactly Mount Everest, but a big adventure for these sheltered youngsters.

When it rained they would stay in their tents, cooking the recipes she'd got them to invent, playing games like Monopoly and even writing up diaries. (Small hope here with Sam and Martin, but big hope with John.) On the way they would visit Edinburgh Castle. Sam would be oblivious and Martin bored stiff, but John was sure to respond...

So the scheme took shape.

Promotion: An Important Member of the Team...

On the appointed morning, armed with all his mountain kit, John dashed round to Dolly's place.

It was daybreak, that early-morning calm before the city roused itself and resumed its noisy and frenetic life. Beaming down from an unsullied blue sky, a benign sun caressed the empty streets with a gentle light. Even the battlefield desolation of Greenwood seemed suffused with optimism – the terminally ill cancer patient given the prospect of recovery. The lush greenery and comfortable old terrace houses of Moorside glowed with a soft radiance promising new horizons and good things to come.

So, indeed, it turned out. Years later, when time had erased the petty squalors of childhood, that Scottish holiday became another

Golden Time wrapped in a roseate mist of nostalgia. A time when everything was new, fresh and simple. The Garden of Eden before the Fall when seeds were planted which blossomed into rich fruits.

It was past seven o'clock when he finally arrived at 27 Fern Avenue, having discovered that there were few buses running so early in the morning. Even so, it was still too early to start ringing Dolly's doorbell. Last Christmas's bollocking for his premature arrival was still a painful memory as was the cold brush-off at the end of this term. If Dolly was going to be his mum, he'd better make her like him and that meant skirting deftly round her changing moods. So he pulled his plastic survival bag out of his rucksack and spread it on the wet lawn and then unrolled his sleeping bag in preparation for one of those 'emergency bivouacs' he'd read about in his *Mountain Survival* book. (Dolly, when she found him was sure to be impressed by that!)

He was just about to bed down when she burst out of the front door in her most fulsome Mother Hen mood. Almost before he realised it, she was hugging him and kissing him.

'Ah, John, I'm *so* pleased that you could come. Now come in and have some breakfast!'

(In some mysterious way he seemed to have done the right thing by coming early this time. You never quite knew with Dolly, did you? What he didn't know was that she had been feeling guilty about Friday's brush-off and was worried about 'losing' him. Nor did he realise just how much she had come to depend on him to give meaning and purpose to her life.)

She fussed round him: 'Fried eggs or scrambled eggs? Baked beans? Mushrooms? Cornflakes or Weetabix?'

Hungrily, he wolfed down the stream of goodies. It was the first proper meal he'd had since the school lunch at the end of term. After Giles' disdainful neglect, he was getting the attention he craved. The centre of attention at last! It was like having a good, hot bath. It was like the old times again.

But after breakfast things were different. The old times, yes, but now he had been promoted. Then everything had been done for you when you went away on holiday. Mrs Bowles had laid out your clothes and packed your bag for you – 'Don't you start packing things, John, you'll just get everything muddled up!' This time it was: 'Wash your plates, John... Now do you see those bundles over there? They're the tents. Can you check them to see if all the poles and pegs are there? ... That's the box with the stoves and the cutlery in it... Can you make sure that everything's there?'

Being bustled around was not wholly unlike what had happened that first night at Gloucester Road, but here it was done patiently and without him being shouted at.

Then Dolly confided in him: 'Now, John, I've a special job for you... Sam and Martin are coming, too. You know what they're like... No, don't start smirking! It's not their fault! ... You'll have to help me out with them. You're not a little boy any more – not with me at any rate...'

A new experience. With Gran and Grandpa you were a delicate piece of china that had to be handled carefully in case it got chipped. At Gloucester Road you were an irrelevant nuisance. Here you were an important member of a team. All in keeping with the fresh and ebullient morning.

Nemesis Strikes Again...

Sam and Martin duly turned up. He eyed their welcome carefully. Friendly and effusive, yes, but no hugs and kisses. He felt a profound relief. Hugs and kisses from Dolly were his special mark of distinction – his property, in fact!

The car was loaded with him in the role of Bill Bleeson as supervisor. (Proper lad now!)

'Now, John,' said Dolly, 'you sit in the front seat with the roadmap. You're the navigator. Turn to page 46 ... We want the road to Hexham and then to Otterburn and the A69 to Edinburgh...'

He swelled almost physically. Responsibility. More promotion! If his gran and grandpa could see him now! If old Mekon could!

Off they went, seemingly whisked away to the golden land of adventure by the fresh and vivid morning. To John, everything seemed transformed – the stately old terrace houses, the brilliant leaves on the trees, even the concrete wilderness of the bypass flyovers. It all seemed to have sprung into life especially for him on that glorious morning. The birth, the biblical version of Creation when all the world was young and fresh.

As the road swept over a low ridge and shook off the last of the suburbs, a new and exciting land began to open up before him. Before long the whole of Northumberland was opening out, green, empty and rumpled, sprinkled from time to time with ancient rocky crags and sprawling away to the brilliant blue domes of the Cheviot Hills, that ancient fastness of the Border Reivers. Beyond lay Scotland the Unknown. Come away! Come away, Denby the Dauntless, hero of the farm raid and climber of mountains, the hidden glens and brooding lochs are waiting for you!

Then came what the Greeks called 'Nemesis', that punishment for overweening pride. That slave in the Roman general's chariot saying, 'Remember you are only a man!' Or in his case, 'Remember you are only a small boy!' He began to feel sick.

He should have asked Dolly for spuke pills... But, then, big lads didn't need spuke pills, did they? He fell silent. A grim gritting of the teeth began. Why, oh why, did *this* have to start when at last he was becoming a proper lad? He began to pray silently: 'Please God, don't let me throw up! Please, I'll give all the wine gums and liquorice allsorts I buy to the poor starving kids in Africa! Promise!'

But obviously God wasn't listening that morning. Suddenly, the ghastly calamity occurred. Out it all came, the whole copious breakfast he'd eaten – the baked beans, the bits of fried egg, the bits of mushroom, the cornflakes; a foul-smelling, sticky green sludge, all down his shirt, over his jeans and all over Dolly's precious roadmap.

Behind him Martin exploded into giggles. It was just what he wanted. Ever since the Adventure Weekend his jealousy of John had smouldered – having to be coaxed up Scafell Pike by that posh git and then being excluded from the Great Escape by Mekon! The humiliation! The injustice! *He* was the one who knew about Great Escapes, not that smarmy little pet of Dolly's! Now the score was even.

'Hey, Miss!' he called out. 'John's been sick all over your map! BLOOOOACH!'

Dorothy responded with her whiplash headmistress voice: 'Martin, you can cut that out RIGHT NOW!'

She pulled off the road into the nearest lay-by. As she eyed the appalling mess, she felt a spurt of fury.

'Oh, John, you *have* gone and done it, haven't you? And all over my precious road map too. That cost thirty pounds, you know! Couldn't you have *said* you were feeling sick?'

No reply from the squalid heap of misery beside her. Then she felt a pang of self-reproach. It was no use getting into a temper. Kids couldn't help this sort of thing. It was her fault. She should have remembered the car-sickness pills. Delta minus from St Aiden's College for her planning!

But redeem the situation by a brisk professional response! Cleaning operations! No recriminations!

'Out you get, John. We'll have your shirt off ... and your jeans. Oh, there's no need to get all squeamish about it! You've got your underpants on and I am a biology teacher, you know. I *do* know what boys have and what girls don't...'

She got the water container and a flannel and a towel out of the boot.

'Now, wipe yourself down... We'll wash these things later on. Now get your spare clothes out of your rucksack...'

As she completed the competent professional job, her anger finally evaporated. The disaster had given her a chance to mother her protégé and in his humiliation he let her do it.

'I'm terribly sorry, Miss...'

'Don't worry, John, I know it wasn't your fault.'

This was followed by a big hug, which they both enjoyed.

A little later it was Martin's turn to be sick – a similar disaster all over the back seat. A repeat professional cleaning operation occurred. Just to stress her lack of favouritism, Dorothy gave Martin a hug. It was not well received. Yes, John *was* different, but she mustn't make her feelings too obvious. Be a professional, not an emotional woman!

Romance

They reached Edinburgh with its castle rising wild and romantic on its tremendous crag.

For John, this was a glimpse of a world of colour and excitement – the old walls of grey stone, the Scottish soldiers in their kilts, the dark passages, the glittering crown of Scotland, the tragic figure of Mary Queen of Scots...that aura of a violent and turbulent past. The only problem was having to put up with Martin who would keep droning on about the 'the SAS in Vietnam' – even when the guide was trying to tell them about a splendid old cannon called Mons Meg. (To keep in Dolly's good books, however, he didn't tell him to shut up.)

After this they had fish and chips in a café in the exotic and

519

exciting High Street and Dorothy went into a chemist's and bought some car-sickness pills.

'Now take two of these, each of you. We don't want any more disasters, do we?' They were just about to drive off when Sam announced that he was 'desperate for the bog'. A long and complicated search had to be undertaken ... which was another lesson in child management for Dorothy. Natural functions loomed large in kids' lives. They covered their fear of their unpredictability with smutty giggles... You had to take this into account when you dealt with them. She was on a learning curve.

An Open and Rocky Land...

The journey resumed.

Doped up by the spuke pills and suddenly tired after the sleepless excitement of the previous night, John slipped into a semi-coma. He was vaguely aware of wild mountains, steeper and more dramatic than the Lake District, a land of brooding chasms and plunging black cliffs.

Late in a purple twilight they arrived in an open and rocky land where they camped amid some sand dunes within earshot of a restless,

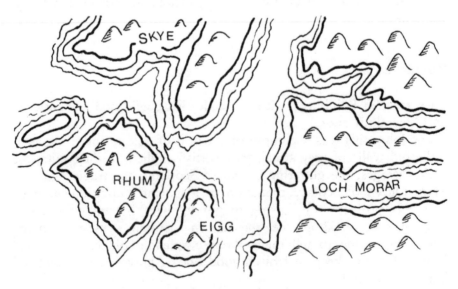

Map of Rhum, Eigg and Loch Morar

pounding sea. The tents were pitched – one for the boys, one for Dolly and a big one for doing things in when it rained. Each boy was given a Trangia stove and a lesson in how to scramble eggs and fry sausages ensued. As the cool and windy darkness closed around them, they crawled into their sleeping bags. After the celebrated 'Farmer Affair' and the subsequent 'firing squad' there was no question of any more 'night operations'.

A New World

The glowing sides of the tent heralded a brilliant dawn.

Under the clear blue sky and, fingered by the long rays of the rising sun, they had their breakfast – another cookery lesson, this time how to prepare porridge oats and make French toast. John hugely enjoyed it, but Martin mumbled to himself about the SAS and 'proper compo rations'.

'Time to go exploring and see what's beyond those sand dunes!' Followed by Dolly, they raced up to the top of the nearest dune.

There for John there was a moment of discovery that made him think he was Christopher Columbus on that climacteric morning in 1492 when he'd first seen that palm-fringed West Indian island. An unexpected new world was revealed. Below was an empty beach of pure white sand, bounded on either side by twisted rocks and small lumpy hills. Heaving and crashing noisily on to it, amid wild and ever-changing swirls of foam, were line after line of shimmering waves. Beyond them a deep-blue sea swept away to the horizon, sprinkled with strange, oddly shaped islands. One was a high plateau ringed by steep cliffs and with a sharp little peak on the far end of it, which made it look like a giant aircraft carrier. Behind it was another island full of wild, craggy mountains, a mass of wrinkles and deep blue chasms. To the right, beyond the glittering waters was a broad tongue of brown land. Behind it, and vividly blue, rose an improbable series of mountains – a steep, spiky range and a vast slab-like mountain in front of it. Far away on the horizon, at the very limit of visibility, he could just discern a line of faint blue hills sticking out of the sea.

It was another of those visions – that glimpse of the Beyond World. The Isles of the Blessed where his perfect gran and granddad were waiting for him.

'Come on, John!' called Martin. 'What are you staring at?'

'Everything! It's ... well, it's so exciting!'

'But it's just an ordinary beach!'

'To you, yes, but then you don't see what I see.'

'What? Have you seen an Argie submarine? Where is it? Where? Point it out!'

'No! No! I haven't seen a submarine!'

'Well, what then?'

'Oh nothing.'

'You're a loony!'

John didn't reply. How could you explain to anybody – let alone to a meathead like Martin – the meaning of what he saw?

And it *was* different. 'Beach' used to mean Brighton or Italy, a crowded place backed by buildings with cafés, fun fairs and ice-cream stalls. This was something else, something glowing and undiscovered ... a deeper and more meaningful place, though he wasn't sure what that 'meaning' was.

He turned to a panting Dolly who had just staggered up to the top of the dune.

'Cor, Miss, just look at that! Look at those islands. Does anybody live there? What are they called?'

'Here,' she replied, handing him a map, 'you tell me.'

He studied the crumpled object for a while, trying to make sense of the seeming confusion of abstract patterns and squiggly lines. There were islands there, yes, but they seemed to have such strange names ...

'That one's called Egg or something,' he said, pointing to the one that looked like an aircraft carrier.

'Eigg,' corrected Dolly, stressing the 'i'.

'And the mountainous one behind it is called ... Rhum.'

'That's right.'

'And that must be Skye. But what are those mountains? They look really fierce ...'

'They're the Coolins, the most dangerous mountains in Britain. It's where the rock climbers go ...'

'Can we go to those islands?'

'Yes, we're going to Rhum.'

'WICKED!'

So a glorious day on the beach ... Rolling down the sand dunes, building a dam across the little stream that trickled over the sands, clambering over the rocks ... Dolly kept on showing them all sorts of interesting things – crabs, worms, mussels, snails... Interesting to John, at least, but less so to Martin who droned on about 'emergency rations' and 'the Argies on Pebble Island' to Sam, who just looked vacant.

Dolly might be a strict old school mam, but she let you do exciting things. That evening, they built a fire on the beach. There, as the sun sank into a crimson sea in a blaze of unbelievable splendour, they cooked their supper.

'We're just like shipwrecked sailors, aren't we?' said John.

Later there followed the thrill of a midnight swim.

His Gran and Granddad were utterly perfect, but they'd never let you do things like this.

For John, it was a glorious day, a perfect golden day when all the world was young and fresh. And not only for John, but for Dorothy, too. Her chosen pupil was responding to her magic – and more exuberantly than she had dared to hope.

Dark Lake... Monsters in the Night?

One fine morning they stuffed their sleeping bags and bivvi bags into their rucksacks, zipped up their tents and piled into the car.

'We're off for an adventure,' said Dolly. 'We're going to Loch Morar.'

'Loch Morar?' queried John. 'What's so special about that?'

'It's very wild,' she replied. 'At the far, eastern end there're no roads, no people, just wild uninhabited mountains. It's where Bonny Prince Charlie wandered after the Battle of Culloden. Just think of it, John, he was wet and cold, always exhausted and with the Redcoats chasing him. He had to trust the few loyal Highlanders who were his friends...'

'Wow! Like me and Sam on the Great Escape...'

'Yes, but in his case it was for real. If he'd been caught, he would have been beheaded... And there's more, too. Loch Morar is the deepest lake in Britain. It's deeper even than Loch Ness. In fact, it's the second deepest lake in Europe...'

'Cor! It hasn't got a monster, has it?'

'Yes it has. It's a much nastier one. It's called the Morag. She's a beautiful woman with bird-like claws who comes out at night and eats people alive...'

'You don't really believe *that*, do you, Miss?'

'Do you believe it, John?'

'Of course not...' (But deep down he wasn't so sure.)

They arrived at the western end of the lake. To John, it was a dark and mysterious place, pregnant with adventure. Here it was fringed with low, wooded hills and studded with small tree-covered islands. Beyond this benign and smiling area, a great sheet of water swept away, vast and blue, into a distant tangle of high, brooding mountains.

'Right,' said Dolly, 'we're going to hire one of these rowing boats and we're going to explore those islands there...'

'Wicked!' exclaimed John. 'I bet nobody's been there! Heaven knows what we might find!'

'We'll have to be careful,' added Martin, looking wise. 'We could find a secret Argie FRP.'

They duly climbed into the boat. Dolly sat in the back and let the boys do the rowing. But as the Jungle Expedition/SBS patrol boat, or whatever, ventured out into the unknown, problems arose. Martin appointed himself 'Supreme Commander' and, positioning himself at the front, issued a stream of orders in the form of unintelligible military acronyms. Sam and John took an oar each and began to row, but while John could keep time, Sam most emphatically couldn't. As a result, they kept going round and round in a big circle.

In the end when it was obvious that the drunken zigzag was getting nowhere and was starting to produce outbursts of temper, Dolly intervened.

'Let me take that oar, Sam...'

As they neared a rocky and anarchically wooded lump, John felt a rush of excitement. The vivid colours of the afternoon, the brilliant sky, the bright green of the trees, the grey, wrinkled rocks... He was an explorer who had discovered a new and unknown archipelago. Who knew what secrets might lie hidden among those tangled moss-covered boulders?

They landed on one island after another, crawling over the rocks and wriggling into the mini caves. Finally, they came to the biggest island, a lumpy tree-covered thing which rose up to a mini-mountain at its far end. Explorer John ran round with his notebook, sketching a crude map of it and naming all the features. The mini-mountain became 'Mount Denby', but, in order not to offend Dolly by being

Denby Island

selfish, he added a 'Davidson Bay' and a 'Hawthorne Cove'. Then he indulged in an orgy of inventiveness – 'Doom Point', 'Secret Cave', 'Silent Harbour'.

Not to be outdone, Martin was also busy naming things on his little map, sprinkling it with acronyms trawled from 'Combat Survival' – FRP, GHQ, RVP and so on.

So eventually the island ended up with a bilingual geography as if it had been settled by two different tribes...

'Let's pretend we're mutineers from the *Bounty*!' cried John, eager to impress Dolly with the names he'd trawled out of his *Great Tales of the Sea* book. 'I'll be Fletcher Christian and you can be Ned Young...'

'No! No!' protested Martin. 'We can be the SAS in Vietnam. I'll be Colonel Jones...'

As the two commanders bustled round in their separate identities, Sam remained seated on a boulder, his face creased up into a blissful smile. He didn't know where he was, but nobody was being horrid to him and that was what counted.

Quietly and contentedly, Dorothy observed the boys' antics and little schemes – just as she'd observed the social behaviour of mice all those years ago at St Aiden's College. When they'd finally wound down, she dropped her premeditated bombshell.

'We'd better make ourselves comfortable because we're going to spend the night here...'

'WICKED!' exclaimed an exultant John. 'Can we light a fire?'

'No you can't because we're not really supposed to be here. We mustn't be seen.'

'Just like I said. We're hiding from Captain Bligh and the Royal Navy.'

'No,' interrupted Martin vehemently, 'we're the SAS hiding from the Argies in the Mekong Delta!'

Dolly produced a Trangia stove and some tins of baked beans, peas and Irish stew and they cooked a meal. Afterwards they washed their dirty mess tins and spoons in the cold waters of the loch and laid out their plastic survival bags and sleeping bags. The sun disappeared in a blaze of crimson. In the long, ever-deepening gloaming, the loch grew mysterious and, as a velvety night slowly engulfed them, the mystery deepened. Who could tell what might be awakening in those lonely woods along the distant shore or lurking in the folds of those dark, untrodden mountains? Or, indeed, what might emerge from the depths of that deep and sinister lake?

They huddled together listening quietly and earnestly as Dolly read them a ghost story. In the deepening gloom they half believed it to be true. In this place who could tell what was true and what was not? . . .

'That monster, Miss,' asked John. 'It doesn't *really* exist, does it?'

'Well, we don't really know, do we?'

'What if we see it?'

'Then you can tell the newspapers all about it and you'll be famous.'

'Hey!' exclaimed John. 'Let's watch out for it!'

'Yeah let's!' echoed Martin.

'Coming, Sam,' said John.

'No, I'm scared of the dark. I'm staying with Miss.'

John was about to say 'shit pants' but, seeing Dolly, he forbore.

While Sam snuggled into his sleeping bag, he and Martin crept up to the top of the island. They gazed out over the brooding blackness of the loch. John began to feel nervous . . . but he couldn't admit it in front of Martin. That vast stretch of water, that fathomless deep, those black and grim mountains . . . all alone on a tiny island in the midst of this hostile immensity. Suppose they went back to Sam and Dolly and found that they weren't there? Just vanished! Perfectly possible!

He nudged Martin: 'What do we do if we see the monster?'

'Shhhhhhh! It might hear us!'

'You think it's real then?'

'Well, Miss said...'

'What if it sees us and comes after us?'

'Shut up, you're making me scared!'

The darkness thickened as clouds covered the moon. A black shroud seemed to envelope them. The dark world was coming alive, preparing for the arrival of something awful. The silence was almost solid...

Suddenly there was a plop from far out in the darkness of the loch. Another. And another... Something was out there. Terrified, John forced himself to peer ahead. The blackness distorted things, making everything big and frightening. He thought he saw a huge shape coming out of the water. Another plop. Then a big splash!

'Oh God, it's coming!'

'HELP!' Martin galloped down to where Dolly was.

John followed him. No point in playing the hero now, not with that nameless horror out there! Mercy of mercies, Dolly and Sam hadn't vanished...

'I think we've seen the monster, Miss! It's real. Can I hold your hand, Miss? PLEASE! I'm scared!'

They both snuggled up to her, burying their faces in her arms. The wind blew. The branches above them creaked. 'Oh God, it's coming!'

A maternal Dorothy grasped her chicks firmly. Eventually, she noticed that they'd both fallen asleep.

Morning came, bright and clear and with it normality. Dorothy found herself lying like a large sow with its piglets all around her. John and Martin were clasping her hands, Sam's head was on her tummy.

They cooked breakfast and rowed back to the shore.

'That wasn't a monster, you know,' said Martin, looking wise. 'It was an Argie submarine on patrol. We'd better alert the MOD.'

John sniggered to himself. How could the Argies possibly get a submarine up that shallow river with its waterfalls that emptied into the sea? Barmy! Pathetic! But he'd better not start teasing Martin or Miss might blow a fit on him...

Internecine Warfare...

Two days of blustery rain followed, confining them to their tents.

John managed to enjoy himself. He wrote a fulsome 'Journal of

Events', drew a chart of the newly discovered 'Denby Archipelago' in Loch Morar and produced a catalogue of 'New Species' found by him in the rock pools beside the sea. He'd been reading about Charles Darwin in his *Great Explorers* book and felt that he, too, could discover a few unknown species of mussels and worms – after all, Darwin couldn't have found them *all*, could he? He even invented some new species of his own.

But, while Sam was lost in his usual haze, Martin grew bored and fretful. John found him increasingly tiresome. Martin always had to be the boss. Martin always knew everything. You could hardly open your mouth before Martin interrupted you and drowned you in a long drivelling speech full of ridiculous army expressions. And it was all such crap! Argie submarines in Loch Morar! A secret Russian base on Rhum! Whatever next? Communist spies disguised as fish? Seagulls collecting info for the Red Army? John felt himself losing patience. 'The kind-hearted little boy' act was becoming harder to sustain with every passing hour...

Adventure on the Shining Sea – But... 'You've got your work cut out with that lot.'

By the third day the storm had blown itself out and a calm and brilliantly clear morning dawned.

'We're going to the Isle of Rhum today!' declared Dolly.

'WICKED!' chorused John.

'Do we *have* to?' moaned Martin.

They packed the big tent into the car and distributed the two smaller ones and the sleeping bags among the rucksacks.

'We're not going to have to *carry* these?' groaned Martin, 'The SAS have helicopters, you know...'

Climbing into the car, they drove along the wriggly road to Mallaig. It was a radiant morning – a pure blue sky dotted with bright white clouds, a restlessly animated sea, the islands vividly clear and all their strange contorted shapes almost lovingly outlined in the warm sunshine.

Mallaig was something new for John. In the old days 'port' had meant Dover, the place where Gran and Granddad took you when you boarded the ship to go to France and then Italy. It was a big place full of hotels, cars and vast concrete 'termini'. Mallaig was utterly different: a tiny place, perched like a seagull's nest on the very edge of a heap of rocky hills and surrounded by excitingly shaped mountains. There was a smell of seaweed and an exhilarating scream of seagulls. The bustle, the thumping vitality... it all seemed to say, 'Come on, John! This is going to be fun!' Dolly parked the car beside the tiny, boat-filled harbour. Lugging their rucksacks, they marched along the small stone jetty past coiled ropes and boxes of richly smelling fish, Martin gasping theatrically and muttering to himself about helicopters.

'Where's the boat?' asked a puzzled John. 'Boat' in his experience meant one of those floating hotel things at Dover which you went to France in and were full of cafés and saloons and where you had to ask somebody the way if you wanted to see the sea.

'There it is,' replied Dolly, pointing to a small thing, little more than an oversized motorboat bobbing about in a hustling crowd of fishing boats.

'Cor! Are we going to sea in *that*? This is going to be exciting!'

Dorothy felt a pang of relief. All along she'd feared that he might start to grizzle and sulk because he'd been expecting one of those Sealink gin palaces full of ice cream and video games. But he'd fulfilled her hopes. Yes, she *did* like him! Far better than Martin who was always wimping and complaining and was such a wet blanket. More, indeed, than a wet blanket: a soggy heap of semi-congealed mud! But, Dorothy, control yourself! You're not to have favourites. You're a professional not an emotional woman.

They went down the steps and, helped by a boatman, clambered aboard. The boat was full of adults who, as soon as they saw the three boys, looked sullen and began to mutter among themselves. 'Not a bunch of kids! We can do without kids!'

A cold, unwelcoming atmosphere enveloped them as they tried to find somewhere to sit. Established like massive boulders on the benches, the adults ostentatiously refused to make room for them as they tried to find somewhere to sit. Eventually, Dorothy found a space near the stern where a large man, draped in expensive hiking kit, reluctantly removed his bulging rucksack from the bench and with an air of pained condescension let them sit next to him.

With a throbbing of the engine, the boat sprang to life and headed out of the harbour and into the wide shining sea beyond. Out into the gleaming unknown... the fresh wind, the sparkling spray, the bouncing movement, the great journey... It was too much for John.

Ignoring Dolly's admonitions not to lose his precious, hard-won seat, he got up and, squeezing his frenetic way past the wheelhouse, rushed towards the front of the boat. Not to be upstaged, Martin followed him. Only Sam remained obediently seated. Dorothy let them go, unwilling to dampen their obvious delight – at least, *John*'s obvious delight! – in the adventure. Anyway, she felt the need to charge her batteries in preparation for the physical and mental exertions that lay ahead.

Pushing past the increasingly irritated adults, John climbed on to the sloping prow of the little boat and tried to dangle his hand in the rushing water.

'For heaven's sake!' growled a middle-aged lady. 'Is nobody going to control that boy?'

'Kids!' sighed a bearded ornithologist, draped with binoculars and peering disapprovingly through a pair of thick, horn-rimmed spectacles. 'They shouldn't really be allowed on boats like this!'

'Quite so,' agreed the woman. 'It doesn't say much for the company, does it? I'll have to make noises in appropriate places...'

It was not long before a flustered boatman approached Dorothy.

'Excuse me, could you control your children, especially that little white-haired one. He'll be overboard in a minute...'

Can't control your kids! Apart from being a paedophile that was about the worst insult a teacher could receive. Stung and embarrassed as the judgemental eyes of the outraged passengers followed her, Dorothy squeezed her way forwards. There on the bow, poised on one leg like *Eros* in Piccadilly, was John.

'Look, Martin, I bet you can't do this!'

'John, come down at once!'

No response from the self-absorbed acrobat.

'John Denby, I AM TALKING TO YOU!'

Still no response.

'Teachers!' declared an unknown male voice from the audience who were eagerly watching the developing pantomime.

In desperation, Dorothy clambered up towards John and grabbed his trouser belt just above his bottom. As she did so, the boat hit a wave and jerked upwards. Together they tumbled down in a tangle of arms and legs and landed in a heap on the deck.

An untidy scuffle occurred as she got up and, holding her trophy firmly by the arm, frogmarched it towards the stern.

'Come on, Martin, you, too!' she snapped.

A vigorous muttering erupted as the audience divided itself into two opposing, but equally paedophobic, groups.

'That woman shouldn't be in charge of children. She can't control them!'

'Look at the way she's manhandling that boy! That's assault. It's a matter for the NSPCC...'

'She wants to give him a bloody good hiding more like!'

They sat down at the back. Dorothy felt sore and humiliated. Her protégé had let her down and in public, too. She turned angrily on him: 'John, if you can't behave yourself, I'll have to send you home!' (The logistics of such an operation she knew to be impossible, but the kid was still at the 'Olympian Adult' stage of development and would take the threat seriously – hopefully!)

John blushed bright red ... being treated like a little kid in front of everybody! It was too awful!

'Little babby! Got to stand in the corner!' jeered Martin on cue. 'He'll be sick next, Miss – BLOOOACH!'

'Martin, there's no need for that!' hissed an exasperated Dorothy.

They sat for a while in a sulky silence. Then the boatman appeared again.

'Look,' he said, pointing to the pouty John, 'if you want, I'll take him into the wheelhouse and he can help us steer the boat. That'll keep him out of trouble and give you a break.'

'All right, John,' ordered a profoundly grateful Dorothy. 'Off you go, but *do behave*! And *do* remember to thank the gentleman afterwards.'

John left in triumph and was soon in the wheelhouse performing before an appreciative audience, steering the boat – or, so he told Danny afterwards, embellishing the drama with the odd gale and perilous reef as a matter of course.

To keep his end up, Martin began a long, rambling lecture to nobody in particular about the SBS in Vietnam. Oblivious of the little dramas around him, Sam beamed vacantly away.

'You've got your work cut out with that lot,' sighed the large, expensively kitted man next to Dorothy, shaking his head dismissively. 'Are you a school party?'

'Yes,' she replied defensively, sensing a sneer in the faintly supercilious tone.

'I thought so. Where are you from?'

'We're a small school in Boldonbridge.'

The man's bushy eyebrows contracted in to an inquisitorial frown: 'You'll be a special school, then?'

'What makes you think that?'

'Well, I'm a teacher myself and I know about kids – normal kids, that is.'

'Well?' Dorothy readied herself for an attack.

'Well, I've been looking at them and, if you don't mind my saying so, they are – well, a bit odd, aren't they?'

Dorothy *did* mind his saying so. In the end they were *her* chicks and any disparagement of them was a disparagement of her. The defensive perimeter was strengthened, the metaphorical wire laid out and the sentries alerted...

'Oh,' she muttered, 'in what way?'

The assault began. 'Well, that one,' he said, pointing to Martin who was busily orating away to empty space, 'is obviously an obsessive.'

Then he pointed to Sam who was sitting with a blissful smile on his face, playing contentedly with his fingers: 'And that one seems a bit autistic ... and the other, that little white-haired fellow, is obviously hyperactive, perhaps even ADS.'

The casual superiority with which he dumped her charges into disparaging slots needled her. 'Oh that one,' she replied, 'he's perfectly normal. Just a bit excited, that's all...'

'That's your word for it, is it? Well, it's hardly what I'd call normal...'

A frosty silence ensued.

Then the attack continued: 'What are you hoping to do with them in a place like this?'

'We're going to Rhum to climb Askival,' she replied defiantly.

An exaggeratedly shocked look spread over the man's face: 'You're not *serious* are you? Don't you know that Askival's a dangerous mountain? I wouldn't take *any* kids up there, certainly not a bunch of oddities. Aren't you being a bit irresponsible?'

'Oh no! They'll be all right! They've all been up mountains before. It's part of our adventure programme!'

The man shook his head: 'You *are* aware, aren't you, that if anything went wrong, you could end up in court? Indeed, you could go to prison if there was a fatality. You're rather putting your head on the block, aren't you?'

Dorothy winced. She was 'aware' – only too well 'aware' in fact! But the man's arrogant negativity grated on her. Couldn't he give her *any* credit for trying to do something positive for these rejects of hers? Apparently not. Not even a smidgeon. And, what was more, how he would just love it if anything went wrong! How he'd just wallow in a fatality, relishing that almost sexual thrill of sanctimony.

She went on to the attack: 'Where do you teach? Presumably, you don't teach oddities?'

'If you must know, I don't.'

'Is it a comprehensive?'

'Good Lord no! I'm spared that.'

'Independent?'

'No, grammar school... Moorhampton Grammar School. Real school. Real pupils. Not just playing around. We get good results, among the best in the country, in fact.'

It was an obvious putdown. He went on to consolidate his victory with a final bombardment: 'To be perfectly frank with you – as one professional to another – you're on a hiding to nothing with this lot. They'll just let you down and you'll be blamed for all their failures. You won't get any thanks. If you want to make a proper career for yourself, go for the better pupils, get the exam results. That's all that matters in the end. That's how you're judged. And, quite honestly, you should think again before you take this lot up a mountain, especially a dangerous mountain like Askival. Don't say you weren't warned.'

'Presumably you don't take school trips, then?'

'Good God no! I've got better things to do with my free time than mess around with kids!'

The conversation fizzled out. They had nothing more to say to each other. No point of contact. Suddenly, Dorothy had one of her flashes of insight: it was Lawrence she was looking at. Look after Number One. Only deal with the best pupils. Take the credit for their successes and call yourself a brilliant teacher. Pick up the easy plaudits. Rejoice in other people's difficulties. See them as a right and proper contrast to your own virtues. And if you were a bit religious be like the Pharisee in the Temple and say... 'I thank God that I am not as other men are.'

But she'd show him – and *how!* Her chicks would succeed and show the world that they were more than just 'oddities'! Yet the seeds of doubt had been sown. That small cloud 'no bigger than a man's hand'. 'Askival's a dangerous mountain'! If something happened? If John went silly and refused to obey her? If he went and got himself killed? How the vultures would swoop! And this morning's signs had not been reassuring. He was in a silly mood...

Secretly, she prayed to herself: 'John, *please*, John, be sensible today. Don't let me down!'

Wherefore Doth the Way of the Wicked Prosper?

The islands grew larger and more dramatic. To the north the Isle of Skye resolved itself into a tremendous range of unexpectedly grand mountains, all bare rock and beetling crags – the celebrated Coolins where 'only experienced climbers went'. Then came Canna, a long, flat-topped island that looked a bit like a stranded whale. Here the boat stopped and a number of passengers got off, including to Dorothy's immense relief, the ghastly Pharisee next to her. She was going to have quite enough problems with her 'oddities' without him hanging around as a sanctimonious and judgmental audience.

Yet, as she watched him lug his hyper-expensive rucksack up the jetty steps, that relief was tinged with resentment. He was probably right. He would rise and she would sink. In the present educational climate his first-class exam results would be deemed 'Excellence' while her very meagre successes – if you could even call them 'successes'! – would be dismissed as 'Incompetence'. He'd caught the right train that was going to the good places: she'd missed it. 'Wherefore doth the way of the wicked prosper?'

On to Adventure Island

Finally, they neared Rhum with its blue, strangely shaped mountains rearing up from the foaming waves. A beaming John emerged from the wheelhouse: 'Cor, that was MAGIC!'

Flashing his 'ingratiating smile', he vigorously shook hands with the three grizzled old boatmen: 'Thanks a bomb! That was MAGIC!'

'Did he behave himself?' asked an anxious Dorothy.

'Och aye! Grand wee wain! Just needs the odd skelp o'er the bum from time to time!'

Clearly, the famous charm had worked. But 'the odd skelp o'er the bum'? It might have to come to that...

They clambered out of the boat, up on to the stone jetty and out

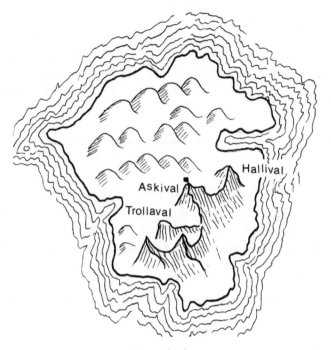

Map of Rhum

on to the unexplored island. Sam was lost in a dream. Martin was sulky and resentful at having to carry a rucksack. John was bouncing round like a highly charged electric eel, seemingly oblivious to the weight of his rucksack. Ahead of them were steep, rough hills, vividly green and all big boulders and long, tufty grass which hinted at the presence of big mountains behind their untidy crests.

After about half a mile they pitched the two tents on a patch of green grass beside a stream and ate the sandwiches and Mars bars that Dolly dished out. Nearby was a grotesque Victorian mansion, a sort of mock castle painted a sickly chocolate brown – the kind of place that could be used as a set for a horror film.

'Does anybody live there?' asked John.

'The owner of the island used to live there in Victorian times,' replied Dolly, 'but now it's deserted.'

'We ought to go and explore it. There could be all sorts of exciting things there. Maybe the old man murdered his wife and buried her in a cellar. Or perhaps he was like Frankenstein, you know, a mad scientist who tried to make human beings by stitching together the legs and arms of people he killed...'

'Crap!' said Martin with a knowing look. 'It's NATO advanced listening post, what they call an FAWP. You won't get anywhere near it because it'll be surrounded by landmines and laser guns...'

'Rubbish! It's just an old ruin that nobody wants.'

'Belt up! You don't know nothing about the Army! You're just a clueless flid!'

'No, I'm not!'

'Yes you are!'

'Aren't!'

'Are!'

Called a clueless flid by Army Barmy, that notorious thickoid and wimp! It was too much for John. All week a suppressed rage had been mounting inside him, filling him up like an over-inflated balloon. The skin of the 'nice and kind little boy' had been stretched ever tighter. Now at last it burst.

'Fuck off, Army Barmy!'

He was about to fling a vicious punch into his fat, grinning face when Dolly grabbed his arm.

'John Denby! We'll have none of that! Control yourself! Now sit down there!

Come on – DO AS YOU'RE TOLD!'

With that she almost threw the reluctant little bundle on to the ground where it sat, steaming like an overheated kettle.

'And you too, Martin and Sam, sit down... Now listen to me. We're going to climb a dangerous mountain, but we can't do it if you're going to fight like a lot of little babies...'

The Day of Judgement?

This was crunch time for Dorothy Watson. The Day of Judgement. She'd climbed lots of mountains before, but this was the first time she'd done it with a bunch of kids. That encounter with the Pharisee on the boat had unsettled her.

'Askival's a dangerous mountain... Aren't you being a bit irresponsible?' She'd spent ages scouring the guide books looking for suitable 'kids' mountains' and the mountains of Rhum seemed to fill the bill. She'd pored over the route in detail, examining all its minutiae. They would start from the campsite, climb up the gentle slopes to the easy peak of Hallval, follow the sharp ridge that connected it to Askival, the highest peak on the island, cross its rocky summit and descend to the high pass that separated it from the tangle of rough mountains that formed the southern ramparts of the island and then cut down to the path which wriggled its way along the eastern coast and return to the campsite. Rugged and scrambly, the route was interesting enough for youngsters without being so technical that it required ropes and harnesses. Neither were the mountains so big and high that they would exhaust her young charges. Exhaustion, she knew, was a highly dangerous state, especially with youngsters who could be full of bounce one minute and on the point of collapse the next. A road-less island would add a final spice of adventure...

But she hadn't actually climbed Askival before and there was one place that worried her, a 'Mauvais Pas', or 'Bad Step', on the ridge between Hallval and Askival. The guide book said there was an 'easy' way round it. She only hoped that 'easy' really *did* mean 'easy' as she understood the word!

The Kids... 'You're not *serious* are you?'

Then there were the kids. 'They'll be all right,' she'd assured the Pharisee. But would they be 'all right'? Would they rise to the occasion? Or would they just go silly? She was in their hands... But what hands! As she eyed the three young scruffs seated on the grass before her, she had a sinking feeling that she was not in control of the situation.

Sam? Few problems here. She could rely on him to do as he was told. He was immensely grateful that somebody was being nice to him for a change. All you had to do was to stop him drifting off into one of his dreams.

Martin? Now there was what St Aiden's College had called a 'challenging pupil'! 'Army Barmy' Martin, a professional ducker-out of everything remotely difficult who wrapped himself in a self-serving fantasy that, in its own way, was every bit as dangerous as a drug addiction. Whatever happened fantasy always came to the rescue. It was so much easier to fantasise than to face the dreary reality that you were a dim clod of a thing with few, if any, positive prospects. For who would employ a lump of self-indulgent flab like Martin Davidson? Certainly not the Armed Forces who had high standards.

If he was ever to make anything of himself, his first overriding task was to bin all that 'Army' rubbish and face up to a few realities. Solid achievement, however humble, was what he needed. And climbing Askival would be a step in the right direction. She remembered Meakin's account of his behaviour on Scafell Pike and shuddered. Suppose that great sack of potatoes just sat down and refused to move?

And, finally, John. A luridly mixed palette here! He was streaks ahead of the others, both physically and mentally. A lad of real promise. But there was that self-willed obstinate streak in him, that dash of arrogance under the cherubic exterior. Supposing the little bundle went bananas and rushed off and got himself killed? Distinctly possible. That 'Farmer Affair' in the Lake District, that bout of disobedience on the boat and now this near-fight with Martin... Despite all the positive things, despite the seeming breakthrough after last winter's Christmas party, despite the fact that he so obviously needed and wanted her, she still had these nagging doubts about him. He was so unlike her other pupils – a rich father, a posh accent, a posh moneyed prep school: was this really the kind of child that she was in business to rescue? Briggs didn't think so for starters, openly accusing her of being exploited by a pampered little manipulator who was exploiting her emotional underbelly. All the last two terms he'd been muttering away. Maybe he was right? ... Was it not time to be a proper professional? Restrain yourself before this male siren drags you down into ruin?

But then... Poor, pathetic little creature, gangbanged in front of a jeering mob by a homosexual thug, having to conceal the fact that he'd been beaten up by his ghastly mother... The small boy who was sick all over himself in the car because he was too ashamed to admit that he suffered from car sickness. And the eager little fellow who responded so well to her attempts at education... *her* special child, entrusted to her keeping by God?

Angel or devil? If only she knew which. But one uncomfortable thing was certain. She loved him with all the passion that she'd loved – and still *did* love – Lawrence.

Traumas and Triumphs

Getting a grip on herself, Dorothy went into headmistress mode.

538

Looking stem and switching on the X-ray eyes, she delivered a short lecture.

'Now this is our big challenge. We're going to climb a difficult and dangerous mountain...'

'WICKED!' came the predictable exclamation from John.

'Do we *have* to?' came the equally predictable groan from Martin.

'Yes, Martin, we do... Now, John, you listen to me, young man. You're *not* to run off and be silly. Mountains are *dangerous* and no place for silly little boys...'

John gave an obedient nod. (But how long would that last?)

Dorothy then outlined her proposed route.

'Not *two* mountains?' groaned Martin. 'You said we only had to climb one!'

'Yes, Martin, two mountains, now get up and get into line behind me. John, you're rear marker.'

'Awwww! Can't I go in front?'

Hint of defiance to come? Tingle of anxiety! 'No, John, you can't. You're in a position of responsibility. I'm relying on you to get Sam and Martin up the mountain...'

At this John stuck his tongue out and made a face at Martin, who winced and clenched his fists.

Unwilling to get bogged down in a tribal war, Dorothy ignored them and they began the 'Great Ascent'.

She led them slantwise up the big, grassy hillside that swept up to the rugged skyline to the south of them. There was no path and the going was rough and tiring, a matter of struggling up a wet, tussocky boulder field and through swampy bits of mush. They climbed with the slow rhythmic plod that Lawrence had taught her on that first, glorious trip to the Lake District all those years ago when life had been so full of hope.

'Are we at the top, yet?'

'No, Sam, not yet...'

'Cor, Miss, how much more of this? I'm knackered!'

'Keep going, Martin, if Sam can do it, then so can you. I'm your sergeant and I'm not accepting any excuses. Think of the Paras yomping over the Falkland Islands...'

'But they had helicopters.'

'No they didn't!' retorted John. 'All the helicopters went down with the *Atlantic Conveyor*.'

'Crap!'

'All right, you two, pack it in!'

Dorothy gave them lots of rests, one after every hundred or so yards: 'We'll get up to that boulder there and have another rest.'

Slow and tortuous, but she was taking no chances. Her ego was wrapped up in the notion of getting *all* of them over the mountains. John, meanwhile, fretted and fumed at the slow pace: they'd never get anywhere at this funereal rate – and all because of fat flid Martin!

At long last they topped the crest of the ridge. There, not very far above them, was a blunt, oddly shaped mountain-top with horizontal cliff bands slanting up to its summit.

'Now, John,' said Dolly, 'tell us what this mountain is called. You've got the map.'

'Hallival, Miss, the first peak on the ridge, 2,365 feet high. But why has it got that funny name?'

'It's something to do with the Vikings. They used to rule the island long ago.'

'Cor, were the Vikings here? Are there any buried ships here, you know like those they found in Denmark?'

'Perhaps there are.'

'Can we go and look for them? Maybe we could find some buried treasure... Please, Miss, this is wicked!'

Yes, she *did* like him, so positive and so full of life!

They clambered on to the rocky and grassy summit. While Sam and Martin sat wearily down, John gambolled round like an excited puppy. A whole new world had burst upon him – a richly blue world of wind, cliffs, mountains and sparkling seas, of strangely shaped islands and wildly dramatic peaks rearing up like broken teeth. It was a vision of wonder – like that mysterious dawn in the Lake District. In front of him was a sharp ridge, a knobbly spine of grass and lumpy rocks which dipped steeply down before surging up to a high wedge-shaped peak – Askival, at 2,663 feet the crown of the island.

'Wow!' he exclaimed. 'It's just like the final ridge on Everest! Bags me Hillary and you Tensing, Miss!'

Dorothy smiled with mixed feelings. John could appreciate the scenic wonders in front of him: the other two might just as well have been at Blackpool or Benidorm. Worse, still: to Martin, that ridge would be an excuse for refusing to move. And, sure enough, right on cue, came the complaint.

'We don't have to climb *that*, do we, Miss?'

'Yes, we do. Remember that I'm your sergeant!'

'But they don't allow women in the Paras... You've no right...'

Dorothy groaned inwardly: could *nothing* ever pierce that armour-plated cocoon of fantasy? Didn't he realise what a *fool* he was?

'Oh come on,' she said, trying to sound cheerful and confident, 'there's nothing to worry about!'

Yet she was worried. That ridge was the crux, the make or break of her educational experiment. They *had* to get over it. But it *was* dangerous. Its sharpness had come as an unexpected shock. It was more serious that she'd expected. There were plenty of places where silly boys could fall and kill themselves. ('Askival? You're not *serious*, are you?' Hubris followed by Nemesis?)

In a strained voice she addressed her little army: 'Now this is the exciting bit, but we've GOT TO BE CAREFUL! Get into line behind me. And PLEASE, NO NONSENSE!'

They picked a slow and careful way along the airy crest, John fretting as Martin stumbled about like a geriatric elephant. All went reasonably well until they came to a big, grey rock, sticking up in front of them like the prow of a battleship. The dreaded 'Mauvais Pas', the 'Bad Step', which Dorothy had read about. It barred their way.

'We can't get up that!' declared Martin triumphantly, relishing an excuse to go down and return to his dream world.

John got frantic. The 'Great Ascent' which he'd been dreaming about for the past few days wrecked by that humanoid snowman? No way! He'd find a way up the obstacle. It was that *Story of Everest* book again. This time he was on the North Face of Everest with Mallory and Irvine in 1924.

'This is just like the Second Step on the North Ridge of Everest,' he said. 'Mallory and Irvine got up it, you know. Look, Miss, I can find a way up it!'

Glory beckoned, the first ascent of Everest! But just then something happened to him. It wasn't a vision as such. He didn't see anything, not in the real world around him, anyway. But he felt it and he saw it with his inner eye as though it really was there. He was at Greenhill on that dreadful Friday, naked, shamed, his most intimate parts exposed to the bestial derision of Freddy Hazlett, crying like a baby, his body squirting disgusting brown liquids over the floor for all to see... 'I HATE YOU! I'M FAR BETTER THAN YOU ARE! ONE DAY I'LL BE FAMOUS!...' Then he heard Giles' scornful voice, loud and clear and so truthful, 'So *that's* what they thought of you! I might have known it.'

God, he'd show them! He just *had* to. He rushed at the smooth, slabby rock. 'JOHN DENBY!' came Dolly's shrill whiplash voice. 'Will you WAIT!'

This was the bit she'd been dreading. The guide book said that there was an easy way round to the right... but was it really there? Carefully, she edged round to the right... and found to her enormous relief that a tumbled rocky slope did, indeed, lead to the crest of the ridge, steep, but presenting no problems. The Great Ascent was assured.

So much for the physical problem. Now she faced the harder psychological problem. On cue, Martin took one look at the slope and said, 'I'm not going up that!'

How to persuade the arch-fantasist to come into the real world? Desperate, she used his mounting vendetta with John – 'divide and rule', that worthy device which had enabled the British to get control of Uganda.

'Oh, come on, Martin, it's easy. John, you show him!'

Hopefully that would shame him into action.

Like the fizz shaken out of a coke can, John bounded up the slope and reached the rocky crest on the skyline.

'WAIT THERE, JOHN!' Dolly shouted up to him. 'DON'T GO ANY FURTHER! THAT'S AN ORDER!'

She repeated the order: 'DON'T GO ANY FURTHER! JUST WAIT THERE!' (But would the little tin of super-heated steam obey her? She was in *his* hands. Alarming thought!)

'Right, Sam, you go next and make sure that John waits for us.'

Sam duly climbed up to the crest. Then she started on the dreary task in hand. 'Come on, Martin, if John can do it, you can do it.'

In dire straits now, Martin used his final deadly weapon. He sat down and started to cry.

'I won't, Miss. I won't.'

Exasperation welled up in Dorothy. Was he just going to sit there and wait till the supposed helicopter arrived? He was so infantile! A great big baby bawling in a pram – 'I WANT! I WILL HAVE!'

Angrily she let fly at him.

'Now come on, Martin! You're just a great big baby! For far too long you've been playing soldiers like a little boy. It's high time you stopped and faced the real world. That slope is the real world!'

No response.

'All right, shall I ask John to come down and kick you in?' (God Almighty, what *would* her tutor at St Aiden's College have thought of that?)

But where appeals to reason didn't work, the threat of violence eventually did. To her huge relief, with a venomously resentful expression, and with a theatrical laboriousness, Martin stood up and faced the slope.

'Right, now put your right hand here and your left foot there... Now up you go. That's it! Well done!'

Gradually, she coaxed the whimpering, self-pitying sack of potatoes, inch by inch, up to the crest. It was, perhaps, her finest hour.

Above them, John was getting more frantic with each passing minute. Again, he'd found himself at Greenhill, naked and degraded with Freddy Hazlett leering at him. Again, he'd heard Giles' mocking voice: 'So *that's* what they thought of you!' Steam boiled up inside him. There before him was an easy ridge leading up to the unclimbed summit of Askival. But not just to Askival, but to the unconquered summit of Everest itself, to fame, glory and redemption... And all to be snatched away from him because of that pathetic, humanoid snowman, Army Barmy! A frenzied madness seized him.

'I'm not waiting any longer,' he told an open-mouthed Sam. 'I'm off!'

'But Miss said...'

'Oh fuck off, Stick Insect!'

With that he bounded off up the rocky humps before him. Soon he stood panting by the summit cairn of Askival. Denby the Dauntless, Hero of the Farmhouse Raid ... on top of the world, lord of all he surveyed! And what a kingdom! Spread out beneath him were the steep and shadowy peaks of Rhum, the knobbly rocks of their summits towering above deep, mysterious valleys. Who knew what secrets might lurk in those hidden depths? To the north, beyond the foaming seas, were the tremendous mountains of Skye, the lordly Coolins. Away to the east, over the strange and contorted Isle of Eigg, was the Scottish mainland, a dark and brooding land of rumpled mountains, wild and waiting to be explored. Far off, in the shining western seas was a line of vividly blue hills. The Lost Isles of the Blessed? The Beyond World where his perfect gran and granddad were waiting for him? Wind, cloud, cliffs, gleaming waves, a boundless sky ... exaltation! No longer the pathetic creature that was sick in cars and cried when he was hit!

Meanwhile, down below Dorothy finally propelled Martin on to the crest of the ridge.

'Well done, Martin! You see you *can* do it if you really try.'

Looking round, she saw Sam, but not John.

'Sam, where's John?'

'Dunno. He just went off.'

A toxic brew of panic and sheer fury overwhelmed her. Worst fears realised! Child lost on a dangerous mountain! In this wild and rugged place anything could happen. At this very moment he could be lying on some inaccessible ledge fatally injured.

The arrogant little brat! How dare he do this to her! And after all she'd done for him, too! Indulged him, bought him Christmas presents, all but adopted him... Her reward? To be made a fool of, dragged to ruin! Game set and match to Briggs and to the Pharisee on the boat... 'Don't say you weren't warned.' Why did those she loved always betray her? First Lawrence and now John? The vengeful fury blazed up.

'Right, you two, we're going on to the top. He's probably there. I'm *very* angry with John! Yes, *very* angry!'

'Will you give him the cane?' asked a hugely delighted Martin.

'Yes, he certainly deserves it!'

'Wicked! I'm looking forward to this!'

Dorothy sighed. Down into the juvenile sewer again! Could she *never* escape? Grimly, they plodded up the heaving and lumpy ridge. Martin was transformed, suddenly energised, positively slobbering with glee at the gross humiliations about to be inflicted on his deadly rival – all the joys of Tyburn Tree!

To Dorothy's enormous relief, they found John sitting by the summit cairn. It was almost as if a painful abscess had been lanced. Then the fury burst forth.

'JOHN DENBY, HOW DARE YOU DISOBEY ME LIKE THIS! WHY DIDN'T YOU WAIT WITH SAM AS YOU WERE TOLD?'

John – alias Denby the Dauntless – stood up. He wasn't going to be shouted at like a little kid in front of kids like Stick Insect and Army Barmy!

'Why do I have to wait for cripples like Stick Insect and Fat Snowman here? I'm much better than they are!'

'That's no answer!'

This kid was right out of hand. She slapped him fiercely across the face.

It stung. The frenzied madness took a hold of him.

'Fuck off! I'm going to climb the next mountain and you can't bloody stop me!' Red-faced and fuming, he strode off.

Open defiance. Open rebellion. Situation well beyond reason. Nasty, cheeky little squirt! Arrogant, snobby little prep-school brat... Blind rage made Dorothy reckless and fiercely strong. She grabbed him by the scruff of the neck, bent him over and laid into his backside with the palm of her hand. One... Two... Three... Four... Five...

She lost count of the blows she rained on to him. It wasn't just John she was pounding. It was Lawrence who had betrayed her. Passion, hate and love in a fiery brew... She'd never 'got physical' like this before. A lifelong accumulation of resentful frustration burst into the open.

Shocked and terrified by the sheer unexpected ferocity of the assault, John yelled out as the blows fell on him: 'OW! OYER! OYER! PLEASE THAT'S ENOUGH!'

No Sydney Carton-going-to-the-guillotine acts this time. Just pain and fright and helplessness in the face of superior strength.

The storm of Dorothy's fury finally blew itself out. Catharsis. Her hand stinging, she finally let the squirming heap drop.

'Now let that be a lesson to you, John Denby. Don't you *ever* defy me again! Now apologise to Sam and Martin for the horrible things you have said to them.'

Abject, shaken and utterly deflated, John mumbled the appropriate mantra.

'Sorry, Sam... Sorry, Martin...'

Then he turned away. Abject despair. Changed back into the squalid little retard that he so hated. Could he *never* break the evil spell? To add to his misery, the tears began to flow. He couldn't help it. It was just like being sick or pissing the bed.

'Yah, look at Big Fart Denby!' jeered Martin. 'He's crying!'

'That's quite enough of that, Martin!' snapped Dorothy. 'If you can't behave, I'll have to spank you, too!'

Slowly, her rage evaporated. Sadness followed. They'd reached the top of the mountain. This should have been a wonderful moment of triumph, of the bonded friendship of achievement. Instead, she was floundering in a juvenile sewer. A jeering Martin – how he'd just loved John's spanking! A miserable and deflated John like a punctured beach ball with all the bounce gone out of him. All the squalors of childhood, exacerbated by personal inadequacies... But,

Dolly, old girl, you've made your bed, you've got to lie on it!

Forcing herself into a simulated bonhomie, she tried to restore the situation.

'Well done, Sam, well done, Martin! And you too, John... Now let's take a photograph to show them back at school.'

They duly posed by the cairn, Martin straightening up his red Para's beret and adjusting his US Marine's badges, Sam vacant and John red-faced and tearful.

'Now we're going down to that pass there and then back along by the sea to our camp.'

She pointed to the west to where the steep, green slopes of Askival tumbled down to a small pass before sweeping up again into the group of high stony mountains that formed the southern rim of the island. Far below a clearly defined path could be seen hugging the coastline.

Slowly and carefully they clambered down the verdant and rocky mountainside.

'Sam! Be careful! Mind that boulder! WATCH OUT!'

A big rock went bouncing down the slope, narrowly missing Martin.

'Sam, don't go into one of your dreams, *please*!'

Remorse

All that was left of John's bravado was a bleak remorse tipped with a nagging anxiety. It was like waking up in the morning after a gorgeous dream. It was the Lake District all over again, but only worse. What *had* he gone and done? Dolly was his protector, the mother he needed, his only protector in an unforgiving world. She'd been kind to him, bought him presents, encouraged him... But in a fit of temper he'd gone and messed everything up! He must make amends. But would she let him? Or would she send him back to... Greenhill?

Unknown to him, however, Dolly was also full of remorse. That tearful heap of misery by the summit cairn! She'd crushed the rebellion all right! Nobody could accuse her of not being in control of her kids! But it was nothing to be proud of. She'd gone and lost her temper and actually committed an assault. Beaten up a defenceless child... And *her* child, too, so full of zest and energy, the answer to her unsaid prayers... The trouble was that it hadn't been normal anger – she could have controlled that – but the sort of anger she'd last felt when she and Lawrence had quarrelled. That intense anger of love that so easily turned to hate and back to love again. That was why she'd lost control of herself. Because she so loved him!

Had she hit him too hard? Had she seriously hurt him? Destroyed the love he'd had for her? Oh, Dolly, what have you gone and done? She'd better start making amends before it was too late. But, hang on, old girl, you're a professional, not an emotional woman! Let him come to you. Don't allow yourself to grovel in front of him. That's weakness ... and weakness leads to disaster!

Reconciliation and Final Triumph

They stumbled down to the level ground of the pass.

'We'll have a rest here and have a snack,' said Dorothy.

They sat down on the rocks while she opened her rucksack and handed them each a Mars bar and a can of coke.

'Give me the litter when you've finished. Don't just throw it away.'

As Sam and Martin dozed in the warm sunshine, John crept up to Dolly, downcast and fearful.

'Please, Miss, I'm very sorry... I just lost my temper. Will you forgive me, please?'

Which, of course, was exactly what Dolly wanted him to say.

'Of course, John, of course! It's all over now!'

A hug and a kiss followed – mercifully unobserved by the somnolent Martin!

'You see, Miss, I just got so excited. It's wicked the way you take us up mountains. I pretended that I was climbing Everest... I didn't want to go down because of Martin. You see Giles tells me I'm a wimp and I wanted to prove that I'm not.'

Another hug.

'Of course I understand you, John. Now you've got to try to understand *me*. You really mustn't run off like that. I don't think you realise just what a responsibility I've got when I take you up mountains. There are lots of people who say that I shouldn't do it with boys like you because you're just too silly – like that man next to us in the boat. Now if you'd got lost or been injured in a fall, the Education Authority back in Boldonbridge wouldn't let me take

547

boys climbing ever again. Do you realise that? I trusted you and you let me down. That was what made me so angry... And you really mustn't say horrid things about Sam and Martin. It's not Christian. I lost my temper, too, you know. That's why I hit you so hard. Did I hurt you?'

'Not half you did! You've got a hard hand.'

'I haven't bruised you, have I?' (Momentary alarm. Hitting kids wasn't a good idea at the best of times. Bruising them in a fit of temper could leave dangerous hostages to fortune... Not what you'd want a school inspector to find out!)

'No! No! No! I'm all right!' (For God's sake, don't *you* start asking to see my bum! I'd die of shame!)

They rested for almost half an hour. While Sam and Martin lay comatose on the warm grass, John grew increasingly restless. He wasn't at all tired. Branching off the pass to the west of them was a dramatically shaped mountain which rose steeply from the north and tumbled over to the south in a line of crags, almost as if it were a gigantic ocean breaker made of tufty grass and big, black rocks.

'Cor, look at that mountain, Miss! What's it called?'

'Trollaval. It's the steepest mountain on the island.'

'Why's it got that name? Trolls were Viking dwarves, weren't they?'

'That's probably why the Vikings called it that. They must have thought that there were trolls there. It could have been a magic place, a sort of forbidden place...'

'Wicked! Are we going to climb it?'

'No, no. I'm afraid we'd never get Martin up that.'

'Awww! Please! The Secret Mountain of the Trolls! I'd love to climb it.'

Affection flowed out of Dorothy. She couldn't help loving him! Then she had her 'Moment of Madness' – or so it seemed to her in the cold light of the following morning!

'All right, John, *you* go and climb it. Yes, by yourself. It's not far, but come back here and *please* don't do anything daft!'

Repairing the broken fence. In a flash she'd understood him. Desperate to prove himself, he'd been sorely tried by Martin's negativity and elephantine ineptitude and had just flipped. Well, give him his head, but make it into a test.

'Now, John, I'm serious. I'm trusting you not to be silly. You're on trust. Breaking trust isn't only wrong, it's also very silly – especially in your case. Do you get me?'

'Of course. Miss! I won't break trust. Promise!'

Elated, he dashed off. Climbing the mountain was fun, a matter of following a knobbly ridge, clambering over big, rounded and mossy boulders and wriggling up muddy, gravelly little gullies. In less than half an hour he was standing by the minute summit cairn, waving frantically to Dolly and luxuriating in his triumph. Then, obedient to her command, he slithered back down the muddy and grassy slopes to the pass.

All the while Dorothy had been on a roller-coaster of panic and elation. Panic as he had disappeared behind a green spur. Sending an eleven-year-old off on his own up a wild and trackless mountain, especially a boy who'd just defied her most stringent orders?! If it all went wrong? Curtains for Dorothy Watson!

But elation when he returned safe and sound, his face flashing that glorious, liquid smile. She'd pulled off a professional coup. Given him a chance to rebuild his bruised ego and wipe out the shame of having had his bottom publicly spanked. Treated him like an adult and he'd responded.

'Well done, John! Very well done!'

The expedition was salvaged.

They went down into a deep, green glen, a sort of gash between the towering mountains, and followed a brawling little river down to the sea. There on the rocks they had more coke and Mars bars while Dorothy heaved a huge sigh of relief. They'd survived the dangerous bit! Now all they had to do was to follow an easy path back to the camp. Even Martin could manage that.

Just then one of those rare moments of magic occurred. A large herd of deer wandered down the glen towards them, led by a magnificent stag with a huge set of antlers.

'Wow! Just look at that!' exclaimed John who'd never seen deer before.

'Don't go too near him, John,' warned Dolly. 'He's the boss of the herd and those other deer are his harem, his wives. He could be aggressive. He doesn't like outsiders who might steal them...'

John was entranced by the sheer regal grandeur of the beast, by its grace, beauty and hidden power.

After a few minutes, the herd moved off, back up the glen. The show was over. 'What a perfect end to our climb!' he exclaimed. 'I never expected to see a sight like that. It's almost as if it had been specially laid on for us!'

So back along the rocky coast, following the path as it wriggled it tortuous way, skirting beaches, cliffs and rocky coves. Above him were the grand and rugged mountains of his conquest, beside him the gleaming, almost living, sea, brilliant and shimmering as the waves crashed nosily onto the rocks. Beyond was the strange island of Eigg with its cliffs and weird mountain peak. A triumphal progress. The temper and the spanked bottom disappeared in a warm glow.

For Dorothy, also, a wonderful walk. Against the odds, she'd pulled it off.

But for Martin a tiresome and quite needlessly long traipse to relative comfort. In his mounting resentment he set up a mutter: 'Dolly's got no right. Need choppers...' For Sam? A sense of belonging, even a sort of heaven... But a day in a café would have been better.

Moment of Truth

The sun disappeared in crimson splendour behind the enclosing western hills. As they cooked their supper, one by one, the stars emerged from the deepening blue dome of the sky. A silence fell, broken only by the soft lapping of the nearby waves. 'That was wicked, Miss!' said John as he crawled into the tent.

'Thank God it's over!' growled Martin. 'I'm not climbing no more mountains. Not ever. Miss can't make me!'

Sam said nothing.

Outside, alone in the gloaming, Dorothy had a moment of truth. Some kids were redeemable: others were not. Don't waste too much time on the latter. Save those who want to be saved.

'So you should be sorry...'

The next morning they packed up their things and went down to the pier to catch the boat back to Mallaig.

A neatly dressed man with a bald head and glasses approached Dorothy, his face contorted with a righteous, paedophobic indignation.

'Are you the leader of the group that climbed Askival yesterday?'

'Yes.'

'Well, you managed to chase a whole herd of deer out of Glen Dibidil, completely ruining a carefully set-up experiment. A vital piece of research was wrecked at the last minute. You really ought to control your kids properly... In fact we shouldn't allow kids on this island at all!'

'I'm terribly sorry... I didn't realise.'

'So you should be sorry. It's set my Ph.D. thesis back at least six months. Rest assured that I shall be reporting this to your Education Authority...'

Dorothy sighed. With kids you just couldn't win. Could you?

The Ghosts of the Night

Time passed. John wrote up his diary, adding an extra thousand feet to the height of Askival and an extra two thousand feet to the height of Trollaval and embellishing the peaks – especially Trollaval – with knife-edge ridges and colossal unclimbed faces. Mallory may have made the first ascent of Everest, but he, Denby the Dauntless, was hot on his heels with the first schoolboy ascent of Trollaval...

So the big, bold lad was firmly established. A scrap with Martin (unseen by Dolly!) in which he was clearly the victor seemed to clinch the issue.

Then, on the last night of the holiday, there was a visitation. From what? Perhaps from that dark, brooding force that the Ancients called Nemesis. 'John Denby, remember that you are still a pathetic little boy and always will be.'

Maybe he was asleep in the tent, maybe he was awake all the time, he didn't really know. Suddenly he was back in Greenwood. Giles and Mary were there looking grim.

'Mrs Watson's dead,' said Giles.

'Yes,' added Mary, 'dead and buried like your grandparents. You're going back to Greenhill to get the punishment that you deserve.'

Freddy Hazlett, Shorly and the whole baying mob appeared: 'Reet! Gerrim lads!'

He turned round and tried to run away, but there, barring his way, was that hideous old tramp that had so terrified him that night in London. They all jeered at him and hooted with laughter as, in his terror, he urinated violently and uncontrollably over himself. He was utterly wretched, stinking, crying like a baby, ashamed and full of self-loathing.

Then he found himself in the darkened tent listening to Martin's grunts and Sam's gentle snores. Which was real, which the dream? Or was it all the same reality? He pushed his hand down his sleeping bag. Everything was wringing wet and stinking. Yes, he *had* pissed himself! The shame! The degradation! What if Martin should find out? Back to being the dirty little retard again! The doom *was* real. Dolly *was* dead.

But, as he lay sobbing to himself, the tent became more real and Greenhill less real. A flash of hope! Maybe Dolly wasn't dead after all? He had to find out. Painfully, he extracted himself from the sodden squalor of his sleeping bag, carefully folding it up to conceal the ghastly secret it contained. Quietly, and desperate not to wake the others, he unzipped the flap of the tent and slipped out into the mysterious world outside. It was dark and cool. The black clouds scurrying over the face of the moon filled him with dread. It was just like the Valkyries of old riding through the heavens to pick up the fallen warriors after a doomed battle – an omen of impending disaster. All was silent except for the gentle rustling of the long grass in the soft wind and the somnolent sigh of the sea as it ceaselessly pounded the nearby shore. Dressed only in his dripping underpants, the night air seemed to sting his wet skin.

There, black and ominous, was Dolly's tent with the terrible secret that might lie within it. Suppose he went in and found that she really was dead? Or, perhaps, that she simply wasn't there any more? It was all so ghastly. He cried a little harder.

In desperation, he unzipped the flap and crawled into the dark interior. There on the camp bed, wrapped up in a sleeping bag, was a prone figure. She was there, but was she alive or dead? Frantically, he shook her shoulder.

'Please, Miss! Please, Miss!'

The figure grunted and rolled over. Immense liberating relief! It was *alive*!

There was a fumble and a torch flashed in his face, momentarily blinding him.

'Oh! It's *you*, John? What on earth do you want?'

'Please, Miss, you're not dead, are you?'

'Don't be silly, John!'

'But you're not going to die, are you?'

'Not for many years yet! But what is all this? You've been crying. What's the matter?'

'I've had a terrible dream. I don't know whether it's true or not.

You were dead and I was being sent back to Greenhill. It's not true, is it?'

'Of course not.'

'But in old times they said dreams were a warning. You know... Joseph and Pharaoh...'

'That's just a lovely old legend.'

'But aren't you getting sick of me? Aren't you going to send me away?'

'Now why should I do that?'

'Well, sometimes I am very bad like I was on Askival. I lose my temper and say silly things. I don't mean to, but ... well, it just happens... And you hit me really hard that last time. It really scared me. I've never seen you like that before. You've never done it to anybody else... Not even to Billy Nolan!' (Bull's eye here! Right into the soft underbelly. Yes, she *had* lost control of herself, laid into him in a fit of uncontrolled fury! It was the first time in all her teaching career that anything like this had ever happened. It was most emphatically *not* something to be proud of. If she'd done it in the classroom, she could have been prosecuted for assault. It was a crime of passion – and that passion was *love*! Love and hate, they were the two interchangeable sides of the same coin. Just look at her and Lawrence!)

There was a pause while the thoughts churned slowly round in her mind, like a clunky old computer sorting out the various permutations and combinations of the problem. Clicks, hums and lights flashing. Eventually, she spoke.

'John, what's the worst thing I can do to you?'

'Beat me in.'

'No, John. Ignore you. Forget that you even exist. I hit you hard because I really cared about you. If I didn't like you, you wouldn't make me angry when you're bad. I'd just not bother with you.'

'Am I very bad then?'

'Of course not, John. You're a very normal boy. All normal boys are bad sometimes.'

'But Mary beats me in for nothing and whatever I do she doesn't like me. I tried very hard to be good to her. I gave her a lovely Christmas present, but she still hates me.'

(Oh how Dorothy was loving all this! Her *own* child was confiding in her! He needed her and he wanted her! In the surge of emotion she became intimate and rashly indiscreet, even 'unprofessional'!)

'It's not *you* she hates, John. It's herself. She's trying to be something that she never can be: the Great Philosopher who's going to change the world. But she isn't a great philosopher. She isn't even clever enough to finish her Ph.D. thesis. She can't face up to this in herself. You're just the football she kicks to relieve her temper. Like a child throwing its teddy round the room when it doesn't get what it wants.'

'But that's pathetic!'

'Of course it is. She's really a child who has never grown up. When she leaves that university environment and enters the real world, she might start to grow up.' (Oh, Dorothy Watson, *do* be careful of what you say in front of a child! You're being very unprofessional. You're letting pent-up emotions get the better of you. You'll only live to regret it!)

The confidences continued: 'I try to be good with Giles, but he just thinks I'm pathetic. He said I deserved what they did to me at Greenhill.'

More 'unprofessional' indiscretions: 'Giles is a very clever man, but he's also ignorant and foolish. Because he's big and clever himself, he has no idea what it's like to be weak and defenceless. In that sense, you're cleverer than he is. You know what it's like. Now just you think what it must be like to *be* Sam – or, Martin, for that matter! You're not very good at things. Everybody laughs at you and tries to kick you in. So whenever you have problems, just think of them. Maybe that's why God has given you problems – to make you understand what the world is really like.'

'So you're not going to send me away then?'

'*Of course* not, John! I love you far too much!'

There was a moment's silence as John braced himself to make his awful confession.

'Please, Miss, there's something I want to tell you. I've been very bad. Really bad. Now, you won't get angry with me, will you? Promise. Promise not to shout at me. Promise not to hit me!' (Dolly's euphoria dissolved in a flash. What *was* this? What had he gone and done in those hours of darkness when he was out of her sight? Smothered poor old Sam in his sleeping bag? Stabbed Martin with his penknife? Raided the nearby farmhouse? Was the dream just a cover for an altogether more serious happening? Was his distressed state merely terror at the anticipated consequences of some appalling crime? She braced herself for the shattering of all her illusions!)

'OK, I promise. Now let's hear the worst.'

'I've pissed my sleeping bag.'

'Is that all?' (That strange, inverted world of children, where messing your pants was a worse crime than stealing, or, even, murder!)

'I'm so ashamed! I'm so ashamed! I didn't mean to. It just happened. Please don't tell the others... Pissing yourself is what little kids do! I'm so ashamed!'

'Of course, I won't tell anybody.'

The tears resumed in earnest: 'But *why* does it keep happening? It never happened all the time I was at Rickerby Hall.' (Come on, Dolly, old lass, you know all about post-traumatic distress disorder! You should have spotted this before! Delta minus from St Aiden's College!)

'You've got a form of illness, John. When people face great fear and terror it alters the chemistry of the body – all those very complicated liquids inside you. That's what causes the nightmares and the bedwetting. Old soldiers often suffer from it...'

'But they're grown-ups, not little kids.'

'That often makes it worse. Mr Meakin knows a man who was a bomber pilot in the war. He won the Distinguished Flying Cross and became a Group Captain, but because of the terrible fear he experienced and the awful things he saw, he often has nightmares and wakes up screaming in the night. Now you've had a bad time and it's upset your chemistry, but you're young and young people get better more quickly than older people. You'll soon be all right.'

(Yes, stability and security is what you need and *I'm* the one who's going to provide you with it! All lingering doubts resolved.)

She was about to give him a hug when she wrinkled up her nose. Yes he *had* wet himself – and not only that either! There were strong hints of that 'other problem downstairs'.

'I think you'd better put some clean underpants on...'

'But they're in my rucksack and if I start getting them out I'll wake Martin and he'll find out.'

'All right, luckily I've got some spare things in my bag...' (Alpha from St Aiden's College for planning: always take lots of spare clothes with you when you go away with kids – they lose things, fall into rivers, drop things into muddy puddles etc., etc., etc...!)

She rummaged for a while and eventually pulled out a towel and a clean pair of drawers.

'Now wipe yourself with this and put these on. Put the dirty things into this polythene bag.'

'Please, don't look – it's embarrassing.'

'All right. I'll turn round.' (She did like his squeamishness. It was so human!)

As he slipped off the offending articles, he saw to his shameful horror and disgust that he hadn't just pissed himself. *That* had happened again! He wept tears of anguish as he wiped himself down and donned the clean drawers. Would it *never* end? But luckily the new drawers were identical to the soiled ones so he wouldn't have to fend off any awkward questions from Martin.

'OK. That's it.'

When Dorothy turned round again and saw the pathetic little white body in front of her, the dam of her pent-up emotions burst and the flood poured out, wilder and more intense than ever before. Poor little scrap! Poor, vulnerable little thing! How desperately he needed her! How she loved him in his vulnerable state! *Why* had it taken her so long to realise it – even after last winter's party when all had seemed clear? Why did she still listen to that ass Briggs? Yes, he was hers!

She hugged him and he responded warmly.

'Now then, John, off you go and try to get some more sleep. We'll deal with the sleeping bag tomorrow.'

'Please, can I stay here? I'm frightened to go back to sleep in case I start dreaming and ... well, it happens again.' (Professional problem here. Let him sleep in your tent, Dolly, and you'll be accused of favouritism. Martin will get even more jealous than he already is. You've got to love 'em *all*, you know! Dilemma.)

Then a bright idea!

'Let's have a midnight feast. It's the last night. Let's get the Trangias out. You get the sausages and chips. I'll brew the cocoa...'

The High Point

So it happened. Midnight terrors dissolved in the job in hand. When all was ready, Martin and Sam were duly roused. The wind had dropped, the pounding of the sea had become a gentle murmur. The moon came out and flooded the sand dunes with a soft, silver glow. There in the exotic setting they feasted. A bond of togetherness formed. It was the high point of the holiday.

Dorothy felt that she had won a great battle, chalked up a big victory. But who would recognise it as a victory, or indeed as anything at all? Not that Pharisee in the boat. Not Professor Stimpson. Not the Education Authority. There were no tangible laurels, no Grade As at O level, not even a winning try in a rugby match.

The Unknown Soldier was alone in his tomb.

42

All's Well That Ends Well?

Rational at Last

That September things settled down. A calm and rational period began.

With Mary gone, Giles was able to swallow his pride and hire a housekeeper. Exploiting the workers, demeaning their intelligence by forcing them to do humdrum and repetitive tasks, humiliating them by making them do the dirty jobs you despised...? It was all these things according to the Social and Political Awareness Group that he chaired at the university. More than that, it was a gross betrayal of the principles of socialism worthy of Ramsay MacDonald...

But, looked at from another angle, it was a classic case of mutual self-interest which satisfied everybody.

Mrs Coburn was a mothering old Geordie housewife who saw the purpose of her life as looking after her 'man' and her 'bairns'. She actually *enjoyed* cleaning up after them and feeding them up. Her two children having grown up and flown the nest, her life had lost much of its purpose. But faced with a domestically incompetent Giles and a messy house, that purpose had been regained. 'Yon bairn wants tekkin in hand!' she declared when she saw a grubby and neglected John.

So 14 Gloucester Road was transformed from a student pad into a respectable dwelling. No more dirty dishes mouldering in the sink, no more fag ends strewn all over the table, no more heaps of dog-sick stew stinking away on the expensive rugs.

For John, the clothes problem was solved. No more muddy rugby shorts floating round in the sink among the unwashed dinner plates, no more mephitic underpants growing mushrooms in the depths of cupboards... From now on it was clean shirts, clean underwear and properly pressed trousers.

The food problem was also solved. No more scraping up spoonfuls of leftover Ukrainian borsch or braving the mysteries of Algerian couscous which had been sitting on the table for two days... No more having to stuff yourself with wine gums and smoky-bacon crisps... There was always a meal waiting for him when he needed it. And it was food he could understand – egg and chips, mince and dumplings, treacle pudding and custard.

Not surprisingly, Mrs Coburn took to John in a big way, inviting him round to her house at intervals and showing him off to her husband and the neighbours. John put on all his charm and wallowed in being the centre of attention.

Giles paid her generously – necessary to rebut any charges of 'exploitation' should his guilty secret get known in inappropriate places. In any case, being very rich, he could afford to. Also, he discovered – like his father – that being munificent was good for his self-esteem.

Not, of course, that any finer points of ideology bothered old Annie Coburn. She could now afford an annual holiday in Benidorm, which pleased her mightily.

A Flourishing Career

Shot of tiresome and petty distractions, Giles could concentrate on more important matters. His monograph was published, he got stuck into his television programmes and he secured the Labour Party nomination for Boldonbridge West. Following Sam Clarke's retirement, he was triumphantly returned to Westminster in the by-election.

Thereafter he spent his weekdays and many of his weekends in London. When he did come back north, most of his time was spent in his constituency office in Greenwood Road.

Sensible Arrangements

All of which suited Dorothy Watson down to the ground. She now had a perfect excuse to keep John at her house during the week. She finally overcame all her 'professional' hesitations and accepted him as her very own child. At weekends and during the holidays she was careful to send him back to Gloucester Road so as to share him with Mrs Coburn and not to appear too possessive.

All of which, also, suited John down to the ground. He'd now got the mum he wanted. Indeed, he found himself with several parents. Mrs Coburn doted on him.

Old George Dawes became a surrogate uncle. He invited him round to see his model railway and a friendship blossomed. 'Eeeee!' exclaimed Mrs Dawes, 'now I've gone an' got two bairns instead of one!' Soon Danny, Fred and Michael were, also, invited round.

His birthday party duly took place at Dolly's place and this time the jamboree went off without a hitch. There was no longer any problem of presents at Christmas. He was showered with them. Mrs Coburn even provided him with a stocking.

A Successful Schoolboy

School life flourished. He became firm friends with Michael and Fred. With Danny an especially close bond developed. They both liked the same things. With Mary gone and Giles away in London, he could invite friends round to Gloucester Road without running the risk of their seeing him being punched and crying like a little baby. He was able to show his trains to Danny while Mrs Coburn provided them with a big tea of crumpets and sticky buns.

With each telling the summer adventures became more dramatic – steering a small boat through a raging storm, the first ascent of the big, unclimbed south wall of Trollaval. The walloping on Askival faded into oblivion. An envious Martin might mutter about it, but who could take a proven pseudo like Army Barmy seriously?

Michael duly gaped in awe. A bevy of new boys arrived at Beaconsfield, more normal than the previous intakes. They, too, were suitably awed. John became the leader of the junior pack – something that could never have happened at Rickerby Hall.

The classwork continued to blossom. Top in all subjects, a clutch of History and Geography projects – 'The Story of Everest', 'The Trans Siberian Railway', 'The Geography of Uganda and the Ruwenzori'. A big part of the annual art exhibition consisted of his work. Two of his paintings fetched up framed in the entrance hall.

Smouldering Frustrations Continue

Even Briggs' hostility seemed to have softened. Underneath, of course, nothing had changed. He still found young Denby repulsive – a pampered and arrogant prep-school brat who'd wrapped his oily little fingers round that gullible ass Dorothy Watson. But he was desperate to move on to a 'proper school' and to do that he needed good references from the old cow. Which, of course meant trying to create the semblance of a good rugby team – and which in turn meant keeping on the right side of her ghastly little protégé.

He didn't know whether to weep or to cheer when he won a crucial match for them against the mighty Marshal Grove, the ultra-posh private school in the area by scoring three tries. Admittedly, it was against the junior fourth reserve team, composed of the school deadbeats and dropouts, but still the victory went down big with the old bitch. 'Well done, James, you're obviously doing a good job with these boys! I really think John deserves a fresh set of rugby colours, don't you?'

Briggs most emphatically *didn't* think so, but dire necessity forced him to comply with a simulated – *very* simulated! – enthusiasm.

He seemed to be trapped. He'd applied for posts at several comprehensives and had been turned down by all of them. Teaching at Beaconsfield seemed to be a kind of professional suicide – 'Abandon hope all ye who teach here.' He resigned himself to a dreary and unfulfilled existence.

Saved

Then one Wednesday evening everything changed. Bored, he'd dropped into the Tabernacle at the end of Ellesmere Road, more out of curiosity than any deep religious impulse. Four hours later he emerged as a 'saved Christian', 'born again' and with a 'mission from God' to cleanse the sick and decadent society of Britain by fighting valiantly against the 'enemies within' which were slowly eating it away: Irreligion, Indiscipline, Drunkenness and Sexual Promiscuity – especially Homosexuality which was everywhere showing its sinister and ugly head. He now knew that his basic assumptions had been correct. God had noticed them and was showing him the way forward. God had work for him to do – even at Beaconsfield. His life now had a purpose.

ARTHUR CLIFFORD

Onwards and Upwards

That year saw a new and very positive development at Beaconsfield. Dorothy made friends with Bob Steadman, the young vicar who'd so successfully managed the Christmas Eve service for her. It was another case of mutual self-interest. *She* wanted to get her pupils properly involved with Christianity. Stuck in a dreary suburban parish with a dwindling congregation of old women, *he* was bored and wanted an outlet for his energy and pedagogic talents. Vigorous, down to earth and full of bounce, he seemed to actually *like* young people and to enjoy their company.

A special Sunday service was arranged and carefully tailored to the needs of the Beaconsfield youngsters. Excited boys dressed up in white robes sang pop songs and swung incense round the place. In the middle of the service they performed little plays written by themselves. A youth club came into being in which creative activities took place. A great long frieze – largely created by John – adorned the red-brick walls of the drab little church. For John God was back again – and much more fun than he'd ever been at Rickerby Hall.

The Adventure Weekends now became an established feature of Beaconsfield life. Steadman joined in and Meakin found his positive, 'can do' approach vastly more acceptable than Briggs' negative 'professionalism'. Another problem solved.

They clambered along the rocky crest of Striding Edge and crossed the bare summit of Helvellyn in the wind and rain. A wet and blustery weekend was spent clinging to their tents on the soggy, rain-swept slopes of the Cheviot... These expeditions were less wildly dramatic than that first legendary trip of yore – no more 'farmhouse raids' or having to escape from 'benders' – but more orderly and instructive.

That summer Dorothy took another group to Scotland. Steadman accompanied them and they hired a motorboat and sailed up to the nethermost end of the deep and dark fjord of Loch Nevis. There, in the pathless wilderness and hemmed in by huge, towering mountains, they camped and climbed the soaring, almost Matterhorn-like, peak of Sgurr na Ciche ... The steep, grey crags, the swirling mists, the dark and brooding waters of the loch ... it all made a deep and lasting impression on John. He and Steadman became firm friends.

Up and Further Up

So it was up and up. The bedwetting stopped, the bad dreams never returned, even *that* faded away. John was a normal boy again. The evil spell was broken.

And it was upwards for others, too. For Dorothy Watson whose school was flourishing and who now had her own child. And for Giles who was making a big impression in Parliament and whose TV series on the British working class was a tremendous success.

A New Role for a Radical

And there was another success in a forgotten corner. A feature appeared in the *Guardian*: 'Up-and-Coming Child Expert Renounces Academic Life'. It transpired that Mary Denby, that 'well-known child development expert', was abandoning a brilliant career to help the deprived children and exploited women in war-torn East Africa. 'Weary of a racist, money-grubbing society', she was going to place her talents at the disposal of a 'more ecologically and socially aware society' which had been so 'cynically exploited by imperialist capitalism'. The Third World Voluntary Work Initiative considered her 'the catch of the decade' – 'She's got all the right ideas... Her passionate and caring radicalism is just what we need to create a better world...'

As she packed her things, Mary relished her new role and looked forward to some 'relevant ethnic experience'.

A Happy Ending?

So for a fleeting moment everybody was happy. There the story should have stopped. If only things could have stayed the way they were that year! If only John could have stayed as he was – an eager little boy, happy, popular and full of promise!

Unfortunately, in this universe we are imprisoned in Time. And Time sweeps us relentlessly on. Nothing lasts. Everything changes. Happy endings rarely happen in this life.

Already, unknown to John, unseen clouds were gathering. Time was bearing an unsuspecting boy into dangerous waters.